DETECTIVES 2

DETECTIVES 2

ASTRO, THE MASTER OF MYSTERIES

GELETT BURGESS

DR. XAVIER WYCHERLEY, THE MIND-READER

MAX RITTENBERG

COACHWHIP PUBLICATIONS

Landisville, Pennsylvania

2 Detectives: Astro, the Master of Mysteries/ Dr. Xavier Wycherley, the Mind-Reader
The Master of Mysteries, by Gelett Burgess (1866-1951), first published 1912.
The Mind-Reader, by Max Rittenberg (1880-1965), first published 1913.
Copyright © 2011 Coachwhip Publications
No claims made on public domain material.

ISBN 1-61646-103-9
ISBN-13 978-1-61646-103-4

CoachwhipBooks.com

CONTENTS

ASTRO, THE MASTER OF MYSTERIES

DR. XAVIER WYCHERLEY, THE MIND-READER

ASTRO, THE MASTER OF MYSTERIES

[*Publisher's Note*: When *The Master of Mysteries* was first published in 1912, it was published anonymously. The Introduction, as you will read, suggests there are three cryptograms hidden in the text. Two of these are known and easily discovered. (The first provides the name of the author, Gelett Burgess.) The third cryptogram remains a puzzle.]

INTRODUCTION

Astro put *The Great Cryptogram* back upon his book-shelf among the other attempts to solve the immortal Shakespeare-Bacon controversy.

"Valeska," he said, turning to his pretty assistant, "it's queer that there appears to be no other book containing a secret message except the Shakespeare folios, isn't it! It seems to me that I have heard it said that Chatterton had a cipher in one of his books, though; that's the only other one I know of. Strange more authors haven't done it!"

"Why?" Valeska asked, looking up from her catalogue. "Why should a writer put anything in that can't go plainly in the body of the book, or, at least, in an introduction?"

"For many reasons: He may be ashamed of the book, or have some other reason for not acknowledging its authorship. It may describe his friends too accurately. It may reveal important secrets. Even if his name does appear on the title page, I can imagine of a number of secret messages he might want to insert for the benefit of those able to understand it."

"Perhaps it has often been done," Valeska suggested. "One wouldn't know, unless one had a reason to suspect the existence of such a thing—and then one would have to be clever enough to read the cipher."

Astro thought it over. "By Jove!" he exclaimed at last, "you're right! Now I think of it there's one particular book, published anonymously, that I've often been curious about. *Clewfinder*,—I think I'll take a look at it."

He went to his book-shelves again and took out the volume, opened it, and ran swiftly over the pages. "Let's see," he said; "if the author wanted his true name known, he would put it in an easy cipher, wouldn't he? But if he didn't want it found out easily, it would be something more complex. This book has had a great sale— it could hardly hurt the man to be suspected of writing it. Let's try the easiest possible method first."

He ran swiftly over the pages. "Well, what d'you think!" he said, looking up. "I knew the man was pretty clever, and fairly versatile, but I never thought of him as the author of such a novel as *Clewfinder*! Just look at it, Valeska."

"You say it's the easiest possible method he has taken?" Valeska said, as she looked over the pages.

"The very easiest."

Valeska studied on it a few minutes, then her face lighted. She hurriedly turned the pages, stopped here and there, and then smiled. "Well, that is a surprise, isn't it! But why didn't he put his name on the title page? I can't understand that!"

"Give me the book!" Astro said, eagerly. "I believe he would be likely to tell that, too!" He took the volume again, and again he ran hurriedly over the pages. "Yes; as I thought," he said, finally. "He has the best of reasons." He handed the book back to his assistant.

"The second cipher, surely, would be written in the second easiest way, shouldn't it?"

Astro nodded. "Naturally."

Valeska sat for a while at her table, her head resting in her hand. Then she slowly turned the leaves, thinking. In a moment she went faster, stopping as before, for a second, occasionally. She went back once, made sure, and recommenced. Finally she smiled. "Yes!" she said. "He's right, too!"

"It may have a third cipher message, too," she suggested, looking at the volume curiously.

Astro thought it over. "Possibly, but that would be for the few, not for the ordinary 'smarty-cats.' I'll see when I have leisure for it. It will probably take a little more time to read it."

"Well," said Valeska, "if other books have contained any such secret messages, it's strange that some one hasn't eventually discovered them."

"That's no doubt because they didn't have modern publishers, who understood the practical psychology of advertising," said Astro.

And he turned to play with his pet white lizard.

MISSING JOHN HUDSON

The Master of Mysteries bent over the onyx lectern for a moment to gaze at the monograph, and then chuckled derisively. "Oh, these German Symbolists!" he said half aloud. "For unadulterated humor, give me a Teuton that has joined the ranks of the metaphysicians. It is hardly to be wondered that ninety per cent. of them have died in madhouses, and that Max Nordau has scheduled the rest of them for suicide!"

He paused again to give a final glance at Ehrenfeld's little book on tone color in vowels. "The letter A," he translated rapidly, "suggests at once bright red, and symbolizes youth, or joy; the letter I is suggestive of sky-blue, and symbolizes intimacy, or love—*et cetera, et cetera.*" He stopped from sheer exasperation. "Poor Arthur Rimbaud! Poor old sodden Verlaine! What crimes are committed in your cause!"

The door opened softly, and he turned to greet a beautiful blond-haired girl who entered.

"Valeska, if I were making up a list of the tonal essences in vowel sounds, I should say the A was yellow, in disagreement with our friend here, Mr. Ehrenfeld. The U would be purple, verging on maroon. By the way, did you happen to notice that woman who was here this afternoon?" He gazed abstractedly at the floor. "It seemed to me," he went on after a few moments' thought, "as if she possessed distinctly purple vibrations, denoting unrest."

"Which one?" was the quick reply. "The one in black satin, with jet ornaments, who wore gold-bowed eye-glasses, and limped?"

"Of course; but I should describe her as a woman who was worried and was jealous of her husband; very suspicious of him; also abnormally anxious for money."

"I didn't talk to her; I was too busy."

"You must do a few palms some day, just to see how you are getting along in your study of the science of human nature. You noticed nothing else about her?"

Valeska put the end of her pencil to her lips and considered it abstractedly for a few moments. "Let me see—" she began. "She carried two books, didn't she?"

"Precisely. One was a Baedeker's *Northern Italy*, and the other was a church report,—Park Avenue Presbyterian. But the point is that she's coming here again, possibly this evening or to-morrow. She was literally perishing with the desire to ask me something which she did not dare to at the time."

At this moment there came a ring at the office doorbell.

"There she is now," went on the mystic. "Did you notice that was a nervous ring? It came twice. She wasn't quite sure the first time whether she had pressed hard enough. Show her in, Valeska."

A few minutes intervened before his visitor appeared, pausing undecidedly on the threshold. "Could I see you for a short time about something of importance?" she questioned.

"Have a seat, madam." Astro had risen, and placed a chair, apparently innocently enough, where the full glare of the drop electric light would illuminate her. His eyes did not appear to survey his client; but under his long lashes they were busy noting detail after detail. She sat down and again hesitated to begin.

"I—I suppose that what I am about to say, sir, will be kept in perfect confidence?"

"Assuredly, madam. You are worried about your husband, I presume."

She started in surprise, looked curiously at him, and then said, "Yes," in a faint tremulous whisper. At once she added, "You told me things this afternoon which were so wonderfully true that I thought I might trust you to give me some help on a far more important affair which has been worrying me for some time. The fact is, Mr. Hudson, my husband, has disappeared. I haven't seen him for over a week."

At this Astro manifested no surprise, and merely remarked, "I was aware that he was away, madam, when I read your palm this afternoon. No doubt I can find him, if that is what you wish; but it may take some time; for I shall have to gaze into my crystals and go into a trance. It will also be necessary for me to go to your house—into his room, in fact—in order that I may first take his atmosphere."

"Oh, I understand," she exclaimed. "To tell the truth, I'm very, very much worried, and anxious to have you go to work as soon as possible. I daren't go to the police; for, after all, there may be nothing serious the matter, and it would cause a lot of talk; and I shouldn't want him ever to know that I'd employed a detective for anything like this. But of course you are different."

"I am 'different,' as you say," responded Astro, smiling. "I shall be able to trace him, no doubt, without any one ever suspecting me. Just when did you see him for the last time?"

"On Tuesday, the tenth."

"And now it is the twentieth. He has had no business troubles?"

"On the contrary, he was doing remarkably well in his real estate business. We've been saving up to go abroad, you see; it has been a plan we've had ever since we were married. It's a sort of delayed honeymoon, I suppose. We hoped to live in Italy for a year." She sighed.

"You are a church-member, I presume?"

"Yes, I go to the Park Avenue Presbyterian church. Mr. Hudson is a deacon there."

"I see. He is well-off, you say?"

"Oh, no; not that. But we have been quite encouraged of late. Mr. Hudson was quite hopeful about our European trip."

"Very well, Mrs. Hudson; I shall be at your house at nine o'clock to-morrow."

Valeska entered the room again as soon as the visitor had left, and looked at the palmist, with a question in her eyes.

Astro waved his hand carelessly. "As I thought," he began, turning to his narghile, lighting it, and blowing the fumes through his nose luxuriously, "John Hudson has disappeared. She asked several pointed questions about him this afternoon, although she thought that she guarded herself well. They are both church-members, and their ambition is to go abroad. He is in the real estate business. Can you put two and two together?"

Valeska's pretty eyebrows creased themselves in thought. "Let me see. Judging from her appearance, they can't have been making very much money in the real estate business. You say they wanted to go to Europe,—wanted to stay a year in Italy, wasn't it?—and wanted all this badly. He'd naturally try to get the money in other ways; perhaps illegitimately. It might even lead him into crime. Being religious, he would naturally want to hide this from his wife. Perhaps he has been suspected and has escaped." She looked up at him anxiously.

"You're improving," said the Seer impassively. "In fact, that's just what I've been thinking myself. What we must find out is, what crime, if any, he has committed. Perhaps he is dead; perhaps he has run away with another woman. We must consider every possibility. Now, I can't very well take you up to the Hudson house, as this is a delicate case; so I wish you'd go over all the newspapers since the tenth and see what you can find that will help us."

At ten o'clock next day Astro appeared in his psychic studio, where appointments with his fashionable clients kept him till two in the afternoon. At that time he called Valeska into his favorite corner of the studio where he did his lounging and studying.

"Well," he asked, "what did you get out of the newspapers?"

"I found so much that it's worse than if I'd found nothing at all,—several murders, an elopement, and a bank robbery. I don't see how any of them help, though. The criminals all seem to be known. Perhaps Hudson was an accomplice."

"My dear girl, never go on general principles; general principles are the refuge of the hopelessly incompetent and inane. If you will follow general principles long enough, you will find yourself in a class that is unlimited in its generalities and hidebound in its principles. If there is no significant detail that dovetails into Hudson's disappearance, we'll simply have to go about it in another way. You will be better able to judge when I tell you what happened this forenoon before I came down to the studio here.

"Mrs. Hudson was ready for me with the news that she had found her husband's check-book, and that it showed him to have an unexpected deposit in the bank of some six thousand dollars. Then she showed me into the bedroom; but as they shared this apartment I thought it unnecessary to look there for anything significant. Hudson's own den was a bare office-like sort of place, small, and furnished with a leather couch, a bookcase, and an old office desk. In this, all the drawers were unlocked except one. I got Mrs. Hudson's permission to pick that lock, and here is what I found." He smiled. "Of course, you understand these were absolutely necessary for me to get my vibrations."

They both laughed at the remark, and he took from his pocket several articles, which he laid upon the table. There were, first, two advertising pictures posed by a pretty woman; evidently the same model in each instance, though used in connection with different products. In one pose the girl held a loaf of bread in her hand; in the other she displayed her gleaming teeth whitened by "Dentabella," a new proprietary toothpaste. She was pretty and quite young. Next was a card, curiously covered with an intricate series of interlaced curves in purple ink,—a beautiful, symmetrical pattern, as accurately drawn as the lathe engraving on a banknote. Last, there was a small printed page containing a calendar with all the months given. Oddly enough, the year was not printed at the top; instead, above the calendar proper appeared the caption, "Number fourteen."

Valeska looked at the collection curiously. "Well," she said at last, "I can't make much of anything except the girl's picture. It looks to me as if Hudson must have some special interest in her, to have two pictures of the same woman. We might find out who she is."

"That's important, surely; unless, of course, we can get hold of a better clue. But do you know what this is?" He held up the card.

"No, it looks to me like a fairy's lace handkerchief design or a sea-shell."

"That is a harmonic curve," said Astro. "Sometimes it's called a vibration curve, and it is traced by a compound or twin elliptic pendulum."

"What's that? I am getting farther away than ever."

"Suppose," continued Astro, "you tie one end of a string to a nail in the ceiling, while the other end is looped up to another nail, also in the ceiling. Now, from the lower point of this V, hang a string with a weight on the end. You observe, the weight will be at the end of a Y, and if you give a rotary motion to the compound pendulum so formed, the weight will travel in an intricate but regular curve, dependent on the relative lengths of the two parts of the pendulum as it swings forward and backward and right and left at the same time. This curve was made by such a one, only more complicated, and arranged so as to trace a line on a plane surface. The curves so formed, curious to say, correspond actually to the musical vibrations of various chords."

"It's interesting, but rather intricate, and I don't see how it helps us much with Hudson," said Valeska. "How about this calendar, and what's the 'Number fourteen' for?"

"That," said the Master of Mysteries, "is a page from a universal calendar; that is, a calendar that can be used for any year. This is the last page of the pamphlet, as it takes just fourteen different diagrams to include all the calendar possibilities,—seven different diagrams in which the year begins on a different day of the week, and another set of seven for the leap years. There's a list in front, probably giving the number of the diagram to be used for each individual year."

"Oh!" exclaimed the girl. "That reminds me, now. I did see something about a 'two-hundred-year calendar.' Where was it? Let me think. Yes, I have it. It was in an account of a body that was found drowned. Stupid of me to overlook that! I'll see if I can find it."

"Get it," Astro said, "while I think this over."

She flew to her file and began to go hurriedly through the sheets of paper. "Here it is! Here it is!" she cried. Then she read breathlessly:

> "The body of an unknown man was found this morning floating in the East River near Thirty-eight Street. The corpse was that of a man of fifty-five or sixty years, and had evidently been in the water some ten days. The lower part of the face was completely covered by a full beard. The body was dressed in a black diagonal cutaway coat and striped trousers, and was doubtless that of a gentleman in reduced circumstances. In the trousers pocket was found a bunch of keys, a small sum of money, and a two-hundred-year calendar. No marks indicating foul play were discovered on the body, which is awaiting identification at the morgue."

"That corresponds in a general way with the description of Hudson that his wife gave me," said Astro. "She had no photograph of him taken within the last twenty years. There's a chance that it may be he, in which case it looks to me like murder; but I'll have to go down to the morgue and see, anyway, on account of the calendar. I think you'd better let me do that alone, while you try to discover something about this 'Dentabella' girl. Come back here as soon as you have located her."

No one would have recognized in the smart, stylishly dressed man who emerged from the studio a half-hour later, the languid picturesque Master of Mysteries, Astro the Seer. He walked briskly along, his eyes eager and alert to every impression. At the morgue he had no difficulty in obtaining permission to view the remains of the man he sought, and to inspect the clothing and the articles that had been found in the pocket.

The body was that of a middle-aged man of benevolent appearance, the face showing weakness rather than resolution in its features. The hands were delicately shaped, with pointed slender fingers. He had been apparently a dreamer, a mystic, rather than a man of vigorous life and practical affairs. Astro turned to inspect the articles displayed before his gaze. The two-hundred-year calendar which had been mentioned in the newspaper corresponded exactly to the page found in Hudson's desk; and on opening it he found that page twenty-nine, containing table number fourteen, had been torn out. What was more remarkable, however, was the fact that with it was a collection of water-soaked, purple-stained cards. Each contained a "harmonic curve," such as had been found in Hudson's drawer. One such coincidence was unusual. Two pointed conclusively to some connection between the two men; if, indeed, the corpse were not that of Hudson himself.

This point, however, was soon settled. Calling up Mrs. Hudson, he found that her husband's hair was scant and brown. The hair of the dead man was strong, slightly curly, and reddish. It was not Hudson.

Astro walked slowly home, plunged in thought, and looked neither to the right nor the left as he advanced. A block before he reached his studio he stopped stock-still for a moment, gazing in front of him; then, with a quick turn, he walked rapidly back, took a cross-town car, and got off at Second Avenue. Along this he hurried till he came to a second-hand bookstore, where on one of the stands outside the window, there was a collection of pamphlets and magazines. He ran his eye over the names: *The Swastika, Universal Brotherhood, Vibrations, The New Wisdom*, and *Cosmos*. He took up one of these and turned to the advertising pages in the rear; then he tried another. It was not till he had read through the *Swastika* that he was satisfied and smiled. He paid for the copy, hailed a passing cab, and was driven to his studio, where Valeska was already waiting for him.

He announced to her at once that the dead man was not Hudson, and gave a brief description of the latter, whereupon she told Astro the story of her own search.

"I didn't find the girl; but I traced her antecedents. First I went to the advertising manager of the 'Dentabella' company, and told him I wanted to get hold of the model he had used in the ad. Finally I wheedled her name out of him—it was Agnes Vivian—and went up to the Harlem address he gave me. The young lady, however, no longer lived there; but I got the woman of the house to talking and found out that our little friend had left without settling her bill. So I intimated that I was looking for Miss Vivian to pay her some money I had borrowed, and in this way got the landlady to tell me everything she could that would help me to locate the missing girl. She had been posing for photographers; but now it seems as if she had got another job. At all events, a gentleman answering to Hudson's description had called on her several times, with the result that one day she had left and had never come back. She had sent for her trunk next day; but the landlady would not let it go, and could not ascertain where it was to be taken. She had an idea, though, that the girl was working on East Thirty-ninth Street somewhere; for she had overheard her telephoning one day previous to her departure. So you see," Valeska concluded, "our friend Hudson has probably left his wife for good and all; or rather for evil, perhaps."

"We'll soon find out," said Astro. "We'll go up and call on him this afternoon."

"What! Have you found out where he is already?"

"I'm inclined to think he's living, temporarily at least, at 198 East Thirty-ninth Street."

"With that girl?" Valeska's eyes blazed.

"Not at all. The only trouble with him is that he loves his wife too much."

Valeska still stared. "That isn't likely,—there are very few men like that nowadays. But I'm very much relieved; for I rather liked the Vivian girl's face; it's attractive."

"Yes," Astro assented, "and Hudson is paying her to be attractive. He has a good business head, this man Hudson. But we must find out first what is the cause of the death of Professor Dove."

"Why, who is he?"

"He is the man whose body is now lying in the morgue."

"How did you find that out?"

"Look at this," said Astro. He pointed to an advertisement in *The Swastika*:

LET ME HELP YOU!
Get into your own Vibration; develop your latent faculties, inherent possibilities; and develop your power, health, success, beauty, and love. Send 50c with name and birth date for trial reading and Vibratory Curve. Prof. Dove, 198 East 39th-St., N. Y.

"And that's what those curves are for, then?" Valeska asked.

"Well, that's what Professor Dove used them for; to mystify his dupes; or, by the looks of him, it's more than likely that he believed in them himself."

"Hudson must have believed in them too, then," she remarked, "or he wouldn't have been keeping them in his desk drawer. Was he a dupe, do you think?"

"You'll recall that Hudson had several of them in his possession. If he had had only one, I'd say he might have been a dupe."

"But what if he did have several?" queried Valeska. "Do you think Hudson murdered the professor?"

"Ah, my dear, that's what I'd like to know myself. I propose that we call at the Vibratory office, or whatever they call it. You see, I doubt if Professor Dove ever had six thousand dollars, or even six thousand cents; he was not worth murdering for his money. One thing is certain, Hudson didn't murder Miss Vivian; and I'm glad of that, for I'd really like to see her. Suppose we go up to Thirty-ninth Street and find out what sort of place it is."

As they walked across town the Master of Mysteries said, "That's a very clever graft, that vibration curve business. The more I think of it, the more I like it. You see, as there are two adjustments,—the length of the upper and the length of the lower pendulum,—you can get an infinite number of vibrations, and consequently an infinite number of curves. Therefore, you can attach any significance you please to the ratio between the two. Suppose, for instance, you divide off the top arm—that corresponds to the upper part of the Y—into inches, and call each inch a certain year. Then divide the lower arm in a similar way into days; say these are eighths of an inch each. If you set your compound pendulum to the two marks—any day and any year—you can produce a curve for any birthday you please, and you can always reproduce it to order. It's a very good plan to have some sort of scientific basis for this kind of thing, on account of the inquisitiveness of the post-office authorities. If you simply have a set of form letters for answers, the chances are that you'll have a fraud order against you and you'll not get your mail— with its desirable money-orders and stamp enclosures."

"And the calendar?"

"Merely to tell easily what day of the week any birthday fell on. For instance, December 22, 1883, was on a Saturday, and so on."

"What I am most interested in is the life readings," said the girl, "and the advice on how to acquire beauty."

"Or love?" Astro added, with a smile.

"I'll try to do that myself. It's more exciting."

From across the street the two now reconnoitered number 198. Below, at the musty stairway, appeared, among other signs, the legend, "Prof. Dove, Astrologer." It was already growing dark, and above, in a window on the third floor, a dim light appeared. The shade was drawn.

"I'm going to investigate more closely," said Astro. "You wait outside here and watch the window. If I raise the shade, come up!"

So saying, he crossed, and ascended the stairs. As he reached the landing, however, he met a young woman coming down, who, at a glance, proved to be the Miss Vivian of the "Dentabella" advertisements. Astro stood still in front of her, barring the way.

"Would you please tell me where Professor Dove is?" he inquired.

"Why, I—I don't know, I'm sure." She looked him up and down curiously.

"Then would you mind telling me where I can find Mr. John Hudson?"

Still she showed no sign of surprise; but drew herself up proudly. "There's no such person in this building that I know of," she asserted.

"I thought I had seen you in Professor Dove's office," continued the crystal-gazer suavely.

Something in his manner now seemed to alarm her. "Indeed! I'm a stranger here. You must be mistaken, really."

"You have never heard of Mr. Hudson?" he went on.

"What right have you to question me in this way?" she demanded boldly; and yet, oddly enough, she did not try to pass him.

"I have the right for two reasons. First, because the post-office is very curious as to the nature of concerns doing a mail-order business, and second, because the police would very much like to know something more concerning the death of Professor Dove."

She scarcely stopped to hear the rest of the sentence before she turned and ran up-stairs. Astro, though he bounded after her in a moment, was a moment too late; for the door was slammed and locked in his face.

"The police!" he heard her cry, and at once there was a commotion in the room. A window was thrown up hurriedly; then all became still. He waited in patience, listening intently. The first sound audible, however, came from the stairway beneath him. Assured that some one was coming up, he turned and saw Valeska beckoning frantically. He tiptoed to her, and she whispered:

"He climbed out through the window into that of the next house! Can't we catch him there?"

"We'll have to, or lose the whole game!" he cried. "It was a bit premature; but perhaps it will be as well, after all. Come along, and—look out for trouble. I'll have to bluff it out now, though I have no desire to impersonate a police officer,—that's a dangerous game. But we must hurry."

In an instant more they were down-stairs and hidden in the entrance of the next building. They had not long to wait. A man, bareheaded and excited, came running down, and would have dashed by, had not Astro's hand immediately clutched him.

"I beg your pardon, Mr. Hudson," said the Master of Mysteries, "but I wish to ask you a few questions."

"Who are you?" The man's voice was full of anxiety.

"A friend," said Astro.

Valeska put out her hand and took that of the frightened old man. "Don't be alarmed, Mr. Hudson. Really you are quite safe with us."

He gazed at her in dull astonishment. "What do you want, any-how?" he exclaimed peevishly, attempting to recover a bold front, though his face was haggard with terror.

"I've found all I really want," Astro replied quietly; "but at the same time I'd like to have my curiosity gratified. What, for instance, do you know concerning the death of Professor Dove?"

Hudson started, and stared in the young man's face. "What! Is he dead? When did he die?"

"He died at about the same time you disappeared from home."

Hudson turned white. "Great God! You don't suspect me of—anything?"

"I'd like to have you explain a few things, that's all," was the quiet response.

"Who are you?" The old man had pulled himself together now, and was more defiant.

"My dear sir," said the Seer calmly, "I am one who has been sent by your wife to discover your whereabouts. As I said, that mission is now accomplished. At the same time you must admit that the circumstances in which I find you are suspicious. You have just escaped from Professor Dove's office, and Professor Dove now lies unidentified in the morgue. You are in possession of a consid-erable sum of money, recently acquired. You are, moreover, found in the company of a very pretty young woman. Surely all this will interest Mrs. Hudson. It remains for you to say how much of it I shall report."

Hudson trembled violently and put his face in his hands. "Oh, my God! you mustn't tell her! You can't! I'm innocent of any crime, so help me God! Wait! Come up to the office, and I'll explain it all."

Astro and Valeska retraced their steps in company with the fugitive, and soon found themselves before the office door. All was dark. Hudson gave three knocks, paused, and then delivered another. The door was opened silently. Miss Vivian stood before them in a dim light. At sight of the two strangers she staggered back.

"Oh!" she cried in alarm. "Are you arrested, Mr. Hudson?"

"I don't know," he answered childishly as he turned up the light.

There was a litter of papers strewn upon the office floor. A long table was piled with letters opened and unopened; there was a typewriter on a stand, a copying-press, a high desk with ledgers, and in a corner, suspended from hooks in the ceiling, the compound pendulum that Astro had described. On the horizontal shelf, fixed to the end of the pendulum, was a white card; and, extending from, a table near by, an arm carrying a glass pen projected so that, when the pendulum was swung, a curve in purple ink was traced on the card. A heavy weight depended from the bottom of the instrument.

Hudson sunk into a chair and groaned. The girl waited without a word, watching him.

Then Valeska approached him. "Mr. Hudson," she said gently, "pray don't take it all so hard. I'm sure that you are innocent, and we'll both help you. If you tell us everything, we can find some way of saving you."

He raised his head and looked at Astro, who nodded in confirmation. Hudson took courage. "The first thing, the most important thing, of course, is to explain about Professor Dove's death. I have no idea how it occurred. Indeed, I didn't know he was dead until you told me. I suspected that something fatal had happened; but I knew nothing definite."

"When did you see him last?"

"Two weeks ago, but Miss Vivian has seen him since then."

The girl took it up. "It was here in this office that I saw him. He was intoxicated, and he frightened me; so I went out and telephoned to Mr. Hudson about it. Then, when I got back, the professor had gone."

"You will understand," hastily explained Hudson, "that Professor Dove, when in his right mind, was a most gentlemanly and kindhearted man; but when he was drunk there was no doing anything with him. I have had several unpleasant experiences with him before. He'd go out and wander all over the town in a sort of daze, talking aloud to himself about his psychic beliefs and all that. He was especially fond of the river, and once we found him sitting away out on a pier and gazing into the water. But I know absolutely nothing about his death, sir, I assure you. Now, about my being here. I'd like to explain—"

"That is not necessary," interrupted Astro, "I know everything I wish to, now."

"What do you mean? What do you know about my private affairs?"

"I'll tell you, Mr. Hudson. First, for a long time you have been anxious to discover some way of making more money than you could in the real estate business. You and your wife wanted to go abroad; and you are very fond of her and naturally wished to please her. Thinking it over and watching the advertisements, you saw that the quickest way to make money was to go into some sort of fortune-telling business and play on the credulity of fools. Knowing of the compound pendulum and the curves it traces so mysteriously, you decided to adopt that as the basis of your graft. You found a willing helper in Professor Dove, who was—well, just a little cracked, and inclined to believe thoroughly in his own psychic powers. You backed him in this enterprise," Astro waved his hand round the room; "but, being a church-member, you naturally couldn't afford to let any one, your wife especially, know of your being engaged in a business that was so undignified and of such dubious morality.

"You advertised, and did so well that you needed more help. You couldn't afford to be known in the matter, and so, when Miss Vivian, here, came to your office to get work, you selected her as assistant. Not wishing to be seen too much in her company, you went to call on her, and finally induced her to help the professor. Then the professor went on one of his periodical debauches, she telephoned to you, and you came down here to straighten out the correspondence, which was becoming larger and more profitable every day. There was more work to it than you at first thought. You had to stay here that night; then you became afraid of Dove's disappearance and of the post-office inspectors. So you buckled down to a night and day job of it until you could clean up the money before you were caught. You are now about ready to quit the affair altogether. Is this correct?"

The old man, who had been listening in great astonishment, assented. "But are you going to report all this to my wife, sir?" he faltered. "It will simply kill her. Can't you keep this from her? I promise to give up the business right now."

Astro drew a telegraph blank from his pocket. There was a message already written on the yellow slip, and he handed it over to Hudson. It read:

> "Rochester, Oct. 21, 4 P. M.
> "Why no letter? Did you receive mine? Return-
> ing Empire State Limited to-night. John."

"Ring for a messenger boy and send this," continued the Master of Mysteries. "She will not know that it isn't a genuine telegram. A woman in her state of mind won't notice anything, I'm sure; and I think if you turn up at the Grand Central, appearing to have come in on that train, she will be there to meet you with open arms."

Tears appeared in the old man's eyes. "I'll do it!" he said. "And to-morrow I'll buy a couple of tickets for Naples. God bless you, sir, for your kindness!"

"And what's to become of me?" spoke up Miss Vivian.

Astro looked at her indulgently. "You may go on with this work here, for all I care," he said. "It's a very tidy little business apparently, and none of my affair. But I advise you rather to apply for a position in Mr. Hudson's office. I don't think, however, that with your face and figure you will have much trouble in getting employment."

"Oh, I'll see to that," said John Hudson.

"Well," Valeska said with relief, as she and Astro left the office, "it's all over now."

"Not at all!" remarked her companion brusquely. "I haven't earned my fee yet. Come into this drug store with me a moment."

He went to the telephone and called up Mrs. John Hudson, "Mrs. Hudson," he said, "I've been consulting my crystals, and have just seen your husband in Rochester. He was taking a train for New York. He had just consummated a real estate deal there which had been very profitable, and I think you will see him safe and sound again to-night. Kindly send my check to the studio. Thank you. Good night."

"My crystals are certainly wonderful," said Astro, laughing.

"Yes," said Valeska, "and I think you're rather wonderful yourself."

THE STOLEN SHAKESPEARE

Hesitating at the door of the studio long enough only to send to Astro a quick surreptitious message with her eyes—indicating, apparently, contempt for the visitor—Valeska announced, "Mr. Barrister," and left the two men alone in the room.

The newcomer looked about a bit foolishly, and then turned to the palmist. "You're Astro, I suppose?"

Astro, in robe and turban, bowed gravely and his glance slumbered.

"Eh—ah—the fact is, sir," continued Barrister, "that I have come here about a peculiar matter, and solely, sir, to please my wife. She has a woman's weakness for anything occult,—anything full of folderol and fake. You see, I don't take any stock in it myself; but—"

"I understand perfectly," said the Master of Mysteries without apparent annoyance. He seemed, in fact, to be bored already.

The other teetered affably on his toes and heels, condescension in his manner. "She had heard that you professed to be some kind of fortune-teller, besides doing this palmistry business. Is that so?"

"I have had occasion at times to use certain powers which are—ah—supposed to be occult. I say 'supposed to be,' out of deference to your manifest feelings in the matter, Mr. Barrister."

"Hum!" said the prospective client quickly. "Well, whether they are or not doesn't matter in this case, as I'm here simply to please my wife. If I didn't come, she'd come, you know. However, if you are able to locate what we want, I'll be willing to acknowledge anything you wish, and pay you accordingly. I suppose you are a medium, then?"

"Some call it that," acknowledged the reserved young man. "I myself assert that I have merely done a few things that others find it too hard to do."

"Such as—"

"Kindly let me look at your hand."

"Bosh!" said Barrister; but he gazed at his own palm, nevertheless, with a new air of curiosity, and after a moment stretched it toward the palmist. "Well, see what you can find in it!" he said.

Astro looked at it negligently; then, under his half-shut lids his eyes sped rapidly over his client's person, the neat business suit beneath the black dress overcoat, the daintily tied scarf, the highly polished shoes, and the general air of careful grooming. Then they returned to the hand before him. Finally, the Seer leaned back listlessly and smiled.

"You went to see Anna Held last night, and were bored. You once had your pockets picked, and will probably have it happen to you again. You are interested in Egyptology—and, apropos, I wish you'd look at my porphyry sphinx there and give me some idea of its age."

Barrister stared, and grew a bit uneasy. Then, apparently to hide his embarrassment, he turned to the carved image and surveyed it with the air of a connoisseur. As he presented his back to the Seer, the latter swiftly stooped over, picked up a return check of a New York theater, good the night before, and slid it into one of the pockets of his silk robe.

"That's about 1400 B. C.," said Barrister easily. "Where on earth did you get hold of it?"

"From my godfather, in Cairo," said the palmist.

"Well," said Barrister, returning, "I've no time now to examine it closely."

"And the matter which worries your wife?" Astro inquired.

Again his visitor hesitated, looked about the room, and gazed again at the sphinx. "Well," he said finally, "I'll tell you." He seated himself and went on: "I have, or rather did have, a First Folio Shakespeare, one of the few good ones of the thirty-seven copies extant. It was stolen from my library yesterday. That's what I want to find—"

"That, and the one who stole it also, I suppose?"

"Er—yes. Yes, certainly."

"An interesting sort of quarry, and rather unusual. Have you been to the police?"

Barrister pursed his lips and shook his head.

"No. You see, there wouldn't be much use in that, would there? I'm afraid the thief, if he found he was suspected, would destroy the book. He can't sell it, anyway; for these folios are as well known to collectors as good race-horses are to touts. He can't get away with it; for every bookman in the world will soon know it if he offers it for sale. I want it back, of course; but it is my wife's idea, this coming to you about it. She gave me the book when we were first married, and so, naturally, I value it at even more than its own great intrinsic value."

"Have you ever had any offers for it?" Astro asked carelessly.

"What? Offers? Oh, no; no indeed; no offers at all. Why should I want to sell it? No, sir! It would be useless for any one to attempt to buy it."

"But nobody is harming you by offering. When did you miss it?"

"Last night, after I came home from the theater. I went to see Anna Held, as you said, though how the mischief you knew it I can't see, and we came home early, disgusted. We happened to be talking about the Folio, and my wife walked to the case and looked for it. It was gone."

"Had the lock been tampered with?"

"Yes, forced. The window had been pried open with a jimmy, too. It was evidently done by a burglar who knew just what he wanted. But it doesn't look like a professional's work; for the book would be too hard to dispose of."

"I see," said Astro. He gazed away into space and puffed at his water-pipe meditatively. "Mr. Barrister, I'll try to find it for you. If I succeed in getting the book or the person who stole it from you, my charge will be five hundred dollars."

"All right," said Barrister, rising. "Will you want to come up to my house and look over the place?"

"I think I can put myself more *en rapport* with the case, if I do; I want to feel the vibrations, so to speak, and no doubt I shall get an impression of the aura of the culprit if I am on the spot. The rest I shall do with the crystals."

Barrister did not conceal his scorn. "Oh, very well," He said, "I suppose it will at least satisfy my wife. When will you be up?"

"To-morrow morning, early. I'll ask you to disturb nothing, and even to keep away from the room until I come."

"There's nothing to disturb," Barrister commented; "but I'll see to it that nobody interferes with your magic." And so saying, he took up his hat, gave the sphinx one last glance, and left the room.

When he was gone the palmist doffed his regalia and yawned. A moment later Valeska reentered the studio. Astro gazed at her reflectively.

"Did you notice that man's watch-charm?" he asked.

"Why, there was something funny about it; but I couldn't make the thing out exactly."

"Did you ever see an Egyptian scarab?"

"Why, yes. But he didn't have one, did he?"

"He used to have one. You know how they mount them,—with a pin through the beetle so it can revolve? The setting and the pin were there; but not the stone. You must look closer next time."

"What else did I miss?" she asked, pouting.

"You didn't say anything about his carrying his purse in his outside overcoat pocket. He will always be an easy mark for the light-fingered gentry if he keeps that up. It's lucky for him that he's rich."

"Oh, he is wealthy, of course! I got that much right, anyway. He looked as if he were very well-off, in fact."

"I should imagine he was, with a First Folio Shakespeare lying loose in his library! That's what we've got to find."

"It's interesting?"

"Interesting! I should say so! It's a regular kidnapping case. Talk about diamonds! Why, they're stupid things. Every one likes diamonds, and they can be cut up into smaller stones and readily disposed of, if you're careful about it. But you can't cut a page out of a First Folio, you can't even hint that you'd like to sell it, without all the world knowing about it. Bookhunters are the most determined and interesting collectors in the world. I know of no passion to equal it."

He walked over to the telephone and called up a leading dealer in rare volumes.

"I wish to ask about a First Folio Shakespeare. Are there any bidders in the open market for a copy?" He wrote down rapidly on a tab as he spoke into the receiver,— "William A. Hepson. Oh, yes, the millionaire. Ah, thank you."

He slammed the instrument down vigorously, snatched up a telegraph blank, rapidly wrote a message, and handed it to Valeska.

She read it aloud:

> "William A. Hepson, Chicago, Ill.—Will you give four thousand dollars for a guaranteed First Folio Shakespeare? Wire reply to Jane Gore, 181 East 18th Street, New York."

"Why!" she exclaimed. "Have you located it already?"

"Not quite. But I have an idea, and this will help, if we get an answer by to-morrow morning."

"Who is he?"

"He's a Chicago beef packer who offered four thousand dollars for the book a while ago; but, curiously enough, he was in town this week."

"Is he in the city now?"

"That's what I should like very much to know myself. In the meantime, send this, get the answer at your place, and bring it to me in the morning. Then we'll go up and see Mrs. Barrister."

Valeska appeared next morning with a yellow envelope. "He refuses your offer," she said.

"Good!" exclaimed the Master of Mysteries, rubbing his hands in satisfaction. "He has the Folio, then, as I suspected. Now, to work! This case already begins to offer delicate little labyrinths which are nothing short of delicious to the analytical mind. We'll lose no time getting out to Mrs. Barrister's, and I want you to use your eyes better than you did last night. I expect you to see everything that I don't. Remember to watch me, though, and be ready for instructions. Notice any signal that I may happen to give you. For instance, if I raise my eyes to the ceiling, my next look will be at what I want you to notice. If I touch anything, you're to take it and look at it carefully, and follow what I say next. If I cough, you're to create some diversion so that I shan't be noticed for a few moments."

Valeska laughed. "You'll be doing a trance next. Funny how well the bluff always works, isn't it?"

Astro frowned. "My dear," he said pompously, "there are waves of the ether,—N-rays, X-rays, actinic and ultraviolet vibrations, to which I am exceedingly susceptible. I have an inner sense and an esoteric knowledge of life and its mysteries that is hidden from all who have not lived for cycles and eons in solitude and contemplation with the Mahatmas of the Himalayas!"

Valeska, instead of being impressed, broke into a rippling laugh as they went up the avenue.

The Barristers lived in a large, solemn brownstone house off Fifth Avenue, one of a hundred similar domiciles, heavily furnished, dim, close, lusterless, quiet, warm. Astro and his assistant waited in the reception-room till Mrs. Barrister appeared. She was large, plumply built, with gray hair artfully pompadoured and undulated, and a pleasant, though not very intelligent smile; a woman that still kept herself well and carried herself well, treasuring the last remains of what had been a comfortable prettiness. She greeted them cordially.

"I'm so glad you've come!" she announced. "Seems as if I couldn't wait any longer; for I felt sure that you could help us if anybody could, and I do feel so terribly about this robbery! You know it was my wedding gift to Mr. Barrister. My husband agreed with me that it wasn't exactly a case for the police, and we don't want any more talk about it than is absolutely necessary. I've heard so much about you, Mr. Astro; for a great many of my friends have gone to you, and you told them such remarkable things! Then that case of your finding the Sacarnet sapphire gave me considerable confidence in you. Why, my own mother once recovered a purse she had lost, by going to a medium about it!" She bustled about amiably.

"Now, I suppose you want to see the library, don't you? You know Mr. Barrister doesn't believe in any thing supernatural, and he wouldn't stay. But I'll show you in."

During this long speech, Valeska's eyes traveled over Mrs. Barrister's portly person; but the Master of Mysteries seemed rapt in thought, abstracted and inattentive. He rose now, however, and followed through the folding doors into the library beyond. The shades had been drawn as if a death had occurred; she raised them, showing a square room, every wall lined with glass-covered book-cases. She went up to one, beside a window, and threw open a door. It was as if she were displaying a rifled tomb.

"Here is where it was kept,—right in there. You can see the marks of a chisel or something near the lock. The frame was pried open. Isn't it dreadful? That book was like an only child to us!"

Astro apparently gave it scarcely a glance. "Mrs. Barrister," he said, "I'll ask you kindly to leave me here alone for fifteen minutes. I am extraordinarily sensitive to vibrations; but I must be undisturbed while I concentrate my mind sufficiently to induce the proper psychic conditions. Meanwhile my assistant will stay with you."

Mrs. Barrister was impressed, and withdrew without further questioning. The door of the library was shut, and the two women sat down by a window in the reception-room. Valeska immediately began her own line of investigation.

"When did you last see the book?" she asked.

"Thursday afternoon at about four o'clock I showed it to a caller, and then locked the case as usual. We got home from the theater that night a little after ten, and went almost immediately to the library, as we had been having a discussion about one of the lines in *Macbeth*. Then we saw that the book was gone."

"Do you know of any one having entered the room, besides yourself and Mr. Barrister, between four and ten?"

"Mary, my maid, was in with the tea things; that's all I know."

"And you don't suspect her?"

"Oh, no! She has been with me for years."

"And the caller?"

Mrs. Barrister thought for a moment before answering. Then she said, "It was a Mr. White. I confess I don't like him very well. But he's more a friend of my husband's than mine. In fact, my husband came in before Mr. White left; so I went up-stairs and left the two men alone. I had an idea there was some trouble between them."

"Does your husband belong to any club?"

"Yes, the Booklovers, and the Stage Club. So does Mr. White. Why?"

"Oh," said Valeska carelessly, "Mr. Barrister seemed such a man of the world,—just the man to belong to clubs, you know. But who showed Mr. White out the door?"

"Why, Mr. Barrister went with him himself. You see, it couldn't have been possible for Mr. White to have concealed the book; it's quite large, you know?"

"You have looked everywhere, of course?"

"Oh, yes. We went immediately to work, searched Mary's room at her request, and then everywhere else in the house. It simply isn't here."

At this moment Astro opened the door and walked silently into the room.

"Oh," Mrs. Barrister suddenly exclaimed, "I quite forgot to tell Mr. Astro something that I'm sure is important! It's a clue we discovered while we were searching the library after we had found the scratches and the broken lock of the case. Here it is!" She drew a scrap of paper from her purse and handed it to him. It was evidently the corner of a letter, and bore a few words written in violet ink.

The palmist held it lightly in his hand for a moment, then asked, "Has any one else had this, except you?"

"Oh, yes. Mr. Barrister himself found it, and, of course, he examined it carefully; but he could make nothing of it."

Astro cast his eyes to the ceiling, and then down on the paper again. He pressed it to his forehead, then handed it to his assistant.

"I shall have to wait until the last influences are evaporated, leaving the original personality of the writer to assert itself." He whirled quickly about, placed his hand to his lips, and coughed.

"Oh, Mrs. Barrister!" Valeska exclaimed. "Look at this paper again for a moment. Come to the light by the window here. It seemed to me I saw a watermark that showed through when I held it to the light. See if you can see it." As she spoke she drew the woman into the bay-window so that she stood with her back to the room.

Astro stepped quickly over to a bookcase against the wall, and, keeping his eyes carefully on Mrs. Barrister, reached to the top of one of the shelves. Four or five books protruded about an inch from the rest of the line. Astro's hand curved over these and down behind until it touched the shelf. Before Mrs. Barrister had turned again, his hand was withdrawn. He spoke sharply.

"Could you lend me a screw-driver?"

"Certainly." She rang for the maid, who appeared, and was sent on the errand. In a few minutes she returned.

"I'm very sorry, Mrs. Barrister, but I can't find it. We always keep it in the kitchen closet; but it's not there now."

"I thought so," said Astro. "But one question, Mary, before you go. First, let me see your palm."

The girl held out her hand timidly, with wonder in her face.

The Master of Mysteries felt of it tentatively, then looked directly into her eyes. "Mary," he said, "where were you after dinner-time on Thursday; from then until Mr. and Mrs. Barrister returned home?"

"In the kitchen with the cook most of the time, sir. I went up into the dining-room beside the library once or twice, though."

"You heard nothing unusual?"

"Nothing at all, sir."

"How did you get that violet stain on your finger?"

Mary looked at it calmly. "It was from writing a letter the other day. I couldn't get it all off."

"I think I have stayed as long as is necessary," said Astro, turning to Mrs. Barrister, "and now, if you'll excuse me, I'll go. I shall report to your husband as soon as I find anything."

Leaving with his assistant, he walked slowly down the front steps. As soon as they were out of sight of the windows, he said, "Well, what did you find out while I was investigating, Valeska?"

She narrated the conversation while Astro walked thoughtfully beside her, his eyes roaming from side to side, until they lighted upon a line of ash barrels near the curb. He stopped.

"See here, Valeska!" he exclaimed suddenly. "I wish you'd go into this house and find out in some way how long these barrels have been standing here. It's a shame the way the Board of Health neglects its duties. Do you see? Tell them you have been sent by a Civic Reform committee to find out if there's any complaint."

He walked on, smiling to himself. "Entirely too clever," he murmured; "so clever that it's positively stupid!" He approached the ash cans and surveyed their contents. From the top of one he gingerly drew out a torn sheet of paper. Another barrel showed, among its overflowing contents, several tin cans, a shoe, a lot of broken bottles, and a mass of sawdust. He gave them a hard look, then sauntered on till Valeska caught up with him.

"Those barrels have been out since Thursday," she said.

He smiled and made no comment. "Now," he said, "what I want you to do is to call on this Mr. White. You had better be getting subscriptions for a book. Get one for a sample at some shop,—something rather silly too—*Bibliophiles and Their Hobbies*—and you are to find out White's private opinion of Barrister. Barrister, you understand, has already subscribed. You may work it up any way you like, only be sure to get some expression of opinion."

It was almost noon before Valeska returned from her errand, and, as by this time the palmist's outer office was filled with waiting clients, it was the lunch hour before she could speak to him.

"I shall have to raise my fee again," he said. "Ten dollars a reading doesn't seem to stop them at all. I'll make them come only by appointment after this. But what did you find out?"

The girl's eyes sparkled with news. "Hepson's our man,—Hepson via White, I guess. Hepson saw Barrister, too, at the club the other morning. Hepson's gone; but White—"

"Hepson, Hepson, Hepson!" mimicked the Seer, with a smile at her eagerness. "But pray give us more news about White."

Valeska laughed. "Well, he's awfully sore on Barrister for some reason. He believes Mr. Barrister's a fool, I gather."

"He isn't in love with Mrs. Barrister, is he?"

"No! He's in love with himself, I think. He said, for one thing, that Barrister knew no more about books than he did about poker."

"Poker! How's that?"

"Why, I told him I had sold several copies to members of the Stage Club,—I got their names out of the *Blue Book*, and knew they played pretty hard there,—so we got to chatting about our luck. You see, I told him I liked to play myself, and he began telling me how successful he always was. Then he said he had hard work with some of his friends to collect the gambling debts they owed him."

"I see." The Master of Mysteries turned into his den, and Valeska followed him.

"Why, what's this?" she asked, pointing to a large, flat, heavy parcel on the table. "Why, it's addressed to Mr. Hepson in Chicago! Oh! have you found the Folio already?"

Astro smiled. "I told you some time ago that Hepson already had it. But this is getting warm."

Valeska fingered the package. "It looks just like a big atlas wrapped up."

"It is," said Astro. "I bought it at a book-shop after I left you."

"What in the world do you want to send it to Hepson for, then?"

"I don't particularly. But I should like to show it to the clerk at a certain branch office of the Adams Express Company here."

"Oh, I do wish you'd explain!" Valeska exclaimed.

"I'd rather let you do a little thinking for yourself. You have seen White. You know that Hepson was in town. You have heard Barrister's story. Nothing could be simpler. For instance, how

about Mary the maid, and the violet ink stains? What would you
make of that?" He stopped a moment, smiling. "I will tell you, however, that I found the screw-driver that was used to open the bookcase with and to force the window with; for it wasn't a jimmy at all."

"Where was it?"

"You recall when I gave you the signal to distract Mrs. Barrister's attention? You did it very cleverly. At that moment I was more
interested in the appearance of several books in a case in the library than I was in the scrap of paper. The instrument, badly bent
and twisted, was behind those projecting books."

"Oh!" Valeska studied at it. "No wonder Mary couldn't find it!
Then it must have been Mary, after all. But why didn't she throw
the screw-driver away? Perhaps she thought it would be missed,
and wanted a chance to have it straightened out."

"Perhaps so," said Astro dryly.

"But what about the scrap of paper, then?" asked the girl. "Have
you made anything of that?"

"A good deal," replied the Master. "For instance, here's the rest
of the sheet," and he took from his pocket the portion that he had
removed from the ash barrel. "Does that give you a clue?"

She studied a moment. "Now, wait! Don't tell me, please! Your
rule is, 'Ask yourself what there is about this crime that distin-
guishes it from others. How is it different from the ordinary run of
things? Then seize upon that difference, be it great or small, and
proceed logically and analytically in any direction it offers.' But
what is different? It's all different, it seems to me."

"Well, you work it out, and I'll go down and try to find an express office in which a flat parcel addressed to a Chicago millionaire will have been noticed. You may turn away any people who
come for a reading. This is going to bring in more money than I
thought, and it will pay to follow it up while it's hot."

Valeska met him at the front door when he returned, and said
in a low voice, "Mr. Barrister is here."

"Certainly," said Astro. "I telephoned him to be here at four
o'clock."

"Then you are finished?"

"You'll see."

"I found out that White had left town to-day," she announced.

"Aha!" said the Seer cryptically.

He went in and bowed gravely to Barrister in the reception-room. Valeska busied herself at her desk and watched under her brows. Astro took his accustomed seat on the divan.

"Mr. Barrister," he said, after a pause, "I am sorry to say that I have been unable to find either the Folio or the thief."

The other immediately rose, shaking his head emphatically and triumphantly. "I thought as much," he said. "This is what all this charlatanry usually amounts to. You're all alike,—you can impose upon credulous women; but when it comes actually to accomplishing anything, you can't deliver the goods. However, I've satisfied my wife, at any rate. I suppose there will be no charge in these circumstances, Mr. Astro?"

The Master of Mysteries twirled his thumbs and spoke dreamily. "On the contrary, Mr. Barrister, my services on this case will cost you just one thousand dollars."

His client stared at him indignantly. His brow drew down. "What in the world do you mean, sir? One thousand dollars!"

"One thousand dollars is my fee. I can give you a blank check if you haven't your book with you."

"But you've discovered nothing."

"I said that I had not found the book or the thief."

"And yet your fee, if you had found either, was to have been only five hundred! I don't understand what you are driving at, sir!"

Astro recrossed his legs and gave his client gaze for gaze. He spoke now very deliberately. His languorous tone had given place to a crisp hard enunciation. "Mr. Barrister," he said, "what you say is true. You understand me perfectly. If I had told you the name of the thief and the location of the book, I should have charged you only five hundred dollars. My price for not telling is one thousand. Do you understand me now?"

He took up a crystal sphere and began to regard it fixedly.

Barrister's face had changed from perplexity to anger, and then to a sudden comprehension. He dropped his head and gazed at the carpet, standing for some moments irresolute and dismayed. Finally he walked to the desk, took the blank check that Valeska handed to him, and dipped his pen into the ink. He looked up.

"You never expect to find the culprit, I suppose?" he asked, with a strange expression on his face.

"I never expect to," answered the Seer.

Barrister signed his name and handed over the check. "You are a most extraordinary young man, sir!" he snarled, and left the room, slamming the door behind him.

Valeska stared, her brows knitted. "Wait a minute! I've almost got it! It was Barrister himself who stole the book—his own book—"

"Which his wife had given him when they were married; don't forget that," said Astro.

"Yes; so, of course, he wouldn't want her to know he had been mean enough to dispose of it. She is still in love with him, I could see that, and she's a sentimental old thing, too. So he had to mimic a burglary, did he?"

"And very stupidly he did it,—with an ordinary screw-driver which he didn't have sense enough to destroy."

"But why did he want the book? What did he do with it?"

"Made arrangements with Hepson that morning; stole it that afternoon. Gambling debt. You found that out yourself from White, who had been forcing Barrister for the money, and was sore because he wouldn't pay up. Barrister is sadly in need of ready cash; I found that out from his bank. And Hepson offered him three thousand for his Folio."

"Then Hepson has the book now?"

"Or it's on its way there. That's the reason he turned our telegraph offer down. He wasn't interested, because Barrister had already sold him his copy."

"How did you know that?"

"Let me ask you one question. What was there about this case that was different from most affairs like it?"

Valeska pondered. "Why, it seems to me strange that Barrister didn't call in the police at once."

"Precisely. If he had, he was afraid he would have trouble, and Hepson might be investigated. It's easy enough now for Barrister to keep his wife from knowing anything of the sale; and Hepson will be glad enough at getting the book to say nothing about it for a year or two. There was my start. It seemed queer that Barrister, losing so valuable a treasure, shouldn't report it at once and have it traced, and all the dealers notified. His wife's belief in the occult was what got him safely over the necessity of calling in the police. I didn't like the way he protested so much that nobody had offered to buy his Folio. It seemed to back up my suspicion."

"I rather suspected Mary," commented Valeska, "when I saw the violet stains on her fingers just like the ink on the scrap of paper. By the way, where did you get the rest of that paper, and what does it mean? It quite led me astray."

"Which was precisely what it was intended to do. Our friend Mr. Barrister tried not only to hide his own tracks, but to create false ones in order to befuddle any detective who tackled the job. I noticed the violet writing as we came past the ash barrels. So, I presume, did Barrister when he came home after committing the robbery. 'Aha!' he said to himself, 'here's a chance to fool any detective that comes hunting for clues. I'll give him clues!' So he took the piece, tore off a part, and carefully left it on the floor. I confess that was clever; for as his finding of it in the ash can was entirely accidental, no one knows where such a trail might have led to. But the trouble is that such a man always goes too far, especially when he has to work in a hurry. Now, there's the case of the boots, for instance."

"But I didn't see any boots."

"I saw one in the ash barrel,—a left shoe. When I looked out the window that was supposed to have been forced, I saw the prints of a right boot; but it had nails in the heel arranged just as its brother in the barrel had. Of course Barrister took the shoe out of the barrel and used it to make the footprints of a supposititious burglar."

"Why," exclaimed the girl, "it's just as wonderful as if you had really done it with crystal gazing! But I don't see how you could be sure, after all. There was White, who might have been Hepson's tool."

"Yes, I had two lines I might have worked on,—White as well as Barrister,—but White had been winning plenty of money, and is well-off, anyway. He wouldn't go around jimmying windows to get things, either."

"Still, I insist you had nothing that absolutely connected Barrister with his own misdeeds."

"Hadn't I? If you had gone into about ten branch express offices in the downtown district as I had, you'd have found out. You recall my package? It was just the same size as the Folio. I finally found the office that I was looking for, and said to the clerk, 'I sent a package to Mr. Hepson two days ago, and he telegraphs that it hasn't been received. So I'm sending this. I wish you'd look it up and see what's the matter. It's from Renold M. White.' Well, the clerk looked over his record of carbon duplicate receipts, and said, 'There was a package sent from a Mr. Barrister to a Mr. Hepson in Chicago; but none from White.' So I said, 'Never mind,' and left."

The two sat in silence for some time. At last the Master of Mysteries spoke:

"There is just one thing I don't like about this case of the theft of the First Folio Shakespeare."

"What's that?" asked Valeska.

"This is the first time I go on record as not having run down my quarry; but it has paid fairly well—for two days' work." And he smiled as he took up an antique volume of the *Kabala*.

THE MACDOUGAL STREET AFFAIR

Entering the room slowly, grave and distinguished in his flowing silken robes, Astro did not glance at his visitor till he had seated himself in a picturesque pose upon the divan. Then, taking up the silver mouthpiece of his water-pipe, he gave a long sober look at the stranger.

"It's a pity you are unhappily married," he said, gazing languidly at the red and gold ceiling above him. He seemed to pay little attention to the thick hairy hand of his client, which lay limp on the velvet cushion.

Opposite him the bull-necked, red-faced man sat staring in amazement, no longer wearing the contemptuous, amused expression with which he had entered the astrological parlors of the slim, romantic-looking, young man in the turban. Like many another unbeliever who had come to test Astro in that very room, his look had changed gradually from scorn to interest, until now his eyes were fixed on the palmist with eager curiosity and perplexity.

"No doubt it's her fault," Astro continued; "for she is indifferent and selfish. It might be better if you were to let it come to an actual quarrel, and be separated." He reached for his narghile, and took a long bubbling whiff of perfumed smoke, as if, as far as he was concerned, the matter had been weighed and settled.

There came at this moment the sound of a muffled electric bell. His client still gazed stupidly in front of him, but said nothing. He did not seem to notice the signal.

Astro, however, rose and went to a pair of black velvet curtains hanging at one side of the wall behind his visitor's back. There was a mirror hung above which reflected the stocky form of the man at the little table, the bulge of a revolver in his hip pocket, and the round head with its short cropped hair. The head did not turn. Astro parted the hangings deftly and peered within. On a level with his eyes was a small square window, lighted from behind. Against the glass a sheet of paper was fastened, and on it was written in a feminine scrawl, "Plain-clothes man. Working on the Macdougal Street dynamite case."

Valeska smiled at him from the secret cabinet.

Astro picked up a magnifying-glass, dropped the curtains, and returned to his client. Seating himself, he looked carefully at the lines in the detective's palm; after which he took a small crystal sphere from a drawer in the table, set it on the cushion, and seemed to lose himself in prolonged contemplation of the mysteries hidden within it. His vis-à-vis fidgeted restlessly.

"You are a busy man indeed," commented Astro, half aloud. "Not only are you keeping your eye on the crooks around the Rennick Hotel, and investigating several pool-room layouts, but you come up here in reality to see if my place is, as you would call it, 'on the square.' How on earth you have time for all this, when you are so puzzled about the Macdougal Street business, is more than I can see. You must be a man of extraordinary resource."

The officer stared like a child at the dreamy-eyed Oriental before him. "Gosh!" he said almost plaintively. Then he rose and thrust his big hairy hands into his pockets. "Say, what do you know about that dynamite affair, anyway?" he asked.

Astro smiled. "Nothing. I'm too busy to trouble about things that are not any of my business."

"But what if it was your business?" continued the policeman eagerly. "What if I made it an object to you?"

Astro assumed a dramatic air of omnipotence.

"Ah!" answered the Seer. "No doubt I could tell you anything you wished to know."

The man drew out a pocketbook. "See here," he said, tapping it, "I ain't rich by any means; but I'm up against it on this case, and if you can look into them glasses and give me a tip, I'll make it worth your while."

Astro laughed. "Oh, it's not quite so simple as that. You must understand, my dear sir, that I can do absolutely nothing without coming into direct personal contact with the vibrations emanating from the scene or from the individual. I can tell about you, because you happen to be before me; but I should have to be present at the place in order to become sensitive to the occult influences that have permeated the vicinity of the crime. Do you understand?"

The officer evidently did not understand; but he was in nowise deterred from making use of this power that had so impressed him. "I'll take you up there," he offered.

"Very well," said Astro. "I'll help you on this case, Mr. —"

"McGraw."

"—McGraw, with the distinct understanding, however, that I am to be left to do what I like, undisturbed and unwatched. Utter abstraction, my dear sir, the harmony of the Tatvic Rhythm, is in all instances absolutely necessary. I see the invisible; I hear the inaudible; I touch the intangible."

The detective stood like a cow gazing on an eighth wonder of the world. "All right," he said lamely. "When'll you come?"

"At three this afternoon. Meet me in front of the place—number 950, isn't it? That's right. But first I should like to know what you have learned about the matter."

"Well, it's just this way. There's a chap at number 950 named Pietro Gallino. He has a wholesale wine and grocery shop, and does a considerable importing business; he also acts as a sort of local banker. Two weeks ago he got a letter that was made up of words torn out of a newspaper, telling him to leave a thousand dollars in ten-dollar bills underneath a certain bench by the arch into Washington Square. He was to put it there the next night, or else his place would be blown up. He went dippy about it, of course, and reported it to the police right away. We told him to put up a dummy package and carry out instructions. He did that and the place was watched. Nobody came, of course. The next day there was an explosion in front of his store, and it smashed up the windows and doors good and plenty. Then he got another letter, something like the first one, only he was to put the money in a certain fire bucket on the third floor of a building at 231 Vestry Street. Somebody came that time! but, with three exits to the building and us watching every one of them, we couldn't nab our man. The next day there was an explosion on top of Gallino's building, and then came this last letter."

He took from his pocketbook a sheet of paper, folded. On it were pasted irregular fragments from the advertising pages of a newspaper. It read as follows:

> "Have a thousand dollars with you, day and
> night. We will tell you how to pay before the twelfth.
> If any more tricks, will blow you to pieces sure!"

It was signed with the dread insignia of the Black Hand,—a skull and cross-bones and a rudely drawn hand.

Astro looked at it carelessly, pressed it to his forehead, fingered it sensitively, and then put it in his pocket with composure. "Very well. I get from this letter, even now, a subtle impression, and when I encounter these vibrations in the flesh I shall immediately recognize them. The criminal has a violet soul, tending toward purple. Purples are malicious and very dangerous. This aura distresses me." And he foppishly sniffed at a bottle of smelling-salts.

The effect of this was not lost on McGraw. "I don't know how the mischief you get wise," said the dazed officer; "but it don't matter how you turn the trick, just so you deliver the goods. I'll see you at three then. And be mighty careful of that paper!"

Astro nodded impassively as his visitor left. Then he pressed an electric button, and Valeska Wynne, his young assistant, entered the room with a free and easy, graceful, girlish stride. She smiled quickly, and lifted her eyebrows at the departing plain-clothes man.

"Easy enough to tip you that time," she remarked, "I passed him on the stairs with a policeman, and caught a few words. Anything in him?"

"No money; but it's a good advertisement, and it gets me in with the police, so that I shall be able to rely on them for help from time to time. Did you notice the chalk on his sleeve?"

"Sure; but I didn't have time to tell you, and I knew you'd get that. Billiard cue, I suppose?"

"Hardly—not in this Broadway neighborhood; though it's possible. Billiard-cue chalk hereabout is generally green in color. That white stuff probably means a bucket-shop. He's been nosing round illegal race-track, gambling places, I imagine. At least I told him so, and it took. Notice the dab of gilt paint on his vest?"

"No," answered the girl.

"They're rebronzing the furnishings and decorations in the Rennick lobby to-day. Inasmuch as that is the notorious hotel for crooks of all descriptions, I saw at a glance that he had been there. Did you observe his handkerchief?"

"Oh, yes," said she eagerly, glad at last to have caught one point in the train of the master's deduction. "It was a small one—a woman's, of course."

"And the top button of his coat?"

"No." Valeska's face fell.

"Sewed on with fine copper wire instead of thread. What do you make of that?" He surveyed her quizzically.

She puckered her pretty face for a moment, then raised her fair blue eyes interrogatively. "They seem contradictory, don't they? The handkerchief would suggest marriage; unless it's a souvenir—"

"No. He used it too strenuously, I'm afraid, for any sentiment to be attached to it; his only emotion seemed to be disgust at its size—or lack of size. His wife's, of course. She's alive, and with him, or her handkerchiefs wouldn't be where he'd pick one up in a hurry; probably mixed in with his when the laundry came home."

"It might be his sister's," suggested the girl.

"Why didn't she sew his buttons on for him, then? Oh, it's simple enough. But your tip was what really helped me most with McGraw—that's his name—after all. He wants me to help him solve the Macdougal Street mystery."

In a few minutes Astro went over the history of the affair, and laid the last threatening letter on the table. Valeska inspected it carefully.

"The pieces are all cut from the advertising pages of *The Era*," she said finally.

"Good! Except these two, which, you see, instead of being cut, are torn along the edge. Not much of a clue, but worth remembering."

"What do you know about the Black Hand?" Valeska asked.

"As much as any one, and that is—nothing. Even Petrosini, the greatest of metropolitan Italian sleuths, said that there was no such thing. Warburton, on *Immigration*, has some very interesting chapters concerning the bloodthirsty Sicilian and his criminal organization, all of which have been corroborated in the recent Camorra and Mafia trials. But here in America there is really no Black Hand; although the rather melodramatic name is made use of from time to time by individuals bent on extortion. It is a great terrorizer. In this instance, the work is clearly that of one person. The affair looks simple. I'll get my vibrations easily enough; you just see if I don't! It isn't half so difficult as that interior epicycloid I was at work on last night. Be ready at three o'clock."

Until that time Astro the Seer was characteristically picturesque. Curious women listened to his talk about them in delight, men came with ill-disguised scorn and left the studio in admiration, and through it all he gazed into crystals, and intoned cabalistic words. When the last client, however, had disappeared, Astro threw off his turban and robe, yawned prodigiously, and became his real, alert, keen-eyed self. With Valeska Wynne he walked rapidly down Fifth Avenue, across Washington Square, and along Macdougal Street to number 950, where he found McGraw awaiting him in some impatience. At once the mask fell again over Astro's handsome poetic face; no summer saunterer seemed ever more idle or indifferent.

"Ah, here you are, sir," said the detective with evident relief as he tipped his hat to Valeska. "And here's the joint."

The house still showed signs of the recent outrage. The broken frames of the front windows were boarded up, and several beams held the tottering lumber in place. The sidewalk was not yet repaired, but had been hastily covered with loose planks. Evidently the bomb thrower had created a terrific disturbance. Every pane of glass in the building was shattered. As a result of the latest attempt upon Gallino's life, the whole top of the store was a mass of broken timber in front; the back part of the roof seemed not to have been disturbed. A small group of silent wide-eyed Italians hung about the place, eying the evidences of destruction in awe.

Astro scarcely gave the place a glance; but, accompanied by McGraw and Valeska, entered the store and spoke a few commonplaces to the proprietor, who, with hunted face, gazed anxiously at the officer. Valeska's eyes roamed vivaciously about the interior, taking in everything.

"Don't you suspect any one?" she asked Gallino at length.

"Yassa, ma'am, I do. I say it ees Tony, my ol' clerk. He ees no good, that-a boy. I fire 'im. That ees-a one week ago. I tell-a da cop; he say-a no. Tony, he live across da street right-a now. He blow me up-a for sure. You wait teel I catch-a heem!"

McGraw laughed easily. "The old man's nutty about it, that's all. We looked up Antonio's record. He had good alibis, too. Nothing to that theory."

Astro seemed to come out of his daze and began to take an interest in the chatter about him. "Well, Mr. McGraw," he announced, as he picked his way daintily among the debris, "I've seen what I care to inspect in this part of the building; now, if you will kindly leave me to wander about the place as I like, I may get those influences and manifestations that will enable me to use my crystals to good advantage."

The bulky officer immediately looked disappointed. He had evidently expected the Master of Mysteries to announce the author of the crime at once; and therefore it was with an unwilling nod that he withdrew.

"I'd like to go up on the roof first," said Astro to the Italian merchant. "It was there, I believe, that the latest explosion occurred."

Gallino showed the way up to a trap-door in the rear, and left Valeska and her companion on the ruined roof.

"Ah, this is more like business!" he said. "Valeska, see what you can find around here that's interesting." Then he walked directly toward the blank wall of the adjoining building. This rose three stories above Gallino's roof, and against it lay a number of pieces of scantling, untouched by the explosion. Over these Astro bent in search, while Valeska, left to herself, inspected the hole that the dynamiter had torn in the middle front of the roof.

"Here we are!" came his voice enthusiastically a moment later. She ran over toward him in surprise, to find him gazing across at the buildings on the other side of the street. Between his thumb and forefinger he held a tiny object.

"I've got it!" he announced, and continued his inspection of the house across the way.

"Got what?" she asked.

"The whole secret, as far as that goes. But specifically, I've got what I came up here for. What did you come up for?"

"Because you did," she confessed. "And, too, on the chance of finding something."

"One doesn't solve mysteries that way, Valeska. There is no use looking for something unless you know what that something is. Have you decided how a bomb was exploded on top of this roof in broad daylight, with people watching the house? Until you've got that, you are nowhere."

"It might have been thrown from the top of a building up there."

"And anybody could have seen it. No. There was only one possible way, besides electric wiring, and here it is." He opened his hand and disclosed a small twisted bullet.

"Oh!" cried the girl. "They put the bomb there and then shot at it."

"Yes. Shot at it—and missed the first time. Now, here we find the place where the first bullet, going wild, hit this piece of scantling. This makes it merely a matter of surveying. If you will stand with the back of your head where the indentation of this bullet is, then sight across the approximate middle of the hole in the roof caused by the explosion, you will probably get some idea of where the bullet came from. What do you see?"

"Well, it might have been aimed from any one of those three windows over there, in the building next to the shirt factory. I should say it came from the second one, where the potted plant is."

"One of them, certainly," answered Astro. "But we shall have to investigate them all, if we are to be conscientious about it, and for that purpose I suggest we look up McGraw again."

As they went down-stairs, Valeska asked, "When did the first explosion occur?"

"At night."

"Then the bomb was merely hurled from the window?"

"Presumably. Nothing could be easier, and, of course, it could not be definitely seen or traced. But here is McGraw; so let us take advantage of his office."

The detective, though delighted to accompany Astro, and especially his pretty assistant, into the house across the street, belittled the possibilities of finding anything there. "I've been into every room on the block, and I saw nothing. But I ain't got the second sight, o' course. All I can say is, I hope you track 'em."

The party went up-stairs into a cheap lodging-house, accompanied by a frightened and voluble landlady, until they reached the third floor fronting on the street. McGraw knocked on the first door; but, getting no answer, motioned the landlady to unlock.

It was a small room, in great disorder, looking as if the tenant had suddenly taken his departure. The bed was unmade, the small bureau was covered with soiled linen, neckties, cigarette stubs, and the like, and a miscellaneous lot of shoes, magazines, newspapers, and rubbish were strewed on the floor. McGraw started to push his way in officiously; but the slim hand of the Seer detained him.

"Kindly wait outside a moment," he commanded. "My assistant and I would prefer to enter alone. The vibrations, you know," he murmured, with a smile. The moment the door was shut behind them, two pairs of eyes ransacked the place, hunting for the things they had already decided to find. Astro's were the first to come to rest on a pile of crumpled newspapers hastily thrown beneath the unkempt bed. In a flash he had seized them and was scanning them one by one. Finally he separated an *Era* from the rest of the sheets, turned it toward Valeska, and smiled. She saw that one page had been torn out.

"The advertising page," he remarked. He drew out the Black Hand letter and compared the torn scraps silently with the journal in his hand, nodded his head in confirmation, then silently opened the door.

"Who lives here?" he asked the woman of the house.

"Antonio Soroni."

Astro turned to the detective. "Arrest him to-night and bring him to my apartments at eight o'clock."

"Did he really do it?" asked McGraw eagerly.

Astro turned away without answering.

"Kindly don't put any questions to him," interrupted Valeska; "for he is now getting in touch with the psychic influences of the place."

"Now for the next room, please," announced the Master of Mysteries, as if suddenly wakening.

"Oh, that's vacant," said the landlady with arms akimbo. "A young girl had it until last Friday; but she's left."

Valeska turned at once. "When was the last explosion, did you say, Mr. McGraw?"

"Thursday."

"And when did you search these rooms?"

"Friday, miss. The girl was here when I came. Fine looker, too, she was. A sort of laundress or seamstress or clerk or something; out of work, she said."

"Well, better look her up too, McGraw," said Astro, "and bring her around with Antonio."

He walked into the empty room, and Valeska followed him. The plain-clothes man and the proprietress awaited patiently until they came out again, some fifteen minutes later. Their faces betrayed nothing whatever concerning their search.

"Now, the third door!" Astro's voice was sharp and commanding. The others pricked up their ears in expectation.

McGraw knocked; but there was no answer. He knocked again, and the listening party caught the sound of unintelligible cursing, heavy and befuddled. At this the officer took the key in haste, threw open the door, and looked inside, his hand on the butt of his revolver. One glance, and he had jumped inside, collaring the man on the bed.

"It's Bull O'Kennery, by all that's holy! Think o' meetin' you this way, Bull! Get up now, an' come along with us; for I've been huntin' you two weeks an' more! Where've you been spendin' your vacation, anyway?"

The prostrate man rubbed his thick knuckles into his eyes and expostulated brokenly with a maudlin drunken accent. In a jiffy McGraw had dragged him upright and placed him against the wall outside, snapping the bracelets on his wrists as he did so. Then the detective turned to Astro.

"This here's Bull, one o' the slickest dips in the burg. There's been a warrant out for his arrest for over two weeks now. He'll be the man we're after, too, most likely. Anyway, he'll have to go up and give an account."

Astro surveyed the disheveled prisoner nonchalantly, took up his hand, examined the palm, the lower lid of his eye, and listened to his heart-beats, his head against the man's chest. "Bah!" he exclaimed with a nauseated shrug of his shoulders, "he's been drunk for sixty hours. Take him away, McGraw. He makes me quite ill. I'll attend to the rest of this alone."

After the detective had led the wretch shuffling down the stairs, the palmist and Valeska entered the room and threw up the blinds. It was a sickening enough abode, smelling vilely of whisky, stale beer, and staler tobacco smoke. A sluggish kerosene lamp still burned weakly on the mantel. Amid the mass of tangled rubbish a bureau drawer stood half open. Astro strode over to it. With a sudden gesture he took out a box of twenty-two caliber cartridges; then a woman's pocketbook, a ten-dollar bill, a piece of old-fashioned paper fractional currency of fifty-cent denomination, and a horn-handled shoe-buttoner.

"I think we're getting at it now!" he exclaimed, his eyes alight with discovery.

"But, for heaven's sake, which one of them did it? Antonio? Bull O'Kennery? Or the girl? Or all three together?"

"Or none of them?" smiled Astro. Suddenly his mood changed as he weighed the bullet thoughtfully in his hand. "It's a very pretty piece of business," he went on. "What was it the old Frenchman said in his wisdom,—*Cherchez la femme?* I'm afraid Mr. Gallino across the street is up against it; unless—hum—well, we'll see what McGraw gets into his net by nightfall."

Valeska never questioned further than the Master wished to answer; for she knew that it merely disturbed the marvelous deductive powers of his brain while they were at work; then, too, he preferred her, as she was, so to speak, still in her student days, to work out her own clues. Later, in case she had erred, he indulgently pointed out her mistakes. It was in some such tacit understanding that they now left the Macdougal Street tenement and made their way back to Astro's cozy studio.

Once there, she could see from the way in which he donned his turban and robe, lighted his water-pipe, and disposed himself on the cushioned divan in his favorite corner, that he had already solved the problem to his own satisfaction. Above the top shelf a row of the ancient Toltec, laughing heads grinned down on him; farther on, brazen implements and slabs of marvelous jade wrought with hieroglyphics gleamed dully, adding their touch of mystery to the man beneath. On the table were the sheets of paper and the dividers and rule with which he had been plotting an intricate curve, and this work he again took up immediately. Valeska withdrew. After an hour's work, heedless of the passage of dinner-time, he smiled, carefully laid aside his instruments, and turned to a plaster cast hung against the wall.

"It is true, then, as I thought, about you, Monsieur Voltaire," he murmured, half aloud. "The line of the upper half of the perimeter of that right ear of yours is a logarithmic spiral, of which the equation is $x^2 = 2ab + y$." He threw back his head and yawned.

Valeska glided in. "McGraw has come with Antonio," she whispered, "and has been waiting half an hour; but I wouldn't interrupt you until you had finished your calculations. Shall I let them in now?"

Astro yawned again, luxuriously. "You are too indulgent of me, my dear girl, I'm very much afraid. The delay may cost Signor Gallino a thousand dollars, possibly his life. Yes, you may show them in."

In another moment the officer appeared, leading by the sleeve a very badly frightened Italian. The moment the latter perceived the gorgeously picturesque figure of the palmist he rushed across the room and sank on the floor, clutching Astro by the knees.

"I no t'row-a da bomb!" he screamed. "I no t'row-a da bomb! *Sacrament'!* I spika da trut'! I no t'row-a bomb, signor! Gallino he give-a me da bounce, *si!* I shake-a-da fist in da face; bot I no t'row-a da bomb!" At that the tears streamed from his wild eyes.

Astro waved his hand impatiently, took up Antonio's hand, and began reading the palm, only to let it drop in a few moments.

"This young lady who roomed next to you," he said gently,— "you liked her, Antonio?"

The accused's eyes beamed. "Ah, *si*, signor! She the fine-a, nice-a girl. She speak-a to me, nice!"

"Very often?"

"Ah, no, signor! She lock herself in da room all-a da time. Some eve she come-a in, get-a da match. Da's all. Read-a da pape', maybe, sometime."

Astro cast a quick significant look at Valeska under his dark brows. "When did she come in and tear out a page from *The Era*, Tony?"

Antonio scratched his head, laboring to remember. "Sometime dees-a last-a wik, early. *Si.* One night she come in, she say, 'Tony, I like-a get-a da posish. You lemme take-a do pape'. I brink 'er back.' I say 'No, I wanta-da pape' for read-a to-night.' She say, 'All-a right; I tear off da one piece.'"

Astro turned to McGraw, "You'd better turn this poor fellow loose, I think. He's innocent enough. I know what I want to know now."

"What *do* you know?" said the detective peevishly. "Seems to me it's time I was put wise to some of this game, ain't it?"

"I'll tell you in ten minutes, if you'll telephone a question to headquarters, or to the proper precinct, and find out if there has been any complaint made of the loss of a pocketbook containing a ten-dollar bill, a fifty-cent piece of the old-fashioned paper currency, and a horn-handled shoe-buttoner. If there has, you'll want your friend Bull O'Kennery for that piece of work, too."

McGraw rose wonderingly and went to the telephone.

Astro called after him, "Tell them that if any one does appear with that complaint, to arrest him immediately and disarm him."

Valeska waited till the detective had gone into the hall. "It was the girl, then. I see!" she cried. "But how in the world did she ever expect to collect the money without being caught?"

"That's the cleverest part of it," answered the Seer meditatively. "You remember that she sent word to him the last time to have a thousand dollars with him night and day, and she'd let him know how to transfer the money?"

"Yes; but she hasn't let him know, so far."

"But she will to-night. You forget that to-morrow is the twelfth, the last day."

Valeska, extremely puzzled even yet as to how a lone girl was to accomplish her design, sat studying the matter over. Before she could reply, however, McGraw came back with an astonished look on his face.

"The girl called at the Mulberry Street Station yesterday and reported that her pocket had been picked. She described the money and the button-hook all right; and I guess if you say so it must be one of Bull's jobs. But it's too late to catch her, I'm afraid."

"What did she look like?" asked Astro.

"Why, that's funny. This Gallino happened to be there, talking to the sergeant about his place bein' blown up, and he recognized her as a girl that used to work in the corner drug store near him. She spoke to him a few minutes, and then left; and Gallino told the sergeant about it."

Astro clapped his hands. "*Selah!*" he exclaimed. "The ether waves have met at last! Wait five minutes. I must consult my crystals."

The two watched him carefully.

Finally he looked up. "We must hurry!" he exclaimed sharply. "To-night a man will come to see Gallino, and as soon as he's alone will demand the thousand dollars."

"A man?" queried Valeska. "I thought it was the girl."

"The girl!" said McGraw in bewilderment. "Well, never mind. Whoever it is, we'll get him—or her. The house is watched."

"Watched!" sneered the Master of Mysteries. "From the outside, I suppose?"

"Certainly," answered McGraw hotly.

"Fools!" answered Astro. "Anybody can enter. You can't keep innocent people out of the house. This man may go in, present a pistol at Gallino's head, get the money, and walk out. Who's to suspect a casual visitor?" He paused a moment to don his street coat. "Gallino may even be chloroformed. We've got to get there at once. Hurry!"

As they hastened along to the cab-stand, McGraw grunted in ill temper, "But who's the man that's after it, I'd like to know?"

He received no answer; nor was a word spoken all the time that they were being driven to Macdougal and Fourth Streets. When they had alighted there, paid their fare, and looked down the dark sidewalk, no one could be observed. Number 950 showed no sign of life. They started to walk briskly toward Gallino's, when suddenly a person emerged from the Italian's doorway and hastened down the steps.

Instantly Astro drew his revolver and shouted to McGraw, "That's the one! Get him!"

At the exclamation, the figure turned on the bottom step, shrank back in surprise, and becoming entangled in the long coat, fell across the balustrade to the stone sidewalk. Instantly, with a frightful roar, a terrific explosion rent the air. Astro and his companions staggered back, and above the crash of falling debris the Master of Mysteries could be heard shouting:

"That's what was meant for Gallino if he hadn't paid to-night!"

Then the three rushed anxiously forward to where the limp figure lay in a distorted knot on the flagging. The clothing had been torn to shreds, and a pool of blood encircled the prostrate form. The body lay face downward; so that the detective had to turn it over. He struck a match and cried in bewilderment:

"Why, it's a girl in man's clothes!"

Astro turned slowly away. "There will be no more bombs exploded in Macdougal Street for a while," he said. "You'd better telephone to the hospital."

THE FANSHAWE GHOST

As it was nearly time for his first client of the day to arrive, Astro the Palmist ended the little lesson in optical anatomy he had been giving to Valeska. He closed the transparent doors of the huge model of the human eye about which he had been talking, and replaced it on a shelf in his laboratory, where it remained, a large livid ball of glass and porcelain, veined with red.

"It's simply wonderful!" Valeska said, staring at it hard.

Astro laughed, and passed into the great studio for his morning consultations. "And yet," he remarked, "Helmholtz says, 'Nature seems to have packed this organ with mistakes.' I'll explain that sometime. Most people do think that the body of man is the consummation of the Maker's skill and wisdom. In point of fact, it is far from being perfect.

"Think of the ants and bees," he went on thoughtfully. "Think of their strength and adaptability! By a mere change of diet a neuter can become a perfect female."

"Do you mean to say that men's bodies are not so good as some of the animals' bodies?" Valeska asked.

"I mean to say that the human machine is imperfect. It contains much that is unnecessary, much that is not well adapted to the struggle for existence."

Astro, now assuming his red silken robe and turban, in preparation for his astral readings, seated himself cross-legged on the divan, and took up the stem of his narghile.

"Wiedersheim," he continued, "has counted one hundred and seven so-called 'vestigial organs'; the remains, that is, of similar but more developed organs that fulfilled a useful function in our simian ancestors. Some of them are still able to perform their physiological functions in a more or less incomplete manner; some survive merely as ancestral relics; and some are actually harmful to the body. Take, for instance, superfluous hairs; they are no longer capable of protecting the body from cold and often do serious harm. Wisdom-teeth are unnecessary to man; their powers of mastication are feeble, and they often cause tumors and diffused suppuration and dental caries. We all know how unnecessary and how dangerous to health the vermiform appendix is.

"Then there are other organs whose powers are almost completely lost. The little tail disappears from the embryo before birth; but there remain the useless muscles of the ear, the unnecessary thirteenth pair of ribs, the weak and imperfect eleventh and twelfth pairs of ribs, which serve no useful purpose, the muscles of the toes, and so on. Why, the colon, or large intestine, the seat of most diseases of the alimentary tract and the nursery of arterial sclerosis, has been pronounced practically useless by Metchnikoff, and in London hospitals the entire colon is often removed."

Valeska stared. "But what are they all there for?" she inquired.

"I suppose their chief use is to shame our vanity. They are undoubted proof of our animal origin, our descent from the anthropoid apes."

Valeska frowned. "I never like to be reminded of that."

"Well, then, of our descent from birds, or reptiles. You have beautiful eyes, my dear; but you can't conceal that little part near the nose which is called the 'semilunar fold.' That is but the remains of the third eyelid you possessed as a bird,—the transparent membrane that eagles draw over the cornea."

The bell rang outside. Astro the Philosopher became, on the instant, Astro the Seer, and dropped into his professional poise,— calm, inert, picturesque, oriental. Valeska retired to another room and began her work of looking carefully over the papers for news of anything that might be of use to the Seer in his conferences. It was her duty to keep in touch with the doings of the day.

For some time she read without interest, making notes occasionally, and from time to time consulting her card catalogue to look up the condensed biographies of persons prominent in society, politics, or finance, adding to the data there collected. She cut clippings, too, and pasted them in a blank book for Astro to look over at his leisure. In the last of the morning papers, her eyes fell on the following paragraph, and she read it with attention:

> No small amount of gossip has been occasioned during the last week or so in the little village of Vandyke, by the rumors of supernatural visitations at the well-known Fanshawe farm, now the residence of Miss Mildred Fanshawe, the last living representative of a prominent old family in the county. While all the servants at the farm deny the sensational reports, and Miss Fanshawe absolutely refuses to be interviewed, the stories afloat make the place famous in the vicinity. According to what can be learned, at least three of the servants at the farm have seen the "Fanshawe ghost," purported to be the spirit of Sally Towers, who was a well-known belle of New York in the 1830's. Sally appears, so it is said, in the walled garden side of the old house, usually with a baby in her arms. Occasionally she is seen on the roof of the dwelling. The Society for Psychical Research is said to be interested, and has asked the privilege of investigating the apparition; but Miss Fanshawe has persistently refused them admittance to the premises, which are now well guarded from intrusion.

Of Miss Fanshawe, Valeska could find no information in her catalogue. But as soon as Astro was free she gave him the clipping, and was not disappointed in his interest.

"It's a case I'd like to handle," he said, when he had read the story. "If Miss Fanshawe does not apply to me for a solution of the mystery, I shall certainly volunteer my services. Perhaps you had better send her a note, anyway."

This Valeska did forthwith, with the result that Miss Fanshawe appeared a few days later at the studio. She confessed herself worried about the stories that had been circulated, because of the unpleasant notoriety she had gained, and the fact that they might depreciate the value of the property, which she wished to sell as soon as possible. The rumors were, she confessed, based on tales which some of her servants had been indiscreet enough to relate. There seemed to be something at the bottom of the affair, and she would be much relieved to have the mystery cleared up.

Miss Mildred Fanshawe was an aristocratic but anemic-looking woman of perhaps thirty years. She was a brunette, with dark hair and eyes, with a lean narrow face, full of nervous energy. Her hands were long and slim; her upper lip was nearly covered with fine hair, almost a mustache, which gave her a distinctly Italian aspect. She talked freely with Astro and Valeska, using gestures like a foreigner.

When she had gone, Astro turned to his assistant. "Well," he said, "I'm curious to know just what you noticed about that woman."

"There is something strange about her—I hardly know what it is," said Valeska. "I noticed, though, for one thing, that she wiggled her ears. I knew a boy once who could do that. I've often tried to; but I can't. Then, her mustache was a great blemish, wasn't it? It's a pity for a woman to have to suffer that. Then, her eyes were queer. What was the matter with them?"

Astro smiled. "And I have been lecturing you upon the eye for a fortnight! It was the 'semilunar fold' I spoke to you about a while ago. It was extraordinarily large."

"So it was, now I recall it. That was funny about her being able to pick up a fork with her toes, like Stevenson at Vailima, wasn't it? I always wanted to live in a country where I could go barefooted. We don't half use our feet, do we?"

"Well—and the ghost? Have you no theory?" Astro asked.

"Already? Of course not! How can we tell any thing till we investigate the premises and see the apparition?"

"Oh, we'll go down, of course; but it's scarcely necessary, I consider."

Valeska's hands fell into her lap with a hopeless gesture. "Oh, dear!" she exclaimed. "I'll never learn anything! How in the world could you learn the secret of the ghost story, just by talking to her?"

"And watching her?" he hinted. "But take her talk, even. What did she say that might be significant?"

"Do you mean about that operation she had for appendicitis?" Valeska considered it thoughtfully. "Let's see. She mentioned the fact that she had her vermiform appendix removed, and it proved to be abnormally large. But that doesn't prove anything to me."

"Think it over. See if you can't put it with what I have told you, and, more important still, read Metchnikoff! I recommend to you his *Prolongation of Life*; but I won't tell you what chapter especially. There you'll find the missing link in the argument. You have already half of my theory, in the doctrine of 'vestigial organs,' which you can apply to Miss Fanshawe's case. The other half I prefer you to work out for yourself. It's the simplest kind of deduction, and needs only corroboration at Fanshawe Farm. Let's see; she asked us to come down next Friday. That gives you three days in which to think it over."

He rose and yawned. "I wish you'd buy me some blue paint and a brush," he added. "Now I must put in a little time on that new somnoform experiment. I think I'm getting at it."

But Valeska had no time to read Metchnikoff that week. Astro's absences from the studio were long and often, and Valeska, who had been preparing herself in palmistry, gave readings to all those clients who did not insist on a personal interview with the Master of Mysteries. It need scarcely be said that most such clients were men. Every moment of her time was occupied until Friday afternoon.

On that day, at four o'clock, she met Astro at the Grand Central Station, and together they took the train for Vandyke village to keep their appointment with Miss Fanshawe.

"How little I know of you, Valeska," Astro said, on the journey down. "Do you realize that it is almost nothing? You applied in answer to my advertisement for an assistant, and you know that it is not my habit to ask personal questions unless it is absolutely necessary. But, to me, you are as mysterious as this Fanshawe ghost we are hunting down. I have always had a queer feeling about you,— that I didn't want to know too much about your history; that it was a prettier situation to be ignorant of everything except this very happy present when we are working together."

"Oh, let's be sure of that, and enjoy it!" she breathed, turning her eyes away. "I am perfectly happy! I only hope that we both shall remain so!"

If Astro had intended by his remarks to give her an opening for a confession, she did not accept it, and he did not insist. Their talk changed to the business that occupied their immediate attention.

Astro carefully reread the newspaper clipping.

"The first thing is, of course, to get the accounts of the servants, and then to see the ghost for ourselves. Finally, we must lay the specter forever."

"I have thought that the phantom might have been impersonated by one of the servants," Valeska suggested.

"With that hypothesis we should seek a motive," he replied.

"I admit that's what has baffled me."

"Well, we must follow every clue, that's all."

Miss Fanshawe's man met them at the station with an open carriage, and Astro, seating himself beside the driver, immediately began to draw him out on the subject of the ghost. The man was Irish, and willing to talk. He himself, however, had not seen the spirit, though he believed implicitly in its existence. John, the stableman, had seen it, however, and Genevieve, Miss Fanshawe's maid. The third witness, an old woman who had been cook, had left the place, refusing to remain in a haunted house.

Miss Fanshawe greeted them hospitably and had them shown to their rooms by Genevieve. Before dressing for dinner Astro and Valeska had the story from her. She took them herself into the garden and pointed out the scene of the visitation.

A high brick wall screened the place from the street and enclosed it on three sides. The garden was laid out formally, with
brick walks along the two axes of the rectangular space, and a cir-
cular pool with a fountain in the middle. The fourth side was shut off
by the brick wall of the house itself, which there rose two stories in
height. Along the south wall was planted a thicket of high bushes,
interspersed with trees. This wall ran into the side of the house
just below Miss Fanshawe's own chamber, whose window showed
some nine feet above. The maid's room was next. The northern wall
was flush with the front of the house, which was decorated with a
portico two stories in height. Above that was the sloping roof.

"I've seen it walking up and down many a time, from my window over there," said Genevieve. "It always disappears in the
bushes over there," and she pointed to the southern wall. "Once I
saw it on the very top of the roof, waving its arms. Yes, it almost
always carries a baby, and it's always in white, shroudlike. It always scares me stiff; but I won't leave Miss Fanshawe for it nor
anything like it."

"It's a queer thing that you and John are the only ones here
who have ever seen it," said Valeska, looking at her fixedly.

"Oh, the cook has seen it, many's the time," said Genevieve.

"But the cook left."

"Yes, and good reason why, too! It came at her with a run once,
and like to scratch her eyes out!"

"It's queer that Miss Fanshawe has never seen it."

"Ah, and I hope she never will, the poor dear! It'll be for no
good if she does. It comes to warn her, I'm thinking."

John the stableman's tale was almost the same. He, too, had
seen the ghost on the roof of the house, and running swiftly along
the garden walk, and often with the baby. In the year he had been
employed at Fanshawe Farm he had seen it, he thought, at least a
dozen times. He appeared to share Genevieve's superstitious terrors and had never dared to pursue the specter.

All this, of course, Miss Fanshawe had heard before, and with
Astro and Valeska she discussed the probability of her servants
possibly having conspired to give the house a bad name. But no

motive for that was apparent, and Genevieve's devotion seemed sincere. The talk had already begun to wear on her. She showed many signs of nervousness, becoming at times almost hysterical. Seeing this, Astro changed the subject, and nothing more was said of his purpose there.

That night he took his place with Valeska at the end of the garden, away from the house, to watch. He had come prepared to spend several days; for the chances were against their seeing anything the first time, though the appearances had, according to John, become much more frequent of late. So, bundled in wraps, the two took their seats on a bench at the end of the path. From here, most of the house windows were screened from them; but a clear vista up the center of the garden was illuminated by a moon beyond its first quarter. Miss Fanshawe, pleading indisposition, had retired to her room early. Beyond the seat there was a small door in the wall, opening on a path leading to the stable. Directly in front of where they sat was an old-fashioned sun-dial. It was altogether a romantic spot, one well fitted for a tryst, natural or supernatural. Perhaps Valeska thought it too romantic, for after sitting with Astro for a while she rose and paced impatiently up and down. He did not try to keep her with him. Her nearness seemed dangerous to his concentration of mind, to his watchfulness.

At ten o'clock a sound behind him attracted his attention. Valeska was some distance away, and he did not call her, but stole to the small door in the wall and looked out. What he saw made him smile. He returned and, with a low whistle, called his assistant.

"We might learn some things from Genevieve and John," he said a little sadly, "even if we don't learn much about the ghost from them."

"Have you seen them?" she exclaimed.

"They were bidding each other good night at the stable door."

"Then," said Valeska, "it's my opinion that we'll see the ghost within a quarter of an hour. Let's sit down now and watch."

They took their places on the bench again, and her hand stole into his. Was it the suggestion she had received from the servants'

love-making, or did she begin to fear the specter? With all his cleverness, Astro could not decide.

But suddenly she sprang up, and now there was no doubt of
her alarm.

"There it is!" she exclaimed in a harsh whisper, pointing toward the shrubbery at the south wall.

There it was at last, indeed,—a seemingly sheeted form, bearing something that looked like a little child in its arms, stealing
down the path! It approached them noiselessly. In the shadow of
the trees it showed too indistinct for identification at that distance.
Astro rose abruptly and took a step toward the house, when immediately the thing sped rapidly away. Astro broke into a run; but
when he came to the house nothing was to be seen.

He went back to reassure Valeska, who stood, staring, trembling with excitement, but without fear. Hardly had he reached her,
however, when her voice rang out again.

"There! On the roof!" she cried.

Astro looked and beheld the figure gliding swiftly along the top
of the building. The vision lasted only a moment, then disappeared.

He spoke sharply. "Valeska, run up to Miss Fanshawe's room
and awaken her! Tell her I want her to see this!"

Valeska ran up the brick walk, passed through a door in the
middle of the south wall, and entered the house. The halls had been
left lighted, and she found her way easily to Miss Fanshawe's room.
Here she knocked on the door, at first softly, then with increasing
vehemence. Trying the door, she found it locked. No one answered.

She flew down-stairs again, and was about to go for Astro, when
a sound attracted her attention. Down the hall, toward the back
stairs, she saw something or some one pass and disappear. Her
thoughts flew to Genevieve, and, with a new desire to awaken Miss
Fanshawe, she went up-stairs again and knocked.

This time there was a noise inside the chamber,—a rattle, a chair
being moved,—and in a few moments the door was partly opened
and Miss Fanshawe looked out. At the same moment Genevieve
appeared in the upper hall.

For a moment Valeska could not decide what to say. If, as she suspected, Genevieve had been, in some strange way, impersonating the phantom, she dared not tell of it before her. She slipped inside Miss Fanshawe's room, which was not lighted.

"We have seen the ghost, and Astro wished you to come out; but it is undoubtedly too late now. I wish your door had been unlocked, so I might have awakened you without making so much noise."

Miss Fanshawe wrung her hands. Her long black hair streamed over her white night-dress; the costume and her aspect of extreme disarray made her figure almost grotesque.

"It's terrible, terrible!" she moaned. "I don't see why I should be tortured so. I don't want to see it! I couldn't bear it!" She broke into a violent fit of sobbing.

Genevieve knocked at the door and entered. "I'll attend to her, miss," she said to Valeska. "I'm used to her when she has the hysterics, and I can calm her down if you'll only leave us."

There seemed nothing better to do, and Valeska went downstairs and passed into the garden again. Astro strode up to her, a lighted cigar in his mouth.

"Well?"

Valeska narrated what had happened.

"We mustn't be caught that way again. I'll ask her to leave the door unlocked to-morrow night. Well, there's nothing further to do to-night. I propose that we turn in."

"But have you found out who or what it is?" Valeska asked, still trembling with the excitement.

Astro smiled. "I'll have a trap for the ghost tomorrow, and if she appears you'll see. It's only a question of how to do it delicately and safely. But it's most amusing. I think I was never so entertained."

"Why, did you see it after I left?" she asked.

"I should say I did! It was as good as a circus. But you must go to bed. Good night."

As they went out into the garden the next night, Astro showed Valeska a nickeled brass cylinder he had concealed in his inside pocket.

"Here's what an automobilist calls an oil gun," he explained. "It works like a large syringe, and is loaded with blue paint. I might also mention that the lightning-rod running up and down the house wall side of those windows is already painted bright blue. If I don't succeed in shooting our extremely lively little friend the spook with this gun, I expect the lightning-rod to streak her up with blue stripes sufficient for identification."

Valeska gazed at the moonlit house in wonder. "The lightning-rod!" she exclaimed. "It isn't possible for any one to climb up there! Do you mean to say—"

"Wait, and you'll see some of the prettiest ground and lofty tumbling outside of vaudeville," was his reply.

"But it runs up beside Genevieve's window! It isn't possible for that girl to climb down from there into the garden."

"It also runs beside Miss Fanshawe's window. It may be possible for her. I assure you, she's an athlete."

"But how could any human being get on the roof so quickly?"

"If you'll go round there, you'll see. Once you climb the north wall, you can almost reach the first balcony. Up the column to the second is easy enough. On the other side there's a stout ivy vine that makes a practical ladder to the very top."

"But why, why, why?" Valeska almost wailed the words.

"Ah, you haven't read Metchnikoff."

Then, suddenly he cried, "Look!" and seized her arm.

They were standing beside the central pool now, and he pointed to Miss Fanshawe's window, clearly visible from this part of the garden. The moonlight struck the glass as the sash was raised. A form looked out, climbed rapidly across the sill, lowered itself till it hung by the hands, and then dropped lightly to the top of the garden wall. Quick as had been its appearance and disappearance, something was visible, tucked under one arm. While they stood fascinated, a white object appeared on the grass of the garden plot, the figure of a woman with hair streaming about her shoulders, apparently carrying a child. She came a few steps toward them, then retreated swiftly and made for the bushes by the north wall. In another instant she appeared atop the wall, and swung up to the first balcony of the portico, still bearing her burden. A few minutes more, and she reappeared on the roof.

"Quick, now!" cried Astro. "Run up to Miss Fanshawe's room and go in and wait for her to return. I'll hide in the bushes by the south wall and pop her full of blue paint. If I miss, there's the lightning-rod, her only way to enter the room."

"But what shall I say—how can I accuse her of it?"

Astro stopped suddenly and looked at her. "Why, my dear, I forgot. Is it possible you haven't guessed it yet? Miss Fanshawe is asleep. It's somnambulism, that's all. But hurry! Make any excuse if she's awake; if she's not, don't awaken her. Let her go to bed herself."

Valeska flew into the house and up-stairs. Miss Fanshawe had kept her promise and had left her door unlocked. Valeska entered.

The window was still up. There was no one in the bed. One pillow was missing. On the instant Valeska understood the secret of the baby that the specter was supposed to carry.

She slipped into the corner and waited. In a few moments a form appeared in the window, blocking out the light. A wriggle and a twist, and it sprang lightly in, and Miss Fanshawe stood revealed in the moonlight, in her night-dress, now streaked and spattered with blue stains. In her arms she still held the pillow, as a mother holds her babe. Her eyes stared straight before her without power of sight.

Valeska, more moved by this uncanny vision than if it had been a supernatural visitation, stole silently away and rejoined the Master.

"I don't see how it was possible, even though I saw it with my own eyes!" she said, as they sat down on the bench to talk it over before sleeping. "A frail woman like that to climb to the second story up a rod, to the roof even! I've heard stories of somnambulists before, but this is miraculous!"

"If you had read Metchnikoff," said Astro, smoking calmly, "you would have found that such a case as this is not rare; and you would have discovered the explanation. The fact is that in somnambulism and in hysteria persons often revert atavistically to the characteristics of their simian ancestors. They are often able to jump and run and climb and even chatter like apes while in this abnormal condition. Miss Fanshawe, as we had already observed, possesses many still active functions of her monkey ancestry, which in most men and women have become atrophied with disuse. Her appendix was large, like those of the apes. She bore traces of this also in the hair on her lip, in her ability to use her ears, in the development of the muscles of her toes. It was evident to me, at my first glance at her, that she was, if not abnormal, at least peculiar. In her waking state, of course, she is a highly refined and cultured lady. Under the influence of hysteria, or in this strange somnambulistic condition, she merely reverts to type. You know that newborn babies can hang from their hands, like monkeys, but soon lose that power. Miss Fanshawe loses her extraordinary agility in her waking moments, and regains it while asleep."

"But why the blue paint?" said Valeska. "If you knew the secret of the Fanshawe ghost, why didn't you tell her at first?"

"Would you have believed it possible?" he asked smiling.

Valeska confessed she would not

"Neither would Miss Fanshawe. And besides, it would have been necessary to explain the origin of my suspicions. No woman would care to be told that she resembled an ape, and I don't intend to explain Metchnikoff's theory to her or to point out her vestigial organs which are not quite vestigial. No, I'll merely tell her she walks in her sleep, as is proved by the blue paint on her nightdress, and advise her either to lock the window when she retires or to have a companion to watch her. I don't think any one will see the ghost again.

"I wonder," he added thoughtfully, as they walked toward the house, "if, after all, I hadn't better begin to investigate the ghost of your past, little girl!" He took her hand affectionately.

"Well, you won't find any vestigial signs in that, anyway," she answered, gently drawing away her hand. "And," she added, "I'm glad I can't wiggle my ears or pick up things with my toes. I'd rather be a lady even while asleep. I'm quite satisfied with my body, thank you, just as it is."

THE DENTON BOUDOIR MYSTERY

Underneath a shaded, swinging, bronze lamp in his favorite corner of the studio, the Master of Mysteries sat with half-closed eyes, seeming to drowse over a huge vellum-bound folio whose leaves bore lines of Arabic characters. But, though his dreamy eyes appeared heavy and dull, his index finger sped with such rapidity from line to line as to reveal that the palmist was eagerly absorbed in the message of those antique parchment pages. Behind him loomed the damasks and embroidered hangings with which the room was adorned; in a corner hung a gilded censer breathing its delicate aromatic perfume; an astrolabe occupied a small table at one hand, and near it lay a strange assortment of queer instruments picked up by the Seer in his vagabond travels,—the dread "spider" of the Inquisition, the *Angoise* "pear," a set of fearsome thumbscrews, strips of human hide, and other such horrors.

"So," he murmured contemplatively, "Ptolemy was a Torquemada himself, in a good many ways. That's interesting; and it confirms an old theory of mine. To think that many persons don't believe in metempsychosis—and do believe in the signs of the zodiac!" His thin lips parted in a smile. He had turned to his book again, and had read for a few minutes, when his whole attitude changed. He sat upright; his eyes gleamed with interest. Voices were heard outside in the office, where his assistant was still working. He listened intently; then with a quick movement of his right hand touched a button, and the room was flooded with

light. It was the first sight of a new client that often told Astro
more than an hour's interview.

"Wait a moment till I announce you!" Valeska was exclaiming.
"The Master can not be interrupted in his work. It is impossible. I
could not do it for the President himself!"

"I must see him immediately! I tell you I must see him!" a man's
voice replied. "By heaven! I'll break in by main force!"

Another moment, and the black velvet portières leading to the
waiting-room were violently flung aside, and a flushed and excited
young man of about thirty years strode into the apartment. Behind him the face of Valeska Wynne appeared in the doorway, with
an alarmed expression.

Astro sat, in turban and silken robe, reading, apparently unmoved by this interruption. When the young man stopped in the
center of the room, the Seer slowly raised his olive-hued face to
the visitor, and a smoldering glance shot from his dark eyes, in a
mute question. The young man took a few steps nearer, and broke
out again:

"See here! You've got to take this case!" he exclaimed appeal-
ingly. "I am at my wits' ends. I'll go mad if you don't help me; no
one else can solve it. You're the only man in New York that can
explain this mystery. For God's sake, sir, tell me you'll do it!" He
dropped in exhaustion into an armchair, looking anxiously at the
crystal-gazer. The fingers of one hand twitched nervously, while
his other fist was clenched. His forehead was lined with vertical
wrinkles.

Astro, still unperturbed, looked at him gravely, his quick eye
darting from point to point of the young man's clothing. Finally he
said languidly, with an almost imperceptible foreign accent, "My
dear sir, the Turks have a proverb, 'He who is in a hurry is already
half mad.' If you were in such haste to see me, you should have
taken a cab to come here, instead of a street-car."

The young man pulled himself together, sat up, and stared hard
at the Seer. Then his face relaxed, as he said, with a tone of great
relief, nodding his head, "That's wonderful! It's exactly what I
did. Oh, I know you can do it, if you only will! The police are all

stupid,—there isn't a man with a brain on the whole force, I believe. You're the man to help me!"

Astro made a graceful gesture with his long slender hand. "It is not a question of brains, my dear sir. It is a question of the right comprehension of the forces of the occult, of undeveloped senses and powers. Men need sign-boards to show them the way from town to town. The birds wing their straight paths by instinct. It is my fortune to be sensitive to vibrations that most minds do not register. Where you see a body, I see a spirit, a life, an invisible color. All these esoteric laws have been known by the priestcraft of the occult for ages. Nothing is hidden from the Inner Eye."

"I don't know how you get it," the young man interrupted. "I believe that there are many things we don't understand yet, and that some men are developed beyond their fellows. I've studied mysticism myself, and that's why I came directly to you. I want the mystery of my sweetheart's death cleared up, and the hellish scoundrel that killed her executed. Until that is accomplished, my life will stop, or I'll go insane. The police can prove nothing, even on their own suspect. What motive there could have been for such a crime I can't imagine; it seems so unnecessary, so monstrous!" He had worked himself again into a fever of excitement.

Astro rose and walked over to his visitor. Placing his thumbs on two muscles in the young man's neck, near the spinal column, he manipulated the flesh for a few moments. His client's hysteria gradually subsided, and he became calmer.

"Now," said Astro, sinking back into his chair and taking up the amber mouthpiece of his water-pipe, "give me the details of your story from the beginning. You need not mind my assistant; she is quite in my confidence and may be trusted implicitly."

Valeska had entered, and sat at a table prepared to take notes of the conversation. Astro's eyes turned indulgently on the pretty blond head as it bent seriously over the writing pad.

The young man spoke now as if he had the history already clearly mapped out in his mind. He used occasional impulsive gestures, displaying an ardent and intense temperament.

"My name is Edward Masson. For three months I have been engaged to marry Miss Elizabeth Denton, of Hamphurst, Long Island. That is, I was, until three days ago, when we had a quarrel,— nothing to speak of, really, you know, but the match was temporarily broken off. It would have come out all right, I'm sure. I intended to make it up with her. I was prepared to make any compromise whatever; for I was crazy about her. She was my whole life." He paused and put his hands across his eyes.

Valeska looked across to the Master, her own eyes already swimming with tears of sympathy. Astro, however, showed no sign, and puffed tranquilly at his hookah, waiting for Masson to become more calm. In the anteroom a great clock broke the silence with a ringing melodious chime and struck the hour of six in booming notes.

Masson looked up with a tense face. "That next day she was murdered!" he said brokenly. "She was found dead in her boudoir on the second floor of her house, just before dinner-time, at about dusk. Both doors were locked; but the double windows were open. The police say she was strangled. Think of it! God! she was beautiful! How could any one have done it? It seems impossible, even now that she is dead. There were slight marks on her throat that looked like finger prints. I didn't see them,—there was lace around her neck when I saw her, in her casket. Oh, God!" He rose and paced up and down the room restlessly, his eyes cast down.

"What have the police done?" Astro inquired gently.

"They've arrested Miss Denton's maid. She had a key to Elizabeth's room, it seems, and some of the servants thought they heard her talking in the room. I think that's the strongest point against her. But I doubt if she did it. It was too brutal. I must run down the real murderer and have it proved beyond the possibility of a doubt. I can't rest till that's done."

He turned almost savagely to the quiet figure of the palmist. "Can't you do it? You can see things in crystals; you know the secret laws of nature; you lead a life of study and research with the old adepts. Can't you do this for me?"

Astro smiled subtly. "My dear Mr. Masson," he said, "I do not ordinarily concern myself with such affairs. Those who wish come to me, and I, of my knowledge of the Laws of Being, can reveal what is hidden. Such agonizing experiences as yours are distracting to the student of the Higher Way."

"I'm rich!" Masson broke in. "I'll pay you anything you wish! Make your price—one thousand, two, anything! Only help me! My God, man! you were a part of the world once. Can't you remember what it means to love a beautiful woman and want to marry her?"

"I remember—only too well. It was partly on that account that I hesitated. But I'll forget myself and consent to assist you."

The young man sank into a chair again, with gratitude in his poise. "You'll want to go down to Hamphurst?" he asked.

"Certainly. I must get the vibrations of the scene itself before I seek the murderer. He has left behind him emanations that will rapidly evaporate. I shall go down to-morrow if you will accompany me. Tonight I shall go to the Tombs and see Miss Denton's maid. She, too, must be studied by one who is sensitive to aura. My friend McGraw will be able to get permission for that, no doubt."

He shot a glance at Valeska as he mentioned the inspector's name. She replied with a fluttering smile and was serious again.

Young Masson buttoned up his overcoat, and with an embarrassed, hesitating manner, did his best to express his thanks. Astro cut short his stammering sentences, laid his own hand with a friendly gesture on Masson's shoulder, and guided him out of the room. At parting it was agreed that they should meet on the nine-twelve train for Hamphurst.

The palmist walked back to the studio, shut off all lights but the one in his favorite corner, and sat down in silence. Valeska waited for him to speak.

"Not bad for two days' work," he said finally, smiling.

"Are you sure you can do it?" she asked, raising her golden brows.

"My dear," he replied, taking up his water-pipe again, "am I not a Mahatma of the Fourth Sphere, and were not the divine laws of cosmic life revealed to me while I was a chela on the heights of the Himalayas?"

Valeska broke into a silvery laugh. "Do you know," she said, "that patter of yours is almost as becoming as that turban and robe. But, to be serious, have you any clue as yet?"

Astro did not answer for a moment; then he said meaningly, "The principle by which muscle reading can be accomplished is this: The person that is held moves in a minute circle until he finds the point of least resistance to his motion. He moves, then, in this line as long as his holders unconsciously guide him in that direction. The same principle is true of any problem of this sort. Let us wait, until we are guided by something that seems characteristic of this special crime. The street-car business was simple enough to you, I suppose?"

Valeska pouted. "Oh, I'm not altogether a fool. Why, he had a Broadway transfer in his hand when he came in here. He was in too much of a hurry to take a cross-town car for the four blocks."

The Seer chuckled. "But now we'd better go to work. I'll see the maid first. There's no need of your going. You'd better get back to your work on the zodiac. Look up Napoleon's notes on the subject. His was the biggest intellect the stars ever fooled. It will teach you how to fool lesser ones. But get a good night's rest. There'll be something more to search for at Hamphurst to-morrow. I'll look over the papers and see what is known about this murder. Masson was too excited to tell half."

After reading for a half-hour, Astro yawned, shook himself, and changed from the cynical psychologist to a man of keen brisk manner and alert glance. His green limousine, which was always kept waiting at the door of the studio, took him rapidly down-town. A half-hour later he was looking through the cell door at Marie Dubois, the French maid of the late Miss Denton.

She was eager to talk and volubly protested her innocence. Astro let her run on without questions, until she had finally told all she knew of the affair, which was little enough, apparently. She had started up to Miss Denton's room at about half past six to get a cashmere shawl which was to be sent to the cleaner's. Half-way up the side stairs she had stopped, hearing voices inside the boudoir.

She did not, however, recognize Miss Denton's voice; instead, there was a higher-pitched voice, exclaiming "Great God!" several times. This was followed by laughter; then came a shrill whistle. She heard something like the fall of a body, then footsteps. All this so alarmed her that she ran up and tried the boudoir door. Finding that locked, she called down to the butler, went and got her own key, and asked him to investigate. The voice she had heard seemed like an old woman's. The butler had heard it, and also the chauffeur, who was in the stable across the yard.

"And how about the letters from Mr. Masson to Miss Denton, which were found in your room?" Astro inquired.

"Oh, Mees Denton, she give me zem zat I send to her fiancé!" the girl protested. "Zat same afternoon she make ze *paquet. Mon Dieu!* ze police say I steal ze letters! It ees not so! Nevaire have I seen a man so good like Monsieur Masson to me. He ees gentle-man. Why I steal his letters?" She began to weep.

"Let me see your hand, Marie."

The girl gave him a slender trembling palm. Astro looked at it for a few moments; then he said, "Marie, did Mr. Masson ever make love to you?"

A sudden wave of color flooded the girl's face; but she cried out excitedly, "Nevaire! *Mon Dieu! non, par exemple!* Why should he do zat? Had he not ze beautiful Mees Denton? *Oh, non, Monsieur!*"

Astro smiled cryptically and walked out. The rest of the evening he spent translating certain obscure Hebrew texts from the *Midrash* and comparing them with the published English versions.

On the train down to Hamphurst, next day, Masson was morose and talked but little. He was nervous and impatient to get to the house, watching sullenly out of the window all the way. Valeska did her best to be agreeable; but Astro came out of his reverie only once, to ask:

"Why was the date of your marriage postponed, Mr. Masson?"

Masson scowled, then sighed and shook his head.

"Miss Denton, a month or so ago, was not at all well. The doctors found her heart to be weak. They thought that the excitement of a wedding and its preparation would be too much for her, and feared a collapse."

Astro resumed his abstracted pose. Valeska bent her brows. Masson gazed mournfully out of the window.

Alighting at Hamphurst, they took a carriage and were driven to the Denton house, an old-fashioned, two-and-a-half-story, frame building, painted yellow with white trimmings. It was surrounded with beautiful wine-glass elms which were scattered over the grounds. A wide lawn stretched in front and on one side, with a gravel driveway to the residence and a stable in the rear. The place had an air of quiet peaceful respectability. It seemed to the last degree improbable as the scene of such a tragedy as had been so recently enacted.

The officers had finished their investigations, and the funeral had taken place the day before. An aged aunt of Miss Denton's and the four servants now occupied the house. Astro and his assistant were introduced to the old lady, then went immediately up to the boudoir where the body had been found. Here, at Astro's request, the exact situation discovered at that time was explained by James, the man-of-all-work, whom Marie had referred to as the butler.

He pointed out the position in which he had found the corpse. It lay face downward; the hair was somewhat disarranged. The square, cheerful, blue-and-white boudoir was now filled with sunlight streaming in from the high French windows which led to a small balcony outside. Many of Miss Denton's belongings still lay about,—a fold of ribbon, a lace collar, a handkerchief on the bureau; and on a small table, a book face down where she had left it, made it seem as if the owner had only just left the room on some trifling errand.

The old lady silently handed Astro a photograph of her niece,— a beautiful woman of twenty-three, with the frank and winning expression of a young girl. Astro handed it to Valeska, who looked at it in admiration and regret. The aunt explained further that her niece Elizabeth was in a low-necked, white mull dress. She had come down for dinner; but, finding that she had forgotten her handkerchief, had gone back up-stairs to get it. She had not hurried, as dinner had not yet been served. Her aunt did not think it strange that Elizabeth did not return for ten or fifteen minutes. Then she had heard Marie scream to James, and she herself had followed him up, and had been there when he opened the door.

The old lady was too overcome to go further; but James corroborated Masson's previous story. Both doors had been locked and the keys withdrawn. The windows were open. No footprints or traces of any kind had been found outside by the police. James himself had been in the lower front hall at the time, rolling up some rugs, and had heard the sound of voices up-stairs, and had wondered at them. One voice, he thought, sounded much like Marie's. It was about three minutes, he thought, between the time when he heard the voice and the laughter—for he had heard that also—to the moment when Marie called for him to come up. She had appeared much excited.

He was a simple-faced fellow, with an awkward air and a generally shiftless appearance,—the ordinary country youth who has had too little energy to better himself in any way. Astro scarcely gave him a glance, but stood gazing at the door in front of him.

He made a sign finally, and all but Valeska left the room. She shut the door behind them. Then she followed his eyes about the walls and floor.

"I think," said Astro, thoughtfully regarding the window-frame, "that Masson regrets exceedingly having tried to kiss Marie about four days ago. Poor chap!"

Valeska's eyes narrowed. "Oh!" she said. "That was what broke off the engagement?"

"I'm afraid so."

"But was Marie in love with him, too?" she asked eagerly.

Astro's expression was more animated as he replied, "I love, thou lovest, he loves; we love, you love, they love. I think, my dear, that in matters of the heart you know the symptoms better than I, although you were not taught the philosophy of the Yogis by a Hindu fakir. What do you say, pretty priestess?"

"Masson was sincerely in love with Miss Denton. He never cared a snap for Marie."

"I believe you. And yet he kissed her—or tried to. There was no mistaking that blush. It is a common error to suppose that French girls are a whit less modest than their English or American sisters. In point of fact, they are often more so,—more ignorant, more innocent. Marie was carefully brought up; she is still a child. But the Latin races have temperament; they soon learn. Marie is a passionate little thing, quick at loving as at hating, full of revenges and regrets."

"But what has that kiss to do with this murder?"

"That's precisely what I'm here to find out. Permit me to resume my meditation, that my astral vision may be released."

Valeska smiled, and kept silent. It was Astro's way of requesting that he was not to be questioned further until he himself had run down his clue.

It was a quarter of an hour before he spoke; then to say in triumph, "Ho! I have found it! I have at least solved half the mystery." He pointed to three parallel scratches on the frieze, above the picture-molding.

Valeska shook her head, puzzled.

He shrugged his shoulders and went to the window, pointing to a tiny spot on the white frame.

"It's blood!" exclaimed Valeska.

"It's blood; and yet Miss Denton was strangled, and no blood was shed,—none, at least, of hers."

"Whose blood, then, was it?"

"Kindly get out of the window on the balcony, my dear."

She stepped over the low sill, unconsciously placing her left hand on the frame to steady herself. Her fingers touched the paint about two inches below the bloody smutch.

"Well, my dear, it certainly isn't your blood, at least," said Astro.

"Marie's, then? She is taller than I."

"She had no wound on her hand. I examined them both carefully."

"And there was none on James'."

"Nor the aunt's. If you have looked all you wish to, you might go down to the kitchen and talk to the cook. It was said in the paper that she had a bad temper, and had lately quarreled with Miss Denton. To be sure, all good cooks have bad tempers; but, as the police didn't see fit to arrest her, she may possibly be the murderer. See what you can do. I shall remain here for a while. There's much to be done, and I'm in a hurry to earn my thousand dollars."

When Valeska had left, Astro resumed his study of the room, going over it inch by inch, looking again at the window, finally turning to the balcony. The care with which he worked showed that the Master of Mysteries was unusually perplexed. After examining the floor and rail of the balcony, he drew a bird glass from his pocket and spent a half-hour gazing at the elm whose branches stretched toward the window. Off the balcony was another window, from the room next to the boudoir. This, too, he examined carefully. Then he smiled slightly, put up the glass, and re entered the room. It was evident that he had found what he had sought.

Descending to the lower hall, he gave a quick look at doors and windows, then went out into the yard in the rear to the base of the tree he had spent so much time in investigating. He looked now up, and then down. He gazed up at the two windows of the balcony. His eyes were on the great door of the stable when Valeska appeared, her eyes shining.

"The cook has a cut on her left forefinger!" she announced breathlessly. "The second girl says that, just before they discovered the crime, the cook was away from the kitchen for about fifteen minutes. The cook herself says that she had gone out back of the stable to get a few strawberries for her own supper."

"Did she come back with the berries?"

"Yes; but she might have picked them before."

"What shape was the cut on her finger?"

"Why, it was a straight cut, of course. She said she did it slicing ham. But you know she might have gone up-stairs and into the guest-room, which has a window on the same balcony, and—"

"What about the second girl?" Astro interrupted.

Valeska laughed. "She's a country girl, awfully, awfully in love with James. She's frightened to death for fear that he'll be suspected of the murder."

"Did she hear the voices and the laughter?"

"No. Anyway, she was with the aunt most of the time, in the dining-room. It was the cook who did it, I'm sure."

"And how about the whistle? And why should the cook laugh at such a time?"

Valeska's face fell. "Well," she said finally, "for that matter why should any murderer laugh? The whistle might have been a signal to some one outside."

"Except that, in this case, it wasn't. My dear, the laughter and the whistle are the easiest parts of the mystery. What I want to know is, where is the key to the door? It was in the lock when Miss Denton went up-stairs the second time."

"Where, indeed, is it? That would show a good deal."

"If you'll come with me, I'll show it to you. But first I think we had better get Mr. Masson. I may need a little help in a few moments. Will you kindly call him? I'll be in the stable."

As Valeska left, the palmist strolled slowly over to the stable and looked in the great door. In the center of the floor stood a large brown touring-car. A young man in overalls was polishing the brass work.

Astro nodded. "A very fine-looking machine," he offered. "A Lachmore, isn't it?"

The chauffeur grunted and kept on with his work.

"I am a friend of Mr. Masson's," Astro went on, "and I should like to look over this car. I am thinking of getting one myself some day."

Still the young man did not answer except by inarticulate grunts.

Astro drew nearer. "What's the matter with your finger?" he asked abruptly.

The young man looked up, now angrily, as if about to make a discourteous retort. Seeing Masson approaching, however, he replied, "Oh, it got jammed in the machine a day or two ago. What's that to you?"

"I'd like to see it. I can cure it. I am a healer."

Astro extended his hand suavely.

The young man scowled darkly. "Oh, it's not much. No need of bothering you."

By this time Masson had entered with Valeska.

"Mr. Masson," said the Seer, "this young man interests me very much. I have been conscious ever since I arrived at Hamphurst of certain very harsh and painful vibrations. In the boudoir, these grew more intense. I felt something in that room that was neither an odor nor a color, but partook of the nature of both. Now, singularly enough, I find the same influence here, only more active and vibrant. This young man has a peculiar aura. I wonder that you can not perceive it even with one of your five material senses."

The young man stared, more and more uncomfortable at the talk. Finally he dropped his rag, walked round to the back of the car, and took up a heavy wrench.

Astro raised his voice slightly. "Mr. Masson," he said, "I can see this fellow's astral body as well as his material frame. Now, I notice on the forefinger of his left hand, in its astral condition, a small V-shaped cut. I am very anxious to know whether such a corresponding wound is to be found on his fleshly hand. Do you think you could induce him to remove that bandage?"

Masson, mystified, but evidently comprehending that something important was at stake, raised his voice. "Walters," he said, "kindly oblige me by removing that rag from your left hand."

Walters looked up surlily. "I can't, Mr. Masson. It would make it bleed again. It bled like anything when I jammed it in the machine."

"My friend," said Astro genially, "jammed wounds do not bleed to any extent. It is a V-shaped scar then?"

"What of it?" The chauffeur stood poised in a sinister attitude.

"That's what I want to know, too," cried Masson. "By heaven! do you mean that this fellow here had anything—"

Astro raised his hand. "One moment," he interrupted. "First, I want to ask you, Walters, to show me where the gasoline tank is in this car?"

A look of terror swept over the young man's face. He raised the wrench in his hand and rushed at the palmist. Astro avoided him lithely and grappled with him. The man struck out, tore himself free, and dashed for the door. He would have made his escape had not Masson jumped for him. There was another scuffle. Masson, now convinced that he had his sweetheart's murderer before him, fought like a maniac. Astro, who had been thrown to the ground by the force of the blow he had received, now rose, and the next moment drew out a revolver and covered his prisoner.

"Let go, or I shoot you like a dog!" he barked out between his teeth. "Let him go, Masson! This is not for you. The law will attend to him. The man's evil enough; but not so bad as you think. He's no murderer, really."

At these words Walters turned to Astro with a gleam of hope in his eye. "Oh, I'm not, sir! Before God, I had no intention of murdering her! I didn't know I had till afterward. I only tried to keep her from screaming, and she dropped like a log. It was that accursed parrot! Miss Denton was frightened to death, sir, and so was I, pretty near."

Astro spoke sharply. "Valeska, get that halter, and I'll fasten him so he'll be safe till the police can get here."

"A parrot," ejaculated Valeska, as she brought the halter. "Ah, I see! That accounts for the strange, high-pitched voice, the laughter, and the whistling!"

"Get up now, and tell your story!" commanded Astro. "And remember that you speak in the presence of one to whom everything is revealed. At the slightest departure from the truth I shall feel instantly the shifting of your spectrum, and a change in the amplitude of your vibrations. In my crystals I saw the scene; but it was dusk, and the glass was cloudy. Tell me exactly what happened, and if it coincides with my vision you shall have my help in your trial."

"I'll tell the truth, so help me God!" cried Walters. "Listen! It was this way. It was only her money I was after. I had planned it for a week back, knowing just when she left the room empty. I got up the side stairs, and out on the balcony, and into the tree where I could watch her. As soon as she finished dressing and put out the light and went down-stairs, I slid on to the balcony and slipped into the room. Well, I had got her purse and emptied it, when all of a sudden the door opened, and in she came; for I hadn't thought to lock it. She gave a little scream at seeing me there in the dusk, and I grabbed her to keep her from making more noise. Just then

Hades seemed to break loose all around me. There was a voice yelling, 'Great God! Great God!' and then something feathery came scratching and flapping into my face. I put out one hand to ward it off, and got a bite that made me drop my hold of the lady. Then as she fell to the floor, there was a laugh that made my blood run cold. It laughed and laughed fit to kill. I couldn't stand it! I didn't care whether I was caught or not then; I locked the door, climbed out on the tree and got down to the ground. I didn't dare to run away, for fear I'd be suspected! but after I heard how it came out it was all I could stand to stay here. I didn't know what to do about Marie; but I hoped she'd get off some way, for I knew they never could prove it on her. And that's the truth, so help me God! Where the parrot came from I have no idea."

"It belongs in the next neighbor's house, and has been missing for a week," said Masson. "Now I'll go and telephone to the police."

He stopped a moment and looked wistfully at the Seer. "Ah, I knew you could do it," he said. "I wish you could tell me now how ever to be happy again."

"There is no such thing as happiness, my friend," said Astro seriously. "There is no joy but calm, the Eastern books say."

Masson bowed his head. Then, as he left, he remarked, "I shall send you a check in the morning. You will see if I am not grateful."

"What I don't see is, how you knew the key was in the gasoline tank of the auto?" Valeska asked him, on the way to town.

"I am not yet sure that it was, but can you think of any safer place for a chauffeur to hide it?" Astro replied with a smile.

THE LORSSON ELOPEMENT

The Master of Mysteries entered the great studio smiling, and, without removing his overcoat or silk hat, threw himself on the divan and chuckled.

Valeska looked up from her desk with a question in her eyes, though she did not speak. As Astro did not seem inclined to answer, she resumed her work with the finger prints. Each one of these, printed in pale red ink on a small sheet of bristol board, she examined carefully, then with a pencil she traced out the primary figure formed by the capillary lines, starting from the microscopic triangle on the inside of the finger, where the lines, coming from the back, first separated, and then following the curve till it met the corresponding little triangle or "island" on the outside of the finger. The axes of this diagram were then drawn, and the pattern thus defined was entered on the card index as an "invaded loop," an "arched spiral," or a "whorl," according to Galton's classification.

So absorbing was her work that it took her whole attention, and she did not think again of her employer until he spoke aloud. He had thrown off his overcoat and put on his oriental turban and his red silk robe to be ready for patrons. No visitors had yet appeared to interview the palmist, however, and Astro was lazily puffing his narghile.

"Valeska," he said at last, between two long inhalations of the water-pipe, "did you ever try to put out a fire in the grate by covering the front with a blower?"

She laid down her pencil and looked up smiling. "Why, no. It only makes the fire burn the hotter, doesn't it?"

He nodded his head gravely. "Precisely. And yet that's what Mrs. Lorsson is doing with her daughter Ruth."

Valeska waited for something more.

"I had an interesting time there to-day," he went on. "There were a dozen or more pretty well-known society women at her tea, and they were all crazy to have me read their palms, of course. That was all stupid enough, until Ruth Lorsson came in. Have you ever seen her?"

"Oh, yes," said Valeska. "A pretty girl of about eighteen, with dark eyes and dark hair, isn't she? She always looks so innocent that I want to pet her."

"You needn't worry. She has somebody to pet her, if I'm not mistaken. And as for being timid and innocent; well, you never can tell by the looks; that is, unless you see what I saw." He smiled again mysteriously.

"Is she in love then?" Valeska asked.

"Without doubt, by her handwriting, which I saw a sample of— you should have seen the double curve in the crossing of her t's— and by her heart line, too, for that matter; and by her general appearance and demeanor, most decidedly. But I had better proof than all that."

"Why, was *he* there? I could have told in an instant, I'm sure."

"No, *he* wasn't there; but another man was; and, though it was evident that Mrs. Lorsson considers him eligible and is trying to make a match of it, Ruth hates him. Of course you or any bright woman could have seen that as well as I."

"Then how did you find out specifically?"

"Why, in a surreptitious way, I must admit. You know that Mrs. Lorsson wanted to exploit me as the latest fad, and she insisted that I should come in costume. Very well, I was willing to oblige. Mrs. Larsson is rich and influential, and I made out my bill accordingly.

"Well, I was shown up into Miss Ruth's room to dress. There on her secretary I happened to see her blotter covered with figures. If it had been writing, I shouldn't have read it; but I confess that that list of numbers piqued my curiosity, and I looked at it. It wasn't a sum, or anything like that. It occurred to me at first glance that it was a cipher. I don't know why—perhaps because the thing seemed so meaningless. At any rate, it interested me, and I made a copy. Here it is."

He pulled out a note-book and showed Valeska the list:

3	36	91		2	101	91
4	36	91		43	98	91
5	36	91				
				8	341	91
1	81	91		71	96	91
11	61	91				

"What do you make of it?"

"Why, nothing as yet. It's absolutely meaningless." Valeska looked up.

"I agree with you so far. But let me tell you the rest of the story. Ruth is, as you know, a very pretty young girl; but she's more than that—she's clever. Of course the cleverness of eighteen isn't quite so deep as the cleverness of maturity; but I think she is intelligent enough to keep that stepmother of hers guessing. Of course one of the first things I said was that she was in love. Her stepmother denied it so indignantly that I immediately smelled a mouse. Ruth didn't betray herself; but I noticed that the young man who was present immediately began to take notice. He is Sherman Fuller, and, I imagine from what I heard, a millionaire in his own right. Decidedly an eligible! The way Mrs. Lorsson managed him was wonderful. There's no doubt that if she can throw Ruth at his head she'll do it. He seemed to be perfectly willing; but Ruth scarcely looked at him. When she did, it was with scorn. It was easy enough to see how the land lay. She was in love with some one else.

"Well, I had used my eyes pretty well when I was up in her room, and had noticed several things. Among these were, first, a Bible on her book-shelf, a half-filled box of caramels, a copy of *The Star* with one page torn out, and so on. I tried what the spiritualistic mediums call a 'fishing test' on her, saying that I thought she was very religious. She smiled rather cynically; but her stepmother thought it was wonderful. 'Why, Ruth goes up to her room every night after dinner to read her Bible!' she exclaimed. I next informed her that she was fond of sweet things, and her stepmother corroborated me by saying that she bought a box of candy every day or two.

"The rest was easy, and doesn't matter. But I could see that she was strictly chaperoned. She didn't go out of the room without Mrs. Lorsson's asking her where she was going, and from the conversation I inferred that she went nowhere alone. I was certain it was not only mere conventionality. Mrs. Lorsson watches her. As I was going out, a maid brought some letters in on a salver. One was for Miss Ruth. Mrs. Lorsson opened it calmly, as if it were for herself, glanced it over, and handed it to her stepdaughter. I have no doubt that the letters Miss Ruth writes are inspected as well."

"Isn't it awful?" sighed Valeska. "I thought that sort of thing had all gone by nowadays."

"Not when you have a stepdaughter, and an eligible young millionaire to marry her to," said Astro. "That woman is a tyrant and a schemer. There's little love lost in that family, I'm sure. But now look at the cipher again."

"First, let me think," Valeska said thoughtfully, holding the paper in her hand. "Here's a young girl who is having a young man, whom she doesn't like, forced on her. She is probably in love with another; but is not allowed to see him or to write to him. Well, *I'd* manage to communicate with him in some way."

"Yes, and you're clever, for eighteen, and you read the Bible every night after dinner."

"Oh!" Valeska's eyes grew bright. "Then these figures refer to Bible texts? But that was the way our grandmothers wrote, interlarding their messages with Scriptural quotations. I don't really believe Ruth is so religious as that."

"Ah, you don't know your Bible then," Astro rejoined, as he went to a bookcase and took down a copy. "Why, it's the most wonderful book in the world in more ways than one! It not only contains the sum of human and divine wisdom, but almost every message that one might wish to send. Why, it's a ready-made lover's codex! It isn't only the Song of Songs that contains beautiful love messages, I assure you. They're scattered all through the book."

"Then these figures must refer to the chapters and verses," Valeska said, scrutinizing the numbers.

"And the books," Astro added.

Valeska still puzzled over the list of figures. "The numbers seem too high for that."

"And there's our first clue. Now let us examine the columns in detail. We'd naturally expect the number of the book to come first, the chapter next, and the verse last. The highest number in the first row is seventy-one. But there are only sixty-six books in the Bible; so that can't be the number of any book. Taking the second column, we see that the highest number is three hundred forty-one. But the longest book in the Bible, the book of Psalms, has only one hundred and fifty chapters, so that column can't give the chapter numbers—as it is, at least. The third column has only the number ninety-one. That can't be the number of every verse."

He waited for Valeska. She frowned prettily as she studied it out. For some time her look was intense, rapt. Then, as if some idea passed from him to her, her smile came radiantly, and she exclaimed:

"The figures are reversed! What a sly-boots she is!"

Astro smiled also. "Of course I saw that at the first glance. There is a direct corroboration of it plainly evident. In the first place, ninety-one reversed is nineteen, the number in Biblical order of the book of Psalms, which has more personal messages than any other book and second we get the chapter one hundred forty-three, which could come from no other book, of course. Now let us try and see what we get. I'll begin at the top, the sixty-third Psalm, verses three, four, and five." And he read aloud:

> "'Because thy loving kindness is better than life,
> my lips shall praise thee.

"'Thus will I bless thee while I live: I will lift up
my hands in thy name.

"'My soul shall be satisfied as with marrow and
fatness; and my mouth shall praise thee with joyful
lips.'"

"It's pretty, isn't it?" he asked.

The tears had come into Valeska's eyes. "Oh, it's beautiful!"
she exclaimed. "No one could call it sacrilegious, even though she
has used the words that apply to the Almighty for her own lover.
She's a dear! It seems wrong to pry into so charming a secret; but
I'm dying to hear the rest of it."

Astro put down the cipher. "This is evidently only one side of
the correspondence, you must remember. If we are to get it all, we
must find his answers. That's a little more difficult."

"It seems impossible to me," said Valeska. "You only happened
on this. I shouldn't know where to look for his messages."

He sat down and looked at her seriously. "The only way is to use
your imagination and your memory. Put yourself in her place. You
can't trust servants or mails. You are watched everywhere except in
your own room. Think it out; concentrate your mind on the problem."

Valeska dropped her head on her hand thoughtfully, and spoke
as if to herself. "Let's see. I am in my room alone. I read my Bible
and pick out appropriate messages. But how do I get them to him?"
She looked up, puzzled.

"Never mind that now. How does he communicate with you?"

"There's a box of candy there, and a newspaper—" She paused
and then, gazing at him through narrowed eyes, went on. "It must
be through the paper; I can't see any other way possible. No one
would suspect that, if the message were concealed. It might be in
the 'Personal' column."

"That's too easy, and it might be noticed. Besides, *The Star* has
no 'Personals'."

"Then— It couldn't be in a news item; for he wouldn't be sure
of its being inserted, even if he were a reporter. It must be in an
advertisement."

He went into the waiting-room, and returned with a copy of *The Star*.

"Correct," he said. "That's the only possible solution. Now the thing to do is to look through this file of *The Star* and see if we can discover any advertisement that seems suspicious. First, what date shall we lookup?"

Valeska returned to the paper on which the numbers were written. "Well," she said, "if it were I, I should want to have a message as often as possible. If I send him my texts every night, he ought to reply in the morning paper. This paper seems to show four messages. The last one must be yesterday's. That would bring his first advertisement just four days ago—Monday, May twenty-fifth."

He turned to the file, and they looked over the pages together, her chin on his shoulder, Astro's long forefinger hovering at one advertisement after another, his suave voice keeping up a running commentary:

"We'll omit the displayed ads. He's probably poor, or Ruth's stepmother wouldn't object to him; so couldn't afford that, and besides they would be too conspicuous. All the little ones are classified under heads. Let's see: 'Automobiles,'—h'm, all well-known second-hand shops. 'Lawyers,'—nothing there. 'Real Estate, Villa Lots,'—don't see anything, do you? 'Furnished Rooms.' 'Unfurnished Flats,'—let's go carefully here. What we want is three figures. We'll recognize them by the wording, if they're put in on purpose. I don't see anything there. H'm, 'For Sale,'—go slow now! 'Fixtures.' 'Bargains.' 'Typewriters.' 'Sacrifice,'—well! what do you think of that? Eureka!"

His finger stopped at a three-line notice, which read:

FOR SALE
19 vols. of Sir Roger de Coverley, 63 illustrations on wood; $6 and $8 each. G. P. James & Co., Flatiron Bldg.

"Now, isn't that crazy enough to be suspicious? 'Nineteen' again, too,—her favorite number. Who ever heard of Sir Roger de

Coverley, except in the papers of *The Spectator*, anyway? There
you are: 19: 63—6 and 8. Look it up!"

Valeska flew to the Bible and turned to the Psalms, and read
from the sixty-third chapter:

> "'When I remember thee upon my bed, and medi-
> tate on thee in the night watches.
> "'My soul followeth hard after thee: thy right
> hand upholdeth me.'"

"The blessed infants! Isn't it perfectly lovely? Ruth must have
had hard work to answer that; but the one she sent was nearly as
good, wasn't it? Oh, let's find the next one, and get the whole correspondence quick! It's too exciting!"

Astro opened the issue of the twenty-sixth, and scanned the
advertisements carefully. It was some time before they found it,
and several false clues were followed up. Valeska, thinking she had
discovered the secret, would hurriedly take the Bible, only to be
referred to some such text in Ezra as,—

> "'The children of Magbish, an hundred fifty and
> six.
> "'The children of Kirjath-arim, Chephirah, and
> Beeroth, seven hundred and forty and three,—'"

and would go off into peals of laughter. Some of these false
scents led deep into the "Begats"; some led into the whale's belly.

But at last the right one was discovered in the "Second Hand"
column, which read, innocently enough:

> For Sale: 64 good, 1st class, 2d hand tables. Ad-
> dress Chester, *Star Office*.

And, turning, therefore, to the third book of John, chapter one,
verse two, she read aloud:

"'Beloved, I wish above all things that thou mayest prosper and be in health, even as thy soul prospereth.'"

"Now let's arrange the whole correspondence as far as we have it," Valeska suggested, after the four messages were all deciphered. "It certainly is a charming set of love-letters!"

"It may well be, written by the ablest literary men of King James' epoch," said Astro. "You read off the texts, and I'll write them down. It's a relief from solving murder mysteries and dynamite outrages and stolen jewels."

Valeska, having the references checked off, read as follows, insisting that Ruth's lover should be called Chester, from the name in the second advertisement.

Ruth

"'I will love thee, O Lord, my strength. (Ps. 18:1.)

"'Thou wilt shew me the path of life; in thy presence is fulness of joy; at thy right hand there are pleasures for evermore.'" (Ps. 16:11.)

Chester

"'And now I beseech thee, lady, not as though I wrote a new commandment unto thee, but that which we had from the beginning, that we love one another. (2 John, 5.)

"'I stretch forth my hands unto thee: my soul thirsteth after thee, as a thirsty land. *Selah.*'" (Ps. 143:6.)

Ruth

"'I will behave myself wisely in a perfect way. O when wilt thou come unto me? I will walk within my house with a perfect heart. (Ps. 101:2.)

"'My covenant will I not break, nor alter the thing that is gone out of my lips.'" (Ps. 89:34.)

Chester

"'How sweet are thy words unto my taste! yea,
sweeter than honey to my mouth! (Ps. 119:103.)

"'Whom have I in heaven but thee? and there is
none upon earth that I desire beside thee.'" (Ps.
73:25.)

Ruth

"'Cause me to hear thy loving kindness in the
morning; for in thee do I trust: cause me to know
the way wherein I should walk; for I lift up my soul
unto thee. (Ps. 143:8.)

"'And hide not thy face from thy servant; for I
am in trouble; hear me speedily.'" (Ps. 69-17.)

Valeska reread the whole series, and her eyes burned deep.
Astro watched her pretty serious face without a word, waiting for
her comments. The tears glistened in her eyes as she said finally:

"Oh! can't we help them somehow? Surely you can, if you only
will!"

Astro recited whimsically to himself:

> "'They warned him of her,
>   And they warned her of him;
> And the courtship proceeded
>   To go on with a vim!'"

"It's altogether too romantic for us to interfere with. Let them
have their clandestine correspondence; it makes the affair interesting. Wait till we read his reply in to-morrow's *Star*, Valeska.
Perhaps they can manage it themselves."

This was all she could get out of the Master of Mysteries that
day; but she knew from his silent contemplation that he had not
stopped thinking the matter over. She herself puzzled her wits as
to how Ruth had communicated with her lover, until she had to

give it up. She knew that if she waited Astro would solve that mystery, if indeed he had not already found it out.

She came into the studio next morning excitedly. "Oh! isn't it awful?" were her first words. She held the morning *Star* out to him, with an anxious look.

Astro smiled and pointed to another copy which lay on his great table where his astrological charts were spread out. "It's only a lover's quarrel, I think. He's a little jealous of that Sherman Fuller, I imagine."

"Well, that's enough. I should think Chester would be wild!"

"Well," said Astro, yawning, "I'm glad he made one jump out of the Psalms, anyway. I was getting tired of that number nineteen. Job is a good place for a jealous man to look. You'd better add his remarks to our list."

Valeska, therefore, wrote down the following texts, which she had drawn from the advertisement of that morning's paper:

> *Chester*
>   "'I prevented the dawning of the morning, and cried: I hoped in thy word. (Ps. 119:147.)
>   "'Thou holdest mine eyes waking: I am to troubled that I can not speak. (Ps. 77:4.)
>   "'Lover and friend hast thou put far from me, and mine acquaintance into darkness. (Ps. 18:18.)
>   "'When I thought to know this, it was too painful for me. (Ps. 73:16.)
>   "'Why doth thine heart carry thee away? and what do thine eyes wink at ... ? (Job 15:12.)
>   "'Deliver my soul from the sword; my darling from the power of the dog.'" (Ps. 22:20.)

"Surely you'll help them out *now*, won't you?" Valeska pleaded. "We can't let it all be spoiled this way! Think how hard it is for her to explain!"

"Trust *her*," said Astro, shaking his head. "Only I'd like to know how she does it; that's all I want. I propose that we take a walk out to Fifty-third Street this evening. You know she goes up-stairs into her room every night after dinner, say from eight till nine o'clock. I think if we walk up and down in front of that block we may find something doing."

"Oh, I hope we'll find Chester, anyway!" Valeska exclaimed.

They proceeded as he had suggested, that evening, to walk up Fifth Avenue after dinner, reaching Fifty-third Street at a few minutes past eight. Astro pointed out Ruth's window, which was already lighted. Then together they walked slowly up and down on the opposite side of the street, keeping the house well in view.

They had not been there for more than ten minutes, when the sash was suddenly thrown up in Ruth Lorsson's room. They could see her form silhouetted against the light. A white something was thrown out, and fell on the sidewalk. Immediately a man emerged from the shadow of the adjacent doorway, ran down the steps, picked up the white package, and walked rapidly up the street.

"It's Chester!" Valeska exclaimed.

"Yes, we must find out where he lives and who he is," was Astro's reply. "You had better go home, and I'll follow him."

The man had walked off so rapidly that she saw it would be useless to attempt to keep up with him, much less overtake him, and she tried to stifle her disappointment as Astro, leaving her, walked quickly up the street. As Chester walked, she saw him tear something from the package he carried. Then another white piece dropped. She followed far enough to discover what the fragments were—the sides of an empty candy box which Ruth Lorsson had thrown into the street. Her message had indubitably been written on the bottom, since he had thrown all the rest away.

"I see now why Miss Ruth is so fond of candy," Valeska said to herself. "A note thrown from the window would be too dangerous and too hard to find. It's ridiculously simple! I think I'm growing fond of that girl."

Next day Astro appeared at the studio with the information that the young man's name was indeed Chester; that he was an artist or illustrator for magazines; and that he lived on the south side of Washington Square.

"He's getting into a terrible state," said Valeska. "Did you read his advertisement this morning? It was under 'Lawyers' this time."

"I haven't had time to look over *The Star*. What is it?"

Valeska read from her list the last addition:

"'For thou hast made him most blessed forever; thou hast made him exceeding glad with thy countenance. (Ps. 21:6.)

"'Thou hast given him his heart's desire, and hast not withholden the request of his lips. *Selah*. (Ps. 21:2.)

"'Yea, they opened their mouth wide against me, and said, Aha, aha, our eye hath seen it. (Ps. 35:21.)

"'I am troubled; I am bowed down greatly; I go mourning all the day long.'" (Ps. 38:6.)

"Poor devil!" Astro grew serious. "I did see a paragraph in *Town Gossip* this morning about a Fifty-third Street belle who was about to make a brilliant match. It was thinly disguised, and evidently referred to Ruth Lorsson."

"He evidently believes she is engaged," said Valeska; "but I don't. No girl would give up such a romantic lover."

"Now," said Astro, "the question is: How are we going to get hold of her side of the correspondence? I'm getting as interested in this affair as if I were paid for it. The fact that there is a misunderstanding does alter the matter too, and I don't see but that we'll have to straighten it out if we can. I've thought of a way to get hold of to-night's message by a trick. It may work, and it may not. Of course it's rather low of us to interfere with their private post-office; but we may be able to make that up to them later. Anyway, it will make it exciting for them. I'm going to bait a box myself," he went on, "and place it on the sidewalk at a quarter of eight. Chester will arrive and think that for some reason she has already thrown it out, and he'll take it and make off. Then, when she throws her own box out, we'll grab it."

The temptation was too great for Valeska's curiosity, and she gave a hesitating consent, on the agreement that it should be tried only once. "But you'll have to put a message on the box, or he'll know there's something wrong," she said.

"Turn to Psalms 102. I think that will not compromise her too much," Astro said.

> "'My heart is smitten and withered like grass; so that I forget to eat my bread. (Ps. 102:4.)
>
> "'Because of thine indignation and thy wrath: for thou hast lifted me up, and cast me down.'" (Ps. 102:10.)

The ruse succeeded. Shortly after eight o'clock, Chester came walking down the street, spied the box which Astro had placed conspicuously on the sidewalk, examined it quickly, and walked hurriedly away. Fifteen minutes later, Ruth's box dropped from the window. Astro secured it and took it to a near-by lamp post, looked at the figures, and then consulted a small Bible which he drew from his pocket.

"This is too bad," he said to Valeska, who had accompanied him. "I didn't think she'd be so strong. It won't do for him to miss this message, poor chap! Here, read it:"

> "'Deliver me not over unto the will of mine enemies: for false witnesses are risen up against me, and such as breathe out cruelty. (Ps. 27:12.)
>
> "'I have not sat with vain persons, neither will I go in with dissemblers. (Ps. 26:4.)
>
> "'But as for me, I will walk in mine integrity: redeem me, and be merciful unto me.'" (Ps. 26: 11.)

"I'll tell you what'll do," said Astro, "we'll send this down to his house by a messenger boy. He won't know what to make of it; but he won't be able to ask her how it was delivered till it's all over."

The message was sent at once; then, as Astro walked with Valeska to her home, he said:

"We can't do this again; it will make too much trouble. You'll have to see if you can't get into his studio some way and find out what messages he is receiving. You can go and offer yourself as a model. That will give you plenty of time to look about, and you may manage to find the bottoms of the boxes every day. If I know the young man in love, he won't destroy them."

Valeska consented to attempt the adventure, and accordingly set out the next morning after entering on her list the following message deciphered from Chester's advertisement in *The Star*:

> "'Let the lying lips be put to silence; which speak grievous things proudly and contemptuously against the righteous. (Ps. 31:18.)
>
> "'For I said in my haste, I am cut off from before thine eyes: nevertheless thou heardest the voice of my supplications when I cried unto thee. (Ps. 31:22.)
>
> "'In the day when I cried them answeredst me, and strengthenedst me with strength in my soul. (Ps. 138:3.)
>
> "'So foolish was I, and ignorant: I was as a beast before thee.'" (Ps. 73:22.)

Astro worked all day in his studio alone, reading palms and casting horoscopes for his fashionable clients, and during the leisure times between their calls, casting many a glance across to the desk where his pretty blond assistant was wont to look up at him with such animation whenever he spoke. The velvet hangings were dull and shadowy, and the high lights on trophies of arms and tinseled costumes on the wall twinkled through the dusk, when the portières parted, and Valeska, smartly attired, gloved and feathered, appeared. Astro smiled for almost the first time that day. She sank into a deep divan to get her breath. He turned on a light above her head.

"He's a perfect dear!" she said as soon as she could speak. "He isn't at all handsome, in fact he's ugly; but he's the most romantic and kind-hearted chap in the world. I'd trust him anywhere. He has red hair, and twinkling blue eyes, and fine teeth, and so young— why he made me feel eighty years old! It was too easy! I was just what he wanted, and I was intelligent, and he liked my hands." She extended them gracefully for Astro to admire. He kissed her finger-tips.

"It was a funny old place, all full of canvases with their faces to the wall, and dust, and pewter pots, and brushes, and old magazines, and everything. It smelled horribly of tobacco and turpentine; but it was such fun! I didn't have to do much detective work, either. Do you know, the child actually had all those candy-box bottoms nailed in a row on the wall over the mantel-piece! I felt like a thief. There they were, all of them you got the list of, and the one we sent last night, and there was a shabby Bible on his mantelpiece."

"How did he treat you?"

Valeska laughed. "Well, not in a way to make me conceited. Oh, he's in love, all right. He looked at me exactly as if he were purchasing a horse. I almost expected him to open my mouth and examine my teeth to see how old I was. But he was nice, all the same, and delighted to find a model that had brains and could take and hold a pose. My, if I'm not tired, though! I was supposed to be playing on a piano—the table—and looking up mischievously over my shoulder. I ache all over!"

"Of course he didn't say anything significant?"

"No. But he stopped working every little while and began to think; and I knew what that meant. Then he'd go to the window and look out for a long while, and then come back and draw like mad. Oh, he had all the signs! Poor boy!"

"Does he want you to-morrow?"

"Yes, all this week."

"Good! By that time I think we shall have arranged some plan to help him. If I bought a picture or two, it might help, perhaps."

Valeska posed for Chester the six days, returning each evening to the studio to report to Astro, each time more interested in the love-affair. Each day she wrote down the cipher message printed in *The Star*, and the text she found in the studio written on Ruth's candy box. At the end of the week the courtship began to approach a crisis, as the correspondence showed.

Ruth

"'He that worketh deceit shall not dwell within my house; he that telleth lies shall not tarry in my sight. (Ps. 101: 7.)

"'But thou art the same, and thy years shall have no end.'" (Ps. 102:27.)

Chester

"'I will instruct thee and teach thee in the way which thou shall go: I will guide thee with mine eye.'" (Ps. 32:8.)

Ruth

"'And I will delight myself in thy commandments, which I have loved. (Ps. 119:47.)

"'But mine enemies are lively, and they are strong: and they that hate me wrongfully are multiplied. Ps. 38: 19.)

"'All that hate me whisper together against me: against me do they devise my hurt.'" (Ps. 41:7.)

Chester

"'Let not them that are mine enemies wrongfully rejoice over me: neither let them wink with the eye that hate me without a cause. (Ps. 35:19.)

"'Let them be turned back for a reward of their shame that say, Aha, aha.'" (Ps. 70:3.)

Ruth

"'Pull me out of the net that they have laid priv-
ily for me: for thou art my strength. (Ps. 31:4.)

"'Then call thou, and I will answer: or let me
speak and answer thou me.'" (Job 13:22.)

Chester

"'Having many things to write unto you, I would
not write with paper and ink: but I trust to come unto
you, and speak face to face, that our joy may be full.'"
(2 John, 12.)

Ruth

"'They gather themselves together, they hide
themselves, they mark my steps, when they wait for
my soul. (Ps. 56:6.)

"'And I said, Oh that I had wings like a dove! for
then I would fly away, and be at rest. (Ps. 55:6.)

"'I would hasten my escape from the windy storm
and tempest. (Ps. 55:8.)

"'That thy beloved may be delivered; save with
thy right hand, and hear me.'" (Ps. 60:5.)

Chester

"'And it shall be, if thou go with us, yea, it shall
be, that what goodness the Lord shall do unto us,
the same will we do unto thee.'" (Num. 10:32.)

Ruth

"'Then said I, Lo, I come: in the volume of the
book it is written of me. (Ps. 40: 7.)

"'And Ruth said, Intreat me not to leave thee, or
to return from following after thee: for whither thou
goest, I will go; and where thou lodgest, I will lodge:
thy people shall be my people, and thy God my God.'"
(Ruth 1:16.)

"It is getting serious, isn't it?" said Valeska, when she brought the last message of Ruth's. "Poor Chester is half crazy. He's been working like mad to get some illustrations for *The Universal Magazine* done; so as to get money enough to get married on, I suppose. But how in the world they are going to elope, I don't see."

"Love laughs at locksmiths," said Astro.

"But not at stepmothers. All the same, they're going to do it somehow, and I want to see the fun. It's bound to come off in a day or so now. I'm dying to speak of it to Chester and offer to help him; but I'm afraid it would spoil his fun. Hadn't we better just play about on the edge of it, and be ready for anything that happens?"

"It all depends on the next message. You go to the studio to-morrow and see if you can't find out about the elopement."

"All right," said Valeska.

At ten o'clock the next morning Astro received by a messenger a hurriedly penciled note. It read:

> "Something awful has happened! Chester broke his leg last night, and was taken to the hospital; but when it was set (the leg), he insisted on being brought home to the studio. He's almost crazy, and has a fever, and I'm sure the elopement was planned for to-night. I'll get it out of him somehow, and you must tell me what to do. Here's the text he got last night: I can't make it out; so please tell me immediately. V."

The text indicated was from the fifty-ninth Psalm, verse fourteen:

> "'And at evening let them return; and let them make a noise like a dog, and go round about the city.'"

As soon as Astro had looked it up, he put on his hat and coat, and jumping into his green limousine drove to Washington Square.

It was half past eight when Ruth Lorsson raised the shade of her window and threw up the sash. It was raining, and the asphalt pavement shimmered with reflected lights. At the curb opposite her house a taxicab was waiting. She looked at it eagerly.

There came a sudden noise like the barking of a dog repeated three times. Ruth smiled, let down the sash, and drew the shade. Then, stuffing a package wrapped in a towel inside her full blouse, she ran down-stairs.

"Ruth, child! what are you doing?" Mrs. Lorsson's voice came petulantly.

Ruth hovered a moment by the doorway, to say, in a voice that trembled a little, "Oh, I only want to get the Smiths' address from one of their cards on the hall table."

She walked swiftly to the front door, opened it noiselessly, slipped out, and shut it carefully behind her. She had to slam it to make it latch, and the jar frightened her. She fairly flew down the steps now, and ran across the street straight for the cab. The door in its side swung open, and she popped inside. The cab instantly drove off at a furious pace.

There was a dark figure inside. She snuggled up to it deliciously. "Oh, Harry!" she breathed. "At last! Oh, I thought this time never would come!" Then with a little scream she jumped away from him. "Who are you!" she demanded. Her voice rang with terror.

"My dear," said Astro, "don't be frightened. Mr. Chester couldn't come. He has had a slight accident; but not bad enough to prevent his being married tonight. I'm going to have the pleasure of giving you away. I have your bridesmaid all ready at the studio."

"Why, how did you know?" she demanded, staring at him. Then, as an electric light suddenly illuminated the interior of the cab, she recognized the fine picturesque features of the Master of Mysteries, and gave a little sigh of relief. "Oh, it's Astro!" she exclaimed. "You know everything, don't you? Did you see it in your crystal ball?"

He smiled as he replied, "My dear, I saw it in your pretty eyes the first time I saw you."

"But tell me about Harry! Oh, I am so frightened! It must be a bad accident to keep him away—to-night."

He reassured her, and they drove on she, excited, eager with anticipation, fearful of the step she had taken, but more and more confident in Astro's protection. They reached Washington Square, and hurried to the studio. Valeska met them at the door with a smile. For a moment Ruth eyed her suspiciously.

"Your bridesmaid," said Astro.

Ruth, relieved, but anxious for a sight of her lover, darted by with hardly a glance, and ran to the bed where Harry Chester lay, weak, but impatiently awaiting her.

"Oh, Harry!"

"Oh, Ruth!"

Astro and Valeska walked into the hall. "Well," said Astro, "I hope she's satisfied now. She has lost four millions and three magnificent houses, not to speak of a permanent place in smart society."

"For which she'd have to pay all her life," said Valeska. "If you ask me, I'd say she's got a bargain. Come, let's call in the minister! I'm going to wait and see it out!"

THE CALENDON KIDNAPPING CASE

Hardly had Astro's office hours begun, one morning, when Valeska threw back the black velvet portières of the great studio, and motioned her visitors to enter. They came in anxiously—a dignified but careworn haggard man of fifty and his hysterical sobbing wife. Apparently they expected immediately to meet the Master of Mysteries face to face; for they looked curiously about the richly decorated apartment with a hesitating air.

"You'll have to wait a few moments," said the girl in a friendly voice. "The Master is at present rapt in a psychic trance, and cannot be disturbed. Excuse me while I prepare for his awakening. It is dangerous to call him too suddenly; but I know your business is urgent, and I'll do what I can."

With that, she took from a small antique reliquary a handful of green powder and scattered it on a censer. Almost immediately it flared up and sent forth an aromatic smoke. It flickered eerily as she left them. Once alone, she entered a small chamber off the reception-room, and turned on the studio lights from an electric switch.

In the place where she stood now, looking into a large mirror, she could see the visitors, vividly illuminated, as if in a camera obscura. The man sat listlessly staring straight ahead of him without movement of any kind. The woman gazed, with raised eyebrows and a half-startled expression, from one curious object to another. The skull in a corner made her tremble. Her fingers plucked nervously at her wrap. It was evident that she was fearfully distraught.

Astro entered the cabinet and cast his eyes on the glass. His assistant leaned close to him and whispered:

"A kidnapping case. The Calendons' little boy was stolen a week or so ago, don't you remember? It's really dreadful. The police have been unable to locate the child anywhere, and the parents are half crazy about it. She poured it all out to me while they were waiting for you. I do hope you can do something!"

The Seer's eyes were busy in the mirror. "Yes, I know. He's a director in the tobacco trust. I'd have known it, anyway, by that little gold cigar on his watch-charm. A dozen of them were made for souvenirs when the combine was first organized. He hasn't slept for two or three nights. But what's he doing with *The Era*? He'd naturally be a reader of *The Planet*. Oh, I see! The kidnappers, of course, have asked him to communicate with them through the 'Personal' column. So they've begun to work him already. Poor devil!"

It was an agonizing story that fell from the lips of Calendon a little later; one which, in all the sensational events of the Seer's career in the solution of mysteries, long stood out as unique. Used as was Astro to astonishing recitals, there was a ferocity about this crime that astonished him. Calendon recited the details in a voice as hard and strained as a taut wire.

"My five-year-old boy, Harold, has been missing for ten days, having been kidnapped and kept in hiding by the most merciless gang of fiends in New York. I try to restrain myself, sir, in order to tell you the story concisely; but I assure you that it is hard to speak calmly. My child was abducted in Central Park, where he had gone with his nurse. He had strayed a little away from her at the time. I cannot think the crime was committed with her connivance. Nevertheless, she has been closely watched. I have not spared money, I assure you. I at once notified the police, and they have been at work on the case, without results, so far." He paused for a moment, almost overcome.

His wife interrupted him with a cry of anguish pitiful to hear. "Oh, James! how can you sit there and tell all that? Why don't you tell him immediately what has happened to-day? Why don't you show him the terrible thing?" She dropped her face in her hands and sobbed aloud. Valeska, deeply moved herself, tried in vain to comfort her.

Calendon put a trembling hand into his pocket and drew out a package wrapped in paper. Silently he handed it to the palmist. Astro took it and carefully undid the wrapping.

Inside was disclosed a small tin box, such as tobacco of the sliced-plug variety usually comes in. This, opened, showed an object in crumpled oiled paper, packed in the box with cotton-wool. Astro, with a grave expression on his face, picked the thing up and looked carefully at it. With great caution, then he slowly unfolded the paper. It was a child's toe.

For a few minutes not a sound was heard in the studio, save Mrs. Calendon's choking sobs, and the intake of her husband's deep breaths as he endeavored to master his emotion. Astro put aside the gruesome object with its wrappings, and then extended his hand and grasped Calendon's with a strong encouraging pressure.

"Mr. Calendon," he said simply, "I am at your service. I thank God that I have had some success in tracking down worse crimes than this, and what I can do in this matter shall be done without reward. Cheer up, Mr. Calendon; I can help you! Madam, pray accept my sympathy; but master yourself, for I must hear the whole story."

Calendon moistened his lips, pulled himself together, and looked gratefully at the slender poetic figure before him. "I'll tell you the rest of the story now, and I pray to God that you can help!" He turned to his wife, and after she was calmer he proceeded.

"It's devilishly ingenious, sir. What they are holding the boy for is in order to get tips on the market. That's their price. I got from them the third day a typewritten, unsigned letter telling me that if I valued the life of my boy, I should give them inside information of the stock market. They furnished me with a cipher,—an easy one that simply reads backward, and by means of it I communicate with them every morning in the personal column of *The Era*. I am not a stock gambler, sir, although I have a fair knowledge of current Wall Street probabilities, and I soon exhausted what information I had, and it became harder and harder to deliver the goods. You know how these things go: a big deal isn't pulled off every day, and, not being on the inside, I had to get down on my knees to beg for news from the men on the Street who were able to help me. A few have interested themselves in my misfortune and assisted me; but they're a cold-blooded set as a rule. But for a week I kept these bloodsuckers posted as well as I could, and I had good luck with my predictions. They must have made thousands; but still they wouldn't give up the boy. Why should they? They have a good thing, and intend to work it for all it's worth.

"But yesterday—great God!—yesterday I advertised in good faith to buy Continental Zinc. It was selling at 31, and I had figured on a big dividend being declared—so my advice had it—but instead the directors voted to pass it, and the stock fell six points. It rallied later, on the mine reports; but the rise came too late."

He stopped to draw a typewritten slip from his pocket. "Here's what came in the box," he said brokenly, and hid his face in his hands. Mrs. Calendon began weeping afresh.

Astro took the note and read it:

> "This is what we'll do every time you fool us. Be sharp!"

For some time Astro gazed at the sheet of paper, then rose and put it away with the other relics. "Have you the other letter here?"

Calendon took an envelope from his inside pocket and handed it to the palmist.

Astro held the envelope to the light, smelled of it, looked at the flap for a minute with his lens, then placed it on a side table. At last he rose and walked quietly over to a cupboard, from which he took a large crystal ball. This he placed on a black velvet cushion. He gazed into the sphere long and earnestly. It was his way of gaining time for reflection.

The Seer finally drew his long slim hand across his forehead and nodded his head. "There is no one you suspect? No woman?" he asked deliberately.

Calendon shook his head in silence.

"My nurse girl has been completely prostrated by the shock," Mrs. Calendon volunteered. "We are both sure she is innocent."

"There is a woman concerned in this, nevertheless. Now tell me what the police have done. They have tried to trace the buyers of the stocks you tipped off, I presume?"

"Certainly. We have tried to find what persons, if any, have profited by all the tips; but have been unsuccessful. I shall have a list, to-night probably, of all the buyers of Continental Zinc, eliminating, of course, the names of those who have bought for investment. The criminals are undoubtedly speculating on a margin, so there's little use looking up the records of the transfer office."

"You have your tip for to-morrow all ready for the newspaper?"

"Yes, and this time I'm sure it's safe."

"Very well, then, proceed as usual. You have, I suppose, your own detectives working on the case?"

"Yes. Can they do anything for you?"

"I'll telephone you early in the morning," said Astro, rising. "To-night I shall be busy. I shall cast the child's horoscope, and find out the best path to pursue. Kindly give me the exact hour of Harold's birth."

He wrote it down solemnly, then pressed an electric bell. Valeska appeared in the doorway; the visitors followed her into the waiting-room to the outer door.

Before she left, Mrs. Calendon took the girl's hand. "Oh, he's a wonderful man!" she exclaimed. "Somehow I have great faith in him. I'm strengthened already. He seems to know everything. Such eyes!"

Her husband shook his head skeptically and went out without a word.

Astro, meanwhile, had turned eagerly to the things that had been brought him, the lines of his olive face set and determined. From the inspired mystic to the man of practical analytic mind, the transition had been instantaneous. All pose was now dropped. His inspection was so absorbing that he did not notice Valeska's entrance. She did not speak, therefore, and watched him as he pored over the envelope, then at the oiled-paper wrapping of the horrid relic. Half an hour went by, during which the palmist rose several times to pace up and down the length of the dim studio. Once he took down a book from his shelves and ran hurriedly through its pages, stopping to mark a diagram. Valeska tiptoed across, and looked at the volume. It was Galton's *Finger Prints*, a classification of all the known capillary markings of the digital tips. It was an hour before Astro put up his work, much of which time had been spent merely in sitting with half-closed eyes, inert. Then he rose and yawned.

"Well, little girl, a bit of supper wouldn't go bad, would it?" he said gaily. "Afterward, you may sit at my feet, and I shall tell you of my desire to meet a lady that takes snuff, whose left thumb shows an invaded loop with two eyeleted rods; also, of my interest in a gentleman that rolls his own smokes on a *Moule à Cigarettes* and gambles in Continental Zinc."

Valeska shook her head, puzzled.

"You heard what Calendon said, of course?"

"Yes, I was in the cabinet all the time. But of course I haven't studied your evidence yet."

"Nor shall you this night, by Rameses! A crystal-gazer has to make his living on the curiosity of women. Kindly let me enjoy your curiosity this evening; and, that you may not be a loser, I shall explain to you the fallacies in Doctor Lasker's analysis of the Ruy Lopez opening. Meanwhile, let us try some of that new Assyrian jelly which I sent for so long ago. If you wish to add anything more substantial, I won't object, although I am a vegetarian, a Mahatma, an astrologer, a cabalist, a student of Higher Space, and a thorough believer in the doctrine that an ounce of mystery is worth a pound of commonplace. *Selah.* I have spoken."

During the meal, no one would have supposed by his animation that the occult Seer was confronted by the most difficult problem his profession had ever set before him. He joked like a young boy. His pretty assistant was kept in rippling peals of laughter. After dinner he produced a chess-board with ivory men, and the girl puzzled with him over innumerable variations of his favorite opening. They followed this by some of the regular chess problems, ending with several of his own. The last, finally, being too difficult, he left unfinished, sent Valeska home in his motor-car, and himself went to bed.

The next morning Astro looked, the first thing, at *The Era* personals. Calendon's advertisement read as follows:

ERUS: '97 Otog Lliwcirt celen atil opom S. O. C.

"I think," he said thoughtfully, "that it will hardly be dishonorable for me to plunge in Cosmopolitan Electric, so long as I'm not going to let Mr. Calendon pay me for this affair. Let's see. Sold yesterday at 75. If I can get it at five points margin, an investment of one thousand dollars will bring me in about eight hundred. I'll be able to get that Coptic manuscript I have been wanting so long. Now for Mr. Calendon!"

He took his telephone, and was soon in communication with his client. "What have you found out?" he asked.

"Twelve persons bought Continental Zinc," was the answer. "Of these, seven were legitimate investors. I have the names of the other five."

"Very good. Send your chief of detectives up to me in a hurry. There are some investigations they can make while I'm at work on a more important aspect of the case."

"Have you found out anything?" came the anxious inquiry.

"I am on the track. Have courage, and follow instructions. Tell Mrs. Calendon that she will not be disappointed in my work."

After Astro's routine work that day, Valeska came into the studio, unable any longer to control her curiosity.

Astro drew out the evidence in the case and spread it before her. "All life is made up of trivial actions," he began. "Every one of them leaves its little trace. Whether you are tracking a bear by its footprints through the forest, or a criminal through his nefarious deeds, it is the same thing. Both leave their spoor behind. Now examine this letter and envelope carefully."

Valeska took the magnifying-glass and scrutinized both; but was forced to acknowledge her defeat.

Astro took the envelope from her and tilted it to the light. "Do you see a slight mark there?" he asked. "It is the print of a thumb. It is not generally known that a finger pressed on paper will leave an invisible oily impression, especially when the hand has recently been passed through the hair. So it will on glass or any polished surface. Let us develop this print. The ink will cling to the paper except where these oily lines have been in contact with it. An ordinary thumb print would show the lines of the ridges; this will show those of the channels between the ridges."

Dipping a large brush in ink, he swept it lightly over the paper. The ink flowed away from a patch where a little system of concentric lines appeared.

"Lo! the invaded loop!" he announced. "It is a woman's thumb. I saw it yesterday, and copied its fundamental diagram and its core. Now look at the mucilage on the flap. Do you see those tiny grains? Snuff, as I proved by my microscope. The postage-stamp is awry, and half off, and also shows tiny traces of snuff. The woman was in a hurry. The corners of her mouth were stained with the result of her filthy practice. Now for the paper surrounding the toe. Let me smooth it out. Do you see the foldings and indentations that were there before it was used for this purpose? The marks are unmistakable, and by their geometric extension, to any one who has studied stereotomy and the development of surfaces, it shows unmistakably what that object was. See,—the parallel lines, a twisted rumpled area, and here the traces of the milling of a small wheel. A small cigarette machine, such as one buys on the Rue de la Paix, in Paris. This is a long shot, to be sure, but sometimes it is the long shot that brings down the eagle. If I hit the mark this time, I shall never be afraid of making a risky guess again. We shall see."

He was interrupted by the bell. Valeska left him, to introduce a neat and dapper young man, who entered, with a self-satisfied smile, with the report from the detective offices of Nally & Co.

The five purchasers of Continental Zinc bought from the curb market had been traced with some difficulty. A man had been assigned to each buyer, and these had followed the instructions given Nally that morning.

Abraham Kraser, retired Jewish merchant; the purchaser of twenty shares; smoked thick black cigars.

H. V. Linwood, a young club-man and society favorite; insisted on a special brand of Russian cigarettes, costing four dollars a hundred.

William Bartlett Smith, a Westerner staying at the Waldorf-Astoria; smoked a French brier pipe with granulated tobacco.

Lambert F. Owens, a race-track bookie, living in South Orange, New Jersey; could not be traced, but information in regard to him was momentarily expected.

"The fifth man, Paul Stacey, I saw myself," said the detective. "I acted as a newspaper reporter. He's fairly well-known on the Street; but yet I could find out little about him. Nobody knew much; but what they did let out was not very favorable. But I talked to him, and he smokes incessantly. Rolls his own cigarettes with a little nickel-plated machine. Keeps Turkish tobacco loose in his right-hand coat pocket, the instrument in his left. While I was near him he threw away a stub, and I brought it to show you. Here it is."

"Very good," said Astro, squinting at the cigarette butt. "You needn't bother about Owens. Now I want you to shadow this man Stacey wherever he goes. Use as many men for relays as you think necessary; but don't let him give you the slip, as you value your reputation. You understand the importance of this, and how fast we must work if the boy is to be saved."

As the young man left, Astro picked up the evening paper and turned to the reports of the stock market. His eyes ran down the column of figures swiftly, until he came to the line:

2000 Cosmopolitan Electric .... 75 70 72 -3

"Rameses the Great!" he ejaculated. "That will teach me a lesson not to take advantage of my inside information. My margin's wiped out already. Pity I didn't stay with my good intentions! And I an Astrologer of the Fourth Circle! I hope nobody will find that out. Valeska, whatever you do, don't gamble." For a moment he stood contemplating the sheet before him, and then he turned to her with a strange expression.

"Mercy!" he cried, "I forgot. Calendon's tip has gone wrong again! What will happen next? It's horrible!"

He was interrupted by a long ring at the electric bell, and, when Valeska answered it, Calendon plunged into the room, holding a package in one hand. The muscles of his hand were twitching in a frenzy of agony.

"It's come again, oh God!" he cried. "My poor boy! What in heaven's name can we do?" He went up to the palmist fiercely. "See here! you promised me your help! You even gave me encouragement! See what has happened already! How long must this thing go on?"

"Have you opened the package?" Astro asked quietly.

Calendon shuddered. "No. I couldn't!"

"Leave it with me, then. You must wait, Mr. Calendon. I am hard at work. I am certain to succeed. Already I have the man; but it is necessary to prove it. One can't use a crystal vision as evidence in a court of law, you know."

"Who is the scoundrel?" Calendon demanded. "By heaven! I'll tear him limb from limb! I'll kill him! I'll—"

Astro put a restraining hand on the director's arm. "Calm yourself, Mr. Calendon," he said soothingly. "It is not by such means that we'll get the boy. In your present frame of mind I dare not trust you with the man's name. If you make a move now, you may jeopardize your boy's life. He must on no account know that he is suspected. No, play the game, Mr. Calendon, according to the rules the kidnapers have prescribed, and I'll guarantee that soon they'll be playing it according to your own ideas of justice. Get your tip and advertise as usual. You will no doubt have better luck to-morrow."

"To-morrow," said Calendon sadly, "I'm going to throw all my holdings in the Fountainet Company into the market and bear the stock long enough for these devils to get their shameful profits. I can't bear to receive another package. It will mean ruin for me; but I'll not care, if the boy is safe."

It was fortunate for Astro that at that time he was also interested in the astonishing burglaries at Glebe House; for it filled in a tedious forty-eight hours of waiting with considerable excitement. Valeska could see that the Master was profoundly interested in the fate of the young boy, and that it had enlisted all his deepest sympathies. What little leisure they had was occupied with a set of chess problems which Astro was working out for relaxation.

It was a great relief, therefore, when the young detective from Nally's put in his appearance two days later, and made his report.

"We've been hot on Stacey's trail ever since I left you; but with nothing doing of any importance whatever until late yesterday afternoon. Then he took a train to Antwerp, New Jersey. He was met at the station by a carryall containing two women. He rode about for an hour with them, not stopping anywhere at all, and was driven back to the station, and took the six-twelve back to New York, and went direct to his rooms at the Beau Rivage apartments."

"He saw no one else? Not even a man in black, with a black tie?"

"Absolutely no one."

"And who are the women?"

"One is a Mrs. Elizabeth Cutter, widow, lives in a small house on the outskirts of the village; the other, a Miss Easting, lives a mile away. Both live alone."

"Did you get into either house?"

"I tried to, but couldn't make it. They seemed to be very suspicious of strangers. Miss Easting turned the dog on me."

"Did you notice that either of these women took snuff?"

"One of them looked it. She was sallow, and seemed to have smears of brown in the corners of her mouth."

"Which one was it?"

"Mrs. Cutter."

"Very good. That is all. Thank you for what you've done. Good day."

In a flash Astro had sprung to a messenger call on the wall and pressed down the handle. Then he scribbled a message on a telegraph blank and handed it to Valeska. It read as follows:

"Come immediately to the Beau Rivage. Important. P. S."

"Give that to the boy when he comes. Where's my revolver? Good! Telephone immediately to Calendon to take the next train for Antwerp, and meet me at the station. I don't want to miss it." He threw himself into a heavy overcoat, slipped the revolver into a pocket, jammed on his hat, and was off before Valeska could question.

She waited in the studio, however, so absorbed had she become in the mystery, so much she feared that, when Astro did return, it would be with some dreadful news.

It was late in the evening when a telegraph boy arrived with a message for her. Eagerly she tore it open. It read:

"Problem 294: White knight to king's fourth; black rook to queen's bishop's third: white king's rook's pawn to seventh, check; black queen's bishop to king's knight's third, mate. Please file.

A."

Valeska was never more exasperated in her life. Only the solution to a knotty chess problem!

When Calendon alighted on the platform at Antwerp, at eight o'clock that evening, he was met in the shade of the station by Astro and a burly local constable.

"Plenty of time and a clear field, I think," said Astro, his eyes dancing with the anticipation of peril imminent; "and unless I'm very much mistaken in my understanding, Mr. Calendon, I'll have some pleasant news for you before long."

"I hope to heaven you will!" said the old man. "I can't stand this much longer. I've sent Mrs. Calendon to the hospital. Her nerves have quite given away under the strain. I only hope that if we get the boy we'll find the dastard who stole him as well!" His look was grim.

"I am afraid you won't get that opportunity, however," said the mystic, drawing out his watch and pausing to inspect it under a gas lamp. "Mr. Stacey was born under an evil planet and in an evil House of the Heavens. At the present moment he is under arrest in the Beau Rivage apartments. One of his accomplices has just left here for New York, where she will be met by the police. Another will soon be taken. I have been waiting for one more of the gang who is engaged in a shady business hereabouts. We need only him to solve the last shreds of mystery in this affair. I've already seen him in my crystals, dressed in black. It remains to find him on the material plane."

They walked rapidly through the outskirts of the village, past a stretch of open country.

Calendon, nervously excited, spoke only once, to say, "There must have been some change of affairs, Astro; for so far as I can find the gang didn't speculate to-day in the stocks I tipped off in *The Era.* I had a circle of my friends attempting to influence the market; but it got away from them altogether. We simply couldn't sell enough to make any effect. The Fountainet Company common stock jumped seven points, when I sold out, and I'm about fifty thousand ahead of the game. If my son is restored to me, I'll have good cause to be happy to-night." He relapsed into silence.

They were now approaching a lonely house, back from the road, and in utter darkness. Astro strode up to the front door and knocked. There was no response. The constable unlocked the door with a skeleton key, and all three men entered. A lighted kerosene lamp was found in the kitchen. Hardly had it been brought into the front room when Calendon stooped and picked up a child's shirt.

"It's my son's, I'm sure!" he exclaimed in excitement "Harold! Harold!" he cried aloud, and began a hasty search through the rooms. He was followed by Astro and the constable; but, after a thorough inspection, no living thing was found except a canary, which, awakened by the disturbance, warbled shrilly in the sitting-room.

The constable threw open the cellar door, and taking the lamp, stumbled down the narrow steps.

In another moment there came a stifled exclamation from below. Calendon dashed down in terror.

Suddenly, up-stairs, where Astro had momentarily remained, there was heard the sound of footsteps. Then a gruff voice broke out:

"I've got you fellers now! I've tracked you for five days, and now, by hickey, I'll make you pay for it! You'll never snatch another body, curse you!"

There was a shuffling of feet, and Astro's voice rang steadily: "Throw up your hands and drop that gun! You're a pretty character to call names! I think you'll show up well when you're investigated! Constable Jenkins, come up here!" He kicked loudly on the floor.

"By Jove! It's the coroner!" said the constable, appearing in the doorway.

"Is there a body here?" the coroner inquired.

"Yes—why?" Now Calendon appeared, most puzzled and alarmed of all.

"It's all right, Mr. Calendon, we're on their trail now!" said Astro. Calendon groaned.

"Your boy is safe and unmutilated. I have suspected this a long time, but I didn't dare let you hope. Now, Coroner, tell your story."

"Why," he began, turning shamefacedly to the constable, "it's this way, Jim. I was comin' along the road last Friday with my outfit an' three of them poorhouse folks' bodies, y'know, an' blamed if the hind axle didn't break short off about a mile up back o' here. I had to walk clean back to Joe Miller's house for a scantlin' to prop up the axle with, an' I was gone about three-quarters of an hour. When I come back I see one of the coffins was gone,—the little one,—a boy it was. An' I see the axle had been sawed half through with a hack saw. Somebody had laid for me just to steal that—"

"And will you please explain," said Astro suavely, "why you were burying these bodies, for which you are paid by the township, at night?"

The coroner's face fell. "Oh, I was too busy day times," he said lamely.

"I think it had best be looked into, Constable. I can see where our friend the coroner makes a very pretty little income from the medical students, and does the town out of a few burials occasionally. But we must go on, Mr. Calendon. I had hoped that the boy was here. We must hurry to the other house. It's a mile away. We'll take your rig, Coroner, while you attend to the remains in the cellar."

The three men hurried outdoors, and the constable drove at breakneck pace to Miss Easting's house. Arrived there, they knocked loudly, and, there being no immediate answer, the constable entered.

Calendon followed close behind. "Harold! Harold!" he called loudly.

There was no reply; but a door slammed up-stairs, and a pattering of feet was heard. Calendon fairly floundered up and threw open the door. There was still no one in sight; but a tumbled bed showed where some one had lain. A boy's clothes were scattered about the room, a few playthings were on the floor.

Astro, who had followed on the father's heels, made directly for a closed door and wrenched it open. There sat a little boy in his red flannel nightgown, caressing a large glass jar of jam. His round chubby cheeks were stained with strawberry.

Then, before his father could reach for him in exultation, the child exclaimed joyfully, "I don't care. I liked it, and I tooked it, and I eated it, and I don't care! I don't!"

And, after the frightful strain that had been on the three men who gazed down at the boy, they all broke into a hearty laugh.

It was Harold Calendon, and he was perfectly happy. But there were several others there who were happy, too.

MISS DALRYMPLE'S LOCKET

"Oh, dear, she's come to see you again!" said Valeska, making a very pretty picture as she stood in the doorway, framed by the black velvet portières.

Astro the Seer followed his first indulgent look by a second questioning, curious glance. "Who is it?"

She put her head on one side and looked at him coquettishly. "A lady," she said, tossing her head archly, "whom, among all your fashionable clients, I believe you consider the most charming, most delicious, the prettiest, the sweetest, the most—"

Astro laughed and nodded. "Miss Dalrymple?"

"The same. She was here only last week. It is very suspicious! Beware!" She shook a saucy finger at him and disappeared.

The young woman who next entered assuredly justified Valeska's adjectives. Indeed, many more might have been applied to her, though the smile that appeared on Astro's own handsome face best testified to her witchery. She was scarcely twenty years old, and of that dark, winning, dimpled, innocent type that few know how to resist. To this, there was an appealing look that flattered men's vanity. Were her brown eyes or her delectable smiling mouth the more lovely to look upon? Astro himself could not tell. Was it her easy well-bred grace or her ingenuous, girlish candor that most delighted him? He remembered her dainty hands,—perhaps the most exquisite he had ever seen. Now they were hidden in her sable muff. Her little rosy face shone like a flower under her picturesque veiled hat; her figure, slim and charmingly curved, was only partly modified by the smart lines of her black cloth suit.

She looked at him with big eyes and said, "Good afternoon, Mr. Astro. I hope you haven't forgotten me."

"Scarcely," was his reply. His tone was flattering.

She smiled with innocent roguery, her eyes exploring the curious decorations of the great studio. She sniffed daintily at the pleasant smell of myrrh that filled the air as she took the seat he offered her.

"I have come for help," she said. "I'm awfully puzzled about something, and you told me such wonderful things last time I came, that I thought I'd ask you." She showed a line of snow-white little teeth.

The Master rested his head negligently on one slender hand, and nodded gravely.

"It's about a locket," she continued.

"Ah! You have lost one?"

"No, not at all. I have found one!"

Astro raised his eyebrows.

"Oh, you're partly right, too; for it was lost a long time ago, and I have just got it back in a rather remarkable way. You see, it used to belong to my mother. She died last year. I returned only in time to see her for two hours before the end."

"When did you see this locket last?"

"Long before mother died. It disappeared mysteriously when I was abroad. Only yesterday it was returned to me by mail, addressed to me at my house in Yonkers, in a handwriting that I can't recognize."

"Well, I don't see what you are troubled about, then, if you have got it back."

Miss Dalrymple looked thoughtfully at him for a moment, her cheek resting on her white-gloved hand, as if not quite sure how to express what she meant. Finally she said impulsively, "Well, it's something so vague and silly it seems absurd to speak to you about it. But Fanny and I have been talking it over and wondering where it came from, and everything, and we both have a sort of queer feeling that it has something to do, perhaps, with a certain letter my mother once had."

"Wait a moment. Who is Fanny?"

"Oh, she's my maid—and she's a treasure. Indeed, she is more like a friend to me than a maid."

"How long have you had her?"

"Oh, ever since mother died."

The Seer frowned slightly. "Go on,—about the letter."

"You've heard about my father's will, and the lawsuit, haven't you? The papers have had a lot about it."

"Oh, yes, the Dalrymple will case. Let's see—your father was divorced from your mother, wasn't he?"

"Yes; but he wasn't at all happy with the woman he married afterward—she's a vixen—and he always regretted that he had left my mother. This Mrs. Dalrymple is contesting the will that father made in favor of my mother. She isn't satisfied with her widow's third."

"And, by that will, you are the legal heir to the rest of the estate?"

"Of course. But the other side has claimed that it was a forgery, and, as he left all his property to his divorced wife, they have a fair case, unless we can prove that the will was genuine. Unfortunately, though the will is in our possession, having been given to mother, both the witnesses to it are dead."

"I see," said Astro, "and the letter you mentioned?"

"Was from my father to my mother, telling her that he had left her all his property. You see how important it would be to our case; but I haven't been able to find it anywhere."

"Yes, but how does the locket come into it?"

"That's what I don't know myself. That's why I came to you," Miss Dalrymple exclaimed eagerly. "I can't describe why, but I do feel that the locket has something to do with it; for my mother was delirious just before she died, and talked about the letter and the locket. She kept saying that she had been robbed—or perhaps she only feared it. Then the locket was restored so providentially, just in time; for the case is to come to court next week. Then I remember that before I went away mother was very careful of it, and kept it locked up."

"Let me see it," said the Master of Mysteries.

She unbuttoned her coat and took it from a gold chain about her neck,—a small oval gold locket such as was commonly worn in the sixties. The cover, being opened, disclosed a small photograph of a beautiful woman in an old-fashioned round bonnet with roses framing the calm serious face.

Astro inspected it admiringly.

"That's my mother," said Miss Dalrymple, looking over his shoulder.

"It is hardly necessary to explain that. I see now where you get your beauty." With a deft movement of his thumb nail, Astro opened the inner rim and removed the photograph. The back of the paper was covered with Greek letters written microscopically in ink, as follows:

$$\Delta \alpha \nu \; o\lambda \epsilon y \; \alpha\rho \; \theta \epsilon \nu \alpha \; \nu\delta \epsilon \; o\sigma o \nu$$
$$\sigma\lambda \epsilon\rho o s \; \epsilon\beta \nu x \; \lambda \epsilon \pi \; \lambda \nu s \nu \epsilon \; \alpha\rho\lambda \epsilon \; \pi$$
$$o\mu \; \mu\iota \epsilon\rho$$

"Oh!" the girl cried excitedly, "I knew it! I knew there was something to be found out! It's Greek, isn't it? Oh, I hope you read Greek! Do you?"

Astro smiled. "I read Greek as well as I do English; but this, unfortunately, isn't Greek at all."

"Why, isn't it? I know some of the letters myself. Look there—isn't that a Delta, and that Alpha and Pi?"

"Yes, the letters are Greek characters, but they are not Greek words. It's a cipher, Miss Dalrymple."

The girl's face fell. "Oh!" she breathed. In her excitement she was almost leaning on his shoulder. She clasped his arm unconsciously as she added, "Surely you can read it? You have solved so many mysteries; you have such wonderful occult power! I've heard that any cipher ever invented could be solved."

"And so it can. I have solved harder ones than this, I'm sure. Yes, your locket is certainly getting interesting. I'm sorry that I am too busy now to work on it, though. I have several appointments that can't be postponed. Suppose I wire you as soon as I have read it. Or, better, I'll send you the solution direct by a messenger."

"All right. I'll be dying of impatience; so I hope you'll hurry."

"I'll promise it some time to-morrow. But another question: Did your mother read Greek?"

"Oh, yes, she had a magnificent education."

"And how about the second Mrs. Dalrymple?"

The girl's lips curled. "I should say not! Why, she was an ordinary chorus girl when father married her!"

"Well," said the Seer, rising to assume a poetic attitude, "I shall consult my crystals and see what I can find out. If I am not mistaken, though, the will will be probated and you will come into your inheritance. And I shall be the first to congratulate you!"

After a quick friendly hand-shake, like a boy's, Miss Dalrymple walked gracefully out of the room.

As soon as she had left, Astro called his assistant and showed her the cipher. Valeska pored over it without speaking for some time. Finally she sighed and said pathetically, "What a pity I don't know Greek!"

"Cheer up!" said the Master, with a whimsical grimace. "You probably know as much about it as the one who composed this childish little cryptogram did. It has the mark of the tyro upon it."

"Why! how could you tell that?"

"Suppose a Fiji Islander attempted to copy a lot of English—that is, the so-called Latin alphabet. Wouldn't you be able to tell instantly that he was ignorant of the English language? It's the same here. Any one who is used to writing Greek would form the letters easily and swiftly; would write, in short, a pure cursive hand. These Greek letters here are all laboriously copied from some school-book or dictionary."

"Well, who wrote it?"

"My dear Valeska," said Astro soberly, "the infinitesimal vibrations from this locket will, if I absorb myself in contemplation, set up sympathetic waves in my own aura. I am not yet ready to go into a psychic trance. Let us first read the message. It is ridiculously simple. I will first separate the message into words, for what here appears to be a set of words is merely letters run together with a few false spaces between them in order to baffle the first glance."

He took a pad of paper and wrote out the following in Greek characters:

Δανσ λε γαρθεν, αυδεοσουσ
λε ροσε βυχ, λε πλυς γεαλ
λε πομμιερ

When he had finished he looked up at her. "You surely know the Greek alphabet, at least?"

"Of course I know that much. We used to use it in boarding-school to write secret messages in. What girl that's ever had a 'frat' boy for a beau doesn't know the Greek alphabet?"

"Then this should read easily. Kindly write it out, letter for letter."

Valeska studied a minute, and then scribbled out:

> *Dans le garden au dessous le rose buch le plus near le pommier.*

"Partly in English, partly in French, you see," said Astro. "One word, 'buch,' looks like German, but it's not: 'In the garden under the rose bush nearest to the apple tree!' The Greek character Chi was the nearest the writer could get to the English 'sh,' you see, and note the use of the Sigma's, too. How childish to consider this a hard puzzle!"

"It is the location of Mrs. Dalrymple's missing letter, I suppose," ventured Valeska. "I suppose she was afraid it would be stolen, and so buried it there."

"You forget, however, that, if Mrs. Dalrymple was a good Greek scholar, she wouldn't have written this so laboriously."

Valeska looked quickly up at him. "Could some one have found the letter and buried it there for his own purpose?"

"It is possible; but it seems an unnecessary thing to do. The most suspicious thing about the cipher is that it is so easy."

"Then I give it up." Valeska shook her head sadly.

"Don't give up, little girl. Simply keep your mind on the fact that there are clever brains at work upon this unsuspecting young woman." He edged his chair over closer and tapped with his finger on the table. "Look here! Who stole this locket in the first place? Why was it stolen? Was the person who took it the one who returned it? Or was the person who returned it a friend of Miss Dalrymple's? If he or she were, why should the action be done anonymously? Did this person know about the cipher? If so, why leave the cipher there where she could find it and dig up the letter? Several things look suspicious to me. I must go over every point and analyze it. We must, in beginning any case of this sort, cast about immediately and find out who are the actors in the drama, who are the ones who will suffer or be benefited by this chain of circumstances.

"Now," he straightened up abruptly, "we must know more about Miss Dalrymple's household. To-morrow morning you shall make the trip to Yonkers, ostensibly to return her this locket with our solution of the cipher, but actually to enable you to inspect the house, grounds, servants, family history, and the like."

At once Valeska became businesslike. "Anything else?"

"Yes," he said emphatically. "Tell her that on no account whatsoever is she to dig beneath the rose bush until she hears from me! Understand?"

Valeska returned next noon with the information that Miss Dalrymple was in high spirits over the solution of the secret message.

"Did you tell her not to dig up the place until I came?"

"Yes, and she promised to wait."

"Well, what else?"

Valeska sniffed. "I certainly do not like that maid of hers. I may be only a woman without any more analytical brain than a sandsnipe, but I can tell a sniveling hypocrite of my own sex as far as I can see her. There's too much goody-goody talk to suit me. It was 'Yes, dear Miss Dalrymple,' and 'Oh, certainly, Miss Dalrymple,' and, behind her back, 'Isn't Miss Dalrymple the sweetest thing!' When I hear that kind of talk, I look out for a cat."

"You think she's two-faced?"

"Oh, she's a snake in the grass! Tall, lantern-jawed, skinny, smirking thing! As luck would have it, she caught the same train back to town that I did,—or rather she came down on the trolley-car just behind mine,—and I sat about three seats behind her when we got the subway at Kingsbridge. I thought I'd see where she went. It was an express, and she got off at Brooklyn Bridge. That's what kept me so long. I followed her over to Brooklyn."

Astro started. "Brooklyn?" he ejaculated.

"Yes." Valeska was evidently pleased that at last she had made some sort of sensation. "I shadowed her to number 1435 Fulton Avenue, waited half an hour, and, when she didn't come out, hurried back to report."

"Well," Astro spoke with a curious expression, "did you find out who lives there?"

The girl was crestfallen. "No. I entirely forgot that."

He threw it at her pointblank. "Mrs. Myra Dalrymple!"

For a moment she could only gaze at him in astonishment. Then, "Oh!" she cried. "Oh!" Her eyes blazed. "Didn't I say she was a snake? Why, then, Fanny is undoubtedly in the pay of the second wife! Think of it! She's been spying on that sweet innocent girl ever since her mother died, and has carried the news to Mrs. Dalrymple number two. It's outrageous!

"Oh, but—" Valeska sprang up in consternation and faced her master with a look of horror. "I forgot! Why, I translated the cipher to Miss Dalrymple while the maid was in the room! What will happen?"

Astro took up his water-pipe with perfect equanimity. "My dear, you seem to have made several very lucky blunders to-day."

She put her hands to her eyes. "Oh, I don't understand! What about this cipher message? Where did it come from?"

"Let us go at it analytically," he replied calmly. "For the sake of the argument, grant first that the cipher discloses the hiding-place of the lost letter, secreted by the first Mrs. Dalrymple. Very good. Let us suppose, also, as a second hypothesis, that the locket was sent by the second Mrs. Dalrymple, knowing of the cipher. Very good again. Now examine the two theories. Is it likely that such a person as this second wife would place a rival claimant to the estate in possession of the secret? No. Something is wrong, the first hypothesis, or the second. Take your pick. I say the first is wrong,—the cipher does *not* disclose the place of the letter, but the second is right: Mrs. Dalrymple sent it. We know that probably she knew Miss Dalrymple visited me, and believed in my power. She, therefore, intended Miss Dalrymple to dig in that spot, cleverly concealing her instrumentality in the matter. That's why the cipher was made so absurdly easy. Do you think it will be well for Miss Dalrymple to dig there? I don't."

He paused. "Now suppose the second hypothesis to be wrong,— that Mrs. Dalrymple did not send the locket. If any one else did, what reason could he have for making such a mystery of it? It would be absurd."

"I follow all that," said Valeska; "but I can't think why Mrs. Dalrymple would have any motive for inducing Miss Dalrymple to dig in the garden."

"I think you forget the second Mrs. Dalrymple's character. But you can study it out. What I intend to do is to call on Mrs. Dalrymple this evening and find out. I have a very good case against her, I think, and I intend to make her give up that letter, if she has it. Of course it may have been destroyed, but I don't quite believe it. It is common for criminals, especially women, to refrain from actually destroying the very evidence that may convict them. From some scruple or fear they seldom do it. At any rate, I shall frighten her with what I suspect of her actions in the past, and use my positive knowledge of Fanny's services."

"But what is hidden in the garden? Anything? And if so, how did it get there?"

"Was there no one besides Miss Dalrymple and Fanny living in the house? No other servants?"

Valeska shook her head, then reflected for an instant. "I did hear something about a gardener—" She stopped and stared at him.

He nodded. "I think that probably completes the last, link of the chain. At any rate, I'm willing to risk it. Well, I'll go right over to Brooklyn and have it out. Meet me at the Grand Central Station to-night in time for the eleven-thirty-six train for Yonkers, and we'll see the whole thing through this very night."

Valeska's eyes danced. "I'll be there, with my own little revolver! I hope it will be exciting!"

She was at the station at eleven-thirty, and waited until the train had pulled out without seeing the Master. A half-hour and then a full hour passed without his appearance. She had begun to be alarmed seriously, when, at a quarter past one, she saw him walking rapidly across the great waiting-room toward her. She gave an exclamation of relief; but at once he took her arm and ran her toward the subway.

"Hurry!" he cried in a tense voice. "We can't wait for the one-thirty; so we'll have to make it by the subway and change to the trolley. We have no time to lose! It's serious!"

They caught the train with less than a minute's margin; and once settled in the car, Valeska turned to him anxiously.

"I was a fool to let Miss Dalrymple have the translation!" he said. "It was the only serious error I have made in a year. I hope to heaven I may save her yet; but it's a toss-up now!"

"What is it?" Valeska shouted above the shriek of the wheels.

Astro said nothing. Seeing that he was too deeply moved to explain, she pressed him no further, covertly watching his restless nervous gestures and his drawn expression all through the ride until the trolley slowed down at Yonkers and stopped on the main street. A solitary cab was standing beside the curb, its driver dozing on the box.

A fat man was waddling hurriedly ahead of them, signaling with his umbrella to the driver; but Astro, with a rough gesture, threw him aside, ran to the cab, and pushed Valeska quickly inside.

"To Miss Dalrymple's, out on Broadway, and drive like light-ning!" he ordered. Then he jumped in himself, and slammed the door in the face of the enraged fat man who was in quick pursuit. The cab drove off at headlong speed.

Still Valeska kept silent; but now she shared the excitement of the Master, who bit his knuckles nervously as the horse galloped along the avenue high above the river. All she could hear besides the pounding of hoofs was the muttering of the dark man by her side. It seemed an hour's drive, so had the suspense wrought upon her,—tree by tree, lamp by lamp, house by house, they advanced. She was now prepared for anything,—for anything save what hap-pened.

At last the carriage slowed down and came to a stop. Before the driver had a chance to dismount, Astro had dashed out without pay-ing the least attention to his assistant. She hurried after him.

The Dalrymple house stood on the side of the hill, overlooking the quiet moonlit Hudson. It was surrounded by a high wall, over the tops of which showed the thick limbs of a few apple trees. The house loomed beyond, a brick edifice of two stories. The iron gate in the wall was locked, and Astro jerked viciously at the bell.

At this moment, as if he himself had set it off, a loud explosion reverberated through the night. A woman's scream was next heard, rising in a piercing staccato. Then all was silence again. At length a shutter was thrown open at one of the front windows of the house, and a shaft of light made a brilliant path through the deep shadow. A woman's head appeared.

"What is it?" cried Valeska in terror. "Is Miss Dalrymple shot?"

"God knows!" Astro muttered grimly. "Help me over the wall. Give me a foot up, Valeska. We're too late, as I feared; but I must find out what has happened. Driver," he yelled back over his shoul-der, "go for a doctor as quick as you can!"

In an instant he had mounted the top of the wall and dropped to the other side. Valeska heard his footsteps running up the gravel walk. After that she waited some time in silence. The cab had driven off with a clatter.

When, after a wait that seemed interminable, Astro returned, Valeska's eyes stared to see him with Miss Dalrymple, who was apparently unharmed. She wore a long mackintosh cape, covering her night dress, and her hair was disordered. A look of horror on her pretty face made her seem a woman almost for the first time. She unlocked the gate and put her slender white arms about Valeska.

"What has happened?" exclaimed the latter.

"What I feared; only, thank heaven, not to Miss Dalrymple!" was Astro's solemn response. "Come this way and you'll see."

He led the way past an apple tree at the side of the house. A few paces beyond this a great hole was torn in the earth, and, by its jagged appearance and slanting sides, it was evident that it had been made by some explosive. Behind a rose bush lay a woman's body.

"Fanny," said Astro.

Miss Dalrymple sank beside her maid and began to weep silently.

"Do you understand now?" said Astro to his assistant.

"What a fiend!" she cried. "Her stepmother meant this trap for Miss Dalrymple! She buried an infernal machine here! But how was it exploded?"

Astro pointed to the motionless body. "The reason why I did not caution Miss Dalrymple not to show her maid the translation of the cipher was because I wanted the second Mrs. Dalrymple to believe that her hellish trick was going to be successful. I was afraid Miss Dalrymple's curiosity would induce her to dig under the rose bush before I came. To-night I wrung a confession from her stepmother revealing this whole frightful business. That's why I hurried. But I had no idea of Fanny's duplicity. Evidently, though she was a spy for the Brooklyn woman, she did not have her complete confidence. Fanny thought she would get the letter before Miss Dalrymple dug it up, and use it to extort money. You see how well she has succeeded."

"Oh! is she dead?" whispered Valeska.

"Luckily, no; only stunned. Mrs. Myra Dalrymple probably won't have to go to the electric chair for it, though she deserves it richly. But, at least, there will be no more contest over the will. In the first place, I got the letter from her to-night; in the second, if I hadn't, we could prevent her opposition by our knowledge of this crime. She'll leave the country to-morrow."

The cab was now heard. It stopped, and the driver, with a physician, carne running up the walk.

"There has been a little accident here," said Astro suavely. "A buried gasoline tank exploded, and this woman was injured, doctor. Carry her into the house and do what you can for her."

Miss Dalrymple, who had been listening wide-eyed to the conversation, a ravishing figure in the moonlight in her charmingly disheveled state, now put her hand on Astro's arm.

"But I don't understand at all," she said, "except that Fanny has been deceiving me for a year. Do you mean to say that Mrs. Dalrymple put that cipher in the locket herself and sent it to me?"

"Certainly," said Astro, "and a very clever trick it was."

"But why did she do it that way?" the young girl inquired, still baffled. "Why was she so elaborate about it?"

"Because," replied the Master of Mysteries, with a lurking smile, "she knew a great deal more about human nature than you do, and a good deal less than I, that's all!"

NUMBER THIRTEEN

Reclining on a huge velvet divan, puffing at his water-pipe lazily, Astro read to the last page of *Dr. Jekyll and Mr. Hyde*, and then tossed the paper-covered book on the floor with a grunt.

Valeska looked up from her work, ready for his comment.

"If Stevenson had written that book this year, he'd have known more about dissociated personality," he remarked.

"Why, it's nothing but a parable, that's all," Valeska offered.

"Well, it might be more; it might be science as well. The fundamental idea is wrong. We haven't only two souls or personalities apiece, one good, one bad; we have an infinite number, according to modern psychology. Our normal self can break up into any number of combinations of its elements. That is why we are different persons when we're angry, when we dream, when we are drunk or insane."

"But isn't there a subconscious self that runs the body at such times?" said Valeska. "I've been reading about it. Some psychologists call it the 'subliminal' self."

"Rubbish!" Astro rose and walked up and down nervously. "They are not psychologists; they are metaphysicians, and not worth considering. They speak as if there were a sort of secret submerged soul coiled up inside us like a chicken in an egg. An oracle in a well! There is no such thing. We are all of a piece!"

"But how about somnambulists who diagnose their own complaints and predict the course of their illness? How about the

known cases of multiple personality,—Felida X and Miss Beauchamp in Boston? Their alternate selves were distinct and separate."

"You should read *The Journal of Abnormal Psychology*," said
Astro. "Those selves are fortuitous combinations of the normal
self's properties; they are, strictly, part-selves. The subjects are
simply not 'all there'."

"And those post-hypnotic time experiments, too?" she persisted. "I have read of their suggesting that a subject should, just
fifteen hundred and forty-seven minutes afterward, look at his
watch and write down the time. He did it, in every such case."

"And you think he has a subliminal self, a sort of psychic alarm
clock, that telephones to his waking personality? Nonsense! They
managed to tap the mechanical part of his memory, that's all. It's
like looking up a book in a library. There are no co-conscious personalities. What happens in 'automatic writing'? A person holds a
pencil in his hand, and it seems to write of itself. Spirits? Rubbish! A subliminal self? Poppycock! The hand transcribes merely
records of thoughts or memories that have been forgotten or were
unnoticed, that's all. We don't think of half we see and hear; we
pass myriads of faces in the street, for instance; but everything is
recorded, as on a phonographic cylinder, and, under abnormal
conditions, the record may be reproduced."

"Well," said Valeska, "it's all uncanny. Normal psychology is
difficult enough to understand; but when one is four or five different persons I give up. How many am I?" she added merrily, tossing a mischievous glance at him, as she put on her hat and furs.

"You're a million—each nicer than the rest."

"Then I'm glad!" She looked very demure as she walked toward
the door; but she stopped there to smile frankly back at him, then
threw him a good night and vanished.

Astro yawned, went to the bookcase, and returned to the couch
with a book by Leonide Keating. For a while he labored with his
grandiloquent mysticism, with the secret of Om and the central
crystal of the universe; then suddenly he sat erect. A noise in the
outer room had attracted his attention. Another moment told him

that Valeska had returned and was speaking to some one. His name was called.

He went out, to find her with a strange girl, strangely clad. Dark-haired and dark-skinned, handsome, oriental, she was of medium height, with a red shawl drawn about her head, and a short plaid skirt, showing her little feet incased in men's heavy shoes. She had a wild frightened look in her eyes, as Valeska tried to calm her. Her mouth trembled pitifully, and she crouched in an attitude of fear and self-effacement. She looked quickly round at Astro, and ran for the door. Evidently she saw a new terror in him, and trembled all over with excitement. It was all Valeska could do to restrain her.

Astro looked the girl over deliberately, noting every detail of countenance and costume, then he raised his eyebrows.

"It's the strangest thing!" Valeska explained. "I was walking along Thirty-fourth Street when I met her, and as I passed I thought that she was probably some Italian organ-grinder's wife. Then she turned back and ran up to me and seized my hand. She was evidently terribly frightened at something; but she wouldn't speak. I haven't been able to get her to speak yet. She seemed to want my protection; so I brought her back here. Who do you suppose she can be?"

Astro addressed the girl in Italian; but got no response. The girl eyed him as a dog watches the boy who has been torturing him. A question in Russian was as unsuccessful. Greek, Turkish, Yiddish,—she appeared to understand none of these, or else refused to answer. The Master of Mysteries became interested.

"Bring her into the studio," he said to Valeska. "We'll have something to eat here. Perhaps she is hungry. If so, that will gain us her confidence." So saying, he went to the telephone and ordered a dinner for three sent up from a near-by restaurant.

As Valeska gently led the stranger toward the entrance to the studio, the girl suddenly gave a wail, clasped her hands to her bosom, and stared fixedly, in an ecstasy of terror, at the office wall. There was a large one-day calendar there above Valeska's desk, the sheet showing the words, "Thursday, May 13." Astro hurried to the girl's side, watching her keenly. Valeska put her arms about her reassuringly; but it was not till she had drawn her softly away from the sight of the calendar that the girl's perturbation was over. She walked doggedly into the great dim studio, as if half-asleep. Valeska, with friendly insistence, placed her in a comfortable chair. There the girl sat, staring with expressionless face at the light.

"Well," said Valeska, as they watched her, waiting for the dinner to be bought in, "is she deaf, or dumb, or half-witted, or drugged, or what?"

Astro had not taken his eyes from the figure of his mysterious visitor. "She's an oriental, of course. That is why she's afraid of me. She has been through some terrible nervous ordeal, I think. I believe she hasn't had enough to eat. Wait till we have had dinner, and then I'll see what I can do with her. Poor thing! I'm glad it was you and not a police officer who found her, Valeska."

The girl began to look about timidly, but with little apparent curiosity. Valeska undid her shawl from her head. A wave of black, fine, curly hair fell with the covering and made the face more picturesque. She nestled a little closer to her protector; held Valeska's hand to her own cheek. The two, vividly blond and brunette, made a striking picture together.

On Astro's table was a small desk calendar, with a memorandum sheet for each day. He quietly took it up and placed it in the girl's lap. Instantly she had a new fit of terror, and leaped up in alarm. Standing in the full light of the electric lamp, they could see her mouth working convulsively as she stared at the number 13. She started on a run for the door. Valeska, quicker than Astro, caught and held her, and again attempted to soothe her.

"Oh, don't try any more experiments with her yet!" she implored. "The poor thing can't stand it. She is suffering so that it makes my heart ache. What can be the matter?"

"Aphasia, for one thing," said Astro, seating himself a little way off. "She tried to speak hard enough; but she couldn't. The girl is not deaf or dumb, anyway. It is growing decidedly interesting."

By degrees the girl was coaxed back to the chair, and by the time the dinner had been brought in she was more easily persuaded to take a seat at the table beside Valeska. Indeed, it was evident that she was nearly starving. She ate ravenously, with great mouthfuls, picking up the food in her hands. She was not to the manner born, but her prettiness made her solecisms pardonable. Once or twice during the meal she stopped, looked at Valeska, and seemed to be trying to speak; but no words came. Her hunger satisfied, she seemed more tractable and courageous. She looked at Astro without fear. Toward Valeska, she showed the devotion of a dog.

The table cleared away, Astro took a sheet of paper and wrote down the number 13. The girl trembled, but now not so violently. She looked up at Valeska with a mute appeal.

"Don't!" said Valeska.

Astro wrote a column of three figures: 6, 5, and 2. The girl stared at it without intelligence. The Roman numerals XIII did not excite her at all. Next, he wrote the word "thirteen"; she was still unmoved. He spoke the word; no response. Then he placed the paper in front of her, and put the pencil in her hand. She took it with evident familiarity, and her hand trembled. They saw her bite her lip—she was indubitably attempting to communicate with them—but she was unable to make a mark on the sheet.

"H'm!" said Astro thoughtfully. "Agraphia, as well. Now we're getting warmer. I think I shall get it after a while."

"Why, to me it seems more impossible than ever!" Valeska said.

"Strange that we should have just been talking about it," he replied. "It's a case of lost identity, disassociated personality, beyond doubt. I think I can solve the riddle if I can hypnotize her. I'll try."

He did try, but without avail. At his first mesmeric gestures she shrank from him in fear. As he persisted, trying with a crystal ball held in front of and above her eyes, to send her into a hypnotic sleep by means of a partial paralysis of the optic nerve, she resolutely defended herself. The strangeness of his motions aroused her suspicion, and she refused to concentrate her attention sufficiently to be influenced. Direct verbal suggestion, the simplest and most effective method of inducing hypnosis, was of course out of the question, since she did not appear to understand any language he spoke.

"There is only one other method, if even that will succeed," Astro said at last. "If we can get her to write automatically, we may learn something. Her agraphia prevents her writing with her conscious mind. We'll try what is called the method of 'abstraction'. It is a common experiment. One holds his patient absorbed in a conversation that compels his utmost mental capacity,—in Hebrew, for instance, if he understands Hebrew,—and while that is going on some one places a pencil in his hand and whispers in his ear. What you have called the 'subconscious self' communicates by writing, and the normal conscious personality is unaware that he is writing."

"But how can we engage her mind so absorbingly?" Valeska asked hopelessly. "We don't know her language, whatever it may be."

Astro paced the room for several minutes, thinking deeply. He stopped occasionally to look at the girl fixedly, and resumed his contemplation. Finally he went up to her, examined her palms, and his face lighted up.

"I believe she's musical!" he said.

Valeska stared. "But then—"

"We'll see. Have the pencil ready to put in her hand, and the paper on the table by it. Watch her closely, and see if she is affected by the music. If she seems to be, give her the pencil."

With that, he walked to the piano, sat down, and began to play the tenth rhapsody of Liszt. As he swung into the abandon of its more temperamental passages, he seemed himself to be absorbed, to lose himself in the intricate harmonies. He was a skilled and artistic musician. He swayed to and fro, giving himself up physically and mentally to the passion and beauty of the themes, and it was not till the echoes of the last divine chords had ceased reverberating that he slowly turned on the piano stool and seemed to awaken.

"I've got it!" cried Valeska, and, springing up, she ran over and handed him a sheet of paper. It was partly covered with rude drawings, apparently meaningless rough sketches, mingled with attempts at lettering:

He took the sheet eagerly, and went to the table under the electric lamp to scrutinize the figures.

"It's not very promising material, is it?" said Valeska.

"On the contrary, it's a fine beginning; only it will take a bit of doing to make it out."

"I see the fatal 13 has put in its appearance again."

The girl, who had seemed to be in a sort of stupor, now leaned over the table and inspected the sheet. At sight of the figures 13 she gave a moan, and threw her arms about Valeska, trembling all over.

"Poor girl!" said Astro. "I'm afraid there's something big back of all this. She's a Turk, or an Armenian, or a Syrian. See the Turkish flag that she has roughly drawn here? . . . *Babi* . . . Wait!"

He had risen to go to the bookcase, when the girl reached over and would have seized the paper, had not Valeska prevented her. Astro turned to ejaculate:

"*Babi?*" and again, "*Baha-Ullah?*"

The girl quivered; but did not speak.

"She may be a member of the Bahai sect, followers of the Bab, the Incarnation of the Almighty, whose religion is not tolerated by the faithful in Persia. They are all kept to one city, where they live like primitive Christians; indeed, their faith is a mixture of Christianity and Mohammedanism. We'll see. Valeska, she's had enough for to-night. You must take her home and take care of her, and bring her back tomorrow. Until then I must stay up and think it out."

For hours after Valeska had left with her ward, Astro walked up and down the length of the great dim studio. Occasionally he threw himself at full length on the big couch in concentrated thought. At intervals he stood erect, his eyes fixed in abstraction on some trophy of arms on the wall, or gazing into the lucent transparency of his crystal ball. Once or twice he sat down at the table and gazed long at the hieroglyphic marks made on the paper by the strange girl. At three in the morning, he partially undressed and lay down on the couch to sleep. He rose at seven, bathed, and went outdoors for a walk.

When he returned, an hour later, Valeska was in the studio alone. Her eyes were red; she seemed ashamed and self-reproachful.

"The girl has disappeared!" she exclaimed the moment Astro appeared. "When I woke up, she wasn't in the room. She must have risen and dressed while I was asleep. But I found this." She held out a short curved dagger, in a morocco sheath.

Astro, withdrawing the blade, found it was engraved with an Arabic inscription. He read the motto aloud:

"*For the heart of a dog, the tongue of a serpent!*"

"Ah!" he commented, "this may help some. Our little friend apparently isn't so timid as she appeared. But, somehow, this doesn't look like the property of a Babist. In spite of their many persecutions, I believe they are usually non-resistants. Well, Valeska, we'll have to find the girl, now! Come along with me immediately."

His green limousine was already at the door in' waiting. Both jumped in, and as they drove to the southern end of the city Astro explained:

"There are two Syrian quarters in New York. One is in Brooklyn, the other down on Washington Street, near the Battery. We'll go to that one first, and see what we can find there. The Turkish flag reminds me that that is often hung outside stores where they sell Turkish rugs. We'll try that clue afterward."

Reaching Washington Street, the two left the motor-car and walked toward the Battery, past rows of squalid houses. At every corner Astro stopped and gazed about deliberately.

Finally, he seized Valeska's arm with a quick gesture. "Look at that sign!" he exclaimed.

On West Street, facing the Hudson River, but with its rear abutting on a vacant lot on Washington Street, was a huge soap factory. Painted on the dead wall was a sign whose letters were eight or ten feet in height.

Valeska read it aloud: "Use Babrock's Brown Soap." She stopped and looked at Astro in bewilderment. "What about it?""

He drew the drawing from his pocket and pointed out the lettering. "Don't you see?" he cried. "'BABP!' That's a part of the sign, surely. Look at those two buildings on each side of the sign. Now look at this row of houses. From some one of those windows the sign must present the appearance she has drawn. Making the drawing subconsciously, she has merely copied something with which she has been familiar,—seeing it, probably, every day. We must find the window from which the sign looks just like her drawing."

He looked at the sign again carefully, estimating its height and the relative position of the two buildings whose roofs would cut off the first and last group of letters. A rough triangulation led him to a house in the lower part of which was a cobbler's shop. This he entered.

"Are there any rooms to let in this house?" he asked of the man at the bench.

The man nodded. "Go up-stairs and ask at second floor," he replied. "You see Garbon Soumissin; he keeps the house."

Up-stairs went Astro and Valeska, and plunged into a dark narrow hallway. A doorway opened part way and a whiskered man looked out. He had an evil face, blotched with red spots, and wore a fez. He was smoking a Turkish cigarette.

"What you want here?"

"I'd like to look at your front room, third floor."

A murmur of voices came from inside the room. The man turned and growled some foreign oath. Then he turned and looked at Astro with a vicious inquisition.

"All right," he said at last; "you go up. Door open. Three dollars a week."

Astro waited for no more; but ran up the stairs, followed by his assistant. Once out of earshot, he stopped for a moment to pull out the paper again, and pointed to the first drawing on the sheet. "Fez," he said, and looked at her meaningly.

"The old man with the cigarette?"

"Probably. Now we'll find out what they have been up to."

The hall bedroom was incredibly dirty, but contained nothing but a cot bed with vile coverings, a chair, and a crazy wash-stand, over which hung a square cracked mirror. Astro first went to the grimy window and looked out. He pointed to the sign, and Valeska followed his eyes. One of the buildings across the street cut off the first word, "use," and the other, with a small dormer, obscured all after "bab" with the exception of the upper half of the R. It showed, in fact, precisely as the girl had drawn it.

"This is the room, all right. Now let's examine it."

He took up the chair first, and looked it over carefully. Then he pointed to marks on the sides of the back, where the paint was worn smooth. The marks were about an inch wide, and similar ones showed on the legs and on the side rails of the seat.

"This is where straps have chafed the paint," he commented. "She was undoubtedly fastened securely. Did you notice where the marks or bruises were on her?"

"Yes; they were bad enough for me to remember. There were red marks on her wrists and on her arms below her shoulders; and her arms were almost covered with bruises; but small ones."

"Oh, they pinched her, no doubt. Undoubtedly she had a rough time of it, if one may judge the character of the villain with the fez. Well, we must find her. There's no use inquiring here. If they have used this room for a torture chamber, we'll get nothing out of them, and they'll grow suspicious."

They went down-stairs, and, while Valeska waited in the street, Astro drove a bargain with Garbon Soumissin. Luckily the lower hall was dark, and the Turk could not perceive Astro's oriental countenance. But the Master of Mysteries had an important piece of news to tell when he rejoined Valeska,

"They were talking Arabic, or rather Turkish. I heard one of them quote the motto we saw on the dagger. Now I know what they are. Have you heard of the Hunchakists?"

The papers had been so full of one of the recent murders of this dreaded Armenian society, that Valeska knew roughly what the name implied.

"Every country seems to have its guerrilla assassins," said Astro, as they drove up-town. "But the Armenian Hunchakists are more dangerous than any of the others, because they are better organized. Their object is usually extortion. Now we must visit the rug merchants. I'm afraid we're on the track of something serious this time."

Their route led them directly into the heart of the mystery. On Eighteenth Street, where, in front of a Turkish rug store, the crescent of Turkey hung out, there was a great crowd gathered, pressing about the entrance. It took Astro little time to discover the cause of the disturbance. The merchant, Marco Dyorian, had been found, when his shop was opened by his head bookkeeper, lying in a pool of blood in his office, shot in the back. He was not dead, though mortally wounded and unconscious. He was now at the hospital, at the point of death.

A policeman guarded the door, preventing any one from entering. Astro and Valeska caught sight of his cap over the heads of the bystanders, and when the crowd eddied they saw his face.

"Why, it's McGraw!"

"So it is!" said Astro. "What luck!"

They squirmed their way through the crowd, to find the burly police officer who, with Astro's assistance, had been able to gain considerable reputation in connection with the Macdougal Street dynamite outrages. The two were now fast friends. Indeed, McGraw owed his lieutenant's cap to the help of the Master of Mysteries. He therefore welcomed them both with a grin.

"What is the straight of this, McGraw?" Astro asked.

"Hunchakist murder, sure!" responded the lieutenant.

"I thought as much. Who did it?"

"Oh, we got 'em all right this time. No thanks to you, sir, for once, though I'd always be glad of your help. This one's a girl who done it."

Astro and Valeska looked at each other. "A girl?"

"Yes, sir. They'll be bringing her down presently. It's only fifteen minutes ago we got her. She was hiding out in a back closet where nobody thought to look at first. She was in a dead faint."

"What does she look like?"

"Faith, I don't know that myself. I've only just got here with the reserves. But if you stand here, you'll see her come down. There's the wagon already. Stand back there!"

The crowd scattered, and the patrol wagon drove up with a clatter. Several officers jumped out and ran up-stairs.

Astro turned to Valeska and spoke under his breath. "What time did you see her last?"

"I got up about midnight, and she was lying on the couch."

She put her hand on his arm. "Oh, it couldn't have been she!" she exclaimed.

At that moment the officers brought their prisoner down-stairs. It was indeed the girl who had been in the studio the night before, and had gone home with Valeska. Just as the group passed, Astro touched McGraw's shoulder.

"Let me speak to her a moment. I know this girl."

McGraw stared; but his faith in the occult powers of the Seer was so great that he delayed the officers. They stopped for a moment. Astro addressed the girl in Turkish.

"Let me help you," he said.

She looked at him sulkily. But it was not with the blank expressionless face of yesterday. Her brows drew together.

"I don't know you," she said at last.

Valeska pushed forward and took her hand.

"Don't you know this lady?" Astro asked.

The girl stared. Some half-forgotten memory seemed to stir within her. Her lips moved silently as she stared hard at Valeska's face. Then she shook her head, and said, "I don't know."

"I can't keep 'em waiting," McGraw whispered. "Let her go, and you can call at the Tombs to see her again. I'll see that you get in. Go on, now!"

The girl was escorted to the wagon and took her seat, facing the crowd stolidly, an officer on each side of her. Once, before they drove away, her eyes turned to where Valeska stood in the doorway, and the same puzzled expression crossed her face.

"McGraw," said Astro, after the wagon had gone, "how'd you like to get a captain's commission?"

McGraw hastily took him aside. "You don't mean to say you know about this job already?" he asked excitedly.

"I know one thing. A man you want lives at 101 Washington Street, and I think his name is Garbon Soumissin. At any rate, I'd advise you to get right down there immediately and run in every one you find in the house. Hurry up before they've gone!"

McGraw's eyes gleamed. "And you'll coach me then what to do?" he asked.

"Yes."

"All right." Hastily summoning a police sergeant, he gave him a few orders, and then hurried to the station.

"Where was the wounded man taken?" Astro asked the sergeant.

"To the receiving hospital."

"We'll go over there first, then." And Astro and Valeska made their way to the limousine and ordered the driver to the place.

"But," said Valeska, "how queerly she acted! I'm so disappointed that she didn't recognize me, after all I'd done for her. I don't know what to make of it."

"Don't you see? She has waked up. Yesterday she was quite another person, a dissociated personality. She had no memory, and had even lost the power to talk or write. That is often the case. Owing to some severe mental shock, her normal personality was broken up into parts, so to speak. She had just enough of the functions of her mind synthesized to have volition, and that part-self resembled a crazy person. She had been tortured and starved, no doubt in order to force her to commit this crime, by Soumissin. Somehow she managed to escape from that house, and then her reason left her. You found her what she was, half-witted, with only sense enough to appeal to your protection. She had forgotten everything,—everything, that is, except something concerning the number 13. Now the question is, when did she come to herself and her full rationality? Was it when she got up in your room to leave you—"

"Or was it when she got into the rug store?" Valeska added, with a look of horror in her eyes.

"That's the question. Let's hope that Dyorian is conscious by the time we reach the hospital. Everything depends on that!"

Arrived at the hospital, Astro entered the office and asked for the house physician. A few words only were necessary to explain the palmist's right of inquiry, and his description of the Syrian girl's mental condition was of great professional interest to the doctor. He promised to go to the Tombs and see her as soon as possible. Dyorian, it seemed, lay at the point of death; but, finding how important it was to have the exact time of the shooting determined, the doctor consented to go up to the ward and attempt to revive him sufficiently to answer the question. Astro and Valeska waited for him in the office.

It was fifteen minutes before he returned. "I could just barely make him understand," he said, "but I am sure that he did at last. With almost his last breath he whispered, 'Ten o'clock,' adding that he didn't know who shot him. He died before I left the bedside."

Acting on Astro's hint, McGraw not only succeeded in capturing a half-dozen Turks and Armenians in the Washington Street den, but, exercising the "third degree" in a manner for which he was famous, extorted a confession from one of the prisoners. It was the more easy because the man, who had honestly believed himself to be working for the cause of Armenian freedom, discovered that he had been merely the tool of a band of blackmailers and murderers. He had witnessed the cruel torture of the young Syrian girl; but had been told that she was a Turkish spy who was plotting to betray the Armenian cause to the Sublime Porte.

On hearing her alibi, sworn to by Valeska, the girl was released; but she was ten days under the care of the hospital doctor before her nerves were recovered enough for her to be brought to the studio. She had been told of Valeska's kindness; but could remember nothing that had happened since her mind first began to wander under the effects of pain and starvation. But her intuition recognized her protectress without the aid of reason, and she fell on her knees like a slave at Valeska's feet. She could not speak a word of English; but her eyes were sufficiently eloquent to prove her gratitude. She treated Astro as if he were her lord and master, watching him continually.

After she had told of her wakening to her full reason in Valeska's room, she described the terror that had come over her at the thought of Dyorian. The thirteenth was the day set for his murder. Her tormentors had in vain tried to force her to do the deed; but, when they found she was intractable, they had told her that, whether she did it or not, Dyorian should surely die on the thirteenth. It was with the idea of saving him from his fate that she made more strenuous attempts to escape, and, after her memory had gone, the number 13 still inspired her with terror and dread. Wakening at Valeska's, this thought had been her first, and she dressed quietly and stole out of the house to warn him. She had found the rug merchant already shot, and the horror of the scene had in her weak state again deprived her of reason. She had run from the body—and that was all she could remember until she was restored to consciousness by two policemen. Then, her fear of being accused as the murderess had nearly distraught her wits again.

She looked curiously now at the pictures she had drawn while in the state of abstraction, and identified the sign, the fez, the Turkish flag, and the number 13.

"But what is this one?" Astro asked, pointing to the one drawing he had not identified.

The girl shuddered, and reach for Valeska's hand. When she could speak, she explained to Astro.

"It was awful,—you can't know how awful it was till you have tried it. I was three days strapped to that chair, and on the wall right opposite my head was a mirror. I had to look at myself all day. It grew more and more horrible, till I couldn't stand it. By turning my head I could see the sign, but always my own face was in front of me, staring, staring, staring. It grew hideous, sinister, diabolic. After a while it wasn't I, at all. It was a devil leering at me, and I knew he was inside of me looking through my own eyes. Oh, God!" She paused, and looking up at Valeska said simply, "She is lucky. She can look at her face in the glass. I can't ever use a mirror any more. It frightens me."

Astro nodded his head slowly. Then he said, with a faint smile, "Yes, I can fancy no more exquisite torture for a woman to bear."

Then, before he translated the speech to Valeska, he turned to her with a whimsical expression.

"What would you do if you were to be deprived of mirrors of any kind for the rest of your life?"

"I think I'd commit suicide," she replied, blushing.

"There'd be no need for that. I shall always be able to tell you how pretty you are. But now we must cure this little girl. I'm sure that a hypnotic treatment will soon convince her how pretty she is, and she won't be afraid to prove it."

Valeska looked up archly, and added, "Neither shall I!"

THE TROUBLE WITH TULLIVER

"I notice that most of the talk about Tulliver's running for governor has stopped," said Astro, dropping his morning paper and looking over to where Valeska, his assistant, was copying horoscopes from the Master's notes.

"I'm disappointed," she replied. "There seemed to be hope for the regeneration of the city government at last. It is strange how Tulliver has let up on the prosecution of those Brooklyn aldermen, though, isn't it?"

"Strange? How?" Astro gazed at her keenly; but it was perfectly evident that he was confident of his own opinion.

"Why, he began so well and so strenuously; and then, just before the case was to be brought for trial he seems to have dropped the whole thing. It doesn't seem to be like what we know of his character, somehow."

"Do you believe that he's been bribed?" Astro bent his dark brows.

"You never can tell nowadays. But he's such a fighter ordinarily that it looks suspicious. Why, I've heard extraordinary tales of his persistence and his energy. He takes no more sleep than Edison,—he works night and day, and can do usually four times as much work as an ordinary man could in similar circumstances."

Astro nodded his picturesque dark head thoughtfully, and took his customary seat on the divan by his water-pipe. With a toss of his hand he threw his red silken robe about his legs. The moonstone aigret in his oriental turban nodded rhythmically as he thought it over. Finally he said:

"The district attorney has not been bribed, Valeska, I'm sure of that. I have seen him and talked with him. I've studied his hand, his face, his gait, his voice, his gesture. Money can't buy that man. He not only has the energy you speak of, Valeska, he has a tremendous moral force besides. There is no graft in Tulliver. But there's something wrong. This lack of power, just when he ought to strike hardest, is suspicious. It's sinister. I tell you!" he added, rising, as the idea caught and held him with a new force. "This gang of boodlers has got him somehow! It's not a square fight!"

Valeska came up to him, more than commonly moved by his emotion. "Oh!" she exclaimed, taking his hand, "why can't you help him, if there is a plot? I'd like to see you try your hand at something more worthwhile than mere murders and jewel mysteries. You're wasting your talents on such ordinary detective work. Why not offer your services? Why not take up the fight for him, and with him, if it's possible, and help him win? You'll never have a more worthy cause!"

In her excitement her voice had become vibrant, thrilling with a warm personal note not wholly accounted for by her words. Astro perceived it, glanced at her, turned away suddenly. His voice had changed too, when he said:

"Shall I offer my services?"

"Oh, do!"

"You know that it is not my policy nor my custom to do that."

"It's your duty."

He swung round to her and took both her hands in a strong grip. "If you ask me, Valeska, I'll do it."

And so Astro undertook to discover what was the trouble with Tulliver.

It was a delicate proceeding, at first, and it devolved upon Valeska herself to undertake the initial steps. It was three or four days before she had gone over the ground well enough to select the point of attack; but at the end of that time she had made up her mind that Mrs. Tulliver was in the line of least resistance to her efforts.

It did not take long for Valeska to discover that Mrs. Tulliver had a baby, and that the baby had a nurse, that the two went every fine morning to take the air in Central Park. In two days Valeska was there also with a baby borrowed for the occasion. Valeska waited at the corner of Fifth Avenue and East Sixty-fourth Street, until little Alice Tulliver and her nurse came down the steps of the Tulliver house. After that it was easy to make connections in the park and to happen to sit down on the same bench. To any one who watched Valeska's whimsical charm, and pretty expressive face, a confidential acquaintanceship was inevitable and the most natural thing in the world.

In such wise Valeska soon learned that Tulliver was suffering from what the doctors were pleased to term nervous prostration; that he had been advised to take a rest; and that Mrs. Tulliver was much worried over the situation. Mrs. Tulliver was ambitious and took great interest in her husband's political career. There was an atmosphere of great anxiety in the house on Sixty-fourth Street.

Valeska was a willing and sympathetic listener to the nurse's confidence, and watched her chance for interposition. It came unexpectedly the very next day, when Mrs. Tulliver herself came across the two engaged in conversation on a park bench. There was little need for diplomacy. Valeska's attractive manners produced an immediate effect upon Mrs. Tulliver's emotional, intuitive nature; and seeing with her rare perception that frankness was the quickest and easiest method with her, Valeska boldly told her who she was, and offered her services.

Mrs. Tulliver was too full of her own forebodings not to grasp immediately at this unlooked-for hope in her trouble. She confessed that her suspicions had been aroused, and, though they were not shared by her husband, she was convinced that the gang of boodling aldermen, desperate at the prospect of conviction, were making underhanded attacks upon their chief enemy, the district attorney. They were not of a sort to stop at any crime that would rid them of his strenuous prosecution.

Of Astro's fame as Master of Mysteries, Mrs. Tulliver had heard, and she willingly consented to lay the matter before him. His name was already known at the district attorney's office through the many crimes that, in unofficial cooperation with the police, he had pursued and solved.

Her story, after reaching the studio, amply confirmed Astro's suspicions. Tulliver had, the week before the date set for the opening of the trial, worked hard night and day over the data. His material was complex and voluminous; it required all his energy to select the proper points of testimony, to arrange his plan of prosecution, and to divide the work to be done by his assistants. All had gone well till Saturday. He had worked at his office till noon, and then had gone to a barber shop in the vicinity of City Hall Square and been shaved and manicured. That night he had intended going to the house of a friend for an evening's entertainment and relaxation, before beginning on the arduous final preparations for the trial. These last important investigations he had put off till Sunday, thinking that the recreation on Saturday night would help him to devote his whole energy to the case.

On Saturday night he showed extreme lassitude and manifested an unwillingness to go out with his wife. She had induced him to attend the entertainment, however; but, his fatigue increasing, they had both returned early and retired. On Sunday he slept late. He was worried about the case; but felt almost unable to rise and go to work. He had, after breakfast, dragged himself to his study and shut himself up with his papers. There Mrs. Tulliver had found him fast asleep at dinner-time. He made a second attempt to go about his work in the afternoon, and fell asleep a second time, showing extreme exhaustion. At nine o'clock he roused himself sufficiently to ask his wife to telephone to the judge of the court to postpone the case, and to notify his assistants of the necessary delay.

A doctor called on Monday against Tulliver's wishes and diagnosed his lassitude as nervous prostration. He had prescribed a remedy, and after taking it Tulliver had gradually recovered his customary state of health and energy. This attack of exhaustion, however, coming just before an important phase of the case was reached, and the rumors of bribery in connection with the district attorney, which had already been voiced in some of the city papers, had affected him as deeply as they had disturbed Mrs. Tulliver. He showed no disinclination whatever to drop the case; in fact he was more ardent than ever in wishing to bring the boodlers to justice. But already his delays and apparent lack of interest had seriously damaged his political career in the minds of the people.

Astro listened to all this attentively, with only an occasional question. A pretty woman at all times, with a proud, spiritedly-poised head and soft dark eyes, Mrs. Tulliver's distress made her beauty pathetic. It was plainly evident that, much as she was moved by the fear of her husband's illness and the sacrifice of his political future, what affected her still more strongly was the fear of some stain on his reputation; and, perhaps, in the dim shadows of her mind, unacknowledged, but sinisterly insistent, was the specter of a doubt of his probity. She knew well enough the cunning and the ingratiating methods of political corruption, and though she would not admit even to herself that her husband was venal, the horror of this potent secret force prostrated her.

It was Astro himself who gave her back her courage and her faith. She regained her strength at his offers of assistance. As he spoke, slowly, gently, commandingly, as she watched his handsome, mysteriously sentient face, some of his secret power went from him to her. The very strangeness of that face, with its oriental calm, with its oriental wisdom, with its beatific sympathy, gave her trust. She sat, so, watching him, one hand in Valeska's hand, till he had finished.

One question, however, before she left, he put in a way to renew her alarm. "Who is your cook?" he asked.

"Why, we've had her only about nine months; but she came recommended highly. Do you think—"

"Can you see to it that all his food is prepared under your personal supervision, or that he takes his lunches only at large, well-known restaurants?"

She thought she could do both.

"Be careful, then," he said. "And, for the last thing, find out all his movements in what detail you can, both in the past and in the future. Telephone me every day what he intends to do. And, by the way, what is the date set for the opening of the trial?"

"Next Monday."

"Then we haven't much time. But we'll win!"

As she left the great studio Valeska accompanied her to the outer door. Here she paused and clutched the girl's hand. "What did he mean about the cook?" she demanded. "Does he think it can be as bad as that,—that they would try poison?"

"Oh, he's only anxious to take all the precautions possible."

"Then I shall have to tell my husband I have been here."

"As you please," said Valeska. "Only be sure that you have the most powerful defender in New York. Astro has never failed yet."

She returned to the studio, to find Astro already absorbed in a medical book. He had taken down a bound volume of *The Lancet*, and pointed to it. "Look that over carefully and see if you can find that article on the *Pathology of Fatigue*. I can't recall what year it came out; but it was the report of the experiments of an Austrian, I think."

She looked at him in surprise. "You have a theory already?"

"No, not quite; but there is a disturbance in my memory,— there's something I can't quite place, or account for; if I don't try too hard, it will float up unconsciously. That's why I want you to look it up. But our line of investigation is plain."

"The barber?"

"Or the manicure. I didn't dare ask about that. I don't want Tulliver to suspect. Of course she'll tell him everything; I can see that, I expected it. But I must get to that particular barber shop to-day and begin to watch."

"Is it poison, then?"

"Undoubtedly poison; but whether physical or moral I don't yet know."

"But you seemed to be so sure of his honesty."

"I knew she would tell him everything. It was the only way. There is always the chance of corruption. Dishonesty is as much a

disease as cholera. One can become infected by it as well as by a
germ. I said it was my business to know human nature; but no one
can know it, except to be sure that it's liable to all sorts of dangers
and diseases. No one is immune. We can only fight infection of all
sorts. If this man Tulliver is being poisoned, I'll find out how and
by whom, and I'll save him. If he is being corrupted morally, is
there any less reason why I should help him? It may be the first
time in his life—and the last. I know only that I like him, I admire
his wife, and if I can beat that gang I'll do it! *Selah*. I have spoken."

It was late that afternoon when Astro returned from his investigations. By his look, Valeska knew that he was worried. Mrs.
Tulliver had telephoned and said that the district attorney would
be at his office all day and would return directly from there. From
her tone it was evident that her husband did not take the Seer's
assistance so gratefully as she herself did. Astro listened with a
frown.

"Well, I'll save him in spite of himself, then. I confess it looks
dubious. I saw our old friend, Lieutenant McGraw of the detective
force, and he succeeded in finding out for me some of Tulliver's
habits. He patronizes a small barber shop on Broadway, opposite
the post-office, but doesn't go there regularly. Most often drops in
there on Saturdays. I went in and got a shave. There was a tow-
headed manicure in a corner, with about ten pounds of bracelets
and a Marcel wave of the Eighth-Avenue type, crisp as galvanized
iron. I didn't like her, on several counts; I somehow felt wrong
with her. I had my nails attended to, and she was too smooth. She
never refuses an invitation to dinner, that girl.

"Now," he continued, "we can't possibly investigate this thing
from the Brooklyn end. There are too many in that gang of boodlers
for us to follow them all. So we have to trace it back from the district attorney, and find some point of contact with the aldermen.
If Tulliver was bought up, he wouldn't have worked so hard up to
Saturday noon. He would have taken it easy and put his assistants
off. Something must have happened on Saturday, and if anything
happened, whether he was doped or bribed, the only place for it to

have happened was in that barber shop. It's too bad I can't trail her to-night; but I have a positive appointment with Colonel Mixter. You'll have to shadow the manicure. She leaves the shop at six o'clock; so you must hurry."

With that, he threw himself on his divan, spread a pack of cards in front of him, and began "getting Napoleon out of Saint Helena." It was a habit of his when most puzzled with his strange problems to rest his mind occasionally by a game of solitaire. It was a sort of mental bath from which he rose always refreshed and ready for a new attack of the question in hand.

"Did you find that article in *The Lancet?*" he asked as Valeska was preparing to leave the studio.

"No," was her reply; "but I found a reference to it in an article on the anatomy of the vasomotor nerves. The name was Weichardt, wasn't it?"

"By Jove! that's it!" he cried joyfully. "Weichardt, Weichardt!" he repeated the name to himself. "I'll get it now! I'll just let that boil subconsciously a while."

Valeska took the subway down-town, reaching the barber shop just in time to see, through the basement windows, an orange-haired girl putting on her hat behind a screen in the corner. She nodded to the men at the chairs as she passed and came slowly up the steps to the street, still fingering the terrific pompadour that jutted from her forehead. She walked slowly down Broadway, glancing at her watch once, and loitering occasionally at shop-windows. It was evident that she was a bit too early for some appointment. At the corner of Fulton Street she stopped and waited.

It was a long time before a man, smoking a cigar, came up to her and stopped without lifting his hat. Then he took the girl's arm familiarly, and the two walked to the subway entrance again, descended, and took a Brooklyn train, and got off at the Borough station.

Valeska had meanwhile not only kept on their track, but had secured a seat where she could watch them at close range. The man looked like a political heeler, a barkeeper, or a sport. He might indeed have been all three. The two seemed very friendly; the girl's strident laugh sounded more than once through the car. In Brooklyn they went to a flashy restaurant that was generally frequented by the sporting element. The man ordered dinner and wine. As the meal proceeded, the manicure's laugh grew louder, and she became more familiar. It was not a pleasant sight.

From here the two came out upon the electric-lighted sidewalk, debated for a while at the curb, then got into a street-car. At Waverley Avenue they got out and walked up to number 1321. Here, rather to Valeska's surprise, the girl left the man abruptly, ran up the steps, took out a key, and entered. The man walked slowly back, boarded a car, and rode downtown.

Valeska followed him. She got out with him at Preston Street, and from here her task was more difficult. Keeping at a safe distance, however, she saw him stop at a two-story wooden house. At that moment a man, approaching from the other direction with two dogs held in leash, met him. The two entered the house together, and Valeska approached and reconnoitered. As she passed, she heard the dogs barking, and mingled with the noise was the sound of whining, as of animals in pain. The lower windows were dark; but the three above, on the second floor, were lighted. Creeping softly up the steps, Valeska laid her ear to the keyhole and listened. There was a low but distinct sound,—a rumbling as of wheels turning, wheels with a heavy load, as if some machine were being laboriously worked.

Two days passed, and each night Valeska took up the scent, following the manicure girl across to Brooklyn as before. Both times, however, the girl was alone. The first night she dined alone at a little dairy near the Borough station and went to a vaudeville show afterward. The second night she went directly home. The next day was Saturday.

"We seem to have got nothing yet," she said to Astro that morning. "I confess I'm discouraged. If that man I saw is the go-between he covers his tracks well. If he hands her any drug or money it is impossible for us to detect it. If we could only get into that house on Preston Street!"

"That's impossible," said Astro; "it's too well guarded. I've been over there to see it. I was looking for a house to rent, you know, and found out enough to arouse my suspicions. The neighbors are gossiping about the place already. Dogs go in; but don't come out. There are moans and howls all night long, and it's getting to be a scandal. But to-day I hope to find out something definite about the relations that exist between Tulliver and that girl. McGraw has agreed to tip me off when Tulliver goes to the shop, and I think I can get a chance to watch the two together."

Nothing had been heard from Mrs. Tulliver in the meantime. To Valeska's mind that in itself was suspicious. Astro's story when he returned did not relieve her mind.

"I got in after Tulliver," he said, "and was shaved, just managing to miss my turn with the manicure lady. Tulliver had his nails polished, as usual. She brightened up considerably at sight of him. It seemed to me that she was excited. He talked and laughed a little with her; but not enough to prove any great intimacy. She was undoubtedly nervous, however. Once she went behind the screen and did something, I don't know what. But she had ample opportunity to convey a secret message to him without arousing the least suspicion. I confess I'm worried about him."

With this, Valeska had to be content for the time, and she heard no more till Monday morning. Then, upon her arrival at the studio, Astro met her with a black face.

"Tulliver is down again!" he said immediately. "Mrs. Tulliver telephoned yesterday at ten o'clock in the morning, while her husband was asleep. He absolutely refused to work, said he was exhausted, and insisted on taking a nap. He said he wasn't ill at all, only felt tired. It was plain enough that she is fearfully worried now, and will help us out with information whether he objects or not. You had better go and see her and get all the details."

Valeska lost no time in obeying him. Astro threw himself on the divan, refused all comers, and gave himself up to a struggle with his problem. Something in his memory balked. He was usually wonderfully in control of it, and the refusal tantalized him.

Valeska returned at eleven o'clock and reported that Tulliver had gone down to the office, though still listless and blue. Mrs. Tulliver's alarm had increased, and she was now willing to tell all she knew.

"I spoke to her as delicately as I could about the manicure girl," she said. "Mrs. Tulliver seemed a bit worried at the subject. She said that Tulliver had often spoken of her as an original slangy type, whose conversation refreshed him after his hard work. In fact, that was his chief reason for having his nails done there,—so that he could listen to the girl's persiflage, to which he didn't even have to answer. That seemed to be her main talent, in fact; for Mrs. Tulliver said that she had a gift of gab, rather striking looks, and the ability to create a high and showy polish on men's nails. She is clumsy, though. She has managed her scissors so unskilfully that she has cut Mr. Tulliver's fingers twice."

Astro jumped to his feet. "Abracadabra!" he exclaimed, and stood staring at Valeska.

"What's the matter?"

"We're getting on!" He started to walk up and down. "Let me think it over again. I believe I've almost got it. Leave me alone here, and I'll do some deep-sea diving in the abysses of my memory, if you'll pardon the metaphor. You look over the papers while I grope in the recesses."

Valeska left and took up the file of morning papers. She was not gone long, having found something almost immediately that seemed important enough to warrant her interrupting the Master of Mysteries.

"What do you think?" she exclaimed, appearing between the velvet portieres that screened the palmist's vast studio from the reception-room. "That house at number 1321 Preston Street has been raided by the police, at the instigation of the Society for the Prevention of Cruelty to Animals. They entered the place yesterday, and found a sort of treadmill where two dogs were working themselves almost to death, for no apparent reason whatever. There was a bed, a table, and chemical things in one of the rooms of the lower floor; but there was nothing up-stairs but the dogs, the treadmill, and a table that looked as if it had been used for dissection."

Astro had stood listening to every word. As Valeska spoke, his face cleared. A smile appeared on his lips. He threw off his crimson silk robe, tossed his turban into a corner, and on the instant appeared as the virile keen man of activity.

"I have it!" he exclaimed. "It is all over! District Attorney Tulliver will have no more mysterious attacks of fatigue! The boodling Brooklyn aldermen will be prosecuted from now on with all despatch!"

He went up to Valeska, and gently led her to a seat, laughing at the wonder in her eyes.

"Listen," he said. "I had it all deep in my memory; but until this moment I couldn't make connections with it and apply my knowledge to this case. Now I recall everything. Herr Weichardt, a Munich pathologist, some years ago made some experiments which showed that fatigue was an actual pathological condition. In other words, he proved it was a disease, by discovering the germ and inoculating living organisms with it. He took some animals,—pigs, if I recall aright,—made them work till they were almost dead of fatigue, then removed the tired muscles and extracted the serum from them. With this he inoculated other animals. He found that a small dose of his serum culture caused all the characteristic symptoms of fatigue in the patient and that a heavy dose produced even death."

"But how could this gang administer such a poison?"

"Through the manicure, whom they had engaged and paid, of course. All she had to do, after she had received the serum from the man you saw, was to dip her nail scissors into the solution, and then clip the cuticle so as to draw blood. The merest scratch would suffice, and no noticeable sore in the finger would be caused; but the toxic germs would permeate the veins and be distributed all over the body. It was the fact that she had cut Tulliver's finger that aroused my memory; then the story of the treadmill instantly suggested Weichardt's experiments. It was a devilishly subtle plot.

You see, they didn't dare actually to poison him, or give him any easily recognized disease. All they needed was to put him out of business for a day or so at critical moments when they needed time to prepare their fight."

"Then you'll tell Tulliver?"

"Certainly. With the police behind him, he can easily run down the plot and do what he wishes about it. Most likely he'll see that the manicure girl leaves town, and let the rest go."

Valeska looked thoughtfully at the huge crystal ball on an ebony table in front of her and spoke as if to herself. "I wish some other symptoms besides fatigue could be transmitted in that way. One might infuse some of the district attorney's own strenuosity and honesty, for instance, into persons who need moral stamina."

"I can think of better things than that to do." Astro gazed dreamily at the pretty flushed face in front of him. His eyes lingered on the fair curling hair, the lovely curve of the neck, the slenderly graceful, girlish hands, the sensitive mouth, the cunningly molded figure, and he sighed.

"What would you try to give me, if you were undertaking the experiment?" Valeska asked without looking up.

Astro did not answer. Instead he took one more long tender look at her. "I think," he said finally, "that first I shall have to treat myself!"

WHY MRS. BURBANK RAN AWAY

"Surely," said Astro, "until you have solved a woman's emotional equation, there's little use in trying to discover her motive. A woman will kill a man she hates; but she will as often kill a man she loves. Now look at this letter and tell me whether the writer is in love or not." As he spoke, he selected a sheet from the many spread out on his table and handed it to his assistant. Then, taking up the stem of his narghile, he leaned comfortably back on his velvet couch and watched the girl with amusement and fondness. His oriental eyes narrowed, and his olive-skinned, handsome, oval face under the white turban became a mask.

Valeska took up the writing with a pretty gesture and scanned it studiously. She looked up at last with a quick interrogative smile. "She's in love, I think; isn't she?"

"Decidedly!" The Master of Mysteries bowed slowly. "The crossings of the "t's" are almost all in a double curve; it's a sure sign. But you notice that some of them have only a single curve, like the lower arc of a circle."

"Oh, so they have! Why, then, she has had a previous love-affair, hasn't she?"

"Yes. She is sincerely in love now; though she hasn't yet forgotten her first. You see by the regularity of her terminals, too, that she's a faithful friend. But to return to the crossings: let us compare these with some others."

He looked over the collection and drew forth another specimen. "Here you see a woman that has had but one affair, and has quite outlived it. The arc is that of the top of a circle, you see. Here's one who is beginning to be in love. You will observe the same arc as in the first,—a rising curve, but no compound curves. If you thoroughly understand this principle, we'll go on to a study of terminals and gladiated words." As he spoke his face lighted up with enthusiasm.

A bell, softly tinkling, interrupted him. With a sudden gesture he swept all the letters into a heap and tossed them into a drawer. That done, he became again the calm impassive Seer. He drew his red silken robe about him as Valeska rose to answer the bell. He followed her svelte graceful form with alert eyes till she disappeared in the waiting-room; then they fell abstractedly on the slow, gracefully-rising, blue, perfumed smoke of the censer in a corner of the dim studio and remained there until the curtains again parted.

The visitor was a fine military type of man, with white mustache and iron-gray hair, tall and well-built, but with a face drawn and haggard. He strode up to Astro with a determined air. The Seer awaited the first words calmly.

"My name is Burbank," the man began,— "Major Burbank, retired. I have come to you on an important and delicate piece of business, at the advice of a friend who has told me of your reputation for solving mysteries. I trust, sir, that you will consider what I have to say to you as confidential?"

Astro nodded and made an expressive gesture.

"My wife left our home yesterday afternoon, leaving a very painful letter for me. I wish to know, sir, if you think that you can discover her whereabouts for me without precipitating a scandal. I have the greatest wish that this matter should not be known unless it is absolutely necessary."

Astro bowed and pointed to a chair, seating himself as well. "I am ready, sir," he replied. "If you will acquaint me with the details, I think I can do what you wish."

"There are no details," the visitor broke out; "that is, none but this letter. Everything was all right; we were happily married; my wife and I loved each other. We have two children, whom she has abandoned. It's incredible, sir! There is absolutely no reason for it at all, so far as I can see. But look at this, and imagine what I have to suffer!"

He took a letter in an envelope from his pocket and handed it to the Seer.

Astro looked over the envelope carefully then opened the letter and read the following message:

> "My Dear, Dear George—I shall never see you again. Don't try to find me. I'm going to finish a long bitter wretchedness. Forgive me if you can; for I have suffered. Farewell. Ellen."

His eyes ran over the pen strokes carefully. He looked at the back of the envelope again, then held it sensitively in his hands, keeping a serious silence for a few minutes. His gaze became abstracted. For several minutes he did not speak, seemingly falling into a deep reverie. Then he said:

"My dear sir, your wife is still alive, and I think I can find her. But I get from the radiations of this writing a conviction that she is in great mental distress which it is not well for you to break in upon just yet. I should prefer that you permit me to inspect your house and see if I can not discover the reason for this surprising action. By visiting the place where she was last, I shall the more readily be impressed by her magnetism and get the vibrations that have undoubtedly affected her. First of all, I must ask you to send me immediately several photographs of Mrs. Burbank, that I may fix her image in my mind."

Major Burbank had stood looking at him with a tense anxious look. "Is that necessary?" he said, "I had hoped that, if you had the occult power you claim, you could do it more simply."

"If you wish to help her—" Astro shrugged his shoulders.

"Help her! It's just that!" he exclaimed. "I want to save her, even more than I want to find her."

"That goes without saying. Very well. Only a few more questions, so that I may be prepared for whatever influences I may find.

Who lives in your house?" He added, "Including servants, of course."

"Besides my wife and myself, only the cook, a second girl, and a nurse."

"Who are your most frequent visitors?"

"Why, let's see. Ellen has a lot of women friends who run in occasionally, of course."

"No, the men."

The major looked at him sternly. "See here, sir! If you attempt for a moment to hint that—"

"My dear Major Burbank," Astro replied amiably, "I hint at nothing. All I wish is to be able to distinguish between the astral emanations of those who frequent your place. It is possible that Mrs. Burbank was most affected by a woman; but it is not likely."

The major, still frowning, replied: "We lead a very quiet life. My friend Colonel Trevellian is the only close friend of the family. But I must tell you, sir, that my wife has of late confessed to me that she did not like him. It has made it very uncomfortable for me, I assure you. But I saw him only to-day. He can have nothing to do with this disappearance, I'm sure. I have known him for several years quite intimately, and he's the last person—"

"I understand," said Astro dryly; "but has he heard of Mrs. Burbank's disappearance?"

"No, I haven't had the heart to tell him."

"Very good. I should advise you not to. Well, I will call this afternoon. I think we shall be able to satisfy you."

As soon as the visitor had gone, Valeska appeared. Astro handed her Mrs. Burbank's letter, with a curious look. She examined it under the drop-light at the table.

"She is in love; but has had a previous affair, just like that other woman. How curious! And she's suffering from a severe mental strain, too. I heard the major's conversation while I was in the secret closet. It's interesting, isn't it? Do you suppose she has outgrown her feeling for her husband and is in love with his friend now?"

"Or is she in love with her husband and has outgrown her affection for Colonel Trevellian—that's what we have to find out." Astro shook his head.

"You said you knew she was alive, though. How can you be sure that is true?"

"You haven't half examined that envelope," Astro replied abstractedly, as he walked up and down, his chin in his hand, supporting the elbow with his other arm, absorbed in thought.

"It's postmarked New York, though— Oh, I see!" Valeska smiled at him. She had turned back the top flap, which adhered, loosely gummed, and looked at the imprint of the stationer. "Hodge & Durland, Poughkeepsie, N. Y." she read. "She may be there, perhaps. But how did she mail it here in New York?"

"No doubt she gave a porter a dollar at the station to post it when his train got into the city. Perfectly simple. You'll notice that the envelope is badly crumpled and soiled. It has evidently been carried some time in a man's pocket.

"Now," he continued, taking off his robe and turban, "I wish to lose no time; so I'll go right over to the Burbanks', while you wait for the photographs. As soon as they come, take the first train for Poughkeepsie, and see if you can locate Mrs. Burbank. It's unlikely she is still there; yet she may be."

"And if I find her?"

"Keep her in sight, wire me, and await instructions."

"I see." Valeska bent her brows in thought. "If she's gone, of course I'll try to trace her, if I can get it out of the hotel clerks."

"If you can?" Astro, struggling into a long gray overcoat, paused long enough to smile at his assistant. In return she made a mischievous face at him. He blew a kiss to her, and taking his stick and silk hat, left the studio.

His green limousine took him in ten minutes to a brownstone house on West Fifty-second Street, one of a row of gloomily respectable fronts. A butler, impressively solemn, ushered him into the parlor.

Astro was about to sit down when the man said:

"I'm sorry to say that Major Burbank has been unexpectedly called away, sir, and left instructions that you should see anything you wished." His voice dropped in tone as he added somberly, "The fact is, sir, the major had just heard a piece of shocking news. His brother has just committed suicide, sir, and he has gone up to Kingsbridge to see about it, sir. He was very much upset, of course, sir; but he told me to do what was necessary for you. So if you are ready I'll show you everything."

"Is Mrs. Burbank in?" Astro asked.

"No, sir, she is not. I understand an aunt was taken ill and she has gone out of town to attend to her. She left yesterday afternoon, sir, directly after lunch, in a great hurry, sir."

"In a hurry?" Astro repeated, watching the impassive countenance of the servant.

"Yes, sir; so much so that she never stopped to hang up the telephone receiver, sir. I expect the call was from her aunt's people, though she got a letter in the morning that did seem to upset her, too."

"Ah!" The Master of Mysteries knitted his brow, and sat for a few moments without speaking, while the butler stood erect, waiting like a lay figure. Astro looked up at him suddenly, with a keen searching gaze, and for a moment a startled expression passed over the man's face.

"So Mrs. Burbank has gone to her aunt's?" he said deliberately.

"That's what she said, sir."

"Do you believe it?"

The butler shifted his feet uneasily. "It's hardly for me to say, sir."

"See here!" Astro rose and took the fellow by the lapel of his coat. "You're quite right, my man. It isn't for you to suspect anything, of course. But if I know anything about human nature, you are devoted to the major, and you're to be trusted. Now see here! I'm here to help him in this matter; but anything I find out from you shall go no further. Do you understand?"

"Yes, sir," the butler replied uneasily. "The major said I was to obey your instructions to the letter, sir."

"There is one thing that I want to know, my man, and that is, did Mrs. Burbank write to Colonel Trevellian before or since she went away?"

"I can't say, sir, as to that."

The Seer still looked at the man searchingly, as if sending his will and thought through his eyes to fascinate and charm. The man's attitude, as he watched Astro, changed subtly from suspicion to confidence. Gradually he lost the conventional stolidity of the servant and became more human.

"All I want to see is the envelope of that letter," Astro said, watching his man.

The butler hesitated. "I might possibly find out from the colonel's man, sir. I'm well acquainted with him, and I've done him favors in times past."

"See if you can get it; and meanwhile I'll go up into Mrs. Burbank's room."

The butler showed the way up-stairs and left the Master of Mysteries alone. Once the door was shut, Astro gave a swift look about the chamber, then walked to a writing-desk. Everything was in order, and not a letter was visible. From here he turned to the open grate. The fire was out, and only a few ashes remained. These he examined carefully. On the top were a few flakes of carbonized paper, crumpled like black poppy petals. With a deft finger he drew these from the grate and carried them to the desk, placing them on a white blotter. On the wrinkled surface, almost invisible, were some traces of writing, appearing as if slightly embossed on the surface. He could make out only one word, or part of a word: "Kellem." The closest scrutiny revealed no more writing; but on one charred fragment he discovered the remains of a postage-stamp. It was curiously shrunk to half-size, and appeared as a negative, in which all that had been white was black, and the red ink changed to gray.

By the time he had accomplished this delicate manipulation, the butler had returned.

"I found the letter, sir; but it hasn't been opened at all. It seems that the colonel didn't come home last night, and hasn't returned yet. I got it out of William; but he's in a mortal terror, sir, and he wants me to bring it back at once. Do you think it will take you long, sir?"

"About ten minutes; but I shall have to be alone."

"You're not going to open it, sir! It's as much as William's place is worth to be caught at this game."

"No, I won't open it. I only wish to see the writing. Come back in ten minutes, and I'll let you have it back."

As soon as the butler had gone Astro drew from his pocket a bottle of alcohol and a velvet sponge. With this he moistened the envelope, and it became as transparent as tracing-paper. The letter inside was so folded, however, that he could read only one line, in a nervous, hurried handwriting which he recognized as Mrs. Burbank's:

"I can not bear it any longer. If you don't—"

He opened the window, set the envelope in a draft, and waited. In ten minutes he took it up, smelled of it, and went out of the room. The butler was anxiously waiting, and received it with relief.

"One moment, before you go," said Astro. "I'd like to see the nursery and the children."

The butler led the way and opened a door on the third floor. Two children, one about four and the other two years old, were playing on the floor with building blocks, while a nursemaid was busy at the window with some sewing. The butler retired to return the letter.

Astro went to the children and knelt down beside them, showing by his manner that he was not only fond of children but used to them. He did not speak at first, sitting with them, smiling, and playing with the blocks as if he himself was of their age. The elder, a boy, seeing him arranging a pile of blocks, crawled over to watch and help him. As the two sat there together, the other baby stared at Astro. Then she put out her two arms and cried:

"Kellem! Kellem!"

Astro stared in surprise. It was the same word, evidently, that he had found on the ashes of Mrs. Burbank's letter. He turned to the nurse, who apparently had noticed nothing unusual.

"What does she mean by that?" he asked.

"Oh, that 'Kellem, kellem'? Why, I don't know, I'm sure, sir. I fancy it's one of the games they play with Colonel Trevellian. He often comes in here for a romp with the kiddies, and they seem to be fond of him. I've heard Agatha say that before; but, lord! I never thought to wonder about it. It is funny, isn't it?"

Again the child reached out her arms and repeated the words, "Kellem, kellem!"

"Did she ever play that particular game with her mother, nurse?"

"I don't remember, sir, I'm sure. I expect so, though. Seems to me, now I think of it, I did hear Mrs. Burbank trying to break Agatha of it; but no doubt I've got it mixed up."

Astro watched the children for some time; then, after kissing each of the chubby faces, went thoughtfully down-stairs.

He had no sooner reached the hall than the outer door opened, and Burbank entered with a serious expression on his face. He bowed and shook his head sadly.

"My misfortunes are all coming at once, it seems," he said. "My brother is dead, my wife missing. It's too much for me, and I'm afraid I'll have to call in the police and put them on the case. I can't stand it any longer; unless—unless you have discovered some way of helping me," he added.

"When did your brother die?" Astro asked.

"As far as we can learn, early this morning. The gas was turned on in his room, and he was found at eight o'clock, dead from the fumes. They were unable to locate me till four this afternoon, when I went right over and did what was necessary."

"He lived alone, I presume?"

"Yes, not even a servant. The body was discovered by a friend whom he had asked to call, who smelled the gas and had the door broken in. I can't account for it any way."

"Did Mrs. Burbank ever visit his apartment?" Astro asked.

"Yes. Occasionally when he was ill, she went over and took him things necessary." He stopped and stared at the Master. "But you don't suspect that— that there's any connection between Mrs. Burbank's disappearance and my brother's death?"

"I should like to investigate your brother's apartments," said Astro evasively. "I may be able to receive some impression there that will lead me on the track. I have succeeded in harmonizing the vibrations in Mrs. Burbank's apartments, and feel already that I understand her mental condition when she left home. But there is a strange discord there, Mr. Burbank, and I must complete the impression."

"Here is my card, then. I'll write a note asking that you be given the fullest opportunity for investigation on the premises. Of course the body has been taken to the morgue, and the police are in charge of the apartment; but I think you will have no trouble with them."

"One more thing, Mr. Burbank. I'd like to know if Mrs. Burbank was ever hypnotized, that you know of."

"Why, only once, possibly twice, at an evening party here. We did have some rather amusing experiments this fall; but it was nothing but fun, of course."

"And who was it that hypnotized her that time?" asked the Seer.

"Why, my friend Colonel Trevellian. He fancied that he had some power, and did succeed in influencing one or two of the company, my wife included. But nothing further ever came of it, and we never tried it again."

"Has the colonel known your wife long?"

"Yes, since before we were married. But, my dear sir, you don't—"

"Mr. Burbank, at present I am merely holding myself sensitive to whatever influences I come in contact with, that's all. As soon as I have soaked myself in them, so to speak, I shall go into a trance and be guided by subconscious mind. I don't know about these things at all. I observe, I listen, I smell; but what works these impressions out in me is deeper than mere sense or mere ratiocination. You must wait patiently, and hope for the best."

He left Burbank disconsolate in the library, and jumping into his limousine, the Master of Mysteries drove to the studio. Here a telegram awaited him. It was from Valeska:

> "She is in Troy. Shall find her this evening and wire address."

He despatched an answer, and hurrying to the subway, took an express to Kingsbridge.

On the way his face belied the confident patter by which he had imposed upon his client. His eyes were fixed, his mouth set. Occasionally he drew from his pocket a note-book and consulted its contents, staring at the page for minutes at a time. As the train slowed down, he became alert again, and when it stopped he waited only long enough to ask for directions, then walked briskly to Burbank's apartment.

The note insured a grudging admittance, and he was taken up-stairs by an officer into a little flat. The place was meagerly fur-nished as a bachelor's quarters. A look into the kitchen revealed a few utensils and packages of food strewn about in a disorderly manner. The sitting-room was scantily furnished, but in better order. Astro gave it a glance. The chamber where Burbank had died next engrossed his attention. Here he spent a half-hour in elaborate scrutiny. Still he appeared dissatisfied. Excusing himself to the officer, he opened the back door and inspected the platform. Here he saw an ash barrel and a can for refuse. He opened the cover of each in turn. Lighting a match, he looked eagerly into them.

In a moment he had drawn out a broken, hollow, black-rubber cylinder, and after assuring himself that he had all the fragments, slipped them into his overcoat pocket. He then returned inside.

"You have no doubt that the death was caused by suicide, I sup-pose, officer?"

"Of course not. There's no evidence to the contrary that I know of."

"No one was known to have visited him the night before he died?"

"The people down-stairs say they heard footsteps late that night; but it may have been anybody. No body heard the door shut. Or if they had, how was it possible to turn on the gas? The door was locked on the inside, as they found when they burst it in."

"And the rear entrance was locked, too?"

"That, too. It was a suicide, all right."

"Of course. Very well, then, that's all. I'll report to the major. Good night, Officer."

Astro hurried back to the subway station. As he reached the ticket taker he drew a photograph from his pocket and handed it to the man.

"Did you see a woman like this last night, late?"

He looked at it for some time before he answered.

"I wouldn't be sure about that; but I've certainly seen her several times. I can't recall just when was the last time."

"That's all," said Astro, and he handed the man a dollar, ran down-stairs, and boarded the express for down-town.

Another telegram from Valeska was lying under his door when he reached the studio. After reading it, he hastily scribbled two despatches and rang for a messenger. One read:

> "Your child Bobby has been taken ill with pneumonia and is at a private hospital, at number 234 West Thirty-fourth Street. Come at once. Important."

This was addressed to Mrs. Belle Grant, Delmar House, Troy, New York. The other was sent to Valeska Wynne.

> "Follow B. G. wherever she goes, and get acquainted with her if possible but do not let her know you know her."

Then, yawning, he took off his coat, rolled up his shirt-sleeves, and sat down to a table under the electric light. Here he laid out the pieces of the cylinder he had found, and with liquid glue started laboriously to piece them together. One by one he fastened them and warmed them over a Bunsen burner till they were dry. The work was long and arduous, and it was almost daylight before he had finished the job. The cylinder was now complete, except for an irregularly shaped hole at one extremity. With a penknife he trimmed the protruding glue, and then examined the whole through a magnifying-glass. Not till it appeared to satisfy his inspection did he desist. But at last the thing was done, and without undressing he threw himself on the great velvet couch under a trophy of arms and fell sound asleep.

His pet cat Deodar, a handsome black Angora, awakened him at nine o'clock by clawing at his sleeve, and Astro jumped up and went to the telephone. A half-hour later, tubbed, and clad in his flowing red silk robe, his turban and its moonstone clasp on his head, he sipped his thick black coffee and munched his rolls as he read in the morning paper the accounts of the suicide of Edward Burbank. Nothing new to interest him had transpired.

As he sat there the bell rang, and soon a boy in buttons entered, carrying a parcel. Astro opened it, and took from a box a phonograph, which he set on the table. He was a bit excited now, as he fitted his mended cylinder to the drum and started the clockwork.

The wheels whirred; a harsh dry voice announced a song by a well-known comedian. After a preliminary orchestral flourish, the solo began. Astro listened eagerly. The melody was constantly interrupted by discordant explosive noises caused by the joining of the broken pieces; but with these interruptions the song ran on for a while fairly intelligibly. Then there was a splitting series of crackling noises. From the silence following these there came a sudden, loud, monotonous exclamation, "Kellem, kellem, kellem, kell—"

Astro, staring, stopped the machine and reseated himself, to fall into a profound reverie. At times he shook his head. Once he rose to take Mrs. Burbank's letter from a pigeonhole, and scrutinized it long and carefully. At last, with a shrug, he took up his narghile and a volume of French memoirs. Smoking and reading, the time passed away till ten o'clock.

The first visitors were sent away by Buttons. Astro would not be disturbed. At eleven, the telephone bell rang. The Master of Mysteries took up the receiver eagerly.

It was Major Burbank. "I have just received a letter," he said, "and I thought it would be well for you to know the contents. It is from my unfortunate brother Edward, and in it he tells me that he is contemplating suicide. The poor fellow was in ill health and financial straits, and the fact that he had been a care to me seemed to worry him. It's dreadful to think of his having been distressed over the little I was able to do for him; but I feel quite sure that he was not sane when he committed his desperate act. The poor fellow is at rest in peace now, I trust. I almost wish I were."

Astro's expression had changed wonderfully as he heard the news. He hastened to offer his sympathy anew to his client, and assured him that it was only a question of a few hours before his wife would return. This promise seemed to quiet the old man's distress. Astro went back into the studio with a new expression, at once determined and jubilant. He sat down, wrote a note, and despatched it by a messenger boy. This done, he set the phonograph carefully at the beginning of the strange exclamation that interrupted the song on the record, and waited.

In a half-hour Buttons opened the heavy portières, announced "Colonel Trevellian!" and a man walked in.

The visitor looked about scornfully. He was a lean, yellow, bony-faced man, with deep-set eyes and a drooping mustache. He spoke with a drawl. "I believe you requested to see me on a matter of importance and of a confidential nature," he observed languidly.

"I did," Astro replied. "I am about to make a request of you."

"Indeed, you do me a great honor." The man's tone was sarcastic.

Astro scarcely looked at him. "I should be infinitely obliged to you, Colonel Trevellian, if you would consent to pack up your things, leave New York and not return for five years."

The colonel scowled, took a step nearer, and clenched his fist. "You infernal charlatan! if you'll take off that nightgown and sweeping-cap, I'll see that you don't decorate this cozy corner any longer! What the deuce do you mean? By Jove! I'll thrash you and pitch you out of your own window!"

Astro yawned. Then he brought his two hands down on his knees, and his dark alert head was outstretched toward the colonel, on whom he turned two blazing eyes. "Colonel Trevellian," he said in a voice like the rattling of paper, "you have persecuted Mrs. Burbank long enough! If you fancy you understand the art of hypnotic suggestion, I can show you that you're a fool as well as a cur. For her sake I consent to permit you to leave town without informing the major exactly what kind of a cad you are, but you'll have to leave quickly."

The colonel had already lost the most of his nerve; but he made a last attempt to bluster. "What do you mean, sir? I've done nothing at all, I assure you. You're quite mistaken. Why, the major is my best friend!"

"And do you not wish to supplant him as husband of your old sweetheart, Mrs. Burbank?"

"Of course not. It's absurd." The colonel's face was ashen now.

"And you did not suggest, after hypnotizing her and getting her somewhat under your influence, that she—"

The man stared hard at Astro, and his jaw had dropped. "That she—what?" He almost whispered it.

Astro touched the phonograph. "Kellem, kellem, kell—" it ground out raucously.

The colonel stared first at the mechanism, then at the palmist. He dropped a step back, undecided, then, turning suddenly, bolted out of the room.

Astro dropped again into his chair, folded his arms, and drew a long breath.

The hansom drew up at number 234. A woman got out, paid the driver, and looked curiously at the front door. Apparently puzzled, she drew a telegram from her purse and read it over. She was a fine-looking woman of thirty-five, dressed all in black, even to her furs, though she wore no mourning veil. Her only luggage was a small traveling bag. Everything about her stamped her as a woman of culture and influence, if not rich, at least comfortably off. Yet her demeanor was timid, almost frightened.

As she started to ascend the steps, a green motorcar, driving furiously, came down Thirty-fourth Street and drew up suddenly before her. A young girl, fresh and pretty, smartly dressed, and with an air of jaunty confidence, jumped out.

The woman who had first arrived stared at her in astonishment. "Why," she said, "how do you happen to be here?" The look of perplexity and timidity in her eyes deepened now into positive alarm. "Oh!" she breathed, "you're not a detective?"

Valeska took her hand affectionately. "No, my dear Mrs. Burbank, only a friend who wants to help you. I knew that if I told you on the train you'd never come here; so I didn't dare to explain that we had really imposed upon you. Bobby is quite well, I assure you. You needn't worry on his account. And I hope on no other account either; for I'm sure that by this time the Master has been able to straighten things out."

"The Master?" Mrs. Burbank gasped.

"Yes, Astro, the Master of Mysteries, my employer and my friend, as I'm sure he is yours. Your husband secured his services, for no one else would have been able to find you and help you without danger of publicity. Come right up and you'll hear from him that everything is all right."

"Oh, if it only were!" The woman followed Valeska hopelessly.

Ten minutes after that Mrs. Burbank sat smiling in the studio. Astro had told her that there would be nothing more to fear from the persecutor who had made the last few weeks hideous. She had herself confessed everything; how, after that first hypnotic sleep, the colonel had given her persistently—so often that it drove her almost distracted—the horrible suggestion that she kill her husband. She had struggled hard against it; but the iteration of the words "Kill him!" so distorted as to be unintelligible to any one else, coming now in letters, now over the telephone, now from the innocent lips of her own child, had finally unstrung her mind; and, for fear lest in her distress she should actually commit the crime, she had run away to get out of the colonel's power.

"When I went away," she concluded, "I thought I had destroyed every evidence that might enable my husband to know how I had been tormented; that is every piece but one,—the phonograph cylinder. I was afraid I could not destroy that, and feared to leave it in the house. I took it with me when I went to see Edward, hoping that I should find some place to conceal it. But every one seemed to be watching me, and I was too nervous to risk throwing it away. So when I got to Edward's apartment I left it there in the ash barrel. I had intended to tell him everything and ask his advice, but the poor fellow was so blue that I didn't have the heart to worry him with my own troubles and I left him without saying anything."

She looked curiously at Astro. "I can't imagine how you ever found out. It's wonderful!"

Astro's look was cryptic. "My dear Mrs. Burbank," he replied, "such a nervous force as yours is intensely dynamic; it effects a disturbance of the ether, and to one sensitive to such vibration the message-impression is as plain as the ringing of a bell."

Valeska smiled and folded her hands.

"But now what am I to tell my husband?" Mrs. Burbank exclaimed. "If he knows everything he'll want to kill Colonel Trevellian!"

"The colonel will take himself out of harm's way, I'm sure," said Astro. "He has had his warning. There is only one possible way that I know of plausibly explaining your absence."

Valeska looked up swiftly, as if to anticipate his explanation.

"What can I say?" Mrs. Burbank said doubtfully.

"The truth—a woman's last resort." And Astro favored her with a rather cynical smile.

MRS. SELWYN'S EMERALD

Gasping at the splendor of the scene, the wonderful house, the gorgeously-arrayed company, the terrifying magnificence of the servants in livery, Valeska grabbed Astro's arm tightly, trembling. He patted her hand and smiled. A pompous butler bent his head to hear their names, then bellowed them into the salon:

"Monsieur Astro and Miss Wynne!"

As they made their way toward their hostess, the buzz of conversation in the reception-room was for a moment hushed. Women watched through curious eyes the distinguished, picturesque figure of the Master of Mysteries, whispered to one another, and noted critically the face and costume of the beautiful girl who accompanied the lion of the evening. Men glanced with amused contempt at Astro's oriental face, and scrutinized Valeska Wynne more indulgently. The murmur arose again, and the temporary stillness that had followed the announcement of Astro's name gave way to motion, laughter and persiflage.

The room fairly scintillated with lights, reflected from the cut-glass pendants of the silver electroliers, smoldering in the dusky gold carvings, twinkling from the jewels on women's necks and breasts, gleaming from the polished oak parquetry floor. The large double salon of the Selwyns was about half filled; there were not yet too many present to hide the elegance of the highly decorated Louis XIV rooms which enclosed the brilliant company as in an ornate frame. The ceiling, frescoed in the panels with nymphs and cupids, seemed faintly to reflect the life below; the tall mirrors multiplied the complexity of mysterious distances. There was an odor of winter roses which mingled with the perfumes of dainty women. An orchestra sounded languorously from the balcony at the head of the wide staircase.

"I'm delighted!" Mrs. Selwyn exclaimed effusively, leaning gracefully forward with a swanlike movement. She was a deliciously, almost a foolishly pretty creature, with her bright smile accented by a black beauty-spot at the corner of her mouth, her slender little fingers flashing with jewels, her lovely neck and her fair hair. It was hard to believe her a matron.

Astro, in his masculine way as striking a figure as she, presented his assistant. Valeska seemed more human than either. There was little artifice in her appearance; her costume was girlishly simple. One was not tempted even for a moment to let his eyes wander from her earnest pretty face.

"I'm so glad to see you, Miss Wynne!" Mrs. Selwyn scarcely gave her a glance and returned spiritedly to Astro. "My dear," she said archly, "I had no idea that I had captured such a lion. People are simply wild about you! Why, I've made a sensation already by merely inviting you, I assure you! Not that I didn't know you were famous and popular and all that, of course; but, dear me, it's a positive rage! You have no idea what stories I've been hearing about you! They say you can read one's thoughts and go through a stone wall, and eat fire, and conjure the dead—and dear knows what! I'm actually afraid of you!"

"And I of you also, madam,—in that gown."

She spread her hands demurely down her sides and looked up at him from under her lashes. She wore a costume of silken mesh, sheer and delicate, over cloth of silver, touched daringly with black. The top of her corsage was caught together by an immense square-cut emerald, set in small blue diamonds. Mrs. Selwyn was evidently not beyond being pleased at Astro's compliment; but her look suggested an unsatisfied desire.

"They're expecting something wonderful," she hinted.

Astro frowned. "My dear lady—" he began.

She nodded and shook her fan lightly. "Oh, yes, I know. I shan't ask you, of course. I promised. But at the same time if something— anything—should happen, you know, it would be perfectly lovely; and it would make the thing go, wouldn't it? Oh, and there's an Italian countess here, whose hand I'm simply dying to have you read!"

Valeska, smiling amusedly at the hostess' prattle, was about to turn away, when Mrs. Selwyn caught her hand eagerly.

"It was so good of you to come on so unconventional an invitation! We must make you at home. You shall have positively all the men you want; I have armies of 'em to-night. And perhaps," here Mrs. Selwyn became almost coquettish, "you may have more influence with Astro than poor I. Do talk to him! Countess Trixola will be so disappointed if you don't succeed!"

A fresh group of guests here interrupted her, and she turned to welcome them.

Valeska took Astro's arm again, and he led her to a corner of the room where they could view the assembly.

"I see what's coming," he began hurriedly. "I'll be at my wits' end to avoid doing parlor tricks to amuse this crowd, in spite of what Mrs. Selwyn promised. I shan't have much time to attend to you, my dear. But, really, you did beautifully. Nobody would ever imagine that you were born in an East Side tenement. Why, I think you can tell the would-be's and the bounders as quickly as I can, already. It's all worth seeing, and I want you to use your eyes. Watch every little thing as if it were all of the utmost importance and you were to use every bit of information you acquired. But don't on any account lose sight of me, if you can help it, and watch for my signals. Be ready for anything. It's the accidents of life by which we profit, and there is no predicting accidents. Give me the 'up and down' sign if you discover anything particularly interesting. Well, I'll see that you are introduced. I'm going to be mobbed."

"Here's the countess, I'll wager," Valeska said.

A tall, ashen-haired, limp and insipid youth was bearing toward them, escorting a vivacious green-eyed brunette, with a narrow alert face and eyes heavily shadowed. Nearer, those dark eyes seemed a bit hard and glassy; but they were quick. She was considerably made up; but her rouge had been applied cleverly.

Astro had time only to remark out of one corner of his mouth, "Look at her right hand!" and then the countess was fairly bubbling over him.

Valeska gave the hand a glance. It hung, white-gloved, lightly by her side, the first and second fingers tentatively outstretched, the third and fourth curled toward the palm, the thumb projecting.

"You are Astro the Palmist, aren't you?" the woman asked gaily, tipping her head to one side and peeping over her fan. "Mrs. Selwyn said I mustn't bother you; but I *do* hope something extraordinary is going to happen! We're expecting something quite miraculous, after all we've heard about your occult powers!"

"My dear Countess," said Astro a bit cynically, "even saints must have holidays. I'm afraid I am out of miracles to-night."

"But at least you can tell me something about myself before you go?" she insisted.

Astro smiled quizzically. "Surely not in public?"

The pale youth burst into a guffaw.

The countess shook her finger at him airily. "Why, my life is an open book!" she protested.

"Be careful that it's open at a blank page, then."

The pale youth again bellowed and was struck on the shoulder by the countess' fan.

"Oh, I hope I'm naughty enough to be nice," she said demurely.

"Madam," said Astro, with a queer expression, "I doubt if you could be either naughtier or nicer."

"Now, what d'you mean by that?" she cried. "Why, positively I don't know whether it's the best kind of compliment or the worst kind of insult!"

"I leave it to your conscience—and your vanity," said Astro calmly.

She laughed it off and turned to Valeska. "Does he say such enigmatical things to you, too?" she asked.

"Oh, he doesn't dare," said Valeska. "He knows that I'd take them all as compliments."

The group was now joined by others eagerly pressing about them to listen to the dialogue. The fame of the Master of Mysteries had grown wonderfully with the reports of his recent exploits and his reputation as a palmist was almost eclipsed by his fame as a seer and solver of inexplicable problems. The distinction of his appearance and the charm of his manner gave him a personal influence as well, and on this first appearance in society in the role of guest he was, as Mrs. Selwyn had said, an immense success.

Valeska's reception was as flattering. She had passed the ordeal of introduction cleverly. The men flocked to this pretty blond girl with the blue eyes, as to a popular heiress. Unused as she had been to fashionable life, her native wit and confidence, combined with Astro's own support, carried her through with colors flying. The affair soon resolved itself into a rivalry among the women for Astro's whimsical notice, and among the men for Valeska's flashing sallies.

To all hinted requests for character readings, the palmist offered polished and affable excuses. He seemed as much at home in this smart company as in his own picturesque studio. Women gathered about him, fascinated by his romantic personality, and rather pleasantly afraid of his powers as an occultist. Mrs. Selwyn persistently showed him off; but, anxious as she evidently was to make her reception a success, kept to the letter of her promise, and did not ask him to perform any tricks for the company.

The salon filled. The talk became gayer. Astro had no time now to speak confidentially to Valeska; but from time to time he sent her a look, a motion of head or hand, which directed her attention to one or another of the party. The quick-witted girl watched him everywhere he went, and followed his cues on the instant. Long practice had made it easy for her to communicate with him thus; but this was the first public test of her facility. She played their game with a new zest, her bright eyes and high color alone betraying her excitement.

At last supper was announced, and as the company paired off and began to leave for the great dining-room, Astro succeeded in eluding his worshipers and captured Valeska for a few hasty words.

"There's something in the air," he said under his breath. "Can't you feel it? I don't know just what it is, but there is something sinister impending. Don't laugh. This is not mere professional jargon. You know I'm sensitive to this sort of thing. I never felt it more strongly."

"I have felt so too, but I thought it was a mere fancy."

"Cultivate those fancies, my dear; they're the inchoate beginnings of intuitions. Nothing comes by chance. There's a reason for every whim we have, and you must learn to trace it."

"I don't like that green-eyed woman. I wonder if she is really a countess?"

He smiled in amiable derision. "Are you?"

Valeska's eyes dilated. "Who is she?"

"That I don't know. I've tried her with all sorts of traps; but she is too clever."

"Oh, she's bad, I know that; but she fascinates me."

"She came alone, in a hired cab, Mrs. Selwyn told me. They got acquainted through mutual friends in Florence. That's all I know, except—"

He had lowered his voice to a whisper, and was leaning toward Valeska to continue, when the woman in question appeared at the door of the dining-room, cast a sharp glance up the hall, and espied them.

"Aren't you coming in, Monsieur?" She smiled bewitchingly.

"In a moment, Countess."

"I want to know if you're magician enough to tell me what Mrs. Selwyn's punch is made of. It's the most mysterious thing I ever saw."

"If it's as mysterious as you are, my dear Countess, I'll have to admit I can't fathom it."

She dropped a courtesy, tipping her head roguishly to one side, and withdrew. Astro's eyes followed her. He was much amused.

"Looking for some one," Valeska suggested laconically.

Astro nodded. "Oh—did you see that chap with a pompadour and a curled blond mustache?"

"Yes. One eye was bigger than the other,—the right one."

"Watchmaker. Comes from screwing up his right eye in his lens and using it so much. Or possibly— by Jove! a diamond cutter! Queer, isn't it?"

"Decidedly. But they seem to be sure enough of their position here. They're as well received as the other guests."

"There's something awry. I wish I could get it. It's all there in my brain, but I haven't time to think it out, now and here. Never mind. Only wait, and be ready! Come, we'll go in. I'll talk to you later. Here's Mrs. Selwyn now."

Their hostess sailed past on a young man's arm, and, holding out a hand, carried Astro in with her to a seat at the end of the room. Valeska was promptly annexed by Selwyn, a short, puffy little man with mutton-chop whiskers and a fat stomach. He had the air of not being at all at home in his own house. Nobody could seem so harmless and timid as this chubby round-faced host. He might have been an awkward servant, in his endeavors to efface himself. Seeing Valeska left alone, he offered his arm in a sudden access of courage. She was not like the others, and apparently he was not afraid of her.

"Infernal humbug, all this sort of thing!" he grumbled.

"Why, what do you mean?" she answered, a little surprised.

"Having this fool palm-reader here, and all that. Bosh!"

Valeska could scarcely repress a titter. But Selwyn was evidently quite serious about it. Seeing that he had no idea who she was, she humored him.

"It is nonsense, of course," she said gravely; "but I think that Mr. Astro is quite modest about it, don't you?"

"Oh, he's all right,—he has to make a living, I suppose,—but the women make such fools of themselves about him. I might as well give a monkey dinner and be done with it!"

Muttering thus, in an inconsequent, petulant way, he led her into the dining-room, where she was immediately surrounded by men who offered her chairs, plates and refreshments. Selwyn, more than ever disgruntled, retired to the wall, against which he flattened himself, and gloomily regarded the crowd. Valeska, besieged as she was, threw him a smile and a remark occasionally, pitying his discomfort and his timidity.

Meanwhile, her eyes were busy in the room. Once she caught sight of the green-eyed countess talking with the pompadoured man, and she noted a certain surreptitious haste in their encounter. Was it furtive, suggestive, or did she merely fancy it? From them, her glance wandered to the group of which Astro, with Mrs. Selwyn, was the center. The countess joined it, sparkling, vivid, keen. A heavy soggy dowager in black silk, with an astoundingly low-cut dress, plump round neck and innumerable curls in her gray hair, was absorbed in Astro's conversation. A debutante, as fresh as a lily, ingenuous, eager, bright-eyed with curiosity, leaned over his shoulder, holding out her hand for him to read. Valeska heard little gushes of laughter whenever he spoke. She had never before seen him in such a company, and it amazed her to see how he dominated it, how his magnetism radiated and drew one after another into his circle of influence.

So it went on for half an hour, until the party began gradually to leave the room, drifting out in twos and threes, all more or less stimulated by the supper and the champagne to an increasing good fellowship. All, that is, excepting poor Selwyn, who seemed to shrink smaller and smaller. He hardly spoke to anybody, except to apologize to some woman for stepping on her train, or to call a waiter to pass cigars or wine. His round eyes winked continually, and his lips moved as if he were talking to himself. When Valeska looked at him with an arch smile, he beamed like a child upon her for an instant, and the next all the light went out of his face.

She met Astro in the hall, passed him, and caught a sign. It was the "up and down" signal this time, denoting whom she was to observe,—a glance up to the ceiling, and down to his feet. His hand touched his hair with a little flourish. The man with the pompadour! She had it as plain as words could tell it.

She drifted away and sought the man with the pompadour. He was nowhere to be seen. The party was now humming with talk and laughter, and the double salon was crowded. The orchestra swept into a Hungarian rhapsody which seemed to waft a wave of abandon into the room. The men who followed her flirted persistently; it was all she could do now to parry their jests and at the same time keep track of what was going on about her. Astro was standing near the center of the room in a group of wonderfully dressed and dangerously pretty women, each perfect, finished, poised, yet animated and merry. Their little aigrets nodded as they talked and laughed. Selwyn, his hands in his pockets, moodily effaced himself behind the piano in the corner. Every time he saw Valeska, he beamed.

As she stood near the great hall doors, new men were continually brought up to her to be introduced, each with a new compliment or a flippant remark or a joke, each showing a friendly rivalry with the others. Valeska enjoyed it all excitedly. She could hear a nervous pitch in her voice, as she shot her frivolous retorts; but the newness of it all stimulated her. For the moment she lost sight of the pompadoured man. She was gazing across the room to where Mrs. Selwyn stood, when—

Suddenly the lights in the two electric chandeliers went out. The room for an instant seemed as black as night. Several women cried out in fright, and then a light chorus of laughter rippled round the room hysterically. In the instantaneous cessation of talk, a shuffling of feet was for a moment all that was heard.

The picture in Valeska's view remained for a moment in her eyes as clear as a photograph against the darkness; Mrs. Selwyn, merry, jubilant, talking to a fat old man; behind her the dowager, the debutante, the pale youth, all talking together; and a little aloof, the countess, with a strange expression, and her fan pressed to her lips, looking in Valeska's direction—as if she were giving a sign! Then the picture faded; a babble of voices arose. Mounting over them all, rising to a scream, came Mrs. Selwyn's excited cry:

"Oh! Stop! Help! I'm robbed!"

Valeska at the same moment felt a man rush swiftly past her, and there was a sharp twitch at the side of her waist.

Then another voice came like a bark, swift, stern, mandatory, abrupt, angry. "Light up, there, immediately! The switch is at the side of the door. Don't any one dare to move till we have a light!"

At last, after a frightened half-minute, full of whispers and shocked expletives, the lights sprang up again, and showed a room full of shocked agonized faces. Every one looked at his neighbor with startled eyes. A louder buzzing of talk arose, only to cease suddenly again as Selwyn, pushing his way into the middle of the room, took command of the situation, like a general.

"Nobody shall move a step here until we find out what's the matter! My wife has lost her brooch, the Selwyn emerald. You all know it. I insist that every one keep his place until it is found!"

What had awakened to the little man? At the crisis he had changed from a bashful boy into a wilful assertive man, dominating the room with his resolution. The talk swept excitedly about the place now; each questioned his neighbor, or stared spellbound. Meanwhile Selwyn had walked to the folding doors and rolled them shut with a bang. Then, red-faced, with a fierce scowl, he strode back to his wife:

"Now, who was near you, Betty?"

"Oh, I don't remember exactly," she answered hysterically. "All I know is that when the lights went out some one came up to me and I felt a snatch at my corsage—see where the lace is torn! Somebody stole it. It's preposterous!"

"Search everybody!" somebody called out.

"No, no!" cried others.

"See if it hasn't dropped on the floor!"

For a moment every one spoke at once, and the confusion was maddening. Then suddenly clapping his hands for silence, and speaking as sharply as an officer commanding his soldiers, Astro's voice rose over the tumult. He had sprung upon a chair, and his fine head appeared above the throng.

"Mr. Selwyn, let me find the brooch! There will be no trouble, no unpleasantness for any one. Let every one keep his place until I've finished, and I'll promise to discover the emerald."

A clapping of hands all over the room responded to his speech. Instantly the mood of the company relaxed from its nervous strain of uncomfortable embarrassment and suspicion to an amused interest.

But Selwyn shook his head savagely. "No, indeed! None of your parlor tricks, thank you! I will send for the police immediately. Meanwhile, every one in this room is my prisoner. Those who object must necessarily be regarded with suspicion."

"Oh, George!" Mrs. Selwyn pleaded, "do let Astro try it! I'm sure he'll be able to do it. He's so clever, and he has done such marvelous things!"

"Yes, yes! Let him try it!" came from every one.

Selwyn hesitated, looking half-contemptuously at the palmist. "How do you propose to find it?" he asked finally.

Astro put his hand to his head and drew his brows together. "I already feel an influence disturbing this gathering," he said. "I shall be drawn inevitably toward the person who committed the theft, as if by a magnet. Or at least I shall be drawn to the emerald," he added.

"Bosh!" Selwyn exclaimed. "That's all poppycock! What I want is a good detective and a police officer or two to search every man and woman in the room."

At this there came an indignant chorus of protest; the guests stirred uneasily.

"Mr. Selwyn, do you believe in the X-ray?" Astro asked.

The little man grunted, "Yes, I do; but this is no time for a lecture!"

"One moment, please, however! Nobody knows in just what part of the spectrum the X-rays lie, except that they are beyond the ultraviolet. They are visible only with the fluoroscope. Nobody knows just where the so-called actinic rays lie, either. They are invisible also; but they react upon a plate sensitized with nitrate of silver. Where are the N-rays, which emanate from the human body? Nobody knows; but I tell you, Mr. Selwyn, that they are registered in the gray matter of my brain. I am sensitive to them, as no one else has been, consciously, for centuries. And it is that sensitiveness that I propose to utilize. No thought can exist without modifying the molecular structure of the brain cells in the thinker. That change acts upon the ether, and is transmitted in vibratory form. Is it not possible that those ether waves can react upon the molecules in *my* brain and set up a corresponding change to that made by the original thought? Mr. Selwyn, I'll prove it!"

Astro's voice had risen to a strident tone, compelling and incisive. Every one looked at him eagerly. There was a hush. Then a volley of exclamations broke out like a storm, and Selwyn's last objections were swept away.

At last the host, overborne, and himself piqued with curiosity, gave a gesture of acquiescence. Astro stepped down from his chair, with a fixed look in his eyes, and gazed eagerly to right and left. He paused one moment, standing with his hand to his forehead, his little finger pointed upward. Valeska saw and read the signal: "Follow the person I point out!"

He then walked up to the dowager with whom he had been at supper-time. "Will you kindly take off your left glove, Mrs. Postlethwaite?" he asked.

"The idea!" she ejaculated. "Why, what do you mean? Do you dare insinuate that I took Mrs. Selwyn's brooch?"

Her eyes were wide open as a doll's, and her anger was ludicrous to the company who watched her. For the first time since the lights went out, there was a hearty laugh all over the salon.

"Silence!" Astro commanded harshly. He turned to the gaping matron. "Madam, you must do what I ask, and do it quickly, so as not to delay the recovery! If you are innocent you have nothing to fear. If you hesitate, we can't, of course, be blamed for suspecting you."

She stared at him indignantly, muttering to herself, but tugged at her glove nevertheless. He took her bared hand and inspected the palm. Then he took her right hand, gloved as it was, and inspected that.

He left her as suddenly as he had come, however, with no comment whatever, and darted to the young debutante who had also been of his group in the dining-room.

"Quick, Miss Preston!" he said. "Take off your left-hand glove!"

Miss Preston was young enough and thoughtless enough to take the situation lightly, and obeyed him with a smile. He gave her palm a glance, then turned her hand and looked at the back. Then he left her for the pale wan youth. His glove, too, came off his left hand, and his right gloved hand was examined. The man with the pompadour came next, and the same pantomime was enacted. Astro's eyes stayed for a second or two on the man's left coat sleeve; then he passed on.

So he went from one to another, now to a woman, now to a man, until he came to the Countess Trixola. Her eyes had never left him; her hand remained on her breast, as if to hide the beating of her heart. Her eyes were hard and cold but the pupils were dilated. Her upper lip quivered a little.

"Will you kindly remove your glove, Countess? No, your right, if you please. Yes, thank you. Now your left hand, just as it is. Thank you."

He turned swiftly to the next beside her, but before he had examined the hand he had bitten the knuckle of his forefinger, as if in abstraction.

This Valeska noticed, and from that moment regardless of what he was doing, she kept her eyes on the countess. The woman had turned to a companion, and was evidently voicing some sarcastic comment on Astro's methods. As she spoke, she moved insensibly away, and backed toward another group nearer the wall by the windows. The company had now begun to move a little, and her progress was so clever as to be unnoticeable to one who did not specially follow her movements. She passed a few feet nearer the window.

Astro went on steadily, from one person to another, examining palms. In another moment, however, he had stopped dramatically, put both his hands to his forehead, staggered and dropped to the floor. A woman screamed. Two or three men ran up to support him in their arms. A physician elbowed his way through the crowd.

At that moment, while every one was staring at the group that surrounded the Master of Mysteries, Valeska saw the countess move quickly toward the window. There, for a moment, she stood facing the assembly, looking sharply about, her hands behind her back. An instant more, and she had left again and joined the man with the pompadour. She drew him aside and spoke to him. He nodded, looked behind him, and moved away.

Some one was calling for water. A man laid his hand to the door to open it, when Selwyn's voice barked out again. He assumed command again.

"No one leaves this room! This man is not seriously hurt; he hasn't even fainted. It's all a trick to cover his failure. We'll end this nonsense right now, and have in the police!"

Valeska hurried up to the group, pressed in between the bystanders, and knelt beside Astro. "Stand back, please!" she exclaimed. "I know how to attend to him. He has gone into a psychic trance, that's all. The strain was too much for him. He'll be all right in a moment, and will go on with his search." She took his hand, and, unseen by the company, pressed it four times. Astro's eyes opened. He sat up; rose to his feet slowly; trembled; looked about; took a step forward, tentatively. Valeska still held his hand.

"Silence, everybody!" she called out, and held up her right hand with a warning gesture.

Every eye turned to the two, and every tongue was silent, as Astro moved, at first uncertainly, and then with increasing confidence, directly across the room. He stopped before a tall cloisonné vase standing in front of the window, looked at it for a moment stupidly, then lifted it and turned it upside down. Out dropped the Selwyn emerald.

A hurricane of applause burst from the company, hands clapped, and men cried "Bravo!" Mrs. Selwyn rushed forward.

Astro handed her the brooch. She gave one look at it, clasped it to her breast, and then took the palmist's hands with both hers.

"Wonderful!" she exclaimed. "It's perfectly marvel—"

Then her eyes caught a whimsical look in his, saw his cryptic smile, and her face changed. First it grew suddenly blank, then a delighted expression flooded it.

"Why—why, it was a trick! wasn't it? How clever! Oh, it was worth the fright, really! It was the best thing I've ever seen done! I never suspected it for a minute! Oh, thank you so much! I knew you wouldn't be mean enough to refuse altogether. I knew you'd be nice and amuse us some way. But my! you are a wizard, aren't you?"

Selwyn strode forward. "Do you mean to say you cooked this whole thing up, sir? Well, you certainly fooled me, by Jove! Ha, ha! You got us all going, didn't you? Think of that! But you pretty nearly caused a big scandal, I tell you!" He turned to a neighbor and began to talk vociferously about it.

The crowd swarmed about Astro now, each eager to congratulate and to praise. Every one gesticulated, almost screamed at one another, laughing, asking questions without number. Dozens of people, their conventional reserve broken down by the strain of the last few minutes, shook Astro by the hand.

The countess came up, also, to flatter him on his success.

"But you didn't tell me my character after all," she complained playfully.

The glance Astro gave her was cold and sharp. "Madam," he replied, "your character will hardly stand another such test. If you will call at my studio to-morrow, I will give you some advice. When do you expect to return to Italy?"

She gave him a long stare, grew a little pale, but shrugged her shoulders. "Are you in a hurry for me to return, Monsieur?"

"I predict a great misfortune for you, if you remain here for more than a week."

"Thank you very much for your advice, then. You are too kind! Yes, I think I shall be bored to death in this town. I shall go. *Au revoir*, Monsieur! I should like to know you better. We would make fine playmates!"

She smiled, and, as if reluctantly, removed her eyes, and left him.

Mrs. Selwyn drew him aside with eager eyes. "Of course, I know I'm a pig," she said, "but really, Astro, couldn't you get that diamond off the countess' hand and hide it somewhere? It would be such fun, you know! Do be nice and do just one more! They'll talk about my reception forever if you do!"

Astro laughed. "That's one thing I'm afraid I can't do. You see, the countess isn't quite so innocent as you are, Mrs. Selwyn."

"It was a pretty big chance you were taking, seems to me," said Valeska, as Astro drove her home. "Of course she grabbed the stone so tightly that it printed the marks of the facets on her white glove; that part of it was easy. But how could you be sure? You didn't look at half the people's hands."

"You noticed the way she held her fingers when I spoke to you, didn't you? I didn't have time, then, to explain. But I knew by that that she was or had been a pickpocket. The professional dip works with his first two fingers, and almost always carries his hand with them extended, and the other two fingers curled up out of the way."

"But why did you look at her left glove, instead of the right, as you did all the others?"

"I had noticed at supper time that she was left-handed. When I took my long chance, my dear, was when I trusted to you to find out what she did with the brooch. I confess that when I dropped on the floor and waited for your signal, I was rather anxious. It was up to you, then, to make me or break me. But I was sure I could trust you, and you did beautifully."

Valeska herself had been more anxious during that few minutes than she confessed. There was, however, one more thing to be straightened out in her mind.

"What I don't understand is who put out the lights," she remarked. "I forgot to tell you that I was standing near the wall where the electric switch was, and immediately the lights went out some one brushed past me roughly, and something twitched at my waist. I wonder who it was?"

Astro cast a look down at her side and smiled. "Oh, that settles something that bothered me," he said musingly. "Clever little buckles on your corsage, my dear! I wondered how that pompadoured chap happened to have his left coat sleeve cut in such a queer way, but I was too busy to think it out. I wish now I had given both of them over to the police. I expect he's a diamond cutter, fast enough! Mrs. Selwyn is lucky that six or seven different persons won't be wearing pieces of her emerald next year, Valeska."

THE ASSASSINS' CLUB

"Every time I see a gargoyle," said Astro, "I feel a thrill of secret kinship. It's as if I were the only one who understood its mystery. If I were romantic, I would say that in a previous incarnation I had lived in the dark ages. What do you think about gargoyles, Valeska?"

Astro looked up from a book of Viollet-le-Duc's architectural drawings and glanced across to the pretty blond head. His assistant, busy with her card catalogue, where she kept memoranda of the Seer's famous cases, made a delightful picture against the dull crimson hangings of the wall.

She came over to him and looked down across his shoulder at the pictures of the grotesque stone monsters. "Why," she said, "I've seen those horrible cynical old ones on Notre Dame in Paris, that gaze down on the city roofs. I've always wondered why they placed them on beautiful churches."

"It's a deep question," said Astro, his eyes still on the engraving. "But to my mind they symbolize the ancient cult of Wonder. In the Middle Ages men really wondered; they didn't anticipate flying-machines years before they were invented, as we moderns do. They took nothing for granted. Everything in life was a miracle."

Valeska dropped quietly into a seat to listen. Astro had many moods. Sometimes he was the dreamy occult Seer, cryptic, mysterious; again he was the alert man of affairs, keen, logical, worldly. She had seen him, too, in society, affable, bland, jocose. But in this introspective, whimsical, analytic mood she got nearest him and learned something of the true import of his life.

He went on, his eyes half-closed, his red silken robe enveloping him like a shroud, the diamond in his turban glittering as he moved his head. His olive-skinned, picturesque face with its dark eyes was serene and quiet now. A little blue-tailed lizard, one of Astro's many exotic fancies, frisked across the table. He caught it and held it as he talked.

"In the thirteenth century clergy and laity alike believed that the forces of good and evil were almost equally balanced. They worshiped the Almighty, but propitiated Satan as well; so these grotesque beasts leered down from the cornices of the house of God, and watched the holy offices of priests. The devil had his own litany, his own science. They were forbidden practices, but they flourished then among the most intellectual people as they flourish now among the most ignorant. Magic was then a science, now it is a fake. Still, a man's chief desire is to get something for nothing,— to find a short cut to wisdom. The gargoyle is replaced by the dollar mark. So be it! One must earn one's living. *Selah!* I have spoken!"

He looked up with a smile and a boyish twinkle in his eyes. Then his businesslike, cynical self returned. He jumped up, tall and eager, a picturesque oriental figure informed with the stirring life of the West.

"Valeska, I've been reading about the Devil-worshipers of Paris,—the black mass, infant sacrifices, and all that. That's an anachronistic cult. I'd like to know if there really is any genuine survival of the worship of Evil?"

Valeska shuddered. "Oh, that would be horrible!"

"But interesting." He clasped his hands behind him and gazed up at the silver-starred ceiling. "I don't mean degeneracy or insanity, but a man that does evil for the love of it, as they did in the old days. Think, for instance, of the lost art of torture—the science of human suffering—"

"Oh, don't! I hate to have you talk like that!" Valeska put a hand on his arm.

"Very well, I won't." He snapped his fingers as if to rid himself of the thought, and walked into the reception-room adjoining the great studio.

Valeska went back to her work. For some minutes she arranged her cards in their tin box; then, hearing voices outside, she looked up and listened. Then she walked softly across the heavy rugs and, touching a button in the mahogany wainscoting, passed through a secret door.

Scarcely had she disappeared when Astro returned, ushering in a young woman stylishly dressed in brown. When she put aside her veil her face shone out like a portrait, vivid, instinct with grace and a delicate, rare, high-bred beauty, full of character and force. Astro showed her a seat under the electric lamp.

"I thought you would help me if any one could," she was saying, in continuation of her conversation in the reception-room. "If it were anything less vague, I'd speak to mother about it; but it's too strange and elusive. I'm sure he has not been drinking; I would notice that in other ways. And yet he is different, he is not himself. It frightens me."

"Have you spoken to him about it?" Astro asked.

"Yes; but he won't say anything. He evades it, and says he's all right. But I don't dare to marry him till I know what it is that has changed him. I know it seems disloyal to suspect him, but how can I help it?"

"What is Mr. Cameron's business?"

"He's a naval lieutenant, in the construction department at the Brooklyn navy yard. And that is another reason why I'm worried. He has charge of work that is important and secret. If this change—whatever it is—should affect his work, he'd be disgraced; he might even be dishonorably discharged."

"When have you noticed this peculiarity of his? At any particular time?"

"Usually on Sundays, when he almost always comes to call; but sometimes in the middle of the week. At times he talks queerly, almost as if in his sleep, of colors and queer landscapes that have nothing to do with what we are discussing. Sometimes he doesn't even finish his sentences and goes off into a sort of daze for a minute; and then he'll ask my pardon and go on as if nothing had happened."

"And when shall you see him next?"

"He will probably come Saturday afternoon. Usually he stays to dinner, but of late he has been having engagements that prevent."

"All right," said the Seer; "I'll see what I can do. Knowing that he is at your house, I shall be able to orient myself and thereby be more receptive to his astral influence. I shall then be able to ascertain the cause of any psychic disturbance."

The young woman, rising to go, looked at him plaintively. "Oh, I hope I haven't done wrong in telling you about it! But I do love him so I can't bear to see him so changed!"

"My dear Miss Mannering," said Astro kindly, "you need have no fear, I assure you. Your business shall be kept absolutely confidential. With the exception of my assistant, no one shall ever know that you came here."

"Your assistant?" She looked at him doubtfully.

"Miss Wynne."

She seemed surprised. "A lady?" she asked; then, timidly, "Might I see her?"

"Certainly." Astro touched a bell.

In a moment Valeska appeared between the velvet portières, and waited there, her piquant sensitive face questioning his wish, her golden hair brightly illuminated from behind.

Miss Mannering walked to her impulsively and took her hand. "Might I speak to you for a moment?" she asked.

Valeska, giving Astro a glance, led the visitor into the reception-room.

"I had no idea that Astro had a lady assistant," she said. "I feel much better about having told him, now."

Valeska smiled at her and held the hand in both hers. "Oh, I only do some of his routine work," she said; "but he often discusses his important cases with me. I'm sure that he can help you. He is wonderful. I never knew him to fail."

"Miss Wynne," said the visitor, "no one but a woman can understand how distressed I am. I'm sure I can trust you; I can read that in your face. I am always sure of my intuitions. And, now that I have seen you, I'm going to tell you something that I didn't quite dare to tell Astro. I know my fiancé is in some trouble. But what I'm afraid of is too dreadful; it terrifies me! Here! look at this! It dropped out of Mr. Cameron's pocket the last time he called, and I found it after he had gone."

She handed an envelope to Valeska, who looked at it carefully and drew out a single sheet of paper. On this was written in green ink:

"Be at the Assassins' Saturday at seven. Haskell's turn."

"What can that mean?" Miss Mannering whispered. "I didn't dare to show it for fear of getting Bob into trouble in some way. That word 'Assassins'—Oh, it's awful!"

"May I take this letter?" Valeska asked.

"No, I daren't leave it. Mr. Cameron may miss it and ask for it. But you may tell Astro, if you think best."

Valeska gave another glance at the letter and handed it back. "My dear Miss Mannering, don't worry about it," she said, pressing her hand. "It may not be so bad as you fear. Whatever it is, Astro will find it out, you may be sure."

When the visitor had departed, Valeska walked into the studio with the news. Astro listened in silence till she had finished; then he smiled, nodded, and took up his water-pipe lazily.

"The solution of this thing is so simple that I'm surprised it hasn't occurred to you, my dear. But that's because of your lack of experience and the fact that you haven't read so much as I have. But, all the same, there may be something deeper in it than appears now. At any rate the girl is to be helped, and the lieutenant as well; and that we shall do."

"But what about the 'Assassins'?" Valeska inquired anxiously.

"Oh, that's the whole thing, of course. But I think I'll let you study that out yourself. It will be good practice for your reasoning powers. First, let's see if your powers of observation have improved. Tell me all about the letter." He blew out a series of smoke rings and regarded her quizzically.

"Well," Valeska puckered her brows, "it was written on buff-laid linen paper of about ninety pounds weight—very heavy stock, anyway—in an envelope of the same, postmarked Madison Square station, April nineteenth, four P. M. The handwriting was that of a stout middle-aged man, who had just had some serious illness,—a foreigner, hard-working, unscrupulous, dishonest, with no artistic sensibility."

"Bravo! Is that all?"

"No, the stationery came from Perkins & Shaw's. I saw the stamping under the flap."

"Very good. Unfortunately we can't ask there about the Assassins. But perhaps we'll find my ideal criminal after all. The easiest plan will be to follow Cameron to-morrow night. Meanwhile, you had better do some thinking yourself."

Valeska sat down and gazed long into the great open fire, her brows frowning, her hands working mechanically, absorbed in thought. Astro took a small folding chess-board and gracefully amused himself with an intricate problem in the logistics of the game. When at last he had queened his white pawn according to his theory, he looked over at his assistant and smiled to see her seriousness. In that look something seemed to pass from him to her.

"Oh!" she cried, jumping up, "does it begin with an H?"

"More properly with a C," he replied

She shook her head and went at the problem again, and kept at it until it was time to close the studio.

The next afternoon Astro and Valeska waited for two hours across Seventy-eighth Street from Miss Mannering's house before they saw the lieutenant emerge. They had already a good description of him, and had no trouble in recognizing the tall good-looking fellow who at half past six o'clock walked briskly up the street, ran down the stairs to the subway, and took a seat in a down-town local train. Astro and Valeska separated and took seats on the opposite side of the car, watching their man guardedly. At Twenty-third Street he got out, went up to the sidewalk, and walked eastward.

Beyond Fourth Avenue was a row of three-story, old-fashioned, brick houses, back from the street. The lieutenant entered the small iron gate to one of the yards and, taking a key from his pocket, went in the front door of a house. It slammed behind him.

"The headquarters of the Assassins," said Astro calmly, his hands in his overcoat pockets, studying the windows.

"And what next?" asked Valeska.

"We'll wait a while. Come into this next doorway."

On the side of the doorway they now entered was a sign, "Furnished Rooms." It was now after seven o'clock, and had begun to snow. Valeska stood inside the vestibule protected from the weather; Astro waited just outside watching the doorway of number 109. The Twenty-third Street cars clanged noisily by, the din of the traffic muffled by the carpet of snow. The open mouth of the subway sucked in an unsteady stream of wayfarers.

Suddenly Valeska put her hand on Astro's arm. "Does it begin with 'C-o'?" she asked.

He smiled. "No, 'C-a,'" he answered.

"Oh, dear, I thought I had it! But don't tell me! I'm sure I'll work it out, though. But it makes me anxious. Anything might happen on a night like this!"

"Yes, even an assassination."

"You don't fear that, really?" She looked at him in alarm.

"But I do,—assassination of a sort. What else could the letter mean?"

She had not time to answer before the door of the next house opened, and a man buttoned up in a fur-trimmed overcoat came out. He stopped a moment to raise an umbrella, and they could see that he was a stout pasty-faced German of some fifty years, with a curling yellow mustache. He wore spectacles and seemed to be near-sighted.

"There's the man who wrote the letter! Follow him, Valeska! Find out who he is and all that's possible! We must follow every lead."

Valeska was off on the instant, running down the steps and walking swiftly up Twenty-third Street.

Astro lighted a cigar, turned up his collar and waited another half-hour in the doorway. Nobody having entered or left number 109 by that time, he rang the bell of number 111. A Swedish maid came to the door.

"I'd like to see what rooms you have," said Astro.

"The only one is on the third floor rear," she replied, and showed him up two flights of unlighted stairs, steep and narrow, to a small square room, meagerly furnished. Walking to the window, Astro saw that, level with the floor, was a tin-covered roof over an extension in the rear. It stretched along the whole width of the four houses in the row. On this he might easily stand and look into the adjoining windows. Saying that he would move in later, Astro paid the girl for a week's rent in advance, and left the house and walked home.

Valeska next morning came full of news. "The German kept right along Twenty-third Street toward Broadway," she said, "and it occurred to me that I might get him to make the first advances, and get acquainted without being suspected. So I passed him, and very gracefully slipped on the snow and dropped my purse. Then I began looking about on the sidewalk for the money that might have dropped out. My German friend came along and offered to help me. It took some time, and the long and short of it was that we had quite a conversation, and I convinced him that I was respectable. He walked along with me and asked me where I was going. I said that I had intended going to the Hippodrome with a friend; but that I had been detained, and it was so late I thought I'd go home. He proposed having something to eat, and of course I refused. I had to be urged and urged; but the more I refused, the more anxious he was to have me come. Finally, I reluctantly assented to his invitation, and we went to the Café Riche.

"Well, you ought to have seen that German eat,—I mean you ought to have *heard* him eat! I couldn't eat anything myself; but sipped the wine he ordered and coyly led him on, chattering away about myself ingenuously. I had an engagement with Richard Mansfield and a three years' contract at one hundred dollars a week when he died, and was awfully anxious to get another chance. All the money I had was tied up in one of the trust companies, and so on. He kept on eating, taking the biggest mouthfuls I ever saw and leaving half of it on his mustache. Oh, I put in some hard work, I assure you!

"Then he began asking me questions, and wanted to know if I would like to earn some money on the side. Would I? I jumped at it!—five thousand actor folk out of a job this season, you know, and all that. He said I reminded him of his dead daughter—you know I'm always reminding people of somebody— and he thought he could trust me. I cast down my eyes and let him go on.

"He said there was a man he knew who had stolen some confidential papers, and he wanted to get them away from him without publicity. He needed a good clever woman to help him out on the job. I brightened up considerably. He asked me to go home with him so that he could give me a photograph to identify my victim. I said I would; although I confess I was getting nervous, not being quite sure what he was up to. He had begun paying me compliments, and when a German begins to get sentimental—well, you know!

"I took the subway with him, and we went up to One Hundred and Twenty-sixth Street. There was a big apartment hotel there, called the Dahlia,—one of those marble-halled affairs that look as if they were built of a dozen different kinds of fancy soap, with a red carpet and awfully funny oil-paintings and negro hall boys sitting in Renaissance armchairs. I refused to go up-stairs. Well, after a while he came down the elevator and handed me this photograph. What do you think?"

She handed Astro a cabinet photograph. He lifted his fine brows when he looked at it.

"Lieutenant Cameron!"

Valeska nodded. "I'm to scrape up an acquaintance with him, get his confidence, and then report to Herr Beimer for final instructions. I wonder what poor little Miss Mannering would say?"

She took off her sables, her saucy fur toque, and touched up her hair at the great carved mirror at one end of the studio.

Astro sat regarding the portrait in his hand. He looked up to ask, "Did you find out what his business was?"

She whirled round to him. "Oh, I forgot! He's the agent for a big German firm, connected with the Krupps' steel plant. They control the rights to a new magazine pistol. I was awfully interested in machinery, you know. It bored me to death; but I listened half an hour to his description of a new ammunition hoist for battleships."

Astro was suddenly electrified with energy. "Ah!" he exclaimed. "You didn't remember that the Krupps stand in with the German government and have the biggest subsidies and contracts in the world? He wants you to make up to a construction officer in the United States navy, does he? He needs a clever woman! I should say he did! Was Herr Beimer sober?"

"Perfectly, as far as I could see, except for his sentimentality. Of course he was a bit effusive, you know."

"Yes, I see. It wasn't his night. It was Haskell's night, whoever Haskell is! But I think we'll have to hurry. This looks more serious than I thought at first. I shall sleep at number 111 East Twenty-third Street to-night. And meanwhile I have a nice job of forgery for you, Valeska. I wish you'd practice copying this writing till you can write a short note that will pass for Lieutenant Cameron's handwriting."

He took a letter from a drawer. The envelope was addressed to Miss Violet Mannering. Valeska took it and read it over carefully. It was a single sheet, torn from a double page, and read partly as follows:

"I believe that just as everything seems somehow
different at night—when we can see farther than by day;
for can we not see the stars?—when our emotions

GELETT BURGESS

seem freer—so there are two worlds in which it is possible to exist. One is the dreary every-day place of business and duty and pain; the other is free from care or suffering. Don't we enter that occult world at night through our dreams, where there is no such thing as conscience? There are no consequences there! No doubt it's a dangerous place, because it is abnormal; but its exploration is fascinating. Why ignore the fact that it exists as a refuge from the worries of matter-of-fact existence—"

Valeska read it thoughtfully. Her eyes looked through the paper as if into a mist beyond. "No wonder poor Miss Mannering is worried!" she said to herself. She looked at Astro, as if to ask a question. He was busy with a planimeter, calculating the area of a queer irregular polygon drawn on a sheet of parchment. Seeing his tense look, she turned to her study of the manuscript.

As soon as it was dark, Astro opened the window of his room on Twenty-third Street, and walked along the crackling tin roof till he came to the first window of the house occupied by the Assassins. Looking in, he saw a small, bare, hall bedroom, furnished with a cot, a wash-stand, and one chair. The next two windows were lighted. He approached them carefully. Three men were seated at a library table strewn with magazines. All were smoking comfortably. One, Astro recognized as the lieutenant, another as Herr Beimer. The third was a yellow-faced man with red hair, high cheek-bones, and dark eyes deeply set into his skull. In front of him was a plate filled with what looked like caviar sandwiches, cut small and thin.

Herr Beimer said something, at which the others laughed loudly. Then with a flourish, as if drinking their health, Lieutenant Cameron took one of the sandwiches and ate it almost with an air of bravado. Beimer looked at his watch. The lean yellow-faced man walked out of the room. The lieutenant took up an illustrated paper and began to read.

Astro tiptoed carefully back to his room, put on his overcoat, and went down-stairs, walked over to the drug store, and at the telephone booth rang up Valeska.

"Have you written the letter?" he asked.

"Not yet," was the answer.

"Well, you must do it immediately as well as you can. Bring it to number in and ask for Mr. Silverman."

He then went back to his room. Another stealthy glance through the windows of the club showed the two still at the table. Cameron was busy with a pencil and a sheet of paper, explaining something to the German. The yellow-faced man watched them over his book. The lieutenant was evidently talking with a little difficulty; every little while he stopped, and began again with an effort. One leg was twitching at the knee-joint. He supported his head heavily on his hand.

Going back to his room, Astro took a bottle of ammonia from his overcoat pocket and placed it on the sink. Next he poured a white powder from a paper and dissolved it in a tumbler of water, stirring it with a spoon. This done, he took the wash-bowl from the stand and put it on the table beside the bed. Then he sat down to wait for Valeska.

In half an hour she appeared, breathing hard, her cheeks flushed with her haste.

"Here it is," she said, as soon as the maid had left. "It's the best I could do." She handed it over. It read:

> "Please allow the bearer to come in and see me
> on important business at any time he may present
> this. Robert Cameron."

"Good!" said Astro. "Now you must wait here and listen at the window till you hear my whistle. Then come right along the roof to me and be ready for anything."

He started to open the door when she put a hand on his arm. "Does it begin with 'C-a-n'?" she asked breathlessly.

He nodded. "How did you get it?"

"From the lieutenant's letter."

"Of course. Well, it may have begun with 'D-a-n' by this time."

"D-a-n-g-e-r?"

"Perhaps. Be ready!" And he was down-stairs.

At the door of the Assassins' Club, a white-haired negro answered the bell.

Astro presented the letter. "I wish to see Lieutenant Cameron immediately!" he said.

"Ah, don't perzactly know, sah," said the darky. "Mah o'ders is not to leave nobody come in yah. Ah expect Ah'd better say no, sah."

Astro brushed past him and had set his foot on the stair, when a fat face looked down over the balusters. The portly form of Herr Beimer followed it.

"Vat's de madder?" he inquired, as he started down.

Without further parley Astro ran up the stair, and, before there was any time for resistance from the astonished German, grasped him by the knees, and pulling his feet from under him, sent him madly sliding down the stairs. Herr Beimer, swearing a polysyllabic oath, stumbled awkwardly to his feet and set off upstairs again after his attacker. But by this time Astro was at the top of the second flight. He dashed into the square room in the rear where he had seen the group of men. It was empty! Beside it, however, was a small hall bedroom, and here, in his shirt-sleeves, lying in a stupor on the cot, lay Lieutenant Cameron.

Astro sprang to the door and locked it just as the excited German thumped ponderously on the panels. Next he threw up the window and whistled. Then taking the lieutenant in his arms, he succeeded in carrying him to the windowsill. Valeska was already on the roof outside, waiting for him.

"Take his feet!" said Astro under his breath, and so together they managed to get the lieutenant out on the roof and to the window of the chamber in number 111. By this time the man had begun to revive and to protest in word and action against his removal. They paid no heed to him, however, and bundled him into the room and on the bed. Then Astro shook him energetically.

"Wake up, man!" he cried. "Wake up now! You can, if you try! Here! Smell this!" He reached for the ammonia and held it under the lethargic man's nostrils.

The lieutenant turned away his head, coughed, blinked, and partially rose on one arm. "Who are you?" he said, gazing at them in surprise.

"Friends of Miss Mannering's," said Astro.

The lieutenant shook his head, and stared. "What's the matter?" he brought out laboriously.

"I got you away from Beimer—afraid of trouble—want to help you." Astro spoke very distinctly, as if to a deaf man.

The lieutenant felt for his coat, found himself without one, seemed puzzled, and dropped back again limply.

"The—draw—" his voice ended in a mumble.

"Yes, the drawer! What drawer?" Astro asked eagerly.

"Find draw—" The lieutenant seemed to drop asleep.

"I wonder what he means? There's something on his mind. No doubt he has hidden something." Astro looked keenly at Valeska under drawn brows.

"Can't you revive him again?" she asked.

"No use trying the ammonia yet. It seems to have too great a reaction and sends him into a deeper sleep. We'll have to wait till he comes to himself for a moment naturally. You know what it is now, don't you?"

She nodded. "And I found it out, curiously, only from the dictionary. I looked up the word 'assassin,' and found that it came from *Hashashin* or hashish eater. Then I looked up about the Old Man of the Mountain who used to drug his followers with bhang till they would commit any crime, and that led me, of course, to *Cannabis Indica*, or Indian hemp, and I found out all about the effects of hashish."

"Yes, I thought these amateur assassins were innocent enough,—only a club to experiment with hashish; for with a moderate dose the sensations are wonderful, and well worth trying,—but there's more in this than that. What is Beimer up to? That's what I want to know."

"Is he really unconscious now?" Valeska asked, watching the prostrate form of the lieutenant as he lay flushed and breathing, but otherwise inert.

"Not really. He may be dimly aware that we are here; but his will is gone. He won't speak until he rises to the level of volition again. It's a sort of double consciousness, a rhythmic process of alternate sinking into apathy, where he sees visions, and rising into full consciousness when he can talk for a moment. I wish I knew what dose he had. The intervals are about three minutes. I tried hashish when I was in college; but I took such an overdose the last time that I have dreaded to use it again."

The lieutenant now began to mutter, as if talking in his sleep. "I'm tottering on the tops of tall pendulums. . . . The world is full of spiralated mucilages . . . lovely color. . . . In a tunnel now, twisting, turning, violet, green, orange . . . floating . . . floating like a spirit . . . tops of tropic trees . . ."

Suddenly he gasped and sat up, staring hard at them. "What did I say? What was it? Quick! before I go off again! I was saying something."

"Find the drawer," Astro suggested, leaning to him.

"Draw—draw— What was it? Drawings!" he exclaimed. "Beimer wants the drawings! For God's sake, help me! I'm losing it again! Drawings! What is it about drawings?"

"Where did you put them."

"Drawings! Yes. Un-der the—mat—" His eyes closed.

Astro tried again. "Under the mat in the little room?"

The lieutenant stared stupidly. "I forget. Mat— that meant something. I can't get it. Wait till I come up again. . . . All snaky now, like live wires . . . pink and green. . . Ah!" The rest was inaudible.

The moment he had again succumbed to the effects of the drug Astro sprang to the window. He paused there to say sharply:

"Beimer is trying to get some of the lieutenant's navy drawings, that's evident, and has given Cameron a big dose of hashish to keep him quiet till the papers can be found. I think Cameron must have suspected it, and has hidden the blue-prints or whatever they are. I'm going to go through that bedroom and see if they're under the mat. You wait here. He is likely to be unconscious for two or three minutes more now, and I'll just have time." With that, he had leaped out on the roof and was off.

The lieutenant still muttered in a whisper so low that Valeska could make out nothing. She went to the window just as Astro reappeared.

"No mat, nothing but a carpet. Beimer must have got away with them. You'll have to get after him, Valeska, while I pull the lieutenant through. If I know anything about hashish, he's had a terrific dose, and is going to have the worst case of nausea he ever had in his life. I took a look at those hashish sandwiches,—they were fairly loaded with the stuff. His first voyage wasn't a circumstance to the seasickness he'll have in about half an hour. You get right out to Beimer's place and see what you can do with him!"

As Valeska threw on her furs the lieutenant was beginning to rouse again. As she slipped out of the door and ran down-stairs, he sat up on the bed, his eyes glassy, his fists clenched. The effort he was making to gain possession of his mental faculties was evident in his writhing mouth and wild staring eyes. "What was it?" he demanded.

"It's all right," said Astro. "Beimer has the drawings; but we'll get them for you." He turned for the glass of water on the table.

The lieutenant clutched his arm in a fierce grip. "Gods!" he cried. "Help me! The papers were secret plans for fire control. Man, it's ruin for me!"

"You must drink this, first of all," Astro replied, holding the glass to the man's lips. "It's an emetic. We must get this hemp out of your stomach before you can recover."

It was too late. The lieutenant dropped back, now as rigid as a marble statue, only his wild eyes moving. He spoke painfully through his clenched teeth.

"Oh, God!" he murmured. "Take it away! I can't drink it! I'm going through hell!" His brow was furrowed with tense lines as he fought with the deathly nausea that was working in him.

Astro put down the glass and waited. It was evident that nothing could help now, and the drug which had thoroughly impregnated the man's system must work off its own effects.

"It works so—so fast . . . All black now . . . Oh, God! . . . I'm afraid! . . . Afraid . . ." He began to moan.

"You're all right; there's no danger. You're just a little sick, that's all."

"I'm dying! It's no use . . . Tell Violet . . . I'm dead . . . Don't you see, man? I'm dead already . . . The world is full of spiralated mucilages—that's the inner secret of Death—spiral . . . I'm whirling through space . . . Dead!"

Astro smiled. It was, he knew, a common symptom of an overdose of *Cannabis Indica*. There was, as he said, no danger. He waited for the crisis, attending to his patient like a trained nurse. For a while the moaning continued; then Cameron began to curse wildly, like a man with the delirium tremens. Then of a sudden he sat up in bed and the convulsion came. His outraged stomach revolted at the burden it had to bear. During this Astro waited on him kindly, and when the active stage of nausea had passed he laid the lieutenant back on the bed and waited till he sank into a natural sleep. Then he took a small book from his pocket and began to read.

For half an hour he read the little volume of the *Morte d'Arthur*; for another half-hour he sat in a brown study, his eyes fixed on the pattern in the worn carpet. There was a zigzag figure in it which resembled the letter M.

The lieutenant moaned in his sleep, and felt under his bed mechanically with one hand. Astro's eyes followed him.

Then, with his face suddenly illumined, he rose quietly, threw up the window, and passed out on the roof. In less than five minutes he returned with a smile on his lips. He took up the book again and began reading.

It was after midnight when Valeska returned in great disappointment. She took off her coat and looked sadly at the lieutenant, who was now sleeping peacefully.

"It was no use," she said. "Herr Beimer wasn't in, and no one knew when to expect him. I waited as long as I dared; for I hated to come back unsuccessful."

"It was too bad I was so stupid as to send you away out there," said Astro quietly. "I should have taken time to think it over, first.

It came to me an hour after you had left. Here are the blue-prints, safe and untouched."

"Oh!" she exclaimed joyously. "Did he tell you where they were after I left?"

"No, before you left. Didn't you hear him?"

"Under the mat? But I thought you looked and found none there."

"My dear," said Astro, with a whimsical expression on his face, "you should learn to concentrate, to focus your subconscious mind upon itself. The psychic state of receptivity—"

"Oh, bother!" Valeska exclaimed. "Where *were* they, if they weren't under the mat?"

"Under the mattress," he answered.

The lieutenant sat up, now fully recovered, and looked at the two. Astro handed him the blue-prints. He grasped them exultantly. For a while he lay weakly looking at them, saying nothing. Astro put on his overcoat and helped Valeska into her wraps. Just before he opened the door, he turned and said:

"I don't think I need give you any advice, Lieutenant. Go to sleep now, and you'll be all right in the morning. If you have gone through what I did the last time I was an 'assassin,' there is no danger of your ever trying it again. I think that Miss Mannering needn't know about this, certainly I shall not tell her."

"What *does* she know? Did she send you to help me?" the lieutenant asked anxiously.

"She asked my advice, that's all. Unfortunately she saw the name 'Assassins'; but I think you can explain that easily enough, if you don't care to confess the truth."

"How *can* I explain it?" Cameron said thoughtfully.

"Why, tell her that the club met to kill—time," said Astro, "and that at that you are a tolerably successful assassin."

THE LUCK OF THE MERRINGTONS

Late one afternoon in February, a policeman, standing on the corner of Thompson and West Fourth Streets, gazing abstractedly across Washington Square, felt something brushing against his trousers. Looking down, he saw a little child of scarcely three years holding something up to him.

"See! See!" she was saying.

The officer opened his eyes in amazement. In one little fist the baby held a fire opal as large as a robin's egg; in the other was a shriveled black hand.

He grabbed them from the child and questioned her; but her prattle was meaningless. Taking her carefully in charge, he hurried to the station-house and reported the incident to the sergeant at the desk.

Next morning the city papers "played up" the account of the astonishing affair, with a picture of the child, the officer, and the two extraordinary objects with which the baby was found. That afternoon the mother of the little girl came to claim her daughter but was unable to explain the incident. She lived in a tenement on a level with the elevated railroad, on West Third Street, and had missed little Elsa at five o'clock. Inquiries in the neighborhood elicited the fact that Elsa had been seen about four o'clock in the afternoon in the basement tenement of a house across the street, a place used as a cheap laundry. The laundress had noticed the child playing at the wood-pile; but had been too busy to send her home. When she had finished hanging her clothes in the back yard and had returned to the wash-room, the child had gone. The baby had been found by the policeman at a quarter to five. Where she had been in the interim it seemed impossible to discover.

The case was turned over to the detective force, and was eventually taken up by Lieutenant McGraw. He worked at it a day without success, and then, recalling the many services done him by his friend, Astro the Seer, he determined to seek his help. McGraw's earlier experience with the palmist had been at the time of the Macdougal Street dynamite outrages and the Hunchakist murder, mysteries that Astro had solved privately. Assuming the credit of this, McGraw had been promoted and had paid his debt of gratitude to Astro in several ways. He had often secured information for the palmist that no one outside the police force would have been able to obtain. The mutual relation having proved profitable, McGraw did not hesitate to apply to his gifted friend in this case, which had become prominent in the papers.

Astro, free at the time, and rather bored with his ordinary routine of chiromancy and astrologic work, readily undertook the commission. He questioned McGraw on the details of the affair, and dismissed him with a promise to go about the matter immediately.

"It will probably be easy and interesting," he remarked to his assistant, Valeska, who had been present at the interview with McGraw. "It is these cases which are apparently so extraordinary that are most easily solved. Given any remarkable variation in the aspect of a crime, and you know immediately where to begin. This will be only play, I fancy. We'll go right down and look the ground over and see the lay of the land. Of course the important thing is to trace the child's route from the basement laundry, in the middle of the block, to the corner."

"Why, the obvious course would be along two sides of the rectangle,—along West Third Street and up Thompson Street to the Square, wouldn't it?" said Valeska.

"Undoubtedly. And yet, if little Elsa went that way, along the sidewalk, it seems impossible that some one wouldn't have noticed her and remarked the surprising playthings she was holding in her hands."

"She might have only just picked them up, near the corner."

"Very true. We must carefully go over all possible routes and then determine the probabilities. But let's go down and look at the exhibits in the case. I confess I'm curious as to that hand."

Astro's green limousine was entered, and he and his assistant drove immediately to the detective bureau on Allen Street. McGraw welcomed them, and taking them into an inner room, displayed the relics.

The opal was nearly an inch long, a perfect ellipse, shot with colored fires. As it was shifted in the light the play of color was mysterious and surprising. It seemed now suffused with blood; now it glowed with pale green; then a blinding ray of pure yellow shot forth. It seemed to hold impossible distances and atomic cosmic worlds within its shell. It winked like a living thing; it glared and blushed; it was at once baleful and beautiful.

The hand, however, seemed never to have had to do with life or motion. Dried like a mummy, strung with tendons like a turkey's claw, wrinkled, stiff, all color dulled into the hue of earth, it was a horrid thing. Valeska turned away from it in disgust; but Astro still peered at it, examining it, inch by inch, from the long coarse nails to the dissevered wrist.

"Well?" said McGraw.

"A negro's hand," Astro replied. "It has been buried. A man of at least forty. Cut from the arm during life. And yet—" He did not finish the sentence; instead, he said abruptly, "Take us to the laundry."

At the basement McGraw left them, Astro preferring to be alone with Valeska during his investigation. The two entered the cellar after McGraw had introduced them to the proprietor. She pointed out where the child had last been seen, and then went on with her work.

The front of the basement was used for one of the small wood and coal depots common in the poorer districts of New York. Partitioned off with rough boarding was a little chamber where the Italian who sold fuel lived. Behind this was the laundry where two girls, bare-armed, were washing. Two of them lifted a basket of wet linen and went out into the yard with it while Astro and Valeska watched.

In each of these rooms Astro spent considerable time, letting his eyes rove in every direction, searching every foot of the walls, ceiling, and floor. After each survey he gave a nod to Valeska and passed on. The laundry itself occupied more time. He watched the girls at work and their going and coming attentively. Then he went back to the wood-pile and knelt down on the rough floor, crawling here and there, watching, smelling, fingering everything in the vicinity. The track he pursued led back to the little room where the Italian slept. There he spent more time, searching carefully. When he rose and dusted his clothes, he handed Valeska a bent safety-pin.

"Keep that safe," he said. "I think that little Elsa has been playing under the Italian's cot bed."

Hardly had he spoken the words than the stairway was darkened, and a man bearing a loaded basket came down the steps. He put down his load and, seeing strangers, demanded roughly:

"What you doin' here, what?"

"Oh, looking about," said Astro coolly. "I've lost something, and I came here to find it."

The Italian stared. "What you a-lost, what?"

Astro kept his eyes on him. "I've lost a large opal," he said calmly.

The man began to tremble. "Opal! Wha's that?"

"I'll show you." Astro walked into the man's little room and lifted the mattress. Between it and the canvas cover of the cot appeared a small box. On its cover was printed, "Heintz & Co., El Paso, Texas."

"I no gotta eet, I no gotta eet! Sure! De littla babee she stole eet away." The man watched Astro's face apprehensively.

"Where did you get it, anyway," asked the Seer.

"My uncle in Italy, he give it to me," the man protested.

They talked for ten minutes; but the man persisted in this story. Giving up the attempt, Astro was about to return to the laundry, when his eyes fell on the basket the man had been carrying. He stopped and took off a few pieces of kindling, then, after a quick look at the Italian, took something from under the pieces of wood. It was a human skull.

"Perhaps you'll tell me where you got this?" Astro demanded sternly.

The Italian's face brightened. "Oh, a littla boy, he geeve eet to me for ten cent," he said simply.

Astro turned to Valeska with a baffled expression. "In heaven's name what kind of place are we in, where babies play with dead hands and human skulls, to say nothing of giant opals hid in cots?"

"Yes, yes, a littla boy, on Washington Square, sure!" the man repeated.

Astro placed the skull on a shelf and regarded it attentively. For some moments he said nothing; then, shrugging his shoulders, he passed into the laundry. Valeska followed him.

"The man is lying, of course," she said. "But what a barefaced falsehood! Would anything be more improbable?"

"He's lying, it's true," said Astro; "but it may not be all false, nevertheless. We'll have to wait till we finish our examination." And with that, he walked out into the back yard.

The place was half-filled with clothes, drying. The ground was completely bricked over and surrounded by a high fence. On the farther side of this and beyond the yards of the abutters appeared the rear of the houses on South Washington Square, or West Fourth Street, rising four stories high. On the right and left were other yards. Astro began at the right-hand side of the house and examined the fence foot by foot all round the three sides, till he had come back to the house again at the left-hand side. Then he looked up at the windows of the house opposite. A second examination of the fence opposite the laundry took more time. Meanwhile, Valeska followed him and did her best to interpret his movements.

"Well," he said, as he returned to the laundry door, "what have you discovered?"

She spoke eagerly. "Why, there's a hole broken in the fence on the north side, and it seems to me it's big enough for a baby to crawl through. Besides, as the clothes are hung now, it is well hidden, and little Elsa might easily have got through unnoticed."

"Did you notice her footprints beyond, in the earth of the other back yard?"

"No." Valeska was apologetic.

"Well, they are there. Nothing else?"

"Why, no."

"Look again!"

Valeska went carefully along the fence and finally stopped at some vertical scars half-way up the north wall. "What do they mean?" she asked.

"That's the false half of our Italian friend's tale," said Astro. "Never mind them for the present. Now we'll call at the house opposite."

They left the basement and walked round the block, climbed over some excavations in the street, and rang the bell. A buxom, jolly young woman opened the door. Astro asked for rooms to let, preferably in the rear.

"We ain't got but one now," she replied. "That's on the third floor up, and it ain't vacant yet though. You can look at it. Was you married?"

Astro laughed and, ignoring the question, followed the woman up three flights of stairs, followed by his assistant. The landlady threw open a door, and the three entered. Astro gave a quick look around the apartment.

It was in confusion, cluttered with clothing and newspapers, old boots and cooking utensils.

"And he ain't paid me for t'ree weeks yet, neither!" she added. "I give him the bounce two days ago. He come home drunk in my house! I don't keep no lodgers like that!"

"What day was it he came home drunk?" Astro asked.

"Only Thursday. He nearly fell out the window, he was so soused. He had a black eye, too."

"What time was it?"

"Oh, about four o'clock. Look at them rags, now! What d'ye think of that! The pig dog!" She picked up a long dirty strip of cloth on the floor. "Bah!" she cried. "It smells like a graveyard, don't it?"

Astro took the rag and examined it carefully. It smelled strongly of creosote. He laid it on a table, and with a secret sign called Valeska's attention to it. Then he walked to the window, threw up the sash, and looked down.

"It would be a bad drop, wouldn't it?" he said.

The landlady laughed. "I only wish he had fell out!"

"Who lives on the floor below?"

"Oh, a Spaniard and his wife; but they ain't been here for two weeks now. They pay all the same."

"And on the second story?"

"Oh, I live there myself with my dog."

Suddenly Astro exclaimed aloud, "The deuce! I've dropped my hat. How stupid! I'll have to go down in the yard and get it."

"Never mind; I'll go down," said the woman.

Astro, however, insisted, and before she had a chance to offer again he was running down-stairs. A sign to Valeska told her to occupy the woman's attention for a while; and this Valeska did successfully. Finally she and the landlady walked down-stairs, the girl talking with animation, the woman giggling and laughing and showing a set of big good-natured dimples. They waited in the hall for Astro to return.

He shook hands with the landlady cordially. "I'll let you know about the room, if I want it," he said. "But I like the landlady better than I do the room. What are they doing on West Fourth Street?" he continued. "Digging for a new drain?"

"Yes," she said. "All the time they are digging up, somewheres. It makes me tired, this New York! I wish they'd get it finished."

"When will your lodger come back to pack up his things?"

"Oh, I wish I knew my own self. He's a crook, I think, that man; he's got a bad eye. All the time he brings such funny things home. Bags and things, and sometimes watches."

As soon as Astro and Valeska were alone he smiled and said, "Well, it's as easy as I said it was going to be, isn't it? All we have to do now is to search the hospitals."

Valeska thought it over. Then she spoke slowly. "I suppose that rag was wrapped round the hand, wasn't it?"

Astro nodded.

"The man came home drunk—he sat down by the open window and dropped the hand?"

Astro nodded again.

"The baby crawled through the hole in the fence with the opal, I see that. She found the hand in the yard under the window, where it had been dropped. Then, somehow, she passed through the kitchen and came out on West Fourth Street, here, and walked to the corner, where she met the policeman. That's all plain enough. But where did this man get the hand, and where did the Italian get the opal?"

"Take the last question first. You recall the up-and-down marks on the fence?"

Valeska assented. "Oh! The Italian climbed over there?"

"He must have. He must have seen the box drop. He climbed the fence and grabbed the box and didn't notice the hand. Then the baby came along, before this man, who was evidently a pickpocket, awoke from his stupor. You see, he came home with the bag he had snatched—"

"Oh! That was that leather bag with the handle cut?"

"Of course. He went to the window and sat down, unwrapped the dead hand, and dropped it, or placed it in his lap. Then he looked at the opal, and, beginning to drowse, dropped both into the yard. When I went down there I saw footprints, undoubtedly the Italian's, in the earth."

"But that leads nowhere, after all?" said Valeska. "How in the world should an immense opal and a hand be in the bag that was snatched?"

"That's what we have to find out," said Astro.

"And why should the Italian have a human skull in his basket?"

Astro laughed. "That's where the true half of his lie comes in. Undoubtedly a boy did sell it to him. It wasn't till I spoke to the woman about the excavations in the street here that I recalled that Washington Square was in old days the 'Potters Field.' Many graves have been found here, and no doubt the gamins of the neighborhood have watched every shovel and got the skulls there. The Italian fancied it,—thought perhaps he could sell it to some doctor,—and so brought it home. In fact, I think we have eliminated him from the affair altogether. Of course, he'd never dare say he stole the opal."

"And what about searching the hospitals?"

"For the original owner of the bag, of course. The thief came home with a bruised eye. That means he had a fight; but, as he brought off his booty, he must have punished his man pretty badly. Consequently he is now probably in a hospital. We have to look for a man from El Paso; for there is where he got the opal, or at least the box in which it was kept. Well, we'll leave that till to-morrow. I believe I have an engagement for five o'clock, haven't I?"

"Yes. A Miss Merrington."

"Who is she?"

"I haven't found out anything about her. You'll have to hurry."

They got into the limousine and drove rapidly to the studio, where Miss Merrington was waiting. While Valeska busied herself with the file of daily papers she had as yet had no chance to look over, Astro interviewed his visitor in the great studio.

Miss Merrington was a tall willowy brunette, with plenty of humor in her face, well dressed, and evidently fairly well-to-do. She had come, it seemed, on a peculiar errand. In brief, as she told it to Astro, it was this:

Major Merrington, her grandfather, had been a United States Army officer on a special errand in Mexico at the time of Maximilian's regime. He had had the good fortune to be of service to the emperor, who had been duly grateful. In return for his services, the emperor, at their last meeting shortly before the end of Maximilian's tragic career, had rather jocosely offered him his choice of two gifts. The first was a large box of the famous cigarettes of Chiapas, made by an old woman who had been famous for her tobacco for years and had recently died. This cutting off of the already limited supply had increased the value of the genuine cigarettes enormously. Mexicans held them in almost superstitious esteem. They were said to have all kinds of esoteric virtues and to bring extraordinary happiness. The first cigarette, when smoked, was as mild as Virginia's tobacco. The second was always as strong as a black cigar and produced a sort of half-trance, like opium.

The alternative gift was an old Aztec relic. Miss Merrington did not herself know its exact nature; but she did know that all sorts of good luck were attributed to its possession. It was this gift that the major had chosen. "The Luck of the Montezumas" it was called; but, as the "Luck of the Merringtons" its name seemed to be as inapt as it had been to the Aztec emperors. With it, whatever it was, and escorted by a trusted negro slave named Ptolemy, the major had journeyed half-way from Chihuahua to El Paso, when his party was attacked by brigands. Their last stand was made in an adobe ruin, where the major had been killed. What had become of the "Luck of the Merringtons" and what it really was, was what Miss Merrington had come, in a rather skeptical and playful humor, to ask of Astro the Seer.

She had got so far, when a muffled electric bell was faintly heard in the studio. Astro, who had listened attentively, excused himself to get a book of astrologic tables which he said it was necessary for him to consult before he could answer Miss Merrington's question. Around a corner of the book-shelf was a sort of alcove cupboard, hung with black curtains. He parted them, and a glass window was disclosed. Pressed against this was a newspaper showing the "Lost and Found" column. One was ringed about with a blue pencil. It read:

"Lost—A large opal, on Second Avenue, Thursday last, at two P. M. Finder will be paid a generous reward and no questions asked. Henry Merrington, Bellevue Hospital."

Astro dropped the velvet curtains, reached on the shelf for an immense volume bound in heavy leather with silver clasps. He took it to the table near where his visitor sat and threw it open. The pages were parchment, written with beautiful medieval letters, with illuminated initials and many zodiacal diagrams. For some time he turned the leaves thoughtfully; then stopped to ask:

"Do you know the exact date of your grandfather's birth?"

Miss Merrington, unfortunately, did not. He asked, then, for her birthday, which she gave to the hour. Astro turned to another diagram, and taking a pencil, made a few computations.

"H'm. Under the sign Libra, with Mars and Saturn in the ascendant—a daughter of the Ninth House—the moon. Wait a moment. Let me see your palm."

She drew off her glove, and, not a little mystified, but still smiling as at a child's game, showed her hand. Astro gave it a glance, turned it over, doubled the knuckle of the third finger. Then he sat down, nodding his head.

"It's too absurd," he said. "One can't often strike a fact so definitely as this appears. If I'm not mistaken, the 'Luck of the Merringtons' is here in New York. It's—let's see," he looked at his diagram and figures again— "forty-seven, that's right. Violet, indigo, blue, green,—that's fourth,—yellow, orange, red,—that's seven. Green and red— Why, it must be an opal; that's the only stone that's both green and red. It's a fire opal, probably a Mexican gem, not the Austrian milky-blue stone. Curious, isn't it?"

"Yes," she drawled, "if it's true."

"Well, if you'll wait a moment, I may be able to find just where it is."

"Oh, I'll wait a long time to get back the family luck, bad or good," she said.

Astro shut his eyes and remained silent for a time. Then he shuddered, put his hand to his head, and said slowly, "I get the name Allen. Allen Street, that's it. And I see a man in a blue coat guarding it. He has brass buttons—oh, yes, he's a policeman." He shuddered again, and appeared to come to himself. "What did I say?" he asked ingenuously.

Miss Merrington repeated his words.

"Oh, that must mean the detective bureau," said Astro.

"It's perfectly wonderful—at least, if it turns out so!" the woman exclaimed. "I can't wait to find out, though I don't see what I can do. I haven't lost any opal, and I can't pretend to. I only know the old story about the 'Luck of the Merringtons' as my father told it to me. You see, grandfather never told in his letter just what it was. No doubt he was afraid of being robbed of it. But there's one other question I'd like to ask you. I have an older brother who went to Mexico two months ago, and we have had only two letters from him. Can you tell me where he is now?"

"His name is Henry, isn't it?"

Miss Merrington stared. "Why—yes! How did you know?"

"It's my business to know such things," said Astro. "Your brother has had an accident but is not seriously hurt. You will hear from him in a very short time."

"An accident!" Miss Merrington's face paled. "That frightens me dreadfully! Do you know," she went on, "somehow, what happened to my grandfather is so suggestive! My brother went to Mexico on purpose to trace up the 'Luck of the Merringtons.' He had a foolish idea that he could find it. It has always been a family legend only, but we children took it seriously. Lucky or unlucky, we wanted it in our possession. Henry always said that if he ever had time and money for a vacation, he was going to Chihuahua to track down that heirloom, whatever it was. It was because I was so impatient to find out about it that I came to you. I thought you might give me some hint that would help him find it. I wasn't worried at his not writing, because I knew he might be away from the railroad; but I was impatient to have news. And I've heard such things of you, so I thought I'd come, for the fun of it. I never expected you could do anything so specific as this, though. Now I'm worried. Oh, I hope Henry's all right and safe! If he only comes back, I don't care if we don't get the 'Luck of the Merringtons,' though heaven knows we need it badly enough! Our luck couldn't possibly be worse than it is now, I think. I've been a companion for a rich woman for a year; but I can't stand it a day longer, and I'm going to be a stenographer."

"I predict a better fate for you than that," said Astro. "I think the family luck will return. You wait patiently for a few days and see if I'm not right."

Valeska came into the studio as soon as Miss Merrington had gone. "It seems to me you took a long chance," she said, as she sat down.

"My dear," said Astro, throwing himself on the red velvet couch and drawing up his narghile, "I took no chance at all. If this Henry Merrington who advertised is not her brother, the opal is, of course, not the 'Luck of the Merringtons'; but she will never know whether it is or not. If her brother has gone on a rough trip to Mexico, he'll scarcely escape without an accident of some kind, though it may be slight. Whatever he finds as a relic, he can't prove it is the true 'luck,'—can he?—and I'll have the benefit of the doubt. But we must look him up immediately and get his story. I confess I'm still at sea about that hand."

"Why didn't he let his sister know, if he was injured?"

"Probably didn't want to frighten her. Perhaps he was drunk. Now he's lost the 'luck,' he hopes to get it back before she finds out he is here, so as not to disappoint her. But come. I confess I can't wait. We can't get in after eight o'clock."

The two set out, therefore, without waiting for dinner, and after Astro had sent up a card marked "opal," a nurse brought word that her patient could be seen. He had been robbed and sand-bagged, as Astro had surmised. He had lain unconscious for several hours; but was now recuperating, and would need only another day in which to be quite well.

He was frankly curious as to his guests, and could hardly greet them before he had sent away the nurse and demanded their errand. In a few words Astro told him exactly what had happened to the famous opal, without confessing how it had been traced. In as mysterious a manner, he let Merrington know that as a Seer he was aware of the esoteric and magic properties of the stone and its tradition.

Merrington listened with immense interest, delighted to learn that the opal had been found, and that he could probably claim it without a reward. He then took up the story of his quest where his sister had left it.

"I founded my whole hope of finding the thing on what I had heard of Ptolemy, the negro. I knew he was brave and clever and faithful. I always put this murder with the story of the Sancy diamond, which I suppose you know. Baron Sancy, you remember, when told that the messenger who was carrying the celebrated gem had been killed, said, 'Never mind, the Sancy diamond is not lost!' He sent men to disinter the body of the messenger, and found the stone in the stomach of the corpse of his faithful retainer. That's something the way I reasoned it out. It was a wild-goose chase; but I succeeded marvelously. I discovered the place where the attack on my grandfather had been made; I found the very adobe ruin where he had made the last stand. Some of the old people there remembered the story,—how my grandfather had been shot first, and how Ptolemy, defending the wooden door, had his hand chopped off with an ax before the brigands could enter. But no one had heard of any precious stone or other valuable thing that would account for the legend, though everybody in Chihuahua knew the story of the 'cigarettes of Chiapas.'

"Well, it took a month to locate the grave; but, after disinterring several coffins, I found one larger than usual, decayed almost to paper. And when I opened it—which was easy, it was so rotten—there, in the skull, between the upper and lower jaw-bone, was a fire opal as big as the end of my thumb! It was the 'Luck of the Merringtons,' I was sure, if for no other reason because, from that time till it was snatched out of my hand on Second Avenue, things went gorgeously with me. One of my *mosos* put me on to an abandoned claim, an old gold-mine that had been lost for years. In a month I sold out my interests for thirty thousand dollars. Every one in the place became my friend. I found an old schoolmate who insisted on my going into partnership with him, and—on the train coming north, I met the nicest girl in the world!"

He sank back in his cot with a smile. "Now my luck's come back," he added, "I'm going to present the opal to my sister Helen and see what it'll do for her."

"But one thing I don't understand," said Astro. "Did you get nothing but this opal from the grave?"

Merrington did not notice the incongruity of the remark, apparently. "Oh, I forgot!" he exclaimed. "That was a funny thing, too! You know Ptolemy's hand had been buried with him. Something had mummified it, somehow, while the rest of the body was pretty far gone,—nothing, really, but bones and a few tendons. Well, I thought I'd take the dried hand as a relic of poor old Ptolemy. It was ghastly; but I didn't know but that would bring luck, too. But no doubt that was what queered me, after all. I wonder what became of it?"

"You'll find that at the detective bureau, too," said Astro. "If I were you, I'd give it decent and honorable burial."

"I will!" said Merrington. "And by to-morrow afternoon I'm going to appear and surprise my sister. I hope she hasn't worried about me."

"But I always thought opals were unlucky," said Valeska, as she left the hospital with the Master of Mysteries.

"My dear," he replied; "nothing is unlucky, but thinking makes it so; and nothing is lucky but—" He looked at her a bit sadly, adding: "Well, I'm afraid you'd hardly understand."

THE COUNT'S COMEDY

Engrossed in his own thoughts a young man waited in the great dim studio of Astro the Seer, nervously punching the magnificent Turkish rug with the ferrule of his cane. He was young, well groomed and smartly dressed, apparently well-bred. It was evident that he was more worried than impatient.

He looked up with a scowl as Astro, dressed in his red silk robe, wearing his turban with the moonstone clasp, leisurely entered the apartment. For a moment the young man gazed at the Seer as if to estimate the man's caliber and character. Astro said nothing; but, bowing gravely, took his seat on the big couch and lazily lighted his water-pipe, waiting for his visitor to speak.

"I have come to you," the young man said finally, "although I must confess I don't quite believe in occult powers, because I have an idea that you must know considerable about human nature. You certainly see plenty of it."

Astro bowed again, and a faint smile curled his lips.

"I have also heard you called the Master of Mysteries," the young man continued.

Again Astro bowed.

The young man rose and handed the palmist a card. It read, "Mr. John Wallington Shaw."

Astro looked at it and tossed it on the table.

"I suppose you know who I am?"

Astro again bowed.

"It's a part of your business, I suppose. You may have read in the papers also of my sister's engagement to Count D'Ampleri?"

The same sober gesture of assent from the palmist.

Shaw sat down again, shoved his hands into his pockets, crossed his legs, and leaned back. "Mr. Astro," he said, "I have come here on a queer errand. I suppose you see many strange things in your profession, and it seemed to me that your experience would enable you to give me some help. What I want you to do first is to believe something that's nearly incredible."

"My dear sir," said Astro, speaking at last, "nothing is incredible. From what I know of life, the more impossible it seems to be, the more probable it is. For that matter, one has only to read the papers. But seriously, if I can help you in any way, I shall be glad to do so."

Shaw now took a gold cigarette case from his pocket, selected a cigarette, knocked it against his fist, and struck a match. After the first long inhalation he remarked, "You'll promise, then, to believe the extraordinary story I tell you?"

"Mr. Shaw," Astro replied, "it's easy enough for me to perceive that you are a gentleman. I expect an equal amount of perception from you. At any rate, I hardly see why you should come here to tell me an untruth."

"But what I mean is, I'm afraid you'll think I'm—well, a bit crazy. It's simply too ridiculous. Why, I wouldn't believe it myself, hardly!"

"Let's have it. You have really excited my curiosity." Astro folded his arms and looked at Shaw with sharp eyes. "You certainly show no symptoms of derangement yet."

Shaw gave a nervous laugh. "Oh, it isn't I; it's my sister. That's why it is so hard to tell. I assume, of course, that this confession will be kept confidential. Not only that, but I expect you to help me out—for an ample consideration."

Astro bowed. "I have secrets enough in this head of mine to destroy a dozen of the first families of New York," he said a little dryly.

Shaw shrugged his shoulders. "Very well. I'll waste no more time. You'll see how useless it is to appeal to the police, or even to my lawyer. But first, have you heard of the robbery of Mrs. Landor's jewels?"

"Oh, yes. The thief, I believe, has never been discovered. It always seemed to me curious, too, that no reward for their return had ever been offered. But what have they to do with your sister?"

Shaw gazed up at the ceiling, then down at the floor. "Really, I'm almost ashamed to tell the story, it's so confoundedly absurd. We are Westerners, you know, of good, sound, and healthy stock. We're as sane as Shakespeare. No trace of brain storms or paranoia in our family! The thing hasn't gone far; but it will be talked about if I can't stop it; that is, if you can't. I don't know what to do. I'm up a tree. You've got to get hold of whoever's responsible for this thing, and tie them up, some way. It's a serious problem for us."

Astro put his fingers to his lips and yawned.

Shaw took the hint and proceeded abruptly: "Mrs. Landor's jewels are at my house, a whole teapotful of them!"

"Ah! You know the thief, then?"

"No, I don't; nor do I know what the deuce I'm to do with the loot! One thing you are to do is to return it."

"And be accused of the theft myself?"

"Oh, that won't need to follow. They have to be sent back somehow. I don't want my sister to be accused of kleptomania; the other thing is quite bad enough. The idea of a gorilla in a top hat and all that! It would make a pretty scandal if it was found out; I can fancy how people would talk. We have a great many friends, you know." He smiled cynically at the word.

"She is innocent, I presume, then?" said Astro. "But what about the gorilla?"

"There's no use in beating about the bush any longer," said Shaw. "Only, you see, I wanted to make sure of you before I trusted you with the secret. I'll go ahead with it, and if you call it a cock and bull story, I don't see that I can blame you. You see, it was this way: We were down at our country place at Lakeside,—a big, rambling old house with a veranda all round it and long French windows opening out on it. My sister's room has a little balcony; it's on the second floor. She had gone up-stairs to dress for dinner. I was in my own room, a little way down the hall, and my door was closed at the time. We had a lot of company down for the week-end; it was ten days ago."

"Who were there?"

"Oh, the count, of course, and his valet, and the Churches—you know, Simeon Church and his wife—the Raddelle girls, and two or three others. I'll give you a list later, if you like."

"All right, go ahead."

"It happened, as I say, just before dinner; about half past seven. It was quite dark. We don't light up much outside,—there was nothing going on at that time. Well, I heard her door open, and then she was pounding on mine, and she called out, 'John, John! Come here quick!' I opened the door, half-dressed as I was, and she was in a deuce of a funk. She grabbed me by the arm and pulled me down the hall and shut her door. Then she said, 'Oh! what shall I do?' I said, 'What's the matter, Ethel? Have you been robbed?' She was nearly fainting, and I thought she would drop before she could speak. But finally I got it out of her. And her story was a wonder, and that's a fact!"

Shaw, in his excitement, rose and gesticulated.

"She had sent her maid out of the room for something, and had her back to the French window and was stooping to pick up a comb, when she heard the sash open, and she looked around in a fright. There, standing right in front of her, was a big black gorilla, bowing to her."

"H'm!" Astro concealed his amusement.

"Wait! I made her tell me the story half a dozen times, and it was the same each time. The thing had on a silk hat, and a Peter Pan collar, a red necktie, and white kid gloves, and pearl gray spats buttoned around his knees."

Astro could control his mirth no longer, and his grave demeanor exploded in a gust of hilarity. Shaw, despite his anxiety, had to join the laugh.

"What do you think of that for a fairy tale? But that's not half. This baboon—"

"You said gorilla before."

"Well, gorilla, then; it doesn't matter in a nightmare like that. He held a china soup-plate in one hand, and in the other a black bag,—a cloth bag. By Jove! that much I can swear to myself! I've seen it. Well, the chimpanzee thing—"

"I thought it was a baboon."

"How the blazes do I know? I wasn't there, and if I had been I shouldn't have known the difference. It may have been a monkey or an anthropoid ape, for all I know. Anyway, it set the soup-plate down on the dressing-table, and tipped its hat and said, 'Miss Ethel Shaw, I believe?'"

"Ah!" said Astro. "Now we're getting warmer!"

"Warm! He's made it hot enough for poor Ethel, I can tell you! Then, without waiting for an answer,—Ethel was out of her wits by this time, though she half suspected a practical joke, too,—the orang-utan—"

"Or monkey," Astro interjected, smiling.

"Yes, or gibbon perhaps—held out the bag to her. It said, 'From your friends and well-wishers in the lunatic asylum.' Then it did a graceful two-step over to the window, recited 'x^2 plus $2xy$ plus y^2,' and vanished on to the balcony. My sister was so frightened that she dropped the bag, and—bing!—out dropped Mrs. Landor's pearls and brooches and rings and things all over the floor. Now I ask you what kind of a story is *that* to get all about town?" He stared at the Master of Mysteries gloomily.

"Well, it certainly would add to the gaiety of nations," Astro remarked quietly; "but it looks like a pretty slim case if your sister had to rely on it for a defense."

"We'd be laughed out of court," Shaw said.

"Did your sister give you any further description of the creature, anything that could identify the masquerader?"

"Why, she said he was a little knock-kneed, she thought; but that might have been on account of the spats." He grinned sadly, in spite of himself. "Oh, I forgot! By Jove! yes! His breath smelled of garlic, and he wore automobile goggles!"

This was too much for Astro. It was some time before he could take the thing seriously.

Shaw waited patiently until the palmist stopped laughing. "I knew you'd think I was a blanked fool," he said mournfully; "but it's no joke to the Shaw family, I assure you. Anybody would say Ethel was crazy. I did myself, the very first time she told me this yarn. I said, 'Ethel, you're foolish!' But there was the stuff to prove it! Then she began to cry. The worst of it is, the count is absolutely convinced that Ethel is mad.

"As soon as we had dressed and gone down to dinner, Ethel told the story to the whole crowd. Of course we consider D'Ampleri already as virtually a member of the family, and the others are old friends. Oh, their friendship will be tested, all right enough! The count looked shocked and changed the subject pointedly, as if the thing was suspicious. It was perfectly evident that he discredited my sister. It made me foam at the mouth; but what could I do? What can we do now? Ethel, of course, persisted in her story, and the count has grown cooler and cooler ever since. I'm afraid he'll talk. We can keep the others quiet, easily enough. They have skeletons of their own to hide. What do you make of it, anyhow? Is there any way out?"

Astro puffed at his water-pipe for a few moments in silence, as he thought. The smoke, rising in a blue swaying curve, writhed in a faint arabesque against the velvet hangings of the walls. Shaw had begun punching holes in the rug with his cane again. From the portieres leading to the reception-room, where Valeska, Astro's pretty assistant, sat, pretending to work, came a silvery chime of bells as the tall clock struck four. It had begun to grow a little dark. Astro pressed a switch and lighted an electric lamp depending from the ceiling. Instantly the walls glittered with points of light from the embroideries, the weapons, the golden carvings, and other decorations.

"What is your father worth?" the palmist asked.

Shaw seemed to awaken from a daze. "If you had asked me two weeks ago, I'd have said, roughly, four millions, or possibly five. But this recent deal in lead has bit him hard. His shrinkage is nearly seventy-five per cent., I suppose. He was almost ruined, in fact. But if you're in doubt as to your fee, why, that'll be all right. It's worth five thousand dollars to us to have the matter settled. We'd have to pay that in blackmail, I suppose. If you can think of any way to return the jewels and no questions asked and head off this insanity charge, the money's yours."

"Had any dowry been settled on Count D'Ampleri?"

Shaw blushed faintly. "Oh, I say!" he began.

"I'm aware that it's a Continental practice, that's all," Astro said suavely. "It is inevitable with an international marriage, isn't it?"

"Yes. I fought against it as hard as I could; but Ethel can make the governor do anything she likes. Besides, my mother was set on the match, you know, and she helped arrange all that. They do it through lawyers, you know. It isn't quite so crude as it sounds; but it's bad enough. Yes, we arranged to buy the title for Ethel, I suppose." He kept his eyes on the rug in some embarrassment. There was a trace of anger in his tone. It was evident that the affair did not please him in any way.

"Very well. I'll undertake the commission, delicate as it is," Astro said, rising. "I'd like to have the jewels delivered here sometime next week. You had best bring them yourself. I wish also you'd find out just when the Count D'Ampleri arrived in America, and by what boat. I suppose you can tell me the day and hour of your sister's birth?"

Shaw wheeled round on him. "Oh, come, now!" he protested. "I came to you because you know or ought to know most of the weaknesses of human nature; but if you think I take any stock in astrology or occultism—"

"What was the date, did you say?" Astro's voice was hard.

"October 14th, 1885; nine A. M., I believe." Shaw scowled.

"My dear Mr. Shaw," said Astro, "if you give me this commission, you must let me do it my own way. It won't matter to you, I should think, how I do it. You are, I presume, an agnostic. Very good, I am a fatalist. Go to a detective or a doctor, if you prefer modern science. I prefer the ancient lore."

"I came to you because you've done harder things than this," Shaw said to placate the independent Seer. "Go ahead with your cusps and nativities, if you like, only get us out of this fearful mess as safely and quickly as you can."

"I hope to see you on Monday," said Astro, bowing with dignity.

John Wellington Shaw left the room. As soon as he had departed, Valeska entered, laughing, the dimples showing in her cheeks and chin.

Astro's pose had gone. He threw off his robe and turban. "Did you hear the uncouth history?" he asked.

Valeska nodded. "Of all things! Can it be true?"

"Easily. Simple as milk. And at the same time one of the cleverest schemes I ever heard of. It's all straight; that is, all except the jewels. That we'll have to investigate."

"But I don't understand it at all," Valeska pouted.

"Have you happened to hear that Count D'Ampleri has been paying rather too marked attention, for an engaged man, to Miss Belle Miller, the lady whom the cruel wits of the Four Hundred have dubbed the 'Bay Mare'?"

"I knew she was in here one day for a reading."

"And was much interested in my prediction that she was to marry a titled foreigner. I heard the gossip at the Lorssons the day I went to that tea. I never forget items of that sort. They are more important than horoscopes."

"I think I have a glimmer of light now," said Valeska. "The Bay Mare is an heiress, isn't she?"

"Rather! Old man Miller owns half of Buffalo."

"And Shaw is on the verge of failure."

"And the count wants a good excuse to transfer his affections and his hopes of a permanent income. What better escape than to impute insanity to Miss Ethel Shaw? I say it's a merry scheme."

Valeska frowned. "It's horribly cruel!"

"Well, it's infamously Italian, if you like. Fancy one of the Borgias reappearing to grace the twentieth century! But you can't deny it is cleverly worked out. Insanity is one of the best reasons for not marrying, even for a fortune-hunting foreigner. Every one will pity him, instead of blaming him, and he'll walk out of the Shaw family into the arms of the Millers. He only wanted to be well off with the old love before he was on with the new. But I'll forgive him anything for the sake of the automobile goggles."

"And the Peter Pan collar!" cried Valeska, laughing. "Couldn't you hear me giggling in the closet?"

"The Landor jewels, though!" said Astro thoughtfully. "If it wasn't for them, one might suspect that Miss Ethel had taken an overdose of headache powders. Acetanilid does affect the brain, you know."

"The question is, who played the gorilla?"

"Ah, an Italian, I'm afraid. If you'll pardon the pun, I think that garlic puts us on the scent. As I see it, it's a case where our friend McGraw can help us out. I'll try him. There'll be no particular credit in it for him; but, what's just as good, there'll be money."

From an interview with his friend, the police lieutenant, that night Astro found out that no one had been suspected of the robbery of Mrs. Landor's jewels strongly enough to warrant arrest. Ethel Shaw and her fiancé were both present at the Landor reception held on the night when the jewels were stolen. A charge of kleptomania might, therefore, be reasonably preferred against her. As young Shaw had said, such an accusation, coupled with her testimony as to the method by which she obtained the jewels, would deal a serious blow to the Shaws' social aspirations.

McGraw had too often profited by Astro's assistance in puzzling cases not to do his best to help the palmist; but nothing was known by the police about the count or his valet. It was found, however, that, on his passage across the Atlantic in the *Penumbria*, Count D'Ampleri had taken no servant. This of itself was of sufficient importance for Astro to request McGraw to look up the man and furnish a description of him and his circumstances. This, in a few days, revealed the fact that the valet had a dubious reputation, and it was suspected that he had been in prison. McGraw himself was not sure at first; but subsequently a brother officer familiar with the Italian quarter of New York positively identified him as Kneesy Tim, who had done time for second-story work, and was so called among his pals on account of his knock-knees.

It did not take the officer long after that to ascertain through the detective force that Tim had attended the Landor reception as Count D'Ampleri's valet. The line of evidence was now direct. Tim had welded the most important link of it himself by appearing as the bearer of the stolen jewels. His boldness was accounted for, of course, by the fact that he relied on his ludicrous appearance to make Miss Shaw's story incredible, at the same time preventing any identification of himself. In all this it was impossible not to suspect the count of being an accessory; if, indeed, he did not plan the whole thing.

But why had the thief been willing to surrender such valuable booty? If the count were merely after money, here was a treasure in the hands of his accomplice. The answer was an easy one for Astro to solve when Shaw produced the black bag full of Mrs. Landor's heirlooms.

The jewels were all false. Astro's critical eyes needed but one careful look at them. They were marvelous imitations; but of no possible use to any one except the owner who would never be suspected of having hypothecated her celebrated gems. It was evident now why Mrs. Landor—the respectable, aristocratic Mrs. Lemuel Landor, of the Landor jewels—had never offered a reward for their capture. Astro, cynical as he was, familiar as he was with the many hypocrisies of the upper ten of the town, could not help laughing when he held the famous Landor tiara up to Valeska's envious view.

"I'll never believe in anybody or anything again!" she exclaimed. "Did you tell Mr. Shaw?"

"Not after his remarks on my profession," said Astro, with a decided shake of his head. "That's the time he did himself out of a hearty laugh at Mrs. Landor's expense. In any case, I don't believe in ever telling any more than is necessary."

"The count is an ordinary crook, then?"

"I doubt that. Nor is he even an ordinary count. He's a clever bourgeois Frenchman. I have talked with him and know. I imagine that he picked up this fellow Tim to help him play the part, and found out afterward what he was and used him. But that doesn't matter. We have them now on the hip."

"And how are you going to fix him? From what I hear, he is more attentive than ever to the Bay Mare, and people are talking about it."

"That doesn't matter. If Miss Ethel can get rid of him without his telling that ridiculous story, she'll undoubtedly call it good riddance to bad rubbish. And I will fix that."

"How?"

"My dear, if you'll walk up and down on Eighth Avenue, between Thirty-seventh and Thirty-eighth Streets, from twelve till half past to-morrow night, you'll see. And," he continued, smiling to himself, "I think it will be worth your attendance. I think we might ask Shaw to escort you, if he's willing to disguise himself a little, enough so that the count won't recognize him."

"I shall be there," said Valeska.

"I promise a comedy," said Astro. "By the by, it may interest you to know that I have rented a room at number 573 Eighth Avenue."

"Indeed!" said Valeska, raising her brows. "I imagine from your tone that I'm not to ask you any questions; but I would like to know if you are through with McGraw?"

"No, indeed. McGraw is to figure as the *deus ex machina*; also he is to earn two thousand dollars. One he will collect from me, and one from Mrs. Landor, who will be very glad to pay, I imagine, if he acts strictly in a private capacity. In other words, it is not particularly to Mrs. Landor's interest for the public to know that she has sold her jewels and wears paste."

"I begin dimly to comprehend now," Valeska mused. "You will emulate the Mikado of Japan, and 'let the punishment fit the crime'?"

Astro replied, "My dear, in the mutual interaction of telepathic vibrations, one neutralizes the other. Two loud sounds can be made to produce a silence. *Selah. 'Tara ak khaldah maha tara. Abraca-dabra, maha tara.'*"

"Boom-de-ay!" Valeska added gaily.

"Precisely. And, speaking of nonsense, I didn't ask you to get me a pair of white duck trousers and a yellow-striped blazer and an old woman's wig and a green umbrella and a white top hat, did I?" He looked thoughtfully at his finger nails.

"No, you didn't," she replied briskly; "nor a bottle of soothing syrup nor a tombstone."

"Nevertheless, you will do this to-morrow morning, and have them sent to number 573 Eighth Avenue."

"I agree, if you'll only let me add some rubber boots."

"Well, as a special favor, yes. Now run along and I'll get to work. Oh, Tim was arrested to-day, on suspicion of having stolen the Landor jewels. Too bad, isn't it?"

He sat down, thereupon, to write a letter as follows:

> "*Commesso sbaglio gravissimo. Lei è in un gran pericolo. Venga a trovarmi martedì a mezzanotte sullo porta del no. 573 Eighth Avenue. Venga solo. T.*"

He showed it to Valeska and translated:

> "Terrible mistake made. You are in great danger. Meet me Tuesday at midnight in the doorway of number 573 Eighth Avenue. Come alone. T."

Roughly scrawled on brown paper, and put into a plain but dirty envelope, the note was convincing. Tim, at any rate, would not be able to deny it for some time. It was not a message that the Count D'Ampleri would dare ignore.

The Count D'Ampleri did not ignore it. Smart and aristocratic in appearance, though foreign-looking with his Parisian silk hat, his queer trousers, and his waxed and pointed mustache, he was prompt at the rendezvous. Valeska and John Wallington Shaw, drifting slowly down the block, noticed him there waiting in the dusky doorway, looking impatiently up and down, smoking a cigarette. The count seemed to be a bit uneasy. He lighted one cigarette after another.

The two spectators passed again, talking absorbedly one to the other, but watching guardedly as they passed. At the Thirty-seventh Street corner they noticed a man standing, his back against a lamp-post. A child would have known him to be a policeman in plain clothes. His burly figure, his bull neck, the very cut of his mustache, proved it indubitably. He gave them a wink as they passed him. They crossed to the other side of the avenue and walked slowly. As they reached the far end of the block they suddenly stopped. Valeska began to giggle, pointed, and excitedly watched the scene across the street. Shaw seized her arm and hurried her over the crossing and to the front of the doorway. The little drama was almost over. As they stopped, staring, a fantastic figure retreated, entered the door, and banged it behind him.

They were laughing at the count's discomfiture as McGraw came up. He took his cue like an actor, and walking up to the count grabbed him fiercely by the arm.

"Now then," he said harshly, "what you a-doin' here? What's that you got there?" He pointed to a black bag the Italian still held in his hand.

"Who are you, anyway?" said the count angrily. "Vat beesness of yours? Tell me that!"

"I'll show you!" and McGraw threw back his coat and displayed his badge. "See here now! What have you got in that bag at this time of night, hangin' round in this doorway?"

"My God! I don't know myself!" the count exclaimed.

"I'll see, then," said McGraw, and snatching it from him he opened the bag and drew out a diamond tiara.

"You don't know!" he thundered. "We'll see about that at the station-house! Come along with me!"

The count, seeing the jewels, seemed almost ready to faint with surprise and horror. "But I am very innocent!" he wailed. "I am ze Count D'Ampleri. I live at ze Saint Regis! You shall see! Before heaven! I never knew that things was there! It was give me just now, by—by—" He paused, discomfited.

"Well, by whom?" was McGraw's inquiry.

"You will not believe—nobody won't believe—it ees too much! A mad woman she give me zis bag just now zis minute!"

"What kind of a woman? Out with it!"

"Oh! what shall I say? You will not believe. A woman like a man, with white pantaloon, with a topper hat, a yellow jacquette with stripes like zis." He made a pitiful gesture down the front of his coat.

"Aw, g'wan!" said McGraw. "D'you expect me to believe a pipe dream like that? That's the worst I ever heard, and I've heard some thin ones, too!"

"But I tell ze truth, I swear it! She have a green *ombrelle*."

"Any more? Go as far as you like." McGraw's tone was affable.

"She wear big boots of *la gomme*,—what you call it—rubbaire."

McGraw towered above him now, and calmly folded his arms. "No blue whiskers, or purple hat pins stuck in her face, was they? She wasn't chewin' shavin's or had red fire on her hands, I suppose? Lord, man! you got no imagination at all! Why, I can dream out things that would make that old lady seem like a fashion-plate. When I dope 'em out they generally wears armor plate and glass gloves at least. But I guess that'll be about all for you. I'm going to run you in."

The count in despair appealed to Valeska. "But ze lady and ze gentleman, she see ze old woman! Ask them! I am spik ze truth to you!"

Valeska, smothering her laughter, did her best to speak calmly. "We saw nothing at all, officer. The man must be intoxicated."

"Or crazy," Shaw put in wickedly.

"You see nozzing?" the count ejaculated in amazement. Then he dropped in a dejected huddle, nodding his head sillily.

McGraw motioned to Valeska, and nodded toward Thirty-seventh Street.

"Well, I'll have to go," she said, smiling. "You'd better be careful, officer; he may be dangerous." And so saying she walked away with Shaw, who was too nearly hysterical with mirth to speak for a while. When he did, it was to say:

"Will you kindly inform Astro when you see him that I take back what I said about horoscopes and occultism? I am quite sure he will understand."

She repeated the message next day, when she and Astro found themselves alone in the studio. Astro smiled. "If they were all like John Wallington Shaw," he said, "you and I wouldn't make much of a living, little girl." Then he added irrelevantly, "I understand that the Count D'Ampleri is to sail on the *Germanic* next week."

"Oh. Then McGraw let him off?"

"All McGraw wanted was to get his thousand out of Mrs. Landor, and the less talk about it the better. He telephoned me this morning to say that she gave him a very lively half-hour, but paid. By the way, I wonder if Shaw told his sister Ethel how the matter was solved?"

"He said he intended to, before he went to bed."

"Then we may consider the episode closed." Astro took down a volume of Immanuel Kant. Before he began his reading he remarked casually, "It was a narrow escape for all three. I don't know exactly which one to congratulate the most."

"I'd congratulate the old lady with the white duck trousers and the blazer," said Valeska. "I think she had the merriest time of all."

"Yes," said Astro, his eyes twinkling, "I think so myself!"

PRISCILLA'S PRESENTS

The winter afternoon had wrapped itself in darkness before Astro spoke. He had bent for twenty minutes over the chess-board, vividly illumined by an overhead electric lamp, while Valeska's keen eyes watched him attentively. Outside, the clanging of bells and the rattle of cars had grown gradually fainter as the falling snow spread a blanket over the pavements. Within the palmist's studio the two were surrounded by shadowy objects enlivened with twinkling lights caught on the polished points or planes of embroidered patterns or ornaments.

Suddenly Astro rose and switched on a blaze of light. The whole picturesque splendor of the apartment blazed in color, from the heavy tones of the oriental rugs to the gilded coffered ceiling. The walls, half lined with books, surrounded the luxurious furnishings of the studio, which in their elegance and rarity gave the place almost the air of a museum.

"Mate in seven moves!" he announced.

His pretty assistant wrinkled her brows in the attempt to analyze the game. For weeks she had been studying with him the mysteries and complications of the Muzio gambit, and, though she was well along with the strategics of the play, Astro's extraordinary imagination made him mentally able to keep many moves ahead of her. She sighed whimsically and looked up at him. He put his finger on a black ivory piece as he spoke with a droll look in his eyes.

"It all came because of your absurd fondness for the knight!"

"I admit that I am partial to knights," she replied. "I'm always willing to exchange a bishop for one."

"I wonder why?" Astro mused. "No doubt because the knight's move is symbolical of a woman's way of thinking. She loves to jump over things in the logical path of reasoning: one move ahead and one diagonally to the right, one backward and one obliquely to the left, or anyway rather than along a straight line." He laughed a little cynically.

"And do men never think that way?" she asked demurely.

He put his chin in his fist and nodded his head, shaking his waving black hair. "That's queer, too. They do, sometimes. There are types that do, races that do; Orientals, for instance."

"And aren't you oriental?" she asked.

He walked away suddenly and picked up his little white tame lizard from its silver cage. "Oh, Egypt is hardly the Orient. Egypt is—well, it's Egypt, the eternal mystery."

He turned quickly to her. "I never believed you were Irish," he said. "I wonder what you are?"

"Pure troll!" she said nimbly.

"I have solved many mysteries," Astro replied, and now his voice was softer; "but you are the most mysterious of all. Somehow, I hate to know too much about you. Well, let's call you a troll." He picked up the mouthpiece of his narghile.

A bell tinkled. Valeska, after a glance at the Master of Mysteries, pressed a button on the wall. In a moment a boy in buttons entered, carrying a salver, on which were letters. Astro took them up and spread them on the table under the lamp. Valeska looked playfully over his shoulder. Then, with a queer expression on her face, she seated herself.

"All from women!" she commented. "I wish—"

"What?" The Seer wheeled in his chair.

"Never mind." Valeska took up a book.

Astro rapidly opened the envelopes and cast them aside one by one. The last, a letter on heavy blue paper, he read a second time and tossed it over to Valeska.

"Read it aloud," he said. "I want to think."

Valeska read as follows:

"My Dear Astro—You will remember, perhaps, having read my hand some months ago, and having told me some most *wonderful* things about myself. It was all so *marvelous* to me that I though you might be able to help me in a funny thing that has been happening for the last five weeks or so. Of course, I apply to you in *strict confidence*, and I *hope* you will understand."

"Oh, cut all that part out," Astro interrupted, "and all her feminine circumlocutions! Get to the business!"

"Well, then, five weeks ago last Saturday I received a mysterious present of a pair of *beautiful* slippers. I had *no idea* where it came from; but supposed it was from a Mr. Thompson, who had been rather attentive to me. But he denied it. The next Saturday I got another parcel, by mail, containing a *lovely* bound leather album, beautifully tooled. Then I suspected a Mr. Gerrish; but he has denied sending either. Since then, *every Saturday* I have received a parcel by mail, every time a different thing, and I'm simply *wild* to know who is sending these things. If you think you can find out for me, I'll be glad to pay you whatever fee you charge, as I can't *stand* it not to know any longer. If you'll make an appointment, I'll come and see you any time.

"Yours sincerely,

"Priscilla Quarich."

"Isn't it lovely?" Valeska exclaimed. "It's a welcome relief from the murders and robberies and things. I'm glad that there are some benevolent criminals."

"Slippers—album—" the Seer mused. "Too bad she didn't mention the other gifts."

"Why? Do you think it's so very mysterious? It's romantic, of course; but—"

"Five Saturdays in succession—" Astro went on thoughtfully.

"Slippers are a funny present," said Valeska. "You have to know the exact size, of course."

"Thompson—Gerrish—" Astro rose. "This should be your field, Valeska," he said, smiling. "My specialty is the intricacy of the human brain. You ought to know about the human heart. Of course it's a love-affair."

"And of course you know nothing of love," she added.

He tossed the black locks from his brow and gazed at her thoughtfully. "No—of course not." His voice was low; he did not look at her.

Then he threw off his mood. "Write her in answer, Valeska, to this effect: In order to settle this rather delicate question for her, I shall have to meet the two men. Suggest that she invite me to dinner and have them there. You'll be invited, of course. Suppose we make it next Friday. Also, ask her to send me a complete list of the gifts she has received to date, in chronological order."

The next day a letter came from Miss Quarich in reply to Valeska's note. She said that, as her butler was usually away on Fridays, she would prefer to have the dinner on Thursday. "And," she added, "do, please, bring that pretty Miss Wynne, if she will pardon my informality in not calling myself to invite her. But I'm so busy—" etc.

On Thursday evening, therefore, Astro's green car bore the two to Miss Quarich's residence on upper Madison Avenue. They were admitted by the smiling Japanese butler, and, entering the drawing-room, found the two men of the party already waiting.

Thompson, the elder of the two, was a typical man about town, bullet-headed, red-faced, with cropped red mustache, and of a jovial magnetic temperament. Care had scarcely rubbed elbows with Tom Thompson, and he was full of the gossip of the day, cordial, hearty, and evidently innocuous. Gerrish was more suave, with a clever head, egg-shaped, smooth shaved, with a sensitive mouth and smiling eyes.

A moment after, Miss Quarich appeared, attired in the most modern of empire gowns, revealing her slim lithe figure and beautiful neck. She was young and merry, with dark eyes full of coquetry. She welcomed Valeska with a little patronizing snuggle, and held out her hand to Astro, who bent over it and kissed it gracefully. Then their eyes met, and Miss Quarich blushed. It became her charmingly. Valeska, meanwhile, had turned to the men, and her eyes and wits were busy. Sam, the Japanese butler, came in with cocktails on a tray. Neither of the women indulged; but the men drank their healths, each with a characteristic compliment. Then they went into the dining-room.

As Sam, with the crisp, impersonal, quiet dignity of his race, passed from one guest to another serving, both Astro and Valeska watched the company sharply. The Seer showed himself not only *au fait*, but distinguished, as always when he accepted such social invitations.

Once or twice, during the meal, Astro's eyes sought Valeska's, with a questioning expression. The faintest possible shake of the head was his only answer. The two men divided their attention between Miss Quarich and Valeska Wynne with discretion and tact. The talk ran on in social commonplaces, of the theaters, of the newspaper topics of the day, of sporting events. That Astro was anything more than the merest society butterfly, the favorite of the moment, no one would have suspected. Yet again and again he shot his shrewd look across the table at his assistant, and his glance in their secret language pointed her attention to many things.

After the sweets, the women retired up-stairs to Miss Quarich's private sitting-room for their coffee and a few moments of relaxation.

"Well?" said Miss Quarich, passing her golden cigarette case to Valeska.

"They're both immensely interested in you, it seems to me."

Miss Quarich's brows rose. "My dear," she said, "it struck me that *you* came in for some notice also."

Valeska smiled. "But I don't expect to receive a present from either of them on Saturday, however."

Miss Quarich sat up with animation. "It's great fun, of course," she said; "but it's tantalizing. I would never suspect either of them of being romantic. Of course I've had loads of flowers and books and all that sort of thing from men, and both these men have been, as you say, interested—and attentive. In fact, each of them has come dangerously near to—a refusal." She laughed merrily.

"Do you recall having mentioned the size of your shoe to either of them?"

"Not at all; though either might have found out, if he tried hard enough."

"And about the album?"

"Oh, I recall having mentioned one I saw, one night at dinner when they were both there. I must show it to you." She rang a bell at her side, and shortly a maid appeared. "Stebbins, will you bring that album on the table in my room, please?"

When it came, Valeska examined it interestedly. It was made in imitation of the Renaissance volumes that are still decorated and sold in Sienna. The board covers were gilded and painted with quaint pictures of knights and castles, and were bound with leather thongs, fastened with silver-headed nails. Inside were pages of tooled leather, with apertures for photographs. The slippers were also brought, of golden and blue embroidery of a quaint design. But, despite her close scrutiny, Valeska could find no distinguishing mark to hint at the place of their manufacture.

Miss Quarich handed them back finally to her maid. "Wrap them up neatly with the other things on my table, and give the parcel to Samugi. Tell him to give them to Monsieur Astro when he leaves the house. Now, my dear," Miss Quarich said, turning to pour out a cordial, "we must hurry down-stairs. We have been here long enough. I want to hear Astro read the hands of the two men. It ought to be fun. Oh, here's the list of presents up to date. You can give him that yourself."

Astro and Valeska left the house early and drove directly to the studio. She was animated with interest. The mystery was pretty enough to excite her feminine enthusiasm. Astro laughed at her but refused to discuss it till she had entered the studio and opened the paper Miss Quarich had given her, and displayed the whole collection of presents. The list was as follows:

November seventh, pair of slippers; November fourteenth, album; November twenty-first, volume of Montaigne; November twenty-eighth, umbrella; December fifth, six pairs of gloves.

Astro first handled the objects taken from the parcel, and then looked over the list. For ten minutes he said nothing, walking up and down the dim apartment in silence. For a few moments he stood by the window, staring out, thinking. Then, with a smile illuminating his countenance, he returned to the table, glanced again at the list of gifts, and chuckled.

"To-day is Thursday," he remarked. "The day after to-morrow, Miss Quarich will receive—can you guess what?"

"Of course I can't!" said Valeska. "What?"

He dropped his chin into his fist. "Well, she will receive a present of an inkstand; probably of cut glass."

"Really?" Valeska stared at him in amazement.

"Yes, unless he sends another book, which I think unlikely."

"He? Who?"

"Do you mean to say you don't know?"

"How can I? Why how can you, either? You haven't even examined the presents. There's that volume of Montaigne's *Essays*. It would be like Mr. Gerrish to send that; but more like Mr. Thompson to send the gloves. I'm all at sea."

Astro patted her familiarly on the shoulder. "After all my lessons?" he complained humorously. "Never mind, think it over. And look over that list again tomorrow, when you're rested."

The next day, however, brought no hint to Valeska, who, in the intervals of her work, examined the articles one by one, and pored over the list of presents. On Saturday, Miss Quarich rang up the studio. Valeska, in high excitement, listened, and then stared at Astro with a baffled expression.

"Miss Quarich received this morning a parcel containing a cut-glass ink-well!"

Astro laughed silently, and nodded.

For some time Valeska stood gazing at him with a blank look on her face. Then, without a word she went to the table, took up the list of gifts, and, as if mesmerized by Astro's unspoken thought, sat down, took a pencil and began to write:

    Slippers
    Album
    Montaigne
    Umbrella
    Gloves
    Inkstand

"What is that Japanese butler's name?" she demanded.

"Why, Sam, isn't it?"

"You know it isn't. It's Samugi. But how did you know? I only happened to hear Miss Quarich mention it."

"Well, I inquired. I often ask questions. So you've solved the acrostic?"

"Yes, the initials read 'Samugi,' of course. But what does it mean?"

Astro yawned. "It is difficult to interpret the oriental mind; almost as difficult as to understand feminine psychology. What did I tell you the other day? It's a mental knight's move, an indirect message. We'll have to wait."

"But fancy that Jap having the nerve to take such liberties with Miss Quarich!"

"That Japanese is, as I have succeeded in finding out at the consulate, more than Miss Quarich's social equal."

"But he's only a servant!"

"In New York, yes. In Tokio, he's a noble of an old Samurai family. His father is an army officer on General Oku's staff. So may Samugi be, for that matter."

"Then why is he taking a servile position here?"

"Oh, that is done very often. Who knows the reason? Not I, nor do I care. Perhaps he's an army spy, perhaps he's writing a sociological book on the American millionaires, perhaps he is sent by his government for private reasons. But most likely of all he is simply desperately in love with Miss Priscilla Quarich, and has taken this devious oriental method of pressing a hopeless suit."

"Hopeless?" Valeska's eyes snapped.

"Of course. The question now is, what are we to do about it? If Miss Quarich finds out, she, of course, will have him immediately discharged. The only thing is to wait till we get his message definitely."

Valeska tossed her head and walked away. "So you consider yourself an expert in the human heart, do you?" she asked jauntily, as she put on her furs.

"I confess I don't know much about yours," was his retort; and then, as he watched her out of the door he added slowly, "I wish to Heaven I did!"

Three weeks elapsed, Miss Quarich having been put off from day to day on one excuse or another. But each Saturday a new gift had been received. On December twelfth it had been an exquisite inlaid mother-of-pearl lorgnette. On the nineteenth she had received a magnificently-set opal, and the next week a huge box of violets arrived, fresh and fragrant from Morley's. The tenor of the message was now growing evident. According to the presents so far received, it read, "Samugi lov," and it needed little shrewdness to construct from that the probable declaration: "Samugi loves you."

The elegance and costliness of the gifts had already confirmed Astro's opinion of Samugi's condition. It was evident that he had not only birth and social position at home, but wealth as well. He had been shrewd enough to send nothing edible, such as confectionery, which might immediately arouse distrust. His tact was, indeed, most delicate. Should Priscilla Quarich disdain his advances, she need only pretend not to understand the acrostic. He was wise enough not to want to subject her to the embarrassment of refusing an overt offer, in case she should be prejudiced against the Orient. He actually did, it seemed, wish to be loved for himself alone, as the song has it, with no aid from his possession of noble birth.

It became, therefore, a delicate question as to how and when Miss Quarich should be informed of the solution of her problem. As she did not press for it, however, Astro let the matter wait a while, hoping to receive word from her of the gifts that might come. No letter came, however, and he expressed surprise to Valeska.

"I'm not at all surprised," she remarked.

"Please write to her for an account of what she has received since the violets came, and in what order," he said.

This Valeska did, and, in a few days, received the following answer:

> "My Dear Astro—I had almost forgotten that I had asked you to unravel my little mystery, and I'm afraid now that it is hardly worth your while spending much time on it. As you ask, however, I'll tell you that I have received, since I telephoned about the violets, a copy of Undine, an emerald, a pair of opera-glasses, and some other things. Please don't bother about it. It really doesn't matter much. Yours sincerely,
>
> "Priscilla Quarich."

Astro whistled. "I confess I don't know what to make of that," he exclaimed; "but at least it confirms my original prophecy. She hasn't given us all the letters, nor their correct order; but what she does give certainly fill in right. He took a pencil and wrote a line as follows:

"Samugi lov . . . ou."

"But why this sudden lack of interest in the solution of the problem?" he demanded. "Do you suppose that she can have puzzled it out for herself; that perhaps she's so ashamed of it she doesn't want me to know the truth?"

Valeska burst out into a laugh. "I saw Miss Quarich in a cab driving up Lexington Avenue this afternoon," she said; and added slyly, "with a man."

"Thompson, or Gerrish?" said Astro.

"It is Friday, isn't it?" she inquired demurely.

Astro sprang up. "By Jove! Samugi's day off! You don't mean to say she was with Samugi?"

"In a top hat," Valeska added with mirth; "which shows all you know about the human heart. I thought she looked at him rather soulfully that first day at the dinner. Only, I wanted to see what you knew of women."

"Less and less, every day," said he, with a mock mournful look.

The next Monday's paper contained an account of Miss Priscilla Quarich's elopement with her Japanese butler. Samugi's history was given, however, and it was one partly to reconcile the gossips with the scandal of the affair. His noble family, his war record, his academic achievements, all received sensational description. Society exclaimed, shrugged its shoulders, and forgot the affair next week. Astro's bill was paid with a yellow porcelain lion of an ancient dynasty, one of the seven left in the world.

Valeska's birthday came that week. She was in the studio when an expressman entered with a big basket filled with parcels all addressed to her. She opened them first with glee, then with increasing anxiety on her face. When the last package had been unwrapped and the papers carefully put away, she spent some time sitting on the floor gazing at the thirteen several gifts. If there were tears in her eyes, Astro came too late to see them. He did not enter the studio, in fact, until after she had arranged the presents into three rows, in this way.

Astrakhan furs	Lorgnette	Yeats' Poems
Slippers	Opal pin	Opera-glasses
Thimble	Violets	Umbrella
Ruby ring	Emerald brooch	
Orchids	Sash	

At the sound of his step in the outer hall, however, she swept the gifts together in a heap and jumped to her feet .

"Well," he said, as he entered, "I wish you a happy new year, my dear!"

She was still blushing. "Oh," she said, "I've just got so many beautiful, wonderful presents! They're simply lovely; but I can't understand why they were all sent to me at once." She looked away.

"And no idea where they came from, either, I suppose?"

She cast down her eyes. "I suppose only an Oriental would be so munificent—and so mysterious. And I'm sure of one thing—that my Oriental's presents have brought me even more delight than hers did to Priscilla!"

THE HEIR TO SOOTHOID

The mellow baritone of Astro's voice vibrated through the great studio with a note of profound mystery, as he read aloud from Anna Hempstead Branch's poem, *The Pilgrim*:

> "Touch me not, mother, who art thou,
>   To lay a hand on me?
> My soul was driven through sun and moon
>   Ere I was come to thee!"

Then he dropped the book and gazed at Valeska, his assistant, for a while thoughtfully. She was sitting on the floor, propped up by gorgeous cushions, playing with a huge piece of rock-crystal cut in the form of a tetrahedron. A shaft of light fell on her lap, piercing the obscurity of the apartment. The crystal caught and gathered the rays, then broke them, shattering the white light into streaks of brilliant color. At the other end of the room a spot of radiance appeared on the ceiling, splendid with the hues of a rainbow. She looked up to the Master as he ceased reading.

"There's the poet's immemorial challenge to the monist," he said, almost in a reverie. "It's a cry as old as the world, and, I think, idealistic as it is, mystic as it is, with as sure a foundation as that of modern determinism. But this is modern, too. It voices an idea that, though it has long been common to oriental thought, is new to the western civilizations. What relation, after all, is the son to the father? See how sublimely Miss Branch herself answers that passionate question:

> "'If thou came out of the moon and star
> I plucked thee forth by my desire.
> I can hold thee burning in my hand!
> It was my hand that shaped the fire!'"

Astro rose, and, as was his custom when absorbed in any subject, began to walk up and down the room. His keen dark eyes stared straight in front of him without looking at the priceless decorations of the studio. His hands were clasped behind his back across his red silken robe. His turban nodded as he spoke. Valeska watched him eagerly. These philosophic moods, alternating with the active eager phases of his mind, when he was pursuing the track of some almost insoluble mystery, fascinated her. It was at such times, she thought, that he betrayed his real self.

"There's the purely transcendental side," he said. "But the materialistic miracle is as marvelous,—the fact that protoplasm is immortal, that characteristics, physical and mental, are handed down in the infinitesimal cell that persists from generation to generation in the id and the biophore. Tricks of speech and gesture, abnormal formations of the organs of the body, temper, emotion,—all transmitted in that tiny primordial atom! What has science done but induce us to believe the impossible?"

A bronze clock in the anteroom pealed out the hour of ten, preceded by the Westminster chime of four staves of music. Valeska rose, but hesitated, unwilling to interrupt the Seer's soliloquy. But he threw off his absorbed mood, came back to her, and smiled.

"Well," he said, "one must earn one's living. What's on for to-day?"

"You have an appointment with Colonel Mixter at ten."

"Very well. When he comes, show him in. I shall now give an imitation of an oriental adept of the Fifth Circle. Pass me the crystal ball, Valeska, and touch off that incense in the Japanese burner. Am I properly sedate and scornful? Bah! What rubbish it all is—and how it goes with the mob!"

He took his favorite position on the couch, drew up his narghile, and assumed a picturesque attitude. Valeska left him and took her place in the reception-room. In ten minutes she ushered in Colonel Mixter, bowed, and left the two together, dropping the black velvet portieres behind her. She did not, however, remain in the reception-room. Instead, she passed into a room connecting that with the studio, where in a combination of mirrors she could see all that happened and also hear the talk.

The new client was a military-looking man of some fifty years, with iron-gray hair and a curling white mustache. He had an active air, full of strength and character and showing his habit of command. Scrupulously dressed, immaculately clean, well groomed from head to heels, he was what might have been called both handsome and distinguished in appearance. His voice was crisp and hearty.

"May I smoke?" he asked. "Dashed if I can talk without smoking! I have to treat my confounded nerves like a confounded pack of dogs, confound it! Thanks."

In reply, Astro had drawn up his water-pipe and inhaled a long whiff of the aromatic Russian tobacco that smoldered in the bowl. The colonel produced a cigar, bit off the end, and lighted it.

"I suppose you've seen the advertisements of 'Soothoid,' that chewing-gum stuff, all over the town, haven't you?" he began.

Astro nodded gravely.

"Biggest fake on earth," said the colonel, "and the most remunerative. My old uncle invented it, you know. Conceived the brilliantly vile idea of doping ordinary chicle with a tincture of opium and making chewing-gum of it. 'It soothes the nerves,'—I should say it did!— 'Children cry for it,' and all that sort of thing! It's monstrous, of course. It ought to be suppressed by law, and it's only a question of time when this pure-food agitation will knock it out of business. It's a crime against civilization; but all the same it has made four millions for that disreputable old uncle of mine, and now the whole works belong to me. Brings me in eighteen thousand a year. I'm afraid to stop it, and more afraid not to. But that's not the point."

He rolled his cigar from one corner of his mouth to another, flicked a fleck of dust from his spotless trousers, and looked calmly at Astro. The Seer smiled, despite himself, waved his hand dispassionately for the other to proceed, and waited.

"The thing is this," the colonel went on. "I'm an expert on ordnance, and I've traveled all over the world for the government. Never at home from one year's end to another. I came back to find myself immensely rich, last October, and at the same time up against a mystery that it's practically impossible to solve. So I come to you. Understand?"

"Scarcely, as yet," said the Master. "Kindly go on."

"Why, see here. I have a son—or thought I had. Query: Is he my son at all? And if not, who is to inherit the 'Soothoid' millions? That's the question I have to decide right away. I have angina pectoris. I'm likely to die any fine day. I don't want a chap that's no relative of mine to get away with all that money, do I?"

"My dear Colonel," said Astro, "you'll have to give me more information than that, before I decide such a weighty question for you. What do you mean by saying you don't know whether he's your son or not. You mean you suspect—"

The colonel roared. "Oh, lord, no, not that!" he exclaimed. "This is no question of matrimonial infelicity, you know. I'm the father of a child, all right; only, the question is, what child?" He put it very gravely.

"Tell me the whole story." Astro's brows bent on his client.

"Well, then, see here. When the child was born, my wife was in a hospital on Long Island. I wanted her to have the very best of care, especially as I had to be away so much. Well, the night her child was born, the hospital took fire. It spread so quickly that they couldn't get the patients out fast enough. The doctors working over my wife didn't dare leave her, and they worked against time. Just after they finished with her and another case of the same kind, the wing caught, and there was barely time to hustle every one downstairs and outside. Do you see the situation? They had to work quick. Those surgeons showed all sorts of nerve, I can tell you. But in the confusion the two babies were somehow mixed up by the nurse. One was a boy, and one was a girl, born within three minutes

of each other. But which was my child, the boy or the girl? That's
how it stands. You see, at the time nothing was said to me about
any uncertainty. My wife died from the shock; so did the other
woman. The boy was given to me as my baby. I never suspected
that there was any doubt about it, and have brought him up and
educated him as my son."

"But when did you first suspect that he wasn't?" Astro asked.

"Only a month ago. The former nurse told the whole thing. Said
it was on her conscience, and had been for years; so much so that
she had kept track of both children. The little girl was put in an
orphan asylum, as no one came to claim her; then she was adopted
by a family in Newark; and now she's a salesgirl at Bloom's candy
store. Working behind a counter at six a week, by Jove! and may
be my daughter, and the heir to 'Soothoid'! What do you think of
that? Wouldn't you worry?" He shoved his hands into his pockets
and regarded the Master of Mysteries.

"The nurse isn't sure which is which?"

"No. It has been tormenting her conscience for twenty years,
and she had to make a clean breast of it. All she knows is that she
'mixed those babies up'; like Little Buttercup in *Pinafore*. So I've
come to you. Doctors say it positively can't be proved, either way.
I thought you might do it by the palms or crystals or something.
I've seen 'em do some great stunts in India, and I believe there is
something in this occult business. They tell me you have a pretty
good record for that sort of thing here in New York."

The Seer waved his hand modestly. "Does the boy resemble you
in any way?" he asked.

"Why, he does and he doesn't. You know the way things like
that go. I've been told I look like everybody under the sun. I suppose I'm a type. Well, he is, too. Sometimes I think he's like me,
and then I doubt it. There's one funny thing, though. We both of
us sleep with our thumbs curled up inside our fists. Then he has a
second toe longer than his great toe, and so have I. They tell me
that's rare. My father had it too, though. He has blue eyes, and so
have I. Red hair, though, and there's no trace of that in my family
or my wife's, that I know of."

"And the girl—have you seen her?" Astro inquired.

"Of course. Went right down there immediately, and found her behind the counter—selling 'Soothoid,' by Jove! Big pompadour, rats in her hair, brass bangles, and all. What do you expect for six a week, though? If she's my daughter, she'll soon learn how to act the part, don't you worry!"

Astro laughed again. "She hasn't been spoken to about it, I hope?"

"Oh, lord, no! What do you take me for? I wouldn't have her building air castles for the world. I only bought a pound of cheap chocolates and talked to her a little. I've no doubt the poor girl thought I was trying to mash her. She was a nice little thing, though, for all her rats. I liked her, by Jove! I'd like to do something for her in any case, daughter or not. Her name is Miss Maverick."

"Does she resemble you or your wife?"

"Why, the funny part of it is that she does, in a faraway sort of fashion. I noticed that she was left-handed, too, like me. Blue eyes; but her hair was hennaed, so I couldn't tell about that. Cute little thing, she is. Confound it! I did like her immensely, at first sight."

"Well," said the Seer, after reflecting a while, "I must confess that you have set a difficult problem for me. But I think that it can be determined through astral means. No doubt you have consulted some medium already?"

"Oh, they're all a lot of fakers! They told me that the boy was mine and that the girl was, too, both."

"I agree with you. The ordinary mediums are an ignorant and unscrupulous lot. I have occult methods unknown except in the Himalayas. But it will be difficult, I am afraid. But may I ask you what is the matter with your eyes, Colonel?"

The colonel stared. "My eyes? Nothing except a slight astigmatism. I have some glasses; but I seldom wear them. Why?"

"They seem peculiar to me. You know that the eye has been called the 'window of the soul'. The phrase is trite; but it contains a germ of truth. I can tell a great deal from the eye, as much as from the palm or the voice. If you don't mind, I'd like to examine yours with the ophthalmoscope. My methods are my own; but I don't hesitate to make use of the instruments known to modern science. After all, the ophthalmoscope merely enables one to see through the cornea into the retina and the optic plexus."

With that he called in Valeska, who darkened the great studio. Then she turned on a single electric lamp which had a blue-glass bulb. The thread of incandescent wire showed purple. Then, attaching his instrument to the wires, he went up to the colonel and peered through the little slit in the holder. He gazed for some moments in silence, then switched on the lights again.

"Now," he added, "I have to make a request that may seem absurd. You may have heard of divination by moles. It is an almost unknown art; but, while not absolute, there is much to be learned from the relative disposition of such marks on the human body. Casanova, you may recall, if you have read his memoirs, practiced the art, and had a theory regarding the symmetrical distribution of moles. For instance, if one has a mole on the right cheek, there is a probability that there will be another to correspond with it on the left hip. We are tracing, you understand, mere physical heredity. That is all you require, I believe. The relation of souls is far beyond our ken."

"That's true," said the colonel. "People often seem to bear no spiritual relationship to their parents."

"Where the soul comes from will probably always remain unsettled by modern science," Astro agreed. "It is one of the world questions that even Haeckel gave up. Our oriental philosophers have their explanation; but for that one has to know the whole lore of the Vedantic sacred books. But there are laws that govern the transmission of physical characteristics. Now, therefore, if you will kindly step into this room and remove your clothes, I shall chart your birthmarks and compare them with your horoscope."

Ten minutes later the Seer joined Valeska in the studio. In his hand was a little diagram, an outline of the human form shown in four positions, from the front and back, the right and left sides. Little crosses were marked where the moles on the colonel's body appeared. He handed it to his assistant with a wink, and she left immediately. The colonel came in soon after, as faultlessly dressed as ever, and, after a few more questions from Astro, was permitted to take his leave.

"Now," said Astro, when he was again alone with Valeska, "you have a delicate piece of detective work to do. Do you think you can get a position in Bloom's confectionery store and scrape up an acquaintance with Miss Maverick?"

"I shall be delighted to try," was her reply. "I suppose I'll earn six dollars a week at it, won't I?"

"Colonel Mixter is worth millions. I expect it will pay you pretty well."

"Besides being lots of fun!" Valeska's eyes shone. "But, really, it seems to me that there's a much simpler way of settling the question. Why not marry young Mixter to Miss Maverick? Then, whoever is the true heir, he or she'll have the use of the money."

"That is exactly what I propose to do. It's the only solution possible. Heredity can't be proved by any method known to modern science, of course; but we'll have to make three persons believe that it can. I believe I can convince them all. At any rate, it's as pretty a task as the other, and you ought to be able to manage it, if any one can."

"Oh, you can't make a person fall in love so easily as that!" said Valeska, turning away.

"I think *you* could make any one fall in love," he answered, gazing at her.

For a while there was silence between them. Then with apparent effort, he took up the subject they had left.

"The evidence is pretty equally balanced between the two," he said. "The son curls in his thumb in his sleep; but many do that. The same with the long second toe. Both have blue eyes; so that's no test. The girl affects him mentally, or spiritually; but that's merely sentimental evidence. Her sinistrality, of course, amounts to nothing, nor does the faint resemblance he remarked to himself. We have to have some positive physical abnormality in order to appear to prove heredity. Mere probability doesn't count."

"How about finger prints?" Valeska asked.

"We know little of that. We have no records of hereditary transmission in that direction. It's too bad."

"What was the ophthalmoscope test for? And why all that patter of moles and birthmarks?"

"A mere shot in the air! Do you know what I brought down, though? The colonel has an optic disk—that's where the optic nerve comes into the retina—of a most peculiar shape, like an angel's wings. I just stumbled on it, in the hope of finding something peculiar that wouldn't appear to any observer. Also, he has a curious red birthmark of almost the same shape on his left shoulder. I saw it when I was pretending to diagram the moles. Now what we have to do is to examine both youngsters in some way. You'll have to patch up a friendship with the girl, Miss Maverick, while I investigate the boy. His father will help in that. I'll fix it: Have a doctor's sign painted on the door of my laboratory, and with the father's directions, medically inspect the lad for life insurance. That's easy. If we find one of the stigmata, the proof will be strong enough. Should we find two, it may be called positive certainty."

A week afterward found Valeska behind the counter at Bloom's, dressed in white, with a pompadour as big as any of those in the shop, selling candy and soda-water. Her bare arms were heavy with bracelets, her language was slangy and facetious. Her companion at the counter was Miss Maverick, known to the other employees as Bessie. It did not take Valeska long to create a friendship.

Bessie was a demure little miss, who did not by any means tell all she knew to a chance acquaintance. But Valeska asked no questions. Her conversation was a monologue, apparently artless, but cleverly contrived to throw the most suspicious off her guard. She asked Bessie's advice on this and that; she fished for Bessie's compliments; she gave Bessie hardly a chance for a word. A week went by without a move in the desired direction. Then Valeska came to the shop with a tale of misfortune,—of a lost purse and other pathetic details. Bessie offered to share her own room with her. From that moment all was easy. Valeska gradually talked less; Bessie gradually talked more. The two soon became real friends.

Valeska's first report to Astro was sensational. "What do you think?" she announced, "Bessie knows all about the 'Soothoid' affair, and the colonel, and even the colonel's son! One of those mediums gave the whole thing away to her, and tried to get her to stand in with him to claim the heirship of the estate. But she's the squarest little brick in the world, Bessie is! She's a dear; she's pure gold! She has looked up the colonel's business herself, and is all ready to fall in love with the colonel's son, just for himself alone. It's going to be easier than I thought."

"But how about the birthmarks?" Astro inquired.

"Oh, you've no idea how hard it was to find that out, till she had a little touch of rheumatism. Then I offered to rub liniment on her back, and—well, she has a birthmark, something the shape of what you said, an angel's wings."

"What?" Astro cried.

"It's true. And how about Willie Mixter?"

"Well, he has a birthmark, too," said Astro.

Valeska burst into a laugh. "Thereby proving that the earth is round, or something like that, doesn't it? Well, what to do now, I don't see."

"You forget the ophthalmoscope."

"Have you looked at Willie's eyes?"

"Yes, and his optic disk is the ordinary, irregular circle."

"Oh, I'm so glad! Then there's a chance for Bessie's making good for the 'Soothoid' millions."

"If you can get her up here for me to examine her eyes."

"But what if, after all, I can make the match without?"

"Oh, I spoke to the colonel about that. He'd be delighted. He really has taken a fancy to Bessie."

"Then Willie must see her."

"I agree. And I've been thinking that in any case Willie should be told. If he loses his money, he'll have to know, anyway. And I see no reason why he shouldn't know now. He's really a fine chap, a gentleman in every sense of the word. If I know anything of psychology, the thing will appeal to him as immensely romantic."

It was with the keenest interest, therefore, that Valeska, three days later, saw Willie Mixter enter Bloom's, cast his eyes about the shop, and walk toward the counter behind which Bessie Maverick stood. She saw Bessie blush; but the conversation was too low to be overheard. When the time came for the girls to leave the shop, instead of Bessie's accompanying Valeska to their room, she excused herself and went off alone. Valeska followed at a discreet distance. In five minutes she saw Willie Mixter overtake Bessie, and the two walked off like old friends.

The next day he came in again. Valeska asked no questions. Bessie had grown reserved. But she did not go this night, either, to the little dairy place where the two girls usually took their dinner. So it went on for another week, Bessie seeing the rich young fellow two or three times.

That next Sunday, as the two girls sat in their little room on East Nineteenth Street, Bessie began to cry. Valeska's arm was about her neck immediately, and, through her sobs, Bessie came out with the whole story.

"He wants to marry me!" she confessed. "And I love him so much that I won't! I know it's all on account of this miserable money, and he only wants to be fair with me, and divide. I simply can't accept him on that account! He'd think, anyway, I was after him on account of his money, even if I didn't think he was after me only because of his conscience. It's hopeless, my dear, hopeless! I hope I'll die and end it that way! I wish I might never see a package of 'Soothoid' again as long as I live!"

"Oh, of course you'll marry him!" Valeska said. "I'm sure he's in love with you."

"He is not! He talks all the time about our dividing the money; so I'm sure he only wants to arrange it like one of those royal family complications I've read about. I've got to tell some one!" she went on. "I'm breaking my heart with it. I have no mother and no father," here she broke off to stare wildly at Valeska, "unless the colonel is my father; and so I tell you! Oh, dear! it can never be settled! That's the horrible part of it. If that horrid old nurse had only been more careful of us!" and she laughed through her tears hysterically. "What shall I do, Valeska, what shall I do?"

"Do you really want my advice?" Valeska asked.

Bessie snuggled closer to her friend.

"I have a friend," Valeska said slowly, "a man whom I know you can trust. He is the wisest person in the world, it seems to me. He has been my friend a long time. He saved me from what was worse than death."

"Are you in love with him?" Bessie interrupted.

Valeska ignored the remark. "He is a palmist and an astrologer, and I used to work for him. He has solved some of the most astonishing mysteries in this city. He is continually doing good. You can be sure of him."

"What must I do?" Bessie demanded.

"He knows all about you," said Valeska. "The colonel has told him everything, and Astro, my friend, has agreed to help solve the problem. I know I can trust you, when I tell you this. I want you to see him and ask his advice."

"I will!" Bessie rose with determination. "I'll just leave it all to him. He can't make it any worse than to tell me that I'm not the colonel's daughter, and then that will settle it. Let's go and call on him now."

Astro looked up in surprise when he saw the two girls enter the studio. A secret glance from Valeska told him the truth. He nodded, and welcomed the visitor.

"I've told her everything," said Valeska. "She can be trusted. You will take my word for it, I know. And she's ready for the ophthalmoscope test."

"Is it really a proof?" Bessie asked timidly.

"My dear girl," said Astro, "if your optic disk shows itself to be the ordinary circle, nothing whatever will be proved, and the chances are equal as between you and Willie. If, on the contrary it appears like your father's—I mean the colonel's—it will be ten thousand to one that you are descended from him; that you are, in fact, his daughter. Now, Valeska, put down the lights and light the blue bulb."

The room became dim and full of shadows. The incandescent wire of the electric lamp showed a rich purple. Astro took up the instrument, placed it in front of Miss Maverick's eyes and stared through the aperture.

"Come here, Valeska!"

He handed her the ophthalmoscope, adjusted it, and bade her look. Valeska gazed into the retina of Bessie's eye. At first she could distinguish nothing. Slowly she perceived the warm pink back of the eye, and in the center a ruddy spot. It was the optic disk— shaped like an angel's wings! She dropped the instrument and clasped Bessie in her arms.

"Bessie Mixter!" she exclaimed.

"No!" Bessie jumped up, staring. For a moment she stood silent, then she grasped Astro's hand.

"Oh, you won't tell him, will you?" she pleaded. "Promise me you won't ever, ever let him know! I don't want the money! I want Willie to have it, as he's always had it! Don't let him ever, ever know!"

"But it's yours!" Valeska exclaimed.

"I don't care. Don't you understand, Valeska?"

"You mean—"

"Yes!" Bessie cast down her eyes.

"Then you'll marry him, now you know that the money's rightfully yours?"

Bessie drew herself up. "Of course!" she said. "Wouldn't you?"

"It's too much for me," said Astro.

"That," said Valeska, "is because you are only a man."

"I know I'm supposed not to know anything about love," he said gloomily.

"Nothing at all!" Valeska's tone was decisive.

"And I'll have a father after all!" cried Bessie. "That's the best part of it! I've wanted a father all my life. And," she added, "he'll never know, by the way I treat him, that he's missed anything by not having a truly daughter!" She walked toward the telephone. "I'm going to ring up Willie right now," she announced.

Astro watched her keenly. "It would be rather pleasant to have a daughter like that," he muttered to himself, and walked into the laboratory with a thoughtful scowl.

THE TWO MISS MANNINGS

"Be careful, Valeska, don't joggle my arm, now!" said Astro.

They were in the small laboratory that led off the great studio. Here the Seer pursued his studies in physics, chemistry, and pathology. Here he had his microscope, over which he spent most of his leisure. Here, now, he stood before the window, dressed in a linen suit, holding to the light a corked test-tube.

Valeska waited, smiling, ready for a new marvel, a new philosophic theory, some shrewd comment on human nature, or what other thought had sprung from the Master's prolific brain. She looked over his shoulder, letting her chin touch it, even; though she did not often permit herself such intimacy as this.

He did not turn his head. Instead, without speaking he unstopped the tube gently. Immediately in the glass cylinder a tiny miracle appeared. A white ray sprang from the bottom of the colorless liquid. It divided and subdivided, branching in a dozen directions; and as she looked it grew rapidly, until the interior of the vessel was filled as if by magic with a feathery delicate mass of crystals.

"Oh! How very beautiful—how wonderful!" she gasped.

He put the tube into her hand and sat down on the table.

"The tree of Paracelsus," he remarked. "In the olden time it was accounted magic. With that simple experiment with sodium sulphate dukes and kings may have been beguiled, fortunes won, the lives of great men changed. Those were the palmy days for charlatans, Valeska. It paid well to be an alchemist in the Middle Ages; that is, if you escaped being put to death for it."

As she handed back the tube, he gazed on it thoughtfully for a moment; and then, holding it over a Bunsen burner, warmed the tube. In a few moments the crystals began to melt. The tree shrank and disappeared. He gave it a shake, and the solution was transparent again. He set it in a rack and smiled.

Valeska waited, knowing that this was not mere amusement. It was like him to wait for her to fathom, if she could, what he was thinking. But his mind surpassed hers; she could only follow him at times, though oftener than at first. Here she had no clue.

"It's a moral lesson," he said. "It is a parable of human nature and its mysteries. Why do we become absolutely different persons when we are angry? I am, we'll say, like this clear solution, hermetically sealed from the atmosphere of strife. Open the cork, or drop in a crystal of anger. Immediately, without apparent reason, I am changed; but not so beautifully as this. Warm this tree of acrid bitterness that has sprung up, and I melt into good nature again. Reading Paracelsus, the analogy came into my mind. Thus endeth the first lesson."

And, so saying, he stripped off his working clothes, attired himself in gown and turban, and, as he changed his costume, became again the inscrutable calm Seer, ready for his patrons. He walked into the dim studio, took a gyroscope from a tabouret and spun it on a little standard.

Valeska's look followed him. His eyes questioned her. She drew down her fair brows and watched the toy, supported seemingly immune from the power of gravitation as it revolved slowly in its orbit, its wheel flying too fast, too silently, for its motion to be perceived.

She spoke timidly. "Human emotions—the downward pull—governed and held in equilibrium by—"

"The trained mind, the intellect," he suggested. "Very well, Valeska. Very well, indeed! You're coming on." He yawned. "Well, now for work! It's dangerous pushing analogies too far."

"Well, about that young man who came yesterday?"

"Oh, yes. I didn't have time to see him. Besides, it's time you were taking some cases off my hands, and he didn't seem too anxious. I know you prefer men to women." He watched her from the tail of his eye.

"I don't!" she protested, blushing.

Astro seemed pleased. "Well, it's agreeable for them, at any rate. What was the story?"

"Why, it's most romantic! It's perfectly ridiculous, though! He wants you to find a strange woman whom he saw on the subway."

"Why strange?"

"Oh, strange enough in every way. And it's a hard problem, too."

"First, who is he?"

"He's a Mr. Jenson, and he said to ring him up at Madison 2995 between nine and two o'clock. Those are banking hours. And I found out the number was that of the Sixth Avenue National."

"Very good. Go on."

"Well, yesterday at four o'clock, he took a local in the subway at Twenty-third Street. Between Twenty-eighth Street and Thirty-third, an up-town express passed him. You know how, sometimes, two trains keep side by side for a short distance, exactly even, and then the express shoots ahead?"

"Yes. I've often thought of complications arising from two passengers watching each other."

"Which is exactly what happened. Directly opposite his window was a beautiful girl sitting in the express. She seemed fearfully agitated, and looked at him strangely; almost as if she recognized him, though he's sure he has never seen her before. But he had another sort of feeling—an emotion—as if somehow she was something to him,—one might call it a sudden feeling of affinity,—a real love at first sight."

"Oh, in the circumstances she felt safe enough to flirt with him, I suppose."

"Oh, that's impossible; for it seemed evident that she didn't feel safe at all,—in fact that she was in a great danger, and was so distressed that she made a mute appeal to him for help."

"Why to *him?*"

"To him, he thinks, perhaps too sentimentally, because she, too, felt the mysterious affinity,—whatever it is, trust in him, or something. And she asked him to help her."

Astro stared. "Asked him! How, pray? She had only a few moments, and I suppose the windows were shut. They always are, even in summer."

"Yes; but she was really clever. She had a newspaper in her hand. On the front page were the headlines. Here, I have a yesterday's paper."

She took up a copy of the *Gazette* and pointed to the scare-head, "Tammany Will Help Push the New Viaduct," in such a way that only the word "Help" was evident.

"Then," Valeska continued, "she gave him a number, 3324, one digit at a time, on her fingers."

"I see. And Mr. Jenson, I suppose, wants to know the lady's name and address, and what she wanted?"

"Exactly. Of course the number was that of her house; but what street?"

Astro snapped his fingers impatiently. "It was her telephone number. Didn't she make any sign to show the central?"

"Why, just as she got to the 4, the train she was in swept out of sight as his slowed up at the Thirty-third-Street station."

Astro thought for a while. Finally he said, "Take the telephone book and make a list of all the exchanges, first thing. Then we'll have to use our pull with the company to find out the names and addresses of all the 3324's, and send men to investigate. It's merely a question of elimination then. But the question is, what was the matter? That requires thought. What happened yesterday? I suppose you've finished all the papers?"

"Yes; but there was nothing that seemed important to me."

"Then I'll have to look over the files myself. What a bore!"

He went into the waiting-room and began listlessly to turn the sheets. He had not gone far before Valeska heard a low whistle. Running up to him, she saw him reading a news item under the following headings: "Aged Woman Killed in Subway Station. Run

Over by Down-town Express After Falling on Track in View of Crowd."

"Look at that!" he exclaimed. "This happened at a quarter to three o'clock yesterday. The mysterious lady might easily have been at the Fourteenth-Street station at the time of the accident."

"And what does that prove?"

"Nothing yet! but it's a chance for a clue; a queer coincidence, at any rate. I'll take a think, when I have leisure."

He went back to the studio, and, after he had finished reading the palm of his first client, Valeska entered with the list:

Audubon	Cortland	Madison Sq.	Riverside
Barclay	Franklin	Marble	Schuyler
Beekman	Gramercy	Melrose	Spring
Broad	Hanover	Morning Side	Stuyvesant
Bryant	Harlem	Murray Hill	Tremont
Chelsea	John	Orchard	Westchester
City Island	Kingsbridge	Plaza	Williamsbridge
Columbus	Lenox	Rector	Worth

Astro glanced it over, and penciled it as he talked. "We'll first strike out all the stations obviously not in the residence districts where the lady would be likely to live. We may leave out Beekman, Barclay, Broad, City Island, Franklin, Cortland, John, Hanover, Orchard, Rector, and Worth. That leaves us still nineteen numbers to investigate. Now, if the young lady wanted help badly enough to appeal to a casual stranger, and for that purpose tried to communicate her telephone number, it must have been that she was going directly home, and wanted a quick reply. As she was on a subway express at Thirty-third Street, then it couldn't have been either of the Chelsea, Gramercy, Madison Square, Spring, or Stuyvesant districts. The subway does not go near the Harlem, Melrose, Lenox, Tremont, Westchester, or Williamsbridge sections. Let's see, then, what is left: Audubon, Bryant, Columbus, Kingsbridge, Morningside, Riverside, and Murray Hill. Ring up Mr. Potter in the advertising department of the telephone company, and tell him I'd like to find the names and addresses of number 3324 in each of those seven exchanges."

Valeska left the studio on this errand, and, as no client appeared, Astro picked up his Paracelsus and went on with his reading. He had finished the chapter on *Aqueous Vapors* when she returned. He took up her memorandum and looked it over. The Audubon and Kingsbridge addresses he eliminated, for the present, these being apartment-houses with private exchanges. The *Social Register* enabled him to identify the persons in the Morningside, Plaza, and Riverside districts. There were left only three addresses, as follows:

(Bryant, 3324) H. J. Cook, 199 West Forty-fifth Street.
(Columbus, 3324) Peter J. Manning, 521 West Seventy-third Street.
(Murray Hill, 3324) Alpheus Hardy, 118 East Thirty-sixth Street.

"Well," he said, "the last one, Hardy, must go, because if she were going to East Thirty-sixth Street, the lady would have taken a local to Thirty-third-Street station. To-morrow we'll see what we can find out about the Cooks and Mannings. We'll see if my theory is correct. You have a description of the girl, I suppose?"

"Such as it is, not much; though he'd know her, of course, if he saw her again. He was too busy trying to take her message to have noticed or recalled much. He did say she wore chinchilla furs, though, had reddish hair, and either a scar or a deep dimple in her chin."

"I hope it's a dimple," said Astro, taking up his Paracelsus.

Valeska pouted, shook her fist at him, and retired.

The next morning a man purporting to be an agent of the New York Directory Company called at 199 West Forty-fifth Street and asked many questions. He had an affable way with him that quite won the heart of the maid who answered the door. She denied, however, that there was any young woman living in the house, which belonged to H. J. Cook.

That afternoon the same agent called at 521 West Seventy-third Street. He was met by a butler, who treated the agent with cold disdain and refused to commit himself more than to assert that the house was the residence of Peter J. Manning, wholesale wood dealer. The servant thawed out, however, in an interview with a young woman who called later, asking for Miss Manning. Miss Manning, he ventured to say, was out; but was expected back at two o'clock. He had not heard that she had lost any chinchilla furs, but hoped the young lady would return, and if the furs found belonged to Miss Manning, he was sure that the finder would be well rewarded. Yes, he had seen Miss Manning with chinchillas, and it was his opinion that she had them on when she left the house at ten o'clock that morning. He hoped the young lady would call again.

At one o'clock a coupe drew up at the corner of West Seventy-third Street and Broadway and stopped. The curtains were drawn at the side of the carriage, but a man's face occasionally looked out from the little window in the end. Two o'clock passed, and three.

Meanwhile, another coupe had been standing at the corner of West End Avenue, at the other end of the same block. In this also the curtains were drawn; but at times a passing pedestrian caught sight of a young woman's pretty face, with light hair and blue eyes. At about half past two o'clock a woman wearing chinchilla furs passed the carriage. Its occupant immediately alighted and after a word to the driver, followed her. She walked rapidly along Seventy-third Street, and ran up the steps of number 521. The follower did not stop, however, but went to Broadway, spoke to the driver of the waiting cab, and sprang in. It immediately drove off.

At the studio Valeska went immediately to the telephone and rang up Jenson.

"The person you inquired about," she said, "is Miss Margaret Manning, and she is now at 521 West Seventy-third Street. I gave the Master the card-case you left, and with that as a test he went into an astral trance yesterday. While in that state he saw, clairvoyantly, the scene you described, as well as the girl's subsequent movements."

She waited for the reply and then smiled as she answered, "I'm afraid I can not tell you more of her, Mr. Jenson. The Master does not feel that he is at liberty to disclose the secrets revealed to him while in this astral state. Should events prove it advisable, however, he will inform you, as far as is possible. The girl is in trouble; but we must make sure that she desires your assistance before we let you into the details of her life. Yes, please send a check to Astro. One hundred dollars. Thank you."

"Oh, the girl is in trouble, is she, sorceress?" Astro asked languidly, looking up from where he was toying with his pet white lizard.

"Why, of course! What woman isn't?" said Valeska. "Did you ever encounter one who didn't have a secret sorrow, big or little?"

"My dear," and Astro playfully chucked her under the chin, "you are positively learning. You are right, of course. The first thing a charlatan has to learn is that every man likes to be understood, and every woman to be misunderstood. Both like to be considered sensitive, critical, good judges of human nature, and of delicate perceptions. No one objects to being called reckless; but every one dislikes being considered stupid. But, seriously, of course the chances are ten to one that Miss Manning has some pet sorrow, and if she hasn't Jenson will never know. At any rate, we have done our part. We'll see him again, though. Any man who has that affinity idea may be depended upon to do something foolish."

It was two weeks after that, however, before Jenson was heard from. He came in late one afternoon, pink-cheeked and immaculate, in stylish clothes, a clean-shaven, fresh, young man, evidently wealthy. Astro received him gravely. The Seer had on his oriental costume and his most effete manner.

"See here!" the young man began. "You're a wonder, I've got to confess that! I take off my hat to you, Astro. I don't know how you do it, but you certainly deliver the goods. I don't mind telling you that I came to this place as the result of a bet. I saw that girl in the subway and told one of my friends about it. He said, 'You go to Astro; he can do anything.' Of course, I didn't believe it, and all this nonsense about astral trances is rot. All the same, you did find the girl. It was Miss Manning, all right."

"I beg your pardon, Mr. Jenson," Astro's voice was a bit sarcastic, "I presume you did not come here to insult me. I take your exuberance as mere youth. As you know nothing of my methods, it would be courtesy, since they are successful, to accept what explanation I am pleased to offer. But I pass that by."

"I say, you know, I didn't mean to offend you." Jenson was visibly embarrassed.

Without reply, Astro rose and touched a gong. Valeska entered immediately. With a gesture toward the young man, the Seer left the studio.

"I say, I'm sorry!" Jenson began.

"The Master has his moods," said Valeska.

"I wanted to ask his advice."

"You may deal with me; and if he decides to continue with your case I shall let you know." Valeska looked her sweetest, but her voice was crisp and cool.

"Well, the fact is, I've seen Miss Manning three times, and she certainly has got me going. I wanted to talk to Astro about it."

"Talk to me."

"Well, it was this way. I went up to Seventy-third Street and hung around the afternoon you telephoned, and I did succeed in seeing her; but I was across the street, and before I could get to her she had got into a carriage. Well, I've been up there very often since; but I never caught her till about ten days ago. She was walking down the block, and as I passed her she recognized me and stopped. The first thing she said was, 'Can you help me? Will you help me?' I said of course I would. It was romantic. I don't mind saying it was mighty exciting to me. We walked a way, and she told me an extraordinary thing. I can't believe it; indeed, it's impossible. But she believed it, though she said it was impossible, too."

"Well, what was it?"

"Why, she said, 'I'm frightened because something that's obviously impossible is true. One hour ago I was in Chicago!' What do you think of that?"

"I should say that she was insane."

"That was my first idea; but, as you see, she herself admitted that such a thing was impossible, as it takes twenty-four hours to go from Chicago to New York. It was four o'clock. She said she was in Chicago in front of the Auditorium at three."

"Well, what did she expect you to do for her?"

"Why, that wasn't all; she said she had no idea where she was or what she was doing in New York. She didn't even know who the people were she was living with. She remembered having signaled to me on the train. She was lost then, too. She suddenly found herself with a stranger, a man who seemed to think he was her protector; but she was afraid of him. She had just heard him give his telephone number to a friend who had passed through the car. That was all the clue she had to where she was going. So she signaled that to me; but didn't have time to give me the name of the exchange, 'Columbus.' She wanted me to take her to Chicago immediately. I told her that was impossible; but that I'd go the next day with her and take her home. She was afraid of this man's following her. I made an appointment for the next morning. She was to meet me in the Waldorf-Astoria palm-room at ten o'clock."

"And she didn't come, of course?"

"No. I got frightened—thought that something serious was the matter—and called at her house. Sent up my name. She came down and coolly asked to know what I wanted. She pretended not to know me, and I was in a deuce of a situation. I floundered out of it as best I could; told her I had an appointment. She denied it; said she didn't know me, nor what I was talking about. And there you are!" Jenson crossed his legs and gazed at Valeska with big eyes.

"Well, I suppose you wish the Master to explain this?"

"That's what I came here for. I told him the first time I came it was on account of a wager. I bet my friend fifty dollars that Astro couldn't find the girl. Well, I lost. This time I come believing in him. Will you see what you can do? I confess I'm fond of that girl. I've felt it from the beginning, the very first glance. I want to help her. I want to know her, and, you may think it absurd, but I want to marry her." He folded his arms and became almost defiant.

Valeska rose. "Very well. I can promise nothing; but I shall put it before the Master, and, as I said, I shall let you know his decision. Of myself I can do nothing; but I shall try to influence him."

Jenson left, thanking her profusely. Just as he opened the door, he said embarrassedly, "See here; I'd do anything for that girl!"

"Would you really?" Valeska asked, smiling.

"I mean just that,—anything!" And Jenson went out the door with a grim look on his face.

Valeska came back into the studio laughing. "Do tell me what it means!" she exclaimed after she had told the story to Astro.

He yawned. "Isn't Miss Manning calling quite often at number 85 Central Park, South?" he remarked casually, examining his long nails.

"Why, how do you know? I didn't know you had done anything more on the case."

"Oh, very little. It's scarcely necessary."

"But whom is she going to see?"

"Doctor George Herreschoff."

"A specialist?"

"A neurologist."

"I don't understand."

Astro smiled and shook his head indulgently.

"Well, I'll give you a book by Doctor Morton Prince to read. You'll find it as exciting as a novel; I might venture to say as exciting as Mr. Jenson's experience with Miss Manning."

Valeska knew more than to ask further. The Seer usually gave her a hint and let her exert her imagination.

"Don't forget the accident in the subway station at Fourteenth Street. And there's an article in the November number of *The Journal of Abnormal Psychology*," he added.

He rose, went to the book-shelves that lined three walls of the vast studio, took down the book and the little magazine, and gave them to her with a smile. Then he walked into his laboratory to prepare, for her edification, the arbor Jovis, the arbor Dianae, and the arbor Saturnae: the trees of tin, silver, and lead.

He stuck his head out of the door a half-hour later and called over to where Valeska was reading under a lamp, "Your friend Jenson will never marry that girl he's after!"

"Oh, won't he?"

"No; she's going to disappear."

Valeska stared at him in wonder. Her look changed to amazement when he added:

"But he may marry Margaret Manning."

"Why, she *is* Margaret Manning," she replied, still puzzled.

"No, she isn't," he said, laughing, and shut the door of the laboratory.

The next day Jenson telephoned to the studio. Valeska came back from her conversation with him, leaving the receiver off the hook. "He says he has met Miss Manning again, and she still is urging him to take her to Chicago. But he has begun to be suspicious of her, and doubts if he ought to do it. He wants your advice."

Astro smiled. "You might tell him what I told you yesterday."

"Ah! but what's the use if he hasn't read *The Dissociation of a Personality?*"

"Then suppose you advise him to call on Doctor Herreschoff and ask his advice."

"Shall I, really? Who is he?"

"The most famous specialist on nervous diseases in America, who knows more of multiple or dissociated personality than any one living."

"Oh, I see. I'll tell him." And Valeska returned to the telephone to repeat the address.

"You understand now?" Astro asked.

"Of course. Miss Manning has a dual personality. In her normal state she does not, of course, recall Mr. Jenson. In her secondary state she appealed to him for help."

"Because she literally did not know where she was," added Astro. "Doubtless, from his story, while she was in Chicago her own normal self, she changed into the secondary character, in which she did not even know her own brother. She alternated between the two states, which may be called the A and the B. It is often the case that a mental or physical shock entirely changes the personality. That's what I thought of on reading of the accident at the subway station. No doubt she witnessed the accident. The shock broke up her personality, changed A, her normal state, into B. She had, no doubt, been B before, in Chicago. But, finding herself with a man she did not recognize, she became alarmed. Her impulse was to appeal to the first likely-looking stranger for help. Somehow she was attracted to Jenson, and so she signaled to him."

"Then she was B again when she asked him to take her to Chicago?"

"Certainly. Of course she must have gone to Chicago between the time he saw her on the train and when he met her in the street. She recalled having been in Chicago at three o'clock. She must have changed almost immediately, and taken the train soon afterward. Then, upon arriving in New York, something threw her back into the B state again. Owing to her amnesia, while in the secondary state, she forgot all that had happened, and thought it was the same day that she was in Chicago. But when he called at the house, she had changed back to her normal condition. All that is evident from his story. It is as evident that such a case would be brought to Doctor Herreschoff for treatment, and doubtless he will be very glad to meet Jenson, who knows something of what has happened to her in this abnormal, or B, state. The doctor will undoubtedly treat her hypnotically and restore her to a permanently normal personality."

"And that's how Mr. Jenson's friend, poor B, will disappear?"

"Yes. There is, properly, no such person. B is merely a *part* of Miss Manning,—Miss Manning with certain faculties, including memory, missing. It's not so interesting a case as that of Miss Beauchamp, which Doctor Prince has written of, nor of the celebrated Felida X, reported by Azan. Of course there are all sorts of dissociations. Some persons break up into three or four separate and intermittent personalities. But Miss Manning is certainly interesting. I'd like to meet her, myself."

"And I'd like to know how poor Jenson's love-affair will turn out," said Valeska. "I'm sorry for him."

"I've no doubt he'll not only lose the girl he has fallen in love with, but he'll be asked to help in putting her out of existence."

"That's simply horrible! He said he'd do anything for her. I wonder if he'd do that? But it's all so mysterious and so impossible! Why, one might as well believe in witchcraft or magic it seems to me."

"It is just exactly what was called witchcraft in the old days. Now we understand it, and it is merely psychology."

Astro rose and pointed to the laboratory. "Do you remember the tree of Paracelsus?" he asked.

Valeska nodded.

"It is like that. In the Middle Ages that experiment was nothing but pure magic. No common person could understand that the clear solution and the mass of crystals were different forms of the same thing,—sulphate of sodium and water. In the same way, no one understood that one person could appear at different times under different forms; it was enchantment. To-day we understand that one's personality is merely the sum of his qualities, emotions and functions. This solid person may break up into other combinations; part of his functions may become synthesized and have a volition of this new group's own character. We see it every day. When we lose our temper we become temporarily dissociated. We say things foreign to our true nature. When we dream, too, we become different in many ways. Occasionally some natures in a state of unstable equilibrium topple over and change their mental and spiritual structure. Then we have such patients as Miss Beauchamp, as Miss Smith, reported by Flournoy, as Mrs. Smead, whom Hyslop describes, or Ansel Bourne, studied by Doctor Hodgson and Professor James. And how many unknown such are confined in insane asylums, who might be easily restored to normality, God knows!"

He had been walking up and down the great studio as he talked. Now he returned to Valeska, and for an instant his hand rested on her blond head.

"There's one thing more potent than mental shock that changes men's personality often enough," he said softly.

She looked up quickly, uncomprehending. "What do you mean?"

"Did I say one thing? There are two things that change a man's character essentially," he went on, looking at her thoughtfully. "One is a profound sorrow; the other is love." He walked away to the window. "Dickens understood that," he threw over his shoulder.

Valeska turned her eyes away from him, then rose and passed into the waiting-room.

Three days after that, Jenson called. He was no longer the blithe and joyous young man of fashion. Instead, he seemed prematurely old. His eyes were softer, his manner less careless.

"It all came true as Astro predicted," he said to Valeska, talking it over; "even to my never marrying the girl I fell in love with. Doctor Herreschoff told me all about her case, and asked my assistance in bringing her back to her true self. In her normal state she does not know me at all; in fact, there is almost a dislike of me, on account of my having been mixed up with her secondary self,—the girl who asked my help. But the doctor thinks my companionship is beneficial, and I have consented to give my assistance. If she appears in her abnormal state, I shall take her to him and have her treated hypnotically. Her changes come less often, and he thinks she will soon be permanently normal."

"You do love her, indeed!" Valeska breathed in admiration.

"Enough to murder her, in a way of speaking, for her own good!" he replied grimly. "But didn't I tell you I would do anything for that girl? Anything! Could anything harder be asked of me than that I should help myself to lose her forever?" He smiled wanly as he spoke.

"Oh, it won't be lost, that sacrifice!" Valeska exclaimed. "She will realize what you have done, in time, and she will—she *must* love you for it! Then it will be she herself, not a mere part of her personality, but the whole woman, who will repay you with her love."

"Perhaps." Jenson rose to go, and stood a moment, sadly thoughtful. "But somehow—confound it, that other girl, you know!—she *was* the one, after all— Well, I've given my word. All I want is her well-being. I'm satisfied. Good-by!" and he wrung Valeska's hand till the tears came into her eyes, though she made no sound.

She came back into the great studio and found Astro gazing abstractedly out of the window. He was so lost in his reverie that he did not notice her approach till she had laid a hand on his shoulder. Then he looked round, startled. His face changed wonderfully and became infinitely tender.

"You were right," she said softly, "there are two things that change human character, love and sorrow. Our poor Mr. Jenson has tasted both, I think."

"It will make a man of him," said Astro. "I hope it may make a man of me!"

He walked into the little laboratory. Into a Florence flask, filled with a solution of lead acetate, he dropped a few pieces of zinc. In an hour there had grown up, exquisitely feathery and foliated, the crystalline tree of lead, the arbor Saturnae of the alchemists, potent with its parable of life.

Valeska found it there after he had left, looked at it a moment, and bit her lip in silence. Then, after a quick timid look about, she took up the flask and gave it a kiss.

VAN ASTEN'S VISITOR

"Unless it stops snowing pretty soon, I think I'll not go to Boston to-night, after all," said young Van Asten, of the law firm of Hipp & Van Asten. He stood looking out a thirteenth-story window, late one December afternoon, watching the big storm which had increased steadily in violence since one o'clock. His hat was tilted on the back of his head and his overcoat collar was turned up about his ears. Keen, quick, and clear-cut, his features showed handsomely in profile. He was the popular member of the firm among his affluent clientele.

"Looks like a blizzard," said the clerk, rummaging in a pasteboard letter-holder.

"Sure. The midnight train is sure either to be stalled or delayed, and I can go on Saturday just as well. I don't care to sit up for hours in a snow-bank." Then he turned suddenly to the clerk. "Say, has anybody from Selvig's been in to-day?" he asked.

"You mean about the Drellmont will case?"

"Yes. By the way young Drellmont spoke yesterday, I rather expect he's getting ready to compromise. He's a fool if he doesn't; and a bigger fool to expect me to show him the will, too!"

"Nobody's been in," said the clerk laconically.

Van Asten went out and plowed his way through rising drifts to the subway station. By six o'clock he was at the Gavel Club, and by eight had finished his dinner. Several games of pool, a long talk with a visiting Englishman, perusal of the French comic papers, and convivial gossip with late comers from the theaters full of tales of the storm, kept him warm and cheerful till midnight. Then, as the clock struck, he put on his things and went out.

There were few abroad at this hour, and not a carriage or an automobile in sight. The street-car lines had given up trying to keep the tracks clear, and he came across one darkened car abandoned in the snow. He had to fight his way home, struggling through drifts waist high. It was deathly quiet except for the sound of the wind.

He reached his apartment-house at last, and, stamping and shaking himself, climbed four flights of stairs, the elevator being out of order. At his door he stopped, surprised. Under the door there was a thin streak of light.

Van Asten's firm was still too young to enable him to live in the style he had been used to before going into business. His apartment consisted of only four rooms,—a large, L-shaped studio, a bedroom, and, off the entrance hall, on one side a bath-room, and on the other a kitchenet. A woman came in every morning to clean up the place; except for that, he was alone.

He distinctly remembered that no light had been left burning when he had left the place at ten o'clock that morning. What, then, could the light mean? No one save the janitor had a key to the place. His thought went naturally to burglars. He hesitated for some moments, wondering what to do. It was late to summon the janitor for assistance, and he would appear foolish if nothing serious had happened. He determined to investigate alone, and, prepared for an immediate struggle, he put his key quietly into the door and turned the latch. The door opened without noise, and he could see through the one opposite into the long studio.

There, a woman in mink furs stood, with her back to him, beside the great table. She was bending over, as if taking something from a bag.

The tension of suspense that had knotted Van Asten's muscles and nerves gave way to a little laugh. The romance of the encounter amused him keenly, though his curiosity was doubly alert. He took a step forward.

At the sound of his footsteps, the woman looked round quickly, and for a minute stood staring at him with an expression of alarm.

Her hand went to her heart. She was a beautiful woman of twenty-three, dressed with elegance. She was a vivid blonde, with masses of heavy yellow hair, blue eyes and slender hands. For a single moment she stood there, immobile; then, to Van Asten's amazement, she ran forward and threw her arms about his neck and pressed her lips to his cheek.

"Oh, Paul! I'm *so* glad you've come! I didn't know what to do! I was afraid I'd have to stay here all night alone! Where in the world have you been?"

Van Asten calmly disentangled himself from her embrace and took another look at her face. She was blushing violently. "Will you kindly tell me, first of all, who you are?"

"Why, Paul! What in the world do you mean?"

"I mean I haven't the pleasure of your acquaintance, and naturally I have a little curiosity about a visitor at this hour."

For a second or two she gazed at him steadily, her lips parted. "Are you drunk, Paul?" she demanded finally.

"I'm not drunk. I simply don't know you. Why should I?"

"You don't know your own sister!" she exclaimed in a vibrant intense tone. Then she took a backward step, as if she feared him.

"My sister is in Boston." He stared at her with a frown and folded his arms. "What's your little game, anyway?"

"You don't know your own sister!" she repeated helplessly. Then she staggered back and sunk into a chair, hiding her face in her hands, and began to weep.

"You are not my sister, and you know it as well as I do! What do you want here, anyway?" he demanded, still standing, staring at her.

"Why, I want to stay here, of course! I've just come from Boston to visit you!" She suddenly sprang up. "The idea! It's a stupid practical joke you're playing on me, of course. Come, Paul, drop it, please! I'm tired, and want to go to bed. Where are you going to put me?"

"I'm going to put you outdoors!" he retorted.

"In this awful blizzard?" she demanded. She smiled sadly through her tears. The effect was really dazzling; but Van Asten kept his head.

He stopped and reflected for a few moments. Then, without taking his eyes from her, he took off his hat and overcoat, tossed them aside, and sat down. He tried hard to appear calm.

"Now," he continued, "I insist that you drop this masquerade and tell me immediately who you are and how you came here. You're either crazy, or it's some sort of blackmailing game. If you know anything about my sister, you know you don't in the least resemble her; and if you know anything about me, you know I haven't any money. So, out with it, quick!"

"I've told you!" she said, and loosed another pathetic smile at him.

He frowned impatiently. "Then you *are* crazy!"

"No, I'm afraid *you* are!"

The deadlock continued for some minutes before either spoke again. Then he began more quietly. "I don't know what's the matter with you. It's too much for me. But, of course, I can't let you stay here. Neither can I put you out into this storm. The only thing I can think of is to telephone to some one to come here. But no woman could get here to-night, even if she should be willing to. I confess I don't know what to do with you."

"It's perfectly all right," she answered sweetly. "I'm your sister, and surely you should be willing to let me have your room for to-night. You can sleep on that big couch round the corner of the studio, and you'll be sober in the morning. When you wake up, you'll probably recognize me. I won't be hard on you, my dear. Only, really, you ought to be careful what you drink." She rose, walked over to him, and patted his head.

He jumped up abruptly and walked away, opened his bedroom door, and stood there for a moment. "Come in here!" he commanded.

"All right, Paul!" she answered with extravagant humility, and, casting down her eyes, walked into the room. Just before she closed the door she came near him again.

"Aren't you going to kiss me good night, Paul, dear?" she asked.

Without answering her he pulled the door to, and heard her swiftly lock it on the inside. Then, still frowning, he walked up and down the long studio for ten minutes. Once or twice he stopped outside the door to listen, but heard nothing. Later she called out "Good night, Paul!" to him in blithe accents. He bit his lip and resumed his promenade, more worried than ever. The thing was uncanny. He no longer accepted the situation as romantic; he felt decidedly uncomfortable and embarrassed. Some one was making a fool of him, or worse.

Suddenly a thought came to him, and he went to the telephone and spoke as low as possible, "Madison, 5555!"

For fully three minutes he waited without receiving a reply.

"Madison 5555 doesn't answer," came the word at last.

"Ring 'em up again!" He spoke a bit more loudly.

In two minutes more he heard, "Hello!"

"Is this Astro?"

"Yes. What the deuce—"

"Wait a minute and I'll explain."

"Well, hurry up! You've got me up out of bed."

"I'm Paul Van Asten, and am at my apartment at the Elton, 444 West Twenty-first Street. I've just come home and found a strange woman in my place. She says she's my sister. Pretty and all that, well dressed, and not otherwise obviously mad. But she worries me. I can't put her out; and she won't go, anyway. What'll I do? Could you possibly come over here? It's mighty embarrassing."

There was a pause, then this inquiry, "Did you find her before she saw you?"

"Yes, opened the door and there she was."

"What was she doing?"

"Standing up, looking into a bag, or something."

"Dressed for the street?"

"Yes, it looked as if she had just come in."

"Did you say how long she had been there?"

"I think she did say she'd waited some time."

"Where is she now?"

"Locked in my bedroom."

"Good. I'll come right over. I can't get a cab in this blizzard; so it may take half or three quarters of an hour."

"All right. But for heaven's sake, hurry! I don't know what she'll do next!"

"Oh, wait. Describe her, please!"

"A blonde, with yellow hair, and lots of it. Rather small, with blue eyes. Mink stole and muff."

"All right. Good-by. I'll hurry."

Van Asten hung up the receiver with a sigh of relief. He had heard much of Astro the Seer and his marvelous solution of mysteries, but the young lawyer did not place much faith in these sensational tales. Astro was, however, a close student of human nature, and, if not intuitive, at least shrewd, and his knowledge of society, and his willingness to undertake any case, however delicate, made him a desirable companion in so embarrassing a crisis.

Van Asten threw himself into a chair commanding a view of the bedroom door and took up a book. No sound came from his chamber. From all that could be gathered, his erratic visitor had gone to bed and to sleep. Now that he was sure of a tactful and clever companion, he rather looked forward to seeing the girl again. He could at last permit his imagination to play with the situation. It might be, after all, a romance—who could tell? The girl was pretty and cultured. No great scandal could ensue with two men there; and somehow, with his luck or his astuteness, Astro would bring the affair to a pleasant solution. A half-hour went by. Van Asten yawned, read a little, and again fell into a reverie. It was three-quarters of an hour before the electric bell sounded. Van Asten ran to the door, threw it open, and Astro, covered with snow, picturesque in slouch hat and Inverness cape, entered.

"Well," he said amusedly, stamping his feet, "when did she leave?"

"She didn't!" said Van Asten. "She's in that room now."

"Oh, didn't she?" Astro shrugged his shoulders and walked toward the bedroom door. "Well, let's see her."

"But, heavens! you mustn't open that door! She's probably in bed and asleep! And besides, the door's locked."

"So it is," said Astro, trying the handle. "I shall have to ask you for a button-hook."

"I haven't any except one in that room."

Astro reflected a moment. Then he asked, "Have you any canned goods in your larder?"

"I have some canned chicken, I believe. Why?"

"And a gas-stove, I presume?"

"Yes." Van Asten looked puzzled, but led the way to the kitchenet. He took down a tin of chicken and handed it to the Seer.

Astro removed the key fastened to the top for the purpose of opening the tin, then went to the stove and lighted a burner. He heated the split wire till it was red-hot; then, taking a pair of small pliers from his pocket, bent the end into a right angle. Returning to the chamber door, he inserted this rough skeleton key into the lock.

"I'll take the responsibility of awakening or disturbing your visitor," he said, smiling at Van Asten. "You must give me full authority to do what I please."

As he spoke he was trying the lock. After some unsuccessful attempts, the bolt shot back. He turned the handle and threw open the door. "Light up!" he commanded sharply.

Van Asten, more embarrassed than ever, stepped to the switch on the wall, and the room was immediately illuminated. Then, staring about him, and finally at Astro, he stammered, "By Jove! She has gone, hasn't she?"

"Of course. You didn't really expect her to spend the night, did you?"

"Well, that's what she said she was going to do. I'm glad she didn't, I confess. Unless—" then he stopped suddenly. "By Jove!" he ejaculated. "Could she have been a burglar?" His eyes roved round the room in trace of corroboration of his surmise, and fell upon a partly raised window which gave on an inner court, or air-shaft.

"Could she have escaped that way?" He ran to the window and threw up the sash.

As he did so, Astro stooped to the floor and picked up a hair-pin, glanced at it, and put it into his pocket. It was of silver, fully six inches long, evidently specially made for a woman with an immense mass of hair. He said nothing of his discovery, however, but followed Van Asten to the window.

"She could hardly have got out that way," said the young lawyer.

"It's unlikely," Astro assented; "but I see you have an electric reading lamp. I wonder if it will reach to the window?"

He took it from the table, and, finding that the wire was long enough; held it above his head outside the window and looked down to the bottom of the court.

"I don't see her," Van Asten laughed.

If Astro saw anything, he did not mention it. He drew himself in, replaced the lamp, and pulled down the sash.

"I didn't expect to see her hanging by the hair of her head, like Absalom," he remarked. "But," he added casually, "what kind of hair did she have?"

"Yellow hair, pounds and pounds of it, apparently, though you never can tell nowadays, when all the women are wearing rats."

"Where is your telephone?" the Seer inquired.

Van Asten led the way back into the studio. Around the corner, out of sight of the chamber door, the receiver stood on his library table.

"She got out while you were talking to me," said Astro. "That's plain enough. Now, the question is, what's missing?"

"By Jove! That's true! But I didn't notice any disturbance. Hold on!" he stood for a moment with his eyes fixed. "The Drellmont will! Good lord! if she came for *that*—" Instead of finishing, he ran back to the chamber. Astro followed him quickly enough to find him at a writing-desk there, rummaging through the pigeonholes.

He stopped and exclaimed, "Thank the Lord!" and held up a package of papers. "Here it is, safe enough. It wasn't that she wanted, at any rate."

"What about the Drellmont will?" Astro inquired casually.

"Why, I took it home yesterday to study on the case with it. You've heard of Albert Drellmont, of course?"

"The millionaire? Yes."

"Then you know he had a scapegrace son, who went to the bad a year or so ago. Well, this is the will disinheriting him. Old Drellmont had made another only a few months before, leaving his son the bulk of his property. Young Drellmont has been trying to bluff his way into the fortune, by claiming his legacy under the old will and asserting this to be a forgery. This, you see, is in favor of his half-sister." He handed the document to Astro, who took it and examined it carefully.

"Drellmont's attorneys are a sharp lot; but Drellmont himself hasn't a cent, and I don't see how he can afford to fight the case, considering what little show he has against his sister. In fact, I've been expecting an offer to compromise. He came in this morning and wanted to see our will. Of course I shouldn't have showed it to him if I had had it; but I told him it was here. If it had been stolen, we should have been up against it, though we should have won in the end."

"What was the date of the former will?"

"January 1, 1908."

"And this, I see, is just six months later, July 1, 1908."

"Yes, it was made after Drellmont, junior, had that affair with a chorus girl. The papers were full of it. After that, he went West and got into more scrapes. I understand the police are after him now. My client, Miss Drellmont, has wanted to compromise, just to get rid of him, but I wouldn't have it."

"I see." Astro spoke abstractedly as he handed back the document. He was sitting near the secretary, and, as he listened, had picked up a red blotter that lay on the desk. As he rose, he kept it in his hand, and when Van Asten put the will away Astro put the blotter into his pocket.

There was a strange light in his eyes, however, as he gazed at the young lawyer. It was as if he were analyzing him, deliberately, scientifically, reading his character in his features, one by one, weighing his soul in the balance.

"Well, I think I can't do anything more now," he said, finally. "I'll try to get home before the drifts have got any higher. If you miss anything else, telephone me. You might inquire of the janitor, too. He may know how your visitor got in."

"What do you think she wanted, anyway?" said Van Asten.

"Ah! I can't tell you that—yet. But there are evil vibrations here. I feel wrong. She wanted no good, you may be sure of that. I shall try the crystals and go into a psychic trance."

Van Asten smiled. It did not escape Astro's notice.

"Having engaged my services," he said calmly, "I shall expect you to follow my instructions to the letter. I can help you; and I think you need more aid than you imagine."

Van Asten immediately became serious. "I believe you do know something," he said. "Well, I don't care how you find out. I know I can trust you. Let me know what to do, and I'll do it."

As Astro opened the outer door of the Elton, the drifts were two feet high. The snow drove in gusts of fine icy particles, and it was bitterly cold. The flakes came in squalls, driving clouds before them; one could scarcely stand upright against the blast. He bent his head forward and fought his way. Before he had gone a block his hands and ears were almost frozen. Another block, and he sought refuge in a doorway to beat himself, rub his ears, and stamp a little warmth into his feet.

There was a drift filling a corner of the doorway, and, as his eyes fell on it, he saw a black patch beneath. Brushing the snow aside, he came upon a woman, unconscious with the cold. She was dressed in black, and wore mink furs. Her heavy yellow hair was fastened with long silver pins.

Bending over her, he tried to restore her to consciousness; but it was impossible. Her hands and feet were indubitably frozen, and she had succumbed to the exposure. The covering of snow had, in a way, protected her; but the case was desperate. What was there to do? Outside in the street there were no signs of life. Had the doorway been that of a residence, he might have rung the bell and appealed to the mercy of the residents. But it was the entrance to a small office building, and no one would be in at this hour. Astro was ten blocks from his studio. He had reasons for wanting to be alone with the girl. A little scrap of mink fur he had found caught in the outer doorway of the Elton fitted suspiciously with a torn place at the end of this woman's astrakhan stole, and her hairpins matched the one in his pocket.

A gray splotch came into view down the avenue. It was a two-horse carriage, laboring painfully into the teeth of the blizzard. As it approached, Astro ran out and bribed or bullied the driver into taking him and the woman to Thirty-fourth Street. It took half an hour, and more than once the man on the box stopped and protested that he would have to give it up. But they finally arrived at number 234, and, taking the inanimate form in his arms, Astro carried her up-stairs.

His first action, after depositing her on a sofa, was to ring for a doctor. His next was to telephone to Valeska, and urge her to attempt to come immediately to the studio. Then he returned to his charge.

She still gripped a leather bag in her frozen hands. Astro separated the stiffened fingers and put the bag away. Next, he got brandy and forced it down her throat. Wrapping her in warm blankets, he chafed her hands with snow till the doctor arrived. Leaving the two alone for a few minutes, he opened the bag quickly. It contained several bills, a bunch of keys, a handkerchief, and a penciled note. This he opened. The note-paper was imprinted with the name of the Swastika Hotel. It read as follows:

> "The job must be done to-night, or it will be too late. S. will give up to-morrow. Do it if you can, let me know immediately here. P. D."

Valeska, living only two blocks away, succeeded in arriving at the studio by four o'clock in the morning. By the time she came in Astro and the doctor had restored their patient to consciousness and the use of her limbs. The woman was, however, weak and suffering. Rest was enjoined, and the doctor left definite instructions that she was to remain in bed all day.

"What I want you to do, Valeska," said Astro, "is, when this lady awakens, to talk with her long enough to study her voice. By nine o'clock you must be able to give an imitation of it that will pass over a telephone wire without being detected."

He proceeded, then, to narrate the whole story of the night, from the time he was awakened by Van Asten's message. Valeska listened attentively.

GELETT BURGESS

"You say that when you looked down the air-shaft you saw a broken bottle at the bottom?"

"Yes, almost hidden by the snow. And here's another clue." He took the blotter from his pocket and passed it to her. "Do you see anything significant in that?" he asked.

"There's a spot where the ink that was on it has disappeared," she said. "But I don't quite see what that means. You say the date of his will was all right, wasn't it? I thought first that she might have gone down there to alter the date, and so make the old will valid."

"But, in that case, the marks of the erasure, even if done with Labarraque's solution or any of the readymade ink destroyers, would have proved that it had been tampered with."

"That's so. Well, I'll think it over. But do you know who this girl is, yet?"

"She's a friend of Paul Drellmont's, and no doubt his tool." Astro passed over the note he had found in the bag.

"I see. I'm to report to him, then, over the telephone, in her voice, that the thing has been done?"

"By no means. You're to tell him that you failed."

Valeska bent her brows over the riddle. "Well, I hope I won't have to go into details."

"No, he'll be satisfied. You see, this is his last card. If she failed, he'll not care to fight the will case any longer. He knows he's beaten, and he can't pay his lawyers. He'll offer to compromise, and I shall tell Van Asten to make a reasonable offer."

"The girl failed, then, in whatever she went for?"

"No, she succeeded."

"Then won't Drellmont find out about it, and make more trouble?"

"I hope he'll leave immediately. If he accepts a sum of money to compromise, I think he'll quit New York without delay."

"Oh! And you expect to keep this girl hidden away from him till then?"

"Exactly. This blizzard was a godsend for Van Asten and Miss Drellmont."

"Well, I don't understand yet what she went to his rooms for, but I'll do my part."

It was just nine o'clock, and the unknown girl was again sleeping quietly, when Valeska rang up the Swastika Hotel and inquired for Drellmont. After a moment there was a reply.

"It's me, Paul," she said. "I'm awfully sorry; but I couldn't get down there and do the business." Valeska dropped the receiver with a shocked expression.

"What did he say?" Astro asked.

"I refuse to tell you." Valeska put up the instrument and rose.

"Didn't he even ask where you were?"

"No, indeed."

"Then it's as I suspected. Drellmont has been playing on this girl; making love to her, probably, in order to use her as his tool. Now she's failed, he has no further use for her. Well, I think it serves her right. Perhaps it will teach her a lesson. Now, I'll give my instructions to Van Asten."

He rang up the lawyer. After the conversation he returned to Valeska and said:

"He's agreed to compromise, if Drellmont calls. The janitor told him this lady presented a typewritten note, with his name forged to it, inviting her to wait in his apartment for him. That's how she got in there. I suggested that he hint at prosecuting Drellmont for blackmail, on the strength of that episode, and he has agreed to suggest to the rascal that he leave town immediately as one of the conditions of the compromise. But it's a ticklish game, altogether. I don't know whether I ought to explain everything to Van Asten or not."

"Why, I should think he ought to know," said Valeska.

"Why, then, you haven't solved the mystery of the lady's errand?" he asked.

"I confess I haven't."

"Well, then, I'll tell you. It's so ingenious and simple that you'd probably never get it alone. The fact is, that she went down there to erase the date on the will. This she did, and then wrote in the *same date,*—July 1, 1908. I saw it immediately I cast my eyes on the document. When I saw the broken bottle at the foot of the air-shaft, I suspected that she had thrown away some damaging evidence. When I noticed that spot on the blotter where the ink had been bleached, I was sure of it. The only question, then, was whether Van Asten himself hadn't taken the paper home to tamper with it. But, as the date was right, of course, he couldn't have."

"What was her, or rather Drellmont's, reason for putting in the same date, then?"

"Why, so that when the will was probated they could call attention to the erasure and subsequent rewriting. That would cast suspicion on the whole document and no doubt the first will would be accepted as legal."

"Oh, it *was* simple, wasn't it? But you didn't tell Van Asten?"

"No, not yet. I want him to offer the will for probate as it is. You see, it is undoubtedly genuine; but if it had been tampered with, he'd never be willing to handle it. I got that from my study of his character. I'm going to take the responsibility on myself. If Drellmont leaves town before he can communicate with this lady, whoever she is, he'll never know that she succeeded, and Van Asten and Miss Drellmont will be safe. When this blond lady finds that she has been abandoned, she won't care to play into his hands, especially as it may get her into trouble herself."

Late that afternoon, as Valeska was busy in the laboratory off the studio, she saw the girl pass swiftly toward the waiting-room. Valeska waited and listened.

"Give me Madison Square 2615 . . . Hello! Is Mr. Drellmont there? . . . He's left? Why that's impossible! . . . This afternoon? Where did he go? ... No address? . . . Are you *sure?*" The receiver went on the hook with a snap.

Valeska waited to see what she would do next. A few minutes later she stole to the portières and looked into the waiting-room. No one was there!

"Well," said Astro, "you should have followed her. That girl was clever. Any one who could act as well as she did with Van Asten would be a valuable assistant. I might have used her."

Valeska's fine lips curled. "I think one assistant is enough for you, sir! She was altogether too blond. I always distrust that kind!"

The Seer smiled. "Well, as for that, I prefer blondes, myself."

He took a step toward her, but she evaded him, and sought refuge in the office. Not, however, before she had paused in the doorway to shake her finger and ask, mischievously: "Are you *perfectly* sure?"

THE MIDDLEBURY MURDER

Returning, late one night, from an investigation which had carried them down to the Battery, Astro the Seer and Valeska were suddenly nearly thrown from their seats by a sudden stop of the green limousine.

They were driving along Canal Street, and, as the vicinity was apparently deserted, the Seer of secrets looked in surprise from the window to see what was the matter.

A police officer was speaking in tones of command to the chauffeur. Astro, recognizing him as Lieutenant McGraw, smiled in relief. The police officer came to the window with his hat in his hand.

"I beg your pardon, sir, but I recognized your car, so I just ordered your man to stop. I wanted to speak to you a moment. Ah, Miss Wynne, it's glad I am to see you!"

Valeska gave him her hand and a smile.

"I've just been called from the office," said McGraw, "on a case that may be interesting, as I know how you like mysteries. Perhaps you might help me out, even." And Officer McGraw winked elaborately. "When it comes to giving a crook the third degree, or raiding a joint, I'm there with the goods; but this looks like a murder, and murders are sometimes—"

"I see," said Astro suavely. "Well, if you can get in here, we'll go with you. Where is it?"

"Just around the corner, here, at the Aspen wall building on Grand Street." And, after Astro had given the order to the driver, McGraw went on. "You see, the night watchman has just telephoned for an officer, as something suspicious has happened. He seemed excited, and it may turn out something doing, or it may not."

"Well, I'll be glad to be first on the ground, at any rate," said Astro. "That ought to make it easier to solve, if it should happen to be a mystery."

He had scarcely finished when the car drew up at the entrance to the Aspenwall building. A full-bearded man in jumper and over-alls was waiting scowling in the doorway. He came immediately forward.

"There's a murder or a suicide been committed here, I'm afraid," he began; "but I didn't want to do anything till I had the police, to be on the safe side. It's up on the tenth story, in Mr. Middlebury's office."

"Has any one left the building since you telephoned?"

"No, I made sure of that. The elevator boy thought he heard a shot fired, and I went around to all the lighted offices. They were all right except at Middlebury's office, where there was no answer when I knocked. The door was locked."

"How many tenants are in the building now?"

"There have only been two or three here to-night, and some went before this thing happened. There's only one I know of,—Mr. Moffett, on the ninth. I think he's there yet. I spoke to him a little while ago."

"Better ring for a couple more men, McGraw," said Astro.

After the party had entered the corridor, McGraw rang up the office, then returned to the elevator. The boy had just come out, and was standing with white scared face in the corridor. He was a thin anemic youth of eighteen, with red hair and roving, pale blue eyes with dilated pupils.

"Now, young fellow," said McGraw, "what do you know about this?"

"Nothing, sir. Only, I thought I heard a shot fired, and I called Thompson."

"You didn't go up yourself?"

"No, only to take Thompson. I waited in the car while he knocked on the door."

"Where did you find Thompson?"

"On the fifth floor. I went down to the boiler-room at first, thinking he was there; then I tried each floor till I found him."

"What time did you hear the report?"

"About half past eleven o'clock."

"How many people have you taken up on the elevator this evening?"

"Only one or two. Mr. Moffett went up to his office on the ninth at eight o'clock or so—he must be there now—Mr. Smythe, on the fourth; but he left at ten o'clock, about. I don't remember the others."

Astro now turned to the night watchman, Thompson, a heavy-set hairy man, who stood with his mouth open, listening as if fascinated.

"What have you been doing this evening, Thompson?"

"Why, I had a bite of lunch in the boiler-room at about eight o'clock. Then at nine I made my rounds to see if everything was all right. I have to look for signs of fires or burglars or anything wrong, you know."

"How many offices were lighted up?"

"Smythe's and Moffett's and Mr. Middlebury's; that's all I remember, sir."

"Where were you when this boy called you?"

"On the stairs, going up to the sixth floor."

"This is the only elevator running at night?"

"Yes, sir. I'm supposed to keep run of this boy and see that he stays till midnight."

At this moment two officers appeared at the entrance. Astro turned to McGraw. "Tell them to keep hidden outside," he said, "and nab any one leaving the building. Now we'll go up and see what has happened."

As the five entered the car, Astro, whose look had fallen on the rubber matting on the floor, moved over nearer the elevator boy, and, pushing him a little aside, picked up a slip of paper on which he had been standing. It proved to be blank; but the Seer, after scrutinizing it, put it away in his pocketbook. The boy slammed the door and the car started up the shaft. Astro touched the boy's arm. "Stop at the ninth floor!" he commanded. The elevator boy looked up in surprise; but pulled the lever and threw open the hall door.

"You wait here," said Astro to Thompson and the lad. "Come on, McGraw. We'll see Moffett first."

They walked down the hall and around a corner till they came to a lighted door. Astro, without knocking, threw the door wide open. It was a small room, and at a roll-top desk a man jumped up quickly in consternation. In one hand he held a revolver, in the other a cleaning instrument. A box of cartridges was open beside him. He stared at his unexpected visitors.

"Good evening, Mr. Moffett," said Astro. "What are you doing with that pistol?"

"Why—I'm—cleaning it," said Moffett. The pistol dropped from his hand as he spoke, and he turned white at the scrutiny of his interlocutor.

The Seer gazed for a moment without speaking at the small, smooth-shaven, anxious-looking man who confronted him. He wore iron spectacles and was shabbily dressed. His thin bony hands trembled visibly.

"Did you fire that pistol this evening?"

"Why, no—of course not!"

"What were you cleaning it for?"

"Why—I always carry it when I go home. I live out at Kingsbridge, and there have been so many hold-ups—"

"Did you hear a shot fired in this building to-night?"

"Good God, no!" Moffett's alarm increased. He put his hand to his head. "You don't mean—there's anything happened?" he faltered.

Instead of answering, Astro walked over, picked up the revolver from the floor, and examined it. The chambers were empty. Next, he looked at the box of cartridges. Five were missing. Of these, four were scattered on the desk.

"When did you fire this gun last?" he demanded.

"Last night—at a cat," said Moffett.

McGraw laughed aloud.

Astro went to the window, threw up the sash, and looked out. The roof of the adjoining building was only two stories below. He gave it a glance, then lowered the window and walked to the door.

"Will I bring him along, sir?" said McGraw.

"No, leave him alone. Mr. Moffett, remain here till we come for you, please." And with that, Astro went out. In the hall he turned to McGraw.

"You don't mind my taking charge of this?" he asked.

"You bet I don't!" McGraw exclaimed. "But I don't see why you want Moffett to make a get-away."

"He can't get past the men down-stairs, can he?"

"That's right. But did you see any empty cartridge shells on the roof below?"

"No. We'll have to examine the roof later. Now we'll go up to Middlebury's office. We've lost too much time already."

"Have you a key to Middlebury's office, Thompson?" he asked on reentering the elevator.

"No, sir. Mr. Middlebury lost one of his office keys this week, and was given the duplicate the superintendent had till another one could be made for him."

"What did he need two for?"

"One was for his stenographer, I believe."

"Oh, he had a typewriter, then?" said Astro.

The elevator boy interrupted. "He had one, but she left to-day."

"How do you know that?" Astro turned to the youth with a keen gaze.

The elevator boy cowered under his inspection. "Why—she told me so, that's all."

The elevator had reached the tenth floor and stopped. The boy threw open the door and the party stepped out.

Almost opposite the elevator, across a narrow hall, appeared a lighted door, on which was painted the legend: "John Middlebury, Architect and Landscape Gardener." Above it was a transom tilted half open.

"Give me a leg up," said Astro, and, placing his foot in Thompson's big hand, he raised himself to the height of the lintel and looked in. He stayed there for a few minutes, then dropped to the floor again.

"Well, it's a murder, fast enough," he said to McGraw.

"We'll have to bust down the door, then," said the officer.

"Unless the boy can crawl through the transom."

"No, I can't!" exclaimed the boy. "It's too narrow."

"You try it," said Astro.

"I don't dare to!" the lad whimpered.

McGraw laid a heavy hand on his shoulder. "Now, then, my son, go to it, and no talk!"

With that, he lifted the lad bodily to a handhold on the lintel. "Hurry up, now, Dennis!" said Thompson gruffly, and the boy struggled through the opening, pulled his legs inside, and dropped to the floor. In a moment he opened the door and stood as white as paper, trembling in horror.

Beyond a counter that shut off the front part of the office, below a large drafting table in the center of the room, the body of a man lay on its back, the arms outstretched on the floor. The eyes were shut, and one hand still held a small black rubber drawing triangle. The counter shut off a view of his feet. He was a man of some thirty years, with black mustache and sparse beard, a handsome picturesque type of slightly foreign appearance.

Astro passed through the little door in the counter with McGraw, and together they bent over the body.

"There's no blood at all!" said the officer in amazement. "What is it, anyway? He can't be shot!"

Astro made no reply for some moments, but examined every detail of the body with care. At last he rose. "Thompson," he said, "have you a gun?"

"Why, no sir!" Thompson spoke anxiously. "At least, I ain't got any with me. I got one down in the boiler-room, though. I don't carry it all the time, sir."

"Go down and get it!" Astro spoke sharply. "Bring it to me! No, Dennis, you stay right here. Thompson, take the elevator down yourself. Tell the officers to telephone for a doctor."

GELETT BURGESS

The watchman left without a word, shaking his head. The elevator boy sat down on a chair outside the counter and gazed dismally into the corridor.

Astro stood for several minutes silently looking about the room. His eyes went from the drawing-board, where the perspective view of a country residence had been roughly sketched in pencil, past the ground-glass windows which admitted light from a side hall opposite the elevator, to the doors of an inner room. Valeska's eyes followed his in careful search of the room.

McGraw still stared in amazement at the body, looking for some sign of a bullet wound, but without success. At last he arose, and gazed long at Astro.

"He's dead, all right," he said finally; "but hanged if I can see what killed him! Could it be suicide? Perhaps we can find some poison, somewhere. Look in the dressing-room."

"He's shot," said Astro, without looking at the corpse. "Valeska, see what you can find in the private office in there." He pointed to the inner door.

As she started to go in through the door in the counter, her foot struck a strip of cardboard that shot in along the floor. Astro glanced at it, then stooped and picked up an advertising calendar. He walked to the waiting space outside and began to examine the wall carefully. The elevator boy's eyes followed him listlessly. The Seer stopped near the hall door and fixed his eyes on a small hole in the woodwork. Then he went back to the drawing-board and examined it attentively. There was a large black blot on it where evidently a bottle of India ink had been spilled. The paper was fastened down with thumb-tacks in the form of wire spirals. He drew one out and put it into his pocket.

Suddenly Valeska called out, "There has been a woman in here to-night!"

Astro and McGraw hurried into the private office. Valeska was standing by a small set bowl in the corner and held up a tiny gold ring.

"Do you see?" she exclaimed. "The bowl is full of soap-suds and dirty water. She must have left in a hurry without stopping for her ring."

"Ah, it was a woman shot him," said McGraw.

Astro examined it, took a long look about the room, tried the private door that led to the branch hall, and then went back to the architect's office. "What was Mr. Middlebury's stenographer's name?" he asked of the elevator boy.

"Miss Wilson." Dennis looked up with a look of alarm.

"What time did you take her up in the elevator?"

"I didn't take her up at all, to-night!" was the response; but his eye wandered away from his examiner.

"I took her down, though, when she left here, at five o'clock."

"It's queer she should leave her ring here, then, and dirty water in the bowl."

"Perhaps it was another woman," the boy ventured.

"Perhaps it was. Did you carry up any other?"

"Why, I think I did; but I can't quite remember. I think she went out again, though."

"You have a remarkably poor memory," said Astro acidly.

The door was now flung open again, and Thompson appeared. He showed signs of the greatest distress, his eyes staring, and his mouth lax.

"The gun has gone!" he exclaimed, and stood gazing helplessly at McGraw.

"It has! Then I'll have to arrest you," said the officer, and he took a pair of handcuffs from his pocket. "Hold out your hands, my man!"

Astro apparently paid no attention to this scene, and walked again into the office and stood looking at the body. "You'd better get Moffett and take them both down-stairs. I'll look about a bit. When the doctor comes, send him up. Send some one to look at the roof under Moffett's window to see if he can find an empty cartridge. Keep a watch out yourself for any one going down-stairs."

When McGraw had gone with his prisoner, Valeska approached the Seer and gazed timidly at the body of Middlebury.

"Look at his left eye," said Astro soberly.

GELETT BURGESS

Valeska shudderingly did so. "There's the tiniest drop of blood there!" she exclaimed. "It's a strange case and would puzzle any one who hadn't brains. I wonder what poor old McGraw would have done alone?"

Astro smiled grimly.

"Do you know who did it?" Valeska asked breathlessly.

"Of course."

"What, already? It seems impossible. There are three persons to suspect, aren't there?"

"Who are they?"

"Why, Moffett and the watchman and the mysterious woman who was undoubtedly here to-night."

"That woman is still in the building. I saw her hiding by a corner of the stairway as we came up; but I didn't mention it, as I knew the men below would get her if she attempted to escape."

"Which one did it, then?"

"That's what I shall have to prove before I leave the building. I'm sure enough; but I need evidence. Just at present what worries me is, how did that calendar happen to fall down from the wall where it was fastened with one of these spiral thumb-tacks?' He pointed to those on the drawing-board.

At this moment they heard the bell of the elevator, which now was standing at the floor below while McGraw made his second arrest, begin to ring furiously. Astro ran out into the hall and listened. In a moment McGraw entered the car with his two men and the car descended. The dial in the front of the shaft showed its descent to the fifth floor; then the marker stopped.

Astro pointed to it. "They've captured the girl," he said. "We'll wait for Miss Wilson in the office; I'm not through with my investigation yet."

He walked rapidly back, passed the body, and reentered the private office. Sitting down at the desk in the corner, he began a rapid investigation of the pigeonholes. Suddenly he held up an envelope on which was printed, "James Moffett, Aspenwall Bldg., New York City." Opening this, he took out a letter and read it aloud:

"My Dear Middlebury: I can't wait any longer for
that money. You'll positively have to pay it by the
fifteenth or there'll be trouble for you sure. I'd like
an immediate answer. J. Moffett."

"Looks bad for Moffett, doesn't it?" said the Seer, putting the
note into his pocket. "But look at this! Here's something worse."

He had just opened a small drawer and looked in. As he spoke he
held up a revolver. "One cartridge used. I'm sorry for Miss Wilson."

"And the night watchman's pistol yet to be accounted for!" said
Valeska.

"Oh, I think I can account for that, all right," said Astro. "I'll
locate that as soon as I get the time. Here comes the latest suspect. See what you make of her. You know women."

The elevator door opened with a snap, and McGraw, holding a
young woman by the wrist, entered the outer office. She was a pretty
blonde, her eyes now red with weeping. She wore a neat blue tailor-
made suit and stylish hat. The elevator boy came in behind her
and gazed at her hungrily.

"We found her on the fifth floor trying to get down," said
McGraw. "She has acknowledged that she was up in Middlebury's
office this evening."

Astro turned swiftly to the elevator boy. "What did you say you
hadn't taken her up for?" he demanded.

"Oh, God! I knew she was up there; but I didn't take her up;
she walked up-stairs. I hoped she'd get away and nobody'd know.
I thought she'd gone already."

"And you wanted to shield her? Why?"

Dennis hung his head. Then he muttered shamefully, "Because
I'm in love with her, sir, that's why! And I didn't want her to get
into trouble. She didn't do it, sir. I'll swear she didn't shoot him!"
He looked down at the body in horror, then turned his eyes away
and began to sob hysterically.

"Well, then, Miss Wilson, what have you to say for yourself?"

She had taken one look at the corpse also, and had turned away,
her tears breaking forth afresh. Between her gasps she told her story:

"Mr. Middlebury was too attentive to me, I thought, and then yesterday he kissed me. He said he wanted to marry me; but I didn't believe it. So I told him I was going to leave. I did leave to-day, and never expected to come back here. Mr. Middlebury had paid me, and everything, only I found I had forgotten my house keys. So I had dinner down-town and then came back here, because I knew Mr. Middlebury would be working late alone in the office on a rush job he had. I didn't want Dennis to know I went up, because I had told him about Mr. Middlebury's kissing me; so I waited till he went up in the elevator, and then I ran up-stairs, trying to keep out of his sight. Only, he caught me half-way up. Besides, I had to hide from the night watchman, because he had had a quarrel with Mr. Middlebury, and he thought I had complained of him."

"Oh, Thompson had quarreled with Middlebury, had he?" said McGraw meaningly.

"Yes, sir. Middlebury had Thompson discharged. He has to leave at the end of the week, and he was pretty angry about it. But I didn't have anything to do with that at all. It was on account of Thompson's refusing to let Mr. Middlebury have an extra key to the door."

"Where is Thompson?" Astro asked.

"Oh, he's safe enough with my men down on the first floor."

"Well, go ahead with your story, Miss Wilson."

"Why, Mr. Middlebury was awfully nice and apologized for kissing me, and proposed to me again. I didn't know what to say to him; but I was afraid he didn't mean it and was up to some game with me. He tried to hold my hand, and I snatched it away so quick I upset a bottle of India ink he was using. So I went into his private office to wash my hands. While I was in there—" She covered her face with her hands.

"You took a revolver from the desk drawer?" said Astro.

She looked at him in amazement, with widely opened eyes. "A revolver? No! Of course not! I washed my hands at the bowl, and just as I was finishing I heard a pistol-shot, and then I heard Mr. Middlebury fall."

"Did you look into this office?"

"Oh, no; I was so frightened I didn't dare to. I waited a minute till I heard the door slam: then I opened the door to the side hall and ran down-stairs."

"You saw nobody?"

"Not a soul."

"Was the elevator there?"

"Oh, I didn't look! I only wanted to get away as fast as I could. I was afraid that I was going to be suspected and arrested. You see, I knew there was a pistol in the private office, for Mr. Middlebury had shown it to me one day. I thought that if he threatened me I might use it to protect myself with."

"Yes, and that's exactly what you did do, I'm thinking," said McGraw gruffly.

Valeska took Miss Wilson's hand affectionately and pressed it. "Don't be afraid, my dear," she said.

With this friendly help the girl became more calm.

Astro, calm and picturesque, the cape of his Inverness thrown negligently across his shoulder, scrutinized the girl keenly for a few moments. His eyes passed over every detail of her costume, analyzed every feature. He was standing so, mysterious, potent, inscrutable, when his face changed suddenly.

"Do you remember, Miss Wilson, whether there was a small calendar pinned to the wall by the door there when you came in?"

She looked up, her eyes still streaming. "Why, yes, I'm sure there was. That is, I stuck it to the wall with a thumb-tack yesterday, and I don't remember its having been taken down." She looked at him in surprise at his question.

The door opened again, and the doctor, who had obtained a key to another of the elevators, coming up alone, entered the room and gave a curious look around.

"I'm Doctor Flynn," he announced. "What's the trouble?"

"There's your man," said Astro, pointing gravely to the body of Middlebury. "He's been dead an hour or so. You'll find he was shot through the eye. The bullet pierced the brain, and the man bled only internally. Lift his left eyelid and you'll see."

"That's more than I could find out," cried McGraw. "So he was shot, then, for sure. Now, then, who done it?"

"We'll leave the doctor here to make his examination," said the Seer. "We'll take Miss Wilson downstairs. I'm about through, now. I promise you the criminal will confess before you can get the coroner and the patrol wagon here."

Leaving the doctor to his examination of the body, Astro and Valeska walked into the elevator, followed by McGraw, who still held Miss Wilson in his heavy grip. The elevator boy stepped in, shut the door, and the car descended. In the hall of the ground floor an officer was standing with Moffett, and another with Thompson, each of the prisoners being handcuffed. As Astro came up, another policeman hurried in from the front entrance.

"I've found the cartridge," he said, holding up the small copper cylinder. "It was not twenty feet away from Moffett's window, on the roof of the next building."

"Yes, I threw it out of the window. It was just before I cleaned the gun. I told you I shot a cat last night with it."

McGraw laughed in derision.

Astro looked Moffett over quietly and said. "I believe, Mr. Moffett, that Mr. Middlebury owed you some money, did he not?"

"Yes—why?" Then Moffett's face changed to terror.

"And you threatened that he would have trouble if he didn't pay up, did you not?"

"By George! we got the man all right now!" said McGraw.

"I got my pay, though, only yesterday," exclaimed Moffett. "You'll probably find the receipt in Middlebury's pocket, or with his papers."

"Which shows how dangerous it is to judge a man on circumstantial evidence," remarked Astro.

"Well, it's more than we got against the others," McGraw grumbled.

"My dear old chap, I'll show you circumstantial evidence enough to convince you, before I'm through. Besides that, I'll let you listen to an outright confession. Now you had better let Mr.

Moffett depart in peace. He's had a narrow escape. It's lucky some one with psychic perceptions was here to rescue him from the web of circumstance."

"It was the night watchman then, I'll bet on that!" said McGraw.

"Well, we'll take up his case next. Let's see, he owed Middlebury a grudge for having him discharged. He had a pistol; but he can't produce it. What has he done with it?"

They had approached Thompson by this time. The night watchman was listening, trembling in his turn. His face had the color of clay.

"I kept it down-cellar in my table drawer, near the foot of the elevator shaft. I have no idea what has become of it!" he pleaded.

Astro touched the officer who had been holding Moffett. "Take the elevator and go down to the cellar. Open the door of the nearest furnace and look in and see if you can find a gun."

"Is it there?" said McGraw. "How in blazes did you know that, you wizard?"

"Where would you hide a gun better?" said Astro, smiling. "If it isn't there, you'll find it in some corner, or in one of the ash barrels. It doesn't matter much, anyway."

Valeska, meanwhile, was trying to comfort Miss Wilson, who was crying and talking intermittently. The two blondes made a pretty picture together. McGraw, who since his first visit to the Seer's studio, had always admired Valeska, looked on, apparently touched. Finally he could endure his curiosity no longer.

"For God's sake, sir, it ain't the girl, is it?" he asked in a whisper.

Astro laughed, and waited. The elevator boy sat on a bench, a picture of dejection, waiting for the outcome. It was ten minutes before the officer reappeared from the basement. As he threw open the elevator door he showed, hanging from a bent wire, the distorted metal work of a revolver, still glowing a dull red.

"It was just where you said, sir," he explained.

Astro gave a glance at it, then turned to Thompson. "What have you to say?" he asked.

"I don't know how it got there," said Thompson dully.

"I believe this is your last week as watchman here?"

"Yes, sir."

"And it was Mr. Middlebury who caused your discharge?"

"Yes, sir." Thompson stared stupidly at his large feet.

"Then you had good reason to hate him? He is shot, and your revolver thrown into the furnace. It looks bad, my man!"

"I swear to God I'm innocent!" Thompson looked wildly into the impassive face of the Seer.

And, as he did so, Astro's face softened. "I believe you. I think you can take the handcuffs off him, McGraw."

"Take 'em off! Why, he must be the one who done it! Any fool could see that!"

"You're fool enough to, no doubt," said Astro, shrugging his shoulders; "but if you want the credit of detecting the murderer, you'd better free this man and listen to me."

Astro had proved his marvelous powers of deduction or intuition too many times, and too much to McGraw's own advantage, for the officer to refuse.

"It's sure too much for me!" he muttered to himself as he unlocked the handcuffs.

"Well, now we'll have an interview with the real criminal," said Astro, walking over to the two girls.

Miss Wilson, hearing this, looked terrified at him; but there was no expression there that could reassure her. She opened her lips to speak, but could not.

Astro began deliberately, speaking so that his words echoed through the corridor. "Miss Wilson, by your own confession you were in the office of Mr. Middlebury at the time he was shot."

"In the inner office, I was," she ejaculated.

"In the inner office, where there was found a revolver with one cartridge used," added Astro.

The girl nodded, her face pale.

"You have confessed to Dennis, here, that Mr. Middlebury had kissed you and that you were offended. You have confessed that he made a proposal of marriage to-night that you suspected was false and only a game to fool you with."

"Oh, but I'm sure now he was sincere!" Miss Wilson cried. "I am sure he loved me! I'm sorry I suspected him of anything ungentlemanly!"

"Nevertheless, there was a scuffle. He attempted to take your hand. You escaped to the inner room—where the revolver was kept."

"Only to wash my hands!" she wailed.

"Your story is too flimsy," said Astro, his voice suddenly grown harsh, as he turned to McGraw. "Officers, I charge Miss Wilson with the crime of murder! Arrest her and handcuff her!"

Valeska, who had sprung up in surprise and indignation, opened her lips to protest. McGraw, instead of moving forward, had taken a step backward, when Dennis, the elevator boy, jumped up and seized Astro's arm.

"Don't arrest her, don't!" he shrieked. "I done it myself!"

"You done it?" McGraw echoed.

"Yes! Arrest me!" and the boy held out his wrists imploringly.

Astro coolly took out his cigarette case and lighted a cigarette. "Well, McGraw," he said, smiling, "didn't I promise you a confession?"

McGraw, stupefied, clasped the handcuffs on Dennis' wrists. Miss Wilson fell, almost fainting, on the bench, where Valeska put her arm tenderly about her.

"Well, Dennis, you're fairly caught," said Astro. "I've known for some time that you were guilty; but it's so much more satisfactory to have an out-and-out confession. Now I'll trouble you for the key to Middlebury's door." And, so saying, he reached into the boy's trousers pocket and brought forth a small Yale key.

"When did you find it, Dennis?"

"I found it last week, sir, on the floor of my car."

"And you kept it thinking it might come in handy, and perhaps get the night watchman into trouble, eh? So you were jealous of Mr. Middlebury on Miss Wilson's account, were you?"

"Oh, it made me wild, sir! I just couldn't stand it when she told me he had kissed her, and when I saw her going up there to-night I went crazy."

"So you stole Thompson's gun from the cellar, went up when Thompson was on his rounds, opened the door with your key, and shot Mr. Middlebury?"

"Yes, sir!" Dennis' voice was faint.

"Then you ran your car to the cellar, threw the gun into the furnace, then went up and found Thompson and told him you had heard a shot?"

"Yes, sir. Oh, I was crazy! I was crazy about her!"

"And you thought if you said nothing about her she would escape?"

"Yes, sir. For God's sake take me away! I don't ever want to see her again!"

"Patrol wagon's come, sir," said one of the officers, walking up to McGraw. He laid his hand on Dennis' arm.

"One minute, please," said Astro. "Dennis, my boy, will you please hold up your left foot? Thank you!" And as the boy did so Astro removed a spiral wire thumb-tack that was imbedded in the rubber heel of the boot.

"What's that for?" McGraw inquired.

"The law doesn't permit a defendant to plead guilty to a charge of murder. You may need this for evidence when the case is tried." As the elevator boy was led away he looked at him pityingly. "Cocaine," he remarked to McGraw.

"Sure. Dope done it, all right. He was worked up to it. It may do for an insanity defense."

"He's a mattoid. You'll find his parents or grandparents were criminals, poor devil!" The Seer turned to Miss Wilson. "You've had a lucky escape, too, my dear. It's fortunate that I was here."

"Oh, I don't know how to say how grateful I am!" she exclaimed.

"We'll drive you home," Valeska volunteered. "I know this shock has been terrible for you. Do come with us!"

She drew the girl toward the doorway and they bade good night to McGraw. As Astro and the officer waited talking for a moment, the girls entered the green limousine. But, hardly in, Valeska returned to the doorway hurriedly. McGraw had gone inside.

"I can't wait till we've left Miss Wilson," she said. "Do please let me see that paper you picked up in the elevator. I think I see where you got your first clue, now. Dennis, the elevator boy, had stepped on it, hadn't he?"

Astro took the paper from his pocketbook and handed it to his assistant. Faintly indented on its surface was a small spiral.

"Yes, I'll have to confess, Valeska," he said, "that, if it hadn't been for that small scrap of paper, McGraw would have had three prisoners instead of one in custody to-night!"

VENGEANCE OF THE PI RHO NU

"Gracious! It's perfectly wonderful! Why, you've told me things no one has ever known about me." The young woman gazed at Astro with her deep brown eyes—eyes that bespoke feeling rather than intellect.

Then she drew a long breath, as if seeking courage to speak. "There's one thing I'd like to know if you can tell me," she added anxiously, "shall I be married soon?"

Astro leaned back into the shadow and contemplated his client. She was young, vivid, temperamental, and decidedly pretty. But he looked in vain for evidences of a sense of humor. Her level eyebrows were too delicately straight for that. Her lips curved deliciously, but not with whimsicality. There was no doubt about it, Miss Pauline Wister was a bromide; and he must act accordingly.

"Very soon," he answered.

She drew a sigh of relief, and he felt her clasp on his hands relax. "I've been worrying a little," she confessed.

It was evident that she was willing to talk, and Astro waited a moment without answering, bending in closer scrutiny over her palm. He finally put down her hand, nodding his head mysteriously. "I can see that you are in trouble. If I can be of any help, I shall be glad to do what I can."

Miss Wister released her hand and opened her bag, from which she drew a small envelope. Her lips trembled as she looked at the Seer.

"I am to be married to-morrow morning at ten o'clock," she said; "that is, if nothing happens to prevent it." Her fingers clasped the letter more tightly. "I am engaged to Mr. Edward Farralon; but—but I haven't heard from him since yesterday noon!" There were tears in her big brown eyes as she gazed up at him.

As Astro, however, only nodded gravely, she went on. "I tried to telephone to him last night, and he was not at home; at least, he didn't answer. I tried this forenoon, and they told me that he had not been down to his office. And—and I'm to be married tomorrow!" Miss Wister had almost broken into tears.

"You've been seeing him often and quite regularly, I suppose?"

"Oh, yes, every day! That's what makes it seem so strange. Do you think anything can have happened to him? I don't know what to do! I daren't tell any one for fear of making talk, and if he's all right, that would be dreadful. But there's something else—here, look at this letter I got this morning!"

Astro glanced at the envelope she passed him, saw that it was addressed with a typewriter, and took out the single sheet it contained. On this was typewritten the line:

"Beware the Vengeance of the Pi Rho Nu!"

"Well," he said, "that certainly is enough to give a girl the creeps on the day before her wedding. You have no idea what it means, I suppose?"

"No. I'm awfully alarmed; but at the same time—I'll have to tell you—Edward is an awful jollier, and is all the time playing jokes on me; so I never can be sure of anything. He says he's training my sense of humor." Miss Wister smiled sadly. "But the fact that he's missing is different. It frightens me!"

"My dear Miss Wister," Astro said, clasping her hand in assurance, "if you'll leave this to me, I'll promise you that you shall be married promptly on time. You need give yourself no anxiety about it. As it happens, I have nothing else to do, and I shall be glad to help you."

"Oh, I'm so relieved! I knew that if you would only try you could solve the mystery. You know, I used to know Mrs. Chester when she was Ruth Lorsson, and she told me the story of how you helped her. It was that made me want to tell you."

Astro smiled. "Yes, I confess love-affairs do rather amuse me, and I'm always willing to help straighten them out. So, if you're willing to do exactly as I say, I'll take this on."

"Oh, I'll do anything!"

"It may cost considerable money, too."

"But think of having trouble with my wedding! It's awful! Why, I don't know but I ought to countermand the invitations! Of course, I don't want to unless it's necessary; it's a terrible thing to do."

"Go right ahead, and trust to me. I'll promise to have Mr. Farralon on time. Is it at a church?"

"No, we're to be married at my house, 5678 Lexington Avenue."

"All right. Where is Mr. Farralon's office?"

"Eighteen West Thirty-second Street. He's the American agent for a Belgian rubber firm, you know, and has only a small place for a headquarters."

"He's a college man, I suppose?"

"Yes, Stapleton University, '04."

"Who is to be his best man?"

"Why, Mr. Stringer, a classmate of his. He's a lawyer; a patent lawyer, I think. I've told him about Edward's disappearance, and he's promised to find him to-day; but I thought—"

"You'd make sure?" Astro smiled as he rose. "Mr. Stringer knew nothing, I suppose? Did he offer to come and see you about it?"

"Yes; said he'd be up this afternoon."

"Very well. Let me know if he's found out anything. Meanwhile, be ready to do anything I request. I'll consult my crystal ball immediately. Valeska!" he called, raising his voice. "Show Miss Wister out, please."

His guest had no sooner left than Astro took up the telephone. He called for Edward Masson, a man whose friendship he had won at the time of the solution of the famous Denton boudoir murder mystery. Of the conversation that ensued, Valeska, returning to the palmist's studio, heard only one side.

"Is this Mr. Masson? . . . You're a Stapleton University man, aren't you, Masson? . . . Were there any local secret fraternities there along from 1901 to 1904? . . . What was the name of it? . . . The Pi Rho Nu? . . . Can you get me a list of the members? . . . Rather lively crowd, eh? . . . Well, thank you, but you'll have to hurry. Telephone me here as soon as you can."

He hung up the receiver and turned to Valeska. "We have but little time, and there's much to be done. I can't explain till later. You'd better wait here till Masson telephones, and stay till I come. I'm off right away. Ring up Lieutenant McGraw, and ask him if he can get me a burglar's jimmy, and also ask him to investigate the Belgian Rubber Syndicate's office, 18 West Thirty-second Street. See if there's anything crooked about it. I'll be back as soon as I can. Oh! If Masson rings up soon, go out to Miss Wister's house, look it over outside, and hurry back and be ready to report the lay of the land."

Two minutes after that, Astro was in a green motorcar headed for West Thirty-second Street. Here he alighted and went in through a narrow doorway. There was a narrow hall with a single elevator, and a flight of stairs leading upward. A list of names on the wall showed that the office of "Edward Farralon, American Agent, Belgian Rubber Syndicate," occupied room twelve, on the third floor. Astro pressed the bell, and shortly afterward the elevator door rolled open. A red-headed man in shirt sleeves was inside.

"Mr. Farralon has an office here?" said the Seer.

"Yep; but he ain't in."

"Been in to-day?"

"Nope."

"Here yesterday?"

"Yep."

"Did you see him go out last night?"

"Nope. He worked rather late, though, I think. He prob'ly walked down-stairs. The elevator boy skipped last night; so the box wa'n't working. I'm the janitor; just running the car till they can get another boy."

"Ah! So the elevator boy skipped, did he? What was his name?"

"Mickey Flynn. He'll have hard work getting another job, if I can prevent it, leaving me in the lurch like that!"

"Do you know where he lives?"

"Out on East One Hundred and Fifty-sixth Street, I believe. Let's see, I believe I got it writ down in my pocketbook somewhere. Did you want him?"

"I dropped a package in the car yesterday, or in Mr. Farralon's office, I don't know which. If I can't get into Farralon's office, I want to see the boy, in case he found it."

"Well, you'll never get it, then, I'll bet! But I'll give a look and see if I can find the address. Let's see. He come here about two months back." He looked over the greasy pages of the note-book till he found the page. "Here it is: 1575 East One Hundred and Fifty-sixth. That's right. Well, I hope you'll find your package, sir."

Astro went back to the cab and drove immediately to the address. It was a tenement swarming with children, and he was directed to the fifth floor, where, at his knock, the door was opened by Mickey himself. It took only a short talk to convince the boy that he would avoid trouble if he told what he knew immediately, and he explained his disappearance from his post of duty with considerable anxiety.

"I was in de box up to eight o'clock, all right. Along about then two swell chaps come into de hall and asked me was Mr. Farralon up-stairs. Yes, I says, he was. Then one o' de chaps peeled t'ree tens off n a roll o' bills and shoved it into me fist. 'Beat it out'n dis here!' he says. 'Go chase a new job,' he says, 'an' lose yourself! Dis here is give you so you don't come back for a week,' he says. Well, I didn't ask no questions. It looked like a easy way to make t'irty to me, an' I got me coat an' piked out in a hurry, and went up to de Circle T'eater to see de show. An dat's all I know."

"How did they come?" Astro asked.

"In a buzz wagon. I copped dat off all right. Say, I'll give you de number for anoder ten."

"You'll give it to me without that, or I'll have you arrested! I'm a detective!" the Seer threatened.

Mickey's eyes grew big; he was evidently a hero worshiper. He fumbled in his pocket and drew out a bit of newspaper. On it was scrawled the number 11115.

"Dat's de mark, all right," he explained. "Say, I'm goin' to be a 'teck myself when I grow up. Will youse give me a job?"

Astro laughed. "If you'd had sense enough to wait and see what those two men did, I'd give you a job right now," he said.

Mickey groaned. "Gee!" he exclaimed. "W'y didn't I t'ink o' dat? I was dopin' out w'at I'd do wit' de money. I was crazy to see a show."

"Well, what did the men look like, then, if you're such a good detective?"

Mickey brightened visibly as he replied, "Say, I got dat, all right. Look a-here! One was a tall guy wit' specs and a little mustache and, gee! w'at a neck! De other was built like Jim Jeffries,—stocky an' heavy. Looked like he could punch, all right! Mout' full o' gold teeth, he had. De other chap called him Frank."

"Was there any one in the car when you left?"

"Dey was a ch'uffer dere, all bungled up so I couldn't reckernize him, wit' goggles and one o' dem hairy coats."

"All right. That's worth the ten you wanted, I think." And Astro passed over the bill and started down-stairs.

Mickey leaned over the rail and shouted, "Say, boss, de tall guy had a leather bag!"

Astro nodded and regained his car. "Drive to the nearest big automobile dealer," he ordered.

The car stopped before the Aeromobile warerooms. Astro got out and asked to see the automobile list. In two minutes he had found that the car registered number 11115 was owned by Frank Brigham of number 1212 Charles Street, in Greenwich village, New York. A look at the telephone book showed Brigham's business to be brokerage, and his office to be 1000 Wall Street. Astro reentered the cab and returned to the studio.

Valeska was not in the place. A boy in buttons informed him that she had left a half-hour ago, after having answered the telephone.

A package had come from Lieutenant McGraw. Astro opened it, and took out a burglar's jimmy and a note. It read:

"Be careful; but if you get in bad, let me know.
Belg. Rub. Synd. O. K, as far as I can find out.
                                                      "McGraw."

It was a quarter of an hour before he heard Valeska enter.

"Did Masson give you any names?" was his first inquiry.

"Yes; Mr. Paul Stringer of Flatbush, Mr. Richard Hanbury of Albany, Mr. Frank Brigham."

"Of 1212 Charles Street?"

"Yes!" Valeska looked at him in wonder.

"And what about Miss Wister's house? You've been out there, I fancy?"

"Yes. It's a five-story brick dwelling. It's on the corner."

"What about the other houses in the block?"

"I have the names of the owners from the *Social Register*, all except one, which is vacant and for sale."

"Real estate agents?"

"Swan & Dowell. 3421 Broadway."

"Very good. Telephone right out there for an appointment; then hire that house and pay in advance for one month. Tell them you'll sign a lease if the place is satisfactory. Use any excuse you need. Just where is it?"

"At the other end of the block, on the corner of the next street."

"All right. Then, as soon as possible, look up Stringer—he's Farralon's best man—and see where he goes to-night. Find him, and don't lose sight of him! I'll have to work quickly, if I'm going to keep my word to Miss Wister."

"You think Stringer knows something of it?"

"He hasn't been to see Miss Wister, and that's suspicious. I telephoned to her and to his office. He hasn't been there. They say he's out of town. That means he doesn't want to be found; but you must try to find him. Miss Wister will give you a description. Now I'm off!"

He ran down-stairs and jumped into the waiting cab. In less than twenty minutes he was at Frank Brigham's Wall Street office. Inquiring of the office boy, he discovered that Brigham was in; but, instead of waiting, Astro took the elevator down to the street. There was an automobile waiting by the curb, and he looked at the number. It was 11115! He went back to his taxicab.

"Can you keep up with that car?" he asked, pointing to Brigham's machine and handing the chauffeur a five-dollar bill.

The man touched his cap and grinned. "I'll do it or get pinched for speeding!" he answered.

Astro got into the cab and waited, watching through a slit side of the curtain window. Within five minutes Brigham appeared with a tall thin man in eye-glasses, wearing a small, black, close-cropped mustache. They entered the tonneau of the automobile, and the car moved off, followed by the taxicab. Winding in and out of the up-town traffic, the car was easily followed until it stopped at the Hotel Saint Nemo, where the two men alighted. Astro followed them to the grillroom, waited till they had seated themselves, and took a table not too far away to watch them.

Cocktails for three were brought. Astro's eyes narrowed as he awaited the third conspirator. In a few minutes he appeared, and the Seer of secrets had time to make up his mind that he was the missing best man before his suspicion was corroborated by Valeska's unobtrusive appearance in the doorway. He gave her a sign that she could safely join him, and she came to his table as if she had been expected.

"How do you suppose I got him?" she asked jubilantly. "I called him up on the telephone, and some one asked my name. I replied, 'Pi Rho Nu.' It was a sudden inspiration, though I haven't the least idea what it means. As soon as he answered, I hung up, and got to his apartment-house as soon as I could. He took a hansom, and I had no trouble in following him. Who are these men?"

"Brigham and Doctor Hanbury," said Astro. "At least I imagine that the one they've been calling 'Doc' is Richard Hanbury. I wish they'd talk a little louder."

"Wait till they've finished those cocktails," said Valeska sapiently.

The three men were already laughing uproariously. One was telling a story, marking imaginary circles on his cheeks as he spoke.

At the close of the narration all three lifted their glasses and drank a health.

"Was that 'To the ride'?"

"Not quite." Astro was seated nearer to the group.

At nine o'clock the men showed signs of being about to leave the dining-room, and Astro and Valeska had just time to make their exit first without being observed.

"I'll have to continue the chase alone," he said. "You'd better try and find out what you can from Farralon's apartment. See his man, if you can. You can act the French maid for that. Any valet will talk, if he thinks you come from some woman. As for me, I may be in the police court for burglary by to-morrow morning; and so, if I'm not at the studio by eight o'clock, you'd better see Lieutenant McGraw. Here they come, now! Good-by!"

In another minute his cab had again taken up the chase of car 11115. They sped north, crossed the park, turned into Seventy-second Street, and finally flew at full speed straight out the Broadway boulevard. Here the little taxicab had hard work following; but kept on and on, nearly to Kingsbridge. Here the open drawbridge enabled Astro to catch up. Beyond that, the car turned sharply to the right and went a hundred yards, stopping before a large brick building that stood alone. It bore the sign of a sewing-machine company but was apparently deserted, though a light shone from one of the upper floors.

Astro, whose driver had stopped the cab at a safe distance, got out and walked on cautiously. Luckily it was dark and cloudy. As he went up the steps to the door, he could still hear the voices of the men who had just entered. The door was ajar. Instantly he slipped inside, and, suspecting that the doorkeeper would return after he had shown his guests the way, he dodged into a vacant room off the hall.

Here he waited nearly an hour, and, hiding close to the door, heard several visitors arrive, saw them give the hailing sign and pass up-stairs. At about eleven o'clock the watchman looked at his watch, lighted his pipe, and walked into the room opposite, evidently to sleep. This was the time, if any time were safe, to investigate the upper floors.

Up one floor he crept softly, found all dark, and listened. From higher up came now the sounds of laughter, of singing, and an occasional cheer. He crept up the next flight; the noise grew louder. He opened a door at the right of the landing, and found a large hall, once used for machinery. The pounding of feet on the ceiling told him that the men he had seen enter were immediately above. He paced the room, and found it to be a hundred feet by fifty. Opposite the long row of shuttered windows was another door. This he entered, and found a small room, evidently once used for an office, with a fireplace, mantel, and one window.

Step by step he now ascended the next flight of stairs, the sounds of revelry growing louder every minute. A glance above showed a streak of light through the half-opened door. A nearer approach showed another door, corresponding to that of the office he had noticed below. He darted up to the landing, put his hand to the handle of this door, and it opened easily. Passing in, he closed it behind him and looked about.

There was a cot bed with a pair of blankets drawn up against the wall, a basket of food, and a pitcher of water and many beer bottles on a table. A fireplace on the other wall corresponded to the one he had seen below. Astro stole to the keyhole of the door leading into the hall and listened. A smile came to his lips.

"Brigham! Brigham!" the company was yelling.

From his post Astro could see only the broad back of Brigham in the light of many candles; but he could hear perfectly the speech that followed.

"Brothers of the Pi Rho Nu," Brigham began, "far be it from me to try to make a speech to-night—as you know I can't! But I'll take my turn in testifying to the utter depravity of the prisoner."

Cries of "Hear, hear!" interrupted him, and after they were stilled Brigham went on.

"The event is now a piece of the history of the Pi Rho Nu; but I'll briefly state the facts. Two years ago I was married."

"How delightful to be married!" the crowd began to sing.

"And it was my fond intention to pass my honeymoon in an automobile. In fact, it was begun all right, and I'd have been safe if I had contented myself with driving only daytimes. But on my very first evening—we were married at noon—I was held up by a band of desperadoes on the road from Albany to Troy. I should have been able to take care of all of them with my fists; but I could never look a gun in the muzzle calmly. The result was that I was tied up with Mrs. Brigham and carried into a lonely house. She was put into one room, and I into another. Gentlemen, I ask you to picture my feelings that night, as I heard scream after scream coming from the room adjacent for hours unending. It was only because I knew my bride had been carried safely away to the nearest hotel that I was able to sleep at all. So, gentlemen, I demand the penalty of—"

"Death!" shouted the rest in a chorus of laughter, after which there were calls for "Doc Hanbury." Hanbury was invisible from Astro's peep-hole, but his voice rose clearly.

"I also was married," he began, and was also interrupted by the popular chorus; "but under painful and embarrassing circumstances," he continued. "The afternoon of the wedding my flat was entered and I was garroted by two masked men. I was tied to a chair, and then one of them painted my face deliberately but too fancifully with iodine. He painted my cheeks in circles, gentlemen, and my brow was a picturesque plaid of squares. Those of you who were present at the ceremony possibly remarked the grease paint that attempted too unsuccessfully to cover my shame. I had to do it. You can't explain an absence from your own wedding except by—"

"Death!" came the jovial chorus.

One after another proceeded to testify, each constantly interrupted by the hilarious members of the fraternity.

Astro had heard enough. It was evident that Farralon, the master spirit of the association and fiercest of its practical jokers, had met his just deserts. Just what they would do with him, Astro could not guess; but that the bridegroom would need a friend was not to be doubted. How was he to be helped? Astro determined to complete his investigation of the building before he decided. Undoubtedly the gang would make a night of it in the house and keep Farralon a prisoner till the last moment, if indeed they did not prevent the ceremony. The Seer took an electric torch from his pocket and stole up-stairs.

The floor was planned like those below, with the same big hall, the small office, and fireplace. As it was in the office that Farralon was to be locked, evidently, when his fraternity members had departed, Astro looked over the little room carefully. The iron shutters were barred and immovable. There was only one safe means of communicating with the prisoner after he was left alone,— by way of the chimney. Astro took the jimmy from his pocket and set to work inside the fireplace, to open a hole on each side. Which of the two flues ran down into the next floor it was impossible to tell. He must be ready for both. It took two hours of hard work to get the bricks out; but by the time the company were racketing down-stairs Astro had the satisfaction of perceiving a faint light deep down in one of the openings. It was now only a question of waiting till Farralon was alone, and hailing him. To find out what was going on, he had started down-stairs when he heard voices. A man was still in the larger room speaking through the closed door of the office.

"Don't you try and make a row now, or we'll come in and make you quit! You keep quiet, Farralon! I'm going to turn in now. So long, old man! Dream of your bride and a happy wedding!" and after turning the key in the door he rolled over on a cot in the hall. In a few minutes he was snoring.

Astro stole up-stairs and put his mouth to the hole, calling Farralon. No answer came. Then he sat down on the floor, took off his sock, and raveled out a long line of silk. Next, he wrote a short note, fastened the paper into his pocket-knife, and tied the line to it. This he let cautiously down the hole, and jangled it softly at the bottom. In a few minutes he felt the line pulled taut. Farralon took the note, read it, and came back.

"Who's up there?" he called up in a loud whisper.

"A friend!" Astro replied.

And thereupon ensued a long dialogue; after which the Seer of Secrets, chuckling to himself mightily, stole down-stairs and out the door, found his still waiting taxicab, and was driven rapidly back to the city. It was four o'clock when he threw himself, exhausted, on the great couch in his studio.

At half past nine that forenoon, Astro and Valeska stood behind the inside shutters of the parlor window at number 5652 Lexington Avenue. It was the house that Valeska had rented at the other end of the block in which Miss Wister lived.

A large furniture van stood in front of the door. A long table was on the sidewalk, standing parallel to the curb. Two men in overalls walked in and out of the house occasionally.

Astro looked at his watch. "About time for the show," he remarked. "How is Miss Wister standing the suspense?"

Valeska giggled. "I don't think she slept a wink last night, and when I got to her this morning she was almost frantic. I don't think that even now she considers herself safe. You see, she doesn't know you so well as I do. If you told me I was to be married today, I'd believe it!"

Astro turned to her with a sudden look in his eyes. "If I told you that you were to be married next month, would you believe it?" he demanded.

"Ah, but you're not going to tell me that!" said Valeska, putting away his hand gently. "But it was impossible to get Miss Wister to see the funny side of it all. I'm afraid that young Mr. Farralon is going to have a hard time getting some things into her head."

"Well, her heart is accessible, at any rate," Astro replied. His gaze returned to the window. "It's queer the Pi Rho Nu aren't here. We have mighty little time to get him ready. I believe they're going to wait till the last minute. No, by Jove! there they come now!" He rapped on the window sharply to the men on the sidewalk, who immediately put their hands to the table.

At the other end of the block, where a long awning stretched from the door of the Wister house to the sidewalk and a curious crowd had gathered, a large red automobile—number 11115—had stopped just as he spoke. It was full of men. One got out, then another, then another. As the fourth stepped on the sidewalk, however, there was a sudden commotion. A man dropped. Two others seemed fighting. They were joined by two more, who jumped from the car. Another dropped, and another, and then—

Sprinting down the block came a wild fantastic creature, half in man's clothes, half in woman's, with ribbons streaming, with short skirts flapping, fighting his way with excited gestures through the passers-by, knocking down several as he strove. Behind him instantly followed the crowd, led by the men who had risen to their feet. As the fugitive came up to the house where Astro and Valeska waited, the men on the sidewalk swung the long table round and the mob dashed against the barrier. One or two hurdled it; the rest ran round the ends. But the moment's handicap gave the fugitive just time to rush up the front steps and enter the doorway before the doors were closed and bolted behind him.

"Quick! Follow me!" exclaimed Astro. He could hardly speak from laughter; but the man followed him with curses, raving like a wild beast. Up three flights of stairs they raced, entered a small closet, and scrambled up a ladder.

"Now it's a plain track to the scuttle of the Wister house," said Astro. "You'll find a ladder three houses beyond here. You have just eight minutes to dress in. Your clothes are all laid out in Wister's room, and the ring is in the pocket of your waistcoat. There'll be no best man. I'll wait here to make ready for your getaway."

"My get-away!" cried Farralon wildly. "For heaven's sake! isn't it over yet? Is there any more of this confounded practical joke?"

"More!" said Astro smiling. "You ought to know the capacity of the Pi Rho Nu. There's a hack covered with ribbons which I've had ready at the door, and there's a brass band and a demonstration waiting at the pier that will make you feel as if you were a crown prince."

Farralon wilted. "Well, I guess I'll get what's coming to me this time," he said, grinning feebly.

"No, you won't. You'll escape on Miss Wister's account. I've got it all fixed. As soon as you can, after the ceremony, you and your wife are to go upstairs. Say you're going to leave in the cab at the door in half an hour and drive by way of the Christopher Street ferry to Hoboken. Then get up to the roof, come back here, just as you are, and I'll give you your instructions!"

"But my trunks, and Kitty's my clothes, and everything—"

"Everything is ready in that furniture van at the door. Now hurry! You've wasted two minutes!"

Farralon darted across the roof at reckless speed. Astro watched, with a lingering smile, till the groom disappeared over the edge of the roof of the third house beyond. Then he descended into the house again. Valeska was arranging a queer collection of clothes in a rear room up-stairs.

"Is everything ready?" he asked.

She burst out laughing. "There's a bride's going-away costume for you!" she exclaimed, holding up a blue gingham skirt, a purple-checked blouse, and a bandana kerchief.

"Well, be prepared for a quick change, then. I'll go to the roof and be ready to help the bride down."

Astro had begun to be anxious by the time the bridal couple reappeared. It was fully an hour before he saw the happy pair approach, clambering lightly over the roof. Then Farralon gave a whoop, and the two came up laughing.

They laughed as she stumbled down the ladder; they roared as—Astro with the bridegroom in the front room, and Valeska with the bride in the rear—the pair changed their clothes for the emigrant costumes that were ready. Then down-stairs they went, Astro carrying two large suitcases filled with the wedding clothes. At the door he stopped them and went to the window to reconnoiter. The Brigham automobile was still standing at the curb, near to the hack which was fairly white with ribbons and bridal flags.

"Take this chair now," said Astro.

Farralon took one end of a Morris chair and Mrs. Farralon the other. There was no one on the sidewalk at this end of the block, though a crowd was collected in front of the Wister residence, preparing for the fun of throwing rice and old shoes. The couple were unnoticed as they lifted the chair into the van and then climbed in themselves. The two teamsters followed with the suit cases, and in another minute the van was safely off. Astro and Valeska waved a discreet adieu behind the shutters of the empty house.

Astro took from his pocket a check for a thousand dollars and handed it to Valeska. "I think I deserve more credit than the clergyman," he said. "But now we must follow them and see how it all comes out."

The members of the Pi Rho Nu had hurried to the ferry as soon as the bridegroom's escape was suspected. They roamed all over the boat, passing the furniture van several times in their search.

As soon as the boat was in the slip the gay fraternity hurried to the pier where the *Carothian* lay with steam up. Here a brass band was in readiness to serenade the couple. The fraternity swarmed aboard the steamer and pushed their quest everywhere—save into the third-class cabin, where the bridal couple, disguised as steerage passengers, sat and laughed till the gangplank was raised. Then Astro and Valeska, near the baffled members of the crestfallen Pi Rho Nu, awaited the denouement.

Just before the last line was cast off, the couple, dressed perfectly now, appeared at the rail of the promenade deck, waving their handkerchiefs merrily. A shout went up from the Pi Rho Nu.

Stringer, who was standing near Astro, turned to his companion. "Well," he said, "they fooled us, after all. But when he gets into his stateroom it'll look like a small grain elevator. There's a good ton of rice on the floor and in the mattresses. He'll get his on the way across! Hooray for the Pi Rho Nu!"

Valeska smiled as if she were pleased; and also as if she were a little envious, too.

THE LADY IN TAUPE

"Excuse me if I appear to patronize you," said the young man, "but you certainly are clever." He twisted up his blond mustache, nodded his head slowly, and smiled.

"My very dear sir," said Astro calmly, "what you call my cleverness is the product of innate gifts, years of study, and infinite thought and contemplation. You are the clever one."

"How so?" The palmist's client raised his eyebrows, as a woman might. His deep blue eyes sparkled, lighted with a strong sense of humor.

"Clever to have come here—for the purpose you did. I assure you that you could have found no better place, though I confess I shall be sorry to have my studio reproduced. I shall have to re-decorate it."

"What do you think I came here for, then?" Some of the self-assurance had vanished from the young man's face.

Astro looked about calmly and pointed with the stem of his narghile as he spoke. "That granite Thoth could be easily imitated in papier-mâché. One can hire rugs, and pay for the rent by advertising on the program. There should be a door there, R. U. E., of course, and the divan should be brought down front so that your leading lady can sit on it and look up over her shoulder when her lover leans on the back of it. You can't escape that sort of love scene, you know, in a modern drama."

The young man laughed heartily. Then he said, "By Jove! you've struck it! I am an actor."

"No, you're not," said Astro. "You're a playwright, and a successful one."

The young man jumped up and banged his fist on the table. "What do you think of that!" he exclaimed.

Astro smiled cryptically. Then, "With considerable literary ambition, as well."

His client sat down again as suddenly, and stared at the Seer. "See here! I want to tell you something. I had no idea of coming to you for advice. All I wanted was local color, as you've discovered. I wanted hints as to setting, props, and business. I wanted a good characterization. And, by Jove! I wish you'd play my Granthope! But never mind that. I'd just like to ask you a question about a queer experience I've had lately. You've convinced me that you know some things."

Astro handed him a small silver box. "Have one of my cigarettes," he said. "There are not more than four or five hundred left in the world. They were given me by an army officer who once helped Diaz. Now go on with your story."

"My name is Pinkard, Lionel Pinkard," said the young man, "and, as you discovered, I am a playwright. I've written a book, too—that is, it's almost finished—and it's going to make a sensation—in more ways than one. Plays are all right for making money; but half the audience doesn't know or care who's the author. I confess I want fame. By Jove! that cigarette is sweet! A bit too mild, though, for me. Well,—let's see,—it was after *A Run of Luck* was put on. I was working on *The Chameleon*—that was when I first saw the Lady in Taupe."

"The Lady in Taupe!" Astro repeated the phrase with humor.

"That's what I called her. She always used to wear that color— 'taupe,' you know—a sort of purplish-gray, something like what they call 'London smoke,' only lighter. A gown with good lines, too. She always wore it, usually with black lynx furs."

"Where did you see her?"

"Everywhere; that's the funny part of it. This very day I saw her breakfasting at Mouquin's, at the next table. She's always near me. About two months ago she began. I say began, because it has happened too often to be accidental. She passed me in the street. Next day she stood on a corner waiting for a car. A mighty pretty girl, too—small head—you know how that makes a girl look taller and helps her figure; most women are built like dwarfs nowadays— deep brown eyes, a delicious mouth, and a touch of originality in her expression on account of a small scar on the left side of her chin. It's positively a beauty-spot, more like a dimple than a scar, and it crinkles up when she smiles. Well, I've run into her almost every day since then—and she's never moved an eyelash to show she recognized me. But she's up to something. She's always right in my way and never notices me. She's got me going, there's no doubt about that."

"Have you ever followed her?"

"Yes, I confess I've tried several times; but she has always given me the slip, or else I was clumsy."

"Well, what do you wish me to do about it?"

"I want to know what the lady's up to."

"That's simple enough. She wants to get an engagement."

"Why doesn't she ask me, then?"

"Ah, no doubt she will. She wants to make an impression, first. You know what a hard struggle it is for a girl without influence to get an engagement. She wants to get you curious, interested. I fancy she's heard you are to have a new play produced, and though the author doesn't always have much to say as to the cast, you are established and could probably help her."

"That's true enough. In my contracts I reserve a power of veto as to members of the cast, and I naturally have some weight, though there's a terrific amount of influence in these things. But it seems an elaborate method, I must say!"

"Well, I've heard of how the girls have to struggle. It strikes me she's clever. I'm curious to know what she will say when her time comes."

"So am I. I hope she'll spring her trap soon."

"And how is your book coming on?"

"Nearly finished. It's more or less of an exposé of society, and I hope will make talk. I'll send you a copy; that is, if your diagnosis proves correct in regard to the Lady in Taupe. If not, my dear Astro, I shall conclude you are merely a clever guesser."

The tone was such that Astro could not be offended at the banter. He rose smilingly to show Pinkard out. The young man gave Valeska, who was busy in the waiting-room, a sharp glance as he left.

"How did you know he was a playwright?" she asked the Master.

"I was in my laboratory when he came into the room, and watched him unobserved. He took in the whole studio at a glance, very interestedly. He went back to the door to get the effect as it would appear in a stage set, from the orchestra. He viewed it, as few do, as a whole, not in detail. Almost every one who enters inspects the curios and furnishings one by one. He summed up the general effect. By his appearance I knew him to be a man with brains. Few men of business can afford the time for a morning call, unless they wish some definite information. He had not the appearance of the idle rich; yet he was well-off. A literary man can use his inventive faculty not more than four hours a day without excessive fatigue; consequently he has time left in which to amuse himself. And finally, when he opened his coat for a pencil, I saw a typewritten manuscript in his inside pocket."

"He might have been an actor."

"It was not a part in a play that he had; they're bound up in smaller shape. Besides, he had none of the vanity of the actor. He was so sure of himself that he didn't feel the need of impressing any one."

"He might have been reading a play for a friend."

"The manuscript was full of pencil corrections. It was not a final draft, and would be almost undecipherable, except to the author. But, as far as that goes, almost every man who writes has an unfinished play up his sleeve. It was a safe guess."

"Well, what of the Lady in Taupe, then? I'm interested in her."

"What I surmised is probably true; but I suspect something deeper than that. It's a bit elaborate, as he said. It's a clever scheme, and may turn out to be still cleverer than it looks."

"I'd like to have a look at her. It takes a woman to read women."

GELETT BURGESS

"True. I believe it would be amusing to have you see her. The more I think of it, the more curious I am. I'll tell you. I'll ring Pinkard up and find out what he's going to do to-morrow."

He took up the telephone that evening and had a short conversation with the playwright. The next morning he said to Valeska:

"Pinkard will leave his house on West Seventy-fifth Street to-day at about ten o'clock, go to Dayton's office, lunch at the Grill Club, attend a rehearsal of his play *Wild-fire* at the Monster Theater in the afternoon, then go to the Park Riding Academy, dine at the Grill Club, and go to see Marlowe this evening at the Broadway. Knowing his itinerary, you can't miss him, and you'll probably see her, as she hasn't appeared for two days, and seldom misses it longer than that."

That evening Valeska returned with her report. "I saw her!" she exclaimed exultantly. "She's a beauty, too! I liked her at first sight. I followed him to Dayton's office, and she met him in Forty-second Street, almost the first thing."

"Where did she go?"

"That's the queer part of it. After she had passed him she waited on the corner of Forty-second and Broadway. An automobile came along with a lady in it—a really swell girl—stopped, and the Lady in Taupe got in. What do you think of that?"

"Number of the automobile?"

Valeska consulted a paper in her purse. "99,954."

Astro went into the little library in his waiting-room and took down the automobile list for the state of New York. He looked up the number, and then whistled softly. "Why, that was Helen Van Amsterdam!"

Valeska's eyebrows rose. "The heiress?"

"It must have been. That's the number of the Van Amsterdam's automobile, at least."

"Then I don't see why the Lady in Taupe should be looking for an engagement, if she has such rich friends."

"Oh, that doesn't signify. But there's something queer about it. Well, we can't take any more time; I have too many important things to attend to. We'll just file that information for reference. We may hear from Pinkard again."

He did hear from Pinkard, in fact, within the week. The playwright came in one morning, as handsome, confident, and debonair as ever. He took a new critical look at the studio, then sat down as Astro came in, and said:

"Well, the Lady of Taupe has called on me at last!"

"Yes?"

"You were quite right—as far as you went. She wanted a part in the cast of *The Chameleon*, and waxed eloquent over her attempts to get an engagement. You should have heard her talk! That girl has magnetism, all right. She played as pretty a scene, for an hour, in my library as I've ever watched on the stage. She did imitations of Mansfield and Cissy Loftus and Warfield and Barrymore; she told dramatic little stories; she discussed the psychology of audiences, the technique of the drama, and the very metaphysics of acting. I never heard such talk in my life; but—" He closed his eyes and smiled.

"Ah, but!" said Astro. "There was something else, then?"

"I should say so! After she had left, I went into my study, and found that it had been visited by burglars."

Astro betrayed no surprise; but his brows bent into a new tense curve. He leaned forward and looked at Pinkard intently. "And what was missing? Wait!" He suddenly raised a warning finger. "Don't tell me! I'll get it, perhaps—I have a feeling." He dropped his head into his hands for a few moments, then looked at Pinkard through half-shut eyes. "Not the manuscript of your new book?"

Pinkard slapped his hand on his knee. "By Jove! you've got it! See here, you'll have to take this on!"

"Anything else gone?"

"Nothing. I had a little safe in the wall, but it was untouched."

"A very pretty game, indeed."

"Wasn't it slick? Of course, she held me there while they worked it. I can't imagine how they ever got in, though. The back door shows no sign of having been forced, it was bolted on the inside.

No fire-escapes available. It's a small apartment-house, and rather old-fashioned. But why any one should want that manuscript, I don't know."

"You have no other copy?"

"No, I wrote it on the typewriter myself, and was too lazy to make carbon copies. I haven't even my first draft of the thing. And I wouldn't attempt to rewrite it for all my hopes of fame and fortune! I'm no Carlyle. I've simply got to get it back! And there's no use going to the police for a thing like that, as you ought to know. If it isn't diamonds or money, they'll do nothing."

"Tell me something about the novel."

"Why, I hadn't decided upon a name yet; but it was by way of being a social satire. I've been about a good deal, you know, in New York, and know the fastest part of the smart set, and not a few of the others. It was pretty frank, an exposé, really, as I told you. Of course, I have toned it down in some places and raised things to a higher power in others. It's a bit sensational; but I've taken good care to change episodes and details so that no one of the characters could be identified. I'm not altogether a cad. But it's all true to life; what might happen any day in New York, and seen from the inside, too."

"How many people know that you were writing it?"

"Oh, I've made no secret of it. Any one who wanted to could have found out."

"Very well. I'll be up this afternoon to look about. The Lady in Taupe called in the evening, I take it?"

"Yes, at about eight o'clock. I'm seldom in at that hour. I can't imagine how she should know I was at home. Funny thing, too, I have almost always met her in the forenoon, usually within a half-hour of the time I left my flat."

"Did you promise her a place in *The Chameleon?*"

"Why, I said I'd do what I could. She interested me, and might go well for my heavy woman, though a bit too young. But of course, now, I'll see that she doesn't get in. It's not likely that she'll let me see her again, anyway."

"On the contrary," said Astro, "you'll see her as much as ever."

Astro and Valeska called at the Vanberg apartments that after-noon at three o'clock and went carefully over Pinkard's rooms. To Valeska's surprise, their call lasted only fifteen minutes, and then Astro, pleading another engagement, took his leave. She did not question him, being busy trying to puzzle out the mystery for her-self; but, when he stopped at the front door down-stairs and rang the janitor's bell, she gave a little cry of triumph.

"Oh, I begin to see!" she exclaimed.

"I should hope so! It's too ridiculously simple. Half the flat burglaries in New York are done that way."

"But who helped? She couldn't do it alone."

"That's what we'll have to make sure of. I can only guess, just now. But here's the janitor. Have you any flats to rent in the building?"

The janitor looked them over before replying. "Well, there's a party wants to move out if she can find a good tenant to sublet to," he said.

"May we see the apartment?"

"She's not in, I think; but I guess it'll be all right. She's in a great hurry to rent, and I promised to help her. It's up on the third floor."

Valeska pressed Astro's arm in glee. Pinkard lived on the third floor! They were taken up, and the door unlocked.

"She's been here only a little while," said the janitor. "She didn't move in all her furniture; but you can get an idea what the place is like."

They walked rapidly through the place. Only one room was fit-ted up, and that but scantily, with only the requisites. The kitchen contained a few utensils, and it was evident that the occupant of the apartment took her meals outside. Astro walked to the dumb-waiter and lifted the sliding door. Opposite, only three feet away, was the corresponding door into Pinkard's kitchen. A glance at Valeska was hardly necessary. She nodded her head emphatically.

"Who lives here?" Astro asked.

"A Miss Demming. She's an actress, I hear. A pretty girl she is, too."

"Well, I'll come and see her. Much obliged, I'm sure."

"Do you think you will take it?" the janitor asked.

"I'm afraid it's too small," said the Seer, as they went out.

They were hesitating in the vestibule, and the janitor had left them, when Valeska exclaimed, "Why, there she is now!"

Astro looked out. A very pretty woman was walking toward them. By Pinkard's description alone he would have known her, even in her spring costume, for the Lady in Taupe. She held her head erect, ran up the steps, and, as they made way for her, entered the vestibule. Astro turned in time to see her open the letter-box of the third-floor suite. She took a key from her pocketbook, unlocked the door, and went upstairs without looking behind her. "Which," said Astro, smiling, "explains how she is able to know so easily when Pinkard is at home, and when he leaves to walk abroad."

"And how the flat was entered while she held him spellbound with her talk," added Valeska.

"But not how she is able to afford an eighty-five-dollar a month flat when she's out of a job," Astro scowled.

"Nor who it was who climbed across the shaft, entered Pinkard's kitchen, and ransacked his study."

Astro finished, "For further particulars I think we'll have to apply to Miss Van Amsterdam."

"Oh!" said Valeska.

"I forgot to tell you that Pinkard was once engaged to Miss Van Amsterdam. She threw him over in a particularly nasty way two years ago, when she was engaged for a time to Count Vinola."

"How did you find that out?"

"The steward of the Grill Club owns a half interest in the Peerless Restaurant, though few of the members know it. I lunched there this noon, and gave him some tips on the stock market. Now that Mr. Calendon is a power in Wall Street, he doesn't forget his friends. The steward was duly grateful, and told me several interesting things. I shall cultivate him in the future."

"Ah!" Valeska looked up, smiling. "So Miss Van Amsterdam was afraid of being exposed in his book, was she? Well, I hope she'll read the manuscript quickly."

"Yes," said Astro, as they walked back to the studio, "I hardly think it will be necessary for us to do anything more. I venture to make a prophecy. The Lady in Taupe will call on Pinkard again within three days, and the manuscript will be returned. See if I'm not right. I'm going to write Pinkard to that effect to-night, and enclose my bill for one hundred dollars."

It was four days afterward when Pinkard made his third appearance at the studio, smiling broadly. "By Jove, Astro!" he said, "I wish really you'd tell me how you did it! I need it for my play. I'll swear it's too much for me!"

"Well, what happened?"

"I don't see why I need tell you, by Jove!" Pinkard shook his head. "You've certainly got your crystal ball well trained. I wish I could make my character Granthope as sensational as you are. I've got your studio all right; but I think I'll have to get you to take the part. You could make an audience believe anything. Of course I got the manuscript back, as you said I should."

"Is your play cast yet?"

Pinkard laughed outright. "Part of it. What do you think? We've signed the Lady in Taupe for the heavy woman, after all. She's an adventuress, all right! Talk about romance in every-day life! She made a grandstand play with me for fair!"

"Do tell me about it."

"Well, last night she turned up again, as bold as brass. I taxed her with being accessory to a felony, and she only laughed, by Jove! She swore it was all a joke, just to awaken my interest in her, and then she promised that the manuscript would be returned if I gave her a part. Well, the audacity of it tickled me just enough to accept. I wanted to see if it was a bluff. And what do you think? She said, as soon as I consented to the bargain, that I'd find the manuscript on my study table. I raced in immediately, and there it was! Here's your hundred dollars. You're a wizard. Sometimes I suspect that you were in cahoots with the Lady in Taupe and planned the whole thing yourself. But who on earth is she, anyway?"

Astro chuckled good-naturedly. "I'm not wise enough to know that. She is certainly clever, though. If you hadn't engaged her, I think I should."

"Well," said Pinkard, rising to take his leave, "there are tricks in all trades, they say. I won't inquire into yours; but if I want any more sleuthing done, I'll know where to go. I'll certainly send you a box for the opening night of *The Chameleon*. I'm going to re-write that part for the Lady in Taupe, by Jove! It wasn't half good enough for her as it was."

"Well, Valeska," said Astro, "that proves again the value of a knowledge of human nature plus a friend 'below stairs.' I fancy Miss Van Amsterdam must have a rather guilty conscience to be so afraid of the revelations of Pinkard's book. She certainly secured a clever assistant in the Lady in Taupe. It must have cost nearly a thousand dollars to put that little game through. I'd rather like to know, though, whether it was the heiress herself who crawled through the door across the shaft. At any rate, it was lucky for Pinkard that he wasn't a cad, as he said. I'm afraid his book would have never seen the light, else."

Valeska placed her hand lightly on the Seer's shoulder. "But you didn't mean—I mean, you wouldn't *really* have engaged the Lady in Taupe as your assistant—would you?"

His answer was not in words; but Valeska was apparently satisfied. It was evident that she had no longer a fear of any such dilemma.

MRS. STELLERY'S LETTERS

"She must be a beautiful woman, Mrs. Stellery," said Astro.

Stellery looked a little embarrassed. He pulled his blond mustache thoughtfully. "Why—ah—yes; I used to think so, when I first married her. One gets used to a face, you know."

"I see. Still your wife must be charming. At least, her anonymous correspondent seems to think so. He is certainly very complimentary. See here," the Seer picked up one of the letters from the bunch on the table, opened it, and read aloud:

> "It may sound banal to say you're pretty, and yet every woman likes to know that she is. You're far more; you have an original type of beauty. One watches for your smile, hoping it will come soon. And that constellation of dimples in your cheeks!"

Stellery laughed faintly. "Just about the way I used to talk," he acknowledged. "When I first courted her I was quite poetical about those dimples,—named every one after a different star, I believe. Queer this chap has picked up the same idea, though."

It was on Astro's lips to say that the simile was as old as woman's love and man's, but he did not. He turned to another letter, typewritten like the other.

> "You're like a little gray mouse. I wonder if there is any lurking devil in you for me to evoke? With your

351

gray eyes you look so demure! Are you really as quiet
as you seem? I'd like to have a talk with you alone
and see!"

"She has a devil in her, all right," remarked Stellery, "and a
delicious enough one, too! Oh, she can be charming, that mouse!
It's very evident that the fellow who's writing these letters doesn't
know her very well. That's one satisfaction."

Astro took up one more.

> "I saw you at the opera last night. You had more
> style, more apparent culture, more caste, than any
> woman in the house. Once you looked full at me, and
> I wondered what it would seem like to have a wife
> like you. To own you, and be owned by so wonderful
> a creature! How proud I'd be!"

"I remember that night. Mrs. Stellery does look well when she's
dressed up. But curse such audacity! Writing to my wife like that!
It's an outrage, by Jove! You'll see why I don't care to go to the
police with these letters. But they must be stopped, and I must
find out who's doing it!"

"How long has this thing been going on?"

"For two months, now. I have a bunch more of 'em at home
that my wife gave me."

The letters on the table were all written on telegraph blanks
and enclosed in government-stamped envelopes.

"All typewritten like these?"

"No; the first ones were crudely printed in pencil, as if a child
had done them."

"And all of them complimentary?"

"Every one of them."

"How often do they come?"

"Every two or three days. Mrs. Stellery has been away visiting
in Philadelphia the last three weeks, and they followed her down
there. She brought back a whole lot of them to show to me."

"Did she show you the first one when it came?"

Mr. Stellery considered the question a little.

"No, not for some time; not till she had received several, in fact. At first she didn't want to worry me, she said; then she decided that I ought to know about them, anyway. Some of the first ones were left in the letter-box, but most of them have been sent through the mails."

"Does Mrs. Stellery seem to be much worried at receiving them?"

"Decidedly. Of course, it isn't as if they were as unpleasant as anonymous letters sometimes are. But she didn't want me to go to you about them, and thought that they'd stop coming after a while. In point of fact she hasn't had any this week; but I want to find out who's responsible for them; and, from what I've heard of you, you're the one to do it."

"I see." Astro let his chin fall into his palms and stared at the table in silence for some time.

Stellery walked up and down, examining the furnishings of the studio. He picked up a gold stiletto and fingered it, walked to the wall and looked at an antique bit of tapestry, smiled at Astro's white lizard in its cage, and returned to the Seer, who looked up to say:

"It's queer that a man who professes to admire her so much doesn't have the courage to tell her so, isn't it?" He watched Stellery between half-closed lids.

"You don't know her. My wife is a very proud woman. She'd not stand for it a minute, I'm sure of that. This chap has some romantic notion, or he wants to make trouble. It seems to me the letters are a bit too literary in style, as if he were used to composition. And what he says is true, too! How does he know my wife has dimples in her shoulders, by Jove? How does he know how she looks in an Egyptian scarf? She hasn't worn one since her honeymoon when I got one in Cairo. Why, I might have written those letters myself! Little intimate details that make my blood boil to think of another man's knowing! Little tricks she has I didn't think any one else had ever noticed! It's amazing!"

GELETT BURGESS

"Are you home much of the time?" Astro asked, stacking the letters into a pile on the table.

"Not much; that is, until lately. I'm a busy man, and when I'm at home I try to get rid of some of my outside work. I have a den down next to my library, and often spend the whole evening there. I've been trying to get together a lot of information on the history of Wall Street coups, and it takes about all my spare time. All the relaxation I get, really, is in bridge at the Percentage Club. Why?" He stopped and darted a look at Astro.

"Oh, I only wondered how much time your wife had to herself."

Stellery wheeled on him. "See here! I hope that's no insinuation! My wife is above suspicion, you understand that! Good lord! why should she show me these letters, if she weren't?"

"Oh, my dear sir," said Astro suavely, "don't take it that way! I was wondering if any one were watching her, following her. Nevertheless, I should like to know, also, just whom she sees, and where, and how. You have given me a difficult task, Mr. Stellery, and you must forgive me if I seem curious. But I presume I shall get it all better in my own way. You don't mind my calling on Mrs. Stellery, I imagine?"

"Why, of course not. She'll be glad to see you, I suppose. But, of course, it's a delicate matter, and she's naturally sensitive."

"Very good." Astro rose, tall and distinguished. A veil seemed to be drawn before his eyes, masking all expression; as if, having learned all he could of his client, he was anxious to be alone to solve the problem.

Stellery seemed to feel the change of atmosphere. He reached for his hat, shook hands, and left the studio.

"How do you diagnose him, Valeska?" Astro asked his assistant, who had overheard the talk.

"A clever man, absorbed in business, a bit cruel, or at least inclined to be cold and unsympathetic, and yet honorable and loyal at heart. I'd hate to be in love with him! He'd make me suffer. And you?"

Astro smiled cryptically. "You work from your feelings; I from my facts," he said. "Fortunately, we often come out in the same place. But, speaking of facts, try and see what you can make of these letters. It's an amusing complication, and a new variation of the anonymous letter."

Valeska sat down and looked over the pile. As she examined them one by one and threw them into a heap to begin over again, she kept up a running commentary. "Mostly stamped at the Madison Square branch post-office. A few at Station E—that's on West Thirty-second Street, isn't it? One or two at Times Square branch, and one at Station I, One Hundred and Fifth Street. All but that one mailed in the early afternoon. Written on a Rem-Smith typewriter; a pretty old one, I should say, for the alignment is bad. All the small 'o's' register below the line, and all the capital 'N's' above it. And I should say that the writer is not in love with her; only pretending."

"How do you make that out?" Astro smiled curiously.

"I can feel it."

"Too literary?"

"Oh, I can't explain it. Only, I know if I got letters like this I'd throw them in the fire. 'Your gracile hands!'—bosh!"

"Yes, I noticed 'gracile.' It seems to be his pet word. Also 'jimp.' Queer love-letters—I agree with you."

"Love-letters! They're deeper than that!"

"You're right, and there is small possibility of finding the author unless we discover the motive first. There are thousands of persons who might write these letters. What I have to decide is, why should any one of them do it? It may be a mere practical joke. If that's so, it would be done by some one who can watch the effect upon her. In any case, I take it that it must be some one who knows her. What good could it do a stranger?"

"What good could it do a friend or an acquaintance?"

"Flatter a woman with all sorts of intimate original compliments,—not spoken, so that she would have to blush, deny, and reprove; but written, so that she could read and reread them in secret as often as she liked,—arouse her curiosity, a powerful ally;

her sense of the romantic, a still stronger one, and finally unmask yourself as the adorer;—I don't know that it's so bad a way, after all."

"Unless you try it on a woman who shows all the letters to her husband," said Valeska dryly.

"Yes; but how's the writer to know she will? He's probably conceited enough to think she won't."

"There's one other way of discovering the writer,—find a Rem-Smith typewriter with an alignment imperfect in just this way."

"Yes," said Astro. "We might begin and fine-toothcomb the city for it. Still, accidents do happen, luckily for prophets and seers. And, at any rate, that will be the final proof. Well, I'm going to reread the whole bunch, look for some unifying theory—and then call on the lady. I confess I'm curious to see her."

Mrs. Stellery, he was to find, was a woman of by no means an obvious type. Outwardly, it is true, she manifested social grace and experience, was handsome rather than beautiful, with a dark serious face and finely-chiseled features. One would call her aristocratic in looks and manner, and yet behind the conventional aspects in which she showed herself in company, a keen observer would note subtlety after subtlety. That she had a fine mind and a fearless one, was occasionally proved by the flashes of wit and perspicacity that illumined her conversation and colored what might otherwise be a rather bored and repressed, though perfectly polite habit of talk. She seemed aloof, waiting for something interesting, all but effete. Her smile was elusive; but, when it came forth, compelling, captivating, and as soon as it had created that impression, it faded and the weary manner asserted itself again. Only the mouth was temperamental. The gray eyes were well schooled, though velvety soft. She had a trick of half raising one eyebrow, which gave a whimsical relief to her haughty pose. One could fancy her always playing a part and wonder what the real woman would be like. Not very different from other women, after all, if one judged by the quivering lips.

This, at least, is the way Astro described the woman to Valeska later. He was waiting in the reception-room, looking at a novel entitled *The Guerdon*, when Mrs. Stellery entered, one brow delicately arched, as if she had not been quite sure whom she was to find.

He introduced himself, and for a moment she seemed embarrassed and turned the conversation to the novel.

"Have you read it?" she asked. "I met the author. Mr. Askerson, lately in Philadelphia at a dinner, and he sent me the book. I saw him only twice; but he seemed quite an extraordinary man."

Astro turned to the title page, and before finding it noticed the inscription on the fly-leaf, "Viola Stellery: Her Book," a quaint-enough wording to arouse his smile. "A problem?" he asked.

"Love after marriage—the modern theme," she replied.

"I'd like to know his solution."

She merely smiled. It was her only smile during the interview, and the talk passed to the letters.

She had no idea, she said, why she was being so persecuted. The letters were stupid, and apparently meaningless, yet they annoyed her. Their audacity had now begun to worry her, as well. If anything could be done to stop them, she would be glad. Yes, they had ceased coming, for the time being, and perhaps it would be as well to wait and do nothing; but now Mr. Stellery himself was aroused and wished the matter investigated. He was too busy with his press of work to spend much time on the matter. He was a very busy man. Quite absorbed in his work—and she had hoped to go abroad with him in the spring. At present it seemed impossible. And so on the talk ran, while her expression said, "What are you going to do about it? I don't care!"

Then a card was brought in, and she said, "It is Doctor Primfield, my husband's brother-in-law, you know. Married Paul's sister, who died two years ago. He's a physician. We see a good deal of him."

She did not add, "and he bores me"; but the merest drag in her words implied it. In another minute the doctor came brusquely in.

He was a nervous, slim, snapping-eyed man of thirty-five, with a jerky way of speaking and moving. He said, "Hello, Lila!" shook hands, bowed to Astro, and looked at him with a professional eye, seemed to decide that the palmist was all right, flapped himself

GELETT BURGESS

into a seat, screwed his feet round the legs of a chair, and began to talk very fast to his hostess, ignoring Astro.

Mrs. Stellery endeavored to include both guests in the conversation but found it difficult. Astro, seeing that he was in the way, at least of the doctor, withdrew and went back to his studio.

On the way he stopped at a bookstore and bought a copy of *The Guerdon*. Dipping into it, walking down Fifth Avenue, he came across a sentence, reread it, shut the book with a snap, and walked home thinking.

Arrived at the studio, he laid the book open at the page he had read, before Valeska.

"'She laid her soft gracile hands, palms down, on the table,'" she read aloud, and looked up. "Did you find 'jimp', too?"

"You'll have to read the book and see," was his answer. And then he described the interview. "If you find 'jimp' and 'nuance,'— for there are several 'nuances' in the letters,—I think it would be well for you to apply to Askerson for a position as secretary. Only on the chance, a slim enough one,—but all we have at present. But Stellery is right; the letters do sound literary, though Mrs. Stellery is wrong—they are by no means stupid. If I could only think of a motive for a man like Askerson doing such a sentimental thing!"

"He might want to see what she'd do, and use the episode in fiction."

"Yes, that's the trouble. Men have many motives, and often several at a time, really mixed. Women seldom act except with a single definite motive, no matter how they conceal it or even pretend to themselves that it's different. I wonder if the author could possibly be Doctor Primfield."

"Why Doctor Primfield more than another?"

Astro laughed. "There doesn't seem to be any other, yet; and there was something queer in the way he looked at her."

"How did he look at her?"

"This way."

But Valeska, seeing too well what was in his eyes, turned away her own. "Well, I'll read the book," she remarked, leaving.

"And I'll read the letters again."

There were, Valeska found, three "graciles," one "jimp," and two "nuances" in Askerson's novel. In connection with their recurrence in the letters, the coincidence might mean anything or nothing. What was more important was to get a sample of Askerson's typewriting; and to this end Valeska, in the guise of a stenographer in search of work, visited him.

She found Askerson to be the farthest removed from her preconceived idea of a novelist. He was a short, round, and chubby, seraphic-looking young man, with light curly hair and the mien of a preternaturally solemn child. His earnestness seemed absurd masquerading in this juvenile guise; but, once that inconsistency was forgotten, under the spell of his mental power, she found him a most interesting man. He was in the midst of his work, dressed in a pink silk shirt and white duck trousers, his hair a mass of light wavy locks over his eyes, smoking a brier pipe.

He assured her that, though he would like to employ a secretary, he could not afford it. Besides, he was engaged in dramatizing *The Guerdon*, and had to work it out himself on his machine, inch by inch. He had to refuse her request; but seemed willing to talk.

Valeska had prepared for the interview by reading everything of Askerson's that she could find. Among other books, she had discovered a slim book of poems, privately printed during his college days. As a last resort, she used this, hoping to play upon the vanity of the poet in him.

"I heard a girl once recite one of your poems; *Sea Magic*, I think it was called. Do you know where I could get a copy of it?"

He seemed pleased. "I didn't know any one remembered that verse," he said. "It's one of my favorites. If you'll wait, I'll see if I can remember it. I'll typewrite it for you, if you like." He sat down to his machine, puckered his brows, and began to write. He paused once in a while in search of a phrase, which he usually found by a hard glare at the ceiling, and finally finished it and presented her with the sheet.

"Would you mind signing it?" she asked timidly.

He put his name and a flourish at the bottom of the page.

She could scarcely wait till she was in the car to examine the printing. The small "o's" registered a little below the lines; but the capital "N's" were in true alignment.

Astro shrugged his shoulders when he saw it, and pointed silently with the stem of his narghile to the word "gracile" in the last stanza.

Two days after that, a hasty summons came from Stellery over the telephone, at four in the afternoon. He wished Astro to come immediately to the house; but did not care to tell, over the wire, why he was needed.

Astro took a taxicab and went up-town immediately. He found the broker in his den, writing at a big table covered with sheets of paper. On a smaller table stood his typewriter, a sheet, half written, sticking from the roller.

Stellery looked up with a worried expression. "Take a seat," he said. "I want your advice; or, rather, your help. Things have come to a crisis. Brush those papers on the floor anywhere."

As Astro sat down, he noticed a waste-paper basket behind him, a little to the left. As he seated himself, he pushed his chair back a foot or so, so that the basket was within easy reach.

Stellery took a letter from his pocket and passed it over. "Here's what came yesterday," he said.

Astro opened it and read:

> "I simply can't wait any longer! I must see you! You must know, by this time, how madly I am in love with you. I don't dare to speak to you face to face, unless I receive some encouragement. But I want to end this suspense immediately and know my fate! Will you meet me to-morrow afternoon, at six o'clock, at the prescription counter of the Times Square drug store? If you'll be there and will let me speak to you for only five minutes, please leave a candle lighted in the window of your room to-night between ten and eleven o'clock."

"Well, did she light the signal?" said Astro handing back the letter.

Stellery frowned and nodded. "See here, you can imagine how I must feel to have this sort of thing going on!" he said. "And it's enough to make me fairly sick! But I want to trap that man and find out who he is. That's why I sent for you. Mrs. Stellery objected very strongly to lending herself to the scheme in any way. It was all I could do to get her to light the candle; in fact, I had to do that myself. But, after talking it over, and deciding that there was after all no real danger of her compromising herself, she consented to be at the rendezvous this evening at six o'clock. She doesn't seem to be curious—the thing disgusts her—but she wants to put an end to the matter. Of course I can't be seen there, or he'd never appear at all. That's what makes me wild. I'd like to go down and punch that chap's head! Instead, I've got to stay here and wait. I want you to follow her down—nobody will know you have anything to do with it, of course—and find out who it is, if it's some one she doesn't know. Then we'll put that chap in jail, if it's a possible thing!"

He had worked himself into a passion as he talked, and, rising and gesticulating, walked back and forth in the little room.

Astro watched his chance, and, when Stellery's back was turned, reached into the waste-paper basket, drew out a sheet of typewritten paper, crumpled it up in his hand, and slid it into his pocket.

"Is Mrs. Stellery at home?" he asked.

"No; she had an appointment this afternoon. But she'll be at the drug store at six, she promised."

"I wish I had known this before," said Astro. "I should have liked to have my assistant with me."

"I've been trying to get you on the 'phone all day. But, in point of fact, though Mrs. Stellery consented to the signal, I had to argue with her all this morning to get her to meet this man. You can imagine how I feel! I wonder if I've done wrong? Can you fancy how it feels to send your wife to a rendezvous to meet an anonymous correspondent? By Jove! I didn't know how much I loved her, before! You know, I've neglected her shamefully, I suppose.

I've been absorbed in my work, and that's why this sort of thing
has been possible. I suppose people have seen her going about
alone, and have thought perhaps we were estranged, even. And
every thing this damned scoundrel has been writing her is true, by
Jove. She is charming, you can see that! She's one of ten thousand, that woman! I ought to know. Now, at the faintest prospect
of losing her, absurd as that chance is—why, I'm fairly crazy about
her. If I saw that man with her, I don't care who he is, I believe I'd
kill him!"

"Which is another reason for your not going," said Astro, rising.
"There must be no scene. You can trust Mrs. Stellery to make the
talk brief and forcible enough, and, in any case, you may depend
on me to protect her."

It was nearly a quarter to six before he reached Times Square.
He entered the building and started down-stairs toward the subway entrance on his way to the drug store below the street, when a
man brushed past him, almost jostling him off the step in his haste.
The man looked round to apologize; it was Doctor Primfield.

"Oh, I beg your pardon!" he said, and looked at Astro queerly.
"Haven't I met you somewhere?" he added.

Astro recalled the meeting but did not mention his own name.

The doctor appeared to be a little embarrassed. "I've got to catch
a subway train; so you'll have to excuse me," he said. "Otherwise,
I'd like to have a talk. I have some theories of my own about capillary markings on the fingers I'd like to discuss with you. Good day!"
and he was off like a busy squirrel. As he passed the drug-store
entrance Astro noticed that he gave a swift, apparently uneasy look
inside.

Mrs. Stellery, however, had not yet appeared; but at a few minutes before six she walked in the door, handed a prescription to
the clerk at the desk, and seated herself without appearing to recognize the Seer, who lounged at a counter some distance away. She
was beautifully dressed in the prevalent mode, and sat like a fashion-plate, without expression on her proud face, as if bored to
death.

Six o'clock struck, and no one approached her. Fifteen minutes went by, and still she sat, calm and haughty, in her place. Finally, when the prescription was handed her, she walked over to Astro and bowed coldly.

"Do you think it will be any use waiting longer?" she asked.

"Not the slightest," was his reply. "No one will come, I am quite sure."

She looked up at him with a sudden keen expression. "You are sure?" she repeated.

"Quite so, Mrs. Stellery. May I escort you home?"

When they arrived, the servant who opened the door put a note into Mrs. Stellery's hand, saying that it had been delivered by a messenger boy. She tore it open, read it, and passed it to Astro:

> "It was, of course, impossible for me to speak to you, as you were watched."

The next day, as Astro and Valeska were driving up-town, returning from a case that was then puzzling him, he proposed that they rest at Sherry's and take tea there. It was not yet four o'clock, and there was no one else in the room when they entered. Tea, muffins, and jam had hardly been ordered, however, when Valeska suddenly exclaimed:

"Why, there's Mr. Askerson now!"

"And there's Mrs. Stellery as well!" Astro added.

Master and assistant gave each other a quick glance, then turned to the approaching couple. They were earnestly conversing, and did not, apparently, notice that there was any one else in the room as they walked across to the opposite side and sat down. Then Mrs. Stellery cast her gray eyes slowly about the room and met Astro's. He and Valeska could see the color mantle her cheeks as she turned away. Askerson was slower at perceiving who was present; but when at last he noticed Valeska, he turned suddenly and said something to Mrs. Stellery. The latter was too well-bred to turn; perhaps she was too busy in attempting to mask her thoughts in her haughty cold expression. They did not look over again.

"Well, if Mr. Askerson has written those letters, it's about time for him to explain now," said Valeska. "I think he's dear! But why should he take such an elaborate method of making love to her when he can meet her like this whenever he wants to?"

"Perhaps he can't."

"There's no reason why he shouldn't, is there? It's all right."

"Do you think he wrote them?"

"I don't know. If it hadn't been for your meeting Doctor Primfield, I'd be surer. Askerson's typewriter leaves it in doubt.

"Oh, the typewriter, we agreed, was only the final test. What you must seek is a motive."

"Well, then, Askerson is romantic—and a bit afraid of her. Doctor Primfield is practical; but afraid of her husband. Either may be in love with her."

"I don't think you have proved a sufficient motive yet for so extraordinary a course. But, by Jove! look at that! If there isn't Primfield himself!"

It was Primfield, indeed, who entered at that moment, looked about, caught sight of Mrs. Stellery, walked over to her table, and spoke. She reached out her hand and smiled faintly. There were a few words of introduction, and he sat down at their table and lighted a cigarette.

"Now," said Astro, "you have a chance to vindicate your woman's perception. Watch and see which of those two men is in love with her."

Valeska narrowed her eyes and watched. It was five minutes before she said deliberately, "I think neither of them is."

Astro laughed softly. "Well, my dear, I have a better motive than you have yet discovered."

"What is it?" she asked eagerly.

"I won't tell you yet; I'll give you a chance to think it over by yourself. But at ten o'clock to-morrow morning the writer of the Stellery anonymous letters will walk into my studio."

At ten next morning Valeska came swiftly into the laboratory where Astro was experimenting with phosphorescent sulfid of calcium screens. The sight of her face made the Seer smile, it was so puzzled in its expression.

"Mrs. Stellery is here. She says you wished to see her. Are you going to have her meet the author of the letters?"

"Yes," he answered, putting down a varnish brush. "And if you want enlightenment on human nature, I advise you to listen in the anteroom."

He took a piece of crumpled paper covered with typewriting from his pocket and handed it to her. She looked at it carefully; then, as she stood for a moment staring at him, her face changed.

"Oh!" she breathed, and walked rapidly back to the reception-room.

Mrs. Stellery was waiting for him, standing beside the granite Thoth in the center of the studio. Her eyes were fixed blankly; but at his coming she turned a white face suddenly to him.

"You said that you had discovered the authorship of the letters," she said, and her voice was very low. "I'm anxious about it. Do you really know? Are you sure?"

He nodded gravely, motioned her to a seat, and sat down himself. "My dear Mrs. Stellery," he began, "I want you to trust implicitly in my tact and my consideration. I shall do nothing whatever without your consent, you may be sure. Indeed, it was to ask your advice that I sent for you."

She continued staring at him anxiously, and her lips formed the words, "My husband!"

"Mr. Stellery shall know—only what you please to tell him yourself," he answered.

"Then you *do* know!" Her lips were trembling.

"It was my business to find out."

"Who wrote them, then?" she demanded almost fiercely, as if defying him.

"Mrs. Stellery," he replied, "you are a clever woman. Not only that, but you have a profound knowledge of men. And you have a heart that, in its danger, knows how to ally itself with your brain."

"You mean—"

"That you wrote them yourself!"

For a few minutes no one would have recognized her for the proud serene woman of the world. A strong effort of her will brought her back to something like composure; but now she must talk.

"If you knew what I have suffered!" she exclaimed. "We have been growing away from each other for a year. If it had been only a quarrel, we might have made it up; but this was only his careless-ness, his absorption in his business, his thoughtless cruelty. I wanted to arouse him, rekindle his interest in me, make him love me again, if I could. Oh! can't you see? It may not have been right— it was a deceit, I know— but I missed him so!"

"My dear Mrs. Stellery, you needn't justify yourself to me. All I need to say is that I'm sure your ruse has worked."

"Oh, I know it has! But I had some good advice,—it wasn't all sheer woman's wit—Mr. Askerson helped me. I don't know how I came to confide in him—I've seen him so few times—but he wrote most of the letters for me, and I copied them; so they would seem more like a man's letters, you know. But I confess—I don't know what you'll think of my praising myself so—all those intimate per-sonal things were truly my own. Most of them my husband had said to me during our honeymoon. I thought they would be most likely to arouse his jealousy."

"Oh, he's jealous enough," said Astro. "You needn't fear that you haven't succeeded. He has threatened to kill the writer of the letters."

She smiled wistfully. "Well, I hope he won't kill *me* when he finds out I'm the one. And that's the question! I always expected to tell him; but now I'm afraid to. I didn't quite intend to let it go so far, and I don't know how to explain. What shall I do?" She looked up at him with tears in her eyes. There was no haughtiness left, now.

"I think you needn't worry," said Astro, giving her his hand in sympathy; "for I met Mr. Stellery this morning on his way to the office. He told me that he intended to take you abroad immedi-ately. That, he said, would stop this nonsense and give him a chance to get acquainted with you all over again. He said he was sure you had been left alone too much."

"Really?" she said, suddenly smiling. "Oh, then, I'm sure the letters will stop! And," she added softly, "when I've quite won him back, and we're happy again, I'll confess everything." She paused a moment, then spoke as if to herself. "There's a little canal in Venice I love. It's called the Rio Margherita. I think it will be there—in June—just after sunset."

She looked up wistfully as she added, "Oh, I do hope he'll forgive me for being such a schemer!"

BLACK LIGHT

Surely it had been a curious wooing; for Astro, Seer of Secrets, so confident in other matters, so keen in his insight into human nature, so quick to think and bold to act, had shown from the first a strange timidity when it came to a personal relation with Valeska, his assistant. His manner had long been merely brotherly, modified only by his relation as instructor to her. But of late he had begun to make tentative suggestions, as if to try and sound her affection. From these Valeska had instinctively warned him off, and his tact had made him accede to her wishes. It seemed as if he feared to lose her by speaking too soon.

But at last he had spoken. The words had sprung unpremeditated from his lips, on the surging impulse of the moment. Nor were they the fruit of any dramatic moment. Merely the sight of her in a characteristic attitude at the table, her blond head illumined by the electric light, and a sudden terror struck him lest destiny should sweep them apart and write the story of their two years' friendship in the chronicles of the past. So many things in his life had faded like autumn leaves! He *must* be sure of her, sure of having her beside him always, sure of the inspiration of her companionship. The speech came on the instant in a passionate demand.

It had appeared to frighten her for the moment, as if it were a question she had long been dreading. She had asked for time in which to consider it, and he had reluctantly consented. Since then he had not mentioned the subject; but he had watched her silently with fear and constraint in his manner.

Valeska found it hard to explain why she had been unwilling to answer; but, as she went over and over the question, it seemed to her that their friendship had been merely the product of propinquity. They had been thrown together continually, had incurred danger, and had enjoyed victory. How, then, could she be sure that it was no more than friendship, a common interest in their work? Love, she had always thought, should come with a flash of sudden illumination, as a divine gift, as a sudden wonder, convincing in its very mystery. But her feeling—was it not the mere result of a daily comradeship? Was it a fatal irresistible appeal of the soul? She found him aristocratic, generous, talented, finely perceptive, and delicate; but was this all? Her love, if it were love, spoke a commonplace tongue—and she had wanted words of fire. So, for a week, she went over and over the subject, subjecting herself and Astro to a searching criticism, and as yet she had found no answer.

He came into the room one morning, carrying from his laboratory a large black square object, which he set on the table. She looked at it, and then her eyes questioned him.

"It is a lantern of a special kind," he said. "It casts black light."

"Black light!" Her delicate brows rose.

"That's what Doctor Le Bon calls it. You see, the visible spectrum (or all the light we can see) is only about one per cent. of all the vibrant energy emitted by the sun or any other luminous body. Beyond that visible spectrum lie, at one end the ultraviolet rays, and at the other the infra-red. I have here a lighted lantern enclosed in an opaque box, which cuts off all the visible rays, but permits the other ninety-nine per cent. to pass through. The flame inside is now casting rays of black light through the opaque sides,— black, because they are invisible; light, because they will illuminate certain objects.

"I want you to witness an experiment. You recall the celebrated interference experiment of Fresnel, in which light added to light produced darkness? Well, I shall show you how darkness added to darkness may give birth to light. It is Le Bon's discovery. Now come into my dark room, and I'll show it to you."

At the farther end of the laboratory he opened a door which led into a small dark room. Entering this, and closing the laboratory door, he opened one into another dark room beyond, carrying the dark lantern. They both entered the inner dark room, which was ventilated through a circuitous light-proof pipe. The room was absolutely black; but Astro, well used to the place, feeling his way with his hands, set the lantern on a table.

"Upon a shelf here," he said, "is a Chinese image of Buddha, which some weeks ago I coated with phosphorescent sulfid of calcium. By this time all its luminosity is gone, and it is absolutely invisible. But now I shall direct the invisible rays of black light from this lantern upon it. Watch!"

As she waited there in the silence and the dark, Valeska strained her eyes for nearly a minute in vain. Then a faint luminous blur was apparent. It gathered intensity and showed a triangle of violet radiance. In another minute it had taken the form of a squatting Buddha and glowed plainly, the only visible thing in the room.

"It's wonderful!" she breathed.

"Oh, that's not half that can be done with black light," Astro said, as he took the lantern and led the way out. "With it one can photograph objects through an opaque screen, when they are illuminated by ordinary sunlight. By using a screen of sulfid of zinc, and training this black light upon an object, one could see it even at midnight, half a mile away."

When they came out into the great studio, he dropped to his favorite place on the divan and went on. "Phosphorescence, opalescence and fluorescence are queer things, Valeska. They haven't been half understood till lately, when what is called 'the new physics' came into being through the discoveries in radioactivity by Monsieur and Madame Curie. It used to be thought that after a phosphorescent object had remained in the dark for a while and had ceased to be luminous, it ceased its radioactivity, and needed a new bath of light to make it act again. But Le Bon found that it would radiate for months after all visible glow had disappeared. We have proved it with this black light just now."

He had taken up his narghile and sat looking off into space with a mystic expression on his face. It was one of his dreamy, philosophical moments. Valeska recognized the mood and waited for the inevitable parable. For, to Astro the Seer, modern science was but an allegory of the intellect and the emotions. By it he explained even his own charlatanry.

"Isn't it like absence? While our friend is present, he is bathed in the matter-of-fact light of day; he is radiant, luminous. When he disappears, for a time that impression of him lasts, like the phosphorescent glow. Then, the light fades and we begin to forget,— all save those who truly love, who truly know, whose soul can still perceive the mysterious astral black light he radiates through the dark. His influence persists, transmuted from mental into psychic energy. *Selah!*" He dropped his narghile and sat with folded hands, looking at her as if she were miles away. His smile was the calm expression of his own bronze Buddha.

But Valeska took the parable to herself eagerly. "Yes, yes, it's true, and that's just what I need to know before I give you the answer you want! I don't know whether I *really* love you or not,— you're too near me, too intermingled with my life and my work. If I could try that test of absence, if I could wait till your phosphorescence fades out, then I could tell whether or not I was affected by your black light. I'd know then just *what* you were to me—alone in the dark!"

"Shall we try it?" he asked gently. "Shall I disappear for a week, say?"

"Ah, I'm afraid it would take at least a month!" she said.

He laughed. "Well, as long as you like."

"Will you really?"

He bowed gravely. "I shall disappear to-morrow. You may use the studio as you please; and, when you've found out whether or not you can be affected by my psychic black light,—you will let me know."

"Do I care? Do I care enough for him?" Valeska asked herself the next morning as she walked to the studio. She had thought of it almost all night; she had risen with the question on her lips. She had seen him every day for two years. The thought that today, and perhaps for a week or a month, she would not see him, gave her a strange feeling. Was it a relief, or a pain? As yet, she could not decide.

As she entered the studio it seemed strange not to find him there, at first. Then, insensibly she began to find it hard to believe that he was not there. Everything suggested his presence,—the curiosities he had collected, the weapons, the Egyptian sculptures, tapestries, gems,—all evidences of his taste and his researches. She could not rid herself of the feeling that at any moment he might come in. He was near her, somewhere, waiting and watching for her.

But this, she said to herself, was only the effect of the familiar environment in which she had been used to see him. But it became at last too strong, too insistent. Surely she could never decide till she sought a new atmosphere. She was sorry that she had not disappeared, instead of Astro. But at least she could leave the studio and be alone for a while, to think it out. As she opened the outer door, she heard the soft ringing of the electric bell in the studio which warned them of visitors. It still rang as she closed the door, and it gave her an uncanny feeling,—the one spark of life in that dead empty place. She hurried away and walked swiftly toward the park.

"Do I care?" Valeska had little doubt of it when the next morning she walked to the studio. One day had made her sure. She wanted to see Astro again more than she wanted anything in the world! The day before had been empty and vapid. She had scarcely reached the reservoir in the park before she knew what a fool she had been ever to doubt. The product of mere propinquity or not, the feeling she had for him was paramount over every other emotion. She wanted him back, to see him, hear him, and—well, he would find out what else!

Again the empty studio smote her with the strange feeling that, despite the fact that she did not meet him there, he was near her. Now it was a tantalizing thought. Why had she not arranged how to notify him? She had been so sure she would need a month that she had not asked where he was going, and she had now no means of letting him know. It was absurd! Must she wait for him to write?

After all, had she really no means of discovering his whereabouts? She looked eagerly about the studio. For two years she had been his assistant in unraveling mysteries. Why should she not now profit by her apprenticeship? But how?

It came to her then that it was, so to speak, by means of black light that he himself had always worked. Most people saw only the outward and visible signs,—the one per cent. of facts that were luminous and obvious. His delicate mind registered the infra-red rays of psychic action. He vibrated to the ultraviolet waves. Could she not do so as well? She was a woman and had intuitions as well as intellect; she had emotions finer than men's. But her emotions told her somehow, irrationally, that Astro was still there in the studio. She could not believe, quite, in his absence. Everything shrieked his name to her. She could close her eyes and see him before the porphyry sphinx, examining thumb prints at his table, poring over the mimic planets of the orrery, figuring out nativities, gazing into his crystal ball.

That would never do! She must keep her imagination as an instrument with which to work on facts. Where, then, were the facts that could help her? She set herself to investigate the studio thoroughly, inch by inch.

At the first round, she found nothing not in its accustomed place, nothing new, nothing significant. She sat down at his table to think, putting her elbows on the blotter and letting her head drop into her palms. Her eyes fell on the blue blotter. It was changed every morning, ordinarily; but now she noticed pencil markings,—a small square drawn with its diagonals. Would this be mere thoughtless penciling, or perhaps a clue? Next, an envelope lying beside the inkstand attracted her attention. Surely that could mean nothing, and yet, as it lay with its face down, the X shaped cross of its gummed edges suggested the diagonals of the square. Either one alone might have no significance; but the two taken together—the hint, perhaps, repeated? She smiled at the very absurdity of so frail a clue.

Then her eyes dropped to the waste-paper basket. This should have been emptied yesterday morning, yet it contained a few scraps of paper. She stooped and drew them out, one by one. Three were blank. On the fourth she found the following:

"St. Patrick's Cath. . . . . 115 10th-Ave.
Pier 83 N. R. . . . . 320 3d-Ave."

She gave a little cry of triumph. Here at last was something to work on! She considered the addresses carefully. What did they mean? Astro had never mentioned such places; yet the notes were in his crabbed handwriting. She knew of a certainty that the studio had been cleaned the day before yesterday. This writing, then, must have been put into the basket after they had had their talk. If so, then they meant something. The first thing to do was, of course, to look up these localities and see what she could find there. Saint Patrick's Cathedral and the Pier 83 seemed unlikely places to discover news of Astro's whereabouts; but she determined to visit all four before she returned.

She called a taxicab and set out first for Pier 83. This, she found, was at the end of the Forty-second-Street side of the Weehawken ferry. She walked along the wharf, and found a tug laid up there. Besides this, there was no sign of life. What should she do? Ask the tugboat men if they knew where Astro was? That was nonsense! She walked up and down for a half-hour, and discovered nothing which she could possibly twist into evidence. She decided, then, that she would visit the other places, and then, if she found nothing suspicious, return over the ground again.

Saint Patrick's Cathedral next. There it stood, on the corner of the avenue, and she recalled how Astro had once called her attention to its resemblance to a vast Gothic rabbit. The two transepts did resemble a bunny's haunches, and the front towers were like ears. She smiled at the thought; but got no nearer Astro by the pleasantry. She walked inside, sat down on a seat, and thought. What associations could this have with his whereabouts? Why, he was not even a Catholic! He always said he was a Buddhist. Well, if this were a part of the black light his memory emanated, it was black indeed!

In Third Avenue her hopes went up. Number 320 was the entrance to a brick apartment-house. There was a sign indicating that flats were to let, and she rang for the janitor. By him she was shown a very pleasant "four rooms and bath," whose windows were on a level with the elevated railroad; but it was as bare as the palm of one's hand, with no lines she could read. She asked tentatively of the other occupants, and found that all, with the exception of a couple of old men, were married families. Yes, a man had been to look at the flat yesterday; but he had worn a beard. Was this a disguise? But if Astro had come there with the intention of renting a flat temporarily, why should he have left the address in the waste basket? And, moreover, why should he have coupled its address with Pier 83?

There remained only the Tenth Avenue address, and this she found to be a huge unoccupied building with shuttered windows, belonging to a gas company. Opposite was a vacant lot piled with lumber refuse, beams and timbers; on the other side was the gastank's cylindrical bulk. She could find no watchman to give her permission to enter. What pretext could she give for wanting to see the premises, even if she inquired at the office on Eighteenth Street? She could think of none. Better think it over and plan a campaign. She had this much information, at least. Now what she had to do was to find some plausible theory to utilize it.

Back she went to her room and cried herself to sleep, as any other woman would. She missed Astro more than ever. Before, she had a hunger and thirst for his presence; now she wanted his help and protection. Oh, she was sure enough, now! She felt lost without him; she saw how necessary he was to her, how he had made life different, romantic, picturesque.

It was a sad little Valeska that crept to the studio next day. She took up one of the cushions of his divan and kissed it passionately, buried her face in it for a while, then sat resolutely down at his

desk to work out the mystery of his location. The more she thought
of it now, the surer she became that he must have left these clues
on purpose to guide her in her search. It would be like him to test
her that way; there was a sort of humor in it that, at last, she saw.
Well, then, she would be a worthy pupil. She would prove that his
lessons had not been without effect. She, too, would be a seer of
secrets!

With a smile on her lips now, she began the problem. But again
she stopped. It was absurd to think of him as being away. She was
so used to seeing him here in the studio that she could not take
her task seriously. Could not she go into a trance, as he had so
often pretended to, and summon him to her, or project her spirit
to meet his? Could she not perceive the radiance of his secret black
light directly through her intuitions, without this tedious and
stupid analytical logical process? As she sat there she could almost
feel him at her side, leaning over her shoulder, looking from the
door of his laboratory. She looked up with a start from her reverie,
and was a little frightened to find herself alone in the great studio
with its shadowy corners. Then she went back conscientiously to
her study. What was the meaning of the four addresses? It seemed
evident that he could not be in any one of the places; that would
be too easy an explanation of the mystery. Was there any esoteric
significance to the Weehawken ferry or Pier 83? She laughed at
the idea. All she could gather from the addresses was that Astro
was probably in New York. Well, that was something. Her mind
jumped to the square with diagonals, to the cross on the envelope.
How did *they* fit in? Why, for all she knew, the pattern on the carpet, or the legs of the chairs could solve the mystery!

No, there must be *some* relationship between these things. If
these evidences were left purposely, they were correlated one to
another. Her mind went back to memories of Astro. He used to
jump up and walk back and forth as he considered his problems.
So up rose Valeska and began to pace the room.

As she passed the book-shelves, she noticed that one book stuck
out a little from the others. It was a volume of Poe's *Tales*. She

pushed it back and continued her promenade. She went over the addresses again,—Saint Patrick's, Pier 83, 320 Third Avenue, the gas works. It came to her vaguely that these places were about equal distances apart. Now could that mean anything? Then she thought that she could consider them more clearly if she had a map.

She went to the shelf, therefore, took down and unfolded a large map of New York, and laid it on the table. She next took four pins and marked each place. They were indeed equal distances apart; she measured them with a ruler. Then she noticed that they seemed to form a square, and tested it with a little transparent celluloid triangle Astro used for plotting horoscopes, and found it was true. The sides were about a mile and a quarter long. Again she dropped her chin on her palms and her elbows on the table and studied the pins.

But her thoughts wandered. It seemed as if Astro should be there to help her as he always had. She thought, with a smile, that if it were propinquity that had made her love him, propinquity was what she wanted most. But she forced her mind to the subject and remembered the diagram drawn on the blotter of the table. Why, *that* was a square, too! And it had its diagonals drawn. The hint reached her at last and, seizing a pencil and ruler, she drew in the diagonals on the map, and looked curiously to see where they intersected. On Thirty-fourth Street, between Seventh and Eighth Avenues. But the studio itself was at 234 West Thirty-fourth Street.

She jumped up, then, her hand on her beating heart. Her intuitions, then, were true! She had felt the black light of his presence, though he was invisible! He was in the studio, and had been from the first! He had, perhaps, even looked from the doorway, as she had fancied. She trembled as if at the presence of a ghost, and feared to see him.

But where was he? Must she look in every nook and corner? Should she call him out loud? Hungry for him as she was, she could not yet do that; her heart beat too fast. Yet she longed to tear the mystery open and let in the light again—the old-fashioned sunlight of his actual visible presence—and break into tears on his shoulder. She moved across the room on tiptoe now, as if she were guilty of some crime in being there, threw herself on the divan, and tried to think it out.

As she calmed herself, the thought of the book she had replaced on the shelf came to her, and she ran across the studio to take it from its shelf. It fell open of itself to *The Purloined Letter*, and she smiled to herself. That proved her hypothesis to be right. Was not the purloined letter concealed in plain sight, so prominently placed that it escaped the search? Then Astro's hiding-place would be as obvious, if she reasoned aright. Could she solve that as she had solved the other, by her intuitions, by means of his black light?

Black light! The very words were enough to tell her. Where should he be, but in the dark room where she first witnessed his experiment, where the little phosphorescent Buddha, though invisible in the dark, still radiated its mysterious waves of energy?

So it was solved! She hugged herself with delight, and smiled at the prettiness of his plans. How well he knew her and her mental processes—indeed, he must know her very soul, to be so sure of her and her ways! Indeed, he was the Seer of secrets; for he had seen hers before she had discovered it for herself, had waited with patience and tact till she should know and be sure of her own love for him. A wave of impatience to see him, speak to him, touch him, swept over her.

Of course he had retreated to his hiding-place when he had heard the ringing of the bell on the door. She had been there for an hour, and he must be tired of waiting there, well ventilated as the dark room was. So she crossed to the laboratory door, opened the door of the little anteroom, shut it behind her, and put her hand to the inner door, opened it, and listened.

It was black and still. For a moment she almost fainted with the fear that, after all, she might be mistaken and he was not there. Her childhood's terror of the dark returned; but she put it away and tried to speak aloud. Her voice came thin and small in that closed space.

"Astro, I have found you!" she said tremblingly. "I have seen your black light in the dark, and I know, now! I want you, dear!"

She gave a little cry as she felt two arms take her in their grasp. Then the touch of his lips thrilled her, and she laid her head on his shoulder in peace and contentment.

When Astro took her out into the light, it blinded them with sunshine so that they staggered and could hardly see.

The thrilling of the electric bell interrupted them in their dream.

"It is the clergyman and the witnesses," said Astro, smiling. "They are just five minutes ahead of time. I didn't expect you'd find me till eleven o'clock at least!"

DR. XAVIER WYCHERLEY, THE MIND-READER

HIS LIFE TO LIVE OVER AGAIN

"Why not?" quietly remarked the man at the other side of the restaurant table. His voice was cultured, courteous, delicately fined, and held a peculiarly soothing modulation. His age was given by the silvery hair, the drooping shoulders, the finely chiseled, ascetic features. Yet in his eyes—keen, searching, quietly humorous—there was youth.

"Of course it's impossible," answered Sir Miles Chenieston dreamily. Then he pulled himself together with a start, for the man at the opposite side of the table was a complete stranger to him. It was evening; Monte Carlo; the Café de Paris. They were chance companions at the same table on the terrace, that terrace looking over to the milk-white Casino and the palm-fronds of its garden. They had not exchanged a word previously, but the stranger's remark had fitted in so smoothly with the baronet's brown study that his answer had been given quite involuntarily.

Sir Miles now looked at him coldly and murmured the conventional, "I'm afraid I have not the pleasure . . ."

"Nor I," said the stranger. "But it would be a pity to let stupid convention keep us from being of service to one another. My name is Wycherley, Dr. Xavier Wycherley." He passed over a card. "You were saying that you wished you could only have your life to live over again."

"I said nothing, to the best of my belief. Certainly my thoughts were running in that direction."

"Very much the same thing."

384

Chenieston stared at him.

The doctor continued: "Now you are wondering whether I am a madman or merely some kind of trickster new to you. Outwardly I appear to be respectable, and yet— Now it is on the tip of your tongue to tell me I am damned intrusive."

He spoke very quietly and evenly, with an undercurrent of gentle irony. Curiously enough, while his eyes were keenly fixed on the baronet, his left hand was engaged in drawing on a wine list a minute portrait of him, marvellously delicate and accurate. Dr. Wycherley, through long self-training, had acquired the faculty of being able to do two things perfectly at the same time. The drawing showed a man of forty-five, clean-shaven, hair brushed straight back from the forehead with that meticulous carefulness characteristic of the conventional Englishman of position, money and abundant leisure. The eyes were hard and tired; around the mouth were the lines of weary satiety; there was a cold reserve in the set of the features when in repose.

Yet behind the conventional reserve was a sense of humour; and it now came to his rescue as he answered with a smile: "I admit it. I feel that convention would expect me to apologise, but I'm not going to do so. It *is* a damned intrusion, and you know it. Still, let's pass that. You interest me. My name's Chenieston." He took out a card from a card-case in delicately tooled leather.

Dr. Wycherley glanced at the proffered card. "There are not many things that interest you nowadays, Sir Miles. The gaming-table"—he waved his hand in the direction of the *Salle des Jeux*, packed with money-lusting humanity crowding over the green fields of the Goddess Chance— "the gaming-table has no attraction for you; your liqueur has lost its savour; your excellent cigar has gone out from want of attention."

Chenieston looked at it, and then threw it over the balcony of the terrace. "Go on," he said.

"And you wish you had your life to live over again. The world bores you. There are no surprises left. You have tasted everything. There is nothing left to do. It is satiety— No," he added quickly, "I have not been making enquiries about you beforehand. That passing impression of yours is a mistake, though a very natural one. Believe me when I say that I have never seen you before this hour. Nor did I know your name before you gave me your card."

"I believe you," answered Chenieston. The doctor's voice carried unmistakable sincerity. "But I must really keep better control of my features. I *had* flattered myself that my thoughts didn't show on the surface."

"My training has been in the direction of sensing what is below the surface."

"You're a London specialist, I take it?"

"I am a specialist," answered Dr. Wycherley, laying a shade of emphasis on the word, "but my name will not be found on the British register, and my field of action covers the whole world. To-day I am at Monte Carlo, but to-morrow I may be called to Paris, to Berlin, to London, to New York, to Tokio. I go wherever there is call for my services as a mental healer. I am sufficiently selfish to choose, where possible, the exceptional cases—the cases that will add to my knowledge of the human mind. And when I am not actively engaged on a case, I am still studying, as I am now at Monte Carlo."

"Studying?"

"Men and women. Here at Monte Carlo they unmask. . . . But, as I was saying a few minutes ago, why not live your life over again?"

"Mephistopheles is not roaming Monte Carlo," answered Chenieston, "and in any case I don't know that I would care to play Faust. The role had its drawbacks."

"The drawbacks were due to Mephistopheles' ideas of a *quid pro quo*, were they not?"

"I have been frank with you," said Chenieston, brusquely, "and I would like you to be equally frank with me. In plain words, what are you driving at?"

Dr. Wycherley looked out over the black, velvety Mediterranean before answering, sipping his coffee slowly. Then he turned on Chenieston with his dark, penetrating eyes, and answered with quiet emphasis, making the simple phrase carry a world of meaning: "I can give you what you desire."

The baronet looked back at him with suspicion in his eyes. "It's not possible. I don't know you . . ."

"It is possible," was the deliberate answer. "Quite possible. I can give you your life to live over again if you will. . . . But I am not forcing my gifts upon you. One day, perhaps, you may care to come to me. You have my address on the card. I will now bid you good evening."

He rose and bowed courteously in a half-foreign way. Chenieston returned his "good evening" in noncommittal fashion. He followed the doctor with his eyes as the latter left the café and made his way through the garden of the palms to the milk-white terraces that overlook the sea.

"What did it mean," thought Chenieston. Of course there was some trickery underlying it. He felt hurriedly for his pocketbook. It was there intact, and he mentally apologised. The man was a gentleman beyond doubt. Suppose it were really possible to . . . ? No, the idea was impossibly fantastic—ridiculous!

*   *   *   *   *

But the idea was not to be dismissed so lightly. When Dr. Wycherley planted his mental seeds, it was with the skill and experience of a master gardener. All through the winter and ensuing spring the idea started up unbidden into Chenieston's consciousness when he was apparently thinking of other matters. During the summer he fought against the growing obsession, tore up Dr. Wycherley's card, made himself busy with outdoor sports, even tried to interest himself in photography.

His attempt was a failure. The strange doctor had placed a mental finger on the baronet's mind, and the finger pressed upon it ceaselessly. Chenieston was indeed bored by the world—satiated at forty-five. He had title, money, wide estates, health—to outward appearance a man to be envied. But he had no wife or child, brother or sister, and with his distant relatives he was out of sympathy. His short married life of many years ago had been a disastrous episode; for his young wife had quickly plunged into the frivolities of a "smart" set, against his wishes, until they had drifted further and further apart and love had turned to hatred.

Chenieston divorced her—for cause—settled a lump sum on her, and put her out of his life. Since then no other woman had made a niche in his heart. His happiness he would entrust to no other's keeping.

But happiness kept to oneself turns sour—like bread hoarded away. He had sought happiness in selfish pleasures—and found only satiety. He had made a wilderness and called it happiness.

At the end of the summer he was shooting wearily, mechanically, without pleasure, on his Scotch grouse-moor. His house-party included a married couple, the Trevors, whose evident happiness in one another made him bitter. In the gun-room one evening Trevor became confidential concerning his wife. Said he: "The little woman had a bad time of it a year ago—thought I was going to lose her. Nothing organic, you know—mental worry. The loss of our child. Doctors could do nothing. Then we came across an extraordinary fellow—I believe he's got Italian blood in him—anyhow he made my wife a new woman. Lives in a queer little island on an Italian lake—Isola Salvatore it's called. . . .

"Name Wycherley?" asked Chenieston. That had been the solitary address on the doctor's card— "Isola Salvatore" and nothing further.

"Yes. . . . By the way, we never mention the child. It belongs to the past. My wife has forgotten."

"Forgotten!" It sounded incredible.

"Completely."

THE GARDEN OF SPICES

October on Lake Rovellasco is the picked month of the year. Even Chenieston, satiated with the glories of the world, felt stirred by the quiet beauty of the scene as he looked out from the window of his hotel by the lakeside. Rovellasco is not yet an exploited tourist centre. Presently, perhaps, we shall see blatantly advertised "A Week in Rosy Rovellasco for Five Guineas!" and then good-bye to the quiet scene that Sir Miles gazed on.

At the far end, where the mountains crowd down upon the lake and take it to their arms, was a solitary islet deeply wooded. From amongst the trees peeped out a white glimpse of a villa. Chenieston's eyes came back to that white spot again and again. Finally he seemed to arrive at a decision, for he entered his room and started to pack his portmanteau. He was traveling without his man.

He had the bag carried down to the lakeside, and hailed a boatman in halting Italian: "I want you to row me to Isola Salvatore."

The boatman shrank a little and crossed himself hurriedly. "I do not like to," he answered. "No one likes to. He sends a boat ashore himself for his visitors. Perhaps if the signore will wait . . ."

Chenieston unwrapped a couple of five-lire notes from a roll and showed them silently.

The boatman hesitated. His feelings were plainly torn between fear and greed.

Chenieston took out some further loose change from his trouser pocket.

"If I do, signore, you will not ask me to set foot on the island?"

"Very well," answered Chenieston, curtly, and seated himself in the boat. He felt a natural disgust at the boatman's fear, but at the same time a feeling of something uncanny came down upon his own mind like a mist slowly driving over the hills. This man Wycherley must have queer powers. After a while the baronet endeavoured to draw the boatman into conversation, but whenever the questions came round to the subject of Isola Salvatore and its owner, the man evaded them or affected to misunderstand.

As they drew near the islet the boatman suddenly crossed himself and muttered an invocation for heavenly protection.

"What is it?" asked Chenieston, sharply. He strongly objected to all this mystery.

"Look, signore! See for yourself!" The man pointed tremblingly to a small dark object tearing through the water around the island.

"It is a dog—that is all," answered Chenieston. "Why all this fuss about a dog? Certainly it is swimming faster than any dog I have ever seen in the water."

"He is not human, signore! Look, as he approaches, at his eyes!"

The dog tore towards them, but as though unconscious of their presence. The boatman hurriedly rowed out of its way. As it passed, Chenieston noted with something of a shock that only the whites of its eyes were to be seen, although the eyelids were full open.

"You see, signore, he is a hound of hell!"

"Get on!" said Chenieston, brusquely.

As they approached a small landing-stage on the islet, a servant came to meet them. He was clearly foreign, but spoke English quite adequately: "My master bids you welcome, Sir Miles. He expects you, but is unfortunately called away at the moment. He asks you to excuse him until this evening."

Chenieston was for the moment surprised at his name being known to the servant. This was succeeded by the very natural suspicion that there might be some means of communication between the hotel and Isola Salvatore. He had seen too much of the world and its trickeries to take good faith entirely for granted. But as he followed the man into the villa, the atmosphere of peace and restfulness and aloofness from the vanities of the world seeped in upon

Chenieston and made him feel somehow soiled by that momentary suspicion of trickery.

The room assigned to him was furnished with great simplicity but equal good taste. It was paneled entirely in some sweet but faintly scented Eastern wood—Japanese cypress, he afterwards learnt. The floor was bare except for one Persian rug harmonising its age-softened reds and browns with the reddish-brown of the paneling. The wooden bed, excessively simple, had a plain white coverlet over it. The solitary ornament to the room—hung facing the bed as the occupant would wake to see it—was a mezzotint of Botticelli's "Primavera." The eye, leaving this, would turn to the wide-open veranda windows looking upon the lake curving down in gentle folds of bay to the little town of Rovellasco at the far end.

The simplicity and dignity of that room brought an inward feeling of humility to the world-weary man as he entered. The room was a silent rebuke to the suspicion which had momentarily entered his thoughts. For a second time he made a mental apology to Dr. Wycherley.

Until dinner Chenieston wandered about the garden of the house—a garden of botanical wonders. The ends of the earth seemed to have been ransacked for strange trees and plants with which to clothe the isle—camphor-trees, pepper-trees, palm-trees, trees of strange spices; cedars of Lebanon and deodars from the Himalayas and cryptomerias from the Far East; pines from the Rockies and eucalypti from New Zealand; wonderful vines and creepers everywhere. It was a veritable isle of spices. It breathed of peace and forgetfulness. Chenieston felt strangely soothed in spirit.

After a dinner simple but in perfect gastronomic taste, the baronet took his cigar to a seat under a giant magnolia, looking out over the dark lake and the snow peaks to the north. He fell into a reverie from which he was roused by suddenly finding Dr. Wycherley smoking a cigarette beside him in silence.

"Excuse my not coming to welcome you before," said the doctor. "I had to go to New York last night—a patient of mine whose wealth is a curse to her."

"I hope you had a pleasant trip," answered Chenieston, conventionally. Then he became aware of the extraordinary statement made by the doctor and added hurriedly: "I thought for the moment you said New York."

"Yes, that is what I said—of course, I did not mean in body."

"You seem to have made a curious reputation for yourself in these parts," said Chenieston, brusquely.

The doctor smiled and answered with gentle irony: "I treated some of the peasants round here— 'cast out devils' and so forth. They were very undecided whether to class me as an archangel or a lieutenant of Lucifer's; finally they settled on the latter."

"Your dog . . ."

"Ah, yes, you met Rolf taking his four o'clock constitutional. I should explain that he has a perfect horror of the water in the ordinary way. When he was a puppy somebody tried to drown him, and I came to his rescue—nothing will induce him to go into the water now."

"He looked as if he were swimming in his sleep—it was very queer."

"Precisely. Post-hypnotic suggestion—ordered somnambulism, if you prefer it. It is good for his health to take a daily swim . . . that suggests undeveloped possibilities in everyday life, does it not, draught horses, mules, elephants, and so on? You take my meaning?"

With his left hand Dr. Wycherley was making delicate experiments with the almost human leaves of a "sensitive mimosa," though all the time his eyes were fixed on his guest.

Chenieston drew himself together sharply and began: "That was not quite what I came to see you about."

"There is no need for you to go into a detailed explanation. I sensed that when you arrived at the lakeside yesterday. You want to hear more—to continue our Monte Carlo conversation. Especially you want to know just precisely what I can offer you, and, to put it bluntly, what my terms are."

"There seems no need for me to hold up my side of the conversation."

Dr. Wycherley smiled again. "Not just at present. This is of course elementary and quite preliminary. Later on, should you wish to try the experiment, I shall ask you to talk for days at a time. . . . To begin with, what are my terms for giving you your life over again? Not money, for of that I have ample for my simple needs. Not influence or power, for that I can build for myself. No, my demands are less material." He paused.

"Well, what can I give you?"

"Data."

"I don't follow you."

"Scientific data—material for my life-work, psychological research. I should ask you to report progress. To bring, say twice a year, the book of your life for my inspection. *I want to know what a man would do with his second life.*"

"There are devilish possibilities in that," answered Chenieston, setting his teeth.

"Precisely. If I don't inspire you with confidence, you would be an utterly weak fool to trust yourself in my hands for an instant. If I were a poor man, the temptation might be irresistible; if I were a criminal man, the consequences might be horrible; if I were an enemy of Society, the consequences might be appalling. It is for you, a man of the world, to make up your mind what sort of a man I am. On the one hand you have the evidence of the peasants around here; on the other hand . . ."

"I met the Trevors," interrupted Chenieston.

"That was a very simple case—like the amputation of a finger to a surgeon. Your case, I would warn you frankly, would be more in the nature of a major internal operation. Have you the courage?"

"Explain to me what you would do."

Dr. Wycherley threw away his cigarette. "Let us get at fundamentals—let me show you the psychological basis of happiness. Happiness is just contentment—neither riches nor power can of themselves give a man happiness. Happiness comes from within. The world laughs at the millionaire who says that he wishes he were poor and obscure—but *he* speaks from experience. He has bought dearly the knowledge I now place before you. Happiness is just contentment; and contentment is based on illusion. Contentment sees the good and ignores the evil. Contentment forgets. Contentment makes every day a new age, a wonderful experience opening out vistas of a rose-strewn future. *You* live in the past—every new experience as it arises is stale to you because you mentally compare it with the past. You have seen everything, tasted everything, done everything. Your experience is a daily burden to you.

"Now suppose you could forget all that had happened to you from twenty-one to—shall we say forty-five? The world would be a new place to you; your life would be before and not behind you. You would be a young man in mind again."

"But not in body," interrupted Chenieston.

"No, one cannot altogether put back the development of the body. But 'a man is as young as he feels' is an old saying, and a very true one. I know boys of fifty—I expect you know some also. The mind reacts on the body."

"To have a blank page from twenty-one to forty-five would hold its disadvantages," said the baronet, thoughtfully.

"Precisely. Therein lies the difficulty of the operation. One has to cut out only what is deleterious. It is like removing a great cancerous growth from the body. One must use the scalpel very warily. It is not an operation for the raw medical student. You place your mental life in the hands of the trained surgeon . . . if you have faith in him. That is why I said a little while ago that I should ask you to talk for days at a time. Your past life would have to be laid bare to me, and to my judgment you would have to confide the decision of what should be cut out and what left in place. There is the matter in a nutshell."

"You propose to hack at my mind, my Ego, my individuality?"

"There you betray an ignorance of psychology. You confuse several distinct issues. I cannot touch your Ego or higher self—*we* call it the 'consciousness'—I can only operate on your lower self, the 'sub-consciousness,' the warden of your memories. In the hypnotic state we converse and treat only with the patient's sub-consciousness."

"Then where does the higher self go to?"

"Where does it go to in sleep, I ask you in return? But let me lend you a scientific book to-night which will put the matter before you in detail."

"Thanks," said Chenieston. "I'll read it. Tomorrow I will give you my decision."

*   *   *   *   *

In after days the month that Chenieston spent on Isola Salvatore seemed to him like a hazy dreamland. He remembered vaguely that Dr. Wycherley had placed him at evenfall of the second day under the great magnolia, stretched out in a gloriously easy chair, and had suspended in front of and above him an imprisoned firefly. On this he had to concentrate his gaze until tired eyelids closed down over tired eyes. Meanwhile the doctor was talking to him—quietly, evenly, soothingly. Sleep had stolen upon him—smooth, restful, heavenly sleep.

He had no direct knowledge of what had happened to him in sleep, but Dr. Wycherley told him that he was then talking *en rapport* with his sub-consciousness for hours at a time, bringing out his past life, ordering forgetfulness of this, allowing remembrance of that.

The month was to Chenieston at once an eternity and a moment.

In the intervals between the hypnotic trances he had written and signed long documents for the instruction of his lawyers, his bankers and his stewards, directing the disposal of his estates amongst his distant relatives and various charities, should he not return again to his world. He was to give out that he had gone to a vague somewhere to shoot big game—a handy excuse—and he was to start life afresh under a new name and with a few thousands only as capital. He was to be one of the world's workers.

He began to grow a beard to change his outward identity, and Dr. Wycherley spent long hours training up within him a new voice while in the hypnotic state. Change the voice and you make a man unrecognisable to his friends.

When Stephen Carruthers—this was the name agreed upon—left Isola Salvatore he staggered mentally as a man staggers bodily when he leaves the nursing home. His past life was mainly a blank to him, though there remained certain memories which Dr. Wycherley had judged advisable. There were sudden gaps in his memory stitched together and working unsmoothly, as the muscles work unsmoothly where the surgeon has used the knife. Queer flashes of unconnected incidents came upon him every now and then, dazzling him. He felt horribly helpless.

The doctor accompanied him to land and stayed with him at intervals for some months while they roamed the Continent together. Gradually Carruthers began to feel his feet—to speak metaphorically—and a great happiness surged over him. Everything was new, fresh, unexplored. The Riviera had before seemed to him a string of pleasure-cities painted like the cheeks and lips of a painted woman—a horrible rouged outrage upon Nature; now he saw the good and not the evil, and it was fresh to him and very pleasant to his eyes. The blood within him danced and sparkled like champagne. He thought and spoke as a youngster fresh from college.

Carruthers was a new man.

THE ZEAL OF THE SCIENTIST

At the age of forty-five—to outward appearance—a man cannot very well study for and enter one of the close professions. The few oldish men who do walk the hospitals or eat dinners at the Temple are regarded by the world with good-natured, rather contemptuous pity. Carruthers, finding himself in possession of a few thousand pounds only, insufficient to live on idly but offering possibilities for earning an income, chose to enter business, which has no age-barrier.

He returned to London. As far as his memory went, he had not seen it since he was a boy of twenty-one or so, and to his eyes great changes had taken place. They struck him sharply like a blow in the face delivered in the dark; at first he was confused and deafened. It took time for him to adjust himself.

Queer flashes of sub-conscious memory stirred him to actions which were meaningless to his understanding. One day, for instance, he found himself walking mechanically up the steps of a mansion in Berkeley Square and ringing the bell. A butler appeared and asked him his business. Suddenly, to his painful confusion, Carruthers discovered that he had no business there, had no reason to be walking up those steps and ringing that bell. He pulled himself together, and for the sake of saying something asked if the master of the house were in. The butler, looking at him suspiciously as someone of dubious intentions, replied that Sir Miles Chenieston was abroad, and edged him down the steps again. The name seemed somehow familiar to Carruthers, but he could not place the connection. It was one of many worrying episodes.

With part of his money he bought a share in a small publishing firm, and in the interest of the work the scars in his memory were smoothed out of conscious thought. The semi-professional aspect of the publishing business appealed to his natural instincts; and since his partner, Bailey by name, was easy to get on with, the work gave him keen pleasure. "Office hours" meant nothing to him, often he would stay on at Booksellers' Row long after the clerks had left and the neighbouring offices were cold and dark, and the grey ghosts of little old caretakers came out of their daylight hiding-places to dust and sweep. He was keen to build up the business into a large organisation.

"How young you are!" said Bailey to him one day, half chaffingly, half enviously. "I declare you make me feel like an old fogey."

"I *am* young," answered Carruthers. "Why shouldn't I be? Everything is so new and fresh; life rushes into one full-tide. Isn't it the same with you?"

"I wish I knew your secret."

"What secret?" Carruthers felt, for a brief fraction of a second, a queer mental confusion that was like a sudden stab of pain. "I haven't got secrets, my dear fellow."

"I only meant the secret of your perpetual youth," his partner hastened to explain. The subject dropped.

Twice a year, spring and autumn, Carruthers took a holiday from work and journeyed to the islet on Lake Rovellasco in unconscious fulfilment of his contract with Dr. Wycherley. Some force within him impelled him to steep himself in the waters of peace, to feel the garden of spices close around him and take him to itself in an ecstasy of joy unutterable. He yielded himself to the soothing passes of the mental healer—all unconscious he laid his soul bare to the gaze of Dr. Wycherley, who studied him as the biologist studies the growth of some strange new organism.

The mental healer was a combination of scientist and humanitarian which is far from usual. As the latter, his warm human sympathies went out unceasingly to the weak, the oppressed, the suffering, the sick of body and the sick of mind. But as a scientist he would for the time being forget the patient in the subject.

Carruthers in the hypnotic state was a *subject* of absorbing interest to the doctor, and he did not scruple to probe the man's most
inner, most intimate feelings. He had explained that frankly to the
baronet before the latter had consented to undergo the mental
operation. "I want to know what a man would do with his second
life," the doctor had said. In return for this new life he was giving
to Carruthers, he was acquiring scientific data which were priceless beyond money. Carruthers was to him alternately a friend and
a subject for scientific exploration.

The doctor no longer made suggestions to his subject while in
the hypnotic state. He had no desire or intention to direct
Carruthers' actions. He merely wished to observe, as an exceptionally privileged spectator, what Carruthers would make of his second life, and the study of the man gave him the keenest scientific
pleasure. The world-weary idler, the parasite on the toil of other
men and women, was becoming transformed to a worker amongst
the common labours of humanity, and in his work he was acquiring a new set of feelings, emotions, main-springs of action which
to Dr. Wycherley were of intense interest.

But what would happen when the inevitable woman came into
Carruthers' life? The doctor knew intimately of the former marriage and its unhappy ending, of the baronet's aloofness from
women except of the superficial plane of the *flâneur* who seeks a
temporary, sensual amusement. Chenieston had dallied with many
women, but had given his inner self to none but the wife he had
divorced and put out of his life. Could he, in his new personality,
be stirred by real love, or would the Chenieston career have killed
that possibility? Could the mental regeneration extend to that most
intimate, most sacred of a man's emotions, or would a woman still
be to Carruthers, as to Chenieston, a mere plaything for a few idle
weeks?

When the inevitable did happen, it was, to the keen pleasure
of Dr. Wycherley the scientist, on one of Carruthers' visits to the
island. Carruthers spent his holidays in fishing, bathing and row-
ing amongst the peaceful solitudes of Lake Rovellasco. He made
great friends with Rolf, who, barring only the bathe, was ready to

accompany him anywhere. Rolf was a big, shaggy-haired English sheep-dog, born for friendship.

It was on a lake excursion that the inevitable happened. The occasion was pure chance—one of those sudden squalls that occasionally sweep down in fury on Lake Rovellasco from the snow-peaks, and toss the waters as a farmer pitchforks the hay. She was alone in a light skiff with a local boatman, who unexpectedly lost an oar, lost nerve, and implored help from above.

Carruthers, not far off, saw the danger and rowed hard to help, Rolf barking eagerly on the front seat. Nothing could have been worse for the boatman's peace of mind. Abandoning the other oar, he grovelled on the floor of the boat, while the waves slapped in angrily.

"Can you catch a rope?" shouted Carruthers.

Mrs. Mannering pluckily climbed over the prostrate boatman to the front of the skiff, caught the rope not unskilfully and tied it to a ring. With the skiff in tow, Carruthers faced the wind and kept head to waves for an hour or more until the squall died away and the sun came out to smooth down the waters.

It was natural for Carruthers to call at her hotel next day to make polite enquiries. But it was more than mere politeness that took him; he had felt strangely attracted towards this woman no longer young, no longer beautiful, and occupying the position of a paid nurse to a testy old gentleman with half-a-dozen imaginary ailments. Something stronger than himself made him linger beyond the time of a conventional call—made him row over to land the next day, and the day after, contriving to meet Helen Mannering on the water-front where the lace work and the wood-mosaic work shops display their allurements, and all the little world of Rovellasco saunters.

He even suffered gladly the querulous egoism of Colonel Padgett so that he might be near Mrs. Mannering. Dr. Wycherley, to whom nothing was hidden, spoke to him in gentle sympathy one evening when Carruthers sat musing under his favourite magnolia-tree,

"A woman in a thousand," said the doctor.

"In a million," answered Carruthers.

There was silence, a silence of mutual understanding.

"Why not?" asked the doctor. His sensitive left hand was rapidly drawing a tiny portrait, a very perfect miniature, of Mrs. Mannering on a scrap of paper.

"Yes, why not?" echoed Carruthers. "It's a dog's life for her. . . . I could make her ideally happy. . . . There's sympathy between us beyond anything I've ever felt. . . . You believe in the idea of one's affinity, Doctor?"

"I do not know," returned Dr. Wycherley, gravely and slowly. "As a scientist I say that I do not know. One feels that it is true, but there is no evidence. If there is only one affinity for each of us in all this wide world, what are the chances of meeting? Infinitesimal. . . . No, there is no evidence. It is one of my problems."

So Carruthers took courage in hand and contrived his opportunity.

The witchery of night on lake and mountain was around them as they stood by a corner of a balcony, far enough away from the few other guests of the hotel to give them solitude. They had been talking disjointedly, with many intervals of silence, speaking now and again of topics which touched them in common—art, music, books, especially, books, for Carruthers was now whole-heartedly an enthusiast in the field of publishing.

Then came the moment when his voice changed from the ease of impersonal topics, and went deeper in tone, as a man's voice does when he has to speak of emotions which touch him as sacred.

"Colonel Padgett tells me you are to move on soon," he said.

Mrs. Mannering realised the significance of the new tone in his voice, and a slight tremor went through her.

"Yes," she answered. "We go to Rome."

"Then I mustn't wait—I mustn't let opportunity slip by. Helen, you know what I have to say to you. We were made for one another. Every fibre in me tells me that's true. I'm fulltide with happiness, and I have to share it. I can share it only with you." He spoke deeply and passionately, breathing fast.

She turned away.

"Helen, I'm not a rich man, but I can give you all the best that's in me. Won't you take me? Look me in the eyes and read me! You can't misunderstand my feelings!"

He caught at her hands; she drew them away, and her voice quivered as she answered:

"I can't, I can't! Don't you read my feelings? Has love blinded you?"

Carruthers felt utterly at sea. "I don't understand at all," he murmured. "I thought your husband was dead. I thought you were free. I thought my feelings were echoing in yours."

"Yes, but—" she paused, searching in his face as though to read some riddle there which eluded her.

"Be frank with me. Be fair to me," he urged. "Have I been too hasty? Too selfish in forcing myself upon you? Don't you realise I'm passionately in love with you, and that means I wouldn't hurt your feelings for worlds. Tell me where my mistake lies. Tell me what you want from me!"

Again she turned away and looked out over the witchery of lake and mountain, as though to seek inspiration or courage from them. When at length she spoke to him, her voice was firm with resolve:

"Don't think that I'm rating lightly what you've offered me. But you are not yourself—this is a moment of madness. If I accepted, it might mean a lifetime's misery—for both of us. When you *awoke*. . . . Look me in the eyes, look at me well!"

Carruthers looked, puzzled, confessed himself at sea: "I don't understand at all. I only see what is very beautiful to me, and what I hold very dear. This is not quixotism. Your position matters nothing to me. I see you for what you are, and I want you—I want you passionately! God, how I want you!"

"Give me till to-morrow," said Helen suddenly.

"To-morrow, then, I come for my answer," he acquiesced.

"We'll say good-night now."

His eyes followed her with hungry longing as she made her way from the balcony to the lighted rooms of the hotel, and he knew that as concerned his own feelings there was no possible mistake. Her hesitation must be the natural one of a woman whose feelings had not kept pace with his own. She was in love with him, but she needed time to make that big final decision.

To-morrow she would say "Yes."

*   *   *   *   *

But in the morning he found only Colonel Padgett, raging fussily and repetitiously:

"By Gad, sir, it's outrageous, positively outrageous! Runs away without saying a word—leaves me to shift for myself! Don't you realise, sir, that she was paid, *paid* to look after me? How am I to go for my morning walk? This will make me seriously ill. I'm feeling damnable twinges already. I never heard of anything so heartless in all my born days. It's outrageous, sir, positively outrageous! I'll put the police on her track! Leaves me a note to say that she has to run away—gives no reason—gives no address. I'll report her to the nursing agency, I'll have her cashiered. I never heard of anything so disgraceful in all my born days!"

"Did Mrs. Mannering leave any note for me?" interrupted Carruthers.

"How do I know? D'you think I've had any time to . . . ?"

But Carruthers had made off to the bureau, where the hotel clerk handed him an envelope which he tore open eagerly in the privacy of a quiet corner. It contained only a little bag of dried herbs and a brief note: "All night I have wrestled with temptation, Miles. I have fought and conquered; I will not spoil your life again. This little bag of herbs will explain to you everything. 'Rosemary for remembrance.' Goodbye. Helen."

He put the bag, *her* bag, to his lips, and in his brain there was as it were a snapping and rending of the stitches that bound up the wounded memory. He had known that little bag of dried herbs before. But where—where? In heaven's name where? He felt the question was driving him mad—the torture was unbearable. At the railway station he discovered that she had taken a ticket for Milan. There was no train in that direction until the afternoon. At Milan the trail would be lost. She might take train again in any one of a dozen directions. What could he do?

Then the soothing shadow of the mental healer came over the glare in his mind, and he rowed feverishly back to Isola Salvatore. Dr. Wycherley's eyes lighted up with the enthusiasm of the scientist as Carruthers explained and showed him the letter.

"Splendid, splendid!" said the doctor. "Your experience is the first direct evidence of the affinity theory, that, so far as my knowledge goes, has ever been obtained. This is well worth the trouble of the experiment!" Then he added with his gentle ironic touch: "The zeal of the scientist—it forgets the patient. Excuse me, Carruthers, for my scientific selfishness. Be quite easy in mind. I will surely find her for you. If you will let me put you to sleep, it will soothe the brain."

"But how can you find her? She's run away deliberately. She'll cover up her tracks. Oh, it's maddening! Preposterous! I tell you there's no reason to it. We're made for one another—suited in every way. There's nothing against me. You know that well. And there's nothing on her side to keep us apart—that I'm sure of, positive of! . . . How can you find her?"

"The bag of herbs," answered the doctor. "It is very personal to her—charged with her personality. Rolf!"

The big shaggy-haired dog trotted up to him, wagging its tail. Dr. Wycherley looked at it eye to eye, and commanded sharply: "Sleep!"

The dog's big round eyes blinked and then closed down. In a few moments the animal sank to the ground and rolled on its side, inert.

"His suggestibility is very highly developed," explained the doctor, "and nowadays a mere command will send him into deep hypnosis. It took me a long, long time to train him. At one time I nearly gave it up in despair; then I hit on a new way to . . . but this would scarcely interest you. I will just say briefly that in hypnosis proper the hyperæsthesia of the senses is of the order four to seven in men and women; that is, their sense perceptions in many cases become four to seven times keener than in the normal working state. That is a matter of everyday knowledge. But what is not generally known is the effect in the case of animals. I have found in them most astonishing magnification of the senses. I will take him to Milan and start him on the trail. He will succeed. Watch!"

He put the bag of herbs to Rolf's nose, and the dog rose slowly and began with closed eyes uncannily to nose the garden for a trail.

"Stop!" commanded the doctor, and the dog obediently stood still, rigid.

"Now let me put you to sleep," suggested Dr. Wycherley gently, and Carruthers acquiesced.

*   *   *   *   *

When Carruthers woke again he found Helen by his side, watching him in silence. He held out his arms: "You're back again. Thank God!"

"Wait," she said softly, "let me explain. Don't you really know me, Miles? Dr. Wycherley tells me you've forgotten, but it seems incredible. I can't understand how you could forget me."

"Miles! Why do you call me Miles?"

"I was your wife."

He looked at her in utter bewilderment, and again that feeling of the rending of stitches in his brain came over him.

"I was your wife," she continued, with a softness in her voice that made his pulses leap. "I was very young—very wilful, very foolish. If only you had been more patient with me—had expected less. You asked too much from a young girl. I wanted to grasp enjoyment with both hands—to bathe in it, to take up great handfuls and let it trickle over me. You were unreasonably jealous of me. I had no harm in my thoughts at first. I only wanted to enjoy the good things of life. But your jealousy drove me to give you real cause for jealousy. My pride was hurt—I wanted to show you that other men valued me. I wanted to pique you and then I was carried away in a whirl of the senses. . . ."

"I don't remember anything like that. Surely, you're imagining . . ."

"You divorced me."

"How could I? I only met you on the lake."

"You settled a sum of money on me for my maintenance. I had expected to marry the man, but after the divorce he cooled towards me, and I realised that I'd been just an amusing episode to him—nothing more. I went away to the Continent to travel and wipe out the thoughts of him. Later I fell in with another man whom I thought I could trust, and I did trust him—implicitly. In short, he was a swindler hunting for easy game, and he tricked me out of the money you'd settled on me. That was the crowning humiliation. I hid myself away from my friends, took up another name, and set to work to make my own living."

"Where's that man who tricked you?" asked Carruthers sharply.

She shook her head. "I doubt if you'll ever find him. But what does it matter now? Let him pass."

"So you took to nursing as a profession?"

"Yes. It made me independent, and helped to give me back some of my self-respect. I'm glad now that I had to turn to it. . . . When I met you here at Rovellasco I didn't recognise you at first—you've changed so, Miles. But gradually the little mannerisms, the little tricks of speech, told me it was you. That evening on the terrace when your voice changed and your innermost self came to ask me. . . . Then I knew for certain. . . . But it was so puzzling to me. How could you forget your own wife, unless it were some form of momentary delusion? I was afraid you would awake presently to recognise me, and then it would mean misery for both of us. I couldn't trust myself to stay any longer near you, so I ran away. Dr. Wycherley traced me to Florence in some extraordinary manner, and when he found me he explained what had happened to your memories. So I came back with him."

"Dear love, you're back again. Nothing else matters." He held out his arms to her.

But she drew back. "Miles, you must realise that you divorced me. Whether you remember it or not, it's a fact which neither of us can gloss over."

"But if I don't remember, what does it all matter? It may be as you say, but it doesn't affect my feelings towards you in the slightest."

"You divorced me for good cause. I want you to realise that."

"I don't remember. Can't you see, Helen, that I don't *want* to remember. Someone told me that to forget is to be happy. He was right. I want only you, Helen. You as you are to-day—as I feel and *know* you are. What has the girl you speak of to do with the woman I love to-day? *She* belongs to the past—*you* belong to the present and the future. . . ."

"We have to live with our past, dear."

"A horrible creed! Let the dead past molder with its dead. Say rather that we have to live with our future. That's my creed, dear love. Won't you make it yours?"

She bent down, and his arms closed around her hungrily. Their lips met.

Presently there came a discreet knock at the door, and the mental healer entered. There was a kindly smile in his eyes as he said:

"I see that I am soon to lose a very interesting patient. He will no longer be coming to visit me at my island."

"We'll both come," answered Helen warmly.

"Yes, but our compact will be ended, for he will have secrets now that even the zeal of the scientist must not intrude upon. Science must step aside—however unwillingly. On behalf of science, I tender a very reluctant good-bye."

"You've done so much for us, and we can't repay it," said Carruthers.

"I am more than repaid already," answered Dr. Wycherley. "I have learnt much from you. What higher reward can any scientist ask for?"

BLIND JUSTICE

Dr. Wycherley's degrees were not the British degrees. In his younger days the prejudice of the English medical profession against anything approaching hypnotism or mental suggestion had been intense. Many fine men of advanced thought had been driven out of the ranks of the profession in England on the score of the practice of hypnotism. To-day, of course, that prejudice has largely been overridden. The Harley Street district has its mental practitioners equally with its specialists in every other line of medicine and surgery. The *Lancet* and the *British Medical Journal*, holding the keys of the profession in their hands, now lend their dignified approval to hypnotic healing.

Dr. Wycherley's early studies had been pursued at Continental cliniques, and when in later years he was offered the honorary degrees which Oxford and Cambridge and Edinburgh bestow on men of European reputation, he steadily refused them. His name was not on the British medical register; nevertheless, he kept a consulting-room in London, and it was his custom to travel there three or four times a year in order to sift over cases which might need his very specialised help, and at the same time afford him new experiences in the work that was his life-passion.

The rooms he occupied when in London were in Adelphi Terrace, that quiet backwater not fifty yards from the tearing hustle of the Strand, and yet in atmosphere a hundred miles away. From the window of his consulting-room he looked down over the soft greenery of the Embankment Gardens, and across the quiet majesty of the Thames carrying its eternal message from hills to sea. Beyond lay South London, a labyrinth of grey, pinched, huddled life, and yet so beautified by the mists of evening as to inspire a Whistler to compose a masterpiece.

Many of Dr. Wycherley's cases naturally came to him through recommendation; but others were of his own seeking. It was in this latter fashion that he became involved in the murder trial of the young artist Neil Lane, of which the inner story was never made public for reasons of state policy. The doctor did not first hear of the case through the newspapers, since he had a strong aversion to the frothy sensationalism and cheap culture of the daily papers, and rarely glanced at them. He heard of the case through a friend of his, a K. C. who held a brief for the defence, and the summary of its strange features given to him by the barrister impelled Dr. Wycherley to attend the Old Bailey for the concluding day of the trial. It seemed as though it might hold some bearing on his own life-work.

*   *   *   *   *

"I will now put my client in the box," said Hatchard, K. C., leader for the defence.

There was an instant stir in court, a vivid quickening of interest. The big moment of the murder trial, to see which fashionable spectators had schemed and cajoled and bribed, was at hand. One could feel the blood pulsing through the court.

Up to now the defence had proceeded on lines dull and unstimulating to an audience which had come to see a man's soul laid naked. Witness after witness had been called to testify to Neil Lane's good character and his more or less friendly relations with the murdered man. What more could the defence do? An alibi was impossible, and the finger-print evidence was damning.

Never did circumstantial evidence point so clearly to the guilty man. Stokes had been murdered in his studio, stabbed in cold blood while he slept on the couch by his studio fire. The weapon was a narrow, vicious-looking thrusting sword which he had brought back from the East and had always kept hanging amongst some other Eastern trophies on the wall by the fireside. It had been plunged into the murdered man's body again and again, and then by some strange oversight or queer whim on the part of the murderer had been carefully placed on the floor by the side of the couch, parallel to it.

A friend of the artist's, a professional model, had testified that on the night of the murder she had called at his rooms and found him alive at 11 o'clock. He had one of his malarial attacks coming on, and had made up a couch, by the right-hand side of his studio fire, on which he was lying down. He had been drinking heavily and taking large doses of quinine, and the girl had found him surly and dazed and out of temper—in no mood for company. So at his request she had mixed him a stiff glass of brandy and hot water, and then left the studio.

Medical evidence had placed the time of the murder between midnight and 2 A.M. No suspicion attached to the girl, who was fortunately able to account for her movements after 11:10 on that night.

Between Stokes' studio and Neil Lane's, was a trail via skylight, roof and parapet, which constituted the damning evidence of the case. It showed beyond human doubt that a man had crept and climbed from one studio to the other, and back again. On the soot of the roof were an abundance of slipper marks and finger-prints. Whose marks were they?

The prosecution claimed that they were Neil Lane's—had apparently proved their point up to the hilt. What surer evidence of guilt could be produced?

And yet officials and spectators, in spite of the overwhelming logic of the situation, were impressed by the open, boyish, impulsive bearing of the prisoner as he stepped eagerly from the dock to the witness-box. Now at last there could be action—personal effort—instead of that terrible wait-and-do-nothing while witness after witness for the Crown had pieced together the chain of merciless evidence which was to hang him.

In Neil Lane was no "iron nerve," no cold calculation of demeanour. He was a mere boy fighting for his life against the relentless machinery of justice—squaring his shoulders and taking a grip of himself in this last desperate effort to escape the gallows. The spectators quivered with the excitement of the chase, as when the hunted animal turns and doubles before the hounds close in upon him and rend him to pieces.

"Tell us now," his counsel was saying, "what you were doing at 9 o'clock on the night of the murder."

"I was in my studio studying a history of Flemish art—Duchesne's. I was tired that evening, and had settled down in my armchair in a dressing-gown and slippers."

"Until what time did you read?"

"Until about 9:30. Then Mr. Gollen came in. I gave him a whisky-and-soda, and we had a short chat."

"How long did he stay?"

"Until about ten."

"You're certain of the time?"

"I remember the clock on my mantelpiece striking the hour soon after he left."

"Did you accompany him to the door?"

"No, we artists aren't so ceremonious, and in any case Mr. Gollen was not a particular friend of mine. I hadn't invited him in. Then I took up my book again."

"Mr. Gollen left at once?"

"I suppose so. I heard the outer door shut to."

"Now I want you to attend to this point very closely. You say that Mr. Gollen left before 10 o'clock. But the evidence given by Mrs. Parker puts the time she heard footsteps going down stairs at between 10:30 and 10:45. Mr. Gollen has stated in evidence that he came to see you after he had called in on Stokes at 9:30, that he left your rooms after 10:30, that he took a cab and reached his club by 11 o'clock, and that he stayed there playing bridge until after 4 A.M. You are quite positive that he left you before 10 o'clock?"

"Absolutely positive. The clock struck ten after he went—that I swear to. Mrs. Parker must have been mistaken."

"What did you do after he left?"

"I began to read again. But I felt tired, and I must have dropped asleep over my book."

"When did you wake again?"

"Some time in the small hours. My fire was down to a few dull cinders. Then I got up from my armchair, feeling a bit dazed, as one does in those circumstances, and went to bed in the next room."

"You were in the same chair?"

"The same chair. My book had dropped on the floor. I had never left the chair."

"You never went out on the parapet, to your knowledge?"

"Never, never!" the young man cried out, turning an appealing face to the jury. "To my knowledge, I never stirred from the armchair! Oh, believe me, I never went to murder Stokes! Why should I do such a thing? In Heaven's name, why? What motive would I have?" His voice rang throughout the court—the cry of a hunted animal.

Hatchard, K. C., mentally patted himself on the back for having stirred up his client to this outburst, which was bound to have a sentimental effect on the jury. In his heart of hearts, he believed that Neil Lane had murdered the other man in a fit of jealous passion, but it is no business of the advocate to wear his heart upon his sleeve.

The Judge intervened with grave impartiality.

"You must answer your counsel's questions," he told the young man, "and leave it to him to make the appeal to the jury."

Hatchard resumed the examination-in-chief on lines which he had decided upon as the only practicable defence. In his final speech he intended to admit frankly that the roof and parapet markings were Neil Lane's, and to urge on the jury with all the suggestive power of which he was such a master that the young fellow, walking in his sleep in his slippers and dressing-gown, had wandered over to the other man's studio and back, but that the actual murder had been committed by some person unknown.

So he sought to draw out from Lane that he was prone to the "brown study" habit, and that, in all probability, he was an occasional somnambulist. The young man eagerly gave affirmative answers to the former line of questioning, and detailed examples of his absent-mindedness, but he was doubtful about the sleep-walking. No one had ever told him about it, and of course he could have no knowledge of it himself. He could only say that it was very probable, which the Judge pointed out was not evidence.

"You had no dreams on the night of the murder while you were asleep by your fire?" pursued counsel.

Lane put his hands to his forehead, and thought deeply.

"No," he answered after a pause. "No, I can't remember anything. I was just asleep in the ordinary way. There may have been dreams, but I don't recollect any."

The leader for the Crown, Garside—keen, polished, hard as glittering steel—rose to cross-examiner

"As to motive, had you no grudge against the deceased?"

Lane flushed perceptibly. "He was not a particular friend of mine, of course, but I hadn't any actual *grudge* against him."

"I put it to you that your affections and his were centred on the same young lady, and that her preference lay in his direction."

"That's true, of course, but it doesn't mean what you imply."

"I put it to you that heated words had passed between you on the subject."

The young man clenched his hands impotently.

"Oh, be fair to me! I admit we had a few words on the matter, but that's utterly different from creeping into a man's rooms at dead of night and murdering him in cold blood!"

"That is a matter for the jury to decide," answered the prosecuting counsel coldly. Then he continued with his merciless probing. "You had threatened to kick the deceased out of your mutual artists' club on one occasion?"

He had been publicly talking of the lady, I don't want to mention her name, in a way no man with any decent feeling could stand, and naturally I resented it."

"Precisely. You felt you had a claim on her affections."

"No, not a claim, though certainly I had some encouragement. But for that matter there were others who had a deep admiration for her as well as myself—Gollen for one."

"The point is immaterial. Now, to take up a different matter. When Mr. Gollen was in your rooms that evening, you gave him a whisky-and-soda?"

"Yes."

"Did you drink yourself?"

"As a matter of civility, yes. But I only had a small drop of whisky."

"Was the whisky left within your reach after he had gone?"

"I suppose so, but I never touched it again. I expect I was too tired or too lazy to put it away. But really I didn't take more than one small glass."

"Have you never taken more than one small glass of an evening?"

"I wasn't drunk, if you mean that!" answered Lane indignantly.

The Judge interposed gravely:

"You must answer counsel's question."

"Well, yes, I suppose I have, occasionally—when there has been a jollification on."

"Then there was nothing to prevent you taking more than one glass on the night of the murder?" "I tell you I didn't!"

"Is it your habit to fall asleep in your armchair?"

"Oh, no. Sometimes I get into a brown study, but I don't fall asleep in my chair and stop there till the small hours of the morning. I don't know why I did on the night of the murder. Heaven knows I wish I had gone out on the bust, or something, so that I could prove an alibi."

"You admit that you sometimes 'go out on the bust,' as you term it?"

"I don't admit it at all!" Lane, deadly pale, was beginning to contradict himself, and Garside, K. C., gave a significant look towards the jury. Feeling was turning against the prisoner once more—to the facts of the case had been added the probable motive and igniting spark.

"When you have 'gone out on the bust,' I take it that you have come home the worse for liquor?" Hatchard jumped up instantly:

"M'lord, I object to that question!"

The Judge allowed his objection, but an impression had been created in the minds of the jury which no formal ruling-out could efface.

Garside adjusted his glasses before making his final merciless stab. Pointing dramatically at the prisoner with outstretched finger, he demanded:

"Tell us now why, if you were not the worse for liquor on the night of the murder—why you scorched the left-hand side of your dressing-gown by the dead man's fire as you stood silently by his couch looking down upon him with the sword ready to thrust?"

A shiver went through the court at the picture conjured up by the advocate's grim words.

Then a warder hastened forward to the prisoner's side; he had fainted.

From the body of the court a man in a long fur coat, with grave, dark eyes and silvery hair, moved swiftly towards the witness box.

"I am a doctor," he said. "My name is Wycherley. Can I be of assistance?"

*   *   *   *   *

The speeches for the defence and for the prosecution had been made: on the one hand eloquent, impassioned, appealing to the heart; and on the other hand cold, hard, mercilessly logical, appealing to the intellect. The Judge had given his summing-up, clear-cut and instinct with the impartiality of British justice, but pointing out emphatically that no shred of evidence had been adduced by the defence to place the murder on to another man's shoulders.

When the jury filed back slowly and gravely into their box after the long wait, everyone in court could see the verdict in their faces. The prisoner went white at his first sight of them.

"What is your verdict, gentlemen—guilty or not guilty?"

"Guilty, my lord; but we strongly recommend him to mercy."

The chaplain moved to the Judge's side. The clerk of arraigns stood up and pronounced the solemn, formal question:

"Prisoner at the bar, have you anything to say why sentence of death should not be passed upon you?"

Neil Lane squared his shoulders and looked the Judge in the face, eye to eye, as man to man.

"My lord," said he, and his voice rang through the court and into men's hearts, "I ask for no 'mercy' of the usual kind. I am innocent, but I would far rather hang by the neck till I am dead than endure the hell of penal servitude for life. As you will one day stand before your God, my lord, be merciful and give me death!"

The Judge took up the black cap placed by his desk.

THE ERRAND OF DEATH

During the days that followed Neil Lane's conviction there were curious rumours current in legal and newspaper circles. Naturally the defence had lodged a formal appeal, and the rumours took the shape that some new and wholly unexpected evidence would be brought before the Judges of the Appeal Court when the case came up for hearing after the customary fortnight.

As with the breed of rumours, they assumed most explicit and circumstantial form as they passed from mouth to mouth. The actual murder had been the work of a woman, a jealous mistress. Lane had seen her in the dead man's studio on the fateful night, and was shielding her by his silence. Stricken with remorse, she had made a confession to her priest, whose religion forbade him to make known her identity. But the police were on her track. And so forth.

The real basis of these fantastic stories lay with Dr. Xavier Wycherley. He had attended the court in pursuit of his life-study, the human mind, the psychological springs of action, but in the course of the trial overwhelming conviction had come upon him of the innocence of Neil Lane. As a humanitarian, he felt impelled to do what lay within his power for the young man.

He was now endeavouring to persuade the Judges of the Appeal Court to step outside the grooves of British justice and create a precedent of a kind that struck the legal mind with horror. Thoroughly convinced himself of the young man's innocence, he had first to carry his conviction into the minds of the two opposing counsel, and then to arrange an interview of a most unprecedented and entirely unofficial nature in the chambers of the Master of the Rolls.

Only his intense conviction, his magnetic personality, and his European reputation had made such an interview possible for a moment.

Lord Thorndyke paced his hearthrug uneasily when he had listened to the doctor's astonishing theory of the crime. The two counsel, Hatchard and Garside, sat silent, with faces composed to legal inscrutability.

"But even granted that your theory were correct, Doctor," Lord Thorndyke was saying, "how would that help matters? The law cannot take cognizance of the action of one human mind on another. If we once admitted such action, we should be plunged back in the old days of witchcraft and the legal horrors of the Middle Ages. Suppose that you could even *bring evidence* of a kind that gave colour to your supposition—what follows? This man, Neil Lane, with an admitted jealousy towards the murdered artist, is stirred up to action in the hypnotic state, and climbs over the roof to kill in actuality the man whom in the ordinary way he would only have killed in thought. But the law can only deal with the facts of the case; the psychological springs of action are outside its purview, except in so far as they mitigate punishment. The law says that he who kills must suffer the penalty of the law, whether he kills in rage and passion, or in cold blood, or under the stimulus of another."

Dr. Wycherley concentrated his keen, penetrating gaze on the finely chiselled face of the old jurist. His voice was low and even, but intense in its sincerity.

"Suppose," he replied, "that Neil Lane had no intention of killing—did not kill?"

"The jury found otherwise."

"The jury could only deal with the facts before them. Grant me this experiment, and who can tell what utterly unsuspected fact might not be brought to light? You, men of the law, have had a lifelong training in the marshalling and judging of the seen and the tangible. I, on the other hand, have had a lifelong training in the judging of the unseen and the intangible.

"I say this, with my reputation at stake, that there are unsuspected factors in the case that, so far, have not been touched by the counsel for the defence and prosecution, anxious as both of them are that justice shall be done. I *know*, as surely as I know that I live, there is that to bring to light which only experiment can give us. Lord Thorndyke, I ask only for an entirely unofficial experiment. Whatever its results may be, their bearing and interpretation will be left unquestioningly in the hands of yourself and your colleagues on the bench. In the name of justice and humanity, I ask for this. It may mean a man's life."

The Master of the Rolls paced up and down in silence, his forehead furrowed in thought. When at length he spoke it was to the counsel for the defence.

"Have I your assurance," he asked, "that the experiment will not be made public, or used for any purpose without the express consent of myself and my colleagues?"

"Certainly, m'lord. We are all agreed upon that essential. On no account must a precedent be created."

"Then," said the old jurist thoughtfully, "I will put the matter before my colleagues."

* * * * *

Dr. Wycherley had gained his point. The experiment had been sanctioned.

Singly and in perfect secrecy, so as to keep the matter away from the avid newspapers, the several participants in the coming proceedings had gathered together in Neil Lane's studio—the Master of the Rolls, the two counsel, an independent medical specialist, the prisoner and a Scotland Yard man in charge of him, and Dr. Wycherley. Round the studio buildings had been posted plainclothes men to prevent any interruption on the one hand, or any attempt at escape on the other.

It was ten o'clock in the evening. Everything had been arranged to repeat the conditions of the night of the murder. Sitting by his studio-fire, in his old armchair, with his old dressing-gown and his slippers on, sat Neil Lane, studying Duchesne's "History of the Flemish School." A single shaded reading-lamp by his side lit up his book; in the outer darkness of the room sat the spectators, in agreement to keep perfect silence and allow Dr. Wycherley's experiment the fairest possible test.

In the studio of the murdered man, in the neighbouring house, a fire blazed and a dummy form lay, stretched upon the couch.

For a full hour they allowed the condemned man to read on, so as to let the environment soak into his spirit once more and prepare the mind for the hypnotic operation. Dr. Wycherley, sitting in the outer darkness, had been spending the waiting moments in making his delicate little left-hand miniatures of Lane, of Lord Thorndyke and of the two counsel, drawn from his memory of the scene in court. These would afterwards be filed away amongst the records of his cases. Now the mental healer moved forward to a place by Neil's side, and asked him to fix his gaze and his full powers of concentration on himself. It was highly, necessary for the experiment that the patient should be sent into deep hypnosis, and accordingly Dr. Wycherley put aside his usual methods of verbal suggestion, and employed with all the power at his command the intensive gaze and the slow hypnotic passes of the older school of mesmerists.

In half an hour Neil's eyes had closed, and his arm stood out rigidly when Dr. Wycherley raised it to a horizontal position. The medical witness came forward with the jurists, and made the usual needle insertions in the arm and the light flashes into the eyes, so as to test the depth of the hypnosis. With a curt nod the specialist expressed his satisfaction at the tests.

Dr. Wycherley put his hand on the sleeping man's forehead.

"It is ten o'clock on the night of the murder. Tell me all that happened after that."

It was a strange, mechanical, far-away voice that replied to him from the body of Neil Lane:

"I take up my book and begin to read again. Presently my thoughts wander, and I fall into a brown study. Somehow I seem to feel in a vague way that a man has entered the room and is standing silently by my side. I do not feel it with my mind, but in a kind of unconscious way. I know that he is making passes over me, but yet I am not sufficiently awake to resist him. Now I seem to feel myself falling under the power of his mind—it is as though his mind were entering into my brain and taking possession of it, side by side with my own mind."

"Do you know who the man is?"

"Now I know that he is Gollen."

"Does he speak to you?"

"Yes; he tells me to obey him, and have no fear. He tells me to stand up, and I do so. He tells me to turn out my lamp, and I do so. Now he tells me that at midnight I am to climb over the roof to Stokes' studio, and kill him. I am horrified at the idea, and I try to resist his suggestion. I tell him that I would never do such a thing."

"What happens then?"

"He tells me that he was only joking, and that I ought to laugh at the joke. I believe him, so I laugh. Now he tells me that Stokes is very ill, and is lying down on his couch by the studio-fire. Unless he is tended he will become worse, and the fault will be mine. I feel sorry for Stokes. Now Gollen tells me that I ought to go at midnight and tend him. I reply that I will go. He gives me detailed instructions as to what I am to do, and leaves me."

"What is the time?"

"It is just after 10:30."

"Do you see this clock on the mantelpiece?"

With closed eyes the young man turned his head towards the mantelpiece, and replied:

"I see it."

"When it strikes midnight you will do exactly as you did on the night of the murder."

"I will do so."

The reading-lamp began to waver and flutter, and, with a gasp, went out. The room was plunged into darkness, except for the eerie flickering of the firelight which showed the watchers dimly to one another. They kept a strained silence whilst the clock ticked its weary way to midnight.

As twelve o'clock struck the sleeping figure in the armchair rose up, and with sightless eyes began to move quickly to the window leading out to the parapet. The Scotland Yard detective responsible for the safety of the condemned man kept close behind him, ready to catch him should he slip on the parapet or roof.

In a whisper Dr. Wycherley suggested to the others that they should go round to the dead man's studio by the usual entrance. As they arrived hurriedly there was a noise heard on the roof, and Neil Lane made his way in by the skylight.

He came to the middle of the room and stared about him with sightless eyes. The watchers shivered at the uncanny deftness of this ghostlike shell of a man with his automaton mind.

"Who is in the room?" asks Dr. Wycherley.

"Stokes."

"Where is he?"

"Gollen told me that he is lying down on his couch by the fire."

"Is there no one else in the room?"

"No one else."

Lord Thorndyke flicked thumb and fore-finger lightly together—a mannerism of his denoting that things were turning out much as he expected. But Neil Lane apparently did not hear him or know that there were watchers of his movements. He went over to the fire, and then moved near to it a small table holding a bottle of brandy, glasses, and a packet of quinine powder.

"Why are you moving the table?" asked Dr. Wycherley at this unexpected action.

The even, mechanical voice of the sleeping man answered him: "Because Gollen told me that Stokes had moved his couch to where the fireplace used to be, and the fireplace to where the couch used to be. . . ."

Lord Thorndyke drew in his breath sharply and moved involuntarily forward.

". . . And so I am taking the table nearer to Stokes' couch in case he were to wake up in the night and want medicine or drink."

Neil Lane went to the wall and placed his hand on a narrow, vicious-looking thrusting sword hanging with some other Eastern trophies.

"What are you doing now?"

"Gollen told me that I would find the poker hanging on the wall. I am to take it down and poke the fire into a big blaze, so that the sick man may have warmth."

The sleeping man took down the sword, handling it as if it were indeed a poker, and started to thrust it vigorously again and again into the dummy form lying on the couch.

"What are you doing now?"

"I am poking the fire into a blaze, as Gollen told me to do. That will make Stokes comfortable for the night, so now I can go back to my rooms."

Placing the sword upon the ground, nearly parallel with the couch, as though he were laying it on a fender, Neil Lane moved across to the skylight and began to climb out, still with sightless eyes.

Lord Thorndyke whispered to Dr. Wycherley: "On the morning the murder was discovered the sword was also found lying parallel to the couch. It was an extraordinary detail."

"And such details are evidence of the highest value," answered the doctor. "In thinking over what you have seen to-night, I would ask you particularly to realise this fact of mental science: that no man or woman can be influenced in a single hypnotic trance to do what is contrary to his or her moral sense. This man Gollen must have been aware of the fact. He made no persistent attempt, judging from what we have seen to-night, to induce young Lane to murder Stokes. He avoided that by a subterfuge. He sent Lane on an errand of death which was ostensibly an errand of mercy."

"I realise that," was the reply of Lord Thorndyke, as he stood looking at the scene of the murder with thoughtful eyes. "I fully realise that. But the legal question raised is one which requires the gravest consideration. To admit as evidence what we have seen to-night would create a most dangerous precedent. I will confess to you that at the moment I cannot see what I am to do in the matter, unless it is contrived to alter Lane's sentence to one of penal servitude."

"An innocent man!"

"It is a tangle apparently without a reasonable solution," mused the Master of the Rolls.

Dr. Wycherley said no more, judging it best to leave the affair to the large-minded sympathies of the jurist.

But the morning brought a most unexpected solution to the problem, cutting clean the Gordian knot. Breaking through his usual rule by glancing at a daily newspaper, Dr. Wycherley's eye was caught by an item of exceptional interest. A brief paragraph told that one of the chief witnesses in the Neil Lane case, a Mr. Gollen, had been dangerously injured in a taxi-cab accident while driving to Charing Cross Station to catch a Continental express. He was now lying in Charing Cross Hospital, and his condition was considered extremely grave.

At once the doctor left his breakfast untouched and hurried off to the hospital. Pleading matters of the utmost urgency, he asked the house-surgeon in charge for a brief private interview with the dying man.

Gollen, swathed in bandages, greeted Dr. Wycherley with a cynical smile. "Another of you specialists?" he enquired banteringly. "You're all no use; I know that quite well. My number's up. But don't imagine for a moment that I'm afraid of death."

Dr. Wycherley gazed at him with his keen, earnest look, and answered very quietly: "Few men are afraid of death—only of the life after death."

Gollen, suddenly sobered, nodded his head in agreement, but then added: "I'm not a 'religious' man. I don't believe in your heaven or hell."

"Is it your belief that the ego will live on after death?"

"That I do believe. It's only my earthly body that I am going to shed."

"Then are you not afraid of meeting Neil Lane in the life hereafter?"

"Neil Lane—what the devil do you mean?" blustered the dying man.

"My poor fellow," answered Dr. Wycherley with a note of real pity in his voice, "I know all that you have been trying to conceal. No one can touch you now; the law is impotent. But will you choose to go to your new life with a double crime shackled to your soul— first Stokes, and now that poor boy who stood in the dock to receive his death sentence for the crime he had never dreamt of committing."

"Stokes deserved all he got and more!" was the bitter answer. "I knew him in the East, and he was a *devil*. He gave me full cause. Yes; he was better out of the world."

"But Neil Lane! What harm did Neil Lane do to you? Can you bear to face him in the hereafter? When you have fled to the uttermost ends of space, and he pursues you still—out in the black void where no star gleams, beyond where the comets wheel on their courses—when his soul and yours come face to face, what will you say to him?"

The dying man kept silence while the clock ticked through a full minute. Then he turned to the doctor and said: "I suppose you want me to sign a confession?"

"Yes; for your own sake as much as for Neil Lane's."

"Well, perhaps you are right. Bring me pen and paper."

With a firm hand he wrote a few lines, and placed below them a signature of characteristic decisiveness.

The true story of the murder of Stokes was never made public in court—the hypnotic experiment was too dangerous a legal precedent to be published at large. But at the Court of Appeal it was put in evidence that Gollen had signed a death-bed confession of guilt; and in due course the announcement was made that his Majesty the King had been graciously pleased to tend a free pardon to Neil Lane.

A ROYAL COMMAND

Home with Dr. Wycherley was always the island and his beloved garden. Next after the study of mind he loved trees—looked
upon them almost as his children. The wonderful collection of trees
and shrubs on Isola Salvatore was a never-ending source of delight and pride to him.

At the moment when the call to Pfalzburg reached him, the
doctor was just preparing to plant in the garden of spices a con-
signment of seedlings from Celebes with the minute care they demanded. He had been looking forward to the arrival and planting
of the newcomers with the keenest pleasure. But there was grave
urgency behind the cold formality of this royal call, and so he must
needs put the anticipated pleasure aside and leave his new children to the care of his gardener.

In translation, this was the message brought to Dr. Wycherley
by a young officer of the royal household:

> PFALZBURG, May 20, 19—
> I am commanded by His Majesty the King to re-
> quest your presence at the earliest possible moment
> at the Palace of Pfalzburg. His Majesty desires to
> consult you.
>
> Von Olmütz
> (Chancellor of the
> Kingdom of Varovia.)

The young officer who had conveyed the message to Isola Salvatore now sat in a chair, considering, with a slight frown, the polish of his boots. The dust of travel was upon them, and it seemed to irk him.

Dr. Wycherley, reluctantly deciding to leave the engrossing occupation of cradling the new seedlings, asked of him: "Do you know how the trains run?"

With military precision the young lieutenant drew out his pocket-book and read in formal, precise tones: "Train from Rovellasco to Brescia at 4:10. Change at Brescia into Milan-Venice train de luxe. Change at Verona into Munich wagon-lit. Change at Munich into Dresden train de luxe. Change at Dresden into Pfalzburg express. Wires ready to send to stationmaster at Milan, Verona, Munich and Dresden to reserve special compartments. Dinner on the Munich train; breakfast at Munich; lunch on Dresden train." He closed the book and returned it to his pocket.

Dr. Wycherley felt urged to stick a mental pin into this very precise young man. Accordingly he asked: "Isn't there one point you have overlooked?"

"So?"

"Our local trains to Brescia are uncertain. We might miss the connection."

The officer gravely drew out his pocket-book again and read: "Emergency wire to stationmaster at Brescia to prepare special train for Verona. Emergency wire to divisional superintendent at Verona to clear the line for special train for Munich." He returned the book to his pocket.

"But that would leave us without dinner anywhere."

Food was a matter Dr. Wycherley gave no concern to; he was merely testing this very precise young man.

For the third time the young officer took out his pocket-book.

"Emergency wire to Hotel Porta Nuova at Verona. Make up best possible dinner for two, and put on special train for Munich."

Dr. Wycherley acknowledged defeat with a smile.

"That is the way Von Moltke won his battles."

The young lieutenant took the compliment with the slightest change of expression, and replied: "Naturally one is always prepared."

But on the long journey to Pfalzburg, Fritz von Lindenau relaxed a little and told the doctor much that he wanted to know of the King Sigmund V's family history, together with his own hopes and ambitions and such of his love affairs as could be related without extensive editing.

Two points von Lindenau had impressed on Dr. Wycherley as being of special importance. The one was that the King desired absolute secrecy, and that it would be advisable for the doctor to pass under another name at Pfalzburg. The second, that the King was quick-tempered and irritable—just as his father, Sigmund IV, had been—and that it would be advisable to humour his caprices. "They are a queer family," commented the young officer, with the familiarity born of his knowledge of Court.

They did not proceed to the central terminus at Pfalzburg, but alighted at Pfalzburg West and drove in a closed carriage to the palace, which is perched high above the city. Without delay, Dr. Wycherley was introduced into the King's private cabinet.

Sigmund V was a man of about forty-five, somewhat small and wizened when seen at close quarters. His official portraits, taken on occasions of State ceremony, decidedly flattered him. His forehead, viewed with out the covering of the eagled helmet, was narrow and receding, and his eyes were ferrety. Further, there was a nervous twitching of the scalp during conversation which was highly unpleasant.

"Sit down, sit down, Dr. Wycherley," said the King in rapid German. "I thought von Olmütz would have met you at the station. You must have missed one another, missed one another. Hope you had a good journey." Then, without waiting for any reply to this perfunctory remark: "I sent for you in the first place because I don't trust any of these Pfalzburg specialists; in the second place, because this is a matter on which I want absolute secrecy. You understand, you understand?"

Your Majesty can rely on my entire discretion."

"It's more than that, more than that. I don't want anybody to know that you have even been called in to advise. No advertisement out of this, you understand, you understand?"

Sigmund V had never been renowned for his tact. Such a remark, to a man of Dr. Wycherley's temperament—a man who neither sought notoriety nor valued it one jot—was almost an insult. But the doctor replied courteously:

"You need have no fear, sir. Whether I take up this case or not, the matter will remain entirely secret with me."

The King raised his eyebrows at Dr. Wycherley's suggestion that he might not take up the case, but there was only a grave seriousness in the doctor's steady gaze. So he continued:

"You know, of course, that my only son, the Crown Prince Karel, is affianced to the Grand Duchess Irma of Weissenrode-Hohenstein. The marriage is to take place in three days, in three days. A very suitable alliance, very suitable in every way. Politically it is vital to the well-being of Varovia. My son and the Grand Duchess are in love with one another, and so everything is plain sailing, plain sailing."

"And what are the objections he has suddenly developed?"

"I didn't say he had any objections. Morbid fancies—that's all they are, morbid fancies." The King's scalp twitched angrily. "So I want you to talk to him, and reason him out of them. It's a matter of the utmost importance to get this nonsense out of his head. That's why I sent for you. Heard of your powers, heard of your powers."

"Is the Crown Prince willing to see me on the matter? The point is important."

"Quite willing, quite willing. No difficulty on that score. In fact, the whole matter is perfectly simple if it's approached in the right way. . . . Of course you must handle him tactfully," added the tactless King.

It was abundantly clear to Dr. Wycherley that any difference of opinion between father and son could easily be widened out into a definite breach. But they would hardly call in a doctor from half across Europe merely to smooth over a family quarrel. Matters must be more serious than the King's words implied.

"When can I see the Crown Prince?" asked Dr. Wycherley.

"Now, of course. No time to lose, no time to lose." He pressed an electric bell. "Lieutenant von Lindenau will show you to my son's study. It's all arranged; he's waiting for you. It's vital for the welfare of the kingdom that this morbid nonsense should be reasoned out of him. But it's got to be done tactfully. By the way, your name in Pfalzburg will be Herr Muller. You understand, you understand?"

The Crown Prince rose from his study armchair to greet Dr. Wycherley. Between father and son there was a striking contrast. Prince Karel was tall and well-built, and his features were moulded on stronger lines than his father's. Altogether there was a breadth of thought behind the boy which was lacking in the King. But the point which riveted Dr. Wycherley's attention were the eyes, deep-set and with a haunting melancholy in them. While the body was the body of an athlete, the mind was the mind of a dreamer.

He spoke in excellent English—accounted for by the souvenirs of Balliol which hung on the walls of his study side by side with the souvenirs of Bonn—and with a voice very pleasant to the ear.

"It was good of you to make this long journey on my account at such short notice," he said as he shook hands. "Did Fritzi look after your comforts properly?"

"He is a model organiser," answered Dr. Wycherley, smilingly. "If he should be lucky enough to get into a war, he will go far. Put him in control of railway transport, your Royal Highness."

"Yes, Fritzi is a good fellow, and cleverer than most people think. Did he tell you much about myself?"

"Only what is to your credit. Now I see that he suppressed little."

Prince Karel shook his head smilingly in depreciation of the compliment. Then his eyes grew grave again, and he replied, with a deep sadness in his voice:

"That little is vital."

"Tell me what is troubling you."

"I fear there is no help that you—or any medical man—can give, but my father insisted on having your professional advice."

"Perhaps the matter is less vital than you think. You have been brooding deeply over it. That is always liable to make the little loom large. Will your Royal Highness give me your hand, so that I may sense the radical or the trivial of your trouble?"

The Prince extended his hand, and Dr. Wycherley took it in his own cool, firm grasp. For many moments he continued to hold it, while he looked deep into the eyes of Prince Karel. At length he said, very gravely:

"What grounds have you for supposing it?"

"Ah, you have guessed?"

"I have sensed."

"The very strongest of grounds—what lies hidden in myself. Ever since I was a boy I have been subject to long fits of melancholy—times when I felt that I would like to slip out of this world of mine and bury myself in a hermit's cell. But during the last twelve months the feeling has slowly changed to another and a very terrible one. When the fits come upon me, I now feel an unaccountable rage stealing inside my brain and gaining possession of my mind. Heaven knows I have struggled against it, but I seem powerless to control the impulse. I see red; I strike out blindly in my rage; I scarcely know what I do! When I have felt this evil obsession coming upon me, I have asked Fritzi to stand by me and see that no harm happens. He's a good fellow, Fritzi, and he has stood by me. Except my father and the Chancellor, no one else but Fritzi knows. I sometimes wonder if the others suspect.

"Last week he was called away, and when he was absent a fit of this strange, sudden anger came upon me. I was alone in his study with my favourite dog. . . . When I had recovered my senses the dog was lying on the hearthrug—there, there!—with his head smashed in! The poker was red with blood!" He shuddered at the recollection. "My poor, faithful dog—I can't bear to think of it!"

"When you became engaged to the Grand Duchess . . ."

"I didn't know then what I know now. It is only lately that I have realised it to the full. At that time I used to think that the fits of melancholy had no special significance. But now I know, and the knowledge is burning into me like vitriol! I love her, Dr. Wycherley, I love her passionately! I wouldn't have harm or sorrow come to her for the world! Oh, God, what am I to do—what am I to do?"

"There are many cases such as yours which have yielded to psychotherapeutic treatment," answered Dr. Wycherley, with deep sympathy in his voice. "Time is required, naturally, and it would not be difficult to arrange that an accident—say, a broken leg—should confine you to your room and postpone the marriage. In a couple of months' time I could give you a more definite opinion. Without wishing to raise false hopes in you, I will say that there is decidedly the possibility of complete cure. Where there is no strong family taint . . ."

The young Prince had been listening to Dr. Wycherley's kindly words with hope dawning in his eyes, but at the last sentence he interrupted fiercely with: "Wait till you hear the worst! You know of my grandfather's death?"

"I know, of course, that King Sigmund IV died of acute scarlet fever, and that he lies buried in the family tomb here in Pfalzburg."

"A dummy form lies buried there. My grandfather is alive!"

"But—"

"Alive and a raving madman! No one knew but the doctor who attended him, now dead, and his keepers," continued the Prince rapidly. "The secret has been well guarded. Four days ago I discovered it by the merest accident. I was out hunting in a distant part of the forest at one of our country estates; I became separated from the others and lost my bearings. At nightfall I came to a forester's hut and entered it to get refreshment and ask my way. For some reason the people of the house were away at the moment, and I unlocked a door in order to find food. As I struck a match in that dark room, the light fell on a man, with a long grey beard, chained down on to a bed. It was my grandfather! It was six years since I had last seen him, but it was he—that I will swear to!" He covered his face with his hands to shut out the horrible vision he had conjured up.

"Is there no possibility that your Royal Highness was mistaken?

"My father denies it; they all deny it. But it was *he*—he called me by a pet name that my grandfather had used for me when I was a little child . . . I quite recognise the political necessity of keeping his madness secret and pretending his death. We have not been a popular dynasty, and the Socialist Party has been growing very powerful in Varovia. If it had been known that Sigmund IV was not merely eccentric, but actually, insane, there would have been a revolution. Of course, I would not be telling of this unless I had absolute confidence in your discretion."

"All that you tell me will be absolutely safe with me. But, once again, there is no possibility of a mistake?"

"None whatever. . . . I believe the keeping of that ghastly secret killed my mother. . . . Now you can realise my feelings, with my marriage only a few days distant. On the one hand the duty to my dynasty and my country; on the other hand the duty to the woman I love and the children that may be ours. Tell me, Doctor, which duty is the greater?"

Dr. Wycherley turned to the window and looked out over the red roofs and the fretted spires of Pfalzburg for some moments before answering. Then he said slowly: "The marriage must not take place."

The young Prince replied sadly: "Ah, you tell me what my own conscience also tells me!"

"Your Royal Highness will be able to do your duty by your country without marrying the Grand Duchess. Under treatment, that unfortunate tendency you speak of may probably be eliminated—certainly kept in check. I see no reason why you may, not be, when the time comes, the best king that Varovia has ever had."

"And the succession?"

"That consideration must be put aside for the present."

"But what am I to say to the woman I love? The truth will break her heart."

"I fear I cannot advise in that. You will know her feelings far better than I."

Prince Karel rose from his chair with a steady determination in his eyes. "I thank you, Dr. Wycherley—I thank you sincerely. I know you have been summoned here to persuade me into a marriage from which my conscience revolts. As *you* have done your higher duty, so will I do mine. Let us come to my father and tell him."

THE DECISION

With the King was the Chancellor, von Olmütz, a man of sixty—stout, bland, smiling, outwardly the personification of easy good nature. Someone in speaking of him to Bismarck had used the epithet "oily." Bismarck's reply had come curt and to the point: "Oiled steel!" For twenty years von Olmütz had stood behind the throne of Varovia and moved the hands and lips of its kings.

Introduced to the doctor, he greeted him with a well-turned compliment: "When his Majesty asked me a few days ago who was the foremost mental healer in Europe, I replied: 'The founder of the *Annalen der Psychologischen Forschungen*, Dr. Xavier Wycherley.' Permit me, Herr Doctor, to tell you how much I value the copies of your journal I have been able to obtain. Perhaps one day you will be so kind as to complete the gaps in my series?"

Dr. Wycherley bowed and replied: "With pleasure. But you will have more to teach me than I you. I confess to coveting the knowledge of men and women that thirty years of diplomacy have given you."

The Chancellor continued blandly: "I had hoped to give myself the pleasure of meeting you on your arrival at Pfalzburg. But apparently our young friend von Lindenau made a stupid mistake in descending at the station of Pfalzburg West. I was, of course, awaiting you at the terminus. You will excuse my apparent discourtesy, Herr Doctor?"

Dr. Wycherley bowed again. Inwardly he was reflecting that the young lieutenant was hardly the man to make stupid mistakes. No doubt he had wanted the doctor to avoid seeing the Chancellor before he had seen the Crown Prince.

Prince Karel brought the conversation sharply to the point at issue: "Dr. Wycherley has meanwhile been enquiring into my case, and he agrees with the conclusion I had arrived at."

The King's scalp twitched angrily.

"What's that, what's that?" he cried, and turned on Dr. Wycherley: "Didn't I tell you plainly that my son's ideas were only morbid nonsense? Your business is to cure, isn't it, isn't it?"

"Where cure is possible, your Majesty."

"As it is here!"

"If sufficient time is allowed, there are good hopes of permanent cure. But marriage must be put aside for some years at least." He spoke quietly but decisively.

"The marriage is arranged for Thursday. It must take place on Thursday! To-morrow the Grand Duchess makes her State entry into the city, into the city!"

The Chancellor interposed smoothly: "The Herr Doctor's examination of the Crown Prince has necessarily been very brief. He will probably desire to look into matters in greater detail before giving his final decision. There are many important aspects that possibly have not yet been brought to his notice."

But Dr. Wycherley ignored the golden bridge that was offered for his retreat. "Your Excellency," he said, "will know that I am not the man to make hasty decisions. My professional advice has been asked, and it is this: that all thoughts of marriage be put aside for some years at least."

Prince Karel added: "That is what my own conscience tells me also."

"And what of your duty to your father?" asked the King. His little, ferrety eyes shot murderous glances at the mental healer. "Isn't it your duty to obey his wishes, to obey his wishes?"

"There are other duties too, father."

The Chancellor moved quickly to interpose between father and son.

"Permit me to explain, sir. I do not think that the Crown Prince thoroughly realises all the aspects of this matter. I have the very deepest sympathy with his scruples of conscience—they do honour to him. But I believe that they blind him to the very serious position in which his proposed action would place us. I have here a report from the Chief of Police." He drew out a folded paper from his pocket, and tapped it significantly as he fixed Prince Karel with his eye. "He tells me that the announcement of the alliance with the Grand Duchess has had a distinctly quieting effect upon the people, and that it has given the Royal Family more popularity—I speak plain words, because the situation demands plain words—more popularity than for many years past. The Socialist element has received a decided set-back. But were this marriage to be cancelled, it is my deep belief—based on a lifetime's knowledge of the people of Varovia—that the political consequences would be *disastrous.* For my part I could only ask that my resignation of the Chancellorship be accepted and that I be permitted to retire and spend my old age in some quieter land."

"You hear that, you hear that?" added King Sigmund to his son.

"The police department wants re-organising," replied the Prince, his lips white and tense.

"So much for internal affairs," pursued the Chancellor relentlessly. "Now for the external aspect. The Weissenrode-Hohensteins are financially of small importance, but through their relationship to most of the Royal Families of Europe the alliance is vital to the political existence of Varovia as an independent kingdom. Is your Royal Highness prepared to see your father degraded to the standing of a mediatised prince? Look at those portraits on the walls surrounding you—Sigmund the Great, Rudolph, Sigmund II, victor at the bloody field of Szczapanacs—what would they think of their descendant who betrayed his dynasty?"

Involuntarily Prince Karel looked up at the grave faces that all had their eyes—or so it seemed—turned upon him. "But our relations with foreign Powers are now friendly?" he argued.

"To outward appearance, yes. In reality—" von Olmütz paused significantly.

With renewed vehemence he went on: "So far we have looked at Varovia's claims upon you—now let us look at the claims of the noble lady who has given you her heart. Are we to send the Grand Duchess back to her country jilted upon her wedding-day—disgraced in the eyes of all her people—a byword in Europe? What excuse have we to offer? That our Crown Prince has wearied of her? That his affections have cooled?"

"We could tell her the truth," interrupted the Prince in a strained whisper.

"And what to her people? Are we to tell them that our Crown Prince fancies he is no fit mate for any woman? Would they believe that? No, they would look on it as the merest excuse. They would believe that Varovia had deliberately insulted the Grand Duchess Irma. Here is the Grand Duchess—" von Olmütz took up a framed photograph from the King's desk— "are you prepared to send this noble lady back to her people insulted and disgraced?

"Come," he took the Prince by the arm and hurried him to the balcony that overlooked the city of Pfalzburg. "See there the arches and the decorations your people have erected to welcome your bride tomorrow! There is the railway-station at which she will arrive. There are the streets through which you will drive to the music of the acclamations of your people. There is the cathedral at which the Archbishop will place her hand in yours and give to you a blessing on the marriage from our Holy Father the Pope. Out there"—he flung his arm wide— "out there in the far distance is the castle of Greiffenfels where even now they prepare for your wedding-night. There you will pass the honeyed days with the noble lady who loves you passionately and is to give you all that your heart desires. Is there no blood in your veins? *Gott in Himmel!* ARE YOU ICE?"

The Crown Prince's face was flushed; his blood ran hot within him. Nervously he clasped and unclasped his hands as he stood on the balcony looking now upon the streets that were being decked for his marriage and now out to the distant horizon.

The Chancellor played his last card. "A special messenger from Weissenrode arrived with a postbag but half an hour ago. For you there is this letter"—he drew it out from his pocket— "the writing is familiar to us all. Open it and see what message your noble lady has for you!"

The young Prince clutched at the letter and kissed it rapturously. The Chancellor came quickly inside the room and said to Dr. Wycherley: "I believe I am correct in stating that the Royal Family of Varovia have no further need of your services. A pleasant journey to you, Herr Doctor!"

Dr. Wycherley bowed in silence and withdrew.

*   *   *   *   *

The three days that followed that momentous interview were days packed with activity for the Crown Prince. There was the arrival of the Grand Duchess Irma at Pfalzburg, her State entry into the city, the dinners and the receptions, the official visits and the official return visits. He had hardly time for thought until he retired to his bed at night, weary from the round of ceremonies and the multitude of pleasant nothings he had had to evolve for each of the important people who were presented to him.

Without a pause the official ceremonies carried him along with them in a breathless rush to his marriage-day. The drive to the cathedral was through a lane of acclamations from his people—right and left he bowed to acknowledge them, bowing as the actor does to a hazy sea of faces on the other side of the glaring footlights. Individual faces were lost in the sea; when he raised his hand to his helmet and smiled up at the fluttering handkerchiefs from balcony or roof, the action was quite mechanical.

It was a huge dream panorama of shoutings and cheerings, of fluttering flags and blazing uniforms, until he found himself walking slowly up the aisle of the cathedral while the solemn organ rolled out its thunderous chords and sent them echoing around the fretted tracery of the great dome. For a moment he faltered; then he looked into the eyes of his bride and his heart leapt to the joy in hers.

A splendid pair of lovers they made as they left the cathedral after the ceremony and drove back to the palace—the people of

Pfalzburg were frantic in their acclamations. One of the very few in all that vast gathering who did not cheer the royal pair was Dr. Wycherley, viewing the procession from the balcony of his hotel. His heart was heavy within him at the thought of the tragedy of the future—of the sacrifice which was being made so that the dynasty should continue in its seat of power.

Upon the woman would the weight of the tragedy fall—upon her and upon the children that might be hers.

Late that evening the Crown Prince and Princess arrived at the castle of Greiffenfels in which their honeymoon was to be spent. The servants in the castle were few. They were to have all the privacy permissible to a royal pair.

Prince Karel and his beautiful bride dined alone in the great dining-room which opens on to the terrace-walk around the battlements of Greiffenfels. They were sipping their coffee, and the attendants had discreetly withdrawn.

"Why are you looking so thoughtful and sad?" asked Irma when a long pause had ensued between them.

"I didn't mean to, Liebchen. My thoughts were wandering," returned the Prince dreamily.

"Tell me what you were thinking of?"

"I was thinking of a solitary hut in the forest of— But what am I saying? That's no matter to dwell upon." He pulled himself together and gazed at his bride with love welling into his eyes. "Tonight, this hour, is the happiest of my life. Is it *your* happiest hour, Liebchen?"

Irma came to him and laid her face upon his shoulder, looking up into his eyes. "Need I say, Kärli?"

He kissed her passionately again and again, crushing her to his breast.

"Oh, you will kill me with your kisses!" she cried in mock fear, and then lovingly returned his kisses.

"Tell me once again, this is the happiest hour of your life?"

"You know it, my loved one!"

"If you had only this hour with me to look back upon, you would regret nothing?"

"What do you mean by saying such a strange thing, Kärli?" she replied, startled. "I want you with me always."

"But this hour would fill you with memories of joy?" he insisted gently.

"Yes—oh, yes!"

He rose from his chair and took out a cigarette-case from his pocket. "I would like to smoke a little on the terrace. Liebchen, you will excuse?"

"Let me come with you—the night is glorious, the stars are singing to us of joy and happiness."

"No, dear, I want this moment alone. I want to persuade myself that all this joy of mine is real. Won't you go to the piano and play for me that which I like so well, 'Star of Eve'?"

"But it is sad!"

"'The sweetest songs are those that tell of saddest thought,'" he quoted, with music in his voice. "Kiss me once again, my beloved, full upon the lips!"

She came to him, and he crushed her again in his arms, raining kisses upon her. With reverence in his eyes he followed her as she moved to the room adjoining to play for him the haunting melody from "Tannhäuser."

Then the Crown Prince Karel, heir to the kingdom of Varovia, left the happiness that was his and walked with firm step and clear eye to the end of the battlements where the shadows are dark.

There was a flower growing in a crevice down the wall, and he leant far over in order to pluck it.

*   *   *   *   *

All that evening of the wedding-day Dr. Wycherley had had a deep sense of tragedy crowding in upon him. To try to banish it from his mind he had made his way to one of the great popular cafés of Pfalzburg, where a tsigane orchestra flung out its gay melodies and the faces of the people radiated happiness.

About eleven o'clock, when he was leaving the restaurant to return to his hotel, there arose a sudden clamor in the streets that carried a very different note to the wild rejoicings of the populace. A crowd was gathering around one of the advertisement pillars on which the newspapers of Pfalzburg display their special news. Every moment its numbers were increasing. "Read it out to us!" they cried.

A man with a loud voice began to read it to the crowd, and fragments came to Dr. Wycherley's ears: "Terrible tragedy! Death of the Crown Prince! A terrible accident has occurred to our beloved Prince Karel on his wedding-night. . . . Apparently he was leaning over the battlements to pluck a flower growing in the wall, and overbalanced himself. . . . The flower was still in his grasp. . . . Medical help was at once sent for. . . . The doctor was of opinion that death must have been practically instantaneous. . . ."

Dr. Wycherley raised his hat reverently.

"There died a prince," he said.

THE COUNTESS PLUNGES

Monte Carlo held a persistent fascination for Dr. Wycherley. Not as a field of fortune, since the doctor never staked money on the tables, but as a laboratory of human feelings, emotions and passions. There is no crowd so cosmopolitan as a Monte Carlo crowd in high season—none so expressive of the complexities of modern civilisation. To the doctor, with his peculiar outlook, they were gathered together from all the great cities of the world for the express purpose of providing him with material for study. Monte Carlo was for him an absorbing morality play—gorgeously staged, produced with sensuous, cynical realism, played by an ever-shifting crowd of actors ranging from the greatest names of the world down to the most beast-like parasites of the underworld.

A hothouse of civilisation, holding rare exotics of delicate beauty and fragrance side by side with brilliant poison-flowers.

It was on one of the doctor's visits to Monte Carlo that he became involved in the case of the Countess Varoczy and the French Government. If one adjective had to be chosen to describe the Countess, it would be unquestionably the word "daring." Daring in dress, in jewels, in play, in mode of life. The scandals around her name were notorious in half-a-dozen capitals of Europe. She flouted public opinion—took keen delight in flouting it. It made women hate her and men flock around her.

That evening when Dr. Wycherley was watching her, the Countess was plunging wildly at the tables. Further, quite a small crowd in the Salon Privé were watching her and her play, and that is unusual at Monte Carlo. For in the gaming-rooms a beautiful woman commands as little attention as a beautiful woman at a race-meeting while the horses are racing. In the Salles des Jeux the horses are always racing. Money reigns. Interest is focused on money—my money primarily, yours secondarily. Men and women become mentally classified as somebodies—those who play; or nobodies—those who watch. As systematists or non-systematists; as cautious or audacious; as lucky or unlucky; as good losers or bad.

It was therefore very definite tribute to the personality, beauty and audacity of the Countess Varoczy that herself and her play were being keenly observed and commented on in the hushed whispers that respect the solemnity of the temple of Mammon. She was apparently flinging money away in limit plunges on single numbers in the midst of her series bets. And yet she was winning—heavily, magnificently. The devil's luck was with her. But whether she won or lost on a *coup* there was no loss of her control and poise. She was magnificently cool. By her side was young De Carteret, lieutenant on the flagship cruiser *La Patrie*, helping her in the collection and changing of her money. Underneath his well-bred restraint one could read a distinct pride in his favored position.

In the background of that cosmopolitan crowd Dr. Wycherley was looking on at the scene with the quiet, intent gaze of the student. He might have been watching the outcome of some laboratory experiment.

There was a touch on his arm, and he turned to find beside him the French Minister for Foreign Affairs, M. Morèze. An elderly man with a white moustache and tufted imperial; well set-up in spite of years, with sure power in his face. That he had kept his post through five successive ministries was proof of his worth.

"My dear Doctor, I did not know you were a student of roulette," he said in French as he shook hands cordially.

"Roulette has no interest for me," returned Dr. Wycherley smilingly. "I have not staked even a five-franc piece for twenty years.

It is men and women that interest me, and I am never tired of watching them. There is always something fresh to discover. Monte Carlo is one of my laboratories."

"How cold-blooded!"

"All keen professional men and women are inevitably cold-blooded in the exercise of their life-study. To the surgeon, you, my dear Morèze, are possibly an interesting specimen of an enlarged supra-renal. To the diplomatist, a model in the art of saying nothing with the most perfect air of bestowing a deep confidence. To the journalist, a column or so of excellent copy. To women, an interesting problem of voluntary celibacy."

"And to yourself?"

"I am asking myself what brings you to Monte Carlo. For your interest in gambling is almost as slight as mine."

The Minister leaned forward confidentially. "You read wonderfully well. I have escaped from Paris for a brief holiday. A few days at my villa at Beaulieu, and then back to work. Ah, work—if only one could cut oneself free!"

Dr. Wycherley smiled. "That confirms a previous remark of mine."

"Which one?"

"Your peculiar interest to the diplomatist."

The Minister lowered his eyes, and Dr. Wycherley, in understanding of his meaning, did not take the matter further.

M. Morèze started another topic. "The Countess," with a glance in her direction, "does she interest you as a laboratory specimen?"

"I am not sure. So far as I have observed her, she falls into type, and the typical is to me uninteresting."

"The immemorial type?"

"Yes, this kind of woman is of all ages. Egypt, Rome, Venice, Spain, Russia—there has always been a Countess Varoczy. The epitome of sex. She reeks of sex."

"Ah, sex! If only the world were sexless . . ."

The doctor completed the sentence for him. ". . . how much easier would be the work of a Minister for Foreign Affairs!"

"You find her 'true to type'—to borrow an expression from the language of the Mendelian?"

"So far. One can almost tell just what she will do or say under any given set of circumstances. The same daring unconventionality on the surface, the same flouting of decent opinion, and yet the same underlying conventionality of thought beneath. Their superstitions, for instance. Would you ever see a Countess Varoczy plunge on the number 13, however sure she might be that it would turn up?"

There was a sudden stir around the table of the Varoczy, a sudden whispered buzz of comment. Both the Minister and the doctor turned to look. The Countess, disdaining all other of the thirty-seven numbers, had just placed a small pile of gold, four louis on top of a five-louis piece—the limit stake—on the square of the number 13 on the green cloth.

The roulette ball had been flicked from the hand of the croupier and was running swiftly around the wall of the roulette board like a finger-click around the whispering gallery of St. Paul's. It began to slow in its course.

"*Rien-n'va-plus*," remarked the croupier in one quick word.

The roulette ball hit against a little metal deflector, rebounded sharply, and tumbled into one of the thirty-seven compartments. Without a spoken word the croupier touched with his rake the number 13 on the green cloth, and began rapidly to pull in the stakes that had lost. The second croupier touched the Countess's pile with his rake to indicate that he was now paying out on it, and then pushed to her notes and gold to the value of thirty-five times her bet. She had won on number 13—and with a limit stake! All eyes were on her, envying, admiring. Young De Carteret glanced around with pride. Even the blasé croupiers looked appreciation of her audacity, and it is rare indeed that they are stirred out of their monotonous boredom.

But there was not the slightest trace of exultation with the Countess—still that same slightly insolent insouciance which goaded men to admiration.

The Minister turned to Dr. Wycherley with a gleam of banter in his voice. "Do you still class her in type?"

The doctor's reply held a seriousness strange in comparison to the triviality of the point: "That is the most startling happening I have seen at the tables this evening. There is always something new to learn in men and women. Yes, it is to me peculiarly interesting."

They watched her in silence for some time, still at her audacious plunging. Then M. Morèze remarked in a casual tone of voice: "You are now interested in the Countess? Good! . . . By the way, the rooms are getting uncomfortably hot, don't you think? Suppose we stroll out on the terrace. You smoke?"

"Occasionally."

"It is relieving to me to hear you have some vice. Shall we stroll out?"

The doctor looked keenly at the Minister for Foreign Affairs. "It would be a great pleasure . . . to do you any service."

It was very quiet out on the terraces—few people could spare time from the gaming-tables to bathe in that wonderful scene. Tall palms, grave in their immobility like Eastern sentinels. . . . The milk-white terraces chalked against the night, velvety-black, and the motionless sea, velvety-black. . . . The tiny port of Monaco below them splashed with the reflection of the lights from the cliff-town. . . . The solitary red light that marks the harbour-mouth. . . . A yacht at anchor with lighted saloon throwing a golden comb of light into the black water. . . . Faint perfumes of exotic flowers floating lazily across the still air. . . . From a distant café the soft, caressing melody of a Viennese waltz touched by maestro artists. . . . Behind them, the milk-white Casino outlined with golden lights. . . . And behind again, the steep, scarped ramparts of mountain that take the Principality under their protection and hold it nestling in their arms against the winds and snows of the North. A picture of fairyland—a wonder of the world.

The Minister had thrown aside his air of casual, dilettante idling. He was now talking very slowly and seriously: ". . . You can indeed do me a service—a great service. And, much more, a service to France and to the Entente which binds your country and mine together. The matter is delicate in the extreme." He paused.

"You have my entire discretion."

"That goes without saying, my dear Doctor." Again he paused in deliberation, and then plunged suddenly into the heart of his subject: "France is being betrayed. For some time past we have been preparing a secret re-organisation of the Navy in preparation for certain eventualities which I need not detail. Our plans must of course be known to the world later on, but at the moment it is vital that they should be kept secret. Yet we have information that they are being sold to a foreign power. And we want to know by whom, to whom, and how. We *must* know."

Dr. Wycherley drew back a little. "Before you proceed further, my dear Morèze, how is such a matter in my province? I am not a detective, but a psychologist."

"That is the very reason why I come to you. The detective work is done, and in any case I should not dream of asking a distinguished scientist to undertake work of that kind. We know this: that the information is being sold from Toulon, by someone in the personnel of the Navy. That has been deduced by a process of elimination. We suspect this: that it is being sold to the Countess Varoczy. We are entirely ignorant of this: how she communicates it to the foreign power in question."

Dr. Wycherley was rolling a second cigarette for himself, left-handedly and with wonderful deftness, for he never even glanced at the operation of his hands. He had trained himself to an unusual independent executive power of the rarely-used half of the cerebral hemisphere. He replied:

"But there are dozens of possible ways—code letters, telegrams, messengers."

"The Monaco police have worked in conjunction with ours. They have not been hampered by scruples. They have opened her letters, altered the wording of her telegrams, spied on almost her every movement, bribed her chauffeur, even burgled her villa in the olive-groves above the town." He pointed to the lights dotting the dark mountainside.

"Wireless telegraphy?"

She has no apparatus. In any case our own installations have been ordered to watch for and pick up any messages."

"By water?"

"We have a spy on her yacht."

"By private interviews?"

The Minister drew out a paper from an inner pocket and un-folded it. "Here is a list of the people who have visited her during the last three weeks. There may be amongst them one who *gives* . . ." There was a note of steel in his voice. ". . . but so far as our suspicions go, not one who *takes*."

He handed the list to Dr. Wycherley, who ran his eye over it non-committally. The Minister continued: "You will see there, re-peated frequently, the names of De Carteret, lieutenant; Falempin, captain of marines; Goncourt, also captain of marines; even Rocanier, rear admiral commanding the cruiser squadron. In Eng-land, my dear Doctor, your people would doubtless hold up their hands in horror at the idea of their naval officers buzzing around a very notorious and very fascinating lady, but that is a matter in which we are happily more tolerant. The moral aspect does not concern us. You will find also the names of many people well-known in what you would call our 'smart set.' . . . But the list does not help us until we know this for certain: does the Countess re-ceive the information, and if so, how does she pass it on? Possibly, I am almost inclined to doubt if she is the intermediary, and so, I have come to Monte Carlo to observe her for myself. Our police suspicions may be entirely wrong; if so, we are wasting time and effort which is vital for the welfare of France. . . . Now, my dear Doctor, for the sake of my country and the sake of the Entente, will you give me your help?"

"How—in what way?"

"You are a psychologist—a mind-reader. I know of your won-derful gift. . . ."

Dr. Wycherley interrupted him with a gesture. "Do not exag-gerate my powers. I am no worker of miracles. The psychic sense is with me only developed to a limited degree. As a Welsh lad, a patient of mine who also possessed the gift, once said: 'The minds of men to-day are like clouded glass.' That expresses it exactly. Sometimes a mind lights up with ardent thought, and one can then read clearly the shadows on the glass; sometimes one can only de-duce from a vague shifting blur. There you have the reason why I am still studying the ways in which men's minds work—so that the vague blurs may tell me so much of a man's inner life as a few lines and bands in a spectrum will tell an astronomer of the life of a distant star. My psychic gift, to accept the analogy, is a very rough and imperfect human spectroscope, and I am still at work on the meanings of the lines and bands."

"Perhaps in this case . . . ?"

"It is just possible. I cannot guarantee success, but I will make the attempt."

"A thousand thanks, my dear Doctor!"

The doctor took out his smoking materials and proceeded to roll himself a third cigarette. But this time he placed two cigarette papers end to end, so that the resulting product was nearly double the ordinary length. Then he lighted it and held it at arm's length, about knee-high, and proceeded to fix his gaze on it.

M. Morèze had been watching this strange proceeding with a very lively interest. "May I ask what you are about to do?"

"I am going to hypnotise myself. . . . The point is here: for some considerable time this evening I have been observing the Countess. That was fortunate for the purpose of this experiment, because I was then entirely neutral and unbiased. If I went to observe her again, I should inevitably be biased by what you have told me. . . . You know, of course, that what one consciously observes is perhaps only a twentieth part of what one sees and hears subconsciously. I am now going to try to recover the other nineteen-twentieths of my sensory impressions."

"Am I to wake you later on?"

"No, when the cigarette burns down to my fingers it will wake me automatically."

He fixed his gaze intently on the glowing end of the cigarette, and presently his eyes closed in a light hypnoidal sleep.

* * * * *

The ash dropped off at intervals as the fire burnt slowly through the tobacco, and when at length the cigarette was down to a stump the heat burnt the doctor's fingers and he awoke with a start.

"What results?" asked the Minister.

The doctor did not reply for nearly a quarter of an hour. He was obviously concentrating intently on what had passed through his mind during sleep. At length he answered: "I see possibilities. Let us go back to the tables. By the way, who was that young fellow by her side?"

"De Carteret, lieutenant on *La Patrie*. The cruiser squadron is now lying at Villefranche, within half-an-hour by train from here. De Carteret is from Normandy, and I will tell you frankly that I do not trust him far. We Frenchmen have an expression, *'fin normand.'*"

"Rear-Admiral Rocanier I have seen in the Casino. He is an oldish man, rather bent and worn, with a scraggy grey beard, is it not so?"

"Precisely."

"Falempin and Goncourt?"

"Just now I believe they are at Toulon. I could have you meet them if you wished."

"Good! Now to the tables."

When they entered the Salon Privé they found that the crowd had melted away from around the table of the Countess. She was now playing rather soberly, staking on black and red and on four or six or eight numbers at a time—*carré* and *transversale* play.

They watched her in silence from a distance, and then Dr. Wycherley remarked suddenly: "I think I should like to try my luck at the tables."

The Minister looked at him in unconcealed surprise. "But I understood you made it a rule not to gamble?"

"I never make rigid rules for myself—life is too complex. Come and help me to collect my winnings, or finance me if I lose too much. I have an idea that my lucky numbers will turn up."

"*Your* lucky numbers!"

"Yes, 13 is one of them. I think I shall stake on 13."

There was a vacant seat at the Countess's table, and Dr. Wycherley took possession of it. As he had indicated, he laid his first stake, a five-franc piece, on the number 13 *en plein*.

By an extraordinary coincidence it won at the first attempt.

"Beginner's luck!" commented the Minister, standing at Dr. Wycherley's side. Young De Carteret, looking up, recognised and bowed to him with empressement. He gave a curious glance, too, at the doctor, a strange figure for a gambler with his silvery hair and the fine face of a man who had given his life to science and humanity. The Countess Varoczy, who had lost on the *coup*, also looked at him with curiosity as the croupier counted out thirty-five times his stake in gold and silver and passed it over to him. But the doctor asked for all in silver—five-franc pieces.

Then, very deliberately, he laid a silver piece on 23, on 4, on 8, and two pieces on 19.

The roulette ball tumbled into compartment 11, and his stakes were swept away.

For the next *coup* he selected 0 for a five-franc piece, 11 for two five-franc pieces, and again 4 and 19.

"You think 11 will come up twice running?" whispered the Minister. "It seems improbable."

"I have a strong feeling it will come up again," answered Dr. Wycherley, and, strangely enough, he proved to be right.

"What extraordinary luck! You almost tempt me to follow your lead!"

"Now to concentrate on the lucky numbers."

"Which are they?"

"13, 23 and 0, 23 being the day of the month."

For a dozen *coups* or more he kept staking on those three numbers, together with sundry bets on black and red and on *transversales*. His curious deliberateness, coupled with his personality of the scientist, made the onlookers think that he was perhaps a mathematician with a new and infallible system, and some of them, including the Countess, began to follow his lead.

But capricious Fortune seemed to have tired of her protégé, and after various ups and downs of luck he finally found himself with but a single five-franc piece remaining out of all his winnings.

"I think I shall stop now," he remarked.

"You ought to have stopped after your second win *en plein*," answered M. Morèze as they made their way out. "Such luck was far too good to continue."

"I am quite satisfied. I have had my little gamble without expense. Now I am beginning to think that roulette is a much more interesting game than I had imagined."

"You have tasted blood!" laughed the Minister. Then he added very seriously, when they were out of earshot of the loungers in the Casino atrium: "What deductions have you made?"

"I would prefer not to speak until I am sure. Please do me this favor: invite the Countess to dine with you to-morrow evening at your villa, and myself also."

"My dear Doctor! Invite a lady I have never met to dine with me, a bachelor and a Minister, at my villa!"

Dr. Wycherley smiled. "With your diplomatic gifts, you will be able to find an excuse for the invitation that will make it appear the most natural thing in the world."

"You set me a problem indeed!"

"And so I enlist your professional interest. Come, you are not to be beaten by a problem in diplomacy!"

The Minister stopped in thought. "I will go back and get an introduction through De Carteret, if you will excuse me."

"Certainly. And please extend a pressing invitation also to De Carteret, Rocanier, Falempin and Goncourt. This is vital."

"Your methods are beyond me, but I will do as you say."

"My methods are open for all the world to read," answered the doctor with his gentle cynicism. "That is why they are so obscure."

THE NUMBER 13

Dr. Wycherley arrived early at the Villa Felicité at Beaulieu. The Minister met him with an open telegram in his hand. "The Countess accepted my invitation last night," he said, "but just an hour ago I received this wire to say that she is suddenly indisposed and begs to be excused."

"Capital!" answered Dr. Wycherley.

"I don't follow you!"

"Beaulieu is well beyond the frontier of the Principality of Monaco, you will note."

M. Morèze looked at him searchingly, perplexity in his eyes. "Have you seen her or met her since last night, or written to her?"

"No, to all those questions. I had an entirely different piece of work on hand—a Monaco doctor I know called me in to help him with a case of his, a Monegasque tradesman with a most extraordinary hallucination of touch. An extremely interesting case. The real cause of the trouble was far removed from the sensory hallucination. We employed the technique of psycho-analysis, and . . . but this would scarcely interest you."

The Minister regarded the doctor somewhat coldly. "Where the safety of France is concerned . . ." he began.

"Please do not imagine I am neglecting the work I had promised to help you with. I had set matters in train, and there was nothing further for me to do until this morning. I hope all four of the naval men will be here to-night."

"All four have accepted. I made the invitation seem as if it had an importance beyond mere sociability."

"Capital! Now, my dear Morèze, if you will allow me, I will go round your garden. Trees are one of my hobbies, and I think I see some fine specimens. What is that strange dwarf tree over there— the leaves are just peeping over the camellia bushes? The scent from it is to me peculiarly attractive."

"It is from Indo-China. I shall have to ask my gardener to tell you the name of it."

"By the way, have you an atlas in your smoking-lounge?"

"In my study I have one."

"Please do me the favor of having it moved to the smoking-lounge. And, for another point, after I have brought the conversation round to the atlas and have threshed out my point in connection with it, will you be good enough to refer to my gift of mind-reading? In the ordinary way I greatly dislike having this exaggerated, but for to-night there are special reasons. And as you know, I do not allow myself to be tied by rigid rules."

"You certainly had beginner's luck at the tables!" answered the Minister, taking the allusion. "But you ought to have stopped at your second win *en plein*. Ah, if we only knew the moment when to stop!"

Dr. Wycherley turned away to examine the dwarf tree with the strange new scent.

Goncourt and Falempin arrived together, having come by the same train. During dinner the doctor carefully observed them as well as the other two, Rocanier and De Carteret, making his quiet deductions and conclusions.

Captain Falempin was a man who spoke little and drank little— an elderly young man who had mastered the art of taking more than he gave. Goncourt, on the other hand, was somewhat flamboyant and Southern in his exuberance, and as the wine passed round he opened his mind freely on any subject that cropped up.

Not until they were all settled in the smoking-lounge over cigars and liqueurs did Dr. Wycherley begin to take command of the conversation, and then it was by a most unexpected turn. He was standing in the open doorway, profile to the rest, a clean-cut silhouette against the lighted veranda. He said very deliberately:

"You Frenchmen are the most inhumane of the civilised nations."

There was an instant chorus of surprise, of dissent, of challenge.

"To prove my point, I need only refer to your penal system. You have abolished the guillotine, and what have you substituted? Penal servitude in the most deadly climates in the world, under conditions of living that are practically inhuman tortures."

"But they have their chance!" protested Goncourt. "In about fifteen years they are released, if their conduct has been good."

"Do any of you know that the death-rate in Guiana amongst the hard labour prisoners is over 10 per cent per annum?" pursued the doctor remorselessly. He picked up an atlas and rapidly turned over the leaves until he had come to a map of the Caribbean Sea, which he laid open on a table before them.

"Here is your French Guiana—one of the most pestilential swamps in the world. Mosquitoes by the myriad; manioc ants avid for human flesh; the *chiques* that burrow under the skin and cause tortures of itching; a score of other insect plagues; and then malaria, dysentery, and yellow fever. Fifteen years! Why, less than ten years is a man's life in penal servitude in Guiana. Ten years of daily, hourly torture!"

His voice had risen in hot indignation. "And then, worse, your Devil's Isle for a traitor—imprisonment for the term of his natural life. Not even the poor ghost of illusory hope that some day release might come! Dreyfus once talked to me of his five years on the Devil's Isle—it made me shudder as no hospital or prison sight has ever done. It was an absolute miracle of will-power that he managed to keep his reason."

"There is no one there now," put in Falempin. (This was some years before Ulmo was sent to life imprisonment on the Isle for selling State secrets.)

"No . . . but it is waiting. And if it were in my power to hand the vilest wretch in the world over to the mercies of your French law, I doubt if I could bring myself to do so!"

There was silence in the room. The Minister struck a match to light a fresh cigar, and the splutter of it cut fiercely into the silence.

Then Dr. Wycherley closed the atlas and returned to his place by the doorway, profile in silhouette—the splendid profile of a man who had given his life to science and humanity.

M. Morèze turned the subject abruptly. "I wonder if you know of the doctor's extraordinary power of mind-reading," he said. "He dislikes to mention it himself, but I have seen him do marvelous things in that direction."

"Do you mean under hypnotism?" asked the Admiral. "That is believable."

"No, just in ordinary life. While we have been sitting here, who knows but what he may have been reading all our inmost thoughts?"

"I confess myself a sceptic. One cannot believe that kind of thing without first-hand evidence."

"Doctor, will you give us a demonstration?" pursued the Minister. "And who will volunteer for the experiment?"

"Thanks!" answered Goncourt with emphatic meaning. "Drag out our little love affairs into the indecent light of day—thanks!" There was a general laugh at this, and the tension was broken.

From the doorway Dr. Wycherley said dreamily:

"As a scientist I read the thoughts of others, and as a humanitarian I keep my knowledge to myself."

Later in the evening, as the party broke up, Rear-Admiral Rocanier offered Dr. Wycherley a lift in his motor-car back to Monte Carlo.

"Many thanks," answered the doctor. And presently: "Shall we take the upper Corniche? There is a glorious view from the hills on such a night as this." And presently again: "I should like to take a rough sketch of this view. Shall we stop for a few moments?"

The Admiral's hand trembled as he grasped his cane, and he drew his cloak around him as though the warm night-air were chilly.

"You are cold," said Dr. Wycherley after a little while. "As a doctor I suggest to you a short, brisk walk. If the car were sent on, we might rejoin it."

And then, walking side by side in the black, velvety night, the mental healer waited patiently for the moment when the Admiral should confess to him.

Three days later M. Morèze asked Dr. Wycherley with veiled impatience whether he had not anything to report, for in the meanwhile the doctor had given no word of his deductions or suspicions.

"It is all settled," answered the doctor, very simply.

"All settled!"

"Yes. Acting in your name, I have ventured to allow the Countess Varoczy twenty-four hours in which to leave the Principality of Monaco and get over the Italian frontier."

"And she has taken your orders?" asked the Minister in blank surprise.

"Otherwise it would have been very uncomfortable for her. Monaco has only an area of a few square miles, and any short motor-ride would have taken her into French territory, where she might have been liable to arrest. She was wise to take my warning."

"But, but—the man? *Who is the man?*"

"I have no intention of revealing his name. Believe me, my dear Morèze, when I say that France has nothing to fear from him. To that I pledge my word."

"Keep a traitor in our Navy? Unthinkable!"

"I have never said that he was of the personnel of your Navy. The list you gave me included a wide range of names."

"But I insist on knowing!"

"So that you may have him sent to the Devil's Isle? No—not through my agency. It is precisely at this point that my professional cold-bloodedness ends and your professional cold-bloodedness begins. You set me a problem in practical psychology which interested me greatly, and I have been fortunate enough to solve it. If I have done any service to France, the knowledge of having done so is sufficient reward for me."

"But your methods of solving it?"

"To tell you that now would be to incriminate the man . . . or woman. Some day, perhaps, when the matter is dead and forgotten—

458   MAX RITTENBERG

if you are then still interested. I admit that then you would be fully entitled to know."

*   *   *   *   *

The occasion came sooner than the doctor had foreseen. Rear-Admiral Rocanier had gone to his death like a brave man during the wreck of *La Patrie* on the cliffs of Majorca, in that memorable gale of November 19th, eight months later. Under seal of confidence, that his memory might not be blackened to his descendants, Dr. Wycherley revealed the full story to the Minister for Foreign Affairs.

"He was infatuated with the Countess with the blind infatuation of an old man. In a young man duty and ambition may together turn the scale against the madness of desire, but in an old man who has reached to his highest post and has no spur of ambition, duty is a poor counterweight. Naturally, with a woman such as the Countess Varoczy, there was a heavy price to pay, and his madness of desire drove him to pay it. He gave me his word, after that evening at your villa, that he would break with his passion and give ample recompense to his country, and I knew that he was speaking from his heart."

"But how did you discover all this?"

"Through the number 13."

"Please explain."

"You remember that on the terrace at Monte Carlo I hypnotised myself in order to recover my full impressions of the Countess. The dominant impression that kept forcing itself upon me was the psychological strangeness of her plunge to the limit on the number 13. In my sleep I went through every play that I had seen her make that evening, *coup* after *coup*, and never once before or again had I seen her stake *en plein* on number 13.

"There must have been some strong reason for that unnatural bet, and I set myself to analyse all possible motives, eliminating them one after another in methodical, scientific fashion. And then suddenly I came to the obvious truth."

"That. . . ."

"That roulette might be a much more interesting game than I had imagined. That it presents the most perfect opportunity for the exchange of cipher messages that one could possibly wish for. Consider. On the green cloth are marked thirty-seven numbers, from 0 to 36 inclusive. That gives you in code your twenty-six letters of the alphabet, your ten numerals, and one number in excess. The number to be eliminated from the code would evidently be the unlucky number 13, and if it were used it must have some very special significance. Now M happens to be the thirteenth letter of the alphabet, and M is the initial letter of your own name. . . ."

"You mean that she was staking out a code message about myself when she plunged to the limit on 13!" interrupted M. Morèze, startled out of himself.

"Precisely. I called back from the storehouse of my memories the other numbers on which she staked *en plein* while we were watching her together, and they pieced together into a flippantly contemptuous message in regard to yourself."

"The devil! What was the message?"

"We need not enter into that. But you can imagine her malicious pleasure in piecing out the message under your very nose. Under the full glare of the lamplight, with a crowd of people watching her every movement, with you yourself keenly studying her!"

The Minister's mouth tightened with suppressed anger. Few men can rise superior to ridicule—especially the ridicule of a woman. He remarked abruptly: "It was a dangerous game to play!"

"I do not agree, my dear Morèze. While your detectives and spies were opening her letters, altering her telegrams, eavesdropping on her private conversations, and even burgling her private bureau, she was in the habit of calmly passing on her information under the full glare of the lamplight, openly for anyone to read. It is the most conventional, the most undangerous form of audacity."

"To whom did she pass it on?"

"Who can say? In that cosmopolitan crowd around the tables it might have been any man or woman. I deduced at once that the code would have to be a very simple one, easily carried in mind, because the accomplice could not dare to take written notes of a cipher message with a dozen people looking over his shoulder. Its simplicity would not endanger its security, for who would guess in the first place that her wild gambling was merely the tapping out of a code message? The alphabet ran from 0 to 26 excluding 13, your special number—and 27 to 36 stood for the ten numerals. Any by-play on *carres, transversales, colonnes* or *chances simples* would be ignored in reading the messages.

"So I returned with you to the tables to play back her code on her. I started, you may remember, with a stake on the number 13, which by pure chance happened to win; I continued, when I saw that I had her attention, with 23, 4, 8 and double 19; I followed it with 0, double 11, 4 and 19. That formed the message 'M. weiss alles,' 'Morèze knows all.'

"Now came the crucial moment: how would she take it? Without a word spoken, without a gesture exchanged, there took place a very pretty bout of thought-fencing. While her face remained a cold mask, her mind was buzzing with perplexity. In my mental spectroscope I saw, so to speak, the lines and bands that I have long since learnt to correlate with perplexity. Her thoughts probably ran in some such fashion as this: Who is that strange old man playing my code? Is he friend or enemy? Is it a bluff or a warning? He seems to be very friendly with Morèze. Or is his staking a matter of pure chance?

"She gave no answer, so I began to hammer home my message, 13, 23, 0—M, w, a. . . 13, 23, 0—M, w, a. . . 13, 23, 0—M, w, a. . . until I had it driven in right on the nerve. Still she was suspicious, and when her answer was at length wrung out of her it was noncommittal—merely a repetition on her part of my M, w, a. But that was sufficient for my purpose, and I then had you invite her to dinner at your villa. That move must again have caused her acute perplexity."

"For a moment she hesitated perceptibly, but she recovered almost at once and accepted rather gushingly," answered the Minister.

"With a woman of that kind, her first thoughts would naturally be for her own safety. She suspected a trap. So she accepted, and then found a convenient indisposition the next day. That placed the matter beyond a doubt. . . . The rest was simple. Probably she had the decency to pass on a warning to the Admiral, and that, coupled with our conversation in your smoking-lounge, drove him inevitably to confession."

The Minister thought in silence for a few moments. Then he said: "I am glad, now, that you would not give up his name. As you said, a keen professional man is always cold-blooded in the exercise of his lifework. I did not appreciate your point of view at the time, but I do now. . . . By the way, your service to France has not yet been suitably rewarded. What honour can I bestow on you? I know that money is out of the question with you, but possibly there is some decoration?"

Dr. Wycherley smiled cordially. "Many thanks, my dear Morèze, but I am going to ask for something much more valuable to me."

"Anything whatever in my power to give. Gladly!"

"That rare tree of yours from Indo-China. I have been coveting it shamelessly. If you could have it transplanted to my garden on Isola Salvatore. . . ?"

"THEY SAY SHE IS BEWITCHED"

She was climbing painfully on her knees the long flight of stone steps that leads from the Grotto of the Vision of Bernadette up to the great double Basilique of Lourdes. With her, helping and encouraging, was her parish priest, Père Bonivet.

"Courage, my child, and faith!" he was whispering. "Have faith, and all will be well. Only faith in Our Lady can cure you."

Out of the crowd of the sick and the dying that had come to Lourdes—the lame, the blind, the palsied, the epileptic, the tuberculous, the cancerous—this peasant girl had above all attracted the attention of Dr. Wycherley. He was there in pursuit of his life-study, psychological research, for at Lourdes there gather, a great multitude of those who are sick in mind. Apart from his study of the cures that earnest faith brings to pass at the Shrine of Notre Dame de Lourdes, many of his previous cases had been garnered there—cases where faith had been powerless to heal the injured mind.

This young peasant girl, scarcely more than a child, now on her knees on the long flight of stone steps, had attracted Dr. Wycherley's attention above all the rest. There was that in her face that lifted her out of the ruck of peasants. Not the beauty of her features, nor her soft, liquid eyes, nor her raven-black hair was it that first caught the attention of the observer, but the spiritual light in her soul that shone through her face as a light shines through wax.

She might have posed as a model for a Joan of Arc when the call first came to her at Domrémy.

Dr. Wycherley watched the girl and the priest on their painful climb to the Basilique, as he had watched them on many days previously; he waited outside the church until they came from their long devotions. In Père Bonivet's face was a look of deep disappointment; in the eyes of the girl was a hardened look, a glitter that had not been there before. The light on her soul no longer shone clear—it was as though a marsh mist had dimmed it with a clammy film.

As the priest was hurrying her to their temporary home in the town, Dr. Wycherley raised his hat and addressed him.

"*Mon père*," he said, "I ask your pardon for this intrusion if it is unwelcome. But I, like yourself, do my humble best to help the weak and the suffering, and I see clearly that your pilgrimage to Lourdes has not brought the benefit you hoped for mademoiselle."

"We must be patient. In God's good time He will vouchsafe His mercies," returned the priest. "But I thank you. I see that you have the good heart."

"If you should need me. . . ." said Dr. Wycherley, and wrote the name of his hotel on his card. Père Bonivet took the card and thanked him courteously.

On the evening of the next day the priest called on Dr. Wycherley in anxious distress of mind.

"I have come," he said, "because I fear that this case is beyond my powers. It may be that I am unworthy—that my soul is too stained with the cares and pettinesses of this world to take my prayers before the Most High. To-night I can do nothing with Jeanne. She has blasphemed against the Holy Name. She will not listen to me! It is terrible, pitiable! And," he lowered his voice to an impressive whisper, "the mark of the beast is coming upon her!" He shuddered at his own words.

Dr. Wycherley drew a chair forward for Père Bonivet. "Will you not sit down and tell me the trouble of mademoiselle? I have studied many cases of diseased mind, and it may be my knowledge can help. She is *hystérique*, is it not so?"

"So the doctor has told us, but in the Landes, where Jeanne Dorthez lives and where I go about the work of my Master, the peasants give it another name—a very terrible name. They say she is possessed—bewitched!

"Myself I believe nothing of that," added the priest hastily. "I am of the modern school, and such things belong to the superstitions of the Middle Ages. So I laid the case of Jeanne Dorthez before Monseigneur the Bishop, and he advised me to take her on a pilgrimage to Lourdes. Out of his own purse our good bishop gave the money that was necessary for us, for Jeanne is but a poor peasant girl, the daughter of a woodcutter of the Landes, and myself I have little to spare."

"If they say she is bewitched, then they must have in mind some man or woman on whom they place suspicion of sorcery."

"You are right, monsieur. They say that Osper Camargo has bewitched her. They whisper many terrible things of Osper Camargo, that he is in league with the Evil One; but you and I, should we put belief in the superstitious chatter of peasants?"

The mental healer did not answer this. "Jeanne is a good girl," he said; "it is plain for all to read. When her attacks come upon her, she changes in mind, is it not so?"

"She changes terribly. To-night she blasphemed against the Holy Name. I greatly fear that she may lose her reason."

"What other signs?"

"Of course, monsieur, it is nonsense what I have now to tell you. But one day the women of the village forced her to be examined, and they whisper that upon her they found places where the prick of a pin was not felt!"

"Those places were of a definite and regular shape?"

"How did monsieur guess? Yes. The shape of the pentacle—that is what they whisper. The doctor at Mont de Marsan could find nothing, and myself I did not believe it. But to-night I have seen the mark of the beast upon her! Red upon her breast!" Again he shuddered, and crossed himself hastily.

Dr. Wycherley looked very thoughtful. "Let us go to see Jeanne," he suggested, and from a traveling medicine-chest slipped a few phials into his pocket.

The girl was lodging near at hand, and in a few minutes they had arrived at the house, a humble dwelling in a little back street of the town. When they were a few yards from the door the figure of a man slipped out quickly from the threshold and into the darkness of an alleyway.

The priest started back. "For a moment I thought that was Osper Camargo! But the light is tricky in this narrow ruelle."

"He has a scrawny beard and a pair of evil-looking eyes?" asked Dr. Wycherley.

"Camargo has that and a nose crushed by the fall of a pine-tree upon his face. It was at the time of the accident—many years ago now—that he ceased to attend Mass, and after that he gradually became feared by the villagers. But of course it could not be Camargo, for he is far from here in the salt-marshes of the Landes. There would be no reason why he should come to Lourdes."

The woman who opened the door to them put her finger to her lips. "S'sh, *mon père*, she is at last asleep! It was with difficulty that we could quiet her."

They moved softly upstairs to the room, and at Dr. Wycherley's request the woman turned back the bed clothes and opened the girl's nightgown.

Above and between her breasts, distinct and unmistakable, was an angry reddish patch of the shape of a pentacle.

"Last night I saw it for the first time!" whispered the woman, with horror in her voice. "To-night it is much redder! Monsieur le Curé, Monsieur le Docteur, what can it mean?"

Jeanne stirred in her sleep, and in her sleep murmured: "I will come. Oh, cease to torment me, for I will come!"

Dr. Wycherley stayed the night through in the girl's room, watching and studying her. Outside the window the Gave de Pau roared unceasingly down its torrential bed. There was menace in its voice.

*   *   *   *   *

Jeanne awoke in the morning with a curious dull glaze in her eyes. She expressed a strong desire to return home to her hamlet of Aureilhac, in spite of the counsels of Père Bonivet still to have patience and faith.

He appealed to Dr. Wycherley, but the latter drew him aside and suggested earnestly: "Let Jeanne have her way, *mon père*. I think it will be for the best. . . . It is upon your lips to tell me that if she will only have faith enough, she will be cured. Yes, but she has not the faith; she has lost heart. . . . Now you are about to ask me what can be hoped for if the pilgrimage to Lourdes has failed."

"You read my thoughts, monsieur!" said the priest in surprise.

"And you, *mon père*, read mine, for you see that I wish for Jeanne only what will be for her good."

"Yes, yes. But if she goes back to the Landes with her faith broken, who can save her from madness? I, alas, am not worthy to do this work for my Master—that I bow my head in sorrow to acknowledge."

"We must work together; I will return with you."

"But her father, Pierre Dorthez, is only a poor woodcutter. In the Landes we are all poor. How could we pay you, monsieur? No doubt you would need many francs—perhaps many hundred francs." To his simple mind the sum loomed vast.

"*Mon père*, you and I have both learnt that the true money lies in the grateful hearts of men and women."

The priest raised his hand in benediction. "I know not if you are of our faith, monsieur, but may the blessing of God be upon you!"

They traveled by slow, cross-country trains to the village of Labouheyre in the middle of the Landes district. It was a hot and sultry day, and the hundred-mile train journey seemed interminable.

Beyond Dax they had come into the true Landes country—great silent pine-forests alternating with wide stretches of sedgy marshland. At Labouheyre their arrival was unexpected, but one of the villagers at once offered to drive them in his ox-cart to Aureilhac. It was an honour to do a service for Père Bonivet.

But Dr. Wycherley noted that the villager took care that Jeanne should not touch him even with her garment.

The two oxen drew them along the great silent highway that runs, level and straight, northwards to Bordeaux, stone-paved like the streets of a town to bear the weight of the lumbering timber-wagons. The oxen plodded along with the slow patience which is theirs.

The silence of the great forest fell upon them. Even in the full light of the afternoon the sombre forest carried something of the grim and awesome. No wonder that for the simple peasants there were still spirits of evil that lurked in its shadows and on Midsummer Eve gathered together for unholy revels out in the marsh of Arjuzanx.

From time to time they would pass a solitary goat-herd lying down on his rough skin coat and dully guarding his little flock of long-haired goats. Once they caught sight of the local postman making his round on the stilts of the Landes to the outlying huts and farms, separated by stretches of marshland impassable on foot.

The ox-cart turned off the highway into a forest track deep-rutted from its winter traffic of heavy timber-wagons. The forest took them to its sombre heart. A grey film began to spread across the sky, shutting out the sunlight. But still it was hot and oppressive.

Late in the afternoon they reached the hamlet of Aureilhac—a few low-roofed wooden houses in a clearing where lean hens scratched for food. Pierre Dorthez, returning from his day's work in the forest, raised his hat to Père Bonivet and greeted them dully. He said little, either of comment or question, but ordered Jeanne to make ready a dinner for the visitors. Himself he would kill a fowl and gather vegetables for the soup.

As the girl set about her work, Dr. Wycherley watched her keenly from his seat in the kitchen that served also as living-room. She was intent on her duties by the *pot-au-feu*, but there was a suppressed excitement underlying her that showed in the twitchings of her hands and the pallor of her face. It was no longer translucent in its whiteness, but of a dull and clammy pallor like the colour of a marsh mist. And in her eyes there was once more the hard glitter. Now and again she would secretly put her hand to her bosom as though to satisfy herself that something of value hidden beneath her dress was still there.

When the simple dinner was over, Dr. Wycherley drew Père Bonivet aside.

"Where does this Osper Camargo live?" he asked. "I wish to see him."

"But surely you do not believe in these superstitions of the ignorant peasants, monsieur?"

"In my studies I have met many strange things, and I try to keep the open mind. I would see this man for myself."

"He lives in a solitary hut out on the marshes on the marsh of Arjuzanx. But do not go to-night, for the way is treacherous!"

"I must go to-night, *mon père*—or it may be too late. Can one of the villagers show me the path?"

"At night-time they would not dare to."

"Can I find it for myself?"

"On the stilts there are many paths, but on foot only one that is safe. If you are determined to go, I must lead you there myself."

"Thank you—I accept your help willingly. But I shall ask you to return without me and keep guard over Jeanne while I am away."

The last gleams of the setting sun shone from between an angry bank of clouds as they came out of the forest on to the marshland. The pools, stagnant with slime, turned to blood, then grew dark and chill.

"It may be a bad night, monsieur," said the priest warningly. "See how the clouds have massed in the west, over the Bay of Biscay!"

"If necessary, I will spend the night with Osper Camargo," answered Dr. Wycherley quietly.

A tortuous path amongst the firmer parts of the marshland brought them within sight of a low hut. It was surrounded by a few stunted trees on ground a little above the general level. Around them again were the dark sedges, whispering amongst themselves, and the chill, dank pools of slime. A marsh bird called to its mate with a strange, eerie cry.

"Is the way straight from here onwards?" asked Dr. Wycherley at length.

"Yes, you have but to follow the path. Only be careful that you sound around you with your stick should the foot tread on ground that gives."

"Then I would ask you to return at once to guard Jeanne. If necessary, give her bromide from the tablets in this phial. See to it that she does not leave the house to-night. *Au revoir, mon père.*"

THE HUT ON THE MARSH

The hut was silent and lightless. After knocking at the door fruitlessly, Dr. Wycherley lifted the latch and entered. It was empty save for a lean grey cat that arched her back and spat at him. The bigger of the two rooms, serving as kitchen and bedroom, showed by small signs that it had been unoccupied for days. There was nothing to be done but to wait for the return of the owner, for no one at Aureilhac had been able to tell of his movements.

It was a lonesome, weary vigil. The cat, refusing overtures of friendship, had stalked out into the night. The clock over the fireplace was silent, for it had run down during the owner's absence. Around the room were tokens that this Osper Camargo worked on the superstitions of his neighbours, for conspicuous on the walls were a human skull, dead bats nailed up with outspread wings, snakes and blind-worms preserved in spirit, and other devices common to sorcerers of all ages. A heavy locked chest doubtless contained more of his paraphernalia.

But to Dr. Wycherley the most significant object in the room was hung above the bed where the peasant of the Landes would place his crucifix.

It was a small pentacle in hammered iron.

For many hours the doctor waited patiently in the lightless hut. For times such as this he had trained himself to a habit of deep thought that lost count of place and time, but yet was alert to the least unusual sign. He had made his brain his servant to an extent far beyond the usual with men.

His thoughts ran on the records in hieroglyphic that have come down to us of the sorcerers of ancient Egypt, the men who claimed that they could use the gods to work their will. He had spent many interesting hours with Professor Clovis Marnier, the great Egyptologist, listening to his demonstration of the meaning of the hieroglyphs.

There was a sound out, of the darkness—a plash in a distant pool. At the instant his watchful senses had flashed the message to his brain, and he was awake and alert. But he kept still in his chair.

The sounds came nearer. The door opened, and a man entered with a lantern, under his arm a pair of stilts slimy from the marsh pools. Placing the lantern on a table, he began to lay sticks on the dead ashes of the hearth, the grey cat rubbing affectionately round: his legs. He had a ragged, scrawny beard and moustache, and his nose was crushed in the way Père Bonivet had described. A face with evil lines—an evil mind behind it.

He had not seen Dr. Wycherley. When at length he caught sight of him, sitting quietly, in the chair in a corner of the room, he started violently and called out in the harsh, twanging dialect of the Landes: "*Sangrediable*, get on your knees!"

The doctor made no reply, but sat still.

"Who are you?" cried Camargo, flashing the lantern upon him.

"Peace, brother!" answered Dr. Wycherley. "Peace to you in the names of Khabbakhel and Knouriphariza, our masters."

"But I don't know you! What are you doing here?"

"We have met in the plane of the spirit," answered Dr. Wycherley courteously. "Though I live afar off, I have long wished to visit you and learn of your wisdom."

The man was clearly puzzled. Suspicion lay behind his narrow eyes. And yet his vanity was touched. Dr. Wycherley had allowed no trace of irony or ridicule to appear in his words. They had a tone of grave deference in them.

Osper Camargo twisted his hands uneasily. Finally he hit on a satisfactory answer: "You want to buy wisdom from me—*hein?*"

"Come!" remonstrated the doctor. "Payment between brothers of the craft?"

"If you want to learn, you pay!"

"Very well," answered the doctor, with assumed reluctance, and drew out a gold piece from his pocket.

The man's eyes glittered cunningly.

"Not enough!"

"This I will give you beforehand, and again a louis when you have shown me what I do not know already." He showed a second gold piece.

"Do you know the incantation that brings the sickness upon the oxen? Or the incantation that drives the goats to madness? With them one can make money."

"Those," answered Dr. Wycherley, "are elementary. I had hoped to see bigger proof of your powers. Even in my land they speak of the spells you can lay on man or woman."

Osper Camargo's pride was awakened.

"They speak well, for I have those powers, and I use them. But," a cunning glitter came again into his eyes, "I work within the law. Whatever I do, it is such that the law cannot touch me. Oh, I am careful!"

"We have all to be prudent. A friend of mine, the great sorcerer Smith, doubtless you have heard of him, desired greatly a young girl of his neighbourhood, but she was of tender years, and the law of his country would not permit that he cast spells to bring her to his side. So he waited."

"As I have waited!" cried Camargo fiercely. "As I have waited these long years! If the mother would have none of me, the child shall—and willingly! It is my right! Everything is prepared!"

With a dramatic gesture he drew out a key from his pocket and opened the heavy oaken chest. The upper part of it was filled with dresses and dress material. There was silk and good cambric in the heap. He plunged his hands into it, fondling the garments, letting them rustle through his fingers.

"A fine trousseau for the bride," commented Dr. Wycherley. "She should be well pleased."

"A bride? Maybe yes or maybe no. Of one girl one may get tired. Why tie oneself up with the law?" He shut the lid of the chest and turned the key. "But that is not the only reason why I desire her. No, no. There is another reason, a stronger reason—a reason that you of the craft should well know!"

Now it was Dr. Wycherley's turn to be puzzled. He thought he had gauged the man's mainspring of action. His motive was surely horrible enough—what worse could lie behind? And yet it must be something within the law, for the man was plainly stating truth as to his devilish prudence.

To gain time, Dr. Wycherley asked: "What is her name?"

"Ask at Aureilhac," answered Camargo. "They will tell you quickly enough!"

There was a note of triumph in his tone that expressed the near fulfilment of his desire. From the law he had nothing to fear, for the law takes no cognizance of wizardry as such, and it was plain that he had no fear of man's intervention. Perhaps they could keep the girl away from his hut for a week, two weeks, a month even—but what of that? He had waited many long years. He could wait a little longer if necessary. Small wonder that Osper Camargo boasted openly of his desires.

"You do not know my second motive!" mocked the sorcerer.

Dr. Wycherley replied deferentially:

"No, I am but a learner at the craft, and you are a master. I have come from afar to drink of your wisdom."

"This much will I show you. To-day I procured it, and it completes the preparations that are necessary."

He flashed a small corked glass tube from his pocket, and quickly returned it to its shelter. In the fitful light from the lantern Dr. Wycherley could only gather the impression that it contained the dried ear of some cereal—barley or perhaps rye. It puzzled him still further. The thought of poison passed across his mind, but this he at once put aside. Osper Camargo was a coward at heart and would never risk the vengeance of the law in that way. But if not poison, what could it mean? A dried ear of barley—or perhaps rye.

"You speak of your powers," said Dr. Wycherley, "but you give me no proof. It may be that this girl is in love with you and will come willingly at your call."

"Ask at Aureilhac!" returned the sorcerer again, licking his lips. "Ask if she has been willing to come. But now I have her in my hands. When I crook my little finger, she will come."

From the west a flash of lightning filled the hut with light, showing with startling distinctness the fire of evil passion in the face of Osper Camargo.

"Shall I give you proof of my power?" he asked fiercely.

"For that I have journeyed from afar, and for that I will pay the further louis," returned the doctor.

The sorcerer set about his preparations quickly, while outside the storm gathered and the distant lightning flashed. First he lit a fire on the hearth and into it threw some powder that gave out a strong odour of balsam. Next he took down the small iron pentacle from its nail over the bed, and hung it by a string round the neck of the grey cat. Then he scattered sand on the floor, and on the sand traced a magical enclosure fringed with mystic signs. In the enclosure he placed a small iron vessel containing a slow-burning pastille with a pungent odour, and next to it a rough wax doll, which bore a certain resemblance to Jeanne Dorthez.

His preparations completed, the sorcerer began to recite strange incantations, swaying himself backwards and forwards in time to the words, beginning low and quietly and gradually working himself up to a pitch of hysterical frenzy. Finally he reached the stage where automatism of the lower centres holds sway in the brain. Writhing and foaming at the mouth, he fell in a fit upon the bed. After a little the jerking muscles quieted down; the sorcerer was in a trance.

Dr. Wycherley had watched with intense interest every detail of the fantastic operation, endeavouring to disentangle the essential and the significant from the gibberish of abracadabra and the puerilities of the wax doll. From the first there had been no doubt in his mind that this Osper Camargo was a dangerous man. The problem in hand was: how far did his powers in the realm of the supernormal extend?

The anesthetic patches on the body of Jeanne Dorthez which had seemed of such horrible significance to the goodwives of the neighbourhood—these were a not unusual symptoms of a patient suffering from hysteria. The shape of the patches was probably the result of a post-hypnotic suggestion; the red mark on the breast of the girl could be produced by the same means. At the Salpêtrière Hospital in Paris many such experiments have been carried out. Dr. Wycherley had no doubt whatever that this Osper Camargo had gained influence over her mind and had been working to bend it to his own will—the appearance on her body of the symbolic pentacle would react on her mind and convince her that she belonged to him, body and soul.

But how would Camargo bring her over the marshes that night? How far did his telepathic powers extend, if he possessed them at all?

Dr. Wycherley searched the room for some indication that might have escaped him, and suddenly he found it. It was a negative indication—during the rigamarole of the incantations and the rhythmic swayings the grey cat had slipped out of the room.

At once a vivid mental picture came before his eyes of the cat padding swiftly over the dark path through the marshes—through the forest to the hamlet of Aureilhac—reaching the low wooden house of the Dorthez—scratching at the bedroom window of the girl—Jeanne opening the window at the call and seeing the pentacle around its neck, the sign of her master—dressing swiftly and slipping out of the window—following it back to the marsh of Arjuzanx and the hut of the sorcerer.

How could he wrest the girl from the power of Osper Camargo? It would be difficult in the extreme. With her mind so under the power of the sorcerer, counter-suggestions might be of very little effect. Was there no way in which the law could step in, so that this man's power of working evil would be fettered?

Perhaps there might be some hope of this if he could discover the ulterior purpose at which Camargo had hinted. His eye turned to the oaken chest, and at once he went over to it. In his excitement, Camargo had forgotten to take away the key.

Dr. Wycherley swiftly opened it and turned over the pile of garments, seeking for something hidden in the box which might give him a clue to the great ulterior motive. His hand brushed against parchment, and he drew it out and took it over to the light—a parchment yellow with age and written in faded ink with words of French many centuries old. But it was possible to get its general purport, even if single words here and there conveyed no meaning:

The Potion
Of Which Whosoever Shall Drink Shall
Become Immortal.

It was a lengthy recipe full of such ingredients as the eyes of bats, the powdered forehand of a toad, broth of blindworms, and others nauseating in the extreme, but the culmination of the recipe sent a chill of horror coursing down the doctor's spine. Though he had watched by the bedside of raving madmen, he had never had to listen to imaginings so devilish as this. His eye ran over it hurriedly before he thrust it into his pocket to bring if necessary before a court of law:

". . . *a maiden undefiled, a first-born . . . when she is with child . . . an infusion of the spotted rye . . . the left eye and the right ear . . . see to it that you both drink the potion together. . . .*"

Dr. Wycherley realised as never before the feelings of our ancestors when, centuries ago, they had had to deal with the sorcerers of their age. Small wonder that they had lynched at the stake men who put into practice what had been written on this old parchment. Small wonder that in their zeal to stamp out such devilish imaginings, they had persecuted the innocent as well as the guilty.

Outside the lightning flashed and the thunder tore across the swishing rain, but through the noise Dr. Wycherley sensed a footstep. He moved towards the door, but at the same moment the man on the bed stirred and rose up. He, too, had sensed the presence outside, the presence for which he in his trance was feverishly waiting.

Osper Camargo thrust back the doctor and strode to fling open the door. And as he did so, as he stepped out of the threshold to lay hand on the girl who had come at the call of the grey cat, a blinding flash of lightning, followed on the instant by the roar of thunder from directly overhead, struck upon him.

The sorcerer staggered back, his hands to his eyes, moaning horribly.

Groping, he blundered about the room, and a torrent of blasphemies poured from his lips as he realised what had come upon him. Then, little by little, the stream of imprecations died down, and as the girl moved to his side, shivering in her sodden clothes, Osper cried out pitifully, in a voice so changed from his previous tone that Dr. Wycherley started at it: "Keep away from me, for I am accursed! The judgment of God is upon me. He has struck me blind for my sins!"

He fell on his knees, and as from a little child there came from him the prayer of the Paternoster. One of those strange instantaneous conversions, the rationale of which is so veiled from us, had been witnessed. For a long hour, until exhaustion set in, the sorcerer laid bare his soul before his Maker and prayed for forgiveness. Let it be granted to him that he should work out his salvation in the cell of a monk, sworn to perpetual silence, and he would be content.

* * * * *

When the morning broke through the grey mists of the marshes, Dr. Wycherley and Jeanne Dorthez were leading by the hand over the marsh-path a blind man who murmured continuously the prayers he had learnt in his youth.

Behind them smoke curled up from the hut of the sorcerer that was. Dr. Wycherley had set fire to it so that the ghastly tokens and records it contained might never fall into the hands of any human being.

A MAN'S HONOUR AT STAKE

It would be a second judgment of Paris to have to choose between the rival claims of Isola Salvatore in spring, in summer and in autumn. Dr. Wycherley made no such attempt. He was content to watch the changing seasons in his beloved garden with the feeling that each was bringing to him a new unfolding of his children, the trees and shrubs and flowers. They grew up around him revealing new beauties, more perfect beauties, with each succeeding year.

But he was never content to rest at Isola Salvatore with his garden, his laboratory and his splendid library of psychological science if any call came for his services from outside. His real laboratory was the whole civilised world. Sometimes he would travel to seek new cases; sometimes they would come to him at his London consulting-room or at his island home.

It was one May that Sir Christopher Hemmerde traveled to Lake Rovellasco in order to consult the mental healer. The two men were seated in the garden under the wide-spread branches of a cypress from Cashmere, its weeping foliage blue-green like some giant cyanophyllous seaweed. To one side was a clump of Japanese bamboo so delicately, so ethereally green as to vibrate with a song of youth eternal. Trailing high over a broad-leaved camphor tree from Celebes was a white Banksia rose in full flower, like a bevy of little children scrambling joyously over a good-natured uncle to find what toys and sweets he had brought for them in his many pockets.

"My honour is at stake," said Sir Christopher Hemmerde.

He sat very upright in the chair that had been placed for him—a broad-shouldered, full-blooded man of forty-eight, with a close-trimmed moustache and beard turning from brown to grey, with firm, authoritative look and the poise of a man of power. He was the head of the great banking and financial house of Hemmerde, Maddison and Co., Lothbury, London, E. C. His knighthood stood in recognition of his financial abilities and of the big sums he had given to prominent charities. In a few years' time he would, in the orderly progression of the mayoral candidature, become Lord Mayor of London, titular head of the greatest city in the world.

"A man's honour lies with himself and with his wife," answered Dr. Wycherley, with his little mannerism of veiling a question under a statement.

"In this case, with neither. The case is a most unusual one—a most delicate one. I am very loth to put it in the hands of a detective, and hearing of your peculiar powers of mind-reading, I have come to you."

Dr. Wycherley did not respond to this. Detective work was strongly distasteful to him unless it were to open out fresh experiences in the realm of the human mind. He waited to hear further.

Sir Christopher continued, with more than a little self-importance: "My honour as a business man is involved. As you will know, in a business such as mine, matters are confided to the heads of the firm which must rigorously be kept secret. Now it has happened three times in the last twelve months that private information has leaked out from my office. This last time, it was information that precipitated the disastrous run on the Essex Bank. It is vital that I find the leak—and stop it."

"Surely that is a problem for a business expert," answered the doctor, somewhat coldly. Money matters held no interest whatever for him, and he resented the implication that he was being consulted as a kind of glorified detective, ready to sell his skill to any man for sufficiently high pay.

"No. Because I know that the leak can lie only with one of two men, my partner and my confidential secretary."

"That means three men—your partner, your secretary, and yourself."

"Naturally." The banker brushed aside the correction as of no consequence. "And I must know which."

"I am sorry, but the case is not one I should care to handle."

"Why not, sir?" The banker's face flushed; a vein throbbed angrily in his temple. "I have made a personal journey to Italy to consult you. The affair is one of urgent importance. In a few years I shall in due course be elected to the office of Lord Mayor, and my business reputation is a matter of the utmost concern to myself and to . . ." He stopped short, having tangled his sentence.

"And to . . . ?" urged Dr. Wycherley.

"Well, if I must say it, to the City of London."

"Scarcely that, Sir Christopher. Of the utmost concern to yourself—yes. But to others—why?"

The banker suddenly felt small—a most unusual feeling for him. His hand fidgeted with his collar, and he cleared his throat, uneasily.

"Is there no stronger reason why I should put my time and skill at your service?" continued the doctor.

"Well, I don't know if this reason would appeal to you. On my return to London I propose either to break with my life-long partner, or to dismiss my private secretary, whom I have helped and trusted since he was a lad. Probably it will be the latter, and yet he may be a perfectly innocent man."

"In other words, the honour of three men is involved. That is a stronger reason than your Lord Mayorship, Sir Christopher." The rebuke was gentle but pointed. "One question: there is always the possibility that secrets may leak out through a man's relations—have you eliminated that possibility?"

"In my case, I tell my business secrets to nobody—not even to my wife. I expect the same principle from my associates. If they confide my affairs to their relations, I consider that as criminal as open betrayal."

Dr. Wycherley accompanied the banker back to London, but Sir Christopher felt considerably disappointed in him. He had expected to find a man who could read his every thought at a glance. He had rather expected to buy ready-made miracles at (say) a hundred guineas apiece, with a five per cent discount for cash. He did not realise that the psychic sense of the mental healer required very peculiar conditions for its highest effort, and that it was out of the question to ask him for miraculous readings at any arbitrary moment.

Sir Christopher was grimed with money, and the temperament of the scientist was outside his range of comprehension.

Proceeding by branch lines, they caught the night express at Lugano, and shared a *wagon-lit* over the St. Gothard route, and so by Basle and Chalons to Calais-Dover and London. On the journey, Dr. Wycherley outlined his plan of action:

"I shall want to study Mr. Maddison and Mr. West when they are off guard. That is essential. On guard, a man can control his thoughts—put armour around them. I make no pretension to cope with a mind-armoured man."

"Yes?" said Hemmerde coldly. This scientific freakness made no appeal to him. He would have been much more impressed by the boastings of a charlatan. What he looked for, in fact, was a modern Cagliostro or Nostradamus. Dr. Wycherley realised that to the full, but he had no intention of degrading his science by any cheap and flashy impressiveness.

"Shakespeare has given us the model for this case," pursued the doctor. "Hamlet—the play scene. Hamlet studying the King while the mimic drama is being enacted before them. Is there a play now on in London where the conditions resemble yours?"

The banker thought over this for a little.

"There is a play of Henri Bernstein's called 'The Thief.' I have not seen it, but I understand that the plot hinges on a theft of money at a country house, and that everyone of the house party is under suspicion. But that is hardly a good analogy to my case."

"It may serve. Will you engage a first-circle box?"

"For us four?"

"For you three. I shall sit in a dress-circle seat convenient for observation. Between the acts I may come to you."

"Perhaps it would be less suspicious if I ask Lady Hemmerde to give the invitation?"

"As you please."

"You will stay with us, of course?"

"After the test—yes. But not before. My presence in London ought not to be known."

"The Thief," that big success of the Paris, London and New York stages, was just starting its run at the St. James' Theatre, with George Alexander and Irene Vanbrugh in the chief parts. In his usual scientific thoroughness, Dr. Wycherley made a matinée visit to the play in order to familiarise himself with the plot and its developments before the evening of the arranged theatre-party. He was thus in a position to give undivided attention to the occupants of the first-circle box.

In the two front seats sat Lady Hemmerde and Angus Maddison, Sir Christopher's partner. Behind were Sir Christopher himself and West, his confidential secretary.

Lady Hemmerde was decidedly plain. In spite of her position as the wife of a great banker, she looked a timid, colourless, insignificant little woman, more fitted to act as hostess in a suburban drawing-room than at the Mansion House, which would in due course be her duty. Not knowing that she had been an heiress, and that her whole fortune had been turned over to the banker, Dr. Wycherley wondered why Sir Christopher had married her. It was evident at a glance that she was not a woman to whom the masterful banker would confide the secrets of his business.

Angus Maddison interested the doctor very greatly. He was a tall, lean, sandy Scotchman with keen, quick-moving eyes and an exceptionally keen intellect. The somewhat conscious self-importance of Sir Christopher was entirely absent. Dr. Wycherley docketed him as a self-made man and the brains of the firm.

West, the secretary, formed a complete contrast. He was the typical employee—a man born to lean on others, a man born to carry out orders. The doctor noted the slight deferential droop of the shoulders as he sat beside his employer and benefactor, evidently much flattered by the honour of the evening's invitation.

Previous to the rising of the curtain, the doctor had injected into himself a drug—one of the pyridyl-novocaine derivatives—which has the peculiar effect of temporarily paralysing the auditory nerve. It renders a man deaf for a period of time dependent on the strength of the dose. In this way he screened out of his consciousness the spoken traffic of the stage, and allowed his brain to concentrate on the delicate waves of thought. The action and gestures of the players would tell him at any time of the developments of the plot, so that he could synchronise them with the thoughts they aroused in the minds of the people he was so intently watching.

The doctor leant back in his balcony stall with every muscle relaxed, concentrating on his mental task.

The first act of "The Thief" is merely introductory—a prelude to the great second act, a bedroom scene in which a husband worms out of his wife a confession of her theft. The drama of this second act gripped the whole house to straining tenseness. To look on the rows of faces behind and around one was to realise that the spectators were living in a mimic world forgetful of realities—were living through every emotion of the guilty wife and the horror-stricken husband. When at length the curtain fell on the second act, there was a perceptible interval of silence before the spectators came back to a remembrance that this was acting and that the actors were waiting for their recognition.

Of the whole house there was perhaps not one except Dr. Wycherley who did not then break into heartfelt applause. But the doctor sat silent, working out the significance of the real-life drama which had been unfolded to his keen senses.

*   *   *   *   *

At the close of the play, when the effect of his injection had worn off, Dr. Wycherley made his way to the first-circle box. Sir Christopher introduced him to the three members of his party, and all five drove in the banker's limousine to his sombre, dignified house in Manchester Square, where supper was served them before they separated for the night.

The conversation, limited to surface conventionalities, held little of interest until the supper-party had broken up and Sir Christopher and the doctor were alone in the library.

"Well?" said the former, his tone showing a suppressed impatience for the results of the doctor's investigation. "Have you discovered anything?"

"Yes—part of the truth."

"Who is the betrayer?"

Dr. Wycherley picked out a cigarette from an open box, turning his head away as he did so.

"I know the betrayer," he answered quietly, "but I do not yet know the reason for the betrayal."

"That's of little consequence."

"I am not so sure. It may be of very great consequence."

"Be good enough to tell me what you have discovered, and I shall then be in a position to judge."

"I would prefer to wait a little, Sir Christopher." The banker flushed angrily. Clearly he was not accustomed to having his wishes thwarted. He twitched at his collar as though his nerves were not under control. "Explain yourself, sir!"

Dr. Wycherley, struck by a sudden thought, took up a green-shaded electric lamp from a table near by and held it up so that its light fell full on the banker's face.

"Please be still for a moment," he ordered. "I want to examine you."

The surprise of the action held the banker speechless for a moment.

"Have you ever suffered from nerve derangement?"

"I? But . . . ! Whatever has this to do with my own question?"

"Possibly a good deal. Have you ever consulted a nerve specialist?"

"Never! Why should I? I'm perfectly healthy."

Dr. Wycherley replaced the lamp on its table. His studious silence made direct contradiction to Sir Christopher's statement.

"You think I ought to have my nerves looked into?" faltered the banker.

"I should certainly advise it."

"Then will . . . will you examine me?"

"I am here not as a doctor but as a detective," answered the mental healer. "That was, I think, the role you assigned to me. I will therefore give you the name of a nerve specialist, and I would strongly advise you to call on him to-morrow."

He scribbled a name and address on a sheet of paper, and handed it to Sir Christopher.

"But—the betrayer? Am I to infer. . . ? You surely do not mean to suggest that I, that I myself . . . ? It's absurd! Preposterous! Unbelievable!"

"I think we had better leave further discussion of this matter until after you have seen the specialist," returned Dr. Wycherley with gentle decisiveness. "Meanwhile, it grows late. Shall we say good-night?"

He held out his hand and took leave of his host.

In his bedroom, Sir Christopher opened the communicating door of their rooms in order to talk to his wife while undressing.

"That queer-looking man I brought home to-night tells me I ought to see a nerve specialist," he growled, not troubling himself with a courteous tone of voice in addressing his wife. "Rubbish! Sheer rubbish! Have you noticed anything wrong about me?"

If he could have seen his wife at the moment of that question, he would have seen her turn white and trembling. But there was a wall between them. She answered timidly: "I don't know. I think perhaps . . . perhaps it would be well for you to see the specialist."

Hemmerde strode into his wife's room.

"What's wrong with me?" he demanded.

"Nothing, dear, nothing!" she hastened to reply. "But just as a matter of precaution, perhaps it would be as well. . . . At your age."

Hemmerde made no answer to this. He finished his undressing and went to bed, but before retiring he started the mechanism of a roll-cylinder phonograph in the bedroom. This was to play him to sleep. He had found that it soothed his nerves, and it had now become an established habit of his.

Soon he was sleeping stertorously.

THE ONE WHO BETRAYED

At eleven o'clock the next morning Dr. Wycherley went to call at Manchester Square. As he expected, Sir Christopher was away at business—or perhaps at the Harley Street consultant's. The doctor then asked to see Lady Hemmerde.

She came to him in the great ornate drawing-room, furnished with ponderous decorative effect like some state apartment in a show palace. It was not a woman's room, but a man's—clearly Sir Christopher himself had chosen the furnishings. In this huge room Lady Hemmerde looked even more insignificant and inconsequential than the evening before—a timid, colourless little woman to outward seeming.

But Dr. Wycherley had read deeper into her.

"I had no opportunity of speaking to you alone last night," he began, "so I have taken upon myself to call at this unusual hour. Will you excuse me?"

"Of course—I am always very pleased to welcome any friend of my husband's. Won't you sit down?" answered Lady Hemmerde with colourless conventionality.

"Last night I was acting in your interests," continued the doctor, "and I want you to know how and why."

"You mean about advising my husband to see a specialist?

"Yes."

"I told him that it might be as well to take your advice."

"That, Lady Hemmerde, was merely a side issue."

"I don't understand."

485

"I will explain. But first, let me assure you that what I am going to ask is in no way a prying into your private affairs." The doctor's voice held a world of gentle sympathy. "I do not presume to set myself up as judge. I only want to understand. Tell me this: why did you give away that private knowledge of your husband's which led to the ruin of the Essex Bank?"

Lady Hemmerde quivered like a bird in the hand of a captor. Her cheeks went chalk-white. But she answered:

"You must be making some great mistake. My husband tells me nothing of his private affairs."

"True—but yet you know of them. I will tell you how you know. Sir Christopher traveled to Italy to consult me, and we came back together in a night express. We shared a *wagon-lit* compartment. I then discovered that Sir Christopher talks in his sleep."

"No doubt. But your inference is altogether wrong. My husband and I—I really don't know why I should be telling you these details—my husband and I occupy separate rooms."

There was fire in her words now; she was a woman at bay.

Dr. Wycherley realised that he had failed to make the sympathy contact—that Lady Hemmerde suspected him of hostile intentions. He therefore tried once more to gain her confidence.

"You believe that I am here to accuse you; but, on the contrary, I am here to shield you. Your husband has no suspicion whatever—*at present*—that you have become aware of his business secrets. I have not told him—nor do I wish to tell him. Come, Lady Hemmerde, look close at me and read my sincerity. . . . I know—*I know*—that you learnt from him of the perilous condition of the Essex Bank. I know that you gave it away to someone else. Why you should have done so is frankly inexplicable to me. Your motive is beyond me. Such a betrayal seems altogether opposed to your true self. . . . There must have been some overwhelming reason."

"I tell you again, you are utterly mistaken," she retorted with set lips.

Dr. Wycherley rose quietly and took up his hat.

"You leave me only one inference," he said. "I shall have to report to Sir Christopher this: that if he did not give away his business affairs in his sleep to you, it must have been to—some other woman."

A bitter cry came from Lady Hemmerde: "You are merciless!"

"As a surgeon is merciless."

"Why do you persist in doubting my word? Am I a woman who would betray my own?"

And with that the key to the mystery lay in Dr. Wycherley's hand.

"No, you are not! I see now that you are trying to protect not yourself but someone dear to you. *It is the mother instinct.*"

He had at last touched the right chord. There were tears in her eyes as she cried:

"Can't you see that I've been trying to protect *him?*"

"Whom?"

"My husband!"

Very gently Dr. Wycherley answered:

"Then I am indeed intruding. I ask your forgiveness. I will leave now, and you will not see me again. I shall return at once to my home in Italy."

"No, stay—listen first to what I have to tell. You have divined so much that you had best know all. Sit down and I will tell you. Perhaps you will be able to help me."

She dried her tears and began with a new trust and hope in her voice:

"I have no children, and the mother instinct in me has gone out to my husband. He thinks that he needs no one's help, but I have always been at his elbow without his knowing it, from the day of my marriage when my whole fortune passed into his hands. I have borne him no children, and he seems to feel that he owes nothing to me. . . .

"Two years ago we were in Brussels. One night he left me to go to a theatre—so he said. He did not return to the hotel until six o'clock the next morning. He did not know that I knew, and I said nothing.

"When we returned to London a man and a woman called here one afternoon and asked to see me. She said . . . she said . . . I can't repeat to you what it was she said. It was blackmail. They had even taken a photograph of my husband—a horrible, disgraceful photograph. They wanted money, and I was frightened and gave them what I had in return for a promise of silence."

"I understand now," said Dr. Wycherley gently. "In order that your husband's reputation might be saved—in order that he might become Lord Mayor of London without an open stain on his character—you paid hush-money. Once you had paid, their demands became heavier . . ."

"And at last I had not money enough to satisfy them. As I told you, my whole fortune went to my husband at marriage. . . . So I had to pay them in another way. They suggested that I should give them business information which could be turned into money. Every time they said it was to be the last demand, and every time they lied!"

"You need not tell me more."

"You had best know all. . . . My husband has a peculiar fancy for a phonograph to play him to sleep, and his machine is always in his bedroom at night. One evening, after dinner, we amused ourselves by taking records of our own voices, and amongst those records was one of Mr. Angus Maddison's voice, my husband's partner. . . . I know that Christopher very often muttered a great deal in his sleep. It has something to do, I think, with a hidden nervous affection of his."

"Yes, there would be a decided connection."

"One night, driven to desperation, the thought came to me to creep into Christopher's room and place in the machine the record of Mr. Maddison's voice. I did so, and as soon as he heard it, Christopher began to answer and talk of confidential business matters. And that was how I came to learn his secrets. . . ."

"My dear Lady Hemmerde, I feel more than ever an intruder."

"Can't you help me?" she pleaded.

"I can only advise you to tell your husband everything—*everything*. He must defend his own honour in the way that seems best to him. . . . I wish I could indeed help you, but like every other man I have my many limitations. . . . A man's honour lies with himself and with his wife. You have done what lay in your power to protect him; now he must stand by himself. He must be awakened."

There was the sound of a motor drawing up by the front door.

"That will be your husband. I will say good-bye now. Good-bye, and courage!"

On the doorstep Dr. Wycherley came face to face with Sir Christopher.

"Well, sir?" demanded the latter. "When am I to hear the results?"

"Your wife is waiting to tell you," said the mental healer.

"Shall I see you later in the day?"

"I have an important call to Cambridge."

"But . . . !"

"Your wife is waiting for you, Sir Christopher."

ACCIDENT OR MURDER

The sudden call to Cambridge was in connection with the University department of experimental psychology and psychiatry, then being re-organised. Dr. Wycherley's European reputation in the science of the mind had led to his being invited to Cambridge by the Senate to give his opinion on the new plans, and at the same time to deliver a short series of lectures to the medical faculty of the University.

As a general rule, the doctor hated lectures. Speaking to human beings in the mass means having to address oneself to an average intelligence, to average prejudices and average sympathies—while Dr. Wycherley was at his best in dealing with the *individual* intelligence, prejudices or sympathies. He almost preferred the trouble of speaking to fifty people separately to the ineffectiveness of addressing them *en masse*. Public addresses constrained him, and he had a little touch of human vanity which made him disagreeably conscious that lectures did not do him justice.

However, in this case he had consented to speak because it was an unique opportunity to hit out from the shoulder at the conservatism of the British medical profession in general and the 'Varsity don in particular. Oxford and Cambridge were at that time, as regards mind-conscience, far behind the schools and clinics of the Continent and the States. He intended to tell Cambridge so in words that they would probably never forgive but certainly would never forget.

This series of lectures, arresting in their boldness if unpalatable to the majority of his audience, kept Dr. Wycherley in the University city from the end of May to the end of June. It was thus that he came indirectly in contact with the mysterious death of Professor Creighton Adams, which took place during "Mays Week." The tragic occurrence was heightened by its contrast with the joyous festivities of that glorious week when Cambridge is a kaleidoscope of flannel-clad young heroes and dainty English girlhood, with the requisite escort of parents and aunts and uncles; when the days and nights are a whirl of luncheon parties and riverings, dances and suppers, flirtations and quickly-born romances.

Professor Creighton Adams had been found in a huddled heap on the floor of the "sloth room" in the Cambridge Biological Museum shortly after nine o'clock on the morning of Thursday, June 4th. Weston, the museum attendant, had discovered the body when he unlocked the doors of the museum and was proceeding with the routine of his morning duties.

The corpse was cold and stark, set in a death rigor for many hours past. That the cause of death was strangulation, Weston saw at a glance. The claw-marks around the neck carried their own grim tale.

Weston gave the alarm at once. The doors of the museum were closed, and police and doctor were at once sent for. White-faced in spite of his service in the Army and his record at the shambles of Dargai, the attendant led them to the huddled form lying in the silence of the sloth room, surrounded by cases of skeletons, mounted specimens in the open, and many oddments relative to the animal group of tree-sloths and ground-sloths.

This room—on the ground floor—was in the making. It was the special domain of Professor Adams, who had a world-wide reputation in the morphology and physiology of the South American fauna. In fact, the specimens in the unfinished room were largely his own spoils from the expedition to the Upper Amazon which he had headed with such striking success a year previously. He had brought back in particular several hides, skeletons and preserved limbs of a new giant sloth hitherto unknown to science. It was closely allied to the monster fossil sloths of the pleistocene epoch, though only half their size. Still, a formidable beast some five feet in length.

Professor Adams had also managed by unusual good luck to bring a living specimen of his new find back to Cambridge. In order to study its habits closely, he kept it caged in one room of his private research suite, also on the ground floor.

Scarcely had the group of officials reached the dead body of the professor, when loud cries for help echoed through the building from a room somewhere below them. Most of them rushed towards the stone staircase leading to the basement, and down the steps, pell-mell, in the direction of the sounds.

It was in the whale room that they found Haines, a laboratory assistant, battering fiercely with a chair at the heaving, palpitating body of a giant sloth. He had managed to split its skull, and blood was streaming over the grey fur—patched with blue-green from the algae which curiously make their habitation on the bodies of the sloths, like mould on the trunks of trees.

The limbs, armed with vicious curved triple claws, splayed around in the animal's death agony. Then it rolled over on the floor and lay still. Haines, a man of fifty odd, panting stertorously from the terror of the fight, gasped out broken words of explanation:

"Brute was hiding . . . in here . . . flew at me . . . muster got loose . . . somehow . . . vicious beast!"

"He's killed the professor."

"Killed the . . . professor! . . . Good God!"

"How did it get loose?" This from the inspector of police.

Haines looked at him speechlessly for a moment. Then the answer: "How should I know?"

Arthur Lethbridge, a demonstrator of zoology and a co-worker with the dead professor, put in a word:

"The cage is on the floor above, in the research rooms."

The group went quickly upstairs to inspect the iron-barred cage. Then they were joined by the doctor, who had been examining the corpse minutely.

"Professor Adams has been dead some nine or ten hours," he said. "The animal must have broken loose last night."

But it was not a case of *breaking* loose. The inspector pointed out that the lock was intact, and that the animal must have simply pushed up the bar of the cage-door, swung it open, and walked out. It must be by some oversight that the key had not been turned in the lock.

"Who has the key of the cage?" asked the inspector.

Weston replied: "The professor always kept it himself. Sometimes he'd go into the cage and pet the animal. A mad thing to do, I call it."

They went back to the body, and the inspector searched the pockets of the dead man for the key. He found it on a ring with some other keys of the laboratories, and was replacing the bunch when young Mrs. Adams burst in upon them.

The scene of grief that followed was painful in the extreme, and the group of men tiptoed away until the inspector of police alone was left with her. This beautiful, frail young girl had been married only two months to the professor. Last night, when he had been working late at the museum, she had been dancing at one of the many college balls of "Mays Week." His death must have taken place while the gaiety was at its height. The thought of that contrast stabbed her with remorse. In the agony of the moment she magnified her very natural love of gaiety to a callous heartlessness. She tortured herself with the thought that if she had stayed at home, and he with her, this tragedy would never have occurred.

The inspector remained respectfully silent until the grief-stricken girl addressed to him a broken question:

"When . . . how . . . how did it happen?"

The inspector explained the facts to her as he knew them, concluding with: "It looks, madam, as if the professor must have left the cage unlocked by accident."

Then it was that Blanche Adams burst out with her passionate accusation:

"I don't believe it! Someone let the animal loose! My husband has been murdered!"

*   *   *   *   *

While the tragedy had aroused Dr. Wycherley's interest, in view of Mrs. Adams' impassioned accusation, he was not directly concerned in the matter until one evening in late June when his gyp brought him a card with the inscription: "J. Hammerton Clark. Scotland Yard."

The doctor occupied temporarily a suite of those rooms in Neville's Court, Trinity, which are reserved for distinguished guests of the college. He gave orders to have the detective shown in to the oak-paneled study where he was now engaged in drafting out his final lecture of the series.

J. Hammerton Clark was a man of consequence in his own world, and his manner showed that he realised it to the full. He had the inquisitorial eyes of the cross-examining counsel, a dark moustache curtaining the expression of his mouth, and an authoritative bearing. In age he was something under forty.

"Well, sir," he began, and the inflexion on the word "sir" was that of equal addressing equal, "you are no doubt wondering why a Scotland Yard man should be calling on you?"

"For help," returned the doctor with his quiet smile. "This is not the first time I have been approached by the police."

A shade disconcerted, the detective continued: "No doubt you know that we Scotland Yard men can't interfere in these country murders until the county police definitely call us in. By the time I arrived here, the local people had bungled the Adams case into a horrible mess."

"Quite probable. But why should you expect me to be interested in such a matter? I have many duties of my own to attend to, and, frankly, police work as such makes no appeal to me."

"This case *will* interest you, sir," answered J. Hammerton Clark boldly, though the word "sir" was now inflected as from one addressing a superior.

"Why, pray?"

"I went to your last lecture. A fine lecture, that! As a practical man, I thoroughly agree with what you said about the neglect in England of psychology in relation to crime."

Dr. Wycherley would have been less than human if he had not been inwardly gratified at this appreciation.

"Well?" he asked. "Why should this case specially appeal to me?"

"Because the one break in my chain is the criminal's motive. The murder seems purposeless."

"You are certain that it was murder and not accident?"

"No. I'll be perfectly open with you. If I can't find a motive for the crime, I shall have to let it go as accident."

"Then you want me to help you run some man's neck into the hangman's noose?"

"Remember, sir, 'Every unpunished crime is the parent of further crime,'" quoted the detective from a standard legal work. He continued slyly: "It may interest you to know that the criminal is at the present moment in Neville's Court."

The doctor pushed aside the draft notes of his lecture, and J. Hammerton Clark knew that at last he had secured complete attention.

"Would you like me to give you a resumé of the case as I see it?" he asked.

"Yes."

"Professor Adams was a brilliant, erratic genius," began the detective. "He appears to have kept women strictly out of his life until the age of forty-six. On his forty-sixth birthday he suddenly married a young girl of twenty-two. She is fond of gaiety, and the balls of 'Mays Week' keep her steadily enjoying herself. On the evening in question, the professor resolves to make a night of it in his museum. . . ."

Dr. Wycherley frowned a little at this flippant way of stating the case, and the detective, quick to notice expressions, sobered his words.

". . . to work late over his zoological specimens. Someone who knows of this resolve borrows the professor's bunch of keys on some pretext or other; unlocks the door of the cage where the giant sloth is kept; returns the keys; and then goes away in the full expectation that the beast will break loose and attack the professor."

"I understood that Professor Adams made a pet of the animal," commented the doctor. "Why should it attack him?"

"Probably the animal was stirred up in some way, by the man who let it loose. However, that's a detail. The main point is this: who stood to gain by the murder of the professor? What was the motive of the crime? I went first on the usual *cherchez la femme*. Mrs. Adams, a young girl who might certainly be described as 'beautiful,' would have had other admirers besides a professor forty-six years old. I found out that Mr. Arthur Lethbridge had been greatly attracted by her at one time. She refused him . . ."

The detective paused to give dramatic point to his words, then continued:

"I look at Mr. Lethbridge, a dreamy, meditative young fellow, highly cultured, highly sensitive, a member of the Eugenics League, a man who has worked hand in hand with the professor for some years past—and I ask myself what on earth he could expect to gain by the professor's death. A man like that could never bring himself to propose marriage to a woman whose husband he had murdered."

"Your next suspect?"

"My next suspect was Haines, the laboratory assistant. A week before his death, Professor Adams had given this fellow a violent dressing-down for disturbing some museum cases. Haines had denied doing this. I look at Haines, a man of fifty-two with a blameless record for twenty years and more at the 'Varsity laboratories, married, happy in his children and his home-life, even tempered, and I ask myself how this man could bring himself to murder the professor in revenge for a mere slanging."

"Your third suspect?"

"My third was a Brazilian student named Ramon Zalazar, a post-graduate man specialising in zoology. He accompanied Professor Adams on that expedition he made to the interior of Brazil. Zalazar is a young man of a fiery, passionate, typically Latin temperament. I tried to connect him with Mrs. Adams, and my enquiries came to nothing. I worked on the theory of revenge, and all my enquiries tended to show that Zalazar and the professor were on excellent terms. I look at the young man, and I ask myself what hidden motive there could be for turning loose a wild beast on a friend."

"These three men could all have been in the museum on the evening of the accident or murder?" queried the doctor.

"Yes. The peculiarity of the case is that the criminal need not have been in the building at the time of the death. It is quite possible that he may have released the animal hours before it attacked the professor. That has made it extremely difficult for me to fix suspicion on any one man on a time consideration."

"But you said that the criminal is now in Neville's Court?"

"Both Lethbridge and Zalazar have rooms around this court, and it happened that as I came across the quadrangle I saw Haines going to the staircase where Lethbridge lives—probably with some message. In other words, the criminal is within a stone's throw of us, because my suspects have narrowed down to those three alone."

"Always assuming murder and not accident."

The detective nodded assent. "My case is practically hopeless unless I can fix the motive. It would give me a new starting-point. That's why I've come to you, sir. This case is one for a trained psychologist, and especially for a man of your known powers."

Dr. Wycherley made a gesture of deprecation. "People weave fairy-tales around my powers. There is nothing supernatural about them. . . . However, I will try what I can sense or deduce. Can you show me the scene of the supposed crime?"

"Now, if you wish it. The museum and research rooms are closed, but I have a complete set of duplicate keys. Now would be the finest time to go over the ground, because Professor Adams was killed somewhere between ten and eleven o'clock at night."

* * * * *

All traces of the tragedy had long since been cleared away from the sloth room, which had been completed by Arthur Lethbridge according to the dead man's plans, and was now thrown open to the general student. But the professor's own research room, and the small room in which he had kept the caged animal, were still very much as they were on the morning of June 4th. Dust had settled over furniture and books, over microscope and bell-jars and gas-oven and rocker microtome, over desk and papers. In one corner lay the broken fragments of a large flower-bowl, with long-dead flowers scattered around.

Dr. Wycherley pointed to it questioningly.

"Professor Adams was a man of hasty temper," answered the detective.

Another thought arose. "Were any of his private papers taken?"

"As far as we know, they were not. But it's impossible to say definitely."

"Will you leave me alone in this room for, say, half an hour?"

The detective withdrew, and Dr. Wycherley, switching off the lights and placing himself in the dead man's desk-chair, gave himself up to that state of intense receptivity in which the radiations of outside thought came clearest to his inner senses. Professor Adams had worked in this room for years past, and some faint echo of his thoughts and feelings might linger—might still make itself evident to the consciousness of the mental healer as the characteristic scent of the man might still make itself felt to the keen nose of a hound.

The detective, returning at the end of the half-hour, found Dr. Wycherley in a rigid, semi-hypnotic condition. After some hesitation, he decided to rouse the doctor.

He touched him gently on the shoulder, and the doctor woke with a start, blinking as one who comes out of heavy sleep.

"Well, sir," asked the detective eagerly, "have you arrived at any conclusion?"

Dr. Wycherley remained silent for some considerable time, gathering together the impressions that had come to him during his hypnotic doze.

"Here is a conclusion you are welcome to," he answered at length. "A man who borrows keys from the professor in order to loose the animal, *on the off-chance of its attacking and killing the professor*, would be a half-hearted amateur of a criminal."

J. Hammerton Clark could scarcely conceal his disappointment. This was a deduction he had himself reached long ago; and after Dr. Wycherley's impressive procedure, the results seemed ludicrously trivial.

"Let us go on to the scene of the death," pursued the doctor, and the detective led the way to the sloth room, though now his faith in Dr. Wycherley's "powers" had shrunken woefully.

After the details of the finding of the body had been explained to him, the doctor again asked to be left alone for a half-hour. The detective withdrew with a slightly contemptuous smile under his dark moustache.

When he returned, it was to find that Dr. Wycherley had already awakened from his hypnotic doze, and was now examining the specimens in the cases and in the open with an absorbed interest.

"Any further conclusion?" asked Clark.

"Yes. There was no half-hearted amateur concerned in the professor's death," was the somewhat casual answer, and then, with a flash of the scientist's enthusiasm: "Have you ever seen a more complete and more excellently arranged collection of any animal group? Full mounted specimens, skeletons, hides, limbs, claws, comparisons of hair, charts of geographical distribution, internal organs, diagrams—complete down to the last detail. Splendid!"

"The professor was a genius for detail, no doubt," returned the detective with a bored shrug of his shoulders. "But I can't pretend to be interested in that sort of thing. Those specimens have nothing to do with my case, and as far as I'm concerned, they don't exist. It's getting very late, and if you'll allow me, I'll be returning to my hotel soon."

"I, too, must be getting to my rooms. Let us come away."

When the two men were parting company, the disappointed detective put one last perfunctory question:

"Then I suppose you can offer no suggestion as to motive, if it were a crime and not an accident?"

"The motive is beyond me," returned the doctor.

BETWEEN A MAN AND HIS CONSCIENCE

Dr. Wycherley had spoken literal truth in saying that the motive was beyond him, but the method of the crime was vividly before him, and his thoughts were full of this and the deductions it involved.

"No half-hearted amateur was concerned in the professor's death," he had said to Clark, knowing that the man who had planned the murder had done so with a deliberation of purpose that was as cold as the stern justice of the law, and with a thoroughness that was scientific to the last degree.

The murderer of Professor Adams was a scientist. Haines could definitely be put aside from the case. He could never have planned such a crime. Of the two remaining, Lethbridge and Zalazar, who was the man? The clear course was for the doctor to see each of them in private, and fortified by his new knowledge of the case—knowledge unknown to Hammerton Clark—to force a confession.

Dr. Wycherley was now intensely interested in the case—as a psychologist. The motive of the crime puzzled him, and motives, the mainsprings of human action, were the material of his own scientific province. He had dismissed the detective in order that no bungling hand should make the dissection. For the time being, Dr. Wycherley the humanitarian was completely blanketed behind Dr. Wycherley the scientist.

It was near midnight when he reached Neville's Court, with its open quadrangle flooded with full moon light and its cloisters dark with slumberous shadow. A number of lights from open windows showed that men were still studying or reveling. Term would close in a few days' time, and then all Neville's Court would lie sleeping, save for the activities of gyps and bedmakers, until Long Vacation brought a few of the studious-minded back for quiet work.

Dr. Wycherley went round the cloisters reading the names painted in white at the foot of the narrow oaken stairways, so that he might know where Lethbridge and Zalazar "kept." Then he stepped out into the open quadrangle to find if either, or both, of the two men were still showing a light in their windows. As it happened, lights streamed out from the living-rooms of both; and Arthur Lethbridge was at a window-seat enjoying the coolness of the night-air as he penciled industriously in a notebook.

The doctor recognised the young demonstrator from the brief description that the detective had given, and it seemed that chance was pointing to a visit to Lethbridge first. If that visit drew blank, the doctor would then call on the Brazilian.

It was characteristic of Dr. Wycherley that no question of his own personal safety entered his thoughts. For the purpose of discussing the crime, he was going to call on two men, one of whom had committed a particularly cold-blooded murder; yet the doctor took no precaution for his own safeguard. He simply went upstairs to the rooms of the first man, and knocked at the outer oak.

Lethbridge came to the door—a young man of twenty-eight, clean-cut, muscular, upright, with curious dreamy eyes that seemed to look beyond one into the future.

"What is it?" he asked quietly.

"I must apologise for disturbing you at this late hour. My name is Wycherley. I am temporarily occupying rooms in this court. I happen to be needing a quotation from Hartwell and Stevens' 'Mammalia,' and I judged that you would probably have a copy."

"Certainly, Doctor. I know you by reputation, of course. Please come in."

Lethbridge led the way to his sitting-room, indicated a chair, and handed to the doctor the two bulky volumes of the work in question, together with a pad of scribbling-paper.

There was a silence for some little while as Dr. Wycherley turned to the chapter on the sloth family, and penciled some notes.

Then he remarked as he closed the volume: "I was at the museum to-day viewing some of the specimens. Allow me to congratulate you on the splendid display in the new sloth room. I understand it has been laid out by yourself."

"No credit is due to me," returned the young demonstrator. "I simply followed out the late professor's plans. His thoroughness in such matters amounted to genius."

"I gather that his genius had its counterweight in a highly erratic temperament."

"He had his fits of anger."

"Did it ever strike you that there was more in such outbursts than mere irritability?"

Lethbridge was sitting on the broad window-seat, his back against a cushion at one end, his feet up at the other, re-filling his pipe. He put in a few last threads of the light gold flake with meticulous care, and replied: "One made allowances, and avoided him on his irritable days."

"Did it ever strike you that the professor was on the verge of insanity?" pursued the doctor, and his keen eyes were fixed searchingly on the profile of the young man silhouetted at the window-seat.

Lethbridge put down his feet and turned squarely towards his questioner. "What makes you think that?"

"I know it. I was alone in his room for half-an-hour to-day, and the thoughts of the dead man were still surging and echoing in it. A tangled maze of thoughts coloured with what I recognise as dangerous abnormality."

"Professor Adams is dead," responded the young man with slow and meaning emphasis. "I was his friend and his wife's friend. The whole subject is a painful one to me. Need we discuss it further?"

"As his friend and his wife's friend," answered the doctor firmly, "you owe it to him to help in the bringing to light of his murderer."

"The death was pure accident!"

"You are sure?"

"Everyone knows it except these pig-headed policemen. Can you imagine a would-be murderer borrowing keys from the professor in order to turn loose the animal, on the mere *chance* of the animal killing him? Suppose that had not happened—that the sloth had merely attacked the professor without killing him? Why, the man who let the animal loose would be instantly known!"

"Precisely. Most unscientific."

"That, to my mind, clinches the matter. It was one of those accidents that no one can foresee."

"To my mind also it would clinch the matter, were it not that I know something further—something unknown to the police, something known only to two men, myself and the man who planned the crime."

"What?"

"That the professor was never attacked by the animal at all."

"But the claw-marks on the neck!"

"The professor was strangled by a pair of specimen sloth-claws in the hands of the criminal. He was no half-hearted bungler. He made deadly sure of his work. He killed the professor first, and released the animal later."

"God! What cold-blooded work! . . . But how could you guess this?"

"I was alone in the sloth room for a further half-hour, in a self-induced hypnosis. In that state of mind I am very often able to sense what is beyond the range of the ordinary sense-organs. I had the most vivid impression—not a vision in the ordinary meaning of the term, but an impression on the psychic plane—that a man had hidden, close to where I was sitting, with an absolutely fixed determination to kill the professor with his own hands. Not a surge of revengeful anger; not a blaze of jealous passion; but a cold determination like the stern justice of the law. That is the nearest description I can give you to the impression stamped on my mind."

Lethbridge was leaning forward now in keen eagerness to hear every word of the doctor's. "But in this vision, or whatever you call it, did you see the murder committed?"

"No."

"Then how did you come to that conclusion?"

"That was deduction. When I woke from the hypnotic state, I thought of the claw-marks on Professor Adams' neck, and at the same moment my eye caught a pair of specimen claws in the museum case, carefully arranged, neatly labeled. The label stated that they came from a full-grown animal of the same species as the giant sloth. In other words, that pair of specimen claws would make marks on the neck of the professor identical with the claw-marks of the live sloth. It would account for the tears in the professor's clothing, and for the marks on the floor around."

"But this is all deduction—theory!"

"No. I took out the claws from the museum case, and examined them with a pocket glass. I found that they had been carefully cleaned. Yet not so minutely that every trace of human epidermis had been wiped away."

Lethbridge rose and began to pace the room.

"Leave me to think this over," he said presently. "What you say has given me a great shock. Is there nothing more I can do for you?"

"Thank you, I have the material I want," answered Dr. Wycherley, taking up the notes he had previously made, and preparing to leave "Don't trouble to come to the outer door. I know my way."

"Good night, then."

"Good night."

Dr. Wycherley closed the door of the sitting-room behind him and opened the outer oak. But he did not step out into the stairway. He closed the oak again with a firm bang of the spring-lock, and waited.

After the expiry of sixty seconds, the doctor opened the sitting-room door quickly and walked in.

"I came back for a favourite pencil I left . . ." were the words on his lips, but there was no need for verbal excuse.

Arthur Lethbridge was lying prone on the floor in a dead faint. By sheer will-power he had held himself together so long as the doctor was in the room, but when the latter had apparently passed beyond the outer oak, the overwrought heart had had its way.

* * * * *

"Why are you here again?" was the question from the young demonstrator when he awoke to consciousness to find himself on a couch with Dr. Wycherley holding a moistened handkerchief to his forehead.

"I came back to ask why you killed your friend."

"I . . . killed . . . the professor!" The protest came weakly.

"Yes. And the motive is beyond me. It was not anger; it was not jealousy; it was not revenge. Why did you do it?"

"I didn't!"

"Remember, the facts are known only to you and to myself. The police know nothing as yet of what I said to you to-night. Who shall tell them—you or I?"

"You're trying to torture a confession out of me!"

"You would not confess to what you had not done," replied the doctor firmly.

Lethbridge sat up suddenly. "Neither you nor I shall tell the police," he answered. "If nobody else knows, the death had far better rest at accident."

"Why?"

"Because it was done for her sake."

"Mrs. Adams?"

"Yes, for her sake alone. I had nothing to gain by it. You surely don't think me capable of killing a friend in order to marry his widow?"

"No, I don't think that. But what was exactly your motive?"

"With all your powers of intuition, you seem singularly dense."

"I am still a student of the human mind—only a student," answered the doctor quietly.

"You guessed the two halves of the story. You had only to place them together to make the complete picture." Lethbridge rose, a little unsteadily, and went to his favourite seat by the window-sill, leaning back amongst the cushions.

"Professor Adams," he continued, "was on the verge of insanity. I had known it for a long time past, but it was only recently that his condition of mind became a menace to others. He decided very hastily to marry, and Blanche—Mrs. Adams—a young girl knowing little of the world, agreed to marry him almost without an engagement. I implored the professor not to marry. I pointed out the dangers. I urged his duty to society in general. I urged the eugenic aspect of such a marriage. He refused to listen to any argument of mine. He married Blanche, and they went away for their honeymoon.

"When they returned, his outbursts of temper became more frequent and more violent. You, Doctor, will know well that a man in his condition might be at one and the same time a loving husband and a constant menace. I am not only thinking of the children of such a marriage; I am thinking also of the way in which a man with homicidal mania is liable to attack those nearest and dearest to him."

"Homicidal mania—you were sure of that?"

Lethbridge threw off his coat and turned up the sleeve of his left arm. "Feel here," he said to Dr. Wycherley.

"A badly-set fracture."

"I didn't take it to a doctor. I wanted to keep the affair quiet. I set the arm myself as best I could."

"The professor attacked you?"

"With an iron bar. Quite suddenly and unexpectedly, without the shadow of a cause. After that I had to watch him very warily when we were alone together."

"You could have had him examined by a doctor, and if necessary, put under restraint."

"Yes, and let Blanche be legally chained for life to a madman in an asylum! As the out-of-date laws of this country now stand, that is what would have happened. No divorce possible. A young girl chained to a madman until his death releases her. What a mockery of human liberty! . . . I thought over the matter in every aspect, and I could see only one way out for Blanche. Then I did—what I did. I made very careful arrangements to suggest an accident, and but for your guesses or intuitions or whatever they may be, an accident it would have remained. Now—!" Lethbridge shrugged his shoulders.

Dr. Wycherley remained silent, thinking deeply over the extraordinary motive laid bare in the young man's recital. He did not doubt its essential truth, for every word dovetailed in with what he already knew.

"Well?" asked Lethbridge at length. "What do you propose to do?"

Dr. Wycherley rose and went to the desk where he had copied the notes from the volume of Hartwell and Stevens.

"I came back for a favourite pencil I had left behind. Ah, here it is. . . . As for the rest"—his hand was on the door-handle— "as for the rest, I am going to leave it between you and your conscience."

"Good night, then," said Lethbridge from his window-seat, tonelessly.

"Good night," answered the doctor.

A WANDERER RETURNED

It was following on the strange case of Professor Creighton Adams, in early July, that Dr. Wycherley found himself at Henley Regatta. The life of the 'Varsity had made a distinct appeal to him through its pulsing youth and unshattered enthusiasms, and he wished to see more of it at the great annual river festival. He therefore accepted readily an invitation for Henley Week extended to him by Professor Devene, one of the Trinity dons, and that had led to a chance introduction to Major Fitzalan, who rented a river bungalow at Henley for the season.

The major, on hearing of Dr. Wycherley's reputation as a mind-reader, had asked for his help on a very delicate matter, and the doctor, much interested in the curious story that had been put before him, had consented to do what might lie in his power.

The two of them, with Mrs. Fitzalan, a very capable, carefully-beautiful woman of thirty, were seated on the Henley lawns, gay with pinks and blues of frocks and blazers, sunshades and college ribbons, joyously surgent with the spirit of youth, rippling with young life. In a corner of the lawns sat old Lord Dallas—a blind man drinking in the sounds of joyous youth, and in them remembering his own youth when he too threw soul into the straining oar and drank deep of the cup of victory. There was a race in progress, and as the bands of undergraduates ran by the towpath shouting and cheering on their college crews, a flush came into the old man's face as if he felt his hands once again upon the oar.

By his side sat a tall, dark, heavily-framed man of forty-five—a man with a hard straight eye and a mouth that told of strength in reserve. A silent, guarded man who spoke little, and then in short, abrupt sentences. A reserved, secretive man. He had a habit of gripping the sides of his chair with both hands as though keeping tight grip of his secret thoughts.

After twenty years of wanderings he had come back to claim his place as the son and heir of Lord Dallas, now blind and feeble and with few years of life left to him. That was the *claim* of the stranger.

"It was over twenty years ago that Morton Langdale quarreled with his father and flung out of the house," explained Major Fitzalan in amplification of the previous conversation wherein he had asked for Dr. Wycherley's help. "Nothing was heard of him directly; he never wrote to his relatives. Indirectly we heard that he was fighting with the United States army in the Philippines. Then he disappeared again out of our knowledge. That Philippines episode may be important if it comes to a lawsuit, because we might be able to hunt out someone who knew the real Morton Langdale there."

His wife shook her head in contradiction. "We should stand a very poor chance in a lawsuit. That I'm quite sure of. If my uncle continues to acknowledge him as his son, it will be taken as overwhelming proof. . . . Isn't it a pathetic sight?" she went on indignantly. "There's my uncle, blind and helpless, and there's that mercenary scoundrel using his blindness and his helplessness to bolster up this horrible imposture! If he could only get his deserts!"

"He's clever—devilishly clever," put in the major.

"Yes, he'd squirm out of any tight corner. That's why we ask for your help, Doctor," proceeded Mrs. Fitzalan with strained anxiety in her face. "Mary Devene told us about the marvelous power you have of getting at the back of people's minds, and so—"

Dr. Wycherley interrupted with a gesture of deprecation. "Please don't exaggerate my powers," he said. "I am no wonder-worker—merely a student of the human mind. Still a student."

But Mrs. Fitzalan would allow no self-deprecation on the part of the doctor to stand in her way. She was a woman of strong will, as her husband had long since learnt and submitted to. She proceeded to detail what she had heard from Mary Devene, and concluded by bringing it round to the present case. "If you could manage that kind of thing, Doctor, surely you could find some way of getting at my uncle's mind and showing him what a horrible imposture is being practised? You see, anything we have urged has been discounted by our self-interest. That's the point that's driving me to desperation. When we say this man's an impostor—another 'Roger Tichborne'—the answer comes at once, Major Fitzalan is next heir to the estate and therefore prejudiced. No one will believe that we can act from anything but selfish motives."

"To have our name pass into the hands of a man like that—to see Greeve Hall lorded over by a scoundrel from God knows where! That's what sticks in my throat!" In Major Fitzalan's voice was sincerity unmistakable; there could be no doubt how deeply he felt the wrong that was being done not only to himself but also to his family.

Yet Dr. Wycherley answered with the caution of the scientist: "All this rests on the supposition that we are dealing with an impostor. So far I have heard only your side of the case, and I cannot promise to act until I have fully assured myself—"

"I can give you a dozen proofs, fifty proofs!" interrupted Mrs. Fitzalan. "From the first moment I set eyes on him I felt my suspicions. And then the little points that tell a woman so much. His secretiveness; his constant air of being on guard. Oh, the man has been splendidly coached in his part, and he's devilishly clever, but if my uncle were not blind and a little feeble in mind, he would have seen through him weeks ago. But the crowning proof is this." She glanced around to make sure that there were no eavesdroppers, but indeed no one was taking any notice of them. Then she drew out from her satchel-bag a cheap, common sheet of letter-paper written on in an ill-formed, uneducated hand, and passed it to Dr. Wycherley.

The psychologist examined it very closely after he had read the words, and asked: "How did this come into your hands?"

Major Fitzalan flushed perceptibly as he answered: "We—er—intercepted the letter. I know it sounds a deuced unsporting thing to do, but when you're dealing with a—"

His wife took up his hesitating words in her own decisive fashion: "One has to meet a scoundrel on his own grounds. I've not the slightest compunction in the matter. I felt that letter held the key to the situation, and I was amply justified in getting hold of it. You see what the letter amounts to, Doctor—a veiled threat to extort money from him. No name; no address. Now, no man can be blackmailed without good cause."

Dr. Wycherley did not answer this. His gaze was fixed on old Lord Dallas in the far corner of the lawns. Another race was in progress, and the wild shouting and cheering on the towpath told that it was a neck-and-neck struggle between Trinity Hall, Lord Dallas' own college, and Leander. In his excitement the old man had risen from his chair as though his sightless eyes could see over the heads of the crowd, and quite suddenly he fell back clutching at his chair. The excitement had caught at his heart.

Dr. Wycherley moved forward swiftly to his aid. Morton Langdale (or the man who had taken that name) had laid his father on the grass before the doctor had reached the scene, and was loosening his collar. In one glance he took in Dr. Wycherley and had him mentally classified.

"Thanks," said Langdale abruptly, before a word had been spoken. "You're wanted, Doctor. Give orders, and I'll see them carried out."

* * * * *

Greeve Hall lies a few miles back from the river at Henley, deep bedded in the woods that clothe the hills on the Berkshire side. From the observatory tower—which Lord Dallas had used for his hobby of astronomy—you look out over thicket and park-land

sweeping down in dark green stateliness to the lush meadows where
the Thames winds in and out as a band of splendid silver. A house
and land breathing of old traditions, high ideals, the shaping of
centuries. They fitted well with the fine-strung motto of the
Langdale family, "I hold no shame."

Lord Dallas had been taken back at once to Greeve Hall, and
the mental healer had ordered him complete rest for several days
at least. A fainting attack which would have been of trifling moment for a young man might have serious consequences for an old
man of seventy. With the professional permission of the family
doctor, the mental healer was remaining at Greeve Hall for a few
days until his patient should be entirely restored. He found a willing collaborator in Miss Seton, a distant relation of the family who
for many years past had stayed at Greeve Hall to keep the cares of
his position away from the shoulders of Lord Dallas. She was devoted to him. A sweet, gentle woman, scarcely marked by the passage of forty years—one of those Englishwomen whose lives are
given to good works, which in return give them perennial youth.
An Englishwoman of the countryside, subtly suggestive of laven-
der and rosemary and sweet-william and the other old-world flowers that grow by the south wall in quiet leisure and very pleasant
fragrance.

During his brief stay Dr. Wycherley was closely observing
Morton Langdale. It roused his professional interest to a high pitch.
The man had a mind encased as it were in steel. Though with most
men and women the mental healer could read deep into their
thoughts and emotions, in the case of this man he was strangely
baffled. It was as though Langdale kept tight grip of his thoughts
behind the barrier of his will.

An unusual case, and therefore of peculiar interest to Dr.
Wycherley. He had the zest of the collector for the rare specimen.
He could not rest content until he had it pinned out in his collection, properly classified and labeled. And on his part Langdale
seemed to be studying the doctor guardedly.

In the smoking-room one evening there had been long silences
between them while Langdale sat with his hands tight gripping the

sides of his chair, and Dr. Wycherley rolled cigarette after cigarette in his wonderfully deft left-handed fashion.

Langdale had broken one of the long, heavy silences with the strange, disconnected remark:

"What is the supreme test of courage?"

Dr. Wycherley considered for some moments before replying. "It depends on the individual temperament. To a few, to sacrifice life. To more, to sacrifice love. To most, to sacrifice the choice of life—to take the living death with a smiling face and bear with it uncomplainingly to the end. Think of the men and women who suffer in silence, showing a brave cheerfulness to the world; think of the X-ray martyrs, of Father Damien . . ."

"Yes." There was abrupt agreement in the tone. But Langdale did not add to his monosyllable, and so the doctor continued after a pause:

"One rarely hears of the world's real heroes. They make no headlines for the newspapers. Their living death makes no more stir than a bubble in the stormy Atlantic. Outside their small circle no one knows of them; even within their circle few suspect the sacrifice that has been made."

"Then what good do they do?"

The leading point of these questions was not apparent. But Dr. Wycherley wished keenly to get behind the reserve of this silent, secretive man, and he was glad to keep the apparently purposeless conversation proceeding. He replied: "I am no pessimist. I do not believe theirs is waste effort. There is a mental aura that radiates out from a man that makes for good or evil in others. A silent, unseen urge. There is no name for it; no way of detecting or measuring or analysing it. Yet it is one of the great realities. . . . Do you agree with me?"

"Possibly," was the abrupt answer, and Langdale relapsed into silence again. Presently he fingered his watch, suppressed a yawn, and remarked: "I think I shall be getting off to bed. Please ring for anything you want. . . . Good-night."

When he had left, Dr. Wycherley rolled himself a double-length cigarette, lit it and held it at arm's length, and proceeded to concentrate his gaze upon it. According to his custom when puzzled by a case of observation, he wished to throw himself into a light hypnoidal sleep so as to recover all of the impressions that Langdale's presence had radiated into his sub-conscious mind.

The cigarette burnt slowly through, and when the burning end scorched the doctor's finger-tips he awoke with a start. Then he quickly left the smoking-room and mounted up to the high tower where Lord Dallas carried out his astronomical hobby. The room was now unoccupied. Dr. Wycherley took up a small hand telescope and began methodically to sweep the surrounding woods and park-lands, dark with the night, from the crest of Gleydon Rise down to the lush meadows that border the silver Thames. In his system-atic, scientific fashion he took strip after strip of the territory and searched every star-lit glade for the object he had in mind.

In his light hypnotic sleep there had come to the doctor a strong impression that Langdale was being menaced that evening. Doubt-less it would be something in connection with the anonymous let-ter which Mrs. Fitzalan had shown him. And so, though Dr. Wycherley greatly disliked the idea of shadowing any man, he felt that here was a case where ordinary feelings must be put aside. The happiness of too many people was involved to allow over-fine scruples to stand in the way of his duty to others.

It was a long while before he found the object of his search—a man standing under the shadow of a broad oak-tree, waiting on some appointment. Dr. Wycherley fixed his telescope on a support of cushions and sat down to keep watch. The man was a rough, stocky, strongly muscular figure—probably a sailor or a navvy of some kind. He moved about impatiently under the tree as though he were being kept waiting.

And presently the doctor saw the figure of Morton Langdale moving quietly and unhurriedly down the park-land, under the shadows of the trees and hedges, going to keep appointment. He was unhurried in his movements, as if he were designedly holding his man waiting, but yet he kept closely to the shadows as though secrecy were a vital factor.

When the two men came face to face under the shadow of the oak-tree there was very evident recrimination from the sailor. It was a strangely silent quarrel that Dr. Wycherley was witnessing through his telescope. No sound could come to him from that distance, and he bent every faculty of mind to the task of trying to read what they were saying from the gestures and attitudes.

Words ran high on the part of the sailorman, but Langdale was at first cool and collected. He was trying to beat down the other man by force of will. There was a tense strain of attitude that told of the tense grip of mind. And presently the strain of holding himself in against the jibes or threats passed the breaking-point, and he whipped forward on the sailor with clenched fists and blazing eyes. For a moment the man slunk back, and then there came from him some retort that caused Langdale to drop his fists and droop his shoulders in defeat. He took out his pocket-book and began to count out bank-notes. Dr. Wycherley could see the sailorman eagerly clutching his booty and crinkling the notes one by one to satisfy himself of their genuineness.

Langdale stood moodily under the oak-tree long after the man had left with his plunder. His tall frame drooped—in his attitude was the bitter realisation of moral cowardice. Slowly he began to retrace his way up the park-lands, while Dr. Wycherley watched him concentratedly through his telescope.

"What have you seen, Doctor?" asked a low, gentle voice at his elbow, and he turned to find beside him Miss Dorothy Seton, with a lace shawl thrown around her head against the night air. In her voice there was pitiful anxiety. "What is happening to him?"

"To—?"

"To Morton—to Mr. Langdale. I want to know what it all means, even more than you do! Oh, tell me, what is threatening him, what does all this mystery mean?"

Dr. Wycherley looked back at her with understanding and deep sympathy. "I see. You believe in him."

A flush came into her face, and there was a note of pride in her voice as she answered: "I *know!*"

"You knew Mr. Langdale before he went away, twenty years ago? . . . Ah, I see that you knew him well. More than well. There was understanding between you?"

"He was . . . very dear to me." Her face was turned away into deep shadow. She paused, but the sympathy that had lain in Dr. Wycherley's voice drove her to fuller confidence. "I thought at the time that he cared for me, too. It was just such a night as this when we sat together under the big cedar-tree in the garden at the Henley Week ball. How grave it looks, the old cedar-tree—how heavy with memories! The starlight touched softly on the old branches, as if it were smoothing away the wrinkles of age. The damask roses by the windows of the ballroom were languorous with scent. The orchestra was playing 'Queen of My. Heart.' It was new then—more than twenty years ago. Perhaps to-day it would sound tawdry, but then . . . And there was a light in his eyes that . . . Oh, why am I telling you all this?"

"Because you have my very deep sympathy. Because I would help you in any way possible to me. . . . And you have been waiting for him these twenty years?"

"Yes." Her answer was barely audible. "So that when he came back I knew it was he. How could I be mistaken? And yet he came back cold and distant, and I don't understand. He is so changed— so reserved and secretive. There is some mystery about him, and I don't understand it. Tell me what it is! Are you his friend?"

It was difficult for Dr. Wycherley to answer this. "I am an observer," he said slowly, "a student of men and women. The mystery around Mr. Langdale has intrigued me. But rest assured of this, that so far as it lies within my power to serve you I will do so. Now tell me this: what you have just confided to me, has it passed to anyone else?"

"To no one else. There is something about you, Doctor, that draws one's confidences. Something magnetic, compelling. You are practically a stranger to me, and yet I felt you would understand and sympathise. . . ."

"It is a gift I value very greatly. Yes, you were right to tell me this. It will help more than you can possibly guess. I see a way, a method of making sure!" The doctor's eye was lighting with the enthusiasm of the scientist. "A beautiful method! Of course the technique of psycho-analysis is not new, yet the application would be novel in the extreme. . . . But these details would scarcely interest you. You will excuse the scientific temperament, will you not? I was forgetting to answer your question. You asked what is happening to Mr. Langdale, and I am at liberty to tell you this: he is being blackmailed. As to the causes I am now investigating."

"But he would never have done anything criminal! I know him too well. He is the soul of honour. The Langdales are a race with fine traditions and splendid ideals, and Morton is a true Langdale. You know our motto, 'I hold no shame.'"

"You said that the orchestra was playing 'Queen of My Heart' on that night of the ball, twenty years ago?"

"Yes, but why? How could that possibly help in unraveling the mystery?" she answered in open surprise.

Dr. Wycherley did not answer this directly. "Please mention to no one whatever that we have been talking about Mr. Langdale. This is vital," was all he said.

THE SUPREME TEST OF COURAGE

Major Fitzalan's river bungalow, "Lazyland," lay within easy distance of Greeve Hall. It was a pretty little toy house with its riot of clambering roses and wisteria and its dainty summer rooms paneled in white wood and carpeted with cool green matting. Amongst the Liberty furniture there was one chair in curious contrast to the rest—a stiff plush-covered armchair with the arm-rests in polished nickel like a dentist's chair.

Dr. Wycherley had had it brought from London for a special and important purpose. Out of sight, covered electric wires ran under the matting from the chair to partition wall in white wood and through into a small bedroom behind. And in this small room he had installed—of course with the Fitzalans' permission—an elaborate piece of scientific apparatus connected with the two electric wires that ran to the plush-covered armchair.

The most striking feature of the apparatus was a revolving "drum" wrapped round with soot-blackened paper. Against this rested a very light metal pointer connected electrically with the wires and a battery of Bunsen cells. To the physiologist such a piece of apparatus is very familiar—he uses it in scores of experiments where blood pressure curves or nerve current curves have to be registered.

Major Fitzalan had regarded it with curiosity and a little soldierly contempt for whatever he did not thoroughly understand. Dr. Wycherley was explaining as he fitted up the connections and made his preliminary tests:

"To-night we should be able to get conclusive, incontrovertible evidence on Morton Langdale—or the man who claims his name. He has accepted your wife's invitation to dinner and the informal concert afterwards, and she will manœuvre him into that plush-covered armchair. When he places his two hands on the nickel arm-rests, according to his usual habit, that completes the electric circuit, and we then have a current passing through his body and connected with this metal pointer by relay."

"Surely he would feel the current?" suggested the major doubt-fully.

"No, it is too weak. Sit in the chair and try for yourself."

The host did so, and admitted that there was nothing particu-lar to be felt. "But what happens then?" he enquired.

"The concert goes through according to the programme I have arranged with your wife."

"And then?"

Dr. Wycherley finished with an adjustment of the soot-black-ened cylinder. "A man can hide his feelings and emotions so that not one muscle quivers—so that not the faintest sign appears in face or hands or body-movement—but there is one thing he can-not control. His nerve currents. Any strong emotion in the mind sets up nerve currents, internal electric currents. Your strongly controlled, intensely reserved man may show no faintest outward sign of his feelings, but nevertheless he will reveal himself infallibly through this instrument. There is no evading it; no deceiving it."

"It seems deuced ingenious," said the major.

Dr. Wycherley smiled quizzically. "Meaning that in your opin-ion it is extremely foolish and unpractical?"

The major fumbled with a conventional denial.

"Yet," proceeded the doctor, "it is a method of technique used to-day by the foremost psychologists of the world. On this smoke-blackened drum we shall read to-night the workings that will tell us of Langdale's inmost thoughts."

That evening, when the concert was in full swing, with the guests gaily chatting between the songs and the light music when Morton Langdale, still cold and reserved, sat in the plush-covered armchair and automatically laid his two hands on the metal rests; Dr. Wycherley excused himself and retired to his improvised laboratory behind the partition wall.

The current was in circuit, as his galvanometer showed; it was passing through Langdale's body via the two arms. The doctor set the drum slowly revolving by clockwork with the metal pointer lightly pressing against it and scratching a thin line through the smoky coating.

At the piano Mrs. Fitzalan, by pre-arrangement, had started a popular waltz-air from the musical comedy of the day. The line of the pointer quivered slightly, then ran on evenly. Presently came a war-song—one of the Kipling poems set to music—sung by Hubert Llewellyn, a prominent tenor of the day, who happened to be staying with the Fitzalans for a week-end. And with that there formed on the recording drum a ragged line that mutely testified to the emotions it was arousing behind the cold, passionless face of Morton Langdale.

And when the applause had subsided at the finish of the song, Mrs. Fitzalan laid her hands on the broad, mellow chords that form the introduction to the song from the opera of "Dorothy" that had swept over all England twenty years before with its message of "Why should we wait for to-morrow? You're queen of my heart to-night!"

As Dr. Wycherley watched eagerly the soot-blackened cylinder slowly revolving against the metal pointer, there came a sudden leap in the curve and a quivering ragged line that placed the inscrutable Morton Langdale beyond all doubt as the son of Lord Dallas and the afore-time lover of Dorothy Seton.

*   *   *   *   *

They were walking home together through the starlit parklands to Greeve Hall—Dr. Wycherley and Langdale.

Said the doctor suddenly: "I owe you a very sincere apology."

"For—?"

"For doubting your identity."

"Mrs. Fitzalan had her hopes, I know," answered Langdale evenly. "I have been very much afraid she would get at my father over the matter and worry him. He is old, and I want to keep anxiety away from him."

"Without your knowing it, you have to-night been put to the test."

For the first time Langdale showed open surprise. "How?"

"The details of the method are unimportant. The vital point is that you have *proved yourself*. And I have a message for you: *she* has been waiting for you these twenty years—very patiently and very steadfastly. Ever since that night at the ball . . . sitting out by the big cedar tree in the star-light . . . while the orchestra played to you 'Queen of My Heart.' . . ." The doctor paused and turned round, looking at his companion full in the eyes with his deep, searching gaze.

"My God!" Langdale gripped tight on his stick and was silent for a long while.

Then he burst out, as though the barriers of his self-repression had broken down and the waters of his soul must needs pour out through the shattered gates: "I come back a coward—a proved coward! I had my supreme test, and I failed! It happened in this way: I was in the war in the Philippines, fighting in the United States army. I carried out some risky bits of work, and at the time I thought that was courage. I didn't know the elementary meaning of the word. That kind of thing is child's play." He laughed bitterly at himself.

"Then after the war I fell in love with a very beautiful young Spanish girl—or rather, half Spanish, half Filipino. I was carried out of myself and I married her. My ardor cooled down; hers continued. I went away on a pearling expedition, and when I came back to her the most ghastly discovery possible met my eyes."

He paused in horror of his recollection.

"She had developed leprosy—it had just begun. It is rare out there, but it exists. They quarantined us on San Fêlipe island—she and myself, because I was her husband, and suspect. In six months' time the disease had gained strong hold of her, but I was untouched. Then came my supreme test. The doctors told me I was free of suspicion and could go. Manuela implored me to stay by her—implored me on her knees. But I couldn't bear with the sights of that terrible island, and the thought of staying by her while she slowly consumed away was more than I could stand." In bitter self-abasement he added: "I gave up—quitted—branded myself a coward."

Dr. Wycherley was deeply touched at this confession. He asked gently: "And that is why you are being blackmailed?"

"You know that? . . . No, the man's story is half truth, half lie, and that is where its devilishness comes in. His story is that I was not allowed to go, but that I *escaped* from San Fêlipe. It's a lie. But to think of having such a lie spread around amongst people eager to believe anything to a man's discredit! And especially to have such a lie reach my father's ears! The shock would kill him. So I gave in and paid hush-money. While my father lives I shall go on paying hush-money. After that . . ." He paused significantly, and his hand tightened on his stick.

"Your wife?" questioned Dr. Wycherley.

"She is dead now. Dead these two years. For myself, I have been examined by doctors again and again, and they tell me there is not the remotest suspicion. . . . Now you will begin to realise that if I failed at the test, I have paid for it over and over again in remorse. As to Miss Seton, how could I go to her with this stain on my life, without telling her?"

"Then tell her," answered Dr. Wycherley firmly. "For twenty years she has been waiting. It is her right to know, and knowing, to have choice. For you it is a second test of courage, and if you rise to it you will efface your other failure. . . . See, she is up there in the tower. Her white lace shawl shows by the open window. She waits for you. Go to her."

Langdale gripped the doctor's hand in silent thanks.

THE MYSTERY OF CASTLE KREMENZ

The season at Felsbrunnen was dying.

From the study of the local "bath doctor," Dr. Wycherley looked out over the marble drinking fountain and the half-deserted promenade, sorrowful with the leaves fluttering softly down from the yellowing lindens, yet beautiful in its sorrow.

"So you leave to-night?" said the local man. He had called Dr. Wycherley into consultation over the case of a very rich patient whom he was "nursing."

"Yes. All your patient needs is a spade or a washtub, and someone to drive her to work. A sheer case of gluttony and underwork."

"*Natürlich!* But one does not tell them so. Such patients, properly worked, are little gold-mines. She had a fancy to call in some specialist from a distance—the further away the better—and so I wrote to you in Italy. It will mean a fat cheque for you, and she will be quite happy." He laughed cynically.

But the mental healer turned away in disgust and looked out again over the promenade of the lindens, where the "Kurgäste" strolled slowly up and down. He had a deep pride in his profession, his life-work, and it hurt him keenly to have it treated in this sordid fashion. "My time has been utterly wasted," he replied. "No cheque compensates me for that. From your letter to me at Lake Rovellasco I gathered that you had a case of very special psychological interest; otherwise I should never have made the long journey to here. Your patient is looking for a fortune-teller, not a scientist."

The little man with the Kaiser moustache bristled angrily. "If you want science without pay," he snapped, "you'd better take on a case like the von Hessele girl! That miserable-looking creature over there by the spring. That will give you all the psychological problem you want, and as for pay . . . well, the von Hesseles are as poor as church mice, and they're not wasting money over the fancied illnesses of a paid companion."

Dr. Wycherley replied evenly: "That English girl. Yes, I had been watching her for some time past. There is something very strange about her—something I have not yet settled in my mind. She is young, and yet she conveys to me a deep impression of Autumn. The leaves are falling from her tree of life. Why?"

"She is going the way of the others."

"The others?"

"The other paid companions of the Gräfin von Hessele. They don't seem to last long. Castle Kremenz appears to be an unhealthy place—a very unhealthy place for young girls. But that's none of my business."

"Whose affair is it?"

The little man shrugged his shoulders. "No one's. Yours, if you like. But let me tell you that it's not a poisoning mystery. They seem to fade away, and then they give or get notice. Nothing more. As for the reason, there's the problem for you. The castle is a few miles away from Felsbrunnen. It's a ruined shell of long-ago grandeur, and probably it's ghosts that make it unhealthy. The von Hesseles have always been known as a queer, eccentric family; I daresay they did a few lively murders in their day. You're a collector of ghosts, I hear, so you ought to find yourself in your element at Castle Kremenz." He laughed with an undercurrent of contemptuous malice.

The mental healer took up his hat and stick. Everything this man said and thought grated, jarred on him, and he longed to get away, into the fresh, clean air outside. Abruptly he made some excuse, turned and went out on the promenade of the lindens.

The visitors left at this dying season were nearly all the genuine Kurgäste; the gay element that comes to Felsbrunnen as part of their yearly routine of pleasure had left the yellowing leaves and the tired sun for the glittering shop-windows and the flaunting lights of the cities. Amongst those who lingered by the baths and the fountain was this English girl, the companion to the Gräfin von Hessele, walking slowly up and down with a nickel cup of spring-water in her hand, sipping at it from time to time in a tired, nerveless way. A leaf fluttered down from a linden and softly brushed against her face. She started violently and let the cup slip from her nerveless fingers.

Dr. Wycherley, passing in his walk, came quickly, forward and restored the cup to her with a courtesy somewhat old-world in its elaboration.

She thanked him and said: "It was careless of me, but it's easily remedied. I will get a fresh cupful." And she made to leave.

"No," said Dr. Wycherley.

"I beg your pardon?"

"That leaf was a message."

"I don't understand you."

"A silent warning. It tapped you on the cheek, but it could do no more. See it lying there; pitifully, dumb. Its work is over. Perhaps it was created on purpose to flutter down and warn you. Who knows?"

"What a strange thought! But what warning do you mean?"

"Your health."

"I know, the Graf has told me already. That's why I come here, whenever I can leave the Gräfin, in order to drink the waters."

"What has he told you? . . . Ah, you are wondering why I am asking such a question. I am a doctor, a psychologist—my name is Wycherley. . . . No, I have no motive beyond interest in my life-work and interest in your special case. . . . No, I am not eccentric, or at least I flatter myself I am not. Perhaps it is vanity on my part?"

The girl broke into a smile. "Why, you're reading my thoughts one after another. How strange to be able to do that!"

"I am gifted to a certain extent with the psychic sense, and I have trained it for my special purposes. It has told me so much about you, that I am anxious to learn more. I should let you know, in strict fairness, that I have made enquiries about you. They tell me that you are the companion to the Gräfin von Hessele, that you live a few miles away from here at Castle Kremenz, and that your health has lately been getting worse. I read in you a deep surge of emotions under. . . ."

She stiffened perceptibly, and Dr. Wycherley quickly broke off: "Ah, you feel that I am intrusive, that I am forcing myself upon you! Perhaps I should explain that I have been called across half Europe in consultation to a case here in Felsbrunnen. I arrived yesterday. My intention was to return to-night to my island on Lake Rovellasco. In that case we should probably never meet again, and the warning of your leaf would die stillborn. Yet if I could have been of service to you, I would have postponed my return. . . . As matters stand, it will perhaps be better for me to adhere to my plan."

He raised his hat in a manner somewhat old-world in its courtesy, and made to leave her.

She was clearly torn between conflicting emotions, and not until the doctor had moved away did decision come. Then she took a few quick steps and laid her hand on his arm impulsively. "Doctor, I was ungrateful! Please forgive me! Sometimes my thoughts drive me to do things I don't mean to do. Perhaps it's the melancholy of the castle. My nerves are not right. I imagine things. . . ."

"It is a strong motive that keeps you at Castle Kremenz," said Dr. Wycherley as she hesitated and paused.

The girl shrank slightly as she answered in haste: "Yes, of course I have my living to get, and posts are not easy to find. My name is Margaret McKaye; my dear father was Colonel McKaye of the Black Watch. Perhaps you have heard his name in connection with the Afridi campaign? Unfortunately he had very little to leave us— hence my post as companion."

"Strangely enough, I was in India at the time, on the Border, investigating the so-called occult. I suggested to the authorities a certain novel method of settling the Afridi rising; if my advice had been taken, your father's life would not have been sacrificed."

"But surely you're not a service man!"

"Ah, my dear young lady, you have inherited the military idea that risings are only to be put down with lead and steel. That was precisely the view of the authorities, although every one of them knew that death in battle had not the slightest terror for an Afridi. Now, on the other hand . . . but these details of native habits of thoughts would scarcely interest you. I cannot say that I knew your father, though I dined once at the mess of the Black Watch and met him there. Still, that should serve sufficiently for conventional introduction."

"What did you think of my father when you met him?" asked Miss McKaye with an eager flush on her hitherto white cheeks.

"We scarcely exchanged a dozen words. Naturally I could see at a glance that he was one of those fine, straight, fearless men who will carry out any impossible order without a second's hesitation. A 'Charge of the Light Brigade' man. The type of man who saves England in spite of muddle at the top."

"Yes, that was my father," she meditated.

"Suppose we sit down and discuss your case? I see a quiet seat over there below the terrace of the baths."

"Shall I fill my cup first?" Her tone now was that of patient to doctor. "Of course you believe in the waters?" she added.

"The waters are good for those who believe in them," continued the doctor, with his gentle irony. "To give impressiveness, the bath authorities publish a chemical analysis to eight significant figures. In point of fact, with the method of analysis employed, the limits of error in the most skilled hands are within six significant figures. That is typical of the insincerity of these cure resorts."

Margaret put down her empty cup on the seat, a little reluctantly. The blood had left her face, and it was again white and pinched. Under her eyes were tired hollows, and her eyelids drooped wearily.

Dr. Wycherley was observing her intently, not only with his eyes but also with his inner psychic sense, so sensitive to the vibrations of the minds of others. As if in continuation of his previous remarks, he took up the thread of conversation: "That will indicate to you my own opinion as to the value of the waters. I note that it is opposed to his."

The girl started violently. Her nerves were clearly ill-controlled. "But. . . but . . . ," she stammered, "what do you mean? Whom do you mean? I don't understand you!"

"The Graf von Hessele."

"When did you meet him?"

"I have never met him. I never even knew that he existed until you mentioned him a little while ago. No, you are misjudging me. I have no wish to probe into your private thoughts out of mere curiosity. Only, if I am to act as your medical adviser, I must ask for complete confidence. . . . No, I have no personal motive beyond the pursuit of my life-study, medical psychology."

With her quick changes of mood, Margaret turned to him impulsively: "Indeed I ought to thank you deeply for the interest you are taking in me. I have so few friends that I am very very grateful, believe me. I can feel that you are doing this for me out of pure kindness. Yes, I can trust you! . . . And oh, the relief it would be to have someone to confide in! The melancholy of the castle! Ruin and decay everywhere. The Gräfin sitting motionless in her chair day after day and week after week. Always dressed in white—dead white. Her son, the Graf, always so busy in his laboratory, working at his experiments. No one else to talk to—no visitors; the housekeeper silent and sullen. In the daytime so quiet and still, and then at night! . . ." She broke off abruptly in her torrent of words, and for some moments there was silence between them.

From a yellowing linden another leaf fluttered softly down and settled in the girl's lap.

Dr. Wycherley pointed to it. "Its message," he said, "is to tell me all. Only in that way can I be of real help to you."

Her answer came in a voice lowered almost to a whisper, as though there were watchers to overhear them—invisible watchers from another world: "I wonder if you have ever felt when you have entered a strange house that there is some peculiar atmosphere about it—something indefinable that seems to cling to the place and gradually glide into your mind? It is a feeling I can scarcely put into words, Doctor, but it is a very real feeling."

The mental healer nodded sympathetically.

"Well, it was like that when I first entered the service of the Gräfin at Castle Kremenz. As I passed in by the drawbridge, under the old ruined gate, and into the great half-empty rooms of the castle, something seemed to close in around me and to press itself over my mind—first like a thin, gossamer cobweb, then like a very fine veil, then gradually thicker and thicker until at times I feel it like a blanket weight upon me." Her eyelids drooped as though there were some real physical weight upon them. "And when the blanket moves a tremour goes through me. It is as though someone were trying to pull at my mind, trying to get the fingers upon it; but feebly, just as a tiny baby would pluck at one. Tug . . . tug . . . tug."

"The conditions of your post are easy?"

"I oughtn't to complain. The Gräfin is a confirmed invalid—paralysed in the lower half of the body—and chiefly I am required to read to her in German for hours on end. I go on reading, and she never makes a comment. Sometimes I wonder if she is listening or merely day-dreaming. But my other duties are light, and since posts as companion are difficult to get, I suppose I ought to be thankful to have mine."

"Her son?"

"Graf Otto is a man of about thirty-five. His hobby is chemical research, and he has a laboratory, fitted up in the tower. At least, I understand it is chemical research, for I have never been inside his rooms. He allows no one whatever to enter. He is very reserved, but he is very clever, I know, and he is particularly kind to me. He is always enquiring after my health and having special dishes prepared to build up my strength. He insists, too, on my going to Felsbrunnen to drink the waters whenever his mother can spare me. The Graf is a man I . . . I very much esteem."

Dr. Wycherley made no direct comment. He had already sensed the motive that kept Margaret McKaye chained to her post at Castle Kremenz. But he asked this: "He has never married?"

"No, not to my knowledge." A flush came into her face as she said this, and her eyes were fixed on the pebbles she was digging into with the point of her sunshade.

"One further question: how did you come into the service of the Gräfin?"

"Through the International Agency in London. I knew German well—I was educated in Hanover—and that was my great recommendation. That and the fact that I looked strong and healthy before I came to live here. Of course I know that appearances are deceptive and that people who look strong are not always so. I expect the Graf has been very disappointed in me, though he would never make a complaint in that direction. Before he engaged me in London, at the agency, he required me to go through a medical examination with a Harley Street man."

"The Graf engaged you?"

"Yes, naturally. The Gräfin is a complete invalid, and she does not travel about. I saw her first only when I entered Castle Kremenz, and she looked me over with her quick beady eyes in an instant and said: 'Good. She will serve.' Then she relapsed into her strange day-dreaming again."

"Now to take up a former point: at night-time. . . ?"

Margaret shivered involuntarily as the doctor brought back her thoughts to the point at which she had suddenly broken off some minutes before. She answered: "In the day-time it is so silent and lonely, and then in the night there come the strange whisperings and creakings, and worse, the terrors that move on padded feet and make not the slightest sound! You can feel them approaching you without making the slightest sound, creeping stealthily up to the bed, nearer . . . nearer . . . nearer! Your heart stands still, as you wait for them to touch you! ! Oh, you will think I am talking nonsense, I know. Just the foolish fancies of an overstrung girl."

"On the contrary, I never consider that patients are talking nonsense when they open their hearts to me. Thoughts and fancies are very real things—far bigger realities than people usually allow. What a man or woman thinks is far more important in life than what is said or done. Thoughts are a man's wealth or illth. . . . But haven't you tried special means to give you sound sleep?"

"Indeed, yes! The Graf has been particularly kind to me in that way. He has given me a special prescription to ensure sleep—there's a new discovery of his own in it, I believe. It's wonderful stuff to make one sleep all through the night, though in the morning it sometimes leaves one with a tired feeling. But if it hadn't been for that sleeping mixture, I don't think I could have endured staying on at the castle. . . . Now, Doctor, your eyes have been piercing into me—what do you read, what have you to say to me?"

"First, put your hand in mine." Dr. Wycherley took her hand in his own cool, firm grasp, and held it for many moments, while with closed eyes he concentrated intently on the feelings it brought before his mind—queer rapid flashes of sensation that he had long trained himself to analyse and interpret.

Then he released her hand and said: "This evening I come to the castle to see you in the capacity of an old friend of your father's. We will meet apparently for the first time for many years. You will introduce me to the Gräfin and her son and have me invited to stay to dinner—"

"But you forget my position," interrupted Margaret. "I am only the companion to the Gräfin, and—"

"Conventions are walls of pasteboard—only solid when seen from a distance. If necessary I will invite myself to dinner. Now remember, you have a part to play."

"But a deception of that kind would mean that I was distrusting Graf Otto and his mother! That would scarcely be right after all his—after all their kindnesses to me."

Dr. Wycherley bent his grave dark eyes upon hers.

"You assume," he said, "that the Gräfin and her son and the servants are the only inhabitants of Castle Kremenz."

The girl chilled with sudden horror. "Why, what do you mean? What a strange thought!"

The doctor did not reply to this. He was scribbling rapidly on a scrap of paper with his left hand, making quick rough sketches that were the embodiments of the fragmentary flashes he had sensed with his inner vision.

INSIDE THE CASTLE

The castle lay back amongst the mountains from Felsbrunnen, some four miles by the forest path but nearly eight by road. For the purpose of his plan Dr. Wycherley decided not to hire a carriage or motor, but to walk there. In that way it would be difficult for the Gräfin to refuse hospitality to a stranger arriving late in the afternoon, just before dinnertime. The sky looked uncertain, too, and that made another element in his favor.

For possible eventualities he had brought an electric torch and stowed it away in an inner pocket. If circumstances forced him to return to Felsbrunnen through the black night over a rough forest path, it would prove decidedly useful. Or there might be other uses for it even more important.

As the doctor tramped through the forest of sombre pines, up the mountain-side behind Felsbrunnen, his thoughts were deeply concentrated on the case of Margaret McKaye. Here was a matter fifty times more interesting and more important than the case of gluttony and underwork to which he had been called into consultation.

It still remained a riddle to the mental healer, in spite of what he had unraveled. What was it that was sapping the strength of the young girl—something material in the realm of the physical, or something beyond? The flashes of ghoulish semi-human features that had come to him as he held her hand and put himself *en rapport* with her inner thoughts—what did these refer to?

It was a riddle only to be solved in the fashion of the scientist, by experiment. And where an experiment was concerned, Dr. Wycherley grudged neither time nor thought nor money. The science of mind had for him the passionate interest that money-making has for the financier, cricket or golf for the keen sportsman, collecting for the connoisseur. And where the claims of science and humanity ran concurrently, as in this case of a friendless girl alone in a foreign land, he was trebly interested.

He was now passing down into a cliff-flanked valley on the other side of the mountain from Felsbrunnen. It was late afternoon, sunless, grey as to sky, a mournful spiritless grey. The pines had given place to beeches, reddening with autumn tints, the leaves drooping sorrowfully and now and again fluttering silently down to the undergrowth of tangled briar and wild raspberry. The stillness of the forest was the mournful stillness of the summer that is passing away. A stillness that creeps into the soul of man or woman. A grey silent dirge of the dying year.

The Castle of Kremenz comes suddenly into view as one rounds a corner of the cliff-flanked valley. It is perched high above, but it is almost hidden amongst the tall trees when seen from below. Since the old days when it was the stronghold of a robber baron, standing flauntingly alone, the forest has crept round it in a silent advance, and the weeds and the briars now clutch at the ruined outer walls and creep over into the courtyards.

But the main portion of the castle stands firm against the decay around, and the tower-keep makes a landmark for the valley.

There was a bell to pull at the drawbridge gate that jangled harshly through the empty, weed-grown courtyards. It was answered by a queer little shriveled old manservant who looked very dubiously at a visitor appearing on foot at that hour of the day. Dr. Wycherley asked for the Graf von Hessele, and after a wait of some ten minutes or more the Graf came to see him in the great bare reception-room.

The mental healer had long since learnt to rely on the general trend of first impressions—those heterogeneous sensations that come to one in a rush of feeling before the intellect has time to separate and analyse. In this case the rush of first impressions brought a feeling of deep distrust to Dr. Wycherley; yet on closer analysis there seemed to be little in the way of logical reason for it. The Graf von Hessele was a man of thirty-five, though his studies had bent his shoulders and given him the air of settled middle-age. His features were fine-cut with aristocratic lineage; his voice was coldly courteous; even in his rough laboratory clothes he looked unmistakably a man of breeding and culture.

And there was a certain magnetism of outward personality, difficult to analyse in words, which made understandable Margaret McKaye's silent passion—a passion unreciprocated.

In his hand he held Dr. Wycherley's card, towards which he glanced enquiringly.

"I am passing through Felsbrunnen," explained the doctor. "To-night I leave for Italy. By the merest chance I heard that you have in the castle, as companion to the Gräfin, the daughter of a very old friend of mine, Colonel McKaye. This is my reason for what would otherwise be an unwarrantable intrusion."

"I will give orders to have your coachman or chauffeur looked after while you are seeing Miss McKaye," answered the Graf coldly, after a very slight hesitation. He had a mannerism of pulling at his closely-cropped beard which somehow conveyed an unpleasant impression, though there was no logical reason for it.

"I have neither. As an old man with strong prejudice, I preferred to walk rather than engage a motorcar. But the way has proved longer and more tiring than I expected." The doctor paused significantly.

The Graf affected not to take the meaning of this significant pause, so Dr. Wycherley asked boldly, yet with a courtesy of manner that would have made refusal boorish in the extreme, for what he wanted: "Perhaps I might further intrude on your hospitality? The way has been tiring, and it will be long after dinner-time before I can reach Felsbrunnen. As an old man, my bodily needs are simple."

Dinner in the great half-empty dining-room—paneled in age-black oak and hung with the portraits of the dead and gone von Hesseles, looking down at the diners in the pride of a vanished grandeur—was a meal of deadly silences.

The Gräfin, a woman of fifty-five or so, with aquiline nose and piercing eyes, sat in grim silence in her invalid chair drawn up to the table, robed in dead white. Only at rare intervals did she make a comment, and then its sharpness cut into the air like a whip. Her son conversed with a cold courtesy, barely hiding the fact that he heartily wished the meal over and the doctor on his way back to Felsbrunnen.

Every now and again he pulled at his closely-cropped beard in a way that told of his masked impatience.

But the deadly silences did not displease the doctor. On the contrary, they were helpful to him in his disentangling of the riddle of Castle Kremenz, for while speech is mostly a concealment of thought, silence speaks nakedly to the inner hearing of the sensitive. And by the end of the meal he had made up his mind to his plan of action.

Before leaving, he took a short walk with Margaret round the ruined courtyards in the darkening, star-clouded night.

"I want you to point me out your bedroom," said the doctor.

"That window up above where I have put the box of ferns on the sill."

Dr. Wycherley measured carefully with his eye the distance from the sill to an iron staple bedded in the stone wall below. "It will need at least ten yards," he mused.

"I beg your pardon?"

"Rope. Have you ten yards of rope for the cording of your boxes?"

"Yes, but . . . but . . . ," she stammered, "what do you mean by that? How do you want to use my rope?"

For reply Dr. Wycherley took out his pocket-book and a pencil, and then began to make, left-handedly, a rapid sketch on its pages.

Finally he tore the page out and handed it to Margaret, flashing his electric torch so that she might see clearly what he had drawn on it.

"My father!" she cried. "My dear father. Oh, may I keep this sketch?"

"With pleasure," replied the doctor. "My point is here: your father was one of those fine, fearless soldiers who will carry out any impossible order without an instant's hesitation. From you, his daughter, I ask the same spirit. Have you the courage?"

By the light of the torch Dr. Wycherley could see the flush of understanding and sympathy in her face. He clicked out the light and continued: "I am going to give you orders which are equally 'impossible' in the social sense. To-night I want a rope-ladder hung out from your bedroom window so that I can climb up into your room from this courtyard. I am no longer a young man; a simple rope would be insufficient. I need a rope-ladder. Here is the way in which I want you to make one." He plucked a couple of long grass stems from the weeds in the courtyard and proceeded to show her his meaning. "In that way I shall be able to get to your bed-room later on and watch over you through the night. . . . Yes, I know all this is socially 'impossible,' but social conventions are only of pasteboard importance. Mrs. Grundy is an excellent paste-board person in her proper place. Let us keep her there. . . . To-night you will tell them that your nerves are feeling out of order and that you would like a strong sleeping-draught. You will take that sleeping-draught, lock your bedroom door from the inside, hang out from your window a thin string attached to the rope-ladder, so that I can pull out the rope by its aid, and go off to sleep in perfect confidence. Meanwhile I will take my leave of the Gräfin and her son, and spend the hours of waiting on the path back to Felsbrunnen."

"But, Doctor, it will rain. You might get your death of cold waiting in the forest. I couldn't let you risk that for me."

"There is a disused woodman's hut I noticed on my way here. That will shelter me. Now I want your promise that you will carry out your orders exactly as your father would have carried out his."

THE SECRET OF THE LABORATORY

It was raining with a thin mournful drizzle when a couple of hours later Dr. Wycherley made his way over the broken outer wall where the briars and weeds clambered, and stood in the courtyard of the castle below Margaret's window. He reflected that the rain would help to veil any slight accidental noise he might make, though indeed there was no reason why anyone should be listening.

The string was there, and by its aid he pulled out the rope ladder—a rough, amateurish production, but sufficient for its purpose if well secured inside. That point must be risked.

The ladder held, and soon he was inside the room and taking off his sodden cloak. Margaret lay on her bed, as the electric torch showed him, sleeping with the heavy breathing of the drug-taker. As a matter of experiment the doctor shook her by the shoulders with increasing force, but she only turned over drowsily without waking up. It was evident that the sleeping-draught produced a deep stupor—almost an anæsthesia.

Then he turned to examine the room. Like most of the rooms in Castle Kremenz, it was walled with stone covered over with cement. To relieve the depression Margaret had had some of her own pictures sent over from England to hang on the walls. The door was locked from the inside. The floor was of stone flags, over which rugs had been spread. A strange detail: the legs of the bed were chained to the stone flooring. Chests and wardrobes of black oak stood grimly around with an air of guarding secrets of the forgotten past.

The drizzle of the rain outside made a mournful background of sound.

And for long hours Dr. Wycherley waited in his chair, watching for he knew not what. Into his sensitive mind came impressions which tallied broadly with those that Margaret had described to him, and he knew that there were realities behind them. Once, as he closed his eyes in a light doze, there flashed before his inner vision a procession of grey-robed girls, drooping, listless, mournful, with Autumn in their eyes—a procession which vanished in a flash as he set his mind to study it.

Now he knew one of the reasons for Margaret's intense depression in that sombre environment—a depression that went beyond mere imaginings. The room was peopled not with ghosts, but with *ghosts of thoughts*, with the lingering melancholy of the companions to the Gräfin who had lived in that room before Margaret's time and had faded away as she was fading away. They had gone, but their concentration of thoughts, running all on the same lines, had left behind them a psychic atmosphere of grey melancholy.

Yet that was not all.

There must have been a reason, a tangible reason, for their melancholy and their drooping of life.

If Autumn had come to them young, as it was coming to Margaret, what was the basic cause? What was the meaning of that ghoulish, half-human figure that had flashed before his inner vision while he was holding Margaret's hand?

For long hours Dr. Wycherley waited in tireless patience for what might solve the mystery.

It was going on towards midnight before action came. At first it was a slight noise of creaking that caught his sensitive ear and made him alert and tense on the instant. Then the creaking grew louder, and with a sudden shock the doctor realised as he looked over at the bed that this was sinking slowly to floor-level. He crept nearer to it on hands and knees. It was sinking to floor-level because the stone flags beneath it, to which it was clamped, had sunk below the level of the rest. Machinery was lowering it to a room or wall-chamber underneath. With a chill of horror there came to the doctor a picture of what this must have implied in the olden times when might alone was right, and the laws of hospitality to the stranger within the gates meant little. In the olden times the von Hesseles or their predecessors had been freelance robber barons: perhaps here lay one of the secrets of their past wealth.

But to-day such an explanation was out of the question. Why then was the bed of the young girl being lowered?

It had stopped now, and Dr. Wycherley crept silently to the side of the pit in the flooring from which a dim lantern light struck upwards. With the back of a metal pocket drug-case to act as mirror, he lay flat on the flags and looked by reflection down in the hole.

Down below, by the side of the sleeping girl, still breathing heavily, was Graf Otto, fixing behind her shoulders what seemed to be a hypodermic syringe connected by tubing to a pump-like apparatus. But it was no syringe. Exactly the opposite. In a flash there came to Dr. Wycherley the realization of what the Graf was doing. His apparatus was to suck blood out of the sleeping girl! Already he was starting to work the small hand-pump connected with the suction needle fixed behind her shoulders.

Dr. Wycherley wasted no time in seeking further explanation. Though an old man, he was at the edge of the pit in an instant and had leapt down, straight on to the Graf so as to break his own fall.

There was a snap of a bone and a hoarse cry of terror and pain as the doctor came down full weight on Graf Otto, bent low over his ghoulish work and unaware of the watcher above. Then in a brief struggle the lantern smashed out, the Graf wrenched himself free, and sounds told that he was groping his way out of the pit by some secret passage. Flashing his electric torch, Dr. Wycherley rapidly made sure that Margaret had not been injured in the struggle. She was still stupefied with the sleeping-draught, but unhurt; the doctor left her to follow the Graf.

The pursuit led through a narrow passage at the end of the pit, up a long flight of steps that ran undoubtedly in the thickness of a wall, again along another secret passage, and then suddenly out into a lighted room where a profusion of chemical apparatus told at once that here was Graf Otto's private study. But it was not the apparatus of the research student that took Dr. Wycherley's attention, nor the Graf himself lying on a couch where he had thrown himself fainting from the pain of his broken arm.

It was an old woman sitting in a barred chair in a corner of the room—a chair that held her back from movement. But "old" is an adjective totally inadequate to describe her. Her age must have been far beyond the hundred; in her face were furrows graven as in the image of an Eastern idol. And when she caught sight of the doctor she cried, in a toothless mumble that rose screechingly like the voice of a parrot: "Give me blood. Give me blood! Give me blood!!"

Then her voice went down to a mumble, and again up to the shrill parrot screech, while she clawed to loosen herself from the barred chair with hands like a vulture's, horrible in their fleshlessness.

For a moment Dr. Wycherley recoiled from this terrible, ghoullike creature. But only for a moment, and then he went quickly to the couch where the Graf lay in a faint, and loosened his collar and put his head low to bring him round to consciousness. In a few minutes he had recovered, to find the doctor strapping his broken arm against a wooden retort-clamp, as an improvised splint.

"Who are you?" he asked feebly. And then, with his voice gaining strength as full consciousness returned to him: "Of course—I see now. That *verfluchte* doctor. And what the devil are you doing in my house? How did you get here? What right have you to—?"

Dr. Wycherley interrupted him without ceremony:

"We will leave those questions. First answer mine. Why were you extracting blood from Miss McKaye?

"Come, answer me!" he went on imperiously as the Graf set his teeth in silence. "It was to inject into this . . . this terrible creature, was it not? Why?"

"She was mad for it," answered the Graf sullenly, plucking at his close-cropped beard with his usual unconsciously nervous gesture. "You don't understand the matter; it was the only thing to be done."

"Again, why?"

"It is like the drug habit. When I began years ago, it was only a scientific experiment. You understand me—a scientific experiment. To introduce a fresh strain of phagocytes into the circulation channels, and so prolong her life. But her system began to adjust itself to the injections, and then one had to continue with them. I tell you there was nothing else to be done; she began to scream for the injections. I have to keep her in the sound-padded room above—at the top of the tower."

"Who is she?"

"My great-grand-mother."

"Your great-grand-mother!"

Again there came that toothless mumble from the shriveled figure in the barred chair, rising to the shrill parrot screech.

The Graf started to rise from the couch, saying: "It is four days since the last injection; if she does not get it to-night—"

But Dr. Wycherley thrust him back firmly on to the couch. "You will lie there quietly. In a few moments I will summon someone to attend to you. First I want to know this: how long has this devilish practice been going on in regard to Miss McKaye? Come, I insist on an answer!"

"Since she came," was the reluctant reply.

"How often?"

"It used to be a week. Now it has to be more often. One is forced to it."

"Every few days?"

"Yes." This very reluctantly.

"And you have been draining a young girl of life to keep the spark burning in this old woman? You have been fanning her secret love for you in order to keep her chained here at Castle Kremenz; in order to provide life serum for this horrible . . . creature? No, it's more than that. To provide you with material for your experiments, just as you are using this great-grand-mother of yours as material. Because you yourself hope to live later on by the life serum of others. If you seek an *elixir vitæ*, it is for *yourself!* Answer me, am I right or wrong?"

But Graf Otto had turned his head away—his face was ashen-grey.

Dr. Wycherley rose with a shiver of loathing and made for the secret passage that led back to the pit where Margaret McKaye lay stupefied on the bed. And as he went, there followed on the sound of his footsteps the toothless mumble of the old woman cut into by curt orders from the Graf.

He heard, too, through the arrow slit, the sound of servants clattering over the courtyard to the base of the tower.

* * * * *

It took months of skilled care and attention before Margaret McKaye was brought back again to her former health of body and mind. Dr. Wycherley had taken her to his island on the still waters of Lake Rovellasco, and in that garden of spices she came gradually to forget the shock of learning the true story of the mystery of the Castle, and to thrust out of mind the secret passion for the Graf that had kept her chained at Kremenz against the cry of every other instinct of her nature.

THE VOICE FROM THE OTHER WORLD

Venice had shaken herself free from the blanket-heats of swel-
tering summer, and had plunged relievedly into the clean cool
breezes of October as into a marble swimming-pool of crystal,
cleansing waters. Venice wakes to new life in the fall of the year,
claiming it as her spring. Then her lovers seek her once again to
offer homage. "Non cosi nol mondo; nulla città più bella."

Dr. Wycherley, so ultra-modern in many respects and so old-
fashioned in others, kept a tiny corner of his heart for the old-world
romanticism of Venice, even though it were being snowed over
these days by hordes of hustling tourists, by sea-bathing week-
enders, by cinemas, penny steamboats on the Grand Canal, and
projected subway tubes. Once a year he traveled to Venice from
his home on Lake Rovellasco to breathe in its fragrance of poetry
in stone and marble.

It was one October that he met at Venice an old acquaintance
in the person of Mrs. Trevor Fordyce, the mother of Norman
Fordyce the writer and poet. Dr. Wycherley had known her when
the boy was first adventuring on the broad seas of literature; now
he was famous over two continents.

Mrs. Fordyce had greatly changed. It was not only that time
had frosted her hair and drawn ineffaceable lines on forehead and
cheek; the change went far deeper than that—into the very roots
of her being.

They reclined in a gondola together, and the red-sashed gondolier drove them with slow, even, powerful strokes over the

rippling lagoon towards the Lido. The afternoon sun mingled its warmth with the freshness of the Adriatic breeze to ideal perfection.

"Seven years ago since we first met, here in Venice, my dear friend," she was saying, and there was a half-sigh in her voice. "That was the happiest time of my life. Why won't you scientists invent some elixir which will keep our life at its zenith-point?"

"And who is to say when the zenith-point is reached?"

"We women know."

"Tell me your secret."

"Indefinable. We *know*—what more can I say?"

"Science will not rest content with such an answer."

"Seven years ago my son was struggling for recognition. I was fighting for him, with him, shoulder to shoulder, we two against the world. That was the zenith of happiness. . . . Now he is famous." Her voice sighed like the wind in the leaves of autumnal elms.

"He married."

"When success came, he married. She was all that I could have hoped for in my son's wife. Position; beauty; a sweet nature."

"And yet you hated her?"

"She had taken away my only son."

"I am answered," said the doctor gently.

After a pause Mrs. Fordyce continued: "She died a year ago."

"Then surely he came back to you."

"No!" The word was flung out with the fire of long-repressed emotion. "No; *she keeps him still!*"

The doctor remained silent, with the silence of deep sympathy.

"How you draw out one's inmost confidences!" pursued Mrs. Fordyce. "I find myself telling you things I have told to no one else."

"And why not? Perhaps it may be in my power to advise. . . . Is there a child to link them together?"

"No child. I will tell you all. She keeps him to her by her voice from the other world. She holds him fast to her by a whispered word. 'Dearheart,' she calls him still."

"You mean literally a voice from the other world?"

"Yes, literally. He hears her calling him. Not in dreams, but when awake. He can think of nothing else but her. He is always hoping to establish complete communication with her. His work, his mother, his friends—nothing matters to him now but that one fixed hope."

Dr. Wycherley looked at her keenly.

"At séances?" he asked.

"Yes."

"You believe in spiritualistic séances, after all the exposures of trickery and fraud that have been made?"

"What does it matter what *I* believe? Norman—he believes in them utterly. Nothing can shake his faith since he has heard his dead wife calling. 'Dearheart,' she whispers. A few nights ago she spoke to him at greater length than ever before; she recalled some little point about their honeymoon that could have only been known to themselves. No other living soul could possibly have known of it. It puts trickery out of the question, you see. And yet—"

"And yet you suspect the medium."

"I do, but I have no grounds to go on. She is not a professional medium. She is helping him to establish communication practically without fee. We have come to Venice because she is here."

"Her name?"

"Signora Franchini."

The name conveyed nothing to Dr. Wycherley. It was certainly not that of any well-known professional medium.

"Could I see her?" he asked.

"It might possibly be arranged. But she does not welcome any casual stranger. She might object—she might say that your aura interfered."

Dr. Wycherley nodded. "Very probable."

"Then what do you advise?"

"Your son must make an introduction for me."

* * * * *

Norman Fordyce had the eyes of a dreamer. They held great depths of mystic, fanciful thought. They were gravely courteous, and yet they looked through and beyond one in a way that made lesser men suddenly realise their smallness. His long hair, prematurely touched with grey, fell across his forehead in a broad, careless sweep. He was tall, but a slight stoop, not unpleasant, discounted his height.

All his writings were tinged with a symbolic mysticism and a wonderfully delicate fantasy. It had taken many years for even the cultured public to learn to appreciate the subtle flavor of his writings in prose and poetry, but now he had undoubtedly "arrived"— his name carried weight and his opinions were listened to with respect by the thinkers of two continents. A thin booklet of essays— "The World in Travail"—had even sprung to the position of a "best seller," much to the astonishment of its publishers.

Dr. Wycherley, who had a natural gift for the making of friends, found an unusual difficulty in getting in contact with Norman Fordyce. It was not until they had seen one another for two or three days that he found himself able to approach the subject of the spiritualistic séances.

It was evening, in the Piazza San Marco, after dinner. They sat at a table outside Quadri's, under the broad colonnade of the square, sipping their coffee. Mrs. Fordyce, planning to leave them together, had stopped at her hotel with some slight excuse of a headache.

An orchestra was playing light, gay music in the open square. Around it, visitors in evening dress, hatless, mingled with the strollers of the city. The moon rode high—serene, unclouded.

"Moths," mused the dreamer, as with a slight movement of his tapering fingers he indicated the circling crowd. "What is the soul of a moth? A restless craving for the light of pleasure—a reaching out with gross fingers for what can never be touched without the searing of disillusion. If they would but turn their backs upon the light and seek in the outer darkness for the realities that have no meretricious brilliance. The unseen—the real, the *keenly real!*"

"It needs a sure step to tread the outer darkness," returned Dr. Wycherley, thinking of the spiritualistic experiments.

"But the rewards are great—greater than anything material earth has to offer. To clasp hands across the infinities of space—to thrill to the thoughts of those who have passed into the realm of the untrammeled spirit!"

"I, like yourself, am an enquirer. My life has been spent on the borderland of the known and the unknown. Above all I have learnt this: to tread very warily in the unlighted region. There is firm ground, and there is the quagmire."

"Do you believe, Doctor, in the life after death?"

"I believe—yes. But I have no proof as yet."

"Do you believe that those who have passed over can communicate with us who are left behind?"

"I wait the evidence."

"There is evidence already."

"Inextricably tangled with fraud."

"Not in my own case. I *know*—past all doubting."

"That is a very strong statement."

"I can prove it to you!" said Fordyce with sudden fire.

"How?"

"Come with me to-night to the house of Signora Franchini. I am to have a sitting at ten o'clock."

"She would probably not care for my presence," objected the doctor, knowing that objections would fan the sudden flame he had aroused.

"She would welcome any friend of mine," answered Fordyce, "if he comes in the spirit of genuine enquiry. It is only the grossly material sceptic we object to."

"One must needs be a sceptic before one can be a thorough believer."

"Yes, I agree. It was so in my own case. Come, but do not expect too much from the first sitting. Conditions are not always favourable. We have to learn what the best conditions are. We have to grope in the outer darkness."

"If I come," replied Dr. Wycherley, "you must allow me to come as a scientist."

"And that means—?"

"That I must exhaust all normal explanations before I allow myself the supernormal explanation."

*   *   *   *   *

A gondola threaded them through a labyrinth of narrow waterways overhung by the balconies of dark and silent houses musing on their dead past. The curious warning cry of the gondolier as he steered his craft round a blind corner cut sharply into the silence of the dark water-lanes. Occasionally an answering cry would meet his, and the two black gondolas would steal past one another like two creatures of the night bent on errands of mystery. Here a vine trailed down its long groping fingers over a wall that hid a garden, but mostly their path lay through canyons of dead stone unrelieved by any green of living plant.

The gondolier brought them gently against a flight of stone steps leading from the water-depths up to an oaken door studded with heavy iron bosses. The windows on each side were guarded with a criss-cross of iron railing. It was the ancient palace of some long-dead merchant prince of Venice. The only light in the house came from a window on the second story, stealing out through the chinks of heavy curtains.

Fordyce pulled at a bell-rope of metal, and an answering clang echoed around the canyons of the waterway. After a long wait an aged manservant appeared at the door, holding a lantern in his hand. He led the way into a bare stone entrance-hall and up a broad unlighted flight of steps to the second story.

It was a welcome relief to arrive in the lighted room where the Signora received them. There was little in the way of furniture in the room, and the heavy dark curtains to the windows gave it almost the aspect of a mortuary-chamber, but the lights of the candles in their sockets were at least human and cheering.

The Signora was a woman of forty, well-preserved, with a wealth of lustrous dark hair and enigmatic eyes that held deep reserves under a smile of welcome. Fordyce introduced her to the doctor; the two chatted for some minutes in an interchange of unimportant trivialities. Her words were seemingly frank and open, but Dr. Wycherley, keenly on guard, sought beneath them for the real woman. She spoke English admirably, but with that careful valuation of words which marks one who speaks in a foreign tongue and has not acquired the easy slurring of the native.

"I welcome any enquiry that is unprejudiced," said the Signora, "and especially do I welcome any enquiry that is scientific. There is nothing to conceal. If it please you, Doctor, search the room to satisfy yourself."

"Thank you—I do not think that necessary," replied Dr. Wycherley, knowing that if fraud were afoot, there were a hundred unexpected ways in which it might be carried out.

"All I ask is the open mind and the fair play," pursued the Signora. "There are some who come to a séance to play practical jokes or to tell untruths as to what they see and hear. But in your case, Doctor, I am sure there is nothing of the sort I should fear. You are a scientist—you will be ready to testify even against your previous convictions, if you receive proof."

"Most certainly."

"But you must not expect too much all at once. Conditions are not always favorable. We do not yet know what conditions are the best. We must grope in the darkness, so to say."

The close resemblance of these words to some previous remarks from Fordyce did not escape Dr. Wycherley. Evidently one of the two had borrowed thoughts from the other.

The Signora drew close the heavy black velvet curtains by the windows and the door so as to exclude the faintest trace of light from the outside. She placed three chairs at the points of a triangle, leaving a space a couple of yards wide in the middle. Here she stood upright a long metal horn open at both ends—somewhat like a coaching horn. After asking permission, she extinguished the candles, and the three sat in utter darkness on the chairs at the three points of the triangle.

The darkness was so complete that it was impossible to distinguish one's hand even a few inches away from the eyes. It became almost painful to keep one's eyes open.

The Signora began to croon very gently a lament from the liturgy of the Roman Catholic Church. Her voice was beautifully soft and flexible—with the softness of deep velvet. One's senses sank to rest in its yielding depths.

Then half-an-hour passed in utter silence. Whether the Signora or Fordyce had passed into trance, Dr. Wycherley had no means of telling.

A faint odour began to fill the room—very faint and elusive. Dr. Wycherley strove to name it to himself. It was . . . yes, hawthorn, the sweet smell of an English countryside in May.

Fordyce spoke suddenly, with a huskiness in his voice: "The scent is beginning. She must be near to us now."

"Hush!" said the Signora gently.

Ten minutes passed. The silence began to be oppressive in its insistent pressure on the senses—as though it called for the will to yield itself utterly to the fascination of the darkness and the unknown.

"I see the light—from the direction of the doctor," whispered Fordyce huskily.

Dr. Wycherley turned in his chair. A faint phosphorescent glow was visible in the depths of darkness behind him. It seemed to spread out in rippling waves, and then to die slowly away.

"They are approaching," said the Signora reverently. "Let us prepare our minds to receive their message."

For a quarter of an hour utter silence, utter darkness reigned. Then quite suddenly something in metal touched Dr. Wycherley on the shoulder and clattered to the floor.

"Some spirit wishes to speak to you," said the Signora. "Do not be afraid. Pick up the horn and put it to your ear."

Dr. Wycherley, to give an unprejudiced trial to the séance, groped for and picked up the metal horn, and placed it to his ear.

"What do you hear?" asked Fordyce presently.

"Only a sea-shell murmur from the air-currents in the horn."

"Listen carefully," advised the Signora. "There may be a message for you from some dear one."

"I hear nothing beyond the sea-shell murmur."

"Then place the horn in the middle between us, and we will wait again for the will of the spirits. It is difficult for them to communicate with us—very difficult. We must have patience."

Dr. Wycherley obeyed, and again there ensued a long spell of that will-enslaving silence.

Then the horn touched Fordyce on the shoulder. He picked it up and placed it to his ear, waiting eagerly for the whispered word.

"Who is it?" they heard him ask of the darkness with a wondrous tenderness in his voice.

"Is it Eithne? . . . Do you know who is speaking to you? . . . Yes, my darling, it is Dearheart. Have you some message for me?. . . Our holiday in Gaiway? Yes, yes, I remember. How could I forget it? . . . When the tide trapped us amongst the rocks. Yes, yes. Tell me what I said to you. . . . My Eithne! Oh, my darling wife! Tell me more—tell me more. . . . I can't hear now—your voice is so faint. . . . I can't hear. . . ."

And after an acute silence: "She has gone!"

"I do not think we shall receive any more to-night," said the Signora, and presently she rose to light the candles.

BREAKING THE CHAINS

"Well," said Fordyce eagerly, when they were again in their gondola. "Are you satisfied, Doctor?"

"I am completely satisfied," returned Dr. Wycherley significantly.

"Then you believe at last?"

"First answer me this: you claim that the horn was raised from the ground by spirit agency and not by a human hand? That the scent and the phosphorescent light were not the result of human agency?"

"I do!" replied Fordyce. His every feature conveyed his intense belief in the reality of the séance. "That scent was hawthorn—hers, her favourite scent. The voice was hers—the every inflexion was as she used to speak to me. And what she whispered was only known in detail to us two. No one else on earth could possibly have known the very words I said to her when we were trapped by the tide on that Galway coast. What more complete proof could one ask for?"

Dr. Wycherley sickened as he realised the utter meanness of the medium's trafficking with a man's most sacred feelings. As Mrs. Fordyce had said, her son was rapidly becoming obsessed by this communing in the darkness. The Signora had him definitely in her velvety clutch; what her next move would be was not difficult to guess. So far she had been shrewd enough to keep the money side in the background, but presently, when the hook was ineradicably fixed in her victim . . . !

"It is no proof at all," answered Dr. Wycherley, gently.

"No proof! You mean to imply that there was some trick used? You mean that the Signora could have spoken the words which came from my dead wife? Words known only to Eithne and myself? Oh, you scientific sceptics are too impossible!"

"There was no trick used in that," replied the doctor evenly.

"Then what is your accusation?"

"Merely an elementary mind phenomenon, which you mistake for a voice from the other world. An illusion of the senses."

"Prove it!" cried Fordyce heatedly.

"I will certainly prove it. To-morrow, at midday, in your own room, without any of the meretricious trappings of the séance. We will come back from the outer darkness to the wholesome light of day."

"How?"

"You will see to-morrow, if you are open to obey my instructions," said the doctor firmly, and would give no further detail of his plan.

Fordyce meditated in angry silence during the rest of the journey home. The call of his dead wife was still ringing in his ears against the cold scepticism of the scientist.

"Dearheart!" she had whispered.

*   *   *   *   *

At midday the doctor and Fordyce were alone in the latter's sitting-room. The doctor had drawn the blinds to screen off the full blaze of the sun, and had arranged an easy chair, in which he invited Fordyce to place himself.

The poet did so reluctantly.

"Is this to be some hypnotic trick?" he asked.

"Nothing of the kind," replied the mental healer gently, passing over the implied accusation. "I merely wish you to be comfortable and to let your thoughts centre on your memories of the past. Rest in this chair for half-an-hour. I will leave you alone and return later."

At the end of half-an-hour the doctor entered the room quietly with a large curved sea-shell in his hand.

"Hold this to your ear," he said, "and rest peacefully."

He withdrew to a corner of the room away from the poet's line of sight, and sat down to wait.

Ten minutes had perhaps elapsed when Fordyce spoke out with a tense eagerness in his voice.

"Is it you—is it you, Eithne? . . . Yes, I am here, next to you. Speak your heart to me, dearest! . . . Do I remember the farmhouse on the Galway coast? Yes, yes! . . . The little lamb we found on the mountainside and brought home with us—yes, yes! . . . Oh, Eithne, how your voice thrills me! Tell me more! . . If those days could only come back again! You won't leave me, dearest, will you? Come to my bedside every night and speak to me as you are speaking now. . . . What keeps you from me? . . . I don't understand. I can't hear what you are saying. . . . Your voice is so faint now. . . ."

There was silence, and then Fordyce rose brusquely from his chair. His eyes were alight with joy as he faced the doctor.

"She came to me!" he cried.

Dr. Wycherley shook his head gently. "What you have heard was the echo of your own memories. Your temperament is very highly strung, and you have the power of projecting spoken memories into the shell just as many other people have the power of projecting their visual memories into a crystal."

"I tell you it was her very voice!"

"A vivid echo of memory. Come, Fordyce, you must face realities." The doctor laid a kindly hand on his shoulder. "I know that I am harrowing your feelings with this normal explanation of your experiences. But I am doing it for your own sake—and for the sake of your mother. The dead have their claims upon us, but the claims of the living are greater. . . . Your mother."

Fordyce moved over to his desk and took up a photograph. "I won't believe it!" he flung over his shoulder. "Do you want to take from me my one joy of existence, my one hope? To know her presence is with me; to have her help in all my problems of life; to speak with her constantly without a barrier between us. It must come slowly, as the Signora says, but it will come! Complete communion!" There was rapture in his voice.

Dr. Wycherley realised that he, as well as Mrs. Fordyce, was powerless against the subtle influence of the Signora. She seemed to have coiled her will around that of Norman Fordyce. Only one course remained, if Fordyce were to be saved from the mental breakdown which the doctor clearly foresaw. That course was to go straight to the Franchini woman and try to buy her off.

With a blank cheque in his pocket-book, the doctor took gondola to the dead palace where the Signora had her present dwelling. She received him with the mark of graciousness of a thorough woman of the world, and for some little time they interchanged the conventional nothings that correspond to the elaborate courtesies of two rapier opponents. Finally the doctor steered the conversation round to the object of his visit.

"I have been demonstrating a little psychological experiment to Mr. Fordyce," he said. "I have been repeating for him, in daylight and in his own room, the echo of memory phenomenon which occurred here last night."

The Signora's eyes narrowed.

"Continue," was her only comment.

"He is largely convinced."

"Of what?"

"That it is a phenomena with an entirely normal explanation."

"Indeed?"

"I want you to help me to complete the proof. Of course I recognise that such a service on your part would call for a substantial recognition."

"Please put your meaning more plainly."

"I want to offer you now such a sum as would only come to you very gradually from Mr. Fordyce, even if he were to continue to seek your services as a medium. A present certainty in place of a future uncertainty."

"A bribe!" was the Signora's scornful comment.

With that tone of scorn, the key to the situation lay in Dr.
Wycherley's grasp. Her object lay beyond money. This woman
wanted more than Fordyce's money . . . then she must want *Fordyce
himself.*

But how was this possible—seeing that his devotion to his dead
wife was of the very fibre of his being?

And then, from his wonderful store of knowledge of the mental
cases of the whole world, there came to Dr. Wycherley the remembrance of a parallel, case he had read of in an obscure Russian journal of psychology. A strange, fantastic, almost unbelievable case.
But what had happened once might happen again.

The doctor gave no outward sign of what was passing through
his thoughts. With seemingly shortsighted obstinacy he pressed
the money offer, produced his blank cheque and a fountain pen
ready to fill it in, and received a crushing refusal and an unmistakable hint to terminate his visit.

He took his departure, and returned direct to Fordyce, whom
he found deep in meditation.

"I want to ask you one very personal question," he said. "Do
not answer it unless you choose to do so."

"Ask it," replied Fordyce listlessly.

"Has the Signora ever made evident her infatuation for you?"

Fordyce answered with an indignant denial.

"She will," affirmed the doctor.

"Out of the question!"

"Suppose . . . suppose she were to claim that your dead wife
were becoming materialised in herself—and that the soul of Eithne
Fordyce was being reincarnated in the body of Signora Franchini?
Would you believe such a claim?"

Fordyce stared at him speechlessly.

"That is the warning I have to give you," pursued the mental
healer with deep earnestness. "Continue with your séances if you
feel that they are leading you to a higher plane. But if the Signora
should broach such a suggestion—as I believe she will, very gradually, very subtly—then remember that I gave you warning. Let that
be the test of the quagmire I fear."

*   *   *   *   *

It was some four months later that Dr. Wycherley again met Mrs. Fordyce and her son. The change in Norman was patent—he seemed revivified to new energy and new enthusiasm.

"You are wonderful," said Mrs. Fordyce to the mental healer. "You have given me back my son. But how did you bring it about? He always refuses to tell me just why he broke off abruptly with his séances. They continued after you left Venice, but a fortnight later Norman suddenly took a strong dislike to them and announced his intention never to touch spiritism again. He said it was primarily due to you. But how was it brought about?"

Dr. Wycherley shook his head kindly but firmly. "If your son does not wish to tell you," he answered, "I fear you must not ask the solution from me."

THE HOUR OF ELEVEN

It was on his way back from Madrid, where he had been called into consultation over a mental case in the family of the Minister of Justice—a case important in itself but not specially novel or interesting to record—that Dr. Wycherley had stopped at Barcelona to look up an old acquaintance of his in the person of Superintendent Brennan.

Brennan, late of Scotland Yard, had been appointed by the Spanish Government to a specially-created police post at Barcelona in order to put down for them the anarchist element in that turbulent city. Barcelona with its surrounding province of Catalonia is the Ireland of Spain—distinct in character, aims and aspirations from every other part of the kingdom, always in covert or seething opposition to the central government. Brennan had had to work with the iron fist, and inside six months he was the best-hated man in the city.

The mental healer had called upon him in order to hear how he was progressing in his dangerous new post, and by way of answer the police officer had passed over to him a note written in the dialect of the province and signed with eleven red stars. In translation it ran:

> Eleven o'clock of the night is the hour we have
> fixed upon. Guard yourself as you will, that hour will
> be fatal for you. We strike in the ways you least expect!
>
>   * * * * *
>
>   (Signed) *
>
>   * * * * *

"Melodramatic beggars, aren't they?" said Brennan, with a lightness in his voice that did not ring quite unforced.

Dr. Wycherley examined the note with deep concentration, while the police officer lay back in his armchair and gently stroked his pet cat curled up on his knees and purring in sleepy contentment. This was the famous Charles, the one-time mascot of Scotland Yard, which Brennan had taken with him as a companion to his new sphere of work in Barcelona.

The handwriting of the note was thin, jerky and ill-controlled.

"A fanatic's writing," commented Dr. Wycherley, and closed his eyes in order to sense its inner meaning more vividly. "This is not an idle threat. . . . I feel the intensity of hatred underneath it. . . . The man is burning for revenge."

"There are eleven of them apparently," replied Brennan, referring to the point that each star of the signature was in a different hand.

"Yes, but the central star carries to me the most vivid sensations of hatred. That man is *dangerous*—the others are merely his tools."

"They're a cowardly crew—these Spanish anarchists," said Brennan. "And yet"—he lowered his voice, and the forced lightness had died out of his tones— "and yet they are beginning to get on my nerves a little. I wouldn't say this to anybody but yourself."

The mental healer had the very rare gift of inspiring confidences; there was that in his personality which made people trust in his discretion without hesitancy.

The police officer continued: "That note reached me a week ago. None of my men can trace who wrote it or who posted it. I've put out some pretty strenuous enquiries, as you may imagine, but I can't get the writer. . . . Since I received it, eleven P. M. has certainly been a not too pleasant hour for me. About eleven on Tuesday night, when a strong north-easter was blowing, I was out in the town and had two big tiles miss me by a fraction of an inch. That may have been mere coincidence. But Thursday night about eleven I was fired on from an empty house; Saturday night about eleven I was just in time to discover a time-controlled bomb under my bed and throw it into my water-jug."

His eye involuntarily went up to the clock on his study mantel-piece, a large presentation clock. It was marking half past ten. "It's now Monday night," said Brennan, "and probably something else in the way of a stab in the back is waiting for me at eleven."

Struck by a sudden thought, he jumped up brusquely—upsetting the sleeping Charles—and rushing to the mantelpiece began very cautiously to open the works. But there was no infernal machine concealed inside it, and the police officer returned to his chair with apologies.

"Excuse me. This kind of life makes one nervy. One doesn't know what coward's trick they'll try next. It's much easier to protect other people than to protect oneself. . . . Charles, come here!"

But the cat, grievously offended at the brusque upsetting, stalked off to an open window and made his way into the night.

"That eleven o'clock device is the scheme of an educated man—a man of refinement," said Dr. Wycherley, again studying the note signed with the eleven stars.

Brennan looked up sharply, and then nodded assent. "That's right! If I could get a line on the man! . . . But wouldn't it be possible for you to—what's the word?—psychometrise him from that note?"

"That is exactly what I have been trying to do," returned the mental healer. "But the note is not sufficiently fresh. I merely get the sensation of burning revenge underlying it. If only—" He paused, deep in thought.

"Yes?"

"If only I could obtain some object he has handled quite recently, it might be possible."

"The Saturday night bomb has been destroyed," said Brennan regretfully. "Or it might have helped you."

"Most probably it was placed in your room by one of his confederates—one of the ten other stars of the signature—and in that case it would have been useless for the purpose."

Brennan went over to a sideboard and unlocked it with a Yale key. As he produced a decanter of whisky and a gasogene he remarked significantly: "I usually take a nightcap before going to bed, and I keep the apparatus under lock and key. That's one danger the less."

Finding the gasogene nearly empty, he re-filled it with water from a water-bottle also kept in the locked cupboard, and then looked around for sparklets of compressed gas. Apparently he had run out of them, and so he rang for his English housekeeper and had her bring him a fresh box from the store-cupboard.

Breaking the wrapping of the cardboard box, he took out one of the steel sparklet bulbs and inserted it in the gasogene. The water bubbled violently as it became charged with the gas released from the metal bulb.

Brennan poured himself out a stiff whisky and soda. "I know that I needn't ask you to join me," he said, and raised the glass to his lips.

With a sudden lithe movement most unexpected in an old man, Dr. Wycherley sprang up from his chair and dashed the glass away from the superintendent's lips.

"Look at that brownish vapour in the gasogene! It means re-leased nitrous oxide. . . ."

". . . and poison in the sparklet," finished Brennan grimly, set-ting his square jaws even squarer. "The box was bought in Barcelona. Inside ten minutes we'll have that chemist in hand-cuffs."

He turned to a desk telephone and rung up sharply.

* * * * *

After twelve hours of repeated questioning inside prison walls— questioning conducted by the Spanish police with no gentle hand— they could get nothing of value out of the unfortunate chemist from whose shop the box of sparklets had been bought.

The box had been sold a week ago; by his new assistant; he himself was not in the shop at the time; the new assistant had left suddenly; the name was Fernandez and the address he gave was Calle de los Cuarto Amigos, 62; he himself was known to be a staunch loyalist all his life and a most respectable householder; he knew nothing about the box beyond the cash book entry that it was sold; not if they imprisoned him for life could he tell them more than he was telling them now; etc., etc.

The address of the assistant of course turned out a false one; the description of him was inadequate for identification in a large city such as Barcelona; in brief, the trial proved itself a *cul de sac*.

The evening after the frustrated poisoning, Brennan and the doctor were again in the former's study. Brennan was pacing up and down, his brows furrowed with deep thought, while Charles, from the hearthrug, looked up at his master with the half-closed, watchful eyes of the cat.

Brennan stopped suddenly in his pacing. "Doctor," said he with deep feeling, "you must go. Barcelona is not safe for any friend of mine. They may get me any day now. If it's a bomb, that will mean general destruction, and anyone who's with me will get hurt or killed. You'd better leave Barcelona by the midnight express for Port Vendres and French soil; there's more than an hour to catch your train."

Dr. Wycherley, for reply, said briefly, "Hold out your arm."

The police officer, though wondering at the request, did so.

"See," said the doctor, "how the pulse is shaking your fingers. No," he added quickly, "don't think that I imagine you afraid of these anarchists. It means that you are not in good bodily condition; that the several attempts on your life have affected your nerves; that at this time particularly you need an Englishman by your side. So I remain—until you have settled with the man of the red star."

"But this is police work!" protested Brennan. "I appreciate your pluck immensely, Doctor, but you're not a young man, and—" He hesitated and broke off, wishing above all to avoid hurting the doctor's feelings.

Dr. Wycherley smiled. "That is such a narrow, professional way of looking at the problem. As I see it, from the outside point of view, police guards are not going to help you greatly. You are fighting an exceptional man—a man of brains and refinement—and these Spanish police proceed as if they were dealing with some common workman."

The clock on the mantelpiece struck eleven, and as the chimes carried through the room the two men, actuated by the same thought, listened intently in silence for what might follow.

Brennan at length picked up the broken thread of conversation: "It's good of you, Doctor—I appreciate it immensely. For tonight at least I ought to be safe. The house has been searched from garret to cellar—every nook and cranny. I've got men posted all round. If anyone gets through the cordon it will either be by treachery on the part of my men or by a miracle. . . . Great heavens!" he broke off. "What's the matter with Charles?"

The cat had risen from the hearthrug and with head thrown back was snarling and spitting venomously at, apparently, nothing. Strange detail: its eyes, though wide open, were fixed in a glazed stare as if they were blinded.

For a moment a shiver went through Brennan's broad frame at this uncanny sight. "He's seeing ghosts!" he cried. And then, pulling himself together: "Charles! Charles! Lie down. Back to your rug, sir."

The cat turned its head towards the voice, like a blinded animal, and with a furious bound leapt in the direction of Brennan, claws wide and angry.

Brennan dodged it by an inch or so, but the cat turned in its leap and made back for him. A second leap, and its open claws would have been into him, had not the doctor pushed over a small table in the nick of time and caught its leap in mid-air.

"He's mad!" cried Brennan, and snatching up a poker stunned the animal into insensibility. "Whatever can have happened to the cat?"

Dr. Wycherley was tying its legs together with a handkerchief. He did not answer for a few moments, but cautiously bent down to get the odour of the cat's breath.

"Cannabis indica," he replied. "Indian hemp. Someone must have given it a dose early in the evening."

"The red star man."

"Probably."

"So that it would turn mad and fly at me?"

Dr. Wycherley bent closer over the unconscious animal. "I get traces of another odour like bitter almonds. That would be cyanide. Yes, the claws have been dipped in cyanide. If it had scratched you—"

"Good God! What a devilish scheme!"

"That man must have had the cat in his hands sometime this evening," pursued the doctor, with the zeal of the scientist lighting up his countenance. "Just what we were wanting for the psychometric experience—something that he had recently handled! Splendid, splendid! Now I'll try to get an impression of his appearance."

Brennan looked in amazement at Dr. Wycherley. He did not understand the scientific temperament, and the way in which it would override all ordinary feelings. For the moment Dr. Wycherley had completely forgotten that the murder of his friend had just been frustrated by a hair's breadth; his thoughts were centred on the possibilities of his experiment. For the moment he was the embodiment of the professional experimenter.

Lifting the cat up, he laid it on Brennan's desk, and making sure that the legs of the animal were securely tied against any movement on awakening, proceeded to lay hands upon it with closed eyes, deep in concentration.

Presently his left hand stole towards a scrap of paper on the desk, and Brennan, guessing at his wish, passed over a pencil.

Dr. Wycherley said not a word, but his left hand began to trace on the paper lines and shadings that presently developed into the sketch of a man with a short dark beard and deep-set, fanatical eyes. A scar ran on his forehead from the left eyebrow to the line of the thick, dark hair, diagonally.

Brennan, watching with keen intensity, clenched his fist triumphantly.

"I know that man! Luiz Arrida. He's a lawyer of the city, and has always been reckoned as a loyalist. I've actually worked on committees with him. I'll have him arrested at once."

"No," said Dr. Wycherley, sharply, as Brennan laid hands on the telephone.

The police officer paused in surprise.

AFTERMATH OF REVENGE

It had taken long argument before the doctor had convinced his friend of the essential logic of the extraordinary course of action he proposed. Brennan, with a life service in the police behind him, was naturally inclined to the routine procedure of arrest and public trial and an object-lesson to the revolutionaries. He ignored the fact that many such object-lessons had been demonstrated in the courtyard of the grim prison fortress of Montjuich, and yet had only served to throw fuel on the fires of hatred.

"This Luiz Arrida is an exceptional man," the mental healer had urged. "Let us deal with him in an exceptional way—the psychological way."

Keen discussion had taken place over the general plan and then over the details, but eventually Brennan accepted the strange experiment, more on the weight of Dr. Wycherley's personality than on any conviction of success. In the early hours of the morning the police officer wrote and posted off a letter to Señor Luiz Arrida, asking him to call that afternoon to take directions for the drafting of a will. Since Brennan intended to settle on Spanish soil, the letter explained, he judged it desirable to have a will drawn up according to the Spanish legal formalities.

When at his office desk Arrida opened his morning's mail and read this letter, his first feeling was a grim and silent amusement. So Brennan intended to settle on Spanish soil? Perhaps he would do so in a sense far removed from his intention. It made a pretty jest.

Then came suspicion of the letter. Was it some trap? Well, in that case there would be an automatic pistol in his pocket, and some lively shooting.

But the dominant feeling was a burning hatred of this Englishman who had come to smash an iron fist into the revolutionaries, the patriots of Catalonia. He, Señor Luiz Arrida, was the instrument of God designed to drive the Englishman back to his own land. The scar on his forehead flushed a dull red with the uncontrollable anger surging through his veins. Perhaps that afternoon's meeting might show him some new way to accomplish his purpose.

Yes, he would certainly obey the call.

As he drove in his smart motor-car through the broad central streets of modern Barcelona, slashed yellow and purple with the flooding sunlight on the stone walls of substantial modern business houses, he fingered an automatic pistol in his coat pocket. It was one of those deadly miniature weapons that spit out ten shots in a few seconds. If a finger were laid on him while in the house of the police Commandant, he would deal out death in an instant.

Under the dark archway that led to the *patio*, Arrida pulled a bell that clanged echoingly down cool stone Corridors. For a moment only he had a chill of misgiving at this venturing into the house of his enemy, but quickly reflected that Brennan could scarcely have connected him with an anarchist organisation.

Besides, he had his automatic pistol with him ready for instant use.

Arrida was shown by the manservant into the cool shadows of the patio, where lounge chairs stretched invitingly under blossoming orange trees odorous with scent. To his surprise, he was received by Dr. Wycherley, who introduced himself and offered the visitor a chair.

"The Señor Commandant will be here presently, will he not?" asked Arrida. "No doubt he has been taking a long siesta."

"He is dead," answered the mental healer very simply, while his grave dark eyes read deep into the soul of the lawyer.

Elation, misgiving, triumph, curiosity—all these buzzed through Arrida's brain before the conventional answer framed itself on his lips: "I am extremely grieved to hear it. He was a capable officer and very courageous—a great help to the Government in the quieting of the city. Yes, I am particularly sorry to hear of his death. It must have been very sudden?"

"He died this morning. There was an attack made on him by his pet cat—it went suddenly mad and flew at him. The scratches became poisoned in some manner."

"*Madre de Dios!* What a strange end!"

"The news is being kept very quiet until his successor is appointed," continued Dr. Wycherley. "They have telegraphed to London this morning, and a reply is being awaited. They have offered the post to another famous Scotland Yard man."

Arrida was profoundly startled. He had not reckoned before on such a probability. Surely no man in his senses would take up Brennan's post after what had happened during the past days? And yet, with these mad Englishmen, one never knew what to expect.

"I am telling you all this," pursued the doctor, "because we can trust in your discretion."

"Naturally, naturally! This terrible affair has greatly shocked me. Is there nothing I can do?"

"If there is any legal formality in which you can help us—?"

"Certainly! With the greatest pleasure!"

"Mr. Brennan has been laid out on the couch in a room adjoining. Would you care to see him?"

For a moment a gleam lighted up the eye of the fanatic, but he regained his mask and answered with a conventional, "I should be glad to see the Señor Brennan once again."

In a room with close drawn curtains Brennan lay on a couch covered with a white sheet. Dr. Wycherley led his visitor into the room, and reverently turned back the sheet to uncover the face. It was white and stiff and motionless.

Then he asked quietly: "Shall I leave you with him?"

The lawyer nodded assent, his words sticking in his throat unuttered, and Dr. Wycherley withdrew *to leave a murderer and his victim alone.*

It was a strange whirl of human emotion that eddied in that darkened silent room after the mental healer had left, closing the door behind him. Arrida's veins surged with the passion of triumph as he looked on the still white face of the man he had done to death. Hatred satisfied to the ultimate end—he had the cup of satisfaction filled for him to the brim. He sipped at it lovingly, gloatingly, as he looked on his victim with the eyes of a fanatic.

For a moment he stood motionless drinking in the atmosphere of revenge accomplished.

Then he moved forward to place a hand of triumph on the dead man's face, but before the body he checked himself with a shiver of superstition. Some day, in another world, he would have to answer for that crime before One to whom nothing was hidden. To touch the dead man would, according to the superstitious working of his mind, add to his crime.

His diabolical scheme of the maddened cat and the poisoned claws had succeeded, and now . . . Yes, and now? Brennan was dead, and they had wired to London for another Brennan to take his place.

The same work to do all over again! The thought came to him with a sudden brusque burr of disgust. As Dr. Wycherley had sensed, Arrida was a man of education and refinement, and the reaction after sated revenge came upon him with a sensation almost of nausea. Brennan had been "stabbed in the back," in unfair fight, and the anarchist organisation would expect Arrida to deal with Brennan's successor in the same way.

It was slimy work!

Involuntarily he wiped his hands on his handkerchief. He found that they were clammy with sweat, and a stinging realisation came to him of the silent revolt of the body against the deed it had carried out at the bidding of his will. He had had revenge in full, and now it nauseated him. He dropped on his knees and began to pray.

It was thus that Dr. Wycherley found him as he entered noiselessly with an open telegram in his hand, and he knew by the head bent in genuine supplication what must be the dominant feeling now in the murderer's mind.

Arrida started as though caught in some guilty action, but recovered his composure in an instant and rose quietly to his feet after a few moments.

"Well?" he asked, with the look directed at the open telegram. Dr. Wycherley handed it to him. "As you will see, the offer has been accepted, Mr. Brennan's successor is ready to take up the post in a fortnight's time."

Lawyer-like, Arrida was carefully examining the telegram, but there was no suspicion under his automatic action. The telegram was perfectly genuine, and he realised that with these mad English-men no other result could be expected. If one of them were killed off, another could always be found to take his place.

Dr. Wycherley had moved over to the body to put the sheet back over the face. He gave a sudden exclamation of surprise.

"What is it?" asked Arrida sharply, and his hand went towards his hip-pocket.

"There is colour coming slowly into the face. I feel a return of the pulse. Quick, call the household!"

*   *   *   *   *

Half an hour later, when Brennan had been put to bed and was apparently on his way to a marvelous recovery, Arrida proposed to take his departure. The matter of drafting out a will could of course wait a day or two.

But Dr. Wycherley drawing him aside, asked for a few moments' private conversation, and led the way to the darkened room where the body had been laid out a short time before.

The lawyer, though keenly suspicious of a trap, followed the mental healer and took the chair as requested.

"To begin with," said Dr. Wycherley quietly, "I am an old man and unarmed. Nor are there any watchers of this room."

"I fail to understand," answered Arrida coldly.

"I mean that there will be no necessity to draw that weapon from your pocket."

The lawyer remained silent.

"I know, of course, the share you have had in the administra-tion of cannabis indica to Mr. Brennan's pet cat. I also know of . . . No," he added quickly, "please don't think that I place myself in any judicial capacity. In fact, I have advised the Commandant to take no action against you, of any kind. He has accepted my advice."

The lawyer rose to his feet. "This conversation is meaningless to me. Explain yourself, Señor Doctor!"

Dr. Wycherley shook his head gently. "Let me repeat again that you are free to go when and how you will. There will be no proceedings taken against you. Tell me this, if I am wrong in my deductions, why did I find you a little while ago on your knees praying to your Maker to forgive you your crime of murder?"

He fixed his keen searching eyes on the lawyer, and the latter quivered involuntarily at the truth of what he was hearing.

"You have escaped that crime by what seems a miracle. And you are glad! Your better self had revolted! When you stood in this darkened room alone with your victim, what was your ultimate thought—satisfaction or remorse?"

Arrida had sunk to his seat again and one hand was twitching nervously at a loose thread on his coat sleeve. He uttered not a word.

"You have learnt a great truth," pursued the mental healer earnestly. "That there is no satisfaction in revenge. That revenge accomplished turns bitter in the mouth. Have I not read your innermost thoughts?"

"You are a strange man," answered Arrida hoarsely. "What is it you want from me?"

"Nothing material. I do not ask, I give. All that I desire is that you should realise to the full *the meaning of revenge*. If Mr. Brennan is removed, another takes his place, as you have seen. What good purpose can it serve to plot against his life?"

"The freedom of my country!" replied Arrida, with sincerity ringing in his voice.

"Which you will obtain, if your cause is just, by other and higher means. Assassination is not revolution—no one realises that more clearly than yourself. Your aim is a noble one, but what of the means you have employed? Now give me your hand and tell me that when you fight in future, you fight fair."

Many had said that there was resistless command in the personality of Dr. Wycherley, gentle as his methods might be. Here at least it was proved true, for Luiz Arrida gave his hand in a silence that was deep with sincerity.

When Arrida had left the house, and Dr. Wycherley with a great relief in his heart had returned to the Commandant of Police, the latter asked:

"What happened while I was in that cataleptic trance you put me into? I remember nothing from the time you had me under the influence until the time I woke up in bed."

"What happened?" answered the mental healer thoughtfully. "In brief, the revelation to a man of his own soul."

COURTESAN SANDS

In pursuit of his life-passion, the study of the human mind, Dr. Wycherley had decided one summer on a tramp through Brittany. It is a land of strange superstitions—superstitions that reach back through the centuries beyond the Christian era and link to-day with the age of the Druids and even with the cradle-time of the Aryan races, There live in one corner of Brittany a people who are as it were an outpost of some Mongol race, driftwood left behind by some mighty race wave of invasion over Europe. In their high, prominent cheek-bones and close-set eyes, one can read the wash of the Tartar blood. In their customs and in the strange superstitions they have grafted on to their Christian faith, one can divine the remnants of a religion five thousand years old.

To get close to the people he wished to study, Dr. Wycherley avoided the towns and the hotels, and sought his lodging in wayside farmhouses and fishermen's cottages. It was thus that he came to stay with old Gil Maurtain and his wife and Yvette his grand-niece, in their cottage by the sands of Plouharnez.

Six miles across stretch the sands from Cap Plouharnez to the Bec de Pieuvre; and ten miles out they stretch at the lowest spring tide from river-mouth to beyond the Rock of the Black Virgin.

Sands glittering yellow under blaze of sunlight; sands golden-orange under slant of sunset; sands glistening grey under a sky of scurrying, ragged storm-clouds; sands that attune themselves to every mood of the heavens; sands ever changing under the restless sweep of the tides and yet ever the same; sands that smile to men and lure them and trap them and mock them.

Courtesan sands.

At full-moon tide the whole sands are clothed with the mantle of the ocean, and fishing boats saunter slowly above them dragging in their wake invisible seine-nets. Then the sea will withdraw for mile after mile, unveiling the seductive charms of the sands— smooth, glistening, sensuous. At full ebb of the spring tides a man may walk dryshod the whole ten miles from the shore to the Rock of the Black Virgin, if he choose the right hours and path, and avoid the trickling sand-streams and the treacheries of the known quicksands. Here and there over the wide stretch of the sands are lines of thin poles which act as landmarks to the fishermen and those who drag for eels and crayfish.

Without such guides, even the shrewdest sandsman might fall victim to the clutches of the siren whose bridal bed is the quicksand.

* * * * *

Dr. Wycherley, with his keen intuitive sense, realised from the first evening of his stay with the Maurtains that under the placid, somnolent exterior of the cottage life there smoldered a drama ready to burst into flame at an instant's notice. He sensed it as vividly as a man can sense a coming thunderstorm. On the psychic plane, the air was electric. And so he resolved to remain on at the cottage. His help might be needed.

Old Maurtain was more than agreeable to the extension of the doctor's stay. It meant money, and money was the ruling passion of the old sandsman. While other passions had burnt themselves out, this one had intensified with age. The less he could use money, the more he coveted it.

They were sitting one evening on the wooden seat outside the cottage door, waiting the call to supper, when the old man suddenly raised a gnarled finger and pointed East across the bay.

"See you, it has returned," he exclaimed.

Dr. Wycherley's sight was not so keen as the sandsman, and it was a little time before he could locate the object pointed at—a dark speck flying low across the sands against the background of the cliff named the Bec de Pieuvre.

"An aeroplane."

"A child of the devil," answered Maurtain, with an ugly frown criss-crossing the age-lines on his forehead.

"You say it has *returned?*"

"It was here in May, two months ago."

"No doubt these sands make an excellent ground for trial flights."

"It will bring ill luck upon all of us. I must burn a big candle to the Black Virgin."

"You mean at the shrine on the rock yonder?"

"Yes, the shrine to Notre Dame des Mors. We of the sands call her the Black Virgin."

"Who owns this machine?"

"He is not one of us, but a stranger. He has built himself a shed across the bay. He calls himself André Vic."

"I know the name." It was that of a young professional aviator who had taken part in the Paris-Rome flight—a mechanic rapidly making fame for himself in the aeroplane world.

"It should not be allowed," said the old man sullenly. "The sands are ours. It will spoil the fishing."

"How?"

"The noise of this devil-bird frightens away the fish. They will leave us and find a new home. But besides that, it is unlucky."

Yvette came out of the cottage to tell them of supper ready. She was scarcely eighteen, lithe and slender, contrasting sharply with the other girls of Plouharnez, a type somewhat short and stocky. Her finely-spun fair hair was gathered demurely under her snowy coif like a Quakeress. An artist would have claimed her for a model.

As she came out by the open door, her keen eyes sighted the monoplane, now resting motionless on the sands across the bay. She said nothing.

Dr. Wycherley, noting that she saw and yet made no comment, sensed some connection with the electric restlessness underlying the placid interior of the cottage life.

"It is an aeroplane," he ventured.

"Yes, monsieur," answered Yvette without raising her eyes to his.

They went in to their homely supper, and the old man asked the blessing of God and of the Black Virgin upon the meal. Dr. Wycherley, who respected all religions, bowed his head reverently.

Late that night, when the household should have been fast asleep, Dr. Wycherley awaked to a slight noise in the room adjoining his. Impelled by a sudden instinct, he threw aside the bed-clothes and went to the window.

Yvette, with a dark cloak thrown round her shoulders, was lowering herself out of the window of her room. She dropped lightly to the ground, and began to walk rapidly eastwards along the grass of the foreshore. Presently she turned down to the sands and started to cross them in a line for the Bec de Pieuvre. Dr. Wycherley watched her until she was lost to view in the darkness.

Now he understood one element in the drama of the cottage.

Yvette was early about the house the next morning, at work on her household duties. Although she must have walked twelve miles between midnight and dawn, to her lover across the sands and back, Dr. Wycherley saw in her no signs of fatigue. She was singing softly and happily when he came down to breakfast.

The tide now covered three-quarters of the bay. The waters were a-ripple with a gentle breeze from eastwards.

"I should like to visit the Rock of the Black Virgin," said the doctor to the old sandsman. "Can I hire a boat and someone to accompany me?"

"Certainly, monsieur, that is easily arranged. Yvette will take you out to the Rock. There is a good sailing breeze, and she handles a boat well."

The girl accompanied Dr. Wycherley to the mouth of the tidal stream, a mile or so away, where their boat was moored to a primitive form of wharf. It was a small, stout dinghy with a lugsail. In it the two made out by the winding channel of the stream and so on to the open waters. In a couple of hours they had reached the Rock, and were climbing to the shrine.

Dr. Wycherley, not usually interested in religious emblems except in so far as they bore on his own line of study, showed a strong interest in the sculptured figure that stood in a niche near the summit of the Rock. It was cut from some very hard stone dead-black in colour—a stone quite unlike the grey granite of the rock itself and certainly not to be matched in the whole of Brittany. Dr. Wycherley knew it for the same stone as the mysterious *lapis nigra* of the Forum at Rome, about the origin of which archeologists argue heatedly.

Even more than the stone itself did the figure interest the mental healer. The pose was set and formal; the face hard and sphinx-like.

"Do you believe this is a statue of the Virgin Mary?" he asked of Yvette.

"Of course, monsieur."

"What does the *curé* of your parish think?"

"He has wanted several times to have it taken away, but we of the sands would not let him."

"The face is very cold and hard."

"Now it is so; but sometimes she smiles."

"Smiles?"

"Yes, monsieur, when Our Lady wishes to bring good fortune to anyone." The girl began rapidly to relate stories of good luck amongst the fisherfolk—a record catch, some wreckage washed up on the sands, once the actual wreck of a cargo steamer on the Bec de Pieuvre. All these she attributed to the influence of the Black Virgin. The sincerity of her belief was beyond question.

"I will light my uncle's candle," continued Yvette, "and perhaps Our Lady will be gracious and smile on us."

Old Maurtain had given her a candle to burn before the shrine. He had been careful to scratch his name on it, so that the Black Virgin might know that the offering was his. Yvette now set the candle in a metal casket to one side of and below the figure, and lit it, watching the face of the statue intently.

Against the sunlight the candle struggled feebly, but presently a cloud passed over the sun, and in the semidarkness of the niche where the statue was placed the candle-light flung sharply on to the face of the Black Virgin, altering completely the normal fall of the shadows.

"See, monsieur!" exclaimed the girl joyfully.

Dr. Wycherley nodded his head in silence. The up-flung candle-light had brought a new expression to the cold features of the statue—almost a sardonic smile. The imagination of the fisherfolk would easily construe this to a smile of gracious benediction. There lay the power of the statue—in the auto-suggestion it roused in the minds of the devotees. Feeling themselves to be lucky, it naturally followed that they would put out their best exertions—and so "luck" would come to them. Dr. Wycherley could easily understand that the *curé* of the parish and for that matter, even the bishop of the diocese—would be powerless against the smile of the Black Virgin, this pagan statue from the mists of antiquity.

The cloud passed away from the sun, and the features changed back again to the set, sphinx-like expression of before.

As they started to descend the Rock, a faint whirring noise caused them both to look up to the sky. The aeroplane was soaring far above them at a height of several thousand feet. Suddenly the whirring ceased—the motor had been shut off. The air-craft dipped sharply downwards, and began to descend in a series of spirals. It came down until, like a seagull, its feet almost touched the water, and then with a rasp the motor came into action and the aviator sped off and upwards, waving his hand to the girl on the Rock.

Yvette waved her handkerchief back to him.

"Have you ever been up in the air?" asked the doctor.

"Once, monsieur," answered Yvette, with a deep blush in her cheeks. "But my uncle did not like it."

"He is prejudiced against the aeroplane?"

"Yes, monsieur."

"And he has other views for your future, has he not?"

The girl looked startled. "How did monsieur know that? Did my uncle tell you?"

"No; but I can sometimes read thoughts."

A sudden flaming passion came into Yvette's eyes. "*I hate him!*" she cried.

"Your uncle?"

"No, Etienne!"

Dr. Wycherley waited for her to say more, but seemingly she had repented of her confidence, for she changed the subject at once and spoke only of impersonal matters.

When they returned to the cottage, it was to find a visitor to table—a powerful, hard-bit, dark-haired man of thirty-five or so, with prominent cheek-bones and eyes set close together.

Old Maurtain introduced him as "my friend, Monsieur Etienne Concarnot." A *patron*, he added, meaning that he was an owner of fishing-boats.

*   *   *   *   *

The storm was near at hand.

Dr. Wycherley felt the psychic tension as they sat at table. The *patron's* eyes were constantly on Yvette, but the girl avoided his gaze and answered questions briefly and in a low voice.

After the meal, the household were very evidently waiting for the doctor to withdraw and leave them to themselves, so he took books with him and went out walking around the bay.

Certainly he had no right to interfere in the family affairs of the Maurtains. Yvette must fight her own battle against her people. And yet, if there were any way in which he could help her . . .

He felt a sudden desire to see the young aviator face to face and judge what kind of man he was. Accordingly he made for the hamlet near the mouth of the stream, and engaged a tumbledown carriage at the inn to drive him round to the far side of the bay.

At the end of a tedious, jolting drive, Dr. Wycherley found himself at the field where the young aviator had built his hangar—a long, low shed in galvanised iron. Apparently he lived with his mount, for there was no other building near, and a thin curl of smoke from a chimney on the tin roof suggested a cooking-range somewhere inside.

Dr. Wycherley traversed the field on foot. Through the open door of the hangar he saw two young men intently at work on the wing of the machine, fitting some new stays.

He watched in silence until one of the men looked up abruptly and jerked out:

"Who are you? We don't want any idlers around here!"

The young fellow was clean-shaven, clean-cut in feature, brisk and authoritative, and the impression he gave to the mental healer was that of a healthy young mechanic-athlete very much wrapped up in his work—one of the modern, wholesome young Frenchmen so utterly different from the comic types of the English stage.

It was not a pleasant welcome, but Dr. Wycherley did not resent the words or the tone of voice. This young fellow was on his own ground and quite within his rights to order any stranger. The doctor replied:

"I am a scientist, and I am staying with Gil Maurtain and his wife . . . and Yvette."

Something in the tone of Dr. Wycherley's quiet words seemed to appeal to the young man, for he answered rapidly:

"Good. Any friends of theirs are welcome here. My brother"— jerking his hand towards the other man, younger than himself and less decided in feature and manner. "Want to see my new flier?"

"I should be very much interested."

"It's my own design." He proceeded to expound the points of the machine with enthusiasm.

"I saw you make a splendid flight this morning. You passed very close to me when I was on the Rock of the Black Virgin . . . with Yvette."

André gave a rapid side-glance at the doctor, and then called to his brother:

"Knock off work and make us some coffee."

The brother went off obediently to another room to do so.

"*Dites donc*, what's the point of your coming here?" asked the aviator shrewdly of Dr. Wycherley.

"I come as a friend of Yvette's."

"Oh!" There was suspicion in his exclamation.

"The question I am going to ask is one I have no right to ask, and so you need not answer it unless you choose to. Do you want to marry Yvette?"

"My God, yes!" came the instant response.

"I judged that. Well, you will have to play a strong hand."

"Why?"

"There is a determined rival in the field."

"I know." The young fellow flicked his thumb and finger together in contempt. "Is that all?"

"That is all—at *present*."

"What makes you say that?"

"I feel that—more strongly than words can put it—something big is going to happen—suddenly—like the bursting of a dam. And I am afraid for little Yvette."

Young Vic sobered at this. "Will you be staying on at the cottage until next week?" he asked.

"Probably."

"Then will you send for me at once if I should be wanted? I've got to get this flier ready for the Western Circuit Race. When I've won that, I shall take a bag full of gold to old Maurtain, and empty it all over his table. Then Yvette and I will marry."

"If you were wanted very quickly, it would be difficult to let you know in time. There is no telegraph or telephone from Cap Plouharnez to here."

The young fellow thought this over for some time.

"Here's a plan. I'll get some rockets from the lighthouse, and send them to you at the cottage. If I'm wanted in a hurry, you could fire them off."

"Suppose you were asleep at the time?"

"My brother and I take turns in watching throughout the night. Otherwise these pigs of ignorant Bretons would be wrecking my machine. Myself, I'm from Burgundy. . . . Besides that, I'll ask the lighthouse men—they're friends of mine—to keep an eye open and let me know if you send up a rocket."

With the unconscious selfishness of youth, he had been taking the doctor's interest in his affairs as a mere matter of course. Now, however, he seemed to realise suddenly that behind Dr. Wycherley's modest and unassuming exterior was a man of international reputation—a big man. Deference came into his voice as he continued:

"Monsieur, you are very kind to put yourself to so much trouble for the sake of Yvette and myself. I owe you a thousand thanks. What can I do for you in return? Would you like a flight with me into the clouds one day?"

Dr. Wycherley smiled. "I am an old man," he replied, "and I have long ago come down from the clouds. Earth has more than enough to teach me."

THE GREEN FLARE

That night, old Maurtain was in a state of secretive excitement. Dr. Wycherley, observing him closely, knew that something vital had happened during his absence from the cottage that afternoon— something connected with the sinister figure of Etienne Concarnot.

Long after his usual bedtime, the sandsman sat on the wooden seat outside his cottage, smoking and gazing intently over the sands shrouded in the veil of the night. Dr. Wycherley, from the window of his room above, watched also, but for what he knew not.

About midnight there came a startled exclamation from old Maurtain sitting below on the wooden seat. Far out on the sands, at a distance which the darkness made impossible to judge with accuracy, flared up a vivid grass-green light . . . then died away.

A footstep sounded near at hand. The voice of Etienne Concarnot whispered in triumph:

"Thou seest?"

"I see well," replied Maurtain eagerly. "Thou thinkest it is indeed She?"

"Who else? I tell thee that not only did She smile but also She raised Her hand and pointed . . . out yonder."

"It is wonderful!"

"My grandfather told me of this. It has been a secret in our family. Thou also must keep it secret."

"Indeed, yes."

"Now wait until to-morrow night. At the same hour She will again walk the sands."

"Blessed be Her name!"

"Remember, in what comes of this we share equally!"

"That is well understood."

The two men went into the cottage, and their whispers were lost to Dr. Wycherley.

The mental healer took pencil and paper, and with his left hand began to draw from memory a miniature of the Black Virgin, accurate to the smallest detail. He enclosed it in an envelope addressed to Professor Clovis Marnier of Paris, an archeologist of European reputation and a friend of the doctor's. With the drawing went a brief note:

"Who or what is this? Let me know immediately by telegram."

The next day there came a call for Dr. Wycherley which it was impossible for him to shelve. He was wanted at Nantes in consultation over a mental case. The call had been some days in reaching his present address, and accordingly he hastened to Nantes by the first train.

It was very late that evening when a tedious, cross-country train landed him back at the nearest station to Plouharnez. The dilapidated fly belonging to the local inn-keeper jolted him over the rough *route communale*, through a slowly drizzling rain, to the cottage by the sands. There he found a telegram awaiting him in his room. It read:

Undoubtedly statue of Astarte or goddess with similar attributions in later times was considered goddess of love but original attribution was goddess of fortune human sacrifices were made to win her favour chiefly young maidens.—Marnier.

Goddess of fortune! Was this the key to the mysterious conversation of the night before between Maurtain and the sinister patron of fishing-boats?

Dr. Wycherley went down to the living-room of the cottage to forage for some supper. Although it was very late—past eleven o'clock—both the sandsman and his wife were sitting in the room, talking in low, eager whispers. At his entrance they ceased abruptly.

"A nasty night," ventured the doctor.

"Yes, monsieur," they agreed.

"Can I have some supper?"

"The wife went to fetch it."

"I have bought a little trinket for Yvette," said the doctor presently, as he sat down to table. "Only a trifle, but it may please her. You have no objection to her taking it?"

The old dame answered with a new-born self-importance: "Ah, monsieur, *now* we shall be able to buy her a gold watch and chain and—"

Her husband made a warning gesture, and she stopped short in her sentence.

You have come into a legacy?" asked the doctor, but the question was only to keep conversation going. The realisation had come to him that in some way the threatened storm had broken upon the household, and he was not listening with the organ of hearing, but—if one may strain words—listening with the psychic sense, his power of gathering the thought-vibrations of others.

"Something like that," was the cautious answer of old Maurtain.

Dr. Wycherley deliberately laid down his knife and fork, and with a sudden blaze of white-hot energy flung out this question, full into Maurtain's face:

"*Where is Yvette?*"

The sandsman quivered as though he had received an actual blow.

"That is not your affair!" he retorted with sullen suspicion.

"Where is Yvette?" repeated the doctor imperiously.

Involuntarily the old dame turned her head towards the window of the living-room.

"Out on the sands! On a black night like this! Do you mean to say that you have sent her out on the sands? Why?"

"That is not your—" repeated old Maurtain angrily, but Dr. Wycherley interrupted him with a fire of questions:

"Out to follow the Black Virgin? Out to the green light? Out to the *quicksands?*"

"No, monsieur!" answered the wife with real indignation and at the same time with the deepest conviction in her voice. "To find the buried treasure which Our Blessed Lady will lead her to! That is why Yvette has gone out on the sands! She will mark the spot with a pole, and to-morrow we shall dig up the treasure and be rich—very rich—so rich that we can—"

"You mean that this fellow Concarnot has told you to send her?"

"Yes; he could not go himself, because it is only to a young maiden that Our Lady will reveal the treasure, so we arranged that Yvette should go with a lantern and a long pole—"

Dr. Wycherley did not wait to hear more. It was the time for swift, decisive action. Only two possibilities could save Yvette from Concarnot's fiendish revenge of death amongst the quicksands. He must have arranged carbide flares to lure her out. The girl was going to her death with implicit faith in the guidance of the Black Virgin. Only two possibilities could save her now: a miracle, or rescue by aeroplane.

In his room were Vic's rockets—three of them. He brought them down and rapidly set them up in the foreshore in front of the cottage. A sheltered match set light to the fuse, and with a roar the rocket shot skywards and burst out into a drooping pendant of red stars, blurred by the drizzle of the night. A second followed, and at a few minutes' interval, a third.

While Dr. Wycherley questioned and cross-questioned the two Maurtains, now thoroughly frightened, as to the direction the girl had taken out on the sands when she had left the cottage a couple of hours before, some of the villagers arrived, panting, in hastily-donned clothes, to learn what the firing of the rockets might mean.

Rapidly the doctor organized a search party to follow her footsteps across the waste of sands, uncovered at full ebb.

A low whirring noise made itself heard, growing rapidly louder.

"Shout!" ordered the doctor. "Shout all together, so that he will know where to land."

Presently the rhythmic drone of the Gnome motor ceased abruptly; the air-craft planed down, and with a jerk hit the sands by the cottage and ran along to a stop.

André Vic and his brother jumped off from their seats.

"What's the matter?" shouted André through the drizzle.

Dr. Wycherley ran to meet him with a lantern, explaining in rapid, terse sentences what the call to action meant.

"We'll off to find her—my brother and I!"

"No, let your brother stay behind. I will come."

"You don't know the machine."

"But I know where Yvette has gone. I can pilot you."

It was no time for argument.

"Jump in!" answered the aviator, pointing to the rear seat of the monoplane.

The younger brother held on to the tail until the whirr of the front propeller pulled the machine out of his grasp. Like a swift-running ostrich, the monoplane shot along the sands, and then, swaying slightly from side to side, slid upwards into the air.

It was the first time Dr. Wycherley had been in an aeroplane. The rush of the air blinded him and deafened him and half-choked him. He had to fight for balance and breath before he could call into the speaking-tube a direction for André to steer, There were only two landmarks to make a course by—the light from the Bec de Pieuvre lighthouse, and the vague shape of the Rock blurred almost to invisibility in this black drizzling night. Dr. Wycherley gave a course which was, as best he could judge, the direction of the green light he had seen flare up the evening before. It was in that direction that old Maurtain, urged by the patron of fishing-boats, had sent his grandniece.

But the course was a hopelessly vague one. Flying low, they drove out to the tide-line, and back again, and around, and could discern no trace of Yvette. The lantern she carried would send its light a very feeble distance on such a night, and the girl herself would only be seen if they passed close to her. On that great waste of sands, six miles across and seven miles out at the present ebb-tide, the chance of finding her was pitifully small.

"The tide's on the turn!" cried André into the speaking-tube, after half-an-hour or more of fruitless search. "My God, she's lost!"

To the doctor's memory flashed back the words, "At the same hour She will again walk the sands." Did it mean that Concarnot would again have arranged a carbide flare, coloured green, in order to lure the girl out to the quicksands? If only—

Dr. Wycherley looked at his watch. Close on midnight. This should be the time, if ever.

Yes, there it was! The green flare was throwing out its lure into the night.

"Make for that light!" he called into the speaking-tube.

André gave a sharp turn to his steering wheel, and the monoplane bore swift and straight to the direction of the green flare. A few minutes later, Dr. Wycherley's straining ears caught a faint cry through the racket of the motor.

"We're near her! Circle round and round."

André instantly shut off the motor, and began to plane the machine round in wide circles. With the noise of the motor cut off, Yvette's agonised shrieks for help came clear to them. The young aviator took his distance with splendid judgment, and the monoplane glided down to within a few yards of her, the wheels settling deep into the semi-liquid sands with a jerk that pitched them forward from their seats as though the craft had driven into a ditch.

Rapidly fastening himself to a long rope, the young fellow climbed out from the monoplane and started to plunge across the half-dozen yards of sand to Yvette. She was buried up to the armpits by now, and struggling wildly.

He reached her; grasped at her; and the two together began slowly to sink in the oozing, sucking, slurging sands—in the clutches of the Black Astarte.

Only the rope held them to a bare chance of life, and to pull them to safety they were dependent on the strength of an old man whose muscles were rusted with age. Dr. Wycherley gave of his utmost strength, but he was unequal to a strain which would have tried even a powerful athlete.

André saw that it was hopeless. He started to unbind the rope from himself, in order to fasten it round Yvette and give her the chance of life.

"Wait!" cried the doctor. A sudden inspiration had come to him. He climbed over to the propeller and twisted the end of the rope round its shaft, as though it were the drum of a capstan.

"Hold tight to Yvette!" he warned as he started the ignition of the motor.

The propeller whizzed round as it gathered in the slack of the rope; went slow to the sudden strain; and gradually the two bodies were drawn up to the aircraft—heaved out of the sucking slime, reluctant to lose its prey.

Safe! On board the monoplane, held up by its two broad wings, they could wait until the rising tide should float them off the quick-sands.

In the early morning, when the tide served, a boat came out to take them from the monoplane, and to tow the machine back to land. They put Yvette to bed, so that merciful sleep might smooth over the shock of her terrible experience; but André and his brother set out at once for the home of Etienne Concarnot.

In André's breast-pocket lay curled a dog-whip, and his face was set of purpose.

LABOUR AGAINST CAPITAL

Across the table in Dr. Wycherley's London consulting-room sat a rough, blunt man, secretary to the National Seaman's and Fireman's Union. Now a leader of sailors in their fight against the big capitalists, he had not so long ago been a sailor himself, and the calling still showed in his bearing and in his walk. Jim Cobbold was his name.

"You've seen in the papers, sir, what Lars Larssen intends to do with us?" he was asking.

"I rarely read daily newspapers," returned Dr. Wycherley quietly. "And who is Lars Larssen?"

The secretary of the Union gave a gasp of astonishment. "Surely you're joking, sir? Not know Lars Larssen! Why, he's a millionaire twenty times over!"

"Money-making has no interest for me—anyone can get money in exchange for his scruples."

"But he's the great ship-owner, sir. Started as a cabin-boy on a trawler out of Glos'ter, Massachusetts, and worked his way right up till he owns ships all over the world. Has great offices in London, New York, San Francisco, Rio, Hamburg, Singapore, Nagasaki and goodness knows where not."

"What else is he?"

Jim Cobbold's face darkened as his thoughts of the man surged up within him. "Lars Larssen is Anti-Christ!" he cried fiercely, bringing a rough fist down on Dr. Wycherley's consulting-room table. "He'd grind us all into slavery, just to make more money!

Hasn't he enough of his filthy money already? Hasn't he all the mansions and flunkeys and wine and women he wants? What could he do with more money if he had it? Tell me that!"

Then he added, remembering where he was: "You'll excuse me, sir? I was forgetting myself. It was very kind of you to see me at all, with your time so busy. But you were so good in helping my sister that time—I'll never forget it, sir, and may God reward you if *I* can't!—that I make bold to come and ask you to help us in the fight."

"The Union against Lars Larssen?"

"Against Lars Larssen and the big combine of ship-owners he's getting together. The papers are full of it. He's going to get control of every line in the world worth talking of. When they've got the combine fixed up, he'll crush us out of existence. Oh, I can see quite well what's coming—every Union man's to be kicked into the gutter. You know we're young, and we've not yet found our footing, and Lars Larssen will crush us before we've had time to get strength."

"The Union has certainly my sympathies in the fight," answered Dr. Wycherley, "but wherein can I help? This is no case for a doctor."

Disappointment crept into Jim Cobbold's face and voice. "I know that, sir. But I didn't come here because you're a doctor—I came because I know you've got such wonderful powers. My sister said to me, she said—"

Dr. Wycherley interrupted him with a gesture. "Surely your only chance is to strengthen the Union as rapidly as possible, and get public sympathy on your side?"

"There's no time, sir. If this had come eighteen months later, or even twelve months later! But with your wonderful powers I was kind of hoping—" he paused irresolutely, for he had no definite plan in his mind.

Dr. Wycherley rose and laid a kindly hand on the sailor's shoulder. "I am no worker of miracles," he said. "The Union must not look to me for help—it must win through the efforts of its leader. Fight for public sympathy—get the British public with you."

"Unfortunately it isn't only them, sir. This fight is international. There are all the foreign Unions, too, and we can't get welded together properly."

The doctor's manservant knocked and entered to announce a patient.

"Good-by, sir," said Jim Cobbold, "and thank you all the same." But there was disappointment in his voice, for he had hoped for miracles.

*   *   *   *   *

The newspaper stir over the great shipping combine died down quickly as a storm in party politics turned public attention in another direction. But the fight between Lars Larssen and the world of sailormen went on in grim silence, working underground with a fierce intensity of purpose to an end unsuspected by the Unions or the newspapers, or even the ship-owners whom Lars Larssen was using as tools to work his will.

For Lars Larssen was no ordinary successful man, no ordinary millionaire. The brief description given of him by Jim Cobbold did not do justice to his personality. The son of Scandinavian immigrants to the States, factory-workers, he had run away to sea at the age of thirteen, with the call of the ocean ringing in his ears from the Viking inheritance that was his. But on this was superposed the fierce desire for success that formed the psychical atmosphere of the new American environment. As a boy in the smoke-blackened factory town, he had breathed in the longing to make money—big money—to use men to his own ends, to be a master of masters.

With precocious insight, he quickly learnt that money is made not by those who go out upon the waters, but by those who stay on land and send them hither and thither. He soon gave up the seafaring life and entered a ship-broker's office. He starved himself in order to save money to speculate in shipping reinsurance. An uncanny insight had guided him to rush in when shrewdly prudent business men held aloof.

Always he speculated—took long chances. Always he saw big when other men looked at little points. Again and again he had played his entire capital on ventures that seemed mad risks.

He had emphatically "made good." Each fresh success had given him new confidence in himself and his judgment and his powers, until at the time of the fight with the Unions he was a human dynamo of fierce mental energy. He would allow nothing to stand in his path. Scruples were to him the burdens of fools. He had commercial spies in his pay the world round. Traitors amongst the sailors and firemen and dockers did his will in splitting up opposing forces. To the great end he had in view no means of help was outside his moral pale.

Such was Lars Larssen. He had no wife living—only his boy Olaf remained to him. A fair-haired giant in build, with inscrutable eyes and mouth set grim and straight—such was Lars Larssen.

The battle ground of the fight was the world, and so its importance was masked to those who were not looking upon it with eyes that ranged the wide world. The dockers' strike in Buenos Ayres did not seem to have connection with the lockout in the Pacific coastal trade of North America or the raising of rates in the carrying trade between the Far East and Europe.

It was not until many months later that the guns of the fight sounded loud in the ears of the English public. On some trifling excuse, the International Federation of Ship-Owners had declared a lockout against the English Union—no Union man was to be employed on their vessels. Scratch crews were picked up here and there to work for the freight ships, while fifty thousand English sailors, fighting for their right of manhood, were thrown out to starve. At the seaport towns there were picketings on the part of the Union men, and bloody reprisals on the part of the scratch crews, mostly foreigners, who had been brought by the Federation to help in the lockout.

To direct the fight from near at hand, Lars Larssen had pitched his headquarters at his great London office in Leadenhall Street.

"Mr. Lars Larssen to see you, sir," announced the manservant to Dr. Wycherley in his London consulting-room, some six months after the interview with Jim Cobbold.

Dr. Wycherley had trained himself to exhibit no surprise, but he was certainly surprised at the visit of the great ship-owner. It seemed as though, against his original intentions, he was to be drawn into this fight of masters and men. The piteous distress of the Union sailors and their families had been brought home to him on a recent visit to the slums of Cardiff (where he had picked up the strange case of William Owen Gwynn, madman, poet, genius and dolt), and his broad humanitarian sympathies had been stirred by this unequal struggle of fifty thousand poverty-stricken men against the irresistible millions of the Ship-Owners' Federation.

The words of Jim Cobbold— "Lars Larssen is Anti-Christ!"— were ringing in Dr. Wycherley's ears when the shipping magnate was ushered in.

At once Dr. Wycherley felt the overpowering personality of the man—the fierce mental energies that were held in check within him at the bidding of his will. Here was the strength of a leviathan— balanced, poised, ready to be turned in this direction or that at the will of the controlling ego.

Yet the interview started on easy, frictionless, almost commonplace lines. Lars Larssen had come straight to his point.

"I had heard of your exceptional powers as a psychologist, Dr. Wycherley," he said. "I want the best specialist in the world for this case of mine, so I come to you."

"Have you brought the boy with you?" asked Dr. Wycherley, drawing a rapid mental conclusion.

"In the next room. I'll explain before you see him. He's fourteen. My only child, and I want him to take up my work when I die. That means training out of the ordinary. To take up the work where I leave off wants brains, grit and something beyond them." There was no brag in his tone—Lars Larssen was merely stating facts.

"Training that must mean a heavy burden on childish shoulders," commented Dr. Wycherley.

"Olaf has a weakness that must be cut out of him. It's fear— funk, to put it bluntly."

"He will probably grow out of it."

"He must grow out of it. I killed fear in myself before I was his age—punched and kicked it out of myself by means of the sailors on the *Mary R.* of Glos'ter. Used those men as whetstones. Butted into them till they grew afraid of a cabin-boy! You notice that I limp still? I reckon that limp has been worth some tens of millions of dollars to me."

"And you have been training your boy on the same lines?"

"At his preparatory school I told him to fight every boy in the place until they acknowledged him master. When he used to come home licked and with his tail between his legs, I lammed him with a strap, trying to get grit into him. Don't think I'm a hard father—I'd give my eyes to have Olaf a man that people will respect and fear."

"Yours, then, is the gospel of fear?"

Lars Larssen's eyes narrowed a shade as they looked straight into Dr. Wycherley's. "That's my concern. I'm here to consult you professionally on behalf of my boy. You can name your own fee—I shan't haggle. Can you cut fear out of my boy?"

"That depends on whether it is constitutional or acquired. It also depends on the ulterior object of the operation."

Dr. Wycherley's left hand was making a clean-cut little miniature on a sheet of letter-paper of the grim, powerful face on the other side of the consulting-room table. Lars Larssen glanced at it: "You're an artist, too?" he asked.

"No; scarcely that. I take records of my cases, and it saves time to do it while I'm talking."

"Yes—good! That's a useful trick. Could you teach my boy to do two things at once?"

"I have not yet decided whether I will take up the case or not."

The ship-owner's mouth tightened a shade. He was not used to allowing opposition to his wishes. "Didn't I say you could name your own fee? I come to you because I hear you're the best man at this mental job, and I pay the price you name. It isn't constitutional fear in the boy—it's acquired. His mother was no coward, or I'd never have married her; I'm no coward. When I tell you I'm afraid of nothing on earth or in heaven or in hell, I'm telling you the literal truth. But Olaf, I believe, got frightened by some stupid nurses when he was a little child, and it kind of grew into his brain. I want it cut out. Though I've got detectives guarding him night and day against the Union men—and detectives guarding myself—he's funky of them hurting him or me. Thinks there are spies amongst the detectives. Perhaps there are—but what of that?"

"A bad environment for a boy."

"You could take him away with you to any place you think right."

"I will see your boy first, and then I will discuss my second point," replied Dr. Wycherley.

Olaf was shown in—a fair-haired, delicate-looking lad with hunted eyes. Dr. Wycherley's warm human sympathies went out to him. Only a father obsessed by the idea of domination that was the keynote to the character of Lars Larssen would have insisted on the Spartan régime that had been mapped out for the boy. To Dr. Wycherley it was patent at a glance that the son could never be what the father was trying to mold him into.

"I would like to see your boy alone," said the doctor.

And when Lars Larssen had gone to the waiting-room he settled the lad in a comfortable arm-chair and talked to him quietly and kindly for many minutes, until the flush of understanding in the boy's face showed the doctor that the sympathy contact had been made.

"Tell me now," said Dr. Wycherley, "what is it that you are afraid of. Come, I am your friend, and I wish you nothing but good. Tell me frankly just what you feel. It will not go beyond me. Do you have bad dreams, or is it in the daytime that fears crowd upon you?"

Olaf turned his hunted eyes around towards the door before he whispered: "It's my father I am afraid of!"

"How? In what way?"

But the boy did not dare to answer.

A BATTLE OF WILLS

Dr. Wycherley had asked for an interview at the ship-owner's office. He had a particular reason for wishing to investigate further the mental atmosphere that obsessed Lars Larssen. In the man's own office, surrounded by what he had planned for himself, more could be gleaned than from the inscrutable eyes and the grim, straight mouth.

Dr. Wycherley had found himself drawn into the great fight between Lars Larssen and the sailormen, in spite of his original intentions. The man's dominating personality had made a profound impression upon him. It was no longer the case of a mere financial squabble—for which Dr. Wycherley had a deep contempt born of his study of mind—it was now complicated by the strange relations of father and son. And beyond this was something larger still that Dr. Wycherley sensed with his keen, intuitive perception, though as yet the feeling had not crystallized into the tangible.

In the great building in Leadenhall street which bore the simple business sign of "LARS LARSSEN—SHIPPING," a sign arrogant in its simplicity, was a room on the second floor that quite transcended Dr. Wycherley's experience of business offices. It was a room a hundred feet long and broad in proportion—a room occupying practically the whole of the second floor. A glass-domed roof rose up centrally to the very top of the building.

A few broad tables and some chairs looked almost lost in the room, but the walls were filled with coloured charts of the world, some with scores of flag-pins upon them that doubtless indicated the positions of ships. At the far end of the room, beyond the central dome of light, was a horseshoe table covered with papers and document-baskets and telephone apparatus. In the centre of the horseshoe was placed Lars Larssen's chair. Behind his chair, hung on the wall, was a portrait of Olaf by Sargent.

As Dr. Wycherley was ushered in by a secretary, his first impression was a slight feeling of contempt for the theatrical trick that gave a visitor a self-conscious walk of some thirty yards before he reached his allotted seat at the horseshoe table. Doubtless this device had helped in business deals by bringing nervousness to a man as he walked down the long stretch of room.

But Dr. Wycherley's second impression was of a very different order. At last the vague intuitions that had been floating in his mind gathered coherence. In a flash he saw the inner meaning of this prodigal space.

It was not a mere business office he was in—it was a throne-room.

He recognised now that Jim Cobbold's estimate of Lars Larssen had been ludicrously short of the truth. Here was no man striving after the pleasures of mansions and flunkies, wine and women, amassing money merely to gratify his sensual appetites. It was bigger game that obsessed his thoughts—power, world-power.

"I would congratulate you on your room," he said as he shook hands. "It is an office for a master of men."

Into Lars Larssen's face crept a gleam of pleasure—Dr. Wycherley had touched the vanity that lies in all men. The ship-owner replied: "In every one of my offices around the world is a room like this. I alone make use of it. When I'm away it stands for me. It's my sign.

"Above the dome," he continued, as he saw that Dr. Wycherley was keenly interested and doubtless impressed, "is the Marconi apparatus that keeps me in touch with my ships. They again link me with New York, New York with San Francisco, thence again by ship to Nagasaki, thence to Singapore, to Colombo, to Aden, to Naples, to Hamburg, to London. I'm independent of the wires and the cables."

"As I passed through the offices downstairs," remarked Dr. Wycherley, "they seemed very quiet. Your business routine must go through in very orderly fashion."

"They're quiet in the daytime," replied Lars Larssen, "because the big work of the office is at night. I have two staffs—a day staff and a night staff. Tonight my men will be at work on matters that the ordinary ship-owner would leave for to-morrow. That's been one of my business rules—do to-morrow's work to-day—get ahead of the other man."

Dr. Wycherley fixed his keen, searching eyes on the ship-owner. "When you have attained to the summit of your ambition," he said slowly, "when you are indeed Emperor of the Seven Seas, when the decision of war or peace between kingdom and kingdom lies in your hands because the traffic of food upon the seas is in your hand—what then?"

Lars Larssen flicked with thumb and forefinger at a speck on his sleeve before replying. "Was that an ant?" he said sharply, half to himself.

"No, it was only dust," answered Dr. Wycherley. "When you are Emperor of the Seven Seas—what then?"

"Then I'll flick away those who oppose me as I flicked away that—that speck of dust," was the reply, given in low, tense voice. "I, and my son after me, and his son after him."

"Do you know the story of the little Duc de Reichstadt—l'Aiglon, the son of the great Napoleon?"

"You mean that my son Olaf is another such weakling?" Lars Larssen's face grew dark with anger, but an anger the more to be feared in that it was controlled and directed, that it was held in leash.

"I do mean that."

"You lie!"

"It is apparent to all but yourself."

"You lie!" repeated Larssen harshly. "You're incompetent. You haven't read him right. He's in a funk at present, because he was frightened when he was young. But, by heaven and hell, I'll have it either persuaded out of him or beaten out of him. That's why I came to you—I thought you were skilled in your mental quackery."

Dr. Wycherley drew a sheet of paper towards him and replied without the least change from his ordinary tone of voice: "I can cure your son—if you wish. But my price is a high one."

"Name it."

The doctor scribbled rapidly on the sheet of paper and handed it to the ship-owner. The latter glanced at it, then tore the paper into scraps.

"I thought you said a *price*," said he cuttingly.

"That is my price—that you send a note to the newspapers announcing that the lockout against the English Union is withdrawn, and that you have decided to recognise the various seamen's and firemen's unions in future."

"I pay in money."

"Money is of no value to me—as well offer me cowrie shells."

"I offer you a hundred thousand pounds. Take it or leave it."

"I leave it."

"Very well—I reckon that's an end of the matter."

"That is by no means an end of the matter," returned Dr. Wycherley. "I represent two sets of interests—those of the sailors and those of your son. For the moment let us put the question of the sailors aside. You are killing the boy because of your ins—, your fanatical determination that he shall be like what you imagine yourself to be. You recognise that he is a 'funk,' as you term it—but you don't recognise that he inherits it from yourself."

"I a funk? You must be crazy!"

"Shall I prove it to you?"

"Prove away—if you can."

"Olaf has not told me what he is afraid of but I see it now. He is terrified at the idea of what you want to make him—master of the world. You cannot understand that terror. On the other hand, you were afraid of a tiny ant just now."

Lars Larssen gripped the side of his chair with tense fingers, but he answered not a word.

Dr. Wycherley continued: "Terror of the big and vast, or fear of the tiny and harmless—where lies the essential difference? I intend to show you, Lars Larssen, what Fear means. Yes, to show you what lies within yourself, until you ask pardon of your boy for your scorn of him, and until you give justice to the men who toil for you to build up your millions.

"A little while ago you told me that this great room stands for yourself, and that when your clerks and managers enter it, even though it be empty, they think of you. It was your sign, you said. Well, the sign I put against it is the tiny and the harmless. Whenever you see an ant, Lars Larssen, think of what stands against you!"

Dr. Wycherley rose and took up his hat.

THE "SENDING"

Three days later, Lars Larssen was working late in the evening in his great throne-room, writing cipher messages to be sent by wireless to his houses in the East. He was concentrating intently, working with the fierce concentration to which he had trained his brain. Finally he grew weary, and raised his head to stretch himself.

As his eyes rose, he saw on the opposite side of the table, looking at him gravely, Dr. Wycherley. The doctor was sitting outside the brightness of the electric table lamp, as he had sat on that momentous interview.

Larssen for a moment was spellbound—for no visitor had been announced. Recovering himself, he was about to utter a question, when the figure melted away, before his eyes. He rang his bell sharply for his secretary, who was working in a small room behind his chair.

"Did you hear anything peculiar just now? Anybody go out your way for instance?"

"No, sir. Nothing."

"To-morrow night and in future you will occupy that table over there."

"Yes, sir."

In the morning, as he put on the clothes his valet had laid out for him, a speck on the sleeve of his coat caught his attention. He looked closer. It moved—it was a tiny red ant. He flicked it away sharply.

The next evening he deliberately stayed late at his office again, and again concentrated intently on his work, but looking up occasionally. He wished to reproduce, if possible, the strange hallucination of the night before. He was not afraid of it—he was merely interested.

At the office nothing happened. But as he was stepping into his motor, thinking deeply, a dim figure of someone lurking in the shadows of the car made him draw back with a start. He called the footman to him—one of his paid detectives.

"Get that man out," said he.

The footman quickly pulled a revolver out of his livery and looked inside the car.

"There's no one there, sir."

"Good!" said Larssen evenly. "Drive home." He took out a wax match from the receptacle inside the motor in order to light a cigar. On the match was a tiny ant, and he dropped it hastily. He looked inside the match receptacle—there were several ants there. When he arrived home he ordered the car to be fumigated, and that another one be put into his service. He undressed for bed in a very thoughtful mood.

"That figure inside the car," he meditated. "Looks as if my eyes were going wrong. Better cut out smoking for a bit."

Two days later, returning early in the afternoon from his office, he went to Olaf's playroom. In it he had had a carpenter's bench put up for his boy to make model ships and a pugilist outfit to get him to practice boxing. But Olaf was not engaged in ship-building or in bag-punching—he was intently examining a little flat box with a glass cover.

"What have you got there?" asked his father.

"I bought it at the stores to-day, Dad. Isn't it cute? It's an ant's nest with real ants under glass. One can make all sorts of experiments with them—coloured glasses like Lord Avebury used to do and—"

Lars Larssen snatched up the box and threw it far out of the open window. The boy uttered a cry of surprise and anger.

"Why did you do that, Dad? I wanted to—"

"I hate ants. I don't want you to play with them."

"But why? I like them—they're such bully little fellows."

"I'll tell you why, my son," answered Larssen, with unusual feeling in his voice, "and then perhaps you'll understand. A long time ago, before I married your mother, I was shipwrecked on one of the desolate swamp keys of the Bahamas. They're hateful islands—nothing on them of value except the flamingoes, great blazing pink flamingoes. But the horrible part of it was the ants. They were everywhere on the island—swarming in myriads—ravenous and with big, nipping jaws. They were in our food, in our water, in our clothes, in our sleeping blankets. You woke up at night to find them—ugh!"

"There's one on your waistcoat now!"

Larssen brushed it away as though it were some deadly insect. His face had paled imperceptibly. "Did this come out of your box?" he asked roughly.

"It couldn't have, Dad—the box was closed up tight."

"Well, there oughtn't to be ants wandering loose in this climate."

"There are plenty of them out in the garden, in the long grass parts. But they can't hurt anybody—they're so tiny and harmless." Still he could not understand his father's horror of them.

"My God, what did you say?" Larssen had seized his son's arm.

"I only said they were so tiny and harmless."

"Who told you that?"

"No one. What makes you look so pale, Dad?"

But Lars Larssen did not answer this. "Put on your boxing gloves," he commanded roughly.

The boy reluctantly obeyed.

That night Lars Larssen slept uneasily. A nightmare came to him—a nightmare that froze him with horror. He was back on that desolate key of the Bahamas—this time alone. The swampland was alive with ants—great, fierce, red ants with nipping jaws that grew and grew in size. They advanced upon him as an army—a myriad army deadly of purpose. They had faces now—the faces of ravenous devils! They were going to devour him alive! He strove to fight them, off, but his body and limbs were as paralysed. Now the foremost of them were swarming over him . . . !

He awoke bathed in sweat and trembling in every limb. The moonlight shone into the room in a broad band. Behind the moonstreak, there in the corner of the room, was the figure of Dr. Wycherley looking at him gravely.

Lars Larssen's strength of will forsook him for the moment. Unstrung by the vivid horror of his dream, he threw his arms across his face to shut out the vision, phantom or real. When his ego recovered possession of his brain and he took his arms from before his eyes, nothing was to be seen save the broad band of moonlight.

He turned on the electric light, and for the rest of the night read a novel to keep his thoughts off the ants. When daylight came there would be big decisions to be made, and he must keep a clear head. Resolutely, by sheer concentration of will, he kept his thoughts off the ants.

But his choice of book was an unfortunate one. It turned on the uncanny powers of the Indian fakirs, and one of the incidents dealt with a "sending"—a rain of frogs that the fakir materialized against a royal enemy. He threw away the book and took up another.

In the morning, as he made his way to the office, the clerks noticed an unusual tenseness in his face. His secretary said to him solicitously: "You're not looking quite yourself, sir."

"Nothing the matter."

"I'm glad to hear it."

Larssen pointed suddenly: "What's that crawling over the blue paper on the desk?"

"I don't see anything."

"There, there!"

"That's nothing, sir. Only an insect of some kind." He went to brush it away.

"Have the room fumigated this afternoon."

"Yes, sir."

A deputation from the Sailors' Union called at the office. Larssen refused to see them.

That night he slept with a stout stick by his bedside.

"If he's flesh and blood, I'll kill him," was his thought. But Dr. Wycherley did not appear—only there came to the ship-owner a terrible nightmare wherein he was chained to his desk in his great domed room, and a vast army of ants advanced again and swarmed upon him—into his eyes, his ears, his nostrils . . . !

That week was a week of torture. At night the horrible dreams: by day the ants—here, there, everywhere in unexpected places. Only one or two—never in quantities, and quite harmless, but ants, real ants.

Then came the day when the ants were *no longer real*—when he fancied there were ants where none existed, and his servants and clerks looked at him strangely and seemed glad to get out of his presence as quickly as possible.

But Lars Larssen would not give in. A dozen times, a score of times the temptation came to him to write or send to Dr. Wycherley, and he thrust it aside with his iron will. He would not give in.

Nor would his pride allow him to consult any other doctor. He bought sleeping drugs, and took them in big doses. Sometimes they gave him deep sleep, and sometimes they but intensified the phantasmagoria of his tortured brain.

He left them alone and tried to do without sleep, reading the night through under the glare of the lights.

Then came the night when Olaf awoke shrieking at the sound of revolver shots, and rushed to his father's room to find him gazing wild-eyed at a broken mirror—in his hand a smoking revolver.

"There's nobody here! What are you afraid of, Dad?" he cried.

"Of nothing on earth or in heaven or in hell!" answered his father grimly. "Get back to your room!"

The next day the boy slipped off secretly to Dr. Wycherley's rooms and implored him to come and help his father, who had become so strange in his manner. Dr. Wycherley at once promised, and went to call on the ship-owner at his office.

When he was shown in he was startled at the change in Larssen. The man's eyes were bleared and bloodshot from want of sleep;

his mouth was flanked with lines of tense emotion; he had in a short three weeks aged by ten years. Lars Larssen was an old man.

Dr. Wycherley was moved in spite of himself. His warm human sympathies warred with the stern duties he had had to carry out. This Lars Larssen was an exceptional man, a man beyond the ordinary pale of thought and morals—he must needs be dealt with in an exceptional way. If his gospel were the gospel of fear, he must be shown the fear to which he as well as others was subject. If he claimed the sovereignty of the earth by right of strength of will, if he claimed to trample on ten thousands of his fellow-beings by right of money then he must be shown the weakness of his will and the uselessness of his money.

The phantoms were a simple projection of the subconscious personality which Dr. Wycherley had willed to appear to Lars Larssen. Night after night he had thrown himself into the trance state for this purpose. The projections were entirely an effect of mind on mind—there was nothing material in them. The ants were real, and the explanation of their presence was equally simple—the footman detective was in reality an ally of the sailors.

But these two simple means of working on the ship-owner's mind, acting together and re-enforcing one another, had produced an effect that startled even Dr. Wycherley. He was moved to pity at the havoc they had wrought.

"What have you come for?" snarled the ship-owner.

"To offer you peace with honour."

"I make no terms. D'you think you can move me with your ants and your ghosts?" He laughed mirthlessly.

"Come, let us be frank," said Dr. Wycherley. "You dared me to show you what Fear means—I have done so. If I have been wholly unscrupulous in my methods, that is a point which should earn your respect. The means that were necessary to the purpose I have used, just as you yourself would have used them."

"Get to your point, whatever it is!"

"You have met Fear, and now you can realise your boy's terror at the career you had mapped out for him. Be fair to him; be fair to your sailors. Give to both their liberty of action. See the humanitarian side—crush that Napoleonic obsession which could only bring misery to all. For my part, I promise that the visions shall cease; that there shall be no more of the 'sending' of ants."

"There's an easier way for me to insure that," said Lars Larssen grimly, and drew a revolver from his desk.

Dr. Wycherley tapped the table a little impatiently, a mannerism of his when anything particularly stupid was said. "Come, come, Mr. Larssen, that way leads to nowhere. If you choose to shoot me, you are arrested and hanged. You merely show the world you were *afraid* to let me live. That hasty idea was surely unworthy of you."

Larssen lowered his revolver.

"The proposal I make is one of peace with honour," continued Dr. Wycherley. "Of my own accord I shall stop the 'sending,' and I leave it to you to do the right thing on your own initiative. There are no conditions to my promise."

"Try to get me to give in by a trick—eh?" sneered Lars Larssen in his pride. "Think I'm afraid—eh? I told you before that I fear nothing on earth or in heaven or in hell: I tell you so again. Do what you please. Now get out!"

"My promise still holds good," said Dr. Wycherley as he rose to leave.

*   *   *   *   *

When Olaf went to his father's bedroom the next morning as usual, he found him lying white and cold. He tried to wake his father—in vain.

The doctor certified death from an overdose of chloral. It was proved at the inquest that the deceased had been lately in the habit of taking sleeping drugs, and the jury brought in a verdict of death by misadventure. Only Dr. Wycherley doubted that the verdict was a true one, for he had looked into the soul of the man and had fathomed his overmastering pride.

Lars Larssen had been shown the Fear that lay in himself, and he preferred Death.

ON MEDENHAM DOWN

Two men had toiled up the great green hump of Medenham Down—Travis Kennion, Home Secretary, a man of forty; and his friend Hatchard, the barrister, some years older.

They now stood on its summit, where the hill breaks away sheer into a chalk cliff fronting the fertile plain of the Weald of Kent. Many hundred feet below, it drowsed in the sunshine of a Sunday afternoon in summer, breathing of tranquility and contentment and the peace of humble work carried out dutifully by simple, upright, God-fearing country-folk.

But on the summit above there was raging a conflict of emotion and will between two men of complex temperament—a conflict vital to the future of Travis Kennion. He was a man great in many respects, a man with ideals pitched high, yet with one kink of character which threatened to ruin his career and cut short his splendid services to the nation.

"I've brought you up here," said the K.C., "to try to make you realise your position. Socially and politically you're standing on the brink of a precipice. A few steps more"—he pointed to the cliff at their feet— "and you go down to perdition."

"Analogies," replied Kennion wearily, as he stretched himself on the close-cropped turf, "are all false. No one situation is like any other. I do not admit the precipice in my case."

"But you've seen the same situation in the cases of other men. Parnell and Kitty O'Shea, for instance. The lure of a bright eye and the man throws over position, power, the world's respect, and everything that makes life worth living. As soon as your affair becomes generally known—and it's bound to leak out soon—your parliamentary career will be made impossible for you. It's sheer madness to go on!"

"A very beautiful madness," mused Kennion.

"Who is the woman?" asked Hatchard sharply. It was in a motor-car that he had seen her, at nighttime, and a motor-veil and goggles make ample disguise. All he knew was that she was a woman of their own world, and that his friend was passionately in love with her.

The Home Secretary made no reply. This was not the first time he had been questioned and cross-questioned and reasoned with by the K.C., and he was weary of it all—obstinately, fiercely weary of it.

"If there's no consideration of duty to your party that will move you, think at least of your wife!"

At that Kennion blazed up into sudden anger. "Leave my wife out of it!" he ordered. "You don't understand, and never will! My temperament is so complex that I scarcely understand it myself. I am like a bulb—one covering under another, one under another, right down to a tiny core. At that core is love and respect for my wife. This"—his reference was plain— "this belongs to another layer of my nature."

"Slough it off."

The sudden blaze of anger had died down, and a great weariness had now come into Kennion's voice as he replied: "I can't. . . . I don't think I want to. . . . I only want to be left alone. I've been sleeping badly of late, and I'm tired. There's the worry of my Bill. Is it worth while thrashing it through in face of all the opposition it has roused? That is what I ask myself. Haven't I done enough for my country? Is the fight worth while?"

His voice trailed away.

From far below came the silvery tinkle of bells from the cattle in the lush pastures, and a lark caroled high in the heavens. The fertile Weald lay drowsing in the summer sunshine breathing of tranquility and contentment and peace. Into the soul of the Home

Secretary crept a great longing to go down into the lush meadow-land of life, to give up the fight on the heights and find peace with the woman he loved. To find peace.

Presently he slept.

*   *   *   *   *

Hatchard had wandered off moodily across Medenham Down, slashing with his stick at the heads of the yellow rag-wort. If it would have done any good, he would have thrashed his friend to bring him to a realization of his madness. The lure of a bright eye, and a great man like Travis Kennion was to sacrifice position, power, wife, friends, and his worth to the nation! No logic seemed to move him one iota. Who could battle with such essence of un-reason?

In this mood, concentrating fiercely on his own thoughts, he almost stumbled into Dr. Wycherley, sitting in the shade of a furze-bush and studying a notebook half filled with tiny sketches of men and women—delicate little miniatures where every line expressed inner character.

Greeting Dr. Wycherley cordially, the barrister asked what brought him to Medenham Down.

"The Wishing Well at Tildenstone," answered the mental healer. "A pleasant example of faith-cure—ordinary, perhaps, yet with points of interest. I have been studying a crippled boy in the vil-lage who has suddenly regained the use of his limbs. . . . But what brings you up here? Ah, I see, something more than idle pleasure. I sense the aftermath of a storm. You have been doing battle."

"You're right. And I've lost," answered the K.C., and then a sud-den idea struck him. "Could you take on the fight?"

"Is it within my province?"

"I'll explain, and then you can judge. Of course, what I am going to tell you will be in strictest confidence."

He went into the matter in abundant detail, telling of the situ-ation as he knew it and his fruitless reasonings with the Home Secretary.

"A fine man," commented Dr. Wycherley. "I have the warmest admiration for his work. A statesman—and England has too few statesmen and leaders. Yes, a man thoroughly worth saving from his baser self."

"Can you save him?"

"I can promise nothing. The problem as you set it before me is the most difficult I have ever had to solve."

"Nothing seems to move him," continued Hatchard. "He's one of your so-called 'strong men'—and he'll take advice from no one. Unless he has convinced himself, it seems hopeless to try to convince him."

"There are no 'strong men'—merely a popular fiction," answered Dr. Wycherley with his gentle cynicism. "Every man has his weakness, open or hidden. It is a matter of degree."

"This weakness is the unforgivable one for a politician. Remember Parnell and Kitty O'Shea, and many a lesser man, too! The English public is abominably hypocritical over such affairs."

"There I cannot agree with you. Men to whom power and influence are entrusted are no longer private men. They are placed on a pedestal and are expected to live on a high plane. It is one of the makeweights of power—penalty of position."

"The public attitude is utterly illogical," argued the K.C. "How can a man's private character affect the value of his public work?"

"Illogical, perhaps; but then it is sometimes extremely sensible to be illogical. That is life. You know it from your practice at the Bar. . . . Now when can I meet Kennion?"

"He is over there above the chalk cliff, but asleep at the moment."

"Excellent! A man asleep is a man unmasked. Let us go and study him."

They walked across the down, and for a long time Dr. Wycherley bent over the sleeping man, reading into the lines of his face and gathering impressions of his thoughts that surged out vaguely from his tumbled dreams.

At length the mental healer arose and drew the barrister aside. "I see one bare possibility," he said. "You told me a little while ago that unless he has convinced himself, it would seem hopeless to try to convince him. I confirm that view."

"Well?"

"*We must get him to convince himself.*"

"You have some plan?"

"The dawn of a plan. You are both staying, you told me, at 'The George Inn' at Medenham. This evening I will arrive there as a casual visitor, and you will introduce me not as a mental practitioner, but merely as a man with a special gift of inducing sleep. It is vital that he should not know who I am."

* * * * *

"The George Inn" at Medenham is one of those delightful old hostelries still to be found in the small country towns and some of the villages of rural England. It lies bowered in roses and clambering wisteria and honeysuckle, under the shadow of great oak trees at the foot of Medenham Down. Near by runs the silver Meden, fished by the anglers who come to stay at "The George."

Both the Home Secretary and the barrister had brought rods with them for their week-end stay, and there was no surprise at the arrival in the evening of a silver-haired old man with keen-cut features and dark, grave eyes. No doubt he was also an angler.

Hatchard recognised him as an acquaintance and introduced him to the Home Secretary, and in the starlight they sat out in the porch and chatted leisurely of things that mattered little. But under all this casual conversation—too trivial to need recording—ran strange undercurrents of thought. Early in the evening the Home Secretary had received a telegram. This lay in the outer pocket of his lounge coat, and every now and then his fingers would caress it under cover of the pocket. With the studied calmness of his face—the mask of the man of position—went a bright glitter of the eyes that could not be kept under. While he chatted leisurely on the porch of the inn, his real thoughts were elsewhere, with the woman he loved.

The barrister, also outwardly calm, was watching eagerly for the unfolding of Dr. Wycherley's plan, whatever it might be. All that had been arranged was that Hatchard should support the mental healer in any move he might introduce. Dr. Wycherley, for his part, had kept conversation on the level of the trivial so that Kennion should not suspect his real vocation and draw back into an unassailable shell of defence. First, he had to win confidence. Later . . .

What was that strange sensation, that sense of something impending in the immediate present? It came to the sensitive mind of the mental healer as a rasping against the calm ether of the starlit night in the quiet village. Most of us experience that vague sensation of impending events at one time or other, and sometimes we act upon it against the logic of our reasoning faculties. Dr. Wycherley, with his super-sensitive perceptions, knew better than to neglect the warnings of intuition. He had schooled himself to respect and follow intuition, and in this case he made an excuse to the other two men and set out to walk to the end of the village, out into the lane which connects by a tangle of lanes with the broad highway of the London-Canterbury road. From that direction he sensed the coming of some event which would cut sharply into the peace of the village inn.

Rounding a corner between the high hedges, the glare of a motor-lamp flashed full upon him, and a car braked up on its haunches with a grinding of wheels.

"Is this right for Medenham?" asked the chauffeur. "We've got mixed up in these twisty lanes."

But Dr. Wycherley's eyes had turned to the solitary occupant of the car, a lady. Her veil was thrown back to let the cool night air play on her face, and with a shock he recognised her as Lilith Kennion, the wife of the Home Secretary. The portrait of the beautiful Mrs. Kennion by Shannon had been one of the features of that year's Academy—she as well as her husband was a celebrity. But now there were lines of pain and anxiety in her face, and in a flash Dr. Wycherley realised that she had come to a knowledge of the

situation in which her husband stood and was pressing hot-haste
to his side. In the present mood of the Home Secretary, the meeting would inevitably lead to a clash of wills, perhaps to an open
declaration from which there would be no turning back. The situation lay poised so delicately that one jar would send the balance
crashing downwards.

It was a dangerous move to interpose between husband and
wife at such a crisis of their lives, but Dr. Wycherley resolved to
take it. He had been reading deeply into the character of Travis
Kennion, and he knew that only from *inside*, from the man himself, could help come. Urgings from outside, even from his own
wife, would only drive him deeper into his mad obstinacy.

"This is the way to Medenham," replied Dr. Wycherley, "but I
wish to speak first with Mrs. Kennion." He raised his hat with an
old-world courtesy of manner. "I have something very important
to say to you— something vital. Will you spare me a few moments?"

"Who are you?" asked Lilith Kennion.

"A medical adviser of your husband's," was the answer, whispered so that it might not come to the ears of the chauffeur. "More
than that, a very sincere well-wisher. Will you not send the car
ahead, and let us rejoin it presently?"

There was a magnetism in the personality of the mental healer
that few could resist. His gently-expressed wishes had more than
the force of commands. Lilith Kennion realised the sincerity of this
stranger with the silvery hair and grave dark eyes and told the
chauffeur to drive on for a hundred yards or so and wait.

When the car had moved off, they looked at one another in
silence for a few moments. Dr. Wycherley struck a match and held
it up to his own face, so that she might read what he did not wish
to put into words.

"You know why I am here? You came to intercept me?" she
asked, with a break in her voice that held pathos.

"I know. I sympathise deeply. I have a plan to help Mr. Kennion
against his—his insomnia. If you will trust him to me for a few
days—*trust him implicitly*—I think you will not regret it. He will
sleep well; his nerves will right themselves; he will come back to

you with renewed strength and courage for his fight. Again he will be a strong man doing battle for his Bill against the weak sentimentalists and the envy and malice of public life."

"I could help him . . . perhaps."

"You cannot help him directly—you or anyone else. He has to fight himself, to conquer himself. Strength must come from inside. My plan is to help him to help himself, without his knowing it."

"And I? What am I to do?" Her voice quivered under the strain of belief he was demanding.

"It would be best for you to go away for these few days—far away. To Scotland, say. . . . It is a big sacrifice I am asking of you. But you, like your husband, are on the pedestal of power, and much is demanded from those to whom much is given."

"I don't want power," she burst out impulsively. "I only want . . . my husband. The rest is emptiness."

The glory of the starlit night wrapped itself around them—the meretricious glitter of the great city with its strivings and strugglings was far away. She began to weep very softly and pitifully.

Then with a sudden effort Lilith Kennion drew herself together. "I will trust you," said she bravely, and held out her hand.

Dr. Wycherley raised it to his lips with old-world courtesy, and went to call the car back.

A little later he had returned to the flower-banked porch of "The George," and soon he had managed to introduce the topic of the mystery of sleep. Kennion mentioned wearily that he had been sleeping very badly of late, and the barrister, taking the opening, spoke of his friend's powers to induce sleep.

"If you wish for sound sleep, I can give it you," said Dr. Wycherley.

"I have heard of that kind of thing," returned Kennion. "It sounds to me dangerous."

"It rests with yourself. I do not press my gifts," returned Dr. Wycherley. "To-morrow I shall be tramping on, and we shall probably not meet again. If you wish to break the chain of sleepless nights, I can do it for you now, but not to-morrow night." There was soothing in the voice and Kennion felt drawn to confidence.

He accepted the offer, and presently in the bedroom Dr. Wycherley passed him into the lighter stages of hypnosis.

"And now?" whispered the barrister.

"Now leave us. What I have to do should rest secret even from a friend."

Far into the night the mental healer sat by the bedside of the Home Secretary, speaking softly to the sleeping man of many, many things which he should know and, realise.

THE FORTIETH MILESTONE

The next morning Kennion slept late. Before he awoke, Dr. Wycherley had left the village. The barrister had to return to town for his work, but the Home Secretary announced that he would stay on at Medenham for a few days, to fish peacefully and build up his nerves. Though he had slept heavily, he had been troubled by dreams, and he wanted his brain to be thoroughly clear for his parliamentary duties. For a couple of days his Under-Secretary could take his place.

Hatchard listened to this sceptically. He had his own idea as to why Kennion wished to bury himself in the country, but Dr. Wycherley had insisted explicitly that Kennion should be allowed to work out his own salvation according to his own dictates.

When the barrister had left for London, Kennion made his way to the post office and sent off two long cipher telegrams. One was addressed to the Under-Secretary; the other to a woman. Also he telegraphed to his wife to let her know that he would not be back in town at present.

Later, he took up his rod and flies and went off to the quiet pools of the silver Meden. But his thoughts were not in harmony with the quiet beauty of the rural scene. They buzzed within him, burst up into flame, died down into cold analysis, flared again into impetuous desires. The dreams of last night haunted him vividly and warred with his desires. They had been so extremely real— detailed far beyond the usual vaguenesses of dreamland. They *haunted* him.

617

In a fever of impatience atone moment aflame, the next cold and shivering—he waited for the reply which should come to one of his three telegrams. He returned early to the inn, without a catch, to receive the answering wire.

It had not come. It did not arrive, in fact, until late in the afternoon, and when it came he crumpled it up feverishly in his hands. "Wait," it said in cipher. "To-morrow night, on the Canterbury road, by the fortieth milestone."

He must perforce wait . . . and think . . . and do battle with his thoughts.

That evening he tramped alone far over the swelling downs, and at midnight he lay down exhausted beside a furze-bush and fell into a deep sleep. A sheep-dog came up and nosed him curiously, then moved away. Another of those tramps, no doubt.

Kennion slept heavily, and again there came to him a series of dreams of a vividness that had never previously been within his experience. He awoke at dawn in the cold gray hill-mists, bathed in sweat, and with a mocking voice ringing in his ears:

"*Who are the Unfit?*"

If the day before had been a battle, to-day was an agony of conflict. Duty—desire! Duty—desire! The heights or the meadowland? Which must he choose for the peace that would be lasting? His mind was stretched taut on a rack of his own devising.

And he was alone. No outside influence was there to throw weight into one pan or other of the balance. On himself alone rested the decision.

In his complex nature, that gave him strength rather than weakness. It is so with many of the world's great men, as Dr. Wycherley knew well.

* * * * *

By the fortieth milestone the white highway curves in between the swelling downs and traverses a narrow neck half-way up the hills.

The night was hot and sultry and working up to storm as the Home Secretary went to keep tryst with the woman he loved. She had arrived before him, having left her motor-car on the farther side of the hills and walked back on foot. She was young and dazzlingly beautiful. When he came to her side she gave a little cry of gladness and held out her arms. No one was in sight—the curves of the road gave them solitude.

But Kennion did not take her in his arms. His temples were throbbing, and yet his hands were icy.

"Come to where we can talk without interruption," he said, and pointed to a chalk quarry near at hand.

They went together, in silence.

"This is to say good-bye," he said with a curtness that scarcely masked the surge of feeling within him.

"No, not good-bye," she urged, and twined her arms around his shoulder. Her warm breath was on his cheek; the soft curves of her body rose and fell with breathing.

But Kennion untwined her clasp with hands that quivered, and repeated: "It's good-bye, Vivien. I've decided. . . . For us both."

"Why?" There was sharpness in her voice now—the sharpness of a woman balked in desire. "I have the right to know."

"Yes, you've the right to know. I have seen many things these last two nights."

"Nights!"

"I saw the whisperings in the lobby, the furtive glances. Men looked away when I looked to them to nod greeting. Then I rose in the House to move the third reading of my Bill for the Segregation of the Unfit. There was icy silence. I went through my speech red-hot with passionate enthusiasm for the great service this Bill would render to the nation; but the House was icy. It was as though I were in the dock, and they were my judges. They put up Leveredge to oppose. His speech was mordant—bitingly mocking. 'Who are the Unfit?' he flung at me across the floor of the House. They threw out the Bill. Even my own friends went into the lobby against me."

"Dreams!" she cut in with a whip-lash of scorn. "And even suppose you lost all that for me. Wouldn't it be worth it? We'd go away together to where the world mattered nothing."

"We went away together. We left Lilith breaking her heart against the iron heartlessness of society. We went away together to some distant isle under a tropic sky. The world around us was marvelously beautiful, but there was no satisfaction in its beauty. Feverishly we drowned our hatred of its beauty in the madness of love. There were hectic cases in a desert of meaningless sand. We pretended that the world mattered nothing—that we were all in all to one another. But it was pretence, and we began slowly to loathe one another for the pretence forced upon us. I saw the loathing in your eyes; you in mine. The days grew long to length insufferable—they dragged out into eons of time. . . ."

"Who has been putting these notions into your head?" she asked sharply. "Dreams don't come of themselves."

"No one. That's the vital point of it all. Hatchard had argued with me in his barrister-like way, but it left me unmoved. I'm not a man to go to another for help in the big decisions. No, Vivien, for two days I've scarcely spoken to a soul, and yet these dreams came to me with a vividness that was appalling. And at last I realised." He paused.

"Realised what?"

"That they came from myself—*myself alone*. That they were the inmost thoughts of my complex being—the glimpse of the future that only the inmost mind can perceive. They were myself speaking to myself." His voice was ringing now with conviction—the balance had swung definitely, decisively downwards towards the scale of duty. "But what I've told you is not one-tenth of all the visions of the future that crowded in upon me. The wretched beings cursed by heredity . . . the still more wretched offspring of their marriages . . . the scrofulous, the crook-backed, the epileptic, the paralysed, the imbecile that came into being because my Bill did not pass—they stretched out in endless phantasmagoria that tore at my heart-strings. They looked towards me in silence as they passed by one by one. *They* haunt me!"

A low growl of thunder eddied and echoed among the hills.

"Come!" she said tensely, and plucked at his arm. "Come before the storm breaks. My car's below the hill. We'll talk of this again when we're in shelter. There's a cottage in the Weald I've rented. We shall be alone there. Then we can talk over this in comfort."

"In comfort? No, the decision is for now. I've decided—I go up on the heights of Medenham Down."

"With a storm breaking! You must be mad!" And she looked at him with new eyes, with a dawning horror in her eyes. "Why, you must be . . . Your nerves must be unstrung. . . . No man in his senses would. . . ."

"I've never been more sane than I am at the present moment," answered Kennion. "Don't you understand my feelings after all I've told you?"

"I don't understand at all. You are supposed to be a strong man, and yet a few idle dreams—"

A blaze of lightning cut short her words. In the moment of light the milestone stood out sharply with its "XL miles " in stark shadow against the white stone.

"Forty miles," mused Kennion. "And I have seen forty years of life. It's my milestone."

She looked at him with chilly horror, thinking that his reason had tottered.

"Good-bye!" he said firmly and finally, and strode away and up the green hump of Medenham Down. She watched him for some moments at his steady, purposeful climb, and then she gathered up her skirts to run for shelter against the breaking storm.

But Travis Kennion strode on and up to the summit of Medenham Down, and the rain slashed at him as he stood on the topmost knoll with folded arms, immobile, dreaming great dreams of what he might do for his country in the days to come.

* * * * *

As to Dr. Wycherley's part in the big decision, Kennion never suspected. He could not know how the mental healer had sat by his bedside far into that Sunday night, speaking softly of the many things that had become woven into his dreams to such haunting effect. He could not know that the visions of the future conjured up by his inner consciousness were but the reflex of what had been poured into his ears during the hypnotic sleep. He had judged that they came from himself alone—*he had convinced himself.*

And Dr. Wycherley, on his side, never revealed the secret, even to Lilith Kennion. He saw the happiness of reunion; he saw Kennion's great Bill pass victoriously into law against the fiercest opposition ever known in the House of Commons; and he was content.

It was a triumph for the science of mind, and the keen joy of achievement was his.

Coachwhip Publications

CoachwhipBooks.com

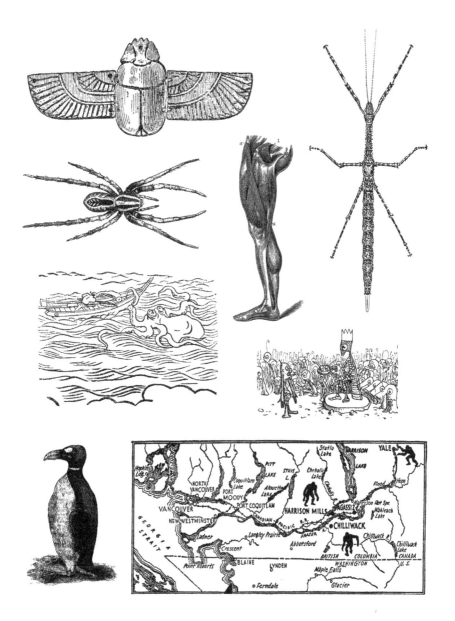

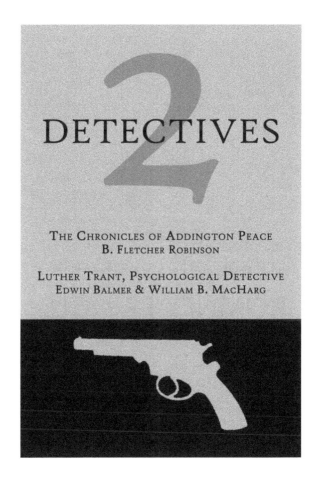

The Chronicles of Addington Peace /
Luther Trant, Psychological Detective

ISBN 1-61646-097-0

THE COMPLETE ADVENTURES OF
ROMNEY PRINGLE

R. AUSTIN FREEMAN &
JOHN J. PITCAIRN
(AS BY CLIFFORD ASHDOWN)

THE COMPLETE ADVENTURES OF
ROMNEY PRINGLE

ISBN 1-61646-090-3

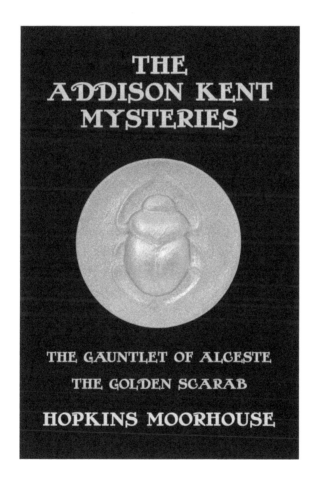

The Addison Kent Mysteries

ISBN 1-61646-080-6

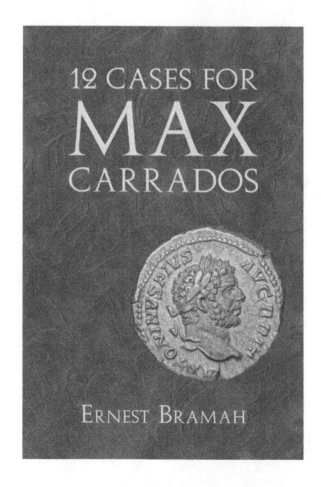

12 CASES FOR MAX CARRADOS

12 Cases for Max Carrados

ISBN 1-61646-018-0

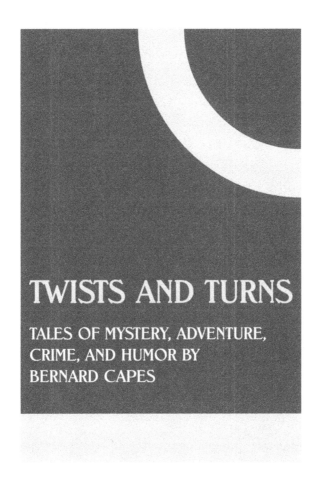

Tales of Mystery, Adventure, Crime,
and Humor by Bernard Capes

ISBN 1-61646-094-6

www.ingramcontent.com/pod-product-compliance
Lightning Source LLC
Chambersburg PA
CBHW021743310125
21212CB00036B/327